BY KATHY TYERS

Firebird: A Trilogy
Shivering World

KATHY TYERS

FIREBIRD

A TRILOGY

BETHANY HOUSE
MINNEAPOLIS, MINNESOTA

Firebird: A Trilogy
Copyright © 2004
Kathy Tyers

Cover design by Lookout Design Group, Inc.

Previously published in three separate volumes:
Firebird copyright © 1999 by Kathy Tyers
Fusion Fire copyright © 2000 by Kathy Tyers
Crown of Fire copyright © 2000 by Kathy Tyers

Published by Bethany House Publishers
11400 Hampshire Avenue South
Bloomington, Minnesota 55438
www.bethanyhouse.com

Bethany House Publishers is a division of
Baker Publishing Group, Grand Rapids, Michigan.

Printed in the United States of America

Library of Congress Cataloging-in-Publication Data

Tyers, Kathy.
    Firebird: a trilogy / by Kathy Tyers.
       p.   cm.

    ISBN 0-7642-2927-3 (pbk.)
    I. Women—Fiction. 2. Love stories, American. 3. Fantasy fiction, American. 4. Christian fiction, American. I. Title.
PS3570.Y4F573   2004
813'.54—dc22
                                                             2004012907

Acknowledgments

Karen, Dave, and the other decision makers at Bethany House—thank you for conceiving this volume.

As always, deep gratitude to my military and medical specialists, General Bob and Doctor Bob, Bill, and Diann. Blessings to Pastor Chris, Pastor Brett, and Chaplain Harry. Special thanks to Martha, Janna, Karen, and Steve.

Thanks and blessings for help, encouragement, and wisdom: Amy, Andrew, April, Basia, Carol, Cheryl, Chris, Clint, Diann, Eddie, Gayla, George, Greg, Harry, Idessa, Jane, Jo, John, Joyce, Karen, Kathy, Kevin, Linda, Lisa, Mark, Marjorie, Marlo, Matthew, Maureen, Michelle, Mike, Peter, Poppa, Rob, Robin, Sharon, Sigmund, Sue, Sylvia, Tana, Vance, and Wynne, and my enthusiastic friends at lady_firebird@yahoogroups.com. It's been an adventure!

Deepest thanks to the holy and merciful One. You give and transcend all stories and songs.

All of the best ideas in this trilogy came from all of you. Any inaccuracies, impossibilities, weak wordings, or accidental perversion of truth are mine alone.

KATHY TYERS is the bestselling author of *Balance Point, The Truce at Bakura,* and *Shivering World.* She has degrees in microbiology and education and lives in Bozeman, Montana, where she plays flute in the Bozeman Symphony Orchestra.

In this whorl of imagined star systems,
God created not Earth but different worlds.

One world's people lived by false doctrine and death.
Light years away, faithful exiles awaited
the Messiah of all creation.

On a third world, they met.

PROLOGUE

Lady Firebird Angelo was trespassing.

Shadowed by her friend Lord Corey Bowman, she squeezed and twisted through a narrow, upright opening between two dusty stone walls. She'd paced off twenty meters in silence. Her eyes had almost adjusted to faint gray light from ahead and behind. Growing up in this palace, she'd explored it thoroughly and cautiously during her childhood. She hadn't tiptoed between these particular walls since she found the gap, four years ago, when she was fifteen. If she remembered right, then in ten meters more—

Something rattled behind her. She froze. If anyone caught her and Corey this deep in the governmental wing, they could be done for. *Powers help us!* she prayed silently.

Slowly, she turned around. Corey crouched three meters away. He pointed at a loose stone and cringed a silent apology.

Time hung suspended, like a laser satellite passing overhead. They waited motionless, hardly even breathing.

Evidently, the Powers weren't feeling vengeful—if those supernatural guides even existed, which Firebird had started to doubt. The soft voices behind the curved inner wall kept droning on, incomprehensible from this point in the hidden passage.

Firebird crept on.

The rough partition on her left enclosed an elliptical chamber. Inside, the highest council in the Netaian planetary systems held its conferences.

Firebird had heard whispered rumors among other cadets at the NPN Academy: that the Netaian Planetary Navy planned to hold military exercises in Federate space, or that an attack was imminent—Federate or Netaian, depending on who had heard whom—or that secret weapons were under development. None of her instructing officers had acknowledged those rumors. They kept their cadets working in blind, busy ignorance.

But this morning, staring out a classroom window-wall, Firebird had seen a silvery shuttle with Federate markings emblazoned on its underside decelerate into Citangelo spaceport. According to a hasty check at her desk terminal, the queen's Electorate had immediately closed this afternoon's session to observers.

Maybe the Federates were protesting those rumored maneuvers, as she guessed—or trying to head off an open confrontation, Corey's assumption. Someone had to find out, on behalf of the second-year cadets. If a war broke out, they'd be in it. During an afternoon hour reserved for studying, Firebird had sneaked home with Corey.

Ahead, light gleamed into their passage through an inner-wall chink. The palace's builders, three hundred years before, had been more concerned with elegance than security. During her privileged childhood, Firebird had found many odd niches in this historic building where walls didn't exactly meet, or where they came together at peculiar angles to create blind passageways. Palace security should have sealed every breach that gave illegitimate access to the electoral chamber. They'd missed this one.

On her next birthday, Firebird would be confirmed as a short-term elector. That was her right, an honor she would receive as an Angelo. Then, she would tell the House Guard and the electoral police about this passage.

But no sooner.

She reached the chink and peered through. Inside the grand chamber's red walls, lined with portraits and gilt bas-relief false pillars, the Netaian systems' twenty-seven electors sat at a U-shaped table that surrounded a small foreign delegation.

Firebird glimpsed the rest of her family. Her oldest sister and confidante, Carradee, sat beside the gilt chair of their mother, Siwann, a strong monarch who was already much more than the traditional electoral figurehead. Beyond Carradee lounged the middle Angelo sister, Phoena, the "beauty of the family" and Siwann's obvious favorite. Though taller and lighter haired than Firebird, Phoena had the same delicate facial features and large, long-lashed dark eyes. They'd often been mistaken for each other, to the disgust of both.

Five strangers stood below the U-shaped table's open foot. The two who'd stepped forward wore dress-white tunics and carried recall pads. One addressed the electors in clipped Old Colonial, the language of most colonized worlds in the Whorl's great half circle of stars. ". . . as a surtax only on nonessential goods," he declared, "such as . . ."

What was this, a trade delegation?

Phoena exchanged disdainful glances with the trade minister, Muirnen Rogonin. Maintaining an indolent slouch, Rogonin—the jowly Duke of Claighbro—flicked two fingers toward the man who'd spoken. "I would see no reason to levy a military assessment against a well-defended system such as Netaia, Admiral. Your logic is flawed."

Admiral. Maybe their business wasn't entirely trade, then—

Corey nudged Firebird from behind. "Hey," he whispered.

Reluctantly, she rolled away from the chink. She pressed against the inner wall, listening closely.

In recent decades, the Federacy had consolidated twenty-three star systems in the local spur of the galactic arm. Netaia, isolated at the Whorl's counterspinward end, had resisted confederation. Despite tight governmental control over their lives, most Netaians lived in proud and comfortable, if xenophobic, prosperity . . . so far as Firebird knew.

As the debate continued, she gradually concluded that the Federates did in fact want to set up a trading protocol. She glowered into the darkness. For this, she'd risked death?

Predictably, the noble electors—the heart of Netaia's spiritual and political power, which Firebird's family served as standard-bearers—were mouthing the same isolationist policies she'd heard all her life. Rogonin's voice rose, boasting about Netaia's high culture, its superbly terraformed ecological diversity, and the absolute lack of necessity of trade with any other planetary system.

All true, Firebird reflected with casual pride. Netaia was a wealthy world with rich resources.

She glanced at Corey. He stared through the chink, his oval face lit softly by fugitive light. Black haired and freckled, he was broadening into manhood, but they never had—never would—become romantically involved. Both were wastlings. Both would die young, as the Powers had decreed for most of these third- and fourth-born noble children. Firebird and Corey had made a pact, years ago, not to make that fate any harder on each other.

She jabbed his midsection. "My turn," she mouthed.

She pressed her face to cold stone and looked enviously on the five Federates. The thought of so many worlds, so much knowledge, frustrated her. She only would see the Federate systems as a military pilot, if at all.

Behind the two ambassadors, an honor guard stood at stiff attention, two armed men in ash gray and one in vivid midnight blue. Ash gray was for Tallis, the Federacy's regional capital. Midnight blue. . . ? Firebird frowned. She ought to remember—

Realization hit her like a laser blast. Midnight blue designated Thyrica. That was only a minor Federate system, but a few Thyrians were genetically engineered telepaths. Was this man one of them, and a spy?

Alarmed, she leaned toward Corey to whisper.

The Thyrian guard turned his head and looked straight at her.

Firebird's jaw dropped. She hadn't made a sound! Her pulse accelerated as the Thyrian stepped back from his formation to touch the arm of a red-jacketed electoral policeman. He whispered into the redjacket's ear, and as he did, she caught a sparkle at the edge of his right shoulder, where the telepaths wore their gold insignia.

She flung herself away from the wall. "Corey, they spotted us!" she whispered. They must move fast . . . and separately. Because she was an Angelo, she stood a better chance of surviving arrest. "Get out the underway," she ordered. "I'll go back through the palace."

As Corey dashed toward a boarded-in cellar hatch, Firebird squeezed back through the narrows. Trying to run silently, she dashed to the passage's end and scrambled up a stone partition. She rolled onto a crawlway, groped for the board they'd left loose, and whisked it aside, then peered down into the public-zone maintenance closet.

So far, so good. The closet was dark. Heart hammering, she lowered herself through the impromptu hatch and then cracked the hall door.

It swung out of her grasp, seized from outside. A massive black-haired man backed across the marble hallway, covering the closet with a deadly service blazer. Kelling Friel, captain of the electoral police, recognized Firebird at the same instant she recognized him. "Lady Firebird," he growled, replacing his blazer in its holster.

She stood a moment, collecting her breath and her wits as she straightened her red-collared Academy blouse. The electoral police carried special authority over Netaia's small wastling class. Firebird had learned years ago— the hard way—that redjackets only honored regal manners, which they encouraged. A few wastlings eventually became heirs, so they all had to be trained, in case they survived to head their families.

She nodded a solemn greeting. "Good afternoon, Captain," she said. "It's only me."

He stepped into the closet, peered into the dark gap in its ceiling, and then frowned. "I think, my lady, that you'd better come inside." He swept a muscular hand up the passway.

Into the chamber? A cold weight settled in Firebird's stomach, but she had to obey. She walked beside him toward the chamber's gilt doors.

Ten powerful families governed Netaia, guarding its traditions of faith and authority. Representing the ancient and holy Powers—its state religion—to the common classes, those ruling families religiously controlled their heirs. Third- and fourth-born noble children could live only until their eldest brothers or sisters secured their titled lines' survival. Then the young wastlings were ordered to seek honorable ends to their lives. Outranked, outnumbered, and constantly chaperoned by electoral police, they had little chance of escaping that sacred duty.

Even earlier, an offensive wastling could be severely disciplined. Fifteen-year-old Lord Liach Stele had faced a firing squad two years ago for incorrigible behavior. Firebird had never liked Liach, but—required to attend his execution—she'd watched with sickened pity and damp palms. She too had been disciplined. Last year, an Academy senior had caught her practicing docking maneuvers on off-limit flight sims. For her punishment, the red-jackets had injected her with Tactol, a sensory hyperstimulant that made every sight, sound, odor, and movement torture for an hour . . .

. . . and then they'd locked her back inside the simulator. Despite the excruciating sensory overload, she'd flown the preprogrammed mission with furious determination. Her all-Academy record still stood.

She wiped her palms on her uniform trousers. Friel's decorative sword harness jingled as he marched her through the chamber's double doors and up toward the U-shaped table. A second red-jacketed electoral policeman fell into step on her other side. Firebird drew a deep breath. Trying to look both submissive and innocent—although she felt neither—she looked up at her mother.

Siwann rose from her gilt chair. An unadorned coronet rode squarely on her coifed hair. With her tailored scarlet dress suit, the effect mimicked a formal portrait. "You have been spying, Firebird," she said. "Alone?"

Firebird was too proud to lie, but she never would've betrayed another wastling, particularly Corey. She stalled for his sake, glancing sidelong at her escorts in their long, gold-edged crimson coats. If she'd been three years younger, she might have tried to kick one of them. But since then, her oldest sister had married and borne her first child. Firebird's life expectancy had already shrunk.

Carradee looked down from the table, biting her lip and raising both eyebrows. Their middle sister, Phoena, merely smirked.

Captain Friel gripped Firebird's arm through the long auburn hair she wore loose over her shoulders. "Answer Her Majesty," he ordered.

Gambling on a few more seconds for Corey, she glanced at the Federates instead. They'd stepped aside, waiting to resume negotiations. The slim Thyrian stood apart from his muscular colleagues, almost as if they answered to him, despite their weathered faces. He looked the youngest, with a straight chin and vividly blue eyes. He stared at Firebird so intently that for an instant, she imagined she could feel his scrutiny. He wore that gold star on his shoulder openly, either flaunting his identity or at least refusing to disguise it.

We see you, she challenged him silently. *We know what you are. Go back where you belong.*

Captain Friel tightened his grip. Firebird faced her mother again and silently prayed to the Powers that the Electorate wouldn't try to impress the Federacy by executing her for espionage. "Your Majesty," she said, lowering her eyes and hoping that by now, Siwann would want to get on with business—or with refusing to do business—and that Corey would've escaped. "I apologize for interrupting. I promise not to observe you again. Ever."

The queen stood, visibly evaluating Firebird's breach of conduct. "This is my youngest daughter," she told the Federates. "She has a history of playing hide-and-search in the palace. I assure you, she is no threat to this meeting's security. However," she added, raising her voice, "you are too old for games, Lady Firebird. You will not be dismissed with just an apology."

Firebird's stomach knotted.

"Friel?" Siwann's voice echoed off the red walls, black marble floor, and domed ceiling. "She will show you her spying place. See that it is made inaccessible."

The captain touched his cap in salute. "Any further orders, Majesty?" he asked blandly.

Firebird met her mother's cold stare. This time, she didn't beg the Powers for mercy. She'd been caught, and she faced the consequences. Phoena's smirk broadened.

"Tactol again," the queen ordered.

Friel grasped Firebird's shoulder. She marched out, breathing slowly and deeply, maintaining a dignified brace until the massive doors boomed behind her. Then her shoulders relaxed. Someday, after Carradee and her prince secured the Angelo inheritance with a second child, she would kneel at the foot of that gold-rimmed electoral table to receive her geis orders. Compared with that virtually inevitable sentence, one miserable hour was nothing. She'd survived Tactol before.

Still, maybe she could distract Captain Friel. "That one's a spy," she muttered ominously, pausing in the great hallway. "The guard in the dark blue tunic."

"We know," Friel answered. "They're going directly back to their shuttle. They won't see anything they can't image from orbit. It's another spy who concerns me now. You."

She followed Friel back up the passway, disgusted. Five years from now she would be dead, guilty only of having been born after Phoena . . . while Phoena still sat on the Electorate, steering Netaian policies. The Powers had decreed their birth order.

Friel paused outside the hall closet where she'd emerged. "Show me your—no. Come this way first. You'll remember this better if we stop in my office."

Firebird's poise slipped at last. Shivering, she resisted the childish urge to plead for a reprieve. She had only one irrational fear, but the redjackets had found it. Injecting instruments—intersprays, sub-Q and intramusc dispersers, and old-fashioned needles—terrified her.

And it had been a trade delegation.

Friel motioned her through an open door. She squared her shoulders. At least Corey had escaped. She wouldn't cringe, wouldn't cry. Wouldn't react at all, if she could help it. She might be only a wastling, but she was an Angelo.

CHAPTER 1

WASTLING

maestoso ma non tanto
majestically, but not too much

A Netaian year had passed since Firebird's first brush with the distant, powerful Federacy.

"... but the phase inducer—*here*—bypasses the third subset of ..."

Firebird dropped her hand into her lap, unable to concentrate. She leaned away from the table and gazed up at a crystal chandelier that lit the palace's private breakfast hall, and she let her mind wander far from the Academy scanbook that glowed on her viewer. In a week, she must be able to reproduce that schematic for a senior-level exam. But tonight, she would appear for an interview with the queen.

In the year since she'd been caught spying, the Netaian Planetary Navy had carried off those rumored maneuvers in Federate space, drawing only a strenuous protest. Her mother's electors had tightened their grip on both high- and low-common classes. Carradee's little daughter had charmed the palace household, and Phoena—

Phoena burst through a swinging door. "You nearly got yourself taken to see Captain Friel again last night," she chanted to Firebird.

Phoena hadn't changed a hair.

Firebird watched over her empty breakfast plate as her middle sister paced the table's length.

"I can't believe you'd be so stupid." Phoena seized a chair across from Firebird and rang for service. Her spring gown shone by morning light, and when Firebird glanced from Phoena's sparkling earrings and necklace up to the chandelier, she couldn't help comparing. As an Academy senior of noble family, Firebird had been allowed to move back to the estate for her final semester. It wasn't far from campus, and this still was her home, for a few last weeks.

"Countervoting the whole Electorate?" Phoena went on. "With a unanimity order? What's the matter with you? Have you forgotten your place?"

This year, Firebird also had learned that her music—she played the high-

headed Netaian small harp, or clairsa—was a passport into the common classes. In quarters of Citangelo that Phoena never had visited, she'd heard ballads that should make any elector nervous. After three hundred years, Netaia
was beginning to chafe under the Electorate's absolute rule and its grip on
the planet's wealth.

Firebird faced her sister squarely. "You know what I think about your
basium project. If I had to do it again, I'd still vote my conscience. You're
not expanding our buffer zone. You only want a threat, a show of power."

"So you said." Phoena buffed her nails on the sleeve of her gown. "We
heard you clearly yesterday."

Firebird laid her palms on the scanbook viewer. "You got your commendation, didn't you? Twenty-six to one."

"One." Phoena lifted an eyebrow. "In your position, I think I'd be trying to live awhile. You're lucky the redjackets haven't already wasted you.
Wastlings who countervote don't last. You're only in there for show, you
know. For your *honor*," she mocked.

Firebird curled her fingers around her viewer. "There's no *honor*," she
echoed, mimicking Phoena's tone, "in threatening worlds that would rather
trade with us than attack us." Phoena's project was secret, and no commoner knew of it. Still, Firebird had used her vote to express her people's
earnestly sung longings to live in free, fair peace.

"You never should have had electing rights to begin with," Phoena
retorted.

The door swung beyond Phoena. Firebird fell silent, toying with her
cruinn cup. Carradee pushed through. A servitor-class attendant followed
the tallest and eldest Angelo sister. A deep green robe draped Carradee's
form, now swollen with a second pregnancy.

Firebird's life expectancy had almost zeroed.

"Carrie," Firebird murmured as the crown princess sank into a cushioned chair held by the servant. "You look exhausted."

Carradee sighed and splayed her fingers on her belly. "With the little
one's dancing all night, it's a wonder I sleep at all. And I'm so worried for
you, Firebird. Why must you try so hard to throw away the time that's left
to you?"

Phoena leaned back and fixed Firebird with dark eyes.

Easy for Phoena to smirk now, Firebird reflected, but it hadn't always
been that way. Phoena had been born a wastling. Firebird was three at the
time and Phoena six, both beginning their indoctrination into their holy
destiny, when their second-born sister had been found smothered. Investigation had implicated the programmer of Lintess's favorite toy, a lifelike

robot snow bear, but—as with the death of their father years later—Firebird harbored suspicions about Phoena that she didn't care to voice.

She watched the scarlet-liveried servitor hurry out. "How can you condone fouling a world, Carradee?" She spread her hands on the tabletop. "Aren't some things worth standing against?"

"But, Firebird—oh!" Carradee grimaced and stroked her stretched belly. "I'll be glad when this is over."

Firebird bit her lip.

Phoena seized the opening like a weapon. "Five weeks," she crowed. "Then there'll be a shift in the family."

Carradee turned pale gray eyes to Phoena in a mute reprimand. Firebird snapped her viewer off. "I'll have longer than that. They'll send me with the invasion force. I would love to fly strike, just once. And I'd rather die flying than . . ." She bit back the comparison. Another wastling had gone recently in a suspicious groundcar accident, but her grief still was too fresh to expose to Phoena. Lord Rendy Gellison had wanted badly to live, had lived hard and wild.

She shook her elbow-length hair behind her slender shoulders and stood to leave. Phoena's breakfast arrived, carried by a mincing white-haired servitor. Netaia's penal laws supplied the noble class with hereditary laborers, who lived caught between the fear of further punishment and the hope that exemplary service would win freedom. Some of the finest musicians Firebird had known, and some of the kindest people, had been servitors.

She snatched up her scanbook and swung out the door. Phoena called after her, "I'll help put the black edging on your portrait."

Firebird paused in the long private hallway to gather up more Academy scan cartridges. As she pocketed them, she shot a wistful look down the gallery, past spiral-legged tables weighted with heirlooms, to the formal portrait Phoena had mentioned: she'd been sixteen and star eyed when it was painted, absorbed in her piloting and her music, years away from this shadow of impending death. The scarlet velvette gown with white sash and diadem made her look queenly, but the artist had painted a mischievous smile between brave chin and proud brown eyes. A scarcely tangible sadness in those two-dimensional eyes always haunted Firebird. Did other people see the flaws in her mask of courage?

She straightened her brownbuck flight jacket in front of a jeweled hallway mirror. *Well*, she told her reflection, *there's an advantage to dying young. People will remember you as pretty*. Humming a defiant ballad from the Coper Rebellion, she dashed off for the Academy.

If Firebird had been born an heir, she'd have had a hard choice between the Citangelo Music Conservatory and the Planetary Naval Academy. She loved flying, though, and had trained hard to develop from a skillful pleasure pilot into a potential naval officer. Noble families considered their wastlings' training as investments in Netaia's glory. When her geis orders came, she'd pay back that advance by making her own contribution to Netaia's greatness, whether or not she approved—or survived—the invasion.

Morning classes were unexceptional. After lunch, she almost crashed into Corey in a passway crowded with cadets. "Easy, Firebird." He stepped back, and his grin faded. "What's wrong? Phoena again?"

"Of course," she muttered. "And Her Majesty, tonight."

"Oh, that's right. I forgot." Lord Corey had taken a surprise growth spurt this year. Pursing his lips in sympathy, he palmed the door panel.

They entered a hushed briefing room. This would be a two-week, special-topic session. These top cadets had waited all term to meet a civilian instructor who'd come in midwinter from the Federate world of Thyrica. Vultor Korda had turned traitor and fled to Netaia, which appalled Firebird: Loyalty was a discipline the Netaian faithful, even wastlings, didn't question. Worse, he was known to be one of the shameful Thyrian telepaths.

She and Corey slipped into adjacent seats and loaded their viewers as the little man scuttled in. Physically, he looked anything but powerful, with a belly that strained the belt of his brown civilian shipboards. His complexion was the fragile white of the academician or the UV-allergic spacer.

Last year, Firebird had learned that his kind descended from a civilization from far above the galactic plane. In a grand bioengineering experiment, they had destroyed their children's genetic integrity . . . then they'd almost annihilated themselves in a horrendous civil war. Only one sizable group of these "starbred" was known to have survived, a few religious mendicants who'd fled the distant Ehret system. They'd made planetfall on the Whorl's north-counterspinward edge, at Thyrica.

Instead of depopulating Thyrica, though, the Ehretan group had adopted strict religious laws to control their powers. Quickly they proved to the Federacy that they were absolutely undeceivable. Since then, they'd insinuated themselves into Federate diplomatic, medical, and intelligence forces.

Maybe one day, they'd bring down the Federacy as their ancestors destroyed Ehret. *Someone should write that song*, Firebird mused.

Standing at his subtronic teaching board, Vultor Korda twisted toward the quarter-circle of seats. "So," he said, "you think Netaia can take Veroh from the Federacy? I happen to think you have a chance."

Corey fingered the edge of his terminal and whispered, "Slimy."

Firebird nodded without taking her eyes off Korda. He struck her as the arrogant kind who compensated for weakness with meanness. His type would deliberately downgrade others—particularly a woman near the top of her class. She shifted uncomfortably.

"You've heard of the Federacy's starbred forces," Korda continued. "'Sentinels,' they call the trained ones. As officers, you'll be more likely to encounter them than your blazer-bait subordinates will. By the way, you won't find a more self-righteous, exclusive group if you see half the Federacy—not that it trusts them. Common people fear what they can't control."

One student protested, "But aren't you—"

Korda waved a hand, dismissing the objection. "Yes. I'm Thyrian, and starbred. But I'm no Sentinel. No one tells me how to control my abilities."

Firebird went rigid. If Korda had such abilities, had he influenced the dangerous decision to attack Veroh? Could he have gone to some of the electors, even to Phoena, and convinced them to try this?

She frowned. Maybe he'd pushed an elector or two. But Phoena's proposal to take Veroh, and Siwann's endorsement, fit their lifelong, belligerent pattern—

Siwann. A tiny time-light blinked on her wristband. Fourteen hundred. She could relax; there was plenty of day left. Vultor Korda launched into a rambling tale of his testing and training under Master Sentinels, then their history.

Then the briefing room went dark. Korda pressed a chip stack into the blocky media unit at midboard, then faced the class. "My topic is Sentinels in military intelligence. If you think you see one of these people, in battle or otherwise, shoot first and make sure of your target after he's dead. Assume you won't get off a second shot. Some of them can levitate your side weapon from the holster."

Firebird's memory served up a year-old image of the electoral chamber. She hadn't seen any levitating, but she'd certainly suspected that Thyrian guard.

A life-size holographic image appeared over the media block. Rotating slowly, it portrayed a handsome black-haired woman who apparently stood taller than half the men in Firebird's cadet class. "This is Captain Ellet Kinsman. She's stationed at Caroli—which governs Veroh, by the way—and rising fast in the ranks. We rate the starbred on the Ehretan Scale according to how strongly they've inherited the altered genes. We're all mixed-blood now, but Kinsman comes from a strong family. She's seventy-five Ehretan Scale out of a rough hundred, which means she can do over half the tricks the original Ehretans could've. You don't want to get near a person like that.

Fortunately, you probably won't encounter Kinsman. She processes information that others collect. Desk worker but still dangerous. Memorize the face, if you have enough room in your memory."

Firebird was already memorizing. The woman resembled her first flight trainer, high in the forehead with a long, aquiline nose. Kinsman's uniform, vividly blue-black with no insignia except a gold shoulder star with four beveled rays, fit Firebird's recollection . . . almost. Something had been different.

The image blurred and vanished. Next appeared a man, older, also black-haired. "Admiral Blair Kinsman is her cousin. Based on Varga. The throwback of the family, about a twenty-five Ehretan Scale. I think he can nudge a few electrons along a wire, if it's early in the day. . . ."

Distracted, Firebird missed several sentences. So they had different skill levels. Where did that put last year's alleged honor guard? She'd finally guessed how he had spotted her; she must've sent off a blast of dismay when she realized just what he was—

"Now, this is trouble." The admiral disappeared in a cloud of static. A younger man's figure materialized in his place, and Firebird gaped. This was the guard! In the chamber, she'd had no time to stare. She did now. Average height, not overly muscled, with hair that was the light russet brown of exotic leta wood. This image's eyes were lost in shadow, but she hadn't forgotten that ice-blue stare.

"This is Wing Colonel Brennen Caldwell," Korda announced. "He's stationed at Regional Headquarters, Tallis, but as a member of the Special Operations force"—Korda scratched the initials SO onto the teaching board—"he has no permanent base. Don't even get close enough to recognize him. He scored an ES ninety-seven, and they haven't had one so high in a hundred years. See the master's star on his shoulder? Eight points, not four."

She nodded. That was the difference. . . .

"Supposedly, Caldwell's the first strong-family Sentinel the Federacy has considered for real rank. Military Sentinels pretend they don't want authority, but the situation is more complex than that. Remember our violent history." Korda paused. "The Federacy uses us, but it's afraid of us. Anyway, Special Ops rotate between fleet and special assignments, so they only serve part of the time with a regular unit."

They'd sent a Special Ops officer here, with a trade delegation? In that case, she—and the electors—had badly underestimated its importance. There'd been a highly skilled telepath in the heart of the Netaian government that day. A shudder flickered down her spine. She wondered what kind of data he'd taken back to Regional HQ, Tallis.

"He's cute," whispered Lady Delia Stele to no one in particular.

Not "cute," Firebird thought, *but compelling—*

Korda flung out both arms. "If that's all you think about, Stele, get out of here. Out! My time is valuable, and I won't waste it on giggly wastlings that anybody can play with but no one will ever marry."

Delia's face, so prettily circled in blond hair, was a study in humiliation. Other cadets glared. Firebird angrily rose halfway out of her seat.

Korda brought up the lights and swung his arms again. "Go ahead, hate me. I can feel it. But I'll be alive next year and most of you will be dead. I only had an hour today, and it's up. But come back tomorrow and I'll show you some things that could give you another week or two." He dove for the exit.

When Firebird saw that Delia was being consoled by several girls (and, Powers bless him, Corey's twin brother, Daley), she slipped out into the passway and headed for the parking garage and her skimmer. For all his sliminess, Vultor Korda had given her a good deal to think about. It roiled in her mind during dinner, which she took alone in her suite.

Telepaths, here. Then and now. What did Korda do when he wasn't teaching? Had the Federacy suspected, over a year ago, that Netaia was moving toward a military invasion? If so, what kind of hair-trigger watch were they keeping on the Netaian systems?

She would mention that to one of the marshals.

After calling her personal girl to remove her leavings, she retreated from her parlor to her music room. A long triangular case lay on her carpet below the studio's window. Carefully she drew out her clairsa. A master-maker's work, its long leta-wood arches had been carved with a pattern of linked knots. Twenty-two metal strings reflected the dying daylight to shine brassy red through her hair's dangling strands.

She spent the hour that remained before her interview cradling it, seated on a low stool with her transcriber running. She was writing a song, one that might be her last.

Almost ninety years before, another queen's wastling had survived to mount the throne. Lady Iarla had set a standard Firebird hoped to match. Manifesting all nine of the holy Powers—Strength, Valor, and Excellence; Knowledge, Fidelity, and Resolve; Authority, Indomitability, and Pride—but also a remarkable compassion, Iarla was a respected figure in Netaia's recent history. The melody Firebird had composed for this ballad was musically solid, and the chords stirred her longings even on a hundredth run-through, but words just wouldn't come. She'd hoped to pass this song on to her friends in downside Citangelo before she left for the invasion.

Then again, there'd been a time when she'd secretly hoped to repeat her great-great-grandmother Iarla's climb to glory. As Carradee's second confinement approached, Firebird had abandoned that hope—but just as a few defiant tunes kept the Coper Rebellion alive, Iarla's name couldn't die as long as someone sang it to honor her.

After four attempts to rhyme a second stanza, Firebird gave up in disgust and ordered the transcriber to shut itself off. She returned the clairsa to its soft case before changing into a fresh Academy uniform.

Flecks of dust had settled on her ornate bedroom bureau. She needed to call Dunna back in to give the suite a good cleaning. Slowly she turned around as if seeing her marble walls and costly furnishings for the first time. Bunking in a cramped Academy dorm had changed her perspective. These elegant rooms had been Iarla's, too. That had always been a point of pride to Firebird. To be Angelo was to be proud.

With dignity that masked her apprehension, she swung down the curved staircase and across an echoing foyer toward the queen's night office.

Siwann had made this appointment weeks ago, which didn't suggest a matter of personal warmth. Loving moments between them had been rare— not that Firebird expected warmth from her mother. No parent could invest her emotions in a wastling child. It was safer to let servitors raise them and redjackets train them.

For two centuries, wastlings had provided Netaia with some of its most notorious daredevil entertainers and naval pilots. Some were heroes in history scanbooks, but unless an older sibling's tragedy elevated them to heir status, none lived past their early twenties. Any who recanted allegiance to the holy Powers and refused their geis orders disappeared, or had fatal accidents, like Lord Rendy Gellison. Firebird wondered sometimes if some who'd vanished had fled the Netaian systems and begun new lives elsewhere. She knew one who'd made the attempt. She had helped. Naturally, she had never heard from him, nor from the high-common-class woman who'd gone with him, but she thought of them occasionally. Had the redjackets found and killed them after Firebird and Corey reported them dead in space, or had they vanished effectively enough?

Her role in the plot nagged her conscience. Aiding their flight had been her one deliberate breach of the rigid, sacred Disciplines. If those holy Powers truly judged the dead, she had doomed herself to linger in the Dark that Cleanses, a purging place where disobedience would be burned from her soul . . . unless the Electorate ordered her to sacrifice herself for Netaia's benefit and glory.

As it would.

Still, she'd enlisted willingly. A soldier's death would cancel all her infractions. She only wished she were bound for a war in which she could give herself gladly, instead of this raid to help set up Phoena's despicable secret project. Rumor made it an environmental weapon that could poison whole regions of a targeted world.

A House Guard admitted her. At the night office's center stood a crystalline globe, grown at zero-g into an incredible likeness of her home world and lit from inside by a white everburner, but Firebird had passed it so many times that it had lost its power to impress her. Beyond it, Siwann sat as stiffly as her bust in the Hall of Queens, erect in a flawlessly tailored black suit. One hand swept a platinum stylus along her desk's inset scribing pad. Siwann had been striking in her day and was rarely caricatured, even by her enemies, except for her lofty haughtiness.

She looked up. "Sit. I'll be with you."

Firebird complied with her usual twinge of awe. Her Majesty's antique leta-wood desk loomed in front of a window draped with shadowy curtains, creating the illusion of tiers of red wings. Gilt-lettered ancient volumes, bound with animal skins, stood in dignified rows along two walls over files of chip stacks, data rods, and scan cartridges. Firebird occupied her waiting time trying to second-guess the Electorate. Would Netaia be preparing to invade Veroh for its unique minerals if the electors had ratified that trade agreement last year? Metal and mineral production and trade, like most Netaian industries, were regulated by electoral underlings. Surely, if Phoena had wanted basium, she could have bought it from the Federacy, if Rogonin's cartel hadn't kept offworld trade strictly illegal.

Siwann switched off her scribing pad at last, then took a white envelope from a drawer and flicked its corner. "Firebird, we have something for you."

"Yes, Your Majesty?" Firebird leaned forward carefully in the massive chair, keeping her posture correct. A graduation gift from Siwann? Unlikely, but possible.

"You will be commissioned next month. Assuming, of course, that you complete your classes."

"That's right." She hoped her mother was joking, or maybe the queen didn't follow her wastling's academic career with the same interest she'd shown in Carradee and Phoena. Firebird, already guaranteed an honorary captaincy as a wastling, had pushed that to a first major's commission with her class and flight evaluations. Top marks on Korda's seminar would win her a special commendation, too. She meant to try for it.

"You're aware that you then will be a first major."

"Yes." Siwann knew! Firebird felt the skin around her eyes wrinkle with smile lines. "My flight trainer tells me I'll be assigned to Raptor Phalanx with a flight team of my own choosing."

"We're glad it makes you happy, Firebird. That makes it easier for us to give you this, as the Disciplines demand." She handed the envelope across her desktop. Firebird fingered it open and found a white paper packet. "Anyone in a combat situation risks capture," explained her mother. "As a first major, you could be a candidate for a particularly thorough interrogation. Think what that would mean to Netaia." She ticked off details on her fingers as if summing up a criminal case; and Netaia's penal system, like its state religion, made few allowances for mercy. "You have been privy to the electoral council for nearly a year. There is your Academy education. Your knowledge of Angelo properties. Military facilities. Defense procedures."

Stricken, Firebird slipped the small packet back into the envelope and let it drop into her lap. She'd held death on the desktop. Her fingertips tingled. "This is poison?"

"You will keep it with you at all times, beginning here and now. For your sake, we hope that you will go out with the navy and finish your days in some exciting episode. We would be proud to see you named in Derwynn's new history series. But if ever it becomes obvious that you cannot avoid being taken prisoner, then your Resolve to use this may be the most important weapon you have carried into battle." She emphasized Resolve, one of the Powers, with regal deliberation—and then dropped her habitual royal plural. "Must I make myself clear, Firebird?"

"Not your orders, Majesty. But—"

"Captain Friel assures me you keep all of the Disciplines and the Charities, and I am glad. Besides guarding your place in history, the Powers will welcome you gloriously into true bliss if you keep this last obligation."

Swallowing a qualm of guilt, Firebird bowed her head. She'd irrevocably broken the Disciplines, helping Jisha and Alef escape. "I understand," she murmured. "But tell me what this is. How it will . . . kill."

"The vernacular is Somnus." Siwann slipped back into the lofty voice that she used at weekly electoral Obediences, when she read from the Disciplines. "It suppresses the involuntary nervous system. Taken orally, it will induce unconsciousness in about five minutes, irreparable brain damage in about fifteen, and finalize in twenty, without discomfort. Your aunt Firebird took it when Carradee was born, as did our mother the queen when we were ready to rule."

Firebird nodded slightly. Such was the duty of a Netaian queen, and she knew about her namesake. The elder Lady Firebird hadn't even waited for the Electorate to issue her geis, but had gone to her suite, eaten a slice of her favorite cream pie, and then poisoned herself as soon as baby Carradee was declared normal and healthy.

Carradee's first little daughter was normal and healthy, too. Firebird loved her as much as she envied her. Princess Iarlet, now three years old, was a beautiful, flirtatious firstborn.

Firebird tucked the packet into her breast pocket. "I shouldn't need this, madam. I intend to have the fastest striking team in the Planetary Navy."

"Fine words for a pacifist."

Didn't Siwann understand? Firebird would never slaughter civilians, but she longed for fame and glory—to let Strength, Valor, and Excellence shine in her actions. "I'll go, Majesty." Firebird rested her hands on her knees. "I know what my orders will be. Just see that they put us on a military target run, not a civilian one, and I swear I'll do my best for you."

"Yes. You will." Siwann's posture softened infinitesimally. "You always do, don't you?"

Grateful for the crumb of royal recognition, Firebird nodded. "Thank you, Mother."

Abruptly Siwann pushed back her chair and stood. "Little Firebird. Come here."

Firebird stood up, unsure of her mother's intentions. "Majesty?"

"Here." The queen flicked her hands. "Come to me."

Hesitantly, Firebird made the circuit of the massive desk into Siwann's outstretched arms. Only when she was not ordered away did she return the embrace.

"My baby," Siwann crooned. "My bright baby."

They swayed back and forth, Firebird holding tightly with painfully stiff shoulders. She didn't know how to react. This outpouring of sentiment made her feel guilty, as if she were taking something from Siwann that rightfully belonged to Carradee and Phoena.

Just as suddenly and inexplicably as she'd called her close, Siwann pulled away. She flicked both hands brusquely. Firebird was dismissed.

CHAPTER 2

COREY

affettuoso
with warmth

The empty foyer lay quiet. As Firebird hurried out of her mother's office, a puff of warm air danced through monolithic doors from the colonnade. She accepted its silent invitation and walked out into a clear summer evening.

She wandered downhill, numbing her dismay with the fragrance of formal flower gardens and a breeze that rustled long, glossy leaves on the drooping fayya trees. Where her path crossed a bridge over an inlet of the second reflecting pool, she stopped and leaned over a railing to throw path pebbles at goggle-eyed skitters. The palace gleamed white behind her, columns and porticoes of semiprecious stone coolly reflecting soft garden lumi-beams. She tossed a pebble idly. Two green-gold fish flitted forward to nip at the sinking stone. The tiny packet that would probably kill her felt heavy and huge in her slim breast pocket.

She'd lived well, she reminded herself. This year, training at the Academy, she'd traveled the solar reach and visited Netaia's buffer systems. She'd had good friends, both noble and common, including some of the best musicians in all three systems. *Plop!* went another pebble. Carradee had been especially gracious. Although besieged by her suitors, Carradee had put off marriage longer than anyone would have expected, had even given Firebird a kind of posterity by naming her firstborn for Iarla, the queen Firebird admired. When Iarlet had been born, Netaia had rejoiced, but dread had settled in Firebird's heart. Soon, another little princess would push her down the succession to the deadly fifth position, and the geis order would come.

Though it couldn't be said out loud, Firebird believed she would have made a more capable monarch than either Carradee or Phoena. She desperately hoped Netaia would remember her that way, and for the courage . . . the Indomitability . . . with which she faced her fate. *Plop!*

She truly was proud to be an Angelo. Three hundred years ago, Netaia had thrown off an invasion from outsystem. Declaring martial law and banding together under the Angelos, who declared themselves limited monarchs, the ten noble families had restored order from anarchy and industry out of planetwide devastation, and they'd elevated reverence for the Powers to an official state religion. The invasion was history, but just as Netaia's distrust of offworlders never had ended, neither had the aristocracy's religiously and judicially enforced stranglehold on its people. Loyalty to the state, and to its noble electors, remained every Netaian's highest duty. That system concentrated vast wealth where it could best be wielded to preserve independence.

Plip! Another pebble disappeared in murky water.

Phoena could marry next. She could have no children, but she would be spared. Firebird bristled, recalling her sister's cruel words over breakfast, and looked skyward.

That bright yellow-orange star was Veroh, target of the pending invasion. Veroh's proximity, and its orientation ninety degrees from Netaia's two buffer systems, made its conquest a logical step in expansion. But though the regime intended to occupy and hold Veroh, its immediate goal was Veroh's basium ore, which the Electorate wanted for the research of Dr. Nella Cleary.

Cleary had come from Veroh, offering talents in strategic ordnance research in return for absolute secrecy—and a price. In personally meeting it, Phoena had startled many electors by exercising a royal prerogative with Siwann's blessing, and had made Cleary the wealthiest commoner on Netaia. Cleary's project would require quantities of basium, a heavy-metal compound mined nowhere in the Netaian systems. Basium had few industrial uses and barely supported Cleary's mining family, but Cleary had developed a way to give it strategic value. If Siwann and Phoena had their way, Netaia would never again need to lower itself by negotiating with the Federacy. *Plip!*

Fortunately, Veroh stood out almost as far toward the tip of the largely Federate Whorl as Netaia itself, hopefully too far for a strong military defense to be economically feasible—*plop*—or so hoped the Netaian marshals. *Plunk!* According to recent intelligence, the Veroh system had only a small self-defense installation and ten support depots. The Federacy was obviously lax. If enough basium concentrate could be seized, the mission would be declared successful, but they would try for conquest. Netaia must grow or stagnate. The invasion would be under way ten days after commissioning.

Firebird would probably die there.

And then?

She stared into the murky water. She'd pondered the written Disciplines for years, but they were vague on the subject of life after death. She had no trouble imagining the terrible purging that might claw her spirit as she served her allotted years in the Dark that Cleanses. She'd probably imagined it too many times. But she'd never adequately imagined bliss, the state of utter joy that she hoped was her ultimate destiny.

She found the Powers themselves hard to imagine, too. Named by an ancient Netaian religion, these nine qualities supposedly enabled the nobles to rule. They existed beyond any person or persons, though, and so—she'd been taught—they could be addressed as gods. They were actually more real than gods, because they were visible. They showed themselves in electors' lives. Their written Disciplines demanded acts of obedience and charity, but as Firebird understood them, the Powers were nothing like . . . persons.

If they existed.

At least it was allowed to have doubts, so long as she never mentioned them. Posterity and the Powers would judge her by all she'd accomplished, not by the depth of her certainty. They demanded obedience, not faith. If Firebird believed in anything, she believed in Netaia and its people. All of them—noble, common, and even the servitors. For them, she was willing to sacrifice herself.

Then what if the Powers didn't exist?

She fingered her pebbles uncomfortably. Then when she died, she would be dead. At least she would never see Phoena again.

She flung a pebble as hard as she could. It bounced off the lawn on the pool's far side.

West of Veroh, the Whorl stars became thicker. Dimmer, more distant than Veroh, she picked out a yellowish spark: Tallis. On Tallis IV, a planet she would never see, the Federacy had established a Regional capital. Nine major civilizations, in two Whorl regions rich with G-spectrum stars, lay under covenance to the Federacy.

Independence made the Netaian rulers proud. Too proud, maybe. Proud enough to attack Veroh, only a protectorate of Federate Caroli, but the treaty ties were there. Firebird hoped the Federacy would let Veroh slip into Netaian hands.

Or did she?

She glanced east. Netaia's second smallest moon, Delaira, crept slowly up over the treetops. Tiny Menarri would soon follow, chasing Delaira in the orbit they shared, sometimes approaching, sometimes dropping back, but never overtaking its larger, sparkling sister.

Firebird felt that way, following Phoena forever, doomed by her birth order. . . .

Splat! went the rest of her pebbles into the water. She climbed the green lawn between drooping fayya and majestic leta trees and stepped up onto the colonnade. Between high white walls and fluted columns, a sentry paused on his rounds. She returned his salute, then went in to bed.

Vultor Korda made the following day's extended session intensely practical. After displaying several more holograms, he shut off the media block and said, "The Sentinels have developed a technique you need to experience. It gives them a critical edge in intelligence gathering. They call it mind-access interrogation."

Out the corner of her eye, Firebird saw Corey scribble on his recall pad.

"It doesn't damage the subject the way psychophysical methods can do, but it's more effective. A Sentinel can send something they call an epsilon carrier wave inside your mind's alpha matrix, where your thoughts and your feelings arise. He can find out anything you know, if he has enough strength, and can plant a relevant suggestion.

"To resist, you must concentrate on something totally irrelevant—your boot heels, or maybe your girl friend. Then you have to hold on like grim death when your mind starts to wander. Because it will. Someone else is trying to direct your thinking. Let's show how it's done, Angelo."

Firebird stiffened. The idea of linking minds, with Vultor Korda or anyone else, repelled her. But she couldn't escape without being cited for disobeying an instructor.

Korda sank onto Corey's desktop. With a slim white hand, he turned Firebird's chin toward him. "Don't be scared, Angelo. That gives me a headache. Look at my eyes. I'm going to be trying to find out your favorite color."

She blinked at him. His eyes were totally irrelevant brown. The sensation started subtly, like pre-nausea prickles at the back of her throat, and then she felt the essence of another person approach, deep beneath her external senses, on a level of awareness she'd never known existed. That other's presence struck her like a stale odor or a string out of tune: it was *wrong*.

"Colors," he whispered.

Suddenly she was panicking, and she saw her best clothes, all crimson.

"That was easy. Red, isn't it? You'll have to be quicker, Angelo. Can you do better, Parkai?"

As he moved on to other cadets, demonstrating and berating, Firebird's hand crept toward the deadly packet in her breast pocket. *Why should I bother to try?* she wondered. *If I were captured, I'd be unconscious before anybody could touch me.* But she coveted that commendation. One day, it would be part of her legend, her own . . . short . . . ballad. She scrutinized each demonstration, scheming how to resist better than anyone else.

In the afternoon, he came back to her. "All right, Red Bird. What's your middle name?"

Staring boldly at his eyes, she stopped down her awareness to a horrendously tricky passage from a clairsa etude she'd recently memorized. Notes danced in her mind as the prickly wave smacked her and ebbed away. Minor chord . . . it had three accidentals . . . descending run . . . arpeggio, two octaves . . .

The wave fell again with more force, and the distasteful otherness cracked her concentration. "Elsbeth," Korda crowed. Firebird opened her eyes to see him backing toward Corey with an odd look in his eye. "Thought you were doing well, didn't you?"

"That is the idea, though?" she asked. "Or did I do something wrong?"

Korda ducked his chin and frowned, studying her. "No, nothing wrong. That's a fair start. We'll try advanced techniques later." He turned to Leita Parkai and said, "Your turn."

Two weeks later, on the day after commissioning, the Netaian Planetary Navy held its traditional officers' ball. With the final flurry of Academy graduation finished and her commendation won despite Vultor Korda's badgering, Firebird intended to dance. She'd let the palace tresser tame her auburn mane into a ladylike coif, smooth to the crown with the back curled stylustight, and then she'd carefully pinned two new ruby rank stars onto the collar of her cobalt blue dress blouse. The marquis-cut stones framed her throat with glimmering light. Her regulation dress shoes concealed a little sharpened stick she'd tucked into her instep, for the sake of an old game. Maybe she could catch Corey off guard one more time, later on.

Nursing a goblet of wine punch and stopping at each group of partygoers, she worked her way down the main ballroom's black marble floor. Tonight the long crimson window curtains were overhung in cobalt blue, and most of the formal furniture and statuary had been moved into storage to make room for dancers. At its far end, a small orchestra filled the dais. Liveried servitors wandered through the crowd dispensing wines, sweets, and steaming, spicy cruinn.

Before she could dance with Corey, she would have to pay her respects to each of the other electors, the marshals, and nearly all her superior officers, all the while watching for heirs with hazing on their minds. Two of her friends had developed ugly, mysterious red blotches on face and throat after talking with Phoena. If those swollen weals felt as nasty as they looked, they would make the uniform's snug collar feel like a garrote.

Major—she was a major now, a career-grade officer! Her fingers stole up to touch one rank star, to assure herself it was real. The music rejoiced with her, a sweep of strings and brass that sang in delight. Dreamily she gazed out over the dance floor and caught sight of Phoena in the arms of a tall, black-haired new officer. . . .

Corey! Firebird halted in midstep. Phoena's hand rested lazily on Corey's shoulder, and she wore a saccharine smile. In Corey's expression Firebird read resigned patience.

A tall couple swept between Firebird and Corey. By the time she caught sight of him again, the dance set had ended. She rushed forward, seized his arm, and pulled him into a crowded corner.

In his fresh haircut, Corey seemed impossibly tall and broad shouldered. Firebird jostled him deeper into the noisy mass. "Did Phoena do anything odd? Quick!"

He shrugged. "She was friendly. That's about as odd as your sister can get."

A passing group drove them closer to the wall, and Firebird guarded her sloshing cup. "What did she do?"

He shrugged and wrinkled his freckled face. "She commented on my haircut—she and everyone else—but she actually played with it."

Seizing Corey's shoulders, Firebird worked around behind him and pulled him down low enough to examine the base of his neck.

A cloth square, almost invisible against his skin, clung just below his hairline. Firebird tore it off and dropped it on the floor.

Rubbing the bared spot, Corey turned around to her. "Skin patch?"

"Absolutely. That's what got Daley and Tor. You may be fine if we got it off in time, but—"

"I will be fine, Firebird. She wouldn't dare debilitate commissioned officers." Corey's black eyes brimmed with mischief. "Too bad you wasted it. I'd like to see your sister in spots. I wonder what she's saving for you."

"So do I." Firebird tapped one foot. "And I wonder where she's carrying them. Surely not next to her skin."

They'd been working sideways out of the congested area. Firebird broke free, pulling Corey along by his hand. "Watch her if you can. I have to make about six more duty calls."

He leaned down and kissed her cheek. "Good luck, Major. And thanks."

She gave him a quick thumbs-up and then recollected her dignity. Devair

Burkenhamn, the navy's massive first marshal, stood alone a few meters away, nibbling a pastry and watching the richly dressed dancers. He'd been her strategies instructor, hard but fair, a high-common-class officer who treated noble wastlings precisely like the other cadets. One of Netaia's aging few who couldn't tolerate the implant capsules that preserved an appearance of youth—and which a wastling never would need—he wore a fringe of silver hair around the back of his skull, far above her eye level. He was a huge man, all muscle. Firebird still wondered if they'd redesigned the tagwing fightercraft's tight cockpit to let him squeeze inside.

"Sir." She saluted, then raised her goblet toward him. "Good evening to you, and my thanks."

He returned the salute and her smile. "Congratulations, Major. Perhaps later you would dance with your marshal."

"Of course, sir." *Major*—he'd said it! She sipped her punch to keep from grinning foolishly. "I have worked for yesterday for so long, I'm astounded to find myself on the other side of it."

He nodded, looking venerable. "Your mother. Give her my respects."

"I will, sir. And my regards to your family." Small talk. She hated it. She wanted to ask, *Have you accepted my flight-team list?* But tonight wasn't the time.

From behind the marshal's bulk, Phoena stepped up. She tapped his elbow. "I'm glad to have caught you together. Firebird." Phoena nodded a mannerly greeting. Her spectacularly interwoven hair and kaleidocolor gown didn't distract Firebird from the narrowing of her eyes that typically presaged some new cruelty.

It might be nothing, Firebird reminded herself. *Get it over with, Phoena.*

Burkenhamn bowed from the waist. "Your Highness, ever your servant."

"Ah," said Phoena, and the bodice of her gown expanded. Body heat, Firebird knew, created the chromatic changes in the fabric—golds, greens, and intense shades of pink. "Thank you. I have a bothersome problem." She traced saffron colorbursts on a sleeve with one fingertip. "It seems that Lady Firebird might not be eligible to accept her officer's commission after all."

"Your Highness," said Marshal Burkenhamn. "Please explain."

Phoena skewered Firebird with a condescending smile and turned sideways, wedging Firebird out of the conversation. "Oh, it may be nothing. Before I forget, has your daughter's mare had her . . ."

Small talk again. What was she working up to? Firebird studied the back of Phoena's hair as her sister prattled on. Several bright clips held the knots in place, and in a pink one . . .

Firebird spotted the patches, hidden precisely where Phoena's habitual primping gesture would put them in her reach, in the lowest hair clip. They looked loose enough to fall free without attracting attention. Gingerly Firebird raised a hand.

At that moment Phoena spoke her name again. "At any rate, it seems there has been suspicion cast on my little sister concerning the deaths of Lord Alef Drake and a commoner named Jisha Teal, last year at about this time."

Momentum carried Firebird's hand forward to pluck out the patches, but her breath caught as Phoena's words registered. Suspicion? What had been found? One patch stuck to her fingers as Phoena stepped back to include her again. Inspired even through her dread, Firebird dropped all the patches into her punch cup and swirled it, remembering one of Phoena's favorite minor indignities.

And Phoena snatched the cup. "Thank you for sharing, Firebird. I was so thirsty." She drank half and then continued. "She and Lord Corey Bowman reported them dead, you'll remember. I'm certain there should be an investigation. I'd have come sooner, Marshal, but decided to save it for tonight. Firebird hates childish pranks, but traditions are important. This seemed an acceptable compromise."

Phoena drank deeply again, but Firebird's moment of revenge was ruined. She felt as if the blood had drained out of her upper body, leaving her with leaden legs and a nonfunctional brain. Because heir limitation was decreed by the Powers, assisting flight was apostasy—a capital crime if the offender belonged to a noble family. If convicted and executed, Firebird would lose her chance to die in battle and redeem herself for eternity. Of course Phoena would save her coup for tonight.

Burkenhamn's massive shoulders pulled back to attention. He bowed again, eyeing Firebird ruefully. "You place it in my hands, Highness?"

Phoena shrugged. "I wouldn't involve underlings in a charge against any member of my family."

"Thank you, Highness. I shall see that all is done for the glory of Netaia."

Phoena curtsied as Firebird clenched her jaw. At that moment His Grace the Trade Minister, Muirnen Rogonin, touched Phoena's shoulder. Nearing sixty, Rogonin had black hair that showed no gray and never would. Fleshy jowls filled out his facial skin and masked any wrinkles his youth implants couldn't arrest.

"Highness, would you honor me with—" His eyes narrowed between folds of flesh. "Highness, are you all right?"

Phoena's entire face was flushing, the shade deepening every second. She touched her left cheek, where a red weal rose visibly, then pulled her finger away as if burned. As she plucked out the pink hair clip, she made a strangled sound and glared at Firebird. "Where are they?" she demanded.

"Oh dear," Firebird murmured as Marshal Burkenhamn extended a solicitous hand to the princess. Another weal was coming up at the base of her throat. "What is it in the air tonight?" Firebird backed away, raising her voice. "Everyone's breaking out!" Nearby heads turned. Someone on Firebird's left snickered.

Phoena threw down Firebird's punch cup, splashing one gawking bystander, and seized Rogonin's arm. Holding a hand over her face, she pulled the duke toward a freshing room.

Firebird saluted Marshal Burkenhamn and then fled back to Corey, while gossip wafted the report of Phoena's humiliation throughout the ballroom.

Firebird and Corey retired outdoors very late. Menarri and Delaira dimly lit the palace grounds, gleaming on the meandering pools and a fayya glade below the colonnade. Along its edge Firebird walked slowly, deep in thought. Every new officer present had congratulated her for scoring on Phoena and wished her luck in the investigation—as had several high commoners, on the sly. Her popularity comforted her.

Proudly she lifted her head, certain that Alef and Jisha had escaped. If Phoena could've reported their arrest, she would have done that—and public suspicion that Firebird had foiled the redjackets would only enhance her legend someday. She honestly didn't think Burkenhamn would order her interrogated. He respected his wastlings. For months, Firebird's commonborn friends had urged her to vanish like Alef and Jisha, but she'd refused. She'd chosen the path of Valor and Pride, Fidelity and Resolve. She wouldn't change her mind now, at the end.

Especially not after yesterday's ceremonies. At last, Netaia had honored her.

Beside a fluted column, Corey vaulted down from the long, bright porch. Firebird silenced thought to listen to the fayya leaves' unending rustle and the *swish-plop* of night-feeding skitters, and joined him. The grassy slope yielded beneath each step, but she kept her shoes on. Although Citangelo's winter would come without her this year, not even for bare feet on the fragrant summer lawn would she dishonor her new dress uniform.

Corey halted under the dark foliage of a fayya tree and turned to gaze down at her. He looked so serious that she almost decided not to go for the stick in her shoe.

But would she have another chance? Leaning forward as if footsore, she reached down and swept up the stick. "Score." She flicked a gold pin on the front of his uniform. "Wake up, Corey."

His mouth crinkled. "Oh, Firebird. That old game."

"Old game," she echoed. "You were glad we'd played it the night Daken Erwin tried to cut you up."

"All right." He reached for her with one hand. "You caught me off guard. Your point. But do you remember the score?"

Oddly, she did. She'd consistently doubled his points over the years at the wastlings' dueling game, but she decided not to remind him. She slid a hand along his shoulder and down one arm, flicking his sleeve stripe. The taller he grew and the more his face matured, the harder she found it to honor that non-romance pact. "Nice suit, Captain. You look your age tonight." Even in midnight shadows, the slick dress fabric gleamed.

Corey didn't seem to be attending. "You too," he murmured absently, staring across the park behind her. "Well," he sighed, "we've arrived, haven't we? 'We who stand on the edge of battle,'" he quoted from the commissioning ceremony. "The victims have come of age. We're ready to be sacrificed, so the others may prosper."

Firebird stepped back, frowning, arms hanging at her sides. "Corey? That's not like you."

He sighed and caught her hand again. "Firebird." She heard unusual sadness in the way he spoke her name. "Usually it's all right. I'd like to go out with a roar, and I'll never need a vanity implant. But . . ." His eyes fixed on the lake again. "I'd rather live. Wouldn't you, really? Marry . . . raise a . . ." He pressed his lips together.

"Family?" she supplied disdainfully.

"Yes," he whispered. He squeezed her fingers, and his gaze came back to hers, uncannily sober for Corey Bowman. "A family, Firebird. I like children."

She stood silenced by the yearning in his voice and a lump that rose in her throat. For an instant, she entertained the forbidden notion. To be represented among those future generations, not merely honored by them, would be sweet. Would their children have had black hair, or auburn. . . ?

She strangled the thought. She couldn't alter heredity. She'd been born an Angelo, not a commoner. A year from now, she would be dead, even if she betrayed her destiny. Why not die heroically instead? That should take her straight into bliss—and history. "Children are for heirs." The words came out more bitterly than she'd intended. She shook herself inwardly, and the mask of self-control settled back into place. "Corey, you're only hurting yourself," she declared. "You know better. And why tonight? Tonight we should just be happy. We did it." She pressed against him, and his hands locked behind her back. A minute later she felt him relax. His familiar, man-scented warmth made her drowsy and comfortable as she rubbed her cheek against the front of his tunic. "Do you know," she murmured after a while, "the one thing I'm going to regret?"

"Mm?" His sharp chin shifted on top of her head. "Now who's doing it?"

She stared over his arm into the distance, toward a starry darkness the garden lumibeams never would touch. "I would've liked to have seen the Federate worlds. Imagine the night sky on Tallis, Corey. Stars everywhere, huge, bright stars. Yellow, red, white . . . Veroh will be a good trip, and farther outsystem than most people ever travel, but the Federacy has so many worlds. I would've liked to have seen them all."

"Of course," he whispered.

"Corey." She slid a hand onto his shoulder. "I do wish . . ."

A flock of nocturnal cardees flew low over the fayya tree, twittering protest at the first pale light appearing over the walls of the palace grounds, and then stillness returned. Firebird held tightly until the melancholy mood passed.

Corey shifted. "Tired?"

"No," she said. "Yes. No." She pushed away. "Let's go in and see if the orchestra has fallen asleep."

CHAPTER 3

VEROH

duo alla rondo
two players alternate carrying the melody

A week after the officers' ball, Firebird reported to Marshal Burkenhamn's office. His aide told her that the investigation had fizzled due to lack of evidence. Phoena's announcement had been a hazing prank after all, a shrewd guess. Burkenhamn apologized personally, but Phoena's influence had earned Firebird's four-ship flight team a place on the first attack wave, a position supposedly assigned at random because of its high risk.

Phoena always was impatient to finish a task, Firebird thought wryly as she ran a spot-checking hand under her tagwing fightercraft's fore wing, one huge golden dart among dozens below the lights of the carrier's number six hangar bay. *But in this case she's only given me what we both wanted.*

Three days after Burkenhamn's apology, Firebird had stared down into the wrinkled red face of a new princess and heir, Kessaree Nyda Laraine Angelo. That infant would live now, and so Firebird must die.

Close behind her, her crew chief in gray coveralls clutched his pocket recorder and called up components for her final checkout. Seventeen minutes remained before launch for attack. The carrier would return to normal space in ten minutes, and in fifteen drop slip-shields over Veroh II.

"Starboard laser cannon," he called.

She caressed the barrel, set close to the fuselage under the fore wing. Finding no external imperfections, she peered into the focusing lens. "Go," she answered, trying to sound detached. Even a mostly honorary first major shouldn't be too excited.

"Shield antennae, particle and slip."

This was it! No longer practice but a check for battle, and she was glad she'd always trained in the way she intended to fight. This felt as automatic as tying back her hair.

She stroked the little projection antennae. They felt secure. "Go," she answered.

"Starboard thrusters."

She moved aft to the second starboard wing, which swept out from the fuselage precisely where the fore wing ended.

The checkout ran perfectly. As she struggled into her life suit just before mounting the cockpit steps, she caught sight of Corey—Captain Lord Corey Adair Bowman—dangling his helmet from one hand and saluting from the stepstand alongside the tagwing behind hers. Mounting the next ladder in line was his brother Daley; behind him, Delia Stele. Firebird waved and climbed aboard, then checked her console.

Seven minutes until launch. . . .

Through the pale blue sky they dropped in final deceleration. The four tagwings made a loose tetra formation on Firebird's main screen, just close enough to support and cover each other. On her display's holographic targeting map, route/risk data for her first assigned target gleamed steadily. Firmly harnessed against her inclined seat, she braced mentally for real combat and gave an order. "Delia, take the generators. Daley, field projectors. Corey, cover me across midline."

The sleek tagwings paired off to strafe the mining colony's support depot, one long squeeze of her side trigger.

A light on her left bluescreen caught her eye—two lights—eight—Verohan interceptors soaring south across the flats, beyond her line of sight but clear marks on her beyond-visual-range BV board. "Twenty-four, we have company," she warned. "Eight bogeys at two-six-six."

An energy-field projector far below and behind exploded, spewing metal fragments into the atmosphere. She gripped her throttle rod as adrenaline made her shout, "Nice shooting, Daley! Now, let's say hello. Pull in. Max shields." She touched a control to extend her energy shields as Corey and Daley pulled in at right and left, low. Delia took the tetra's high slot position.

Firebird concentrated on her BV display, then line-of-sight. The moment the interceptors came into range, they fired laser cannon, but the tagwings' overlapped shields deflected the energy. "Half-eight left . . . now!" directed Firebird. The tagwings looped bubble-down beneath their opposing marks, came up behind, and gave chase. Those old-line atmospheric interceptors, just as awkward as she'd been instructed to expect, split left and right. The Netaian fightercraft followed in loose pairs.

"No cockpit shots," she ordered. "Let them eject if they can. Careful, I don't read particle shields." Every interceptor destroyed cleared the way for the invasion force.

Left hand on the ordnance board, she shot a bull's-eye pattern of ranging bursts while braking to stay above her hindmost enemy's tail. Had the interceptors scattered, she might've had a real fight. These pilots clung together like banam fruit on a tree, keeping their atmospheric shields over-lapped. *All they can really do against better ships*, she reflected, smiling. She fired again. An interceptor fell out of formation, wing shattered on its axis, just beyond the shield overlap that had protected its fuselage.

Just like on the simulator. Still in ideal position, she fired once more. Another interceptor veered away. "Overlap's gone," she called. Corey and Daley took the enemy wingmen, and Firebird watched, satisfied, as Delia scored last. The final interceptor pilot ejected from a smoking craft.

"Now let's finish that depot!" Though her flight gloves dulled the touch, she fingered a star on her inner collar as she brought the tagwing into a tight turnabout. If this went on, she might last long enough to win another pair of the glittering insignia and promotions for her friends.

In her earphone, Delia cried, "I'm right above you, Major!" as she dropped back into slot position of the broad tetra.

Soon the depot was glowing rubble. Firebird circled her team to be cer-tain its warehouses' contents were burning.

At that moment, a voice rumbled in her helmet. "Raptor Phalanx, this is Command and Control. We have a stage one alert. We're confirming three Federate cruisers breaking slip-state just inside Veroh III's orbit. Continue operations."

Squill! she exclaimed silently, dismayed. So much for strategic specula-tion. "Too distant to defend?" And how in Six-alpha had they gotten here so soon?

Something had tripped the hair-trigger watch. With superior Netaian technology and armament, losses had been light. Even Veroh had suffered little damage under the circumstances.

But the Federates' technological edge was assumed in all drills. With the odds more equal, advanced Federate craft against Netaian numbers, the bat-tle could turn grim.

No more mercy shooting. She tried to steel herself. She'd taken her geis at Kessaree's birth, but Delia, Daley, and Corey had no such orders yet. Maybe she could find a way to obey hers and protect them at the same time.

Furthermore, Federate reinforcements couldn't reach this planet for some hours. "Twenty-four, let's take our next target." She touched a cross-program control, sending route/risk data.

"What do we do when *they* get here?" Daley asked.

"Depends where we are. If we can, we'll run for those mountains and lose them in the canyons." A range of glowering pinnacles bordered the red plain. The four golden darts soared toward Firebird's next target. *One more . . . good*, she observed, a weaponry storage dump. They'd burn it before the Federates could use it.

At attack velocity, they covered the distance in minutes. Before surface defenses could get a bead on them, the formation transmuted into a horizontal line. One pass, and those defenses were neutralized. Firebird wheeled the line and returned at ninety degrees from the first pass, targeting three poorly camouflaged armament warehouses.

She ran a loving eye over her control panel. Flying this advanced short-range attack fighter in real combat had been as satisfying as she'd dreamed it would be: watching the horizon spin around her, pressing deep into her seat as ion-drive engines responded to stick and throttle.

Two industrial targets later, Corey spotted them: "Marks at oh-eight-six-five!"

Her BV screen picked them up in another instant. "Roger, Corey. Oh-eight-six-five." Six of them were coming in from Corey's side, two pairs and two loose wingmen. And the speed! These were no Veroh interceptors. "Twenty-four, max shields. Let's run for it." *All we can really do against better ships*, she reflected, pursing her lips. Still at strike speed, her escorts—her friends—roared back into tetra formation. The pinnacles loomed closer, nearly filling Firebird's field of vision, as six ominous pips advanced across her BV board.

In the foremost Federate craft, her opposing strike leader gave an order. "Intercept range, ten seconds. Delta Six, drop out and check on the colonists. Call Med Wing if you have to." One wingman peeled away. Five elegant black Federate intercept fighters streaked on after the Netaians. "Energy wedge. Standard intercept. Commence fire on my mark."

Firebird needed maneuvering speed, but she didn't dare push for it. Once the pursuers came into firing range, only overlapped slip-shields would cover the tagwings' critical spots at engine ports, where the escaping gases' heat warped each single shield. Overlapped flight was slower, but as long as the Federates' lasers were off wavelength from the Netaians' shields, Firebird could hope to turn the counterattackers into prey.

She could see them when she craned her neck, narrow wings perched aft of their long, sleek fuselages, black as jet, flying tight to maximally overlap their shields and firepower. That close, they made a tempting target. She armed a missile and initiated a turn.

They opened fire.

Delia, in high slot position, saw what Firebird could not: All five Federate ships trained their cannon on Corey's fightercraft, at right wing low, where his starboard engine port lay on the unsteady edge of shield overlap. And, incredibly, the shade of those beams began to change.

"Twenty-four," Delia shouted, "they're tuning those lasers! If they hit on our shield wavelength—"

At that instant, Corey's ship exploded with a flash of fusion fire that quickly fell behind.

Delia's anguished voice announced it. "Corey's gone!"

For a moment, Firebird went blind. She couldn't believe or even understand that her best friend had died between two of her heartbeats. She cried denial, though her boards confirmed the gap in formation where Corey had been.

The pursuers roared overhead, gaining altitude, circling tightly to set up for a second kill. The maneuver gave her precious seconds, another chance. She veered back toward the canyons. There, her pilots could split and dodge and maybe trap those Federates.

But why had they overflown? Why hadn't they simply kept firing?

Delta Leader was starbred. Besides his Thyrian ancestors, he descended from Ehretan telepaths who'd reached Thyrica from far north of the galactic plane. Ten seconds ago, a mental shriek had pierced his personal static shields and splintered his concentration. It hadn't originated in his own mind, but in one of those Netaian tagwings.

But that was almost impossible.

He glared at his glowing sensor screens. "Delta Flight, cease fire and pull up."

Normally, he couldn't sense any individual's feelings over that range, even one in emotional extremity. Personality factors must've matched him to this man like a transmitter and a receiver on the same frequency. Even among other Sentinels, he rarely found this kind of connaturality, that deep like-mindedness that led to real brotherhood.

By standing orders for a situation he'd never thought to encounter, he couldn't target that pilot.

But maybe Delta Flight could take him as a resource . . . or even, eventually, a recruit.

He overflew the tagwings and circled high, studying his fleeing enemies through a visual screen skewed far from the horizon by his high-g turn. With most subjects, his best quest pulse over such distances would catch only intense, uncontrolled—

There it was. The lead fightercraft echoed with the anguish he'd sensed.

"We want the number one," he transmitted. "Alive. Delta Three, get high. Relay his catchfield coordinates as soon as I read them. We target the others only if we have to." Another ship veered away, climbing furiously. His compatriots dropped, following in formation as Delta Leader nosed into a precipitous dive.

Firebird's grief became heart-wrenched relief when the Federate fighters pulled up. That turned to terror as they started their second dive.

"Delia, pull into right wing! We need full overlap on those rear shields or we're all dead!"

In close triangle formation, the 24th Flight Team fled for the pinnacles.

Delta Leader plunged groundward, now entirely satisfied as to which Netaian pilot he wanted. *We have a surprise for you*, he thought at his unknowing enemy . . . *mercy*. "Come in high and scatter them," he directed. "Stay with the leader. Chase him out into the open. We'll get a clear fix for the catchfield."

Daley's voice squeaked on the intersquad frequency. "Firebird, they're coming down right on top of us!"

She made a hasty decision just short of the peaks. "Cadence starboard. Go!" One by one, the tagwings sheared under, looping back barely within overlap range. "Heading eight-zero!" she called, and she pulled away at a sharp angle from the pursuers. Her wingmen followed. On the sims, that maneuver would've easily shaken off a pair of Verohan interceptors.

But the Federates kept closing with absolute accuracy. *They're good*, Firebird admitted. Though catching up faster than when they'd taken Corey, they were still holding fire.

Corey . . .

Did they mean to break up her team?

Blast Phoena and her secret project! What a wretched thing to die for—

But it was time. She would give Corey the highest possible tribute and die with him. Her lead position made her the likeliest of a scattered flight team to be chased, especially if she braked for one second. That might help Daley and Delia escape.

"Twenty-four, I'm going to dive. Split nine-zero port and nine-zero starboard on my mark. Maintain full velocity and shake those birds. Get back to the carrier if you can."

"Right, Major," Daley's voice choked.

He knew. He'd take his own geis someday. She kept her voice calm and officerlike. "Daley, you're in charge. Give Carradee . . . my best. Three seconds." She inhaled with a sense of utter unreality. This was only a role, one she'd rehearsed for years. "Go!" she shouted with a plunging, twisting turn away from her wingmen. She cut in her thrust inverters, and her velocity indicator spun down. Daley streaked on to the west, Delia to the east. Once clear of them, she nosed toward the highest pinnacle and shut off her brakes.

Delta Leader smiled behind his visor as the tagwings scattered. "Let the wingmen go," he said.

Firebird checked her display. Good. All four remaining adversaries had locked on to her. Things were happening too quickly now to let her think beyond the moment. At attack speed, her impact should explode her ship and catch theirs in the fireball. She wouldn't feel a thing.

Wait for me, Corey!

She switched off both shielding systems and directed the generator's full output into her engines, accelerating her dive yet more. An alarm light pulsed on her display.

"Delta Three, stand by: point . . . six . . . two, eight, dropping fast. Get him."

A staggering force flattened Firebird against her flight harness. Rattled, she checked her controls. Everything read functional, but she was decelerating hard.

Seconds later, the velocity indicator plunged past zero into the negative range. She was going backward!

Realization slapped her as limp as a dead skitter. Somewhere above, a Federate starship had projected an electromagnetic snare, a catchfield, down into Veroh II's atmosphere. The field had seized her tagwing and was drawing it back into space, toward the Federate ship itself.

She maxed her engines, wrenched the throttle rod in all directions, even tried redirecting her brakes.

Nothing.

She glanced up into pale blue sky and trembled. Her mother's voice spoke from the back of her mind. ". . . If ever it becomes obvious that you cannot avoid being taken prisoner . . ."

Firebird slumped. The packet still lay in her breast pocket.

She hesitated. She'd done everything as ordered, except for that final obedience. It was too late to change her mind. Whether or not there was a bliss, she owed this to Netaia. Her young life had ended.

But with or without the Powers' endorsement, death was a terrible mystery. That blackness seized everything and gave nothing back. She faced it now with a painful abundance of time to consider what she was about to experience.

Irreparable brain damage . . .

There'd be no discomfort. Her mother had promised.

She brought her craft back to the horizontal and shut down its engines, one last act of respect for the tagwing she'd longed to fly into battle. Then she slipped off her right glove and fished out the packet.

She tore off a corner with fumbling hands. Inside, she found a gram or so of tiny white crystals. She hesitated, wishing there were some quicker way to have done with dying. Waiting to fall unconscious would be horrible, each breath a last sweet sip of life. Her handblazer would be hard to reach, though, in the cramped cockpit, and when it came to the choice, that didn't sound any more pleasant.

Wasn't there some escape? Did she really want to die? No! She did not! But capture would be far worse.

Still she waited, not wanting to waste a minute of life if she had only minutes left. The altimeter read higher and higher, and soon she spotted the Federate cruiser against a starry background, looming nearer as the sky darkened. Her ventral screen showed a lone intercept fighter like a black shadow below, circling and slowly climbing. Following her to her doom.

Whoever he was, he'd beaten her.

Stung, she pulled the mask away from her helmet, toasted her unseen adversary with the packet, and tipped the crystals down her throat.

They tasted like salty metal and burned all the way down. With her mask off, the cockpit air already seemed thin. "Done, Your Majesty," she said aloud. Then she bowed her head, shuddered, and breathed slowly.

Nine minutes later, a second catchfield landed Delta Leader in a minor docking bay aboard the Federate cruiser *Horizon*. The space door shuttered closed. Atmosphere swirled in, then techs and carrier crew. Near the inner bulkhead, the golden tagwing rested on another receiving grid.

Eager to face his prisoner eye to eye, he jumped from his ship and hurried to the captured fightercraft. The Netaian hadn't sprung his cockpit. As a deck crewer sprinted alongside and activated the external cockpit release, Delta Leader drew a shock pistol and held it ready.

The bubble swung upward. The hunched shape inside didn't move.

"Unconscious?" guessed the subordinate.

Delta Leader holstered his pistol and leapt up onto the forward triangular wing of the golden dart. Unconscious, he confirmed, and barely breathing. He pulled off the pilot's gold flight helmet.

A long tail of dark auburn hair fell free. This was a woman! He inhaled sharply. White paper fluttered beside her gloved hand. "Call Medical," he cried, grim-voiced. "Suicide attempt."

As the crewer barked into an interlink, he unbuckled the Netaian pilot, lifted her, and jumped down onto the glossy deck, still cradling her against himself, noting the flashing officer's stars, the absence of ID plate, and then her petite, lovely face: small nose, delicate chin, softly flushed cheeks. Brushing soaked auburn hair from her forehead, he knelt and steadied her on one knee. Besides his standing order and the lure of her mental cry, she was a valuable prisoner. This was a high-security matter. He didn't need to hesitate.

Guide me, he prayed hastily. Closing his eyes, he turned inward for his epsilon-energy carrier, then reached out with it to slow her frantically pumping heart as it spread poison through her body. She slipped into tardema-sleep. The medical crew arrived, and he held her there, near death itself, as they readied an ultradialysis unit. One tech cut the heavy outer life suit from her arms and upper chest. He was exquisitely aware of her will, fighting his for the right to escape into the void. The alpha matrix of her personality brushed his own, passionately determined to excel . . . but poised to sacrifice her life.

Two med attendants lifted her out of his arms onto their stretcher, then went to work. Blood-cleansing equipment hissed as it activated. He relaxed his mental stance. The foreign officer rose to normal unconsciousness and her pulse pounded again, rushing poisoned blood to her vital centers but also into four clear catheter tubes at her wrists and her throat, and then into the filtration system. He gripped her forearm. Three meds in yellow tunics watched their instruments. A red light flashed at one corner of the console.

It stopped.

He pulled back his hand. She was out of immediate danger. One attendant turned to him. "She'll need at least an hour on full filtration, sir. We'll take her to the med deck."

Abruptly, weariness caught up with him, and he wondered if the battle had ended. He didn't doubt that the Netaians would be repelled. It was only a matter of time, and maybe soon he could shorten that. Rubbing his face, he said, "Get her under a restraining field before she wakes up. Don't cancel that suicide watch."

Two attendants steered the stretcher away. He stared until the little group disappeared into a corridor.

That face. He knew that woman.

He commandeered an invigorating cup of kass and reported to the command bridge.

"We've taken a prisoner, General Frankin," he announced over a second cup. "First major's insignia. Tried to kill herself when she knew we had her."

"Herself?" echoed General Gorn Frankin, an ebullient acquaintance from Caroli. "They send women on the attack phalanx?"

"They sent this one."

"Took her yourself?"

He nodded.

"I assume you had reason. Do you want to interview her yourself, too?"

"Yes."

That was exactly what he wanted.

SENTINEL

allargando
slowing, increasing volume

As Firebird slowly climbed back to consciousness, she reached out eagerly for sensations, curious about the afterlife. Finally, she'd put her ordeal behind her.

The muffled sounds around her seemed odd, though. Something swished past quickly. Something else clattered. And she ached everywhere, particularly her shoulders. If this was an afterlife, it wasn't the bliss she hoped she'd just earned.

She tried to bring up a hand to rub her eyes, but her arm wouldn't move. Cautiously she opened her eyes and saw a low white ceiling. Something started to beep softly.

Did she . . . could she lie in a restraining field, with a facial-movement sensor?

Unfamiliar medical-looking machines surrounded her. A med attendant gowned in soft yellow walked over and reached down out of Firebird's view. The beeping stopped. Her left leg jerked involuntarily as the restraining field released her.

"Sit up, please, Major," directed the attendant in a vowel-heavy accent. This was a Federate ship!

The attendant supported her elbow as Firebird pushed up off the hard mattress. Walls wheeled around her. She sat still and let her head droop. While waiting for the bulkheads to settle down, she struggled to recall being taken aboard. How could she be here? She'd done everything as ordered. When she swallowed, her throat still burned. She reached up to touch it and found a short, rough strip of tape on the side of her neck . . . then another, at the other side, over her carotid arteries. Numbly she glanced at her wrists. They too were bandaged with tiny, almost invisible strips.

She guessed then what they'd done to her. She'd waited too long to open the packet. This was her fault.

The attendant stood in front of her. "Do you want something to eat?"

Firebird nodded. She waited warily on the edge of the bed, hoping the attendant would leave for half a minute. There must be something in this medical suite that was long and sharp and deadly. Horrified by the implications for Netaia of her capture, she must finish what she'd attempted.

But the woman turned to a servo on the nearest wall, assembled a tray, and handed it to Firebird. She accepted a hot cup of some sort of broth and several soft objects with a texture between bread and crackers. She ate slowly, still a little shaky, and cautious for aftereffects of the poison—which a victim generally didn't need to know, and she'd neglected to research. The broth soothed her throat.

"Enough?" asked the attendant.

Firebird handed back the empty tray. "Thank you."

"All right. Relax for a bit. I need to watch your vitals."

Firebird slumped back down onto the hard surface. She had only two options, suicide or escape. But how? A lean, gray-uniformed man stood at the sick bay's closed door. His breast insignia dispelled her last doubt. That stretched-out parallelogram, with its long red and blue triangles set back to back and edged in gold, was the Federate slash.

Powers help me, she begged. *Get me out!*

Delta Leader strode up a narrow corridor of the starship, carrying his recall pad under one arm. The meds had demanded a two-hour wait for the Netaian major's systems to clear the last toxin. To make any difference in the battle still raging below, he needed to begin soon.

His fellow pilots hadn't quite believed this call-up to Veroh, but he had. After studying the Netaian Electorate in action, he'd predicted this confrontation.

But not the connatural prisoner lying in sick bay. No data on her would go on record yet. He used a special secure shorthand to jog his trained memory. For deep class-three access work, he must first establish an alpha-matrix framework—decode her systems of mental association. Then he could collect every shred of useable intelligence.

But he already guessed that her personality patterns would prove starkly familiar. That cry of grief couldn't have reached him unless she were utterly connatural with him, with her mental functions closely matched to his own. This would be a quick, efficient frameworking.

He passed six pilots wearing Carolinian khaki. They turned and stared. Accustomed to stares, he searched his recollections for clues to his prisoner's identity. Their meeting must've seemed inconsequential. His visual memory was excruciatingly accurate. . . .

As he turned up the medical corridor, a young woman's face finally filled the blank. She wore a dust-smudged cadet's uniform and stood flanked by arrogant, gaudily dressed guardsmen. Though her raised eyebrows and slightly pursed lips suggested meekness, her emotions flamed with defiance.

He frowned. Surely this wasn't his prisoner. That cadet wouldn't be an officer only one year later.

But she'd been the queen's daughter. Entitled, maybe, to preferential promotion, the same way he was as a Master Sentinel.

Whoever she was, Frankin waited on the bridge for information.

The guard in gray finally turned aside for a moment.

Firebird rolled off the bed and sprang toward the door's opening panel, but her legs wouldn't move quickly.

The guard seized her wrist. "None of that, Major," he said firmly. "Unless you'd rather be put on muscle relaxants." He nodded at the yellow-gowned med, who reached for an intramusc injector.

"No . . . that won't be necessary." Firebird's voice shook, though she tried to control it. "No."

Just as the guard let her go, the door slid open. Firebird lunged. She made it through, and she'd almost dodged the first man outside in the passway when her legs buckled, utterly nerveless this time.

The lead Federate caught her by an arm and a shoulder and steadied her upright. "No," he said softly. "Don't do that."

Looking up into startlingly blue eyes, she had an instant of mindless, delighted recognition. It was the Thyrian guard!

Then she heard Vultor Korda's voice echo in the silent corridor. *Wing Colonel Brennen Caldwell. . . . Don't even get close enough to recognize him. . . .*

Firebird cast a frantic glance up the passway. Two guards in Tallan ash gray stood with shock pistols trained on her.

"Come back inside," Caldwell ordered. Though she had no intention of obeying, her legs walked her back through the sick bay's metal door. Korda had explained, but never demonstrated, Sentinel voice-command.

The door slid shut, closing her inside with Wing Colonel Caldwell, the med attendant, and her original Tallan guard. She braced herself against the bed where she'd wakened. This couldn't be happening!

Caldwell set a recall pad on a lab bench, keeping his other hand slightly upraised. He still wore the vivid midnight blue of Thyrian forces. On his right shoulder, as in the hologram, she saw the eight-rayed gold star. When he lowered his free hand, she felt the ethereal cords on her body drop away.

She clenched her own shaking hands. Did he remember her, too?

He dipped his head slightly. "Wing Colonel Brennen Caldwell, of Thyrica."

She avoided his stare. Korda had warned, *Guard your eyes! A Sentinel can use them as doors into your mind.*

After she'd stood still for almost a minute, silently begging that inanimate door to open once more, he said, "Please sit back down, Major. I must ask you some questions." His vowels sang strangely in her ears.

Standing stiff legged, she compressed her lips.

The guard paced back to the door and stood there unmoving—probably trained not to hear, either.

Caldwell raised his hand a few centimeters. "Sit down, please," he repeated.

Though she tried to stay upright, her body obeyed him again.

Colonel Caldwell sank onto a stool that the med assistant slid up to him. "Now," he said, "sit back, Major . . ." He hesitated. "Angelo?"

Firebird glanced at his face, horrified.

"Lady Firebird," he said softly. "We've met."

Powers, no! If he knew her, soon he'd know everything. Her heart pounded, a great weight jumping in her chest as she perched on the edge of that hard bed. That bed with its restraining field . . . and even as she watched, the med readied a life-signs cuff, to monitor her body's responses to interrogation procedures. There'd been a short but tough class on this kind of thing in her senior year.

"How long have you been in service, Your Highness?" Caldwell pushed his stool back half a meter, a gesture she supposed was intended to calm her. "Last year I thought you were only a cadet."

It seemed a harmless, even friendly question, but she could guess at his motive: get her talking, start her remembering things. She shook her head.

"I see."

She eyed his booted feet, planted firmly but casually on the deck. Soon they'd move, and then it would start.

"Sit back, then, Highness," he said, but he didn't command. She found that she could stay upright, so she did, clenching her jaws and gripping her thighs.

"Lady Firebird, please. I'd prefer not to force your defenses."

"I'll give you nothing willingly." She swallowed hard.

The booted heels came together under his knees. "Then sit back," he said, regaining that queer tone of voice, and she swung around to recline. Immediately she found herself frozen again. "The restraining field is only to help me keep my mind on my work," he intoned as the med secured the life-signs cuff around her arm. "I'm not going to harm you. Don't be afraid, Major."

If only she were just a major! She could move only her head. She turned it away.

After another minute's wait, he spoke again. "How long have you been in service, Lady Firebird?"

She pressed her eyes shut. This was the real thing, a terrifying variable Vultor Korda had never introduced in his classes. She called the difficult etude into her mind and focused on it with performance intensity, waiting with the fringe of her attention for that revolting, prickly feeling to begin.

But Vultor Korda had barely started Sentinel training. Brennen Caldwell had won a master's star. Vast weight pressed her toward the deck, driving chinks in her defenses. She accelerated the etude, making it harder to follow, demanding more concentration.

Unexpectedly, the weight lifted. "Someone has breached you before this."

"What?" escaped through her clenched teeth.

"Who trained you in access resistance?" When she tightened her jaw muscles, he went on. "I'm sorry for your sake that they did. That will only make this more uncomfortable."

She stared at a metal ceiling panel. "I have a conscience."

"You've satisfied any reasonable conscience. You tried to crash into a mountain. Then you poisoned yourself. You followed orders, Major Angelo. How long have you been in service?"

She lay stubbornly silent.

"All right," he said softly. "It's your duty, of course. Keep me out for as long as you can. Although . . . it would be more comfortable for you if you'd look this way."

She shut her eyes tightly.

The weight fell onto her again. She bound herself round with a supreme effort of concentration. For long, desperate minutes she felt like a stone on the seashore, trying to hold back a tide that rose swiftly to become a storm surge. She was drowning in darkness, terrified to breathe.

A wave fell that was sharp and warm. She ducked beneath it, rolling inward and aside, and gasped for breath. It fell again, tumbling her head-long. She flailed in the deep. Again. This time, a current propelled her toward rippling light and the piercing sense of another person's presence. She gasped, recognizing her peril. The Sentinel had breached her mind's outer defense. But she still might evade him. She called into her mind her most compelling composition—Iarla's song—but uncannily, her memory sprinted down the long stairway from her practice room toward the electoral chamber.

He'd taken it there. She fled outdoors, toward the gardens, but her thoughts shifted again, to the military, to her commissioning ceremony. She cowered inside the brass band's music.

The Sentinel forced her awareness wide open. Huge, long-faced Devair Burkenhamn bent to pin the second ruby star to her collar, shook her hand, and presented her Academy certificate. She read and reread the special commendation, deeply gratified. At one corner was lettered the commissioning date.

The vision vanished. Limp and disoriented, but shivering with indignation, she roused herself.

Her tormentor exhaled. "You realize I cannot go on that way. Surface access is gentler, but as you see, it can be complex and time-consuming. I have orders of my own."

She looked hastily away from his face. He wore no holster, but a glance at his left wrist confirmed that he—like the big Tallan guard—was armed. Korda had told them about the Sentinels' ceremonial weapon, the crystace.

She was doomed to fail, to betray her people. All of them. A tear rolled from her eye. She couldn't wipe it away, and it trickled toward her ear.

"Perhaps you'd answer this question for anyone, Your Highness. What do your friends call you?"

"Firebird," she choked. "And you had it right before. It's 'Lady,' not 'Highness.'" He brushed away the tear, the touch startling her into volunteering, "It's an awkward name."

"Not so awkward," he said soberly. "I'm called Brennen, or Brenn. Would you do that? Even though . . . this is my duty?"

She wished the outworlder would treat her like an enemy, so she could hate him more deeply. "You must be joking," she grumbled.

"No, Firebird."

Though she stared at the ceiling, from the corner of her eye she saw him take up a stylus and reach for that black recall pad he'd laid down. "You have courage," he said as he wrote. "I respect that."

She swallowed a trace of salt water that had run into her throat.

"Relax now. I will go gently if you'll let me."

She turned her head and tensed up.

He sighed softly. "All right, then. Charna, please dim the light."

The med waved at a panel. She seemed to vanish, leaving only a small luma burning behind Caldwell's left shoulder. Nearer and stronger drew the alien presence, pounding Firebird's awareness like a falling torrent. Inexplicable lights flashed in the dark sick bay. She flung herself against them, trying to fight her way free, to awareness of anything but that invader, but bit by bit he beat down her resistance until all thought was pinned and restrained.

His voice seemed to come from inside her. "Open your eyes." She could no more disobey than cease to exist. The shadowy ceiling reappeared.

"Watch my fingers," he directed softly. Two fingers of his left hand hovered over her face. They seemed to shine in the dim light as he swung them slowly across her field of vision, and back, back once more, then far to one side, and back again. When abruptly he dropped them, her dazed glance was snared by his eyes.

They were brilliant, azure blue. Her last defenses crumbled like sea-walls of sand.

For several minutes, she felt only pressure. Then her mind raced out of control, dizzying and sickening her, first to the Planetary Naval inventory, then ship by ship all that she knew about their armament and defensive hardware. Schematics and illustrations and memories of qualifying flights spun by. She'd been allowed to study most of them. Wastlings didn't survive to face . . . this.

It stopped. The Sentinel turned aside, and she was herself again, exhausted by useless resistance. How could she stop him now? He wrote rapidly on his pad, then touched a final panel. Addressing a wall interlink, he said, "Transmitting." The recall pad ticked an ominous rhythm. Her heart sank. She urged her bruised memory toward Vultor Korda's special session. He'd taught them to concentrate on nothings, blank their minds of anything that truly mattered. If only she'd known nothing about—

As the thought rose, her interrogator seized it. He homed on Dr. Nella Cleary, the co-workers D'Stang and Parkai, and Phoena's passionate calls for the Electorate to support her secret project. Firebird struggled to break the Sentinel's control. She writhed against his restraining field. "No," she pleaded.

When at last he told the med to bring up the room light, she felt as limp as if she'd flown a mission helmetless and unharnessed. He left her under guard to sleep for a while, and returned a few hours later with a small breakfast.

He wasn't settling for the data it would take to win today's battle. He wanted all that she knew.

Humbled but rested, Firebird was freshly determined to resist, knowing now that she couldn't succeed by strength. She relaxed her defenses and let him pass through, watching from a distance as he called back memories of electoral Obediences and secret meetings.

When he moved her focus toward their discussions of planetary defense, she began her resistance. She called up the passionate *intermezzo* of an orchestral suite she loved, bass, tenor, and treble strings soaring together like the skyward rise of sweet flight. Sensitized to his focal point, she felt him touch the music. Effortlessly it swept him along with her, back to neutral ground.

He withdrew roughly.

Disconcerted, she shook loose of the music and the warmth she'd sensed as he flew alongside her. When she could think clearly again, she opened her eyes.

He'd slid his stool back several meters. "Very good." His voice, though not angry, sounded tired and peeved. "You surprise me." He stared at her for quite a while without attempting access again. Then he shifted his stool. "Mind access almost invariably causes revulsion, even nausea, and a clear sense of foreignness. Do you feel those signs?"

Recalling the sessions with Vultor Korda, she grimaced. "No. None of them."

He made a few aimless-looking marks on the recall pad, set down his stylus, then scooted closer and raised his fingers again. "Watch," he commanded.

But she'd finished cooperating. He took no more information on Netaia's main bases until he'd exhausted her again, and then he scanned her mind like a data stack, without drugs or intimidation, and for all her resentment she was glad he didn't need them, for he could have terrified her. Surely by now he'd discovered her irrational fear of injecting instruments, so commonly used by the redjackets and in Netaian interrogation. Firebird's efforts to desensitize herself had only made it worse. She guessed the sick bay's compartments held dozens of the ghastly things.

He soothed instead, flooding her raw nerves with warmth that carried a faint, smoky-sweet savor. Vultor Korda's mental touch had sickened her. This felt like being plunged into a warm ocean permeated with incense.

Forced backward and forward in memory, she lost track of time. At some point, as he sat writing on his recall pad, she tried to guess what a Sentinel could've been and done in the Planetary Navy and the advantages it would've given Netaia.

"I wish you were Netaian," she groaned, meaning nothing disloyal.

"And I wish you were Thyrian. Look this way."

At the next respite, he shocked her with the suggestion that she ask for asylum. Netaia never offered haven to military prisoners. Evidently the Federacy followed a different prisoner-of-war protocol, because he pressed the suggestion four more times. Eventually he switched off his notes and leaned against the lab bench. "I'm sorry, Lady Firebird. Forcing a mind is tiring for both involved."

It was over, then. Over . . . and she'd survived it. She had never felt so ashamed.

He touched a control, and the restraining field collapsed. She stretched stiff joints and muscles.

"I will no longer listen in on your thoughts. You are a sovereign being, and I'm sworn to honor your privacy except when ordered otherwise."

Yesterday, being called "sovereign" would've made Firebird smile. She glanced at the door guard, then faced Caldwell quietly, miserably.

"You should also know," he continued, "that of all the people I have accessed for the Federacy, I've never met a person of your abilities who was so determined to throw away her life. Who exactly did you mean to die for, Lady Firebird?"

An intelligence officer, offering sympathy? She clenched her hands. "I was born to serve the holy Powers. That is our way."

Rotating his stool, he set his recall pad on the lab bench behind him, and then he said somberly, "You've questioned their existence for years. You certainly don't love them."

Firebird glared. Unfair! He knew all her doubts now, all her weaknesses. "They require obedience. Not faith. Definitely not love. They rule through us."

His voice softened. "You intended to die for something you don't love?"

No, not sympathy. He was still interrogating. "It was for Netaia," she said angrily. "To keep from . . . this." *Finish your job, Sentinel. Dispose of me.*

"I understand that. Not your allegiance to gods you don't believe in."

She fingered the tiny red scar that had already formed on her wrist. "Then you probably have no religion, sir."

He raised a dark eyebrow. Then she remembered his ancestry, and the "mendicants" who'd fled Ehret's destruction.

"I'm glad you failed." *To die*, she understood. He still held his stylus in one hand. He tapped the lab bench. "You could still be a help to us. And to yourself."

Firebird refused to react. She didn't want asylum. She was Netaian; she was Angelo. "I have no hostage value, Colonel. I am 'geis,' to be finished. They gave me a death order when I dropped to fifth in the succession."

"Why?" he demanded.

"Because I'm a—"

"Why, by all that's sacred to either of us, do your people kill extra heirs? Why not simply disinherit them?"

"Oh. Now I see what you're asking." She clenched both fists in her lap. This was an unexpected privilege. She'd never hoped for the freedom to explain this as she truly saw it, especially to an enemy officer. It certainly wasn't current intelligence. "We call it a religious obligation, but it didn't start that way. About two hundred years ago, a pair of younger heirs—disinherited under the old custom—led an uprising that nearly succeeded. They were popular," she said, raising her chin, "unlike the ruling regime. The Coper Rebellion was a blot on our history." *Our official history, anyway.* "After it was quelled, the custom was changed. By electoral decree, which gave it the Powers' endorsement. We punish some crimes to the second and third generation. This one, apparently . . . forever."

He shook his head.

Her hopes had died, but her loyalty hadn't. "Flying in a combat squadron was one of my life dreams, Colonel, but I was assigned to the first attack wave to die. First line, right into the defenses, is a common use of wastlings when they have us to spend. If we succeed, we win lasting acclaim. If not . . ." She shrugged. "We die well. 'Only as one obeys at the highest cost to oneself,'" she quoted the Disciplines, "'can one escape the Dark that Cleanses and go straight on to bliss.'"

He frowned, but his eyebrows lifted as if he pitied her.

"Besides," she muttered, "no drone can take out defenses as effectively as a trained wastling pilot."

Bowing his head, he steepled his fingers. Somewhere nearby, a faint mechanical hum changed pitch. "Would you like kass?" he asked.

Firebird shook her head. He touched a control above a servo cubby beside his recall pad. A minute later he pulled out a steaming cup, drained it, and keyed for another. She wrinkled her nose at the Tallan tonic's strong, bitter smell.

"We cannot ignore Netaia any longer," he said. "We need someone who can advise us, who understands Netaian mindset and policies."

"You know everything I do now. What more do you want?"

"I know what you've seen and done and felt recently," he agreed, setting down his cup. "But the will that controls your decisions is not mine to direct. I don't even understand it.

"As we face each other now, the Federacy might respond to a situation one way, while your electoral regime might do something completely different. You could anticipate them. That might help us avoid costly mistakes. Unnecessary deaths," he added.

"What are you suggesting?"

"That you advise us, Lady Firebird. Your loyalty is to your people, not the Electorate."

"I can't betray either of them." She turned away, grimacing. "As if I hadn't already. If Netaia is destroyed in this war, one Netaian will be responsible."

"You don't understand at all, if you believe we would do that. We will never destroy a people . . . not even in war," he added after a pause she understood too well. Shamed by all she'd guessed about Nella Cleary's basium research, she shook her head.

"Are you aware of the greed and deception and the monolithic arrogance that has surrounded you all your life?"

Firebird's cheeks flushed. He might've been quoting her own stunned thoughts when she heard her first suppressed backroom ballad.

Actually, he'd probably done just that.

"Changing that regime could bring freedom and advancement to many Netaians, whatever their history. But, Firebird, I understand your reluctance—if not your actions." He walked away, hands clasped behind his back. "Maybe in time you'll reconsider."

She couldn't keep still. "You're speaking of my family, Colonel. I chose to accept what I was born to become. What do you know about that kind of honor? You're Federate."

"Federate I am," he said softly, "but first, I am something else."

The concept shocked her. Did these Thyrians put their religion before their government?

"Under normal circumstances," he said, "you might have been held under cold stasis until hostilities end, but I wish to treat you differently. As I said, I'm willing to sign asylum papers. Let them be under another name, if you can't come to us openly. Let them be temporary, if you aren't ready to commit yourself. But you need time. You cannot make such a vital choice without adequate information."

Firebird gripped the bed's metal edge. "Thank you, sir," she insisted, "but I still want no more than death with honor. I'll be glad to have it over with."

He drew up sternly. "That's a lie."

"That is obedience," she snapped. "I'm a criminal now."

"You've done nothing wrong," he argued. "If you won't accept asylum, I have to lock you down. I'm sorry. The brigs on this ship are even smaller than the cabins. But you will be anonymous. I can do that for you. Try not to think like a wastling for a few weeks."

She glared. "Are you listening to me think?"

A smile softened his eyes and then vanished. "No. It's an unmistakable sensation, and I don't think you'll forget it. But I'll never force access on you again, unless security is again at stake."

Maybe. But obviously, here as in the electoral chamber, he read her emotions like a scanbook. At every change of her mood, he responded.

"You suggested another name." She sat rigidly, aware that she'd lost another battle. "Make it a common one."

He curled his fingers under his chin. "Marda," he said softly. "No. Mari. Popular, but pretty enough to suit you." He dropped his hand and let his glance linger. "You like it."

She frowned at the door guard, a new one.

"He's heard nothing," Caldwell said. "Now choose a solid Netaian surname. You'll be a political refugee, I think."

Firebird lowered her voice. "Sir, I'm no refugee. I'm a prisoner of war."

He looked at her steadily. "Would you prefer that status?"

She couldn't believe the Federacy offered a choice . . . or was this special treatment from Wing Colonel Caldwell? Netaia kept its war prisoners on subsistence rations, or else had medics cold-stase them. Civilian prisoners, especially political ones, could be transferred to better quarters.

And she was so tired.

"No," she murmured, staring at the deck tiles. "I wouldn't. I . . . appreciate this."

"Then First Major Lady Firebird Angelo," he said softly, "has just vanished."

With a promise of anonymity her only remaining possession, Firebird stepped into a shipboard holding cell about two strides across and watched another dark door slide shut. Sick bay staff had exchanged her cobalt blue shipboards and ruby officer's stars for a green worker's coverall. A servitor's uniform.

As the tide of battle turned over Veroh, Firebird fell onto a rock-hard cot, curled into a fetal ball, and cried bitterly.

CHAPTER 5

MARI

meno mosso
a little less quickly

With a full division of the Federate fleet defending Veroh and a suddenly heavy string of losses, First Marshal Burkenhamn elected the route of discretion and recalled his forces. Firebird wasn't told, but she guessed it. Within a day, another uniformed Sentinel released her from her cell. Anyone who noticed them saw only a small worker-class woman with a long auburn braid that hung over her green coverall and a dark-haired Thyrian who followed protectively.

An atmospheric shuttle, a flattened oval with stubby delta wings, lay against *Horizon* like a yeast bud on its underside. A lift shaft dropped Firebird and her escort from the cruiser's lowest level into a shuttle corridor. They followed a waist-high trail of tiny red lumas to a private cabin.

The Sentinel, First Lieutenant Jonnis Mercell, secured the lock and waved her to an isolated window seat. Mercell looked younger than Colonel Caldwell, with a round face and curly hair. Eyeing his four-rayed star insignia and wondering how their talents differed, she buckled a black harness across her lap and shoulders. Shortly, their shuttle and four others pulled clear of *Horizon* and drifted toward Veroh's main settlement, Twinnich.

Ten flights of sleek black intercept fighters and a trio of tiny messenger ships escorted the shuttles. As they glided toward the red plain, Firebird withdrew into a contemplative haze and stared out the viewport. Her mind and memories still felt raw, almost bruised.

And what about Daley and Delia? Had they been imprisoned too, or killed, or were they on their way home?

As for Corey, at least he'd died instantly. He'd never had to kneel before the electors, between two redjackets, and receive the hated geis. Her chin quivered at that humiliating recollection. Her chest ached with grief.

Jon Mercell leaned toward the oblong window panel. "There." He pointed. "That would be Twinnich."

She followed his gesture, out and down, as the shuttle banked. Twinnich sparkled like bright children's blocks scattered around a cylindrical bin. A slight movement of Mercell's hand focused her attention back inside the cabin. His tunic's deep blue sleeve had risen far enough to reveal one end of a weapon sheath.

He reached across casually to pull the sleeve down and covered the crystace.

Once again she heard Vultor Korda's voice.

"Hollow handgrip, activator stud. Ehrite crystal inside the grip." The slouched little man had straightened enough to sketch on his teaching board with one fingertip. "The crystal is priceless, and even crystallography hasn't explained the chemistry. Imbedded in the handguard is this sonic mechanism. You can hear it if you're close. Like one of those little bugs that flies into your ears . . ." He appeared to grope for the name.

"Bloodletter," Daley offered from his seat behind Corey.

"Yes. Sounds like that. Now, do all you children know why ice floats?"

Corey rolled his eyes.

Korda didn't miss a beat. "That's right. It's lighter than liquid water. Less dense. The molecular bonds in an ice crystal expand when it freezes. Activate a crystace and the same thing happens, only more dramatically. As a certain resonant frequency is sounded, the crystalline bonds lengthen along their beta and gamma axes, and you've suddenly got a crystal as long as your arm, three fingers wide, and with two cutting surfaces exactly one atom thick at the edge. That's sharp."

"So you need a twinbeam blazer," suggested Corey. "Sir," he added, imitating Korda's unflattering tone.

"Hardly. The refractive properties of ehrite scatter cohesive laser waves into harmless beams of light."

"Where are they made?" Delia twisted a blond curl around her ring finger.

"They're not. The Ehretans brought them. Apparently the crystace was invented as a shipboard weapon before the Ehretans developed variable-power energy guns."

Firebird spoke up. "Does the crystal have fracture planes? How can you fight a man carrying one?"

"You can shoot him before he knows you're there."

"Anything else?"

"You might try a shock pistol if you're fast, or a sonic disruptor. But for that, your chance of tuning in the resonant frequency is about as good as hitting one of your moons with a rock. The pitch varies from crystal to crystal."

Speaking of shock pistols . . .

Firebird glanced down to Mercell's holster and confirmed that he carried one of those instead of a blazer. They suspected she'd try to escape, and they were determined not to kill her if she did.

"This'll be your defense base, then?"

"For a small force."

"What about the fleet?"

He flicked one hand in a dismissive gesture. "Sorry. Can't discuss that."

Not that she'd expected it. "Then why are you holding me planetside?"

"Colonel Caldwell wants you there."

That sounded out of character for an intelligence officer. Surely his job was finished. "Don't tell me he's giving orders."

Mercell half smiled. "He is now. They've given him command of the groundside peacekeeping force."

Shocked speechless, she stared out the window again.

A command. They'd rewarded him well.

The shuttle touched down in a shady half-dome landing pod. Mercell let the other passengers debark, then led her through a clear-roofed passage onto a walkway that swept them toward the central tower. Inside, the complex was aging under colonial neglect. Derelict papers and containers, probably dropped in the initial terror of the Netaian attack, were everywhere. Even the tower had a shabby, ill-cared-for atmosphere, as though people who worked or lived there hoped soon to collect their fortunes and move on.

A pitted steel elevator door ground open. The cubicle held a silent old couple wearing shapeless gray coveralls, and two boys midway through their teens in torn and faded short pants and sweat-stained shirts. Firebird stared at the door as the others left two by two. Finally, the door opened on the fifth floor below ground. Mercell touched her shoulder.

A battered brown administration desk stood in this tiled passway. Two men in limp blue uniforms, one tanned and reed-thin with a long, sour face, the other pale skinned and only slightly heavier, slumped behind it. As the elevator grated shut, the pale man snatched a scan cartridge from a tri-D viewer's program port. His darker partner hurried around in front of the desk, carrying a camera recorder and a recall pad in sun-spotted hands.

"Mari Tomma?"

Firebird nodded stiffly, noting as she did that the detention guards avoided approaching the Sentinel too closely. She could sympathize.

The dark man glanced down at his recall pad while she eyed his name-plate, which read Tryseleen. Like the underground passway, he seemed to be aging, declining under a too-long tour of duty. "We didn't get her rank or status in your transmission, Lieutenant."

"She has none."

She envied the Sentinel's ability to lie so smoothly.

Tryseleen took her right hand by her wrist, spread her fingers, and held it against the recall panel. His tan, callused hands scratched hers.

"Mari Tomma." The pale-skinned guard grabbed his colleague's camera and pressed the exposure release without warning. "Have I seen you before?"

Her heart sank. Had she been recognized again? Braiding her hair had been the only feeble disguise she could manage with materials at hand. She studied the grimy floor while Tryseleen finished tapping side panels on the registry. Then he handed it to her for confirmation.

She and Colonel Caldwell had orchestrated a careful harmony of truth and invention. This registry listed her name as Mari Aleen Tomma. That, of course, was wrong. Birthplace Citangelo, Netaia III, Netaia Systems (Independent)—correct. The age looked wrong, but she'd forgotten the conversion factor into Federate annual units. She skipped height and weight to confirm her alleged offense, which had been listed as "political." That wasn't so far afield. But the baldest untruth was her military rank, where Colonel Caldwell had entered N/A.

She nodded.

The short man snatched back his registry pad and strode off down the corridor's left branch. It took Firebird a moment to realize she was expected to follow.

This underground cell had mottled gray walls and smelled vaguely stale. The guard shut her in without instructions, leaving her to examine a network of blemishes that stained the gray floor. At least here she could take several steps. She tried the cot and found it slightly softer, too. Cautiously she lay back and gazed up at a cracked gray-green permastone ceiling.

Were the Powers utterly powerless? This was completely unjust. How could one battle shatter her dreams, kill her dearest friend, and reward her interrogator with the command of a peacekeeping force?

In a stark but private bunk room twelve stories above the detention center, Brennen Caldwell sipped from his half-empty kass cup, grimaced, and thumped the cup onto his desk. It had gone as cold as Thyrian rain.

How long had he stared at that wall?

He cleared away mental images that had held him hypnotized, pushed back his stool, and spun it to face out into the bunk room. Part of the inner-tower security quarter, it had no window, though the walls had been painted off-white to reflect as much light as possible. On the only furnishing other than this data desk, a low cot, his midnight blue duffel lay open.

He should unpack and then stow it to keep moving, keep from staring like a night-slug. A leg muscle twanged as he stepped off the stool.

Only a small, clear packet remained at the bottom of the carryall. He frowned. Evidently he'd unpacked so mechanically he'd forgotten. Through the packet's wrap, gold gleamed. Brennen focused a flicker of epsilon energy into one hand and called the packet to his fingers, then rubbed it thoughtfully. Years ago on Planetfall Day, the quiet commemoration of his Ehretan ancestors' arrival on their world of exile . . .

. . . His memory shifted. His older brother, dark hair still uncombed at breakfast, stood over him as Brennen fumbled to unwrap a small package. (A glimmer of little-brother adoration glowed, and the grown-up Brennen savored it. He hadn't let it pass his trained emotional control in years.) The medallion fell free, a bird of prey plunging with wings swept back almost far enough to touch each other. Delighted, young Brenn held it up in the bright light of his mother's kitchen. On an impulse he flung it high and called, "Fly!" The golden bird hovered for a moment over his outstretched hand. His mother covered her mouth. His father blinked rapidly. "Put that down!" his brother exclaimed. "You can't do that!" The medallion clattered onto the table. . . .

Both brothers had tested for epsilon potential three autumns later, though at twelve Brennen was much younger than the usual applicant. Tarance had tested respectably, particularly in carrier strength, but Brennen was inducted into college on the spot.

: .·. Brennen, slightly older, sat with Master Keeson in college. Head back in a comfortable chair, he struggled to focus static from a tightly modulated epsilon wave between emotion and his awareness. The target sentiment: that burning ache of Tarance's rejection. . . .

Brennen set the medallion on a corner of the gray Verohan data desk. Tarance had abandoned their mutual ambition to travel the Federacy, had gone into psi medicine and bonded a wife of appropriate family, while Brennen finished his schooling. Graduating early, Brennen had risen through the lower ranks of Thyrian forces and then vaulted into Federate service. Before Brennen won the Federacy's Service Crest at Gemina, Tarance had fulfilled a higher obligation. He'd fathered three children, fresh heirs to their small but ancient family's holy promises.

Brennen's own romantic dream, of bonding the perfectly connatural woman within a week of finding her, had faded when he hadn't found her among the women near his age in the starbred families. His enthusiasm had shifted to his career as his twenties passed.

He touched the medallion's beak. It pricked, even through its wrapper. He wore no jewelry but his master's star, but he'd carried this memento wherever the Federacy sent him.

His data desk still displayed a page of pale blue characters on a deeper background. He shut it down.

As on that morning with Tarance, how life could change in an instant! Guarding his emotional threshold, he let the new memory return.

. . . Body steady, mind focused for work, he sat aboard *Horizon* with his prisoner humanely restrained. Ignoring her painful terror, he focused his carrier, made the breaching plunge . . . and failed. Astonished, he made a second effort, then a powerful third.

Braced for suffocating otherness, he found only warmth. As he worked his carrier deeper, her presence grew even more compelling. The interrogation had taken hours to complete, hours, deep in that tantalizingly connatural matrix. . . .

He'd never anticipated this, not even from the power and appeal of her mental cry over Veroh. Her new pseudonym helped his subconscious to separate the identities: Firebird Angelo before that plunge into warmth, Mari Tomma after, and himself, still free . . . but changed.

A provincial aristocrat, sworn to serve unholy Powers? Fine traits, most of them, but not to be worshipped.

Some life events are not in your control. Shamarr Lo Dickin, his father in faith and his sponsoring master, spoke from another pool of memory. *Even you, Brennen. You can refuse to walk any path, for your will and rewards are your own, but some fates will find you.*

Still he recoiled. For years, he'd begged the Eternal Speaker to send him a mate. Could Firebird Angelo—undeniably lovely and fully, deeply connatural, but scarred and tormented—be his answer?

Surely not. He of all people must not join himself to a woman who worshipped false gods. And their connaturality—the deep likemindedness of compatible personalities—didn't require him to set aside his highest priority. Firebird . . . Mari . . . had no inkling of the web of identity, duty, and ambition inside him.

But she'd torn that web apart. Despite her insane belief system, she'd understood and obeyed one of its few truths: self-sacrifice, the determination to serve at all cost. Moreover—he smiled, recalling one final memory he'd observed—she'd found him appealing, at least in a poor quality holo.

. . . Soaring music of winds and strings captured his attention, sweeping him off focus of the interrogation. Her deepest feelings resonated with his own. . . .

Not for years had any subject broken his concentration during the deep class-three access of an intelligence-rated prisoner. What were the odds against their having met in battle and then in person? Thousands, tens of thousands to one?

Odds meant nothing in eternity.

Some fates will find you. . . .

Caught. These new memories wouldn't fade or lie down under a sediment of daily experiences, not if he lived for a century. Nor would her other memories, now his own. They were wastling memories, deep scars left by the nobility's heirs and her fierce longing for fame. She would rather have died than survived to meet him. She still might suicide, to satisfy the terrible guilt that her beliefs and this twist of events had heaped on her.

He forced down the visions, disrupted his emotions, and sank staring, visually and mentally blank, onto the edge of his cot.

Holy One, I've made mistakes before. But this couldn't be your answer!

That evening Tryseleen finished his guard shift by escorting Firebird from her cell to a wide observation deck. Semi-circular and covered with brown viewing glasteel, it commanded a view over Twinnich toward distant gray mountains. Shabby furniture stood in groups, but after she'd passed the door guard, the only signs of life were a dusting of litter and one man, who turned toward her as she stepped off the lift. He stood precisely in the setting sun, so she couldn't see his face, but she recognized Colonel Caldwell's body type and posture.

Out of the sun. He would've made a good pilot.

She wondered if he'd sensed her entrance. Defensively she muted her thoughts as he left the window and crossed to the doors, finally stepping into plain view. His hair, just too dark to be blond, almost touched the high collar of his tunic.

Tryseleen drew up to a stiff salute. His faded blue uniform looked slightly more dignified on straightened shoulders. "You sent for Miss Tomma, sir."

The Sentinel saluted with rather less flair, extended a hand, and introduced himself.

As Tryseleen answered, he gripped Caldwell's smooth hand with his callused one. "Koan Tryseleen of Caroli, sir. Recently of Veroh."

"How long have you been here?"

"Six years, sir. Welcome, sir. We were cert'ly glad when you all turned up. Looked like we were going to be Netaia's next royal buffer system."

Caldwell's glance flicked toward Firebird.

Yes, she grumbled silently, though he'd sworn he would no longer listen in on her thoughts. *That's what they would've been.*

He turned back to Tryseleen. "Off duty now?"

"Yes, sir."

"Would you have an hour to do me a favor?"

Tryseleen, who'd slouched, straightened back up with what Firebird read as pleasure. "I think so, sir."

"I understand Twinnich has a resource center. Would you withdraw five or six good cadet-level scan cartridges on Federate history and a viewer?"

"Of course, sir."

"Bring them to Miss Tomma when you come on duty tomorrow morning."

"Very good, sir." Tryseleen cocked an eyebrow at Firebird. She glanced toward Colonel Caldwell, trying to project her discomfort with Tryseleen's presence.

Caldwell nodded. "That'll be all, Tryseleen. Thank you."

The dark guard strode out. Firebird wandered to the spot where Caldwell had stood, and she gazed out over scattered low outbuildings. Below the sky, now a regal shade of purple, the settlement glimmered with lights, yellow and white on a hodgepodge of quonsets and bunkers.

Caldwell followed. He sat down against the back of a threadbare blue lounger.

She turned to him. "Thank you for the books, sir," she muttered. "And congratulations on your command."

"My name is Brennen." He matched her low volume. "I wanted to ask if you were being treated well."

"Better than I could've expected," she admitted, wondering what he really wanted. More information, no doubt.

"I'm aware that you know little about the Federacy. You shouldn't reject us offhand."

"I'd like to know more about other worlds," she admitted, "other people." Overhead, familiar constellations were appearing in oddly skewed shapes. She looked at . . . Brennen, he wanted to be called, though he hadn't corrected Tryseleen. He stared at a nearby hangar. Surveying his new dominion? "So," she said, "you're not counterattacking yet."

"No." His voice, she noticed incongruously, was mellow but not deep. He'd sing tenor, if he sang at all. "Our mission was to defend the colonists, not to discipline your navy. I don't think Netaia will repeat its mistake."

"Not with your fleet still insystem," she suggested.

Instead of agreeing, he watched a small civilian craft touch down near the hangar.

His silence seemed to imply that the fleet had left. What if it had withdrawn back to Caroli, or Ituri, or wherever that division was based?

Uneasy, she eyed the sky over those distant mountains. Netaia's humiliated marshals would be maintaining close surveillance. If the Federate division had dispersed, she would bet her life—whatever it was worth now—that they'd turn back the strike group and attack Veroh again. She wondered if Caldwell had catalogued that assumption.

Half her mind laughed bitterly at the thought that he might've missed something. The other half, after reminding her this was pure speculation, worked mercilessly onward.

If somehow she were retaken by Netaia, she'd be executed as a traitor . . . which now she was. She'd never forgotten watching Liach Stele collapse in front of that firing squad.

But did she have the courage to ask for the only real alternative?

She shot Brennen Caldwell a guilty glance. He perched loosely on the lounger's back, hands on his knees, following that small craft as it taxied toward a brightly lit hangar.

Maybe he truly wasn't listening. "Brennen," she began. Pleased to hear her voice coming out boldly, she plunged ahead. "I'm grateful for the . . . status you've given me, but after all you've taken, you owe me something. I want the dignity of dying peacefully. I cannot live with the shame of treason."

His smile flattened. "Mari Tomma," he said slowly, "I must tell you three things. First, I'm amazed that the Netaian government is willing to waste someone of your talents, and astounded that you're willing to comply. Sometimes an officer finds it necessary to disobey an order that contradicts all reason.

"Second, you want to be admired." The frown lines softened on his forehead. "Of course. Your people owe you honor already. And there are other kinds of honor, which you've never experienced.

"Finally." He flexed his hands and lowered his voice. "I don't have the authority to sign a capital order on someone of your . . . social rank."

"Who does?"

"The regional council, at Tallis." He challenged her with a pointed stare.

She spoke right through it. "Would you ask them for authorization?"

"Don't even request it."

"Then give me a blade. I know how to use it."

"No," he said.

Her nerve failed. She sighed. "What will my people think of me?"

He laid a hand against the waist-level windowbar. "Your fighter," he said softly, "was launched from *Horizon* on autopilot near the place where you were captured, and targeted with an incendiary. Most of it burned before impact. So you truly have disappeared, Mari. You're free. Your people think you've died, just like . . . Alef and Jisha."

Firebird let the shock charge through her as a four-ship Federate patrol screamed overhead. Free . . . truly? Free to keep living and learning, free to dream—

Caldwell fingered his cuff tab.

No—she mustn't surrender! All her life . . . except that once . . . she'd kept the Disciplines and the Charities. She couldn't falter now. Never again. "I don't want your pity."

"You don't want to die," he pressed. "Your Powers demand obedience, but this practice of heir limitation goes beyond thinking submission. How could any civilized family raise a child for slaughter? Look what it's done to you."

She shifted her feet but met his stare. How dare this man, a common-born offworlder, challenge the Powers and insult her family?

"Once, you hoped to become a leader of your people. Now you mean to be a martyr. You think of death and dying when you could serve, could build, could govern.

"You love music, too. Don't you realize what a gift you have? At the least, as a performer you could bring pleasure into hard lives. Perhaps you could lead a . . . a cultural exchange that would bring your people into Federate prominence.

"But look at you. You're young, lovely, and talented. But 'wastling' is branded across your mind," he finished, plainly exasperated, "and you're proud of it."

"Of course I'm proud of it." She hated his shallow praise even more than his pity. "My honor is at stake, Brennen Caldwell. I insist on obeying my orders, just as you followed yours by interrogating me."

He rose from the lounger, scrutinizing her. "As matters stand, you could effectively vanish. If I sent your request through channels, it would destroy your anonymity, whether or not they granted authorization to execute."

"I'll take that risk."

"It would also end your freedom."

"I've never been free," she muttered. That had only been a terrible temptation. At best, she still was a civilian-rated prisoner.

His jaw tensed, and he closed his eyes. He appeared to be struggling with the decision . . . or was he consulting his Thyrian equivalent of the Powers? If so, she had a chance. He'd claimed to serve them—it—whatever it was, above his Federate government.

"All right," he said at last. "I'll write a request."

She felt her eyes widen.

He walked to a deep black chair and picked up a recall pad, then returned to where Firebird stood. Drawing a stylus, he wrote quickly. He signed the pad and then handed it to her.

She read carefully. It was apologetic and lacked command, but amazingly, it was what she'd requested. "When will you send it?"

"I'd prefer to dump it."

She remained silent. She didn't need an enemy's sympathy.

"Immediately, if that's what you truly want," he said at last.

"That's what I want."

His eyes accused her. She too knew she'd lied, but she clung to the knowledge that only this action would satisfy the Powers and her guilt-wracked conscience.

Frowning, Brennen touched in a numerical code and then hit the SEND panel. The pad clicked for two seconds. That data would travel out with the next scheduled messenger ship, still the fastest means of intersystem communication, until someone developed a way to extend the range of faster-than-light DeepScan com waves. It would reach Tallis in just a few days.

Firebird sat down on the back of a soft chair, considering while the night deepened. She'd settled matters as well as she humanly could, and Brennen Caldwell had done as she asked, against his expressed preference. Placated, her conscience sent her groping for some way to thank him.

What if Netaia did return, trying to destroy Twinnich or, more likely, to take enough basium to finish Cleary's research? The elimination of a Master Sentinel might be a significant accomplishment for Netaia, but if she told him that he was vulnerable to a second attack—if he made sure the Federate division stayed in Verohan space—then the threat of Cleary's allegedly ultimate weapon would come to nothing.

Imagine! Even if the Federacy executed her, she might stop Phoena's research. Fate, or the Powers, had placed her at this pivot point. She cleared her throat.

Brennen glanced at her.

Treason! screeched her conscience. *You promised the Netaian marshals absolute loyalty. You swore an oath. This man, this genetic freak, you owe nothing . . . unless you turn traitor.*

She bit her lip and looked away.

The lift doors opened, and a man in pale blue stepped off. "You're needed, Colonel Caldwell," he said.

Narrow eyed with frustration, Brennen beckoned the door guard. "I'm sorry," he murmured as the Verohan approached. "I must get back to work."

He raised his voice and ordered the guard, "Escort Miss Tomma back to detention."

CHAPTER 6

STRIKE

subito allegro
suddenly fast

In the elliptical electoral chamber on the Angelo palace's ground floor, Count Tel Tellai excused himself from a knot of his peers who were discussing the military invasion. Their talk had degenerated into an argument comparing Netaian and Federate armament. Critically Tel examined a portrait of his ancestor, Count Merdon Tellai, which hung between gilded false pillars on the wall's rich red backdrop. Several shadows seemed poorly placed, and the rendering of the nobleman's diagonal blue sash was clumsy. The brushstrokes, too, seemed . . . hesitant. It hurt his dignity to see his family badly represented.

Surreptitiously, Tel glanced down and smoothed his own sash. Ever conscious that his body had given up growing before he had, Tel understood the importance of appearance. Today his tailor and dresser had chosen a suit of elegant amber sateen. The shade caught the gold veins of the chamber's black marble floor. He looked as if he belonged here.

Satisfied, Tel backed against the chamber's inner wall, between a pair of chairs embroidered with the Drake and Rogonin crèsts, and craned his neck in search of Princess Phoena. Though he was eight years younger than Phoena, he now was the head of his family, and eligible to approach her. To marry a second-born who ranked him as Phoena did, Tel would have to give up his right to bear children for the Tellai name, but that didn't matter. His wastling brother would rejoice . . . and Phoena fascinated him. Besides, he was a count now, with more prestige than many closer to her age. Unquestionably, Phoena noticed rank. His electoral seat, midway up the inner branch of the table, lay apart from the Angelos on the center section, but maybe someday he'd sit higher, a member of the inner circle.

The gilded doors blew open. Phoena, gowned in pale orange, stepped between door guards. Without waiting for a lull in conversation, she cried, "Any word from the forces?" then swept forward. The sight of her blasted all daydreams out of Tel's mind. Orange—the color of Excellence in

Netaia's heraldry—brought flame into her chestnut hair. If ever he found the courage to ask her to sit for an informal portrait, he'd suggest she wear exactly that shade.

He took another step away from the other electors and lifted a gloved hand, trying to catch her eye. "Your Highness."

He had to call twice before she walked his way. The hem of her gown whisked over the floor, and her plunging bodice floated on perfect skin. Tel coughed, unsettled by the sight. "Highness . . ." He paused, catching a breath of woody perfume.

Beside one of thirty false pillars, she stopped and arched her brows. He adored her regal impatience.

"We've received a DeepScan transmission from just outsystem," he explained. "Our forces were initially turned back, but—"

"Firebird? What word of her?"

The poor little wastling. Tel frowned, unable even for Phoena to hide his compassion. Around them, conversations droned on, and he knew that the others cared as little as Phoena that a delightful woman had left them forever. Maybe as he matured, he'd develop a firmer attitude. "They identified her craft—downed. Lord Corey and Lady Delia are missing as well. But with the distances involved, communications are dreadful."

"Downed?" Phoena's dark eyes sparkled. For the first time in Tel's experience, her poise slipped enough that she bit her lower lip. "Are there any other details?"

Her excitement encouraged him. "There was little left but the transponder, Highness. The fightercraft burned almost completely."

Her long lashes fluttered. "Thank you, Tel. That's what I wanted to know." She gathered her skirt, intending to brush past him, toward her seat.

"Highness, wait!" he cried. "There was good news as well. Our retreat wasn't pursued. Reading their weakness, we turned again. The basium . . ."

She seized his arm. "Little cousin, you have a marvelous sense of priorities. Powers bless you." Finally she seemed really to see him, as a fellow elector instead of the boy he'd been. "Are you interested in our research, Count Tellai?"

He rested his free hand on the gilded arm of a chair and tried to strike a strong pose. "I see in it two strokes of genius, Your Highness. One Cleary's, in discovering the, ah, basium principle. The other is yours, of course, in bringing her here. My interest in your mysterious secret is keen, yes."

Phoena gave a rising, tinkling laugh and released his arm. "Everyone wants to know my secret, Count Tel, and it is worth keeping. Within months, we will have power to spare, and the Federacy won't dare dream of subjecting us to any compromise. But until then, I do need support. Quiet support." She shot a glance up the table at Princess Carradee, who'd paused to speak with another nobleman. "There are some, Tel, who are having second thoughts. Who—" She seemed to catch herself before saying too much.

Hastily he murmured, "Highness, you must count on me whatever the circumstances. My house always has looked to the Angelos. I shall look always to you."

She smiled slightly, perhaps remembering her father—Tel's great-uncle. Tel's sire—her father's brother's son—had been more hardhearted than Prince Irion Tellai-Angelo, but he hadn't deserved violent death. The murderer, a disgruntled overseer of their Tiggaree holding, had been executed under torture by the Enforcement Corps, and his family members (those who could be found) sentenced to ten years in dark Hinanna prison, then reduced to servile status for the maximum three generations.

A high-toned bell echoed off the white ceiling. Silenced by the call to order, Tel bowed to the princess. She extended a long, perfect hand. Earnestly he took it on his palm, closed his eyes, and touched his lips to her fingertips.

Brennen walked a zigzag pattern across the command post. Half enclosed by an L of glasteel windows, it had large viewing screens to fill in the panorama's missing sides. At its heart stood a transparent cylinder just over waist high and two meters in diameter. Inside that tri-D well, a relief-figured red sphere mapped Veroh II's surface. Four radio and laser-pulse interlink transceivers followed the well's curve. A ceiling map displayed the stars near Veroh, glimmering faintly above a conference table surrounded by rotating stools.

He walked the pattern again, internalizing every monitor's location. From any point along a captain's walk behind the controllers' stations, he could see all the data he'd need if this force saw further action. From one dead spot near the windows, he could see none of it, only the tri-D well. At any other place, he'd have partial vision.

With that done, though his legs still felt restless, he sat down at a monitor to evaluate his personnel, intelligence, matériel. Contingency plans. Fallback positions. The controller on duty bent over her own console, avoiding his glances.

He found memorizing easy. He needed only to focus his epsilon carrier through his memory and let lists scroll past. Evaluating those resources, though, and planning a defense if that proved necessary, would take concentration. He'd never headed a force any larger than Delta Flight. In the days to come, he must inspire confidence among Verohan men and women. He must know Veroh's defenses, including this room, better than he knew Thyrica's.

The Federate fast track, a system of rapid promotion that was an honor in itself, demanded a defensive major-command assignment without much risk of combat before his next advancement. Here it was, though he hadn't expected it so soon. It would've given him a chance to hide Firebird from the Federacy, for a time—until she'd demanded those papers.

What had she meant to say?

He pushed away from his viewer and eyed yellow-gold Netaia, bright in Veroh's dusty evening sky. Danger had throbbed in her emotions, there on the observation deck. Some specific fear had risen from her past to menace her, and maybe unfortunately, he hadn't found any reason to access that memory. She'd crept to the edge of allowing him inside her defenses and then fled in shame. Had she almost accepted asylum?

Chaos take that twisted, guilt-sick sense of honor! It anchored her to Netaia—

He paused. Did he mean that? Shouldn't she obey the highest law she knew, for now?

Carefully he reviewed the message he'd sent Tallis. Certainly he'd justified the request poorly, but his having sent it would buy her several days to reconsider her fate, meanwhile proving he understood her greatest desire: to show herself faithful, loyal even to death. Regional command would protect her, even from herself, once they knew she was in Federate custody. They would call her to Tallis, and possibly reprimand him for having kept her back. He knew the regional councilors slightly from several brief appearances, during which he'd kept closely attuned to their emotional states, but he'd never violated his codes by attempting even a shallow access. Of seven, he could count on three to show compassion under all circumstances. They would spare her life. But for what future?

A high cloud blotted out the yellow-gold star. He turned from the window, shaking his head. What good were his abilities if he couldn't ease her mind open, show her the false assumptions behind her harsh, legalistic beliefs . . . and then truth?

But that use of epsilon power was strictly forbidden. For the first time, he understood why the urge to guide others could've tempted his ancestors to their downfall. It had been an utter violation of free human will.

A young corporal in Tullan gray appeared alongside him, saluted, and dropped a scan cartridge on his desk. Brennen nodded thanks. The viewer glowed silently, reminding him that although Firebird's military duties might have ended, his hadn't.

Firebird awoke rested, realizing that in the night, her mind had settled the question that had kept her awake for so long. Completion of Cleary's work could cause Netaia's destruction, if the weapon were used, and if the Federacy took appropriate vengeance. In the end, nothing mattered more than her people's welfare: neither her death, nor treason, nor wanting to repay Colonel Caldwell for honoring her wishes. When the guards brought breakfast, she asked them to call him.

Within minutes the gray door slid open. Caldwell entered, clean-chinned and uniformed in crisp contrast to her wrinkled coverall. He strode directly to her side and trapped her eyes. "Good morning, Mari," he greeted her gravely from an arm's length away.

The name caught Firebird by surprise. He didn't need to call her that in private.

"Did you change your mind?" he prompted. "About termination?"

"No. But I must . . . tell you something." This was harder than she'd expected. Much harder. She was about to pass information to the enemy. "You must watch—" She faltered, stepped back, and then started over. "One objective of our attack was to load enough pure basium to finish Dr. Cleary's research."

He nodded gravely.

"If . . . your peacekeeping force were the only Federate strength in this system," she said carefully, "then we'd come back to try again, if not by stealth, then by force. I can almost guarantee that we'd strike here first, at Twinnich."

His dark eyebrows lifted. "You're saying you would expect an attack here, if the fleet has withdrawn."

"I would," she managed.

"Probability?"

Firebird considered the commanding officer that Marshal Burkenhamn had sent, a ranking aristocrat with a noble's attitudes. "Ninety percent," she admitted.

He turned toward the door, then glanced back. As he stared at her face, she felt that smoky flicker touch the fringe of awareness. "Why did you tell me this?"

Firebird wanted to look away, but she couldn't, and suddenly she doubted her motives. Enemy or ally, she didn't want this man dead. He'd shown himself worthy of respect by sending that termination request. She felt no compulsion to speak, but she understood that he'd reject any attempt to fool him.

"The . . . basium project," she said carefully. "I don't like unlimited warfare any more than . . . than I think you do."

"I know that." He touched the locking panel. "But there's probably not much time." As the door slid away, he paused. "Firebird—Mari," he corrected himself oddly, "you, of all people anywhere, are in the best position to fight deployment of that weapon."

"I realized that last night."

"Maybe that's worth living for. If nothing else is."

She smiled wanly. They'd found grounds for agreement at last.

Later that morning, dark-tanned Koan Tryseleen brought a handful of scanbook cartridges and a lap viewer. "I cleaned the file," he commented dryly. "The super wanted to know if my kid was failing school. I don't have a kid." Fingering the brightly labeled cubes, he read her their titles. "*Systems of the Federacy. Federacy of the Free. Transnational Government.* You won't find any of these on Netaia."

Firebird loaded the top cartridge and spun its pages through the viewer. No pictures but plenty of footnotes. It had the look of an Academy text. "Do you know if any of these are particularly good?" she asked.

"No idea. Wait, this looks like one I had. Long time back."

"Well, thank you." She popped out the first cartridge and scrolled another. Glorious tri-Ds and large lettering—junior school history with a patriotic slant.

"Study hard." Tryseleen locked her in again.

Was this how Vultor Korda's treachery began? she wondered bleakly. But she'd always been a voracious reader and student. For hours, she compared indexes and contents. This was the other side . . . from the other side. She read until her eyes ached.

Brennen woke with the memory of a horn blaring in his ears. For an instant he struggled to identify this sterile room. Where. . . ? A luma pulsed on the far wall over an interlink speaker. Fully awake a second later, he sprang off his cot and touched the luma before the klaxon could screech again. "Caldwell."

"Large slip-shield zone approaching, sir. Netaian approach vector."

Too soon! The division had dispersed after repelling Netaia's attack, just as Firebird had suspected. At least he'd left Twinnich on stage-two alert before he turned in. "Call stage three. I'll be right up." Brennen cut the interlink, zipped into a clean uniform, and took a minute to wash his face.

The tingle of depilatory soap helped make up for his shortened sleep. After drying, he stood motionless, composing his inner energies, focusing his spirit. *Guide us all. Keep me on the Path today, and save life.* Then he sprinted out.

Controlled chaos filled the com room—now a war room—and the ancient interlink didn't help. Dropping into his chair, he pressed a panel on the command display.

"Central," said a feminine computer voice.

"Caldwell speaking. Call up another pair of controllers."

"Sir."

He glanced at the tri-D well in the room's center. Only a few bright speckles, friendlies, hovered over the red topo globe. That would soon change.

On his left, a com tech in Tallan gray sat drumming his fingers on his board. Brennen created an energy flicker and dissipated his epsilon shields, a cloud of mental-frequency static with which he constantly and automatically wreathed himself to escape the assault of others' emotions. Chaos blared on that level, too, the nearby tech's anxiety welling over all else.

Brennen cleared his throat to catch that Tallan's attention. "Get me DeepScan to the outsystem scouts. Channel F."

"Sir." The tech's relief at finding something to do leaped out from the background buzz. Brennen's static shields sprang up again. The emotional noise cut off.

"DeepScan, sir," called the tech.

Brennen picked up a headset and clipped it on. "Outsystem? Give me status on that slip zone."

In ten seconds a distant voice hissed in his ear. "Now passing orbit nine, sir."

"Begin regular reports when it reaches six."

At least the Federacy now knew that Netaia had less accurate subspace scanning, and that the approaching force wouldn't spot his scouts, nor Federate reinforcements, if they came in time.

Thanks to Firebird.

He glanced at the dead spot in the room that he had found earlier. Here was a chance to bring his best resource close enough to access on a moment's notice, and show her respect at the same time. It would be highly irregular. . . .

Holy One, would it be right?

He clenched a fist, debating . . . then reached for the interlink.

"Central."

"Detention desk, please."

Firebird hadn't dozed long or well when footsteps awakened her. Disoriented, she sat up on her cot and clutched her thin blanket. A masculine silhouette blocked yellowish light in her cell's open door.

"What is it?" She recognized the faded blue Verohan uniform, though not the man wearing it.

"We're under attack," he answered with thinly covered hostility. "You're Netaian?"

"Yes—"

"I have orders from Colonel Caldwell. You're to be allowed uplevel."

This is it! she thought with a thrill of fear. She jumped off the bed, smoothed her rumpled coverall, and hastily braided her hair.

"Don't get any wise ideas." He unhooked a singlet wrist restraint from his belt and let out a meter of cable, then linked it around her right wrist. "If the colonel trusts a Netaian observer, he needs a psych exam."

Cabled to the guard's heavy belt four minutes later, she stepped from the lift . . . not onto the quiet observation deck she expected but into a room vibrating with activity.

Four transceivers were manned. Controllers curtly relayed reports along the line, onto an overhead star map and into a tri-D well.

She gaped.

"This way," the guard said firmly, positioning his bulk to block her view of the controllers. He led her along a projection wall toward a broad observation window.

She couldn't believe this. On Netaia, even a civilian who accidentally reached an active command center would be instantly imprisoned.

Well . . . according to Verohan records, she *was* a civilian. And imprisoned.

That didn't explain Caldwell's reasoning.

"Sit down." The guard waved her to one of two stools that had been moved near the window. "Move off that stool and you won't move far." He touched the shock pistol on his belt.

"Understood," she said softly.

She craned her neck. From here, she could see nothing that even suggested a security rating, as hard as she tried. She could barely make out the tri-D well. It looked alive with glowing blips, red and gold, that must signify attacking and defending ships.

Brennen Caldwell stood just beyond it, speaking rapidly into a collar mike. He spared her a glance and a nod and went on issuing orders. Golden sparks scattered in the well. As far as she could tell from this distance, Caldwell was arraying his squadrons planetwide but with a treble concentration near Twinnich, to hold off precisely the attack she'd predicted.

He'd done a remarkable job, finding her this spot. She could see the well and the windows. Nothing else.

So she searched the sky for moving pinpoints of light. Those would be the attackers' fightercraft. So far, she saw none.

But she was glad to be above ground. *If Twinnich goes*, she reflected, *I'll die here with the Federates.* She surveyed the heart of the room, enemy headquarters. That Thyrian with the star on his shoulder was her enemy.

Why did she keep forgetting that?

The answer came easily, from another corner of her mind. *Because he has treated you with respect. More than your own commanding officers ever showed. Because he values you . . . alive.*

And she did want to live.

Hours of tracking crawled by. Patterns changed in the tri-D well as scouts' reports returned. The navy had reappeared out of slip-state at some distance from Veroh's surface. As the swarm of red blips started its series of deceleration orbits, Firebird tensed in memory. She'd made that approach so recently. Five days ago? More? *Skim lower to lose speed, but don't overload the heat shielding. Pass again, thicker atmosphere. Eyes on screens for defensive countermeasures.* There had been few. That approach had thrilled her.

This one was agonizing. Now she sat shackled to a target, a colonial outpost that had probably sent a messenger fleeing for reinforcements as soon as she warned Brennen Caldwell. Furthermore, if the Federates hoped to hold Twinnich, they must kill Netaian pilots. Daley might be out there, and Delia.

A small man in quicksilver gray hurried around the controllers and pulled up a third stool. Before he spoke, he too scanned the black sky. There still was no sign of the attack force. In the well, it was in its second orbit and approaching the near side.

Then he cocked a bright brown eye at them. "Vett Zimmer of Tallis," he offered. "Messenger Service. Looks like an exciting day."

"Right," growled the guard. "I'm Deke Lindera of Kilworth, here on Veroh. My friend"—he ran a hand up the cable—"is Mari Tomma of Netaia."

"Oh!" Vett Zimmer drew up a bit and spoke more formally. "You're a prisoner, Mari?"

"Yes. They're being gracious enough to let me observe, instead of waiting below."

"Caldwell," Vett guessed. "Right?"

Firebird glanced at Brennen's back. He peered into the well, tracking incoming ships.

"You'll hear disturbing things about his kind," the messenger captain continued. "But him, I like. About time they gave him a command—but I'll bet fifty gilds he's going to be absolutely dying to be in the air."

"Oh?" Did he hope she'd predict Netaia's strategy? Not for a chatty Federate messenger! "So he flies? I'd assumed he was Intelligence." Assumed. Ha.

Then she remembered the way he'd come out of the sun in the observation deck.

"Both." Vett kept talking. "Special Operations. Those SO people get called off their regular assignments whenever they're needed."

"He's a pilot, too," she repeated. Why should that matter? Then she remembered seeing six black shapes through her cockpit bubble, hearing the shock in Delia's voice. Corey! Could Brennen have. . . ?

She hung her head, unwilling to convict anyone on supposition.

Someone had killed Corey, though. Some Federate, who might still be here.

Evidently she really had been in love with him all along.

Enemy headquarters . . .

Everything suddenly grew still. Brennen turned toward a transceiver, and a voice filled the room. Firebird knew it. Count Dorning Stele, CO of the invasion force, was Delia's elder brother and heir of his house. "Veroh, this is Count Stele, Prime Commander for Raptor Phalanx. Give me your commanding officer," he barked.

"This is Veroh," Brennen answered into his tiny collar mike. "Colonel Caldwell commanding. Break off your attack, or you will be liable to the most serious consequences. I repeat, break off, Count."

Stele spoke again. "Colonel, we will receive one negotiating party of your top people to discuss your surrender and reparations for damage suffered by our navy. You have ten minutes in which to launch a negotiators' shuttle. We will guarantee the safety of those negotiators only."

Firebird clenched her jaw. Dorning Stele had testified against his own brother at Liach's geis trial.

Brennen leaned onto the console. "Count Stele, this base now accommodates a Federate peacekeeping force. Any hostile action on your part will be answered by the Federate fleet upon your home system. I repeat. Any hostile action on your part will be answered by the Federate fleet upon *your home system.*"

"You will be unable to send for additional ships, Colonel," sneered Stele's voice. "We guarantee the safety of one negotiating team. We grant the rest of Veroh no such promise. You have nine minutes in which to launch your shuttle."

So you can shoot it down, Stele? Firebird wondered.

Scarlet blips kept advancing in the tri-D well, with the majority over-passing Twinnich just to the north. Nine minutes crawled by, and then Stele spoke again. "Colonel, your time is up. Have you no one whose life you value enough to send us?"

As he spoke, a Netaian squadron that had trailed the others roared over Twinnich. Federate intercept fighters pursued, and groundside guns finally roared to life, but the overflight, only a hand slap, baffled Firebird.

A different speaker buzzed in an erratic speech rhythm. Brennen made a twisting hand signal to a controller. "Zeta Four. Can I have that again?" he asked his pickup mike.

Silence. Brennen leaned down and did something Firebird couldn't see. A static-charged voice cackled from a large room speaker, ". . . fifth series of battle groups on a five-two heading and the last one due eastward."

In the well, the crimson swarm was dispersing unexpectedly into smaller clusters.

Firebird leaned forward, listening intently, but no more information came. This wasn't the attack she'd expected! Twinnich should be the main target. It was virtually the only military strength in the system.

Brennen spun toward her and lifted his hand. She clutched her stool, clinging to balance as she found herself command-paralyzed and then accessed again. Her memory raced back to briefings, to strategy classes under Stele and Burkenhamn and her other commanding officers.

By the time Caldwell let her go, everyone watching had seen his atten-tion to an alleged civilian refugee. Her guard eyed Brennen, then her, and then drew back to the end of his cable, as if making sure he'd be out of range of any future mind probe. The enthusiastic messenger captain eyed Firebird with bright-eyed curiosity, almost envy. She blinked, struggling furiously to restart her own thoughts.

Brennen turned back to the well.

So this was why he'd brought her into the war room! Would he also betray her presence to Dorning Stele, in spite of his promises? He'd lied on her behalf. Maybe he'd lied to her, too.

Firebird stared angrily at the line of his jaw, which was stern like that of a gamesman who couldn't play until his opponent revealed a strategy. The red speckles were far spread now, sweeping in twenty arches toward night-side as morning light grew in the war room.

A scout transmitted another report. "Twinnich, this is Tau at nine-seven by two. The settlement at one-oh-six has been bombed. Looks like a flasher. I can't get any closer for the dust and the rem count."

Her Verohan guard sprang to his feet, cursing.

Firebird gasped. Her own flight had overpassed that community, a hydroponics plant and a few settlement domes. It had no military significance. Surely it hadn't been flash bombed. Photo-enhanced weapons were forbidden by treaties even Netaia claimed to support. She'd known they were in the arsenal, as weapons of last resort, but she'd had no idea they'd been loaded for this invasion—and these were civilians!

Brennen's eyes caught hers again in the midst of her stricken thoughts. This time, she willingly showed her surprise and horror as he probed for the grim weapons' specs.

He studied the tri-D well, then redeployed a squadron. The Planetary Navy's twenty attack groups could sweep Veroh clean of life before converging on Twinnich. Brennen scattered six squadrons into pairs and sent them to intercept the Netaian advance, but as the Federates spread out to join battle, satellites continued to beam images of settlements bombed to dust clouds, life and structures wiped from Veroh with callous, methodical deliberation. Within hours, Veroh II could be open-air uninhabitable.

Had Dorning Stele planned this massacre all along? Had Marshal Burkenhamn, who Firebird admired for his integrity, authorized it?

Brennen called for a civilian com frequency and ordered every settlement within transport distance evacuated into Twinnich's shielding zone. Soon after that, one controller tuned in a Federate pilot on intersquad frequency, who'd come upon an NPN battle group and found himself outnumbered ten times. "Heavy bomber," he announced, then called off a string of range and bearing coordinates. A controller acknowledged. The pilot continued, "Cover me, Three."

Anxious silence filled the war room. Somewhere, two Federate pilots were taking on twenty tagwings escorting a big loadship.

"Look out, boss, he's dropped a drone."

"I'm on it."

Firebird squeezed her eyes shut, but she couldn't escape the mental image: Some Netaian bombardier sat at station in that loadship's bomb bay. Someone else who'd trained at the NPN Academy, who knew as well as Firebird the long-term effect of each deadly drop.

Could she have done it, even following orders?

She envisioned the warhead's steering rockets igniting, the Federate pilot chasing, his wingman covering him with a cone of laser fire, trying to give him hope of destroying the drone at high enough altitude to spare the targeted settlement.

She barely breathed.

In the war room they waited, but there were no more transmissions from those pilots.

Firebird's Verohan guard cursed again, clenching both fists.

"Attack pairs." Brennen's voice rose crisply. "Random scatter. Pull back. Re-form your squadrons at nine-oh degrees from Twinnich."

CHAPTER 7

STALEMATE

ritardando
gradually slackening in speed

The long Verohan day-cycle passed slowly, every hour bringing a wave of terrorized refugees and a few degrees' retreat toward Twinnich. When Deke Lindera was replaced by another guard, Vett Zimmer took a sleeping capsule and went for some rest. Firebird ate in her tightly guarded corner, but she scarcely tasted the food. Twinnich's particle-shielding dome might protect it from missile attack and radioactive debris, but that was no guarantee against a laser strike, and so many attacking ships swarmed on all sides that a shield overload looked bleakly certain, unless the perimeter could be held at a distance.

Near dusk, Vett Zimmer returned and took a shift wearing the guard belt. The horizon flashed with missile hits and laser cannon fire. Before long, heavy bombers would break through and begin to launch drones.

Firebird deliberately caught Brennen's glance. He was pacing now, with eyes that looked dark, and she knew he shared her grief for the massacred civilians. She spread her hands and shook her head, a helpless gesture. He acknowledged with a nod.

A series of day-bright flashes wrenched all eyes to the westerly projection screen. Another flight of Netaian drones had found targets between Twinnich and a distant mountain range. As the bombs' rumble reached Twinnich, the jagged horizon disappeared behind a rolling dust cloud.

No more refugees would arrive from that direction.

Firebird felt a hand on her shoulder and spun defensively around.

"Don't you want some sleep?" Brennen asked softly as he dropped his hand.

"No." She had to say more. "I'm sorry, Brennen," she murmured. "I never dreamed."

"I know." His forgiving tone wounded her as no rebuke could have. He strode away.

"Look at him," Vett whispered. "He is *dying* to be out in the thick of it. And he can't leave his post."

Firebird smiled ruefully. Maybe a command wasn't such a handsome reward after all. His frustration showed in clenched hands and the set of his jaw.

Stars came out, only a few of them bright enough to pierce the wild interplay of light in Twinnich's smoky sky. In the well, Federate ships scattered, regrouped, and picked off tagwings here and there. Once, Firebird heard the transmissions from a Federate squad that vaporized a pair of drones released by a distant bomber. It seemed as if she were watching a band of children hold off armed giants.

But before long, she realized that she'd seen the Federates score several kills, while not one intercept fighter had fallen since they pulled in to defend Twinnich.

She too longed to seize her tagwing's controls. A triangle of blue-hot engine lights roared overhead, and she watched with passionate envy. Chained, with nothing to do but watch, she felt a traitor to Netaia, and to the Federates a barbarian. She avoided Vett's casual questions until a horrendous, roaring shriek startled her eyes upward. Expecting a bomb, she found herself witnessing the immolation of an entire Netaian flight team, as the tagwings followed their lead pilot directly into the particle shield. It vaporized them, lighting the sky field.

Daley? she mourned. *Delia?*

At last, Dorning Stele apparently came to the conclusion Firebird had drawn hours earlier. The defense of Twinnich was too well coordinated to break. Shortly after midnight, the Netaians withdrew into orbit, settling for a stalemate and a siege.

Brennen finally passed command to a Verohan officer. Sweat soaked and whiskery, he smiled wanly as controllers congratulated him. He snatched a meat pastry from the conference table on his way to the window. "Captain Zimmer, are you willing to try to slip for Ituri? If that other messenger didn't make it, we haven't got a chance."

"Of course." Vett pulled off the guard's belt and held it up, raising both eyebrows.

"I'll bring in a staff guard. Look, Zimmer, I'm not ordering you out. Your chances are almost nil."

"I didn't hear that." Vett's buoyant salute so resembled Corey's—the very last time she'd seen him—that Firebird swallowed hard.

"Thank you." Brennen clapped his shoulder. Vett scurried off.

Two controllers were replaced by a fresh pair as Brennen sagged onto the stool beside Firebird's.

"Your people must've done some spectacular flying," she murmured. "We're still here."

He offered her half of his pastry, and she took it gratefully, too tired to argue.

Shortly after another Verohan guard took the stool beside her, Vett's little messenger ship roared off the breakaway strip. Fifteen minutes later, his dot in the tri-D well vanished in a circle of scarlet blips. She clenched her hands. If this went on, she would burst into tears. The Planetary Navy coiled just out of reach, a venomous snake gathering itself to strike again. Outside, on the dome that shielded Twinnich, ashen fallout slowly settled.

Brennen brushed crumbs off his lap. "I need sleep and so do you," he said bluntly. "I'm taking you back down. Belt," he told the guard. As the Verohan undid the belt's clasps, Brennen raised his voice. "Central? Page me if anything changes."

Cabled to Brennen, Firebird stumbled into the lift cubicle. While they rode, he stared silently at its door. Beside the guards' desk, he released her wrist restraint and removed the belt. Handing them to Deke Lindera, he turned away.

"Colonel. Could I talk to you for a minute?" she called.

His shoulders rose and fell in a deep breath. "All right," he replied without emotion, and he escorted her up the passway to her cell.

If she was exhausted, he must be half dead, but she desperately needed to speak. "Brennen, I can't be a part of that. The ones who ordered that attack aren't my people. The pilots and crews—the ones who went out to fight and die—I still believe in them. But not the Electorate. Not the marshals. The butchers," she added bitterly, rubbing her chafed wrist. "Flash bombs. On civilians."

"What are you saying, Mari?" He sat down on the foot of her cot.

"I think," she began, and then she choked. She tried again. "Brennen, you've been . . ."

No more words came. Sobbing, she buried her face in her hands.

At a hesitant touch on her shoulder, she raised her head to see Brennen, standing and looking down with something in his eyes she hadn't seen before. Gone was the power of command. In its stead was a depth of understanding she'd known only in Corey.

Corey. Dead, as she deeply wished she were.

She fell against Brennen, clutching him and crying. His arms gathered her in as they might hold a child, and he stroked her shoulder with one hand.

Slowly, her tears subsided. Her pride revived, though, mortally wounded. She'd made an idiot of herself in the arms of a Federate colonel, a genetic oddity. What depth would she reach next time?

His grasp loosened as suddenly as her emotions changed. Forcibly reminded of his starbred empathy, she wrenched out of his warm grasp. She hated herself and his humanness. "I wish you'd move me uplevel," she lashed out. "Then, when they break through and flash Twinnich, at least I'll die fast with the rest of you. Do you really think you can hold them off?"

His stare remained compassionate. "The fleet will come. Soon enough, I hope. But I'll find you better quarters as soon as I can."

"The fleet will come," she mocked. *Come on, Sentinel! Since you're human, get angry!* "But meanwhile, Netaia raids the basium mines. They can—"

He shook his head. "Not now. We've made contingency plans. I cannot tell you why, but the mines won't be taken."

Too relieved to fight on, she asked, "But what happens to me if your fleet comes and they won't issue those termination papers?"

"I've given that serious thought. Mari . . . would you want to go home?"

Firebird blinked, passed a hand over her aching eyes, and then shut her gaping mouth. She could return voluntarily. She could face the electors and proudly tell them she'd come back to meet a Netaian fate on her home ground. "You'd let me?"

"Would you go, if I could?"

They'd like that, she reflected grimly. *They love to punish people.* "They want me dead," she reminded him.

"Yes."

Of course he knew. "It doesn't matter. Here or at home, I'm condemned."

"I doubt any Federate termination papers will come at first request, if that's your concern. You're valuable . . . to us."

Firebird interlocked her fingers and squeezed tightly. Could she really choose to live among the Federates, whom she'd been raised to despise, instead of facing the sacrificial death that would satisfy the merciless Powers and their blood-lusting electors?

After what she'd just seen, was there any question? She'd hide on Tallis, or Caroli, or somewhere in deep space, before letting Dorning Stele enjoy watching her die, the way he'd leered at his brother.

"No," she murmured, "I couldn't go home. What they did here was wrong. I want to live. A little longer, at least."

He stood against the far wall, unmoving, unthreatening. "May I take you into protective custody?"

"That makes me sound helpless."

He rubbed his rough chin and nodded.

"Under the circumstances, I suppose I am." She looked down at the cot. She ached to fall onto it. "But what if that authorization to terminate comes through?"

"I don't give the order. Particularly if you've requested asylum. You still haven't," he reminded her.

"All right," she said numbly. She took a deep breath of stale air, and then she spoke the treasonous words. "I'm officially requesting asylum, Colonel Caldwell."

He paced toward the gray metal door. "I'll be back in a minute."

"Oh, Brennen, it'll wait for the morning." She sank onto the thin mattress.

Inside her doorway, he stopped. "I don't want to risk waiting. This won't take long."

He returned carrying a recall pad. She read it carefully, battling to concentrate, to simply stay awake. For three standard months, she would be quartered and cared for, and granted diplomatic immunity, by the Federacy's Tallis Region. During that time, Wing Colonel Brennen D. Caldwell would answer for her safety, and when the period ended, other arrangements would be made. There was a place to record date and time with her own hand, so that if the document were ever published on Netaia, then the Electorate, the marshals, and her mother would know she'd signed only after the slaughter at Veroh.

"So if Twinnich falls and I survive," she observed, "this will record my protest."

"I'll get you a microcopy to keep with you, in case that happens." He drew his stylus from his left cuff and signed the pad.

She'd unbraided her hair while he was gone. It fell over her shoulder as she signed below him and pressed her thumb to the recall panel, confirming her signature. "Thank you," she mumbled.

"I'm glad I can offer it." Against the gray walls his midnight blue uniform looked almost black, and so did the circles under his eyes.

"Are you as exhausted as you look?" he asked.

Aren't you? "I haven't slept well since . . . before we left Netaia," she confessed.

"May I—I could help you with that, if you'd let me."

She eyed him warily. "Sleep only? Nothing else?"

He shook his head. "Nothing else. I promise."

She shrugged permission. He walked forward and gently placed his fingers over her eyes.

All fear and tension dropped away, leaving her too deeply relaxed to wonder what he'd done, or how he'd done it.

"Good night," she whispered. Irresistibly, her eyelids dropped. That was no genetic freak, she reflected in the last uncontrolled instant before she fell soundly asleep. That was a most exceptional man.

CHAPTER 8

REBEL

tempo giusto
in strict time

Firebird was roused midmorning by the pale guard. Fast advance ships of the Federate fleet had arrived from Ituri. She watched from the same stool as before, while Brennen ordered a sortie that caught Netaian attackers between jaws of titanium and steel. Most of the Netaians survived to flee Twinnich. The controllers cheered, but Firebird was achingly aware that it was only a foretaste of things to come. Netaia had used flash bombs on civilians. It was one thing to accept sanctuary for herself, another to consider the kind of retribution Federate technology might inflict on her home world. Her own people.

Brennen left after the battle. From that alone, she knew the defense of Twinnich was over. Little else would be done until more Federate ships reached Veroh. Firebird asked her guard to take her below.

Several of the Second Division's ranking commanders had come ahead with the advance detail. It was late afternoon in Twinnich when Brennen boarded the officers' frigate, a heavily armed, roomy but fast ship.

General Gorn Frankin of Caroli seized his arm at the airlock and pulled him bodily down the dark corridor toward a galley. "Brennen Caldwell! We thought you'd been swizzling killcare when that troop request came through, and I don't mind telling you, if it'd come from anyone else, we'd have sent the psych team instead of warships! What kind of fools attack a peacekeeping force? The clincher was that weird termination request. Was that the pilot you interviewed?"

At a gray galley table ringed with fellow officers, Brennen took a chair. Another Sentinel sat among them, Captain Ellet Kinsman, and he sent her a quick unspoken greeting. She returned it with a burst of feelings, relief foremost among them, but out of respect to the others present, neither added the subvocalized words of mind-to-mind speech.

"Then when we saw Veroh was under attack again," added another officer, "and how hot the atmosphere was, we were afraid they'd dusted you all. I'm with General Frankin. What's going on?"

Brennen accepted a staffer's cup of kass with thanks. "First, I have to know if I worded that termination request weakly enough to have it denied."

"Denied?" Frankin sat down, running one hand across his thick shock of hair. "Shredded!"

Brennen smiled into his mug.

"How in Six-alpha did we get a member of the royal family in custody?"

He explained, beginning with the first battle of Veroh and concluding with Firebird's request for asylum, and when he finished, they were silent. Lowering his static shields, he observed their reactions.

Ellet, tangibly surprised and concerned, spoke first. "You can quiet me if I'm out of line, Colonel, but what do you intend to do with her?"

Yes, what? "I'm waiting for orders. I've only just convinced her she doesn't need to die." *Thank the Holy One!*

"We have no orders for her disposition." Ellet tossed her head, and her chin-length hair shimmered. "What if she's sent back to Netaia?"

"Firing squad, I think." He'd thought hard before offering to return her, down in her cell. If she'd chosen that, his follow-through might have cost him, too—a court-martial.

Instead, just as he'd hoped, she'd repented. She'd distanced herself from her own forces with sincere remorse. He'd rejoiced on the run, bringing back that recall pad before she could change her mind.

"They're that sort, are they?" asked Ellet.

He nodded. "An incomprehensible penal system has propped up their government for decades."

Frankin, tangibly pleased, bounced a fist off the tabletop. "I don't imagine she's anxious for publicity, but think what an advantage she's given us. Maybe now we can settle down those people. So far, Netaians don't strike me as rational people."

"You accessed her?" Ellet asked.

Brennen nodded.

"Is she rational?"

Irritated by the scorn in her voice, he shot her an unguarded glance. He and Ellet shared a faith and a culture, but he didn't like her inflated sense of importance.

She strengthened her own shields, drew up stiffly, and watched his eyes.

Frankin stood. "Caldwell, before we go on, Regional sent you something." He picked up a folded, heatsealed paper from the table and passed it across. Brennen had barely pulled open the seal when Frankin announced, "We've all had crazy experiences with the time lag in communications. Our Sentinel friend commanded the defense of Veroh as a wing colonel, but when Regional found out I'd given him the command, they made him a field general. And I say, well deserved. Congratulations, Brennen."

Holding back a startled smile, Brennen shook Frankin's hand. Then he finished scanning the paper. It offered terse congratulations, the advancement in rank, and a significant pay raise.

The other officers murmured good wishes. Ellet Kinsman's epsilon sense fairly glowed with approval.

One step closer to the High command, he told himself. He tucked the paper into his pocket, briefly wishing he could've worn his new rank's triangular insignia on his collar, like Frankin. A Sentinel could wear only the star.

"Netaia, then." Frankin waved at the nearest bulkhead. A three-dimensional projection of that star system sprang into existence: one major world, two others designated *C* for "colonized," and several deep-space modules. "Full demolition of military resources, and this quarter of the Whorl will sleep easier. General Caldwell, your access intelligence will be critical."

General Caldwell. He liked the sound. He rolled it through his mind once more, then focused on the war. This would mean new responsibilities. "It's all on cross-programmable record aboard the *Horizon*," he said soberly.

"We requisitioned *Horizon* when we heard about your data," Frankin agreed, "but we had no idea your source was this good. The rest of the division should get here in another day. I'd like to speak with Her Highness before leaving Veroh."

Brennen cleared his throat. "Be careful. We still can't rule out suicide. Lady Firebird knows what that data she gave us will mean to Netaia, and she has a capacity for loyalty under circumstances we'd consider impossible. She . . . needs to be shown a worthier cause," he added.

Despite his objective phrasing, Ellet flashed with a jealous horror that he felt plainly.

"Very well . . . General," said a smiling, oblivious officer on his left. "Have you any other advice in dealing with this woman?"

So Ellet had read him correctly, interpreting his concern for Firebird as a personal hope. "Since you asked my advice," he said, "I'd transfer her to Tallis. As quickly as possible."

Firebird spent that day studying *Federacy of the Free*. Brennen Caldwell's likeness in Unit 78 startled her, an old tri-D of a nineteen-year-old second captain they'd decorated for leading a daring raid. Spying a birth date, she did the numbers mentally: He was seven Netaian years older than herself. By this account, just as Vett Zimmer had claimed, he'd been Academy-educated as a fightercraft pilot.

Even as she read from a suspicious mental distance, this Federate history intrigued her. She already knew its beginning, because Netaia had suffered the same catastrophe. Four hundred years ago, Sabba Six-alpha—a binary star between the Whorl's Tallis and Elysia regions—had evolved with only a few months' warning into something that still baffled astrophysicists. Without going nova, it started to spew radiation and high-energy particles in decades-long spurts. Space-faring civilizations were chased to ground for over a century, and much information technology was scrambled or lost. During that long disaster, while advanced civilizations deteriorated all over the Whorl, the Netaian aristocracy had repelled those marauders from out-Whorl space, consolidated power, and then saved Netaia's culture and industry by reviving predisaster technologies.

But as the radiation storms began to subside, the Federate worlds had reestablished free commerce and unrestricted research. According to this account, the Federacy claimed to be primarily a trade and mutual defense organization, founded on justice for all classes, respectful nonaggression between self-governing peoples, and a refusal to unnecessarily deprive anyone of life or liberty.

Firebird glanced up at the cracked ceiling and sighed. Maybe the truth was more complex than this junior-school oversimplification, but she would've gladly served such a government. Years ago she had grieved for her innocence when experienced electors finally bullied her into believing that common people couldn't be ruled by the ideals of her favorite ballads, but only by Strength . . . and the other eight Powers. Her mother had actually tightened the penal system. According to Netaian policy, the Federacy would have to be just as oppressive as the Electorate, or worse, to maintain its grip on so many star systems.

Maybe the electors were wrong. This government didn't claim to be "gripping" at all. The Federate fleet had let the NPN retreat unassailed from its first attack on Veroh. And hadn't Brennen Caldwell, the only Federate she knew even slightly, treated her decently when he could've been arrogant and cruel?

If the electors were wrong, then either the Powers were mistaken, or else they only existed as personal attributes, not as gods. If that were the case, then Firebird Angelo had sacrificed herself for nothing.

Nothing but Netaia. That was some comfort.

Uneasily, she popped out the scan cartridge. The truth couldn't be this simple. There were usually contingencies.

She was struggling through the preface to *Transnational Government*, a weighty volume on the Federacy's sociopolitical-economic structure, when Brennen came into her cell carrying a sealed parcel. He looked like a lord in dress whites. They carried no insignia or decoration but the Federate slash and his Master Sentinel's star.

"Your uniform." He laid it on the cot. "The officers who came with the fleet have arrived planetside. They want to discuss that termination request."

Enough history, enough theory. Her life was at stake. "What will they do?"

"Just talk. They've been in contact with Tallis."

"Does . . . everyone know I'm here, then?"

"Only Regional command and these officers. But they want to discuss making the announcement."

Which would destroy the sweet legend that she'd died a hero. It was false, anyway. Firebird tore the seal on the parcel. "All right," she said. "I'll just be a minute."

She dressed hurriedly but carefully. Early this morning, Brennen had sent down a microcopy of her asylum document, mounted on a plastene card. She slid it into the breast pocket that had once held a white packet, a promise of safety replacing her promise of death.

Official again in cobalt blue with rubies glittering on her collar, she found herself standing straighter than she had for a long while but profoundly uncomfortable. She'd been thinking treasonous thoughts this afternoon, and she'd accepted treasonous amnesty. Forcing a comb through her long hair, she greeted her reflection in the cracked mirror: *Welcome back, Firebird. You were always the rebel of the family at heart, even when you obeyed them.*

She left her hair loose this time.

Brennen stepped back in. The corners of his mouth twitched into a smile that reminded her she was safe, for the moment. "I feel like an officer again," she said. "Almost."

"You look it." He motioned her to lead him down the passway.

At a long table in a small conference room, five more officers in white scrambled to their feet. Undeniably nervous among so much Federate authority, Firebird still felt flattered that they'd met her in dress uniform. She came to attention.

"Your Highness." The nearest man extended his hand.

She clasped it boldly. He didn't look as if he had brought her a death warrant. "Thank you, but that's not my title," she corrected him gravely. "Lady Firebird is correct, or Major Angelo."

"Please, then, sit down, my lady," he suggested.

She took the vacant chair at the head of the table, one self-conscious soldier in cobalt blue facing six in Federate white.

Brennen introduced the officers, but they seemed a blur. The nearest, General Frankin, did nearly all the talking. "I'm not sorry to report that the Regional council didn't authorize your execution, Lady Firebird. General Caldwell says you have now applied for asylum."

General Caldwell.

She shot him a glance. He smiled faintly.

Of course they'd promoted him. He'd held a major command. Battling down her jealousy, she answered with care. "What Netaia did here lies heavily on my conscience, sir. I want to help ensure that this basium project will not be developed, as much for Netaia's sake as for yours." From their lack of reaction, she assumed they'd been told about Cleary's research. Brennen must've released that intelligence. Frankin and the other three men looked thoughtful, although the woman Sentinel—as Firebird stretched her memory, she recalled Captain Kinsman from Korda's holograph—scrutinized her, and even Brennen, through narrowed eyes.

Brennen. A general. Unfair, unbelievable.

But at least he wasn't promoted posthumously.

"We are aware of the basium project," announced Frankin. "We share your determination to see it thwarted. From here, we will proceed to demilitarize Netaia. I say this without malice, Lady Firebird, but your navy will be badly outgunned."

"I understand," she answered, wishing she didn't.

"Do you understand that your name will likely be used in negotiations?" Frankin asked.

This was the price she would pay for survival. Her people would brand her a traitor. Aching, she looked to Brennen. Suddenly his promotion didn't matter at all. He nodded, arching an eyebrow in sympathy.

She focused on Frankin again. "How will you use my name?"

Frankin laid both forearms on the black tabletop. "Your people should know you are safe. Their impression of the Federacy is in transition. We cannot ignore your navy's challenge to peace, but our goal is long-term mutual respect. We will strike quickly and mercifully and then allow your people to return as soon as practicable to home rule.

"We've received your claim that you have no worth as a hostage," he went on, "but be assured, the Federacy takes no hostages. Your presence among us is of great importance because our treatment of you will surely influence the Netaian public, as will your request for asylum."

They cared what the *public* thought. "I hope so," she admitted, "but that will not affect the Electorate."

"You also remain a source of advice and information."

Remembering her interrogation onboard that Federate cruiser, Firebird looked hard at Brennen. He returned this stare frankly. He—or another Sentinel—might be ordered to question her again.

So maybe she'd learn to resist. She lowered her eyes. "You'll tell the Electorate that I asked for amnesty?"

"Only in context of the full account, including your final heroic actions as a squadron leader, and what General Caldwell has called your 'astonishing' effort to resist mind-access."

What? Had she almost succeeded? She glanced to Brennen for confirmation. Again he nodded. The chill on her heart thawed slightly. She turned back to Frankin. "Where are you sending me, then? Netaia will seek my execution."

"We'd prefer to see you transferred to protective custody at Regional command on Tallis. I hope you'll find that acceptable."

"I'm in no position to object." Inwardly she sighed. She would see Tallis after all.

Four of its walls, anyway.

"Very well, then. We'll meet again, Your Highness. Thank you for cooperating."

She winced at his choice of words. *Collaborator!* she berated herself.

Brennen led her away. Once the lift doors closed, she murmured, "General. Congratulations, Brennen."

"Thank you." She heard satisfaction in his voice.

"Expected?"

"Not quite so soon."

Plainly, though, he was on the fast track of promotion.

Down at the battered brown jailer's desk, he asked her to halt. "Gentle men, this officer has accepted asylum and will be traveling to Tallis shortly. Please see that she's treated with respect."

"Sir?" Koan Tryseleen's rangy body straightened.

"Her name is not Tomma. I apologize for deceiving you, but it was done in the best interests of the Federacy." He glanced at Firebird, who stood at loose parade rest. "This is First Major Lady Firebird Angelo, the queen's third daughter."

Tryseleen and his pale associate drew away as though Brennen had announced she had a communicable terminal disease.

She believed that she did. It was called treachery.

Brennen inclined his head toward her end of the corridor. When the door had ground shut behind them, he took her right hand and pressed her fingers. "I'm going on with the fleet as soon as I can pack, and I won't have time to say good-bye later."

"To Netaia?"

"Yes."

In the yellow light, she looked up into his face, finding it hard to imagine that she would be living somewhere in this vast Federacy, but he'd be elsewhere. "Thank you, then. Watch out for yourself."

"I will." He studied her eyes. "You still feel guilty."

"Terribly."

He shook his head. "You've done nothing wrong. You obeyed your orders and more. Please, Mari. Reconsider your . . . deities. There's a higher call on your life now."

Why did he keep calling her that? She clutched his arm. "And please, don't . . ." She choked. How could she plead mercy for Netaia's forces, after Veroh?

His answering expression would haunt her for weeks: lips straight and bland, stress lines crowding his eyes, and a lift to his eyebrows that might have been sympathy or regret, or even pain.

"Be careful," she managed, ". . . General."

He took two steps through the doorway, turned, and saluted her.

The door slid shut.

CHAPTER 9

NETAIA

marziale
martial, marchlike

Too many details needed final attention before Brennen could leave Twinnich in Gorn Frankin's hands. He eyed his shorthand notes. Since this job was no longer simply a peacekeeping command, Frankin—with experience on Caroli's board of protectorates—had the seniority and experience to get the Verohans back on their feet. In retrospect, it almost seemed odd Frankin hadn't taken the original command.

He was glad he'd been ordered out. From memory, and his brief data-collecting mission years ago, he was starting to grasp the Netaian mindset, but now it seemed urgent to know the place in his own flesh. He wasn't quite certain why.

He didn't like assigning Ellet Kinsman to escort Firebird to Tallis, but he had no other qualified woman to send. He had worked on and off with Ellet. About a year ago, she'd offered to exchange a connaturality probe, as unmarried Sentinels could do. He'd declined . . . maybe too politely.

Now he would have to rely on Ellet's vesting vows to keep her from deliberately shaking Firebird's fragile independence. Ellet's loyalty to the Sentinel kindred and her racial pride must make her a teacher, and Firebird's curiosity must cement their relationship.

He wished he could confide his true feelings to Ellet. He'd grown weary of living alone, when most Sentinels shared every emotion with a bond mate; but Ellet's first reaction to public events, without fully knowing his heart, had warned him away again. To Ellet, any outsider was suspect. Inferior.

As if Ellet had caught his thoughts, he felt her step into the com center. Looking up, he imagined Firebird, with her delicate face and long, hot-colored hair, next to Ellet, whose strong nose and slightly concave cheeks represented classic Thyrian features. At his own height and a little more, Ellet would tower over Firebird.

"When do we slip?" she asked, casually resting one hand on his desk. ". . . General?"

He couldn't help smiling slightly. "I'd like you on escort duty, Ellet. Would you take Lady Firebird to Tallis?"

An upside interlink buzzed nearby. Brennen made certain a com tech caught it, then turned back to the other Sentinel. "Minimal security detention," he explained.

Ellet's epsilon cloud had thickened. "Tallis is a choice assignment, but I've been working as Frankin's admin counselor. Don't you feel I should go with him?"

"Frankin will stay on Veroh. He'll have good counsel from Twinnich staff."

An aide hurried past, balancing a tray of kass cups. Brennen watched Ellet without communicating, each wreathed in static no outsider would discern and through which no emotion would pass.

Her face had gone blank. "Something is wrong, Brennen. Would you show me your feelings for her?"

Sentinel ethics dictated that he must grant such a request, and Ellet would need some assurance if he wanted this time to go well for Firebird. He cleared his outer shields and raised feelings that shouldn't distress Ellet: pity, understanding, optimism. Ellet's feathery touch, connatural enough to caress although the otherness felt distinct, swept over his surface emotions.

She pulled back and stood tall. "Brennen, be careful."

Ellet doubtless guessed more than he'd shown her. They both knew he could conceal some emotion under inner, deeper shields she wouldn't even sense. "I am always careful, Ellet."

"Very well," she said softly. "The girl has been through torments, and she could make the Federacy a valuable resource. I'll try to educate her."

"Thank you." Absently he tapped the desk. "I will ask for a full report."

"You'll have it."

Within a day, the rest of the Second Division reached Veroh. A shuttle picked up Firebird, Ellet, and a few other passengers and streaked on to Tallis. From another, Brennen boarded the Federate cruiser *Corona*. Half an hour later the division slipped, bound for Netaia.

The officers met after dinner on *Corona*'s bridge. Admiral Lee Danton, the only Second Division fleet officer to have risen through diplomatic channels, stood at one edge of a tri-D projection of the Netaia system. The tri-D's glow seemed to deepen the cleft in Danton's chin, and it set lights in his sandy hair. Inside a projected sphere, tiny gold and scarlet ship-images stood out against the orbits of Netaia's five stony inner planets.

"So the main strike," Danton continued, "will be the largest division of our forces. Smaller groups will deploy as follows. I'll keep *Corona* just out-system and ensure the Netaians receive no reinforcements—"

Brennen glanced up.

"What, General Caldwell?"

"Sir, they have no outsystem allies."

"They could hire Geminan mercenaries. *Elysia*, with escort," he continued, "to orbit with and isolate the primary intersystem relay station. CNC One, Colonel Nikolas. You'll be on board *Elysia. Deng* . . ."

Leaning against a table-level communications console, Brennen waited out the other tactical assignments. A systemwide strike would require several CNCs, Colonial Neutralization Commanders, but Brennen didn't expect to miss the main battle. He wasn't surprised when Danton called his name for a job he didn't really want.

"*Horizon*, main planetary assault. Field General Caldwell, Atmospheric Commander." He looked up from his recall pad. "General Caldwell, I want you on the main attack with that target data. We do appreciate your understanding of Netaian affairs and locales."

Brennen nodded, frowning. He'd had a major command. He'd fly a bridge from now on, not an intercept fighter. He probably had more combat experience than any other officer here and knew more about Netaia, but the AC would direct the assault on Netaia itself. Today's action would be a kind of warfare he detested, a punitive strike.

He'd been decorated during that kind of battle at Gemina. The Federacy always practiced restraint, but he wouldn't enjoy this assignment. His force would square off against Netaian combatants trying to defend their own bases, their own people. He was glad Mari didn't know what he had to do.

Mari—oddly, in his mind, "Mari" was the woman he knew. Another woman, Firebird, had tried to die for Netaia's glory. She was changing . . . he hoped.

Minutes later, Danton dismissed his staff. General Gulest Vanidar of Tura, the swarthy officer who would command *Horizon*, caught Brennen's glance and beckoned him over. "You'll be on my boat, then." Vanidar's accent, cultured with a slight drawl, suggested a classical education on Elysia, capital of the other Federate region and HQ of Federate High command. "I've never worked with a Sentinel."

Brennen shook his head. "Don't expect anything unusual. Not unless something comes up."

"No . . . telepathic orders across the bridge?"

Brennen shook his head. "I wear a mike like anyone else, General Vanidar."

The firm set of Vanidar's jaw softened slightly. "Then I look forward to working with you."

Bemused and slightly depressed, Brennen searched out his cabin, though a casual friend invited him to join a group for Carolinian dagger play in the R&R center. After Veroh, he needed some uninterrupted rest.

Someone else would lead Delta Flight, he mused as he pulled off his boots. He'd clung to his wings longer than normal, thanks to his SO status. But now—with this promotion—the Federacy finally had invested too much in him to risk him in battle anymore.

This would be strange, though.

He slept a full eleven hours before the attack force's final rendezvous, during which crews were transshipped for battle. The rest of Delta Flight shuttled to a huge fighter carrier escorting *Horizon* while Brennen familiarized himself with a new list of squadron commanders, including his former wingman, the new leader of Delta Flight. Brennen sat beside Vanidar when the battle group accelerated back into slip-state, making its final jump to Netaia.

Count Tel Tellai sat flipping the ends of his blue sash, waiting with twenty-six other men and women around the gold-rimmed electoral table. A tense, garbled outsystem message had interrupted this last afternoon session of the week. It would take several minutes for the electors' DeepScan request for a repeat to reach the system's fringe.

Irritation lines did nothing for Princess Phoena's features. Today she wore a snug, iridescent shipboard-style suit that touched several of propriety's limits, and jewels to cover what it did not. Crown Princess Carradee, in conservative mauve, merely looked concerned, and tailored Siwann held herself with utter calm.

He dropped his sash ends and emulated the queen. He should consider the report his holdings manager had sent up this morning, regarding how a recent early frost might cut profits—

The media block at center table hissed. "Repeating previous transmission. A report has come in from the Veroh strike force, Operation Pinnacle, dated four days past. Our forces had driven back the enemy to Veroh's main settlement and there established a state of siege."

Tel crossed his hands on the smooth, cool table. On his left, Muirnen Rogonin gave a satisfied sigh.

"Concern was then growing, however, regarding an apparent slip-shield zone approaching Veroh from out-spinward. Contingency alert was recommended, allowing for communications lag."

Tel furrowed his brow. Bad news?

First Marshal Burkenhamn stood. His cobalt-blue-swathed bulk seemed wasted on a man who didn't need size to command attention. "Contingency plans have indeed been drawn up by my staff. Our forces are standing alert." The marshal's rich voice heartened Tel. "And let us remember that a slip zone can exist merely as a lingering radiation echo from the great catastrophe, bouncing out of the Whorl or its Eye. That, of course, is our best-case scenario."

"And the worst?" The queen remained as collected as statuary.

Burkenhamn raised a finger. "Because no such slip zone has been observed near the Netaia system by our sensing stations, we assume Netaia is safe for the moment, even if the Federates have sent a force to retake Veroh.

"It is, however, conceivable that Veroh could be already retaken. A force large enough to achieve that could advance in this direction. Because of the buffer systems' location ninety degrees from Veroh, we would have little warning, if any, of an attack. This is—"

Burkenhamn tapped the table to silence a whisperer at the outer branch's far end. "This is, I remind you, merely a worst-case scenario. Let us remember that the Federates hesitated to approach our system at the moment classic strategy would have suggested they strike."

Tel understood less than half of that.

Siwann raised an eyebrow. "Continue."

Burkenhamn bowed from the waist. "Let us then turn to the possibility of Veroh having been finally subdued by our forces—"

Again the media block buzzed, cutting him off.

"Outsystem report," said the clear, nearby voice. "DeepScan channel three. This is a new report. May I broadcast direct?"

"Certainly," Siwann snapped. Silence fell. Tel found himself holding his breath.

The distant voice babbled, all pretense of poise gone. "Subspace wake, passing deep-space module two. Alert. Very large subspace wake—"

Even Tel knew what that meant . . . many ships had entered the Netaian system!

Burkenhamn and Siwann fell on their communication terminals. Carradee's fingers splayed on the tabletop. Phoena clenched a fist and bit down on her thumb, keying furiously with her other hand. Tel wanted to hurry over and stand by her, protect her, but he sat welded to his chair.

Countdown to launch commenced. Brennen had conferred with

squadron commanders—selecting primary targets, establishing refuel and re-arm procedures and contingency plans for possible enemy courses of action. Within minutes, *Horizon* would exit slip-state for normal space. Vanidar sat surrounded by junior officers, reviewing *Horizon*'s own maneuvers and defense plans. Brennen's monitors gleamed with maps that covered both of Netaia's major continents and the sketchy base data Firebird had remembered. Refueling information was one thing; energy-shield wavelengths would've been infinitely more helpful, but she'd had no need to know those.

He felt restless, fidgety. In vivid memory, he was elsewhere:

Helmeted, harnessed, and linked to life support, he had waited inside the cockpit of his intercept fighter. Behind, cabled one after another in a deep chute on the carrier's belly, sat the rest of his flight. Inside other chutes waited more pilots. He'd boarded hours ago, strapping down before the carrier began maximum deceleration, and then slept while he could.

"One minute to normal space reentry. Three minutes to launch. Activate generators."

Brennen obeyed the voice in his helmet with one pull of his gloved hand, then keyed over to intersquad frequency. His inclined seat started to vibrate. Lights sprang to life on the board. "Delta Leader, generator check."

"Two, check."

"Three, check . . ."

The carrier shuddered. Drop point: He'd ridden it twenty times from the cockpit of a carrier fighter, but it still made him nervous. A drop-point malfunction could strand carrier, fighters, and pilots in quasi-orthogonal space.

Seconds continued to melt off on his console chrono, still crossprogrammed into the carrier's main computer. He gripped stick and throttle and cleared his senses one by one with focused bursts of epsilon energy.

The carrier's slip-shields dropped. The computer kicked his docking cables free. He pulled back his throttle. The chute rushed by—dropped away—and his overhead screen lit with stars. A reddish sphere lay ahead, growing visibly. With the momentum from the carrier as well as his own thrust, he carried enough velocity to make the crossing in minutes.

"Shields up," he called; then, "Deuce flight."

Five blips shimmered on his rear screen, jockeying into pairs.

He shook loose of the memory as drop point shuddered the ship, and he formed a silent prayer. *Guide our hearts, guide our hands. Show us mercy and help us show it.*

And wherever Mari is, Holy One, go with her.

As *Horizon* reentered normal space, surveillance screens lit all over the bridge with current data. Mari's was a wealthy world, with rich cities and fertile land masses, but its leaders were greedy for more. Did they know they couldn't win? Better for them if they surrendered quickly . . .

"General Caldwell," snapped Admiral Danton's voice in his left ear.

Brennen wore a collar mike. "Caldwell here," he answered.

"Confirm launch?"

Brennen touched up the carrier's frequency and consulted its main computer. "All fighters launched," he said, barely keeping the wistfulness out of his voice. "No malfunctions."

Within three hours, two of Netaia's seven main land and ice military bases were gone, and its auxiliary spaceports were following. The NPN was utterly outgunned, though its three sea bases might hold out indefinitely. Brennen was redirecting squadrons north toward the Arctica ice base when an alert light flashed on his main deployment screen. He slapped the response panel. "Caldwell," he said.

"Sir, it's a transmission from downside. Holding for you, at General Vanidar's request."

Brennen looked over his shoulder at Vanidar's command chair. Vanidar's voice rumbled in his earphone, "Transmit." After a short pause, he continued. "This is Federate Cruiser *Horizon*, Major General Gulest Vanidar commanding."

"General Vanidar," said a distant voice, "this is Count Dorning Stele, Second Marshal of Netaian Forces. Request cease-fire and negotiations."

"We will negotiate only one conclusion, Count Stele," drawled Vanidar. "You are to surrender. Unconditionally. Do you copy?"

"Copy," Stele responded, but he gave no further answer. Brennen imagined the electors that Firebird remembered, gathered in fancy dress around their ornate table, dithering while they tried to bully their armed forces.

Maybe those without military obligations had fled to country estates.

A squadron commander's voice spoke in Brennen's other ear. Until the cease-fire had actually been called, his job was battle management—and until necessary, Count Stele didn't need to know his location as AC. Brennen touched a panel that sent targeting data down to the squadron leader.

"Affirmative," Stele finally came back. "I am authorized to offer surrender."

Two junior officers cheered. Brennen touched on a com frequency. Two minutes later, he'd diverted the northbound squadrons. By then, Stele and General Vanidar were discussing time and place. They settled on two hours—here, on board *Horizon*—Stele in an unarmed civilian ship, with minimal escort.

As soon as Vanidar cut the transmission, though, Brennen spoke to him on a secured frequency. "General, one caution. Don't trust Dorning Stele. He commanded the Veroh massacre." *And*, he recalled, *consigned his own brother to the execution block.*

Vanidar rose out of his chair. "Thanks for the reminder, General Caldwell. We'll arrange an extra-secure reception."

Brennen waited on the control bridge for Landing Bay Four as Stele's craft slowly approached, pulled in by an auxiliary catchfield. The Netaian ship's exterior looked esthetically sleek, lacking shield projection antennae or weapons ports. A scanner alongside the visual screen confirmed no shipboard weapons, nor even energy shields. It was plainly an elegant civilian shuttle.

Up a corridor behind Brennen's right shoulder, Vanidar and his staff had assembled in a conference room. An extra security contingent, ten guards in Carolinian khaki, waited inside the bay's control bridge with Brennen, along with normal security and maintenance personnel, as the huge space door slowly drifted open. Three of the security people had brought in a weapons scanning arch, which stood at the base of the half flight of stairs outside this vacuum-secured bridge.

If Stele were sincere, this meeting would end the fighting and begin Federate occupation of Netaia. Brennen would like nothing better.

The passenger craft settled onto a receiving grid. The space door slid shut. Normally, the main airlock would be disalarmed and unsealed as soon as the bay held air.

Brennen had ordered it to remain sealed until he gave the order. Some weapons, some explosives, no scanner could pick up.

"Count Stele, this is Airlock Four," he said. "Please wait for security precautions. These are for your protection as well as ours."

"Roger, Airlock Four," clipped a voice Brennen now recognized as Stele's pilot. "Waiting for security."

"Go," Brennen said aside to the Carolinian security crew. They hustled down the half flight of steps and out into the bay. He followed, watching closely. Several crewers formed an honor-guard line along the little ship's hatch. Two others, moving more circumspectly, circled the craft to look for anything blatantly suspicious. The last three steered their scanning arch to a spot between the ship and main airlock. Brennen took a position behind the scan unit.

As the only Sentinel on board, he'd be a final weapons detector. The Netaians could conceivably bring low-tech weapons through a scanner—only fools would try to carry metal-frame blazers or shock pistols, so he doubted they'd try that. But no potential assassin should be able to hide his intention. This time, Brennen had to thank the college's policy makers for his unadorned uniform. The simple midnight blue painted no "Atmospheric Commander" target on him.

Just a "Danger! Telepath!" target, he reflected.

When all seemed secure, he nodded to the security crew's chief, who'd put on dress whites to serve as Stele's escort to the conference room. The chief signaled a communications tech up in the command post.

Ten seconds later, a hatch slid open.

Two crewmen in cobalt blue stepped off first. Then came Stele. He ceremoniously whipped off his hat and clutched it under one arm, half bowed, and accepted the security chief's offered hand. The chief motioned him and his crew toward the honor-guard line, which would steer them to the scanning arch.

Count Dorning Stele's posture remained stiff and straight. His nattily tailored uniform bulged halfway up his chest, suggesting a girdle.

And what else? Brennen wondered. He diffused his epsilon shields as the little procession approached his scanner. Four more Netaian escorts followed Stele, who stepped boldly to a table that had been moved alongside. Arching his neck to look down on all Federates, Stele ceremoniously drew and surrendered a gleaming full-dress dagger. Then his sidearm, an ornamental blazer.

Leaving all six of his escorts behind, he marched through the scanner.

It came up clean. Stele turned back toward his escort.

This was the critical moment. Brennen stepped up and tapped his shoulder. "My Lord Count," he said.

Stele whipped around. Brennen looked into hard brown eyes. There was no time to probe, only to check Stele's emotions.

Stele's mental state hummed with suicidal determination.

Brennen reached into his left cuff for his crystace.

Stele turned again. "Now," he shouted, thrusting his right hand through his uniform's front seam.

Instantly Brennen caught him in voice command, freezing him with his hand inside the breast panel. Stele resisted hard, struggling to pull his hand free.

"Security," Brennen shouted.

Two Carolinian guards hustled up. "Explosives check," Brennen ordered. He heard shouts behind him. He couldn't turn to assist until he'd disarmed Stele.

The Carolinian drew a tiny laser knife and slit both sides of Stele's breast panel. Beneath the cobalt blue fabric, he did wear a girdle, or something like it. Small, heavy-looking packets bulged beneath and alongside it. Another security tech hurried up. Brennen focused an access probe and made a fast, deep breach. "Keep his hand on that detonator," Brennen ordered. "Tape it there if you have to, until it's disarmed. If he lets go, it explodes."

Then he looked out into the bay.

Beyond the weapon scanner, three of Stele's crewmen had drawn twin-beam blazers. Another hurried toward the outer bulkhead, carrying an archaic hunting pistol, a projectile weapon fully capable of holing a ship's hull. Two Carolinians sprinted toward him.

Two—no, three—Netaians lay sprawled on the deck, felled by Federate shock pistols. But two Carolinians also were down. Out in the bay were four large, blocky starter units and the Netaian ship, and somewhere behind them, two of Stele's crewmen had to be hiding. As Brennen watched, one of the Carolinians sprinting toward the saboteur fell heavily.

"Drop your weapons," Brennen called, holding his crystace ready. "You won't be targeted if you surrender."

A head popped out from behind Stele's little ship. Brennen activated the crystace and concentrated on that head. Blazer bolts would arrive at light speed, the moment he saw them fired.

He deflected a shot. Then another. He stepped closer. Where was his backup?

There! . . . Circling behind the Netaian ship. "Drop your weapon!" Brennen shouted again, holding the Netaian's attention until the Carolinian could line him up. The Netaian fired once more, and then the Federate guard dropped him.

Brennen whipped around in time to see the saboteur stand close to the bulkhead and start firing. Once, twice, three times. A horrible sucking sound filled the landing bay.

Brennen sprinted across its surface toward the saboteur. *Come on*, he urged the Netaian covering him. *Show yourself.*

He felt him before he saw him, alongside a blocky charge unit. "Behind Unit Six," Brennen shouted as he readied the crystace. This Netaian must've seen what the crystace could do. He hesitated, probably waiting until Brennen looked distracted. That gave Brennen time to get between him and his partner. Then he turned his head aside, pretending inattention.

The Netaian fired. Brennen leaped aside. The Netaian's shot felled his compatriot. An instant later, another Carolinian got him.

Now Brennen felt the ominous wind. "Repair," he shouted. "Breach in panel . . . four-eight-six," he read off the prominently labeled bulkhead. The landing bay held enough air to keep everyone inside alive for several minutes, even with several small leaks; but minuscule holes could spread, open cracks, and destroy huge sections of the hull. Even the ship itself.

Brennen breathed slowly and deliberately.

Two maintenance men dashed up, steering a cart laden with metal sheets and flexible adhesives.

Leaning into the wind, Brennen strode back toward the inner airlock. Stele stood bare chested, with both hands in wrist restraints. On the deck lay several white packets, sections of cobalt blue fabric, and dozens of short, multicolored detonator wires. One security tech held out a packet to Brennen. "Smells like Glyphex," he said.

Brennen didn't recognize the substance. "Well done. Take it down to Armament for analysis." Then he met Stele's eyes again. "So you were the sacrificial victim," he said coldly. "Did they order you to suicide because of Veroh?"

Stele's shoulders shifted. He was probably trying to pull his wrists free.

Brennen would've felt thoroughly disgusted, except for one thing: Dorning Stele, a commanding officer, would yield up everything Brennen needed to know about those critical undersea bases.

"Take him to sick bay," Brennen ordered. "Suicide watch."

The security team led away its new prisoner. Now, Brennen realized, the fleet must disarm Netaia right down to its last metals manufacturing plant before Admiral Danton could consider a surrender offer.

He no longer dreaded the battle ahead.

con brio
with vigor

By the time Brennen rejoined Vanidar on the command deck, Netaia's navy had launched all remaining ships. The Citangelo quadrant's defenses fell back before a punishing main attack, but on the dark side at Claighbro and the Bruggeman Gap, fewer Federate ships faced a fierce defense.

An alarm clamored. The frame on *Horizon*'s dorsal status screen turned from blue to orange. A voice pealed in his ear, "Topside attack, *Horizon*! Twenty marks, point-zero-zero heading, range nine-seven-nine. ETI two-point-four minutes."

As if piloting his own fighter, Brennen first checked the cruiser's energy shields. Vanidar barked, "Full assault power to topside shields and gunnery." As others relayed the order, Brennen touched an interlink control. "Delta Flight, this is *Horizon*. Major Kirzell, can your quadrant spare the flight to defend the cruiser?"

"Yessir," snapped a familiar voice in his ear.

Brennen clenched a fist at the screen. Withdrawing Delta Flight from the battle to subdue Citangelo might cost more downside lives than it would save up here. Even with the intelligence he'd just taken from Dorning Stele, the Netaians' unorthodox tactics would only worsen their punishment.

"General Caldwell," came a new voice from a small speaker. "Gamma group over sea base three. We're badly outnumbered. I need more high support."

Brennen exhaled sharply and checked a grid for the sea base's newly acquired specs. A glance at the master screens showed his atmospheric forces already spread thin.

Brennen switched his link to Vanidar. "Redeploy Delta Flight to support Gamma group?" He wanted permission for this one, with *Horizon* in danger. As Vanidar gave it and Brennen relayed it, the corporal between them glanced up from her terminal. Sweat glistened on her forehead. Vanidar checked screens, then reached for the interlink board again. "Generator, draw power from all systems but weapons and life support to maintain energy and particle shielding. Status reports every two minutes."

The bridge fell eerily silent. Blinded by the loss of external screens, Brennen held his emotions under control and waited for a possible impact.

A minute later the lights flared on again, and with them the screens and a cacophony from the speakers.

"Take the link, Corporal," ordered Vanidar. The ordnance and shield banks had drained but were rapidly recharging, and the Netaian attack group was peeling away . . . twelve, thirteen, fourteen remaining. Then the group changed course. Brennen blinked. They'd lost thirty percent, but they were coming back. *Their commanders should be spaced!*

In three more passes, the suicide attackers were annihilated. Then Brennen could attend again to the atmospheric battle. The main force finally had neutralized Citangelo; over Claighbro and the Gap bases, the tide was turning again, in his favor. Relaxing slightly, he prepared to finish an unpleasant job.

Crown Princess Carradee Angelo watched tri-D monitors built into a catfooted marble table in her cream-and-gold parlor. On the night side of the world, lightning storms swept the skies. By daylight, tall buildings stood empty, industrial areas evacuated to an unnatural holiday-week stillness— except for outsystem attack ships that dropped in tight formations, destroyed Citangelo's remaining depots and factories, and sped off-screen. Terror strangled the mighty city.

She watched alone. Servitors attended her daughters, and underground somewhere in Citangelo, her husband supervised a communications network. Along the marble wall that separated their living suites, several receiving units had been set on a credenza to let her listen in on his movements, but one by one their voices had gone silent. *This cannot be!* she moaned. *For Veroh and its forsaken basium mines we pay with our homeland? I've already lost a sister.*

The thought of Firebird brought tears. Carradee had tried to see Firebird in her proper light, a wastling who should be honored to pour out her life so young, so much younger than Carradee would be when Iarlet was ready for rule—

Well, yes, Firebird had that nonconformist streak. Carradee tried to smile. She would forgive that streak, given Firebird's fiery doom at Veroh and the way Phoena had tormented her.

The hall door opened without warning. A page in Angelo scarlet slipped in and shut the massive wooden panel behind him.

Hastily Carradee wiped her face dry with a silken hand cloth from her skirt pocket. "Don't you still knock?" she asked wearily. "We are at war, but the world still turns, and the Disciplines help it to do so."

The boy was gulping his own tears. "Pardon, Highness. Please, Highness. Her Majesty is dying."

"Dying?" Carradee cried. She scrambled to her feet.

"She said you'd have only a few minutes, Highness. Please hurry!"

Netaia's only remaining defenses were wheel-borne when Brennen sent reports to Admiral Danton, to General Frankin at Veroh, and to Regional command, then ordered downside silence. Netaia still hadn't officially surrendered. More deep-space forces would soon arrive from Ituri to reinforce this battle group, and Danton was bringing the *Corona* insystem.

Only one duty remained, and then he'd be able to rest. When he shut his eyes, he saw flames and explosions. There would be nightmares tonight.

The sentry at the ship's vault sprang to attention when Brennen stopped at his desk. "It's all over but the talk," Brennen said, "we hope. Item twenty-six seventy-six, please."

Three minutes later he sat on his bunk, examining the parcel. Through a fresh layer of clear wrap, fabric showed cobalt blue, and two ruby stars gleamed like smoldering sparks. Firebird, wearing this uniform at their parting, had bitten back a plea for her people—he'd read it in the cry of her emotions. He knew she would offer almost anything to buy peace for Netaia. Revealing her survival had already been named as part of the price.

He broke the seal and drew out the uniform. From its collar he unclipped the ruby stars, then laid them on a bunkside niche. He made a mental note to find a presentation box and send the rest of the uniform back down with a courier.

Gratefully he began to undress. He'd pulled off one boot when his interlink buzzed. Groaning, he reached for the tab.

"DeepScan transmission for you, sir. Switching on." For a moment the link crackled. "General Caldwell?" came Admiral Danton's voice. "We've been discussing staff for occupation forces. Since you're rather an expert on these people, we were wondering if you could see yourself as lieutenant governor. I need a strong second, someone to do my tough jobs while I work diplomacy. Temporary position. After you clean house, the diplomatic corps can move in someone else. Regional told me to push you, anyway. Want the job?"

Unbelievable. Lieutenant governor? Less than a month ago, he'd had only a flight team to call his own, and that only between intelligence assignments. *"When the fast track accelerates,"* he'd been warned, *"hang on!"*

He spoke to the pickup. "Sir, I accept. I believe I'm slated to assist you when they officially surrender."

"I want their surrender before I go planetside. Major General Mafis will do the honors. He's Diplomat Corps. You speak 'on behalf of the fleet commander,' and when papers are signed planetside, have Mafis announce both our names."

"Good, sir."

"I'll make an official landing soon after. But if they refuse to surrender, I suppose you'll have to convince them they should give up rather than take further losses."

Another strike? "Yes, sir," Brennen muttered.

As he expected, his sleep was haunted by circular dreams of a battle that couldn't end until he'd found every piece of a tridimensional puzzle. The following morning, ship's time, an interlink transmission woke him. "Sir," said an unfamiliar voice, "Major General Mafis has been delayed. We are holding a transmission from downside. He requests you answer."

"I'll be there immediately."

The corporal saluted as he arrived on the bridge. Resting one hand on the back of Vanidar's command chair, Brennen signaled for activation of the main reception screen.

A huge man's image appeared . . . Devair Burkenhamn, he knew from Firebird's memories, as well as Count Dorning Stele's. Accessing Stele's mind had been like bathing in sewage—arrogant, sensual, stifling—but informative. The marshal waited calmly, but Brennen read defeat in his posture. Brennen came to attention and nodded to the corporal. For the first time in sixteen hours, *Horizon* broke downside silence. "Sir," he said curtly. "Field General Brennen Caldwell, speaking for . . ." Yes, he'd been authorized. ". . . the fleet commander."

"Thank you for responding, General." Burkenhamn reached beyond the projection field to retrieve a long scribepaper. "I am First Marshal of Netaian Forces Devair Burkenhamn, authorized by the Electorate to offer complete and unconditional surrender, as you have demanded. When and where will you meet with us to discuss terms?"

Brennen warmed to his unexpected role. This wealthy world lay like a wounded beast on its back, with its military forces wiped out, and—for the moment—under his personal control. He could demand any of several humiliating conciliatory gestures. He felt almost giddy. This sensation must be the pride that corrupted, creating conquerors. He'd been warned to control his ambition, but he'd never guessed it would tempt him this way. "Citangelo spaceport is central," he reminded Burkenhamn.

"It is in ruins."

"I'm sure it's still adequate to handle one shuttle. Clear a landing pad. Meet us there at ten hundred local time. We require a representative from your military, one for the Assembly, one for the Electorate, and, of course, the Crown." That was it, the best statement of strength he could make. "We wish to speak with the queen, sir."

"And we will require—"

Brennen shook his head, aware that he was gloating. "The surrendering party will be treated fairly, but today's terms are not yours to set. Your day will come again, I assure you. The Federacy is anxious to establish normal relations. However, if Netaia tries treachery again, you will pay a high price."

Burkenhamn bowed his head and vanished.

During his next break, Brennen examined the new emotion. He'd made solid command decisions, and personally gathered the intelligence that made victory possible. No other living person could've performed those interrogations so well. Still, he'd been warned never to depend ultimately on his own abilities, but only the One. According to all he'd sworn, he was only a highly effective servant, and even that wouldn't last. Someday—many years in the future if he was careful—his starbred abilities would wane. Before then, he must learn enough wisdom to go on serving well.

So he mustn't let pride enslave him to himself. His people lived as exiles, torn from their home world, because their ancestors had lusted to rule. Now, from Netaia's West Reach to Kierilay Island, from the Cheitt Penin-sula southwest to the fertile DeTar plain, Netaians must bury their dead sons and daughters and rebuild their lives. Imagining Thyrica laid waste, he tried to banish all sense of self-congratulation as he checked Vanidar's shuttle arrangements.

He settled for a deep sense of personal victory.

Three hours later, a saucer-shaped Federate craft settled gently on an area of Citangelo spaceport that had been dozed clear of rubble. Watching out a viewport near the main lock, Brennen saw that the spaceport was in fact largely unusable. Its main tower and outbuildings had been blasted into twisted, tottering shapes of metal and stone. Five rocket craters were dishes of jagged boulders, while its main terminal was glassy slag, framed by the fractured wreckage of a high-speed maglev system.

Brennen reviewed his orders. He would personally notify the Angelo family of Firebird's survival. He must be firm but respectful with Siwann, though he'd have liked to force access and make her understand, through Firebird's memories, how cruelly she'd scarred her third daughter. Grimacing, he straightened his tunic.

Twenty Federate pilots marched off down the shuttle's ramp into escort formation. Major General Clohon Mafis, the diplomat, had arrived on *Horizon* shortly after Burkenhamn's transmission. He followed the guards, carrying a silver scribebook. An albino soldier of the Dengii race from the Whorl's rimward-north quadrant, he stood nearly two meters tall, with white hair brushed sleek and a scarlet tunic thick with decorations.

Brennen came last, finally surveying firsthand the damage that had been wreaked under his command. Unlike Veroh, Netaia had taken no nuclear shelling. Precision bombing of military targets had left the city's civilian skyline, a curious blend of ornate and angular, virtually untouched, though its sun shone a bleary orange through dust and acrid smoke. Less than a quarter mile from the spaceport's skeletal tower, children could play in undamaged gardens.

The approaching Netaian delegates, more than had been requested, eyed him curiously. Standing beside the heavily decorated Mafis, he guessed he looked like an honor guard. Thyrian regs still prohibited him from wearing the honors he'd earned.

Scanning the Netaian group, he abruptly realized Siwann wasn't there. He did see Carradee, standing between two burly House Guards. Both relieved and disappointed, and wondering what consequences must be demanded for Siwann's refusal, he stepped forward with Mafis and let his epsilon shields diffuse. Intimidation by position, his masters had taught him, could control a crowd without overtly menacing anyone. This crowd, however, felt subdued already.

With a long pale hand, Mafis activated a recall pad on a cart brought up by one guard, and he introduced himself and Caldwell to the Netaians. Marshal Burkenhamn faced Mafis as chief of his own delegation, regarding Brennen with unconcealed curiosity.

Brennen guessed Burkenhamn knew the uniform. Firebird had recognized his star even as a cadet.

Mafis spoke. "The terms of your surrender are as follows. Martial law will be enforced. The Regional council has appointed Admiral Lee Danton of the Second Division to be your governor. His official landing shall take place at this time tomorrow. Governor Danton has selected Field General Caldwell, Special Operations, as his lieutenant governor pro tem." He motioned aside, indicating Brennen. "The Netaian Assembly, the Electorate, and the Crown shall hold authority under the planetary governor.

Netaia and both its buffer systems shall remain demilitarized. The Planetary Navy is disbanded until further word, as shall be the Assembly and the Electorate. You shall hold new elections in one month."

Brennen spoke next, quoting lines Danton had written for him. "Because the Federacy has no provision for holding a conquered state, Netaia with her subjugate systems will constitute an independent Federate protectorate, roughly equivalent to the Veroh system." That ought to sting. "You will have no forces of your own, but we will not leave you defenseless." He felt their surprise. Apparently they wouldn't have protected Veroh if they'd taken it. Disgusted, he restored his shields.

Mafis continued. "This document, as we directed in our communiqué, shall be signed by four Netaian representatives. I summon you four to sign the instrument of surrender."

Three men . . . and Crown Princess Carradee . . . came to the cart, their steps raising small dust clouds. The men signed the recall pad first.

Firebird's oldest sister was surprisingly tall, in her late twenties, and still slightly heavy from her recent pregnancy. She held her head and shoulders regally. As Brennen passed her the stylus, he asked so only she could hear, "Was the queen unable to come as we directed, Highness?" He would know if she lied.

"I am now the queen, Excellency, Carradee Second."

Startled by her news and the way she'd addressed him, he eyed her more closely. Her pale gray eyes looked red and puffy; her hands worked nervously at the hem of her fitted brown jacket. "My—our mother, Her Majesty Queen Siwann, left Netaia in our hands two nights ago," she added. She signed neatly, without flourishes, and stepped away.

His private conference would be vastly different from the one he'd anticipated. He caught her elbow. "Your Majesty, I am sorry. May I speak with you alone?"

"Is this something our sister, Princess Phoena, cannot hear?" Carradee turned toward the watching Netaian delegation.

Firebird had loved and trusted Carradee. He resolved to be tactful. Phoena, however, would be a hostile witness. Plainly dressed for once, she glowered over the proceedings.

Trying to manage the throne, was she? Maybe Phoena already was addicted to that conqueror's pride. "Alone, Majesty," he whispered. "For a moment. I mean you no harm. I have news for you to hear first."

Carradee nodded. They walked together through the circle of Federate pilots, away from the shuttle toward the edge of the bulldozed area, followed at a discreet distance by Carradee's House Guards and one uniformed Federate. Back at center stage, General Mafis began to address the crowd and media representatives. He'd written an instructive speech for the occasion, and Brennen had asked him to take his time about finishing.

CHAPTER 11

MAXSEC

tempo 1
at original tempo

As Mafis's voice faded, Brennen cleared his shields again. "How did your mother die?"

Grief and anxiety blurred Carradee's mental state. "She took poison, sir, when it became evident to her that she had led us to a dishonorable defeat."

"Somnus?"

"Yes," she said bleakly. "In no other way could she save her honor and satisfy the Powers."

That gave him his opening. "We've dealt with that poison before, Your Majesty." He drew the tiny presentation box from a pocket of his belt and handed it to her. Suspicious, she held it at a graceful arm's length. "Nothing deadly, madam." He took it back, opened its lid, and returned it into her hand. Ten clear, marquis-cut rubies flashed in the morning light.

As she examined them, he studied her face. Men might kill for Phoena, but Carradee's attractiveness was subtle, touched with humility at the eyes and sadness at the mouth. She would be exactly the kind of queen Netaia needed, if she could hold on to power through these transition years.

Carradee eyed the goldwork on the back of one star, then replaced it on the box's velvette liner. "These are Netaian rank stars, General, as you surely know. Why are they in your possession?"

"They belonged to your sister Lady Firebird." He watched as his verbal missile exploded. Carradee pulsed with grieved dismay, then delight, then confusion.

She gripped the box. "We were told she'd been killed in action, but if that were true, these would have been destroyed."

"She is alive, Majesty."

For a compassionate instant, she let herself smile, but then she drew the inescapable conclusion. Firebird, now her subject, would be a grave concern. "Where is she, General? How is she being treated? Was she . . ." Her already pale cheeks lost all color. ". . . interrogated?"

Brennen glanced toward the crowd. Mafis droned on. He needn't hurry with Carradee. "She is under protective custody, at Regional command on Tallis." A single intercept fighter swept low over the skyline, following the Etlason River toward its midtown confluence with the Tiggaree. "I assure you, she is well treated. But, yes, as a military prisoner, naturally she was interrogated. It was humanely done."

He felt panic replace her concern.

"Your Majesty, that is not the only reason why we were able to take Netaia without prolonged warfare and great loss of life. But may I suggest that many of your people were saved by her capture, and Count Stele's."

She wouldn't be diverted. "She was taken at Veroh, then?"

He related Firebird's suicide attempts and how they'd been thwarted, then her capture and questioning, without mentioning his own role. He'd need to be able to work with Carradee.

She frowned, still plainly displeased with Firebird for revealing vital information.

He asked, "Have you not heard of Ehretan mind access?"

"What is that?"

"I'll show you." She was watching his eyes, and he trapped her easily. She quailed and stepped back, and then, caught, she stood blinking. He probed only enough to confirm that Siwann had truly died and wasn't in hiding. Carradee had stood at her side at the last, silently sorrowing, terrified of the future.

He released her, catching her hand to steady her while she regained her balance. "That is very simple access. Your sister's memory was taken much deeper. I assure you, she did not cooperate."

The line of her lips became hard. "Those who did so should be punished."

He who did so, Brennen observed wryly, *will never recover.* "You'd rather hear that she had been tortured for information?"

Carradee stepped back and studied the dusty ground. When after a minute she spoke again, her words came in a toneless voice. "We would rather have gone on believing that Firebird died well, and is now beyond all of the suffering life dealt her. You and your kind are dangerous, Excellency. You surely will be a powerful lieutenant governor."

He wished he could. "I'll only oversee the establishment of our military governorship and the peacekeeping forces. We Sentinels are allowed to use those abilities only under a few circumstances. You'll see little of them now. The Federacy wishes to help your forces keep order, in the best interests of all concerned."

"Perhaps you mean, 'restore' order."

He detected a grudging respect as she closed her hand around the little box, snapping it shut.

"Many will be glad to hear that Firebird survived," the new queen went on. "She was popular among the people. We . . . I, too, wish her the best. However, the Electorate will be deeply concerned. We do not allow extraneous heirs, sir."

That again! "And your sister Phoena will be unhappy, I think."

Her gray eyes widened.

"We learned many things from Lady Firebird's mind," he said, "on several levels."

Carradee glanced over her shoulder. Phoena stood at the edge of the circle of guards, openly ignoring Mafis's call for unity, still watching Brennen confer with her sister.

Carradee turned back to him. "Be that as it may, General, she must know. I will tell her."

"Of course. Majesty, don't be afraid to contact me if you need to work with the Federacy. You've just been handed an awesome responsibility."

"Thank you," she said, "but that will not be necessary."

He honestly wanted to help her, but they must both follow protocol. As they walked silently back toward the circle, Mafis finished his discourse. Two guards let them through the cordon directly beside Princess Phoena.

"Good morning, Your Highness." Brennen gave Phoena a slight nod.

She raised one eyebrow, coldly looked him up and down, and then turned away.

Exactly as Firebird remembered her . . .

Brennen bowed toward Carradee Second and left them to settle their family affairs.

On Firebird's fifth day on Tallis IV, Captain Ellet Kinsman arrived early at the minimum-security suite where they'd locked her away for safekeeping. Its bedroom and anteroom were small but comfortable, with a magnificent view of Tallis's capital city, Castille. Sitting at a two-seat servo table in one corner of her anteroom, Firebird pulled a pale green audio rod from the player she'd requested. Ellet had kept her under a full news blackout. Determined to stay mentally active, she'd taken up a new field of study: Federate music.

Ellet's midnight blue tunic looked crisper than usual, and Firebird spotted thin lines of brown on her eyelids. Something was up.

"What was that?" Ellet nodded toward the rod.

"A Luxian art song." Firebird hoped Ellet would feel her amusement. The blackout had, at least, forced her deep anguish to lie down and rest. "It came with that assortment from the tower library yesterday morning. The melodies are gorgeous, but the harmony has me baffled." She set the rod back into its case. "Why are you early?"

"You have a meeting with the Regional council uplevel in half an hour. Just an introduction, I believe. They have little time to waste."

"Regional council?" This was a shock. Why would they bother with her now? Surely they'd won their war.

Ellet turned back to the door. "Half an hour."

The tower, where both had been assigned security rooms, was called MaxSec. Ellet had explained that stood for Maximum Security. Eighty stories tall, it was a self-contained fortress, with offices, laboratories, security apartments, and shops, and a sec system developed by the finest minds in the Federacy. Escape would've been impossible. Firebird had examined the broad, gridded window and had even given it a suspicious touch the moment Ellet left her alone. The stun pulse had left her arm limp for an hour. Within a day she'd learned to identify several classes of local aircraft. Traffic flowed steadily in and out of a parking bay above her.

Why the council, today?

News from the war, maybe. *It's over*, she guessed. *What's left of my home?*

Half an hour later, she preceded Ellet from the security lift into a long, lofty chamber. The pale gray ceiling rose three stories, vaulted by pure white stone arches. Air moved freely. They crossed an expanse of silver-flecked stone below empty spectator galleries, then ascended three wide stairs onto a platform large enough to hold a full choral orchestra.

Behind a long, curving table sat the ruling septumvirate of this half of the Federate Whorl. Three civilians sat at the table's right side. One had rough brown skin and sat in a mobility chair, bent nearly double by his hunched back. The white-robed woman at center looked oldest. To her left sat two men and a woman in military uniforms. A blank panel hung over their heads, probably a translation screen.

Ellet stepped forward. "Members of the council, I present to you First Major Lady Firebird Angelo of the Netaia systems."

Firebird made the formal half bow Ellet had suggested, but she felt awkward wearing gray shipboards. This was a full-dress occasion, with people who might eventually set her free.

The robed woman stood. "Good afternoon, Captain Kinsman. Lady Firebird, you are welcome on Tallis. I trust you have been treated well?"

"Yes. Thank you, Your Honor."

"I am Tierna Coll, formerly of the Elysia system. May I introduce Admiral Madden of Caroli, Admiral Baron Fiersson of Luxia, General Voers of Bishda." As she continued, she turned to indicate the civilians on her other side. "Mister Lithib of Oquassa, Madam Kernoweg of Lenguad, and Doctor Gage of Deng."

Firebird repeated her bow. *Coll, Madden, Fiersson, Voers*, she repeated silently. *Lithib, and . . . oh, squill.*

"Our news must be conveyed with sympathy," said Tierna Coll. "First, Netaia has surrendered to Federate forces."

Firebird bowed her head.

"We received that word late yesterday." Tierna Coll's voice was pleasant and commanding, like that of a well-trained alto. "The second news came only an hour ago. Your mother has died, Lady Firebird. She committed suicide. We are sorry."

"Thank you, Your Honor." Firebird couldn't summon up any other reaction. Her emotions seemed dead. Given the surrender and Netaia's traditions, this didn't really surprise her.

Admiral Madden, second from the left, seemed to see her awkwardness. He stopped stroking his blond beard and spread his elbows on the table. "We've been advised that the survival of our patrol holding Veroh resulted in part from a warning you gave. I am certain you have been thanked, but please let us add our sincere gratitude."

She made another small, polite bow. *Madden of Caroli*, she reminded herself. Caroli, Veroh's governing world, could afford magnanimity now.

Madam Kernoweg sat as straight as any military officer, with a strong brow ridge and close-cropped hair. "We have hoped for some time that your home world would covenant to the Federacy, Lady Firebird. Poorer worlds would benefit from its resources. Wealthier systems would carry lighter assessment burdens, while Netaia itself would reap significant rewards. This council has ordered our forces to demonstrate tact and respect in dealing with your government."

Firebird inclined her head, though she doubted Madam Kernoweg would get any positive result if the Federacy ever caved to the Netaian Electorate. Any show of weakness would only encourage defiance. Hadn't they learned that at Veroh?

At Tierna Coll's side, General Voers stood. Gold stars sparkled under the Federate slash on the breast of his coal black uniform. "Lady Firebird, we have before us a report submitted by Field General Caldwell of Special Operations concerning your government's weapons research. The . . . 'Cleary/D'Stang/Parkai Project,'" he read off his recessed terminal. "Is this a special concern of your family, Your Highness?"

Could she assume Brennen had survived another battle to submit that report? No. He would've sent it from Veroh. She restrained her urge to correct Voers' improper address and answered his question. "Princess Phoena sponsored that research, Your Honor."

"It also was supported by the late queen's electoral council, was it not?"

"Yes, sir."

"You were, I understand, a member of that body?"

"Yes, General Voers. An honorary member," she explained, "but with voting rights."

"General Caldwell's report states that you did not support the research. Why not?"

How could she answer without denigrating her family?—which she mustn't do, not here. "Your Honors, I have little official status on Netaia, and I am not authorized to speak for any of its governing bodies. But for myself, I must express my regret for this situation. I am a career military officer by choice, but I was born to the Electorate. I have . . . reservations about some of its decisions." In this bright, alien environment, even those carefully chosen words sounded like treason. If the Powers truly existed, if there actually was life after death, she might spend all eternity in the Dark that Cleanses.

"My lady." Mister Lithib's low, gasping voice seemed appropriate to his deformities. "This report indicates that you might be willing to consider— consider, I say—making a home among Federate peoples. We would find that heartening, after what you've endured. Would you confirm that report?"

Distracted by his appearance, Firebird forgot to worry about her eternal destiny. Lithib's dark, sad eyes were set unnaturally wide. On Netaia, severely deformed newborns were humanely put down; yet this man had risen to interstellar authority. She must rethink still more of Netaia's laws and traditions. "The standard," she said, "by which I've been taught to judge any policy has been, 'Is it good for the Electorate?' Your broader standards are hard for me to grasp." *Especially showing the Netaian regime respect!* "I do not understand how so many peoples can coexist as you claim. But I would like to believe it.

"And yes, I have been treated well here. I can consider remaining. It is difficult, though, to consider forsaking my home and my people."

Voers raised one eyebrow and frowned. She flinched, wondering how she'd offended him.

Tierna Coll spoke again. "That is a decision you need not face for some weeks. The public files of the MaxSec library will remain at your disposal, as will governmental newscans issued to Captain Kinsman, when she has finished reading them." She glanced down at Ellet, who nodded.

"Thank you," Firebird exclaimed.

Tierna Coll barely smiled. "Eventually, we hope to be able to accord you more freedom of information and movement without jeopardizing your safety. Please bear with our protective custody for a time."

Some inflection in Tierna Coll's voice, maybe her use of the royal "we," reminded Firebird suddenly of Siwann. Apprehensively she waited for the deep, dull chest-ache of grief that she always felt when remembering Corey.

It didn't come. She felt only relief tinged with regret, and amazement at having survived her mother after all.

"Lady Firebird, we thank you." Tierna Coll inclined her head.

Firebird imitated the gesture. Ellet touched her arm and led her away.

CHAPTER 12

PROTECTORATE

l'istesso tempo
although the meter changes, the beat remains the
same

Citangelo's day burned out in a sunset still fiery from atmospheric dust. Inside his office on the newly constructed occupation base, Brennen watched a transport decelerate toward the new spaceport north of a rebuilt control tower and new Memorial Gate. It returned Federate goods and gilds for a load of Netaian exports. He wondered who'd bought those first exports—exotic produces, fine arts, military souvenirs.

He turned back to his bluescreen. Like most of his office furnishings, the viewer had come from Caroli. Federate engineers had built the base out of military-depot rubble. Now it was a particle-shielded foothold on this conquered world. His wall shelves held an array of Thyrian pieces—pseudo-Ehretan reproductions, multicolored seashells, holo cubes that depicted Thyrica's vast western rain forest—none of them his own, but furnished to provide a Federate dignity to match the native aristocracy.

That aristocracy's tentacles were everywhere. It had ruled and still controlled manufacturing, research, and commerce, patronized music and the other arts, and had ordered the military. The nobles ruled as tyrannical benefactors, but also, to his distaste, as priests. They represented the nine Powers to their people.

He'd tried to untangle that concept of Powers. He'd thought they were a supernatural pantheon, and evidently they were still considered godlike, but during the isolated years of Six-alpha's space storms, the Netaians' loyalty to their gods had been sublimated into loyalty to the state. Perfect citizenship became its graceless religion. Conformity to the expected Charities and the written Disciplines bought a soul's way to paradise, the afterlife being the only truly "religious" aspect that remained in their religion. If a Netaian didn't make the minimum offerings, the financial base for their welfare system, or keep those laws correctly, a terrifying purgatory awaited.

So for three centuries, the semi-deified nobles had controlled almost every public function. Enforcement Corps officers imposed harsh penalties even for minor violations—recently, passing "seditious" information about offplanet trade had resulted in imprisonment for one offender and a reduction to servitor status for his children. The system still smacked of an older martial law. Governor Danton had decided quickly that disenfranchising the noble class would lead to chaos, so the Electorate had been given back the right to meet, under Federate supervision.

Brennen leaned away from his desk, refusing to sink into self-righteousness. His people had their own dark history. His first genetically altered ancestors had tried to seize power from their nongifted elders. The older generation had fought back. Family by family, they destroyed each other and their world. One priestly family fled rather than fight, taking fifty-one orphaned starbred children onboard.

Some contemporary Sentinels called that faithful remnant's survival a proof that in time, the Eternal Speaker would reveal himself openly again, in a prophesied messenger who would bridge the chasm to eternal peace for all of flawed humankind, on every world.

The prophecy interested Brennen keenly and personally. This messenger, this Word to Come, was to rise from a small Ehretan family that had been known as Carabohd, "honorably called."

If you will it, Holy One.

Netaia needed such a messenger. Firebird needed that peace. He couldn't give it, though. She must find it herself.

Or you must find her. Please.

He adjusted his bluescreen's brightness and checked his day's agenda. Two items remained. A man waited in the hall outside, with his secretary, another aristocrat for scan evaluation. It would be merely a surface emotional check. Brennen had avoided using deep access except in extreme cases.

Already he'd examined the former marshals and several electors. Unanimously, they longed to throw off Federate rule. Meanwhile the low-common class, held down by that penal system, itched to rise against the electors. The high-common majority was caught between and desperate for peace. Most lived in physical comfort, content to endure their less oppressive lack of rights because their co-opted religion and rewritten history had taught them to dread civil chaos. Thanks to those historic invaders and Sabba Six-alpha, even the elected Assembly deferred to the Electorate.

Civil war—the worst threat they feared—was distinctly possible, with so much unrest among low commoners with little to lose. Netaia needed several calm years to begin to see the Federacy as an ally and a stabilizing factor, to ease power away from the nobility, to equalize the distribution of resources.

High-common and noble Netains cherished their independence—he'd heard some of the traditional stories and songs, listening fascinated while performers' fierce nationalistic pride radiated through his downed shields.

But though the Federacy offered stability, it never would stifle independence. Every Federate cultural unit, whether multiplanetary or single-continent, kept its local government and was represented in a Regional senate. His home world answered to Tallis, but Tallis rarely influenced Thyrica's day-to-day affairs. Personal and media contact with other peoples, such as the aristocratic Luxians, would demonstrate this to the Netains, if the Federacy could bring peace and two-way communication.

That, he reminded himself grimly, was how his disobedient ancestors had justified creating telepathy. They'd hoped unrestrained communication would create complete understanding.

They'd forgotten greed. *Thank you for covering our faults, Holy Father and Speaker. Hasten the day when you will remove them.*

He pressed his touchboard to signal his readiness, and then he dropped all epsilon static, the better to read his subject.

Count Tel Tellai stepped into the office's far end. The count's small size and soft features made him look even younger than his eighteen Netain years, which made him twenty-one, Federate. He wore the blue sash of office—father deceased only last year, according to the file glowing on Brennen's bluescreen—extensive agricultural lands, children's hospital. Otherwise dressed hat to heels in black, Tellai walked with measured steps. His antipathy created a nagging unease in Brennen's unshielded senses. "Please take a chair, Count Tellai."

Seated, Tellai looked slightly taller. He brushed dust from velvette trousers and pulled off his narrow-brimmed, fashionable hat. Short, fine boned, and effeminate, Tellai looked the consummate aristocrat.

Projecting the allowable calming assurance, Brennen began. "The purpose of this interview is simple, sir. We need to know your underlying attitude toward the Federacy. Naturally you wish us elsewhere, but for the present we must work together for the good of your people."

He'd repeated the lines several times already and recorded his subjects' responses. Here in private, he could scan conclusively. He could also place a subject under voice command if any tried to attack him.

Tellai didn't seem the attacking sort. Brennen pulled a stylus from his cuff and held it lightly between his hands. "Can you recall, briefly, your feelings toward the Federacy before this crisis set us against each other? Be honest, please. You are in no danger if you tell the truth, even unpleasant truth, but I can recognize deception."

Tellai's long, dark lashes fell closed, and Brennen was startled by a sudden resemblance to Firebird. Was there—? He glanced at his screen and touched for additional data. Yes, the connection was close. Tellai was her second cousin.

The count took several breaths. "I thought very little of the Federacy, Your Excellency. I had my lands to administer; I have been relandscaping my primary residence . . ."

Brennen focused not on the words but on Tellai's underlying emotion. He caught a brief rise of regret, washed out by resentment. Not so different from the others, and Brennen didn't sense the inner strength that might've made him dangerous—unlike the queen's sister.

He'd heard rumors that Phoena stood behind most of Danton's electoral troubles. For the second time, Brennen toyed with the idea of suggesting to Carradee that she ask Phoena to leave off her agitating, leave Citangelo for a while, take a long vacation.

Tellai finished speaking and sat still, blankly apprehensive. Brennen rested his elbows on the desk and said, "In five years, the Netaian systems will be eligible to rise from this occupied protectorate status to full Federate covenance, probably including representation on the Regional council. That covenance would be tremendously beneficial to your defenses and your economy. Free trade would take Netaian goods to many other systems and return substantial wealth to a growing trade class. Assuming for the moment that this came to pass, how would you envision your role in such a society?"

Tellai's slender fingers curled around the hat brim in his lap. "Never in our history has such a thing happened, sir, and it never, never will."

Brennen had to admire the young dandy's sincerity, though fear of how Brennen might retaliate wept in both their minds.

This was no ringleader.

Restoring his epsilon shielding, Brennen shifted his stylus to a writing grip. "Thank you, sir. You may go."

Tellai blinked, opened his mouth—shut it—then scurried to the door. Brennen pressed the key to let him out, then made a line of shorthand notes.

The return of emotional silence felt coolly quiet, but he knew it wouldn't stay pleasant. Since Veroh, solitary spells had gnawed at him. This was the price of having touched absolute connaturality without bonding it, without even telling her how powerfully she attracted him. Blessed Word to Come, how would he say that?

Not as a lord over her people! As he'd created and amended his administrative duties, the conqueror's pride had almost lost its ability to tempt him. The better he knew the conquered Netaians, the more he empathized with most of them.

A message remained on his Crown channel, saved for day's end and a possible follow-up. Carradee Second might reign chiefly as figurehead and standard bearer, but the nobles deferred to her so insistently—in public— that Danton hadn't ordered her to appear for an interview, nor even her troublesome sister Phoena. Danton meant to comply with Regional's orders to show the Crown respect. That would make occupation a tightrope walk, but eventually, it might shift the nobles' attitudes. In three standard years, occupation-moderated free elections, open to all four social classes, would determine whether Netaia joined the Federacy.

He called up Carradee's message. His bluescreen cleared, then filled with pale letters.

> Lieutenant Governor Caldwell, greetings.
>
> You must be aware by now of our tradition of heir limitation. For the present we are willing to accept the Federacy's injunction outlawing the issuance of any new geis.
>
> However, previous to the establishment of your Protectorate, younger scions of noble houses often were granted expensive education and training and the wherewithal to make for themselves a most honorable end. This was considered an investment in the eternal nobility of our homeland.
>
> Our sister Lady Firebird accepted such gifts, but took gross advantage of our investment and reportedly lives now under Federate protection. We and our Electorate deem it reasonable to request that the Federacy repay the house of Angelo the following expenses incurred anticipating her contribution to the homeland's glory, which apparently were squandered. . . .

Brennen gaped. Siwann's electors, still meeting as Carradee's, meant to bill the Federacy for three years of Academy education, all jet and laser-ion fuel thereby consumed, uniform allowance including jeweled rank insignia, and a thirty-million-gild tagwing fightercraft?

Half smiling at the absurdity, he stretched his legs. Federate policy respected others' viewpoints. To the Electorate, the request might seem appropriate.

He checked her request against the governor's reparations budget and decided to defer the matter to Danton, the diplomat. Danton might make a token payment for the sake of Carradee's good feelings. Brennen couldn't have it intimated that he'd asked the Federacy to buy Firebird's freedom.

He would, though. He'd give her all he owned. His life, his hand for protection, his future . . .

But would she take freedom, or forgiveness, as a gift? Did she even know what they meant? Did any Netaian, raised in this merciless mindset? He corralled his emotions and thrust them back down.

The message's postscript astonished him. The tone changed, implying a different author, and suggested the Federacy reduce Firebird to servitor status to pay that debt herself.

Unquestionably Phoena's touch.

He inserted "Can you believe this? See budget 12-C" after the postscript and keyed it onto Danton's agenda for the following morning. Then he shut down his viewer and waved off room lights. Evening was his, to settle another matter. Rumor had just reached him that Vultor Korda, whom he remembered with little respect, lingered in Citangelo. On his own time, he would start a different kind of investigation, to satisfy himself . . . and the Code of Exile that governed the starbred.

Sweating from a packing frenzy, Vultor Korda stowed his last load into a skimmer the electors had given him for his services. "Cheap slugs," he muttered as he buried a roll of Federate gilds in the toe of one shoe. "You could've afforded air transport, but, ah, no, save a little credit for Nella Cleary's lab work."

Exhaust from traffic below his apartment block congealed in chill air. Korda slammed the side trunk and ran back up to his studio for a last plunge into cabinets. Breathing hard, he paused in the doorway. He couldn't see his rented furniture anymore. It lay buried under a jumble of discarded belongings.

"Caldwell," he fumed. At least Phoena had come to warn him. "Why did they have to send that eight-pointed goody-boots?"

"Not a friend of yours?" Phoena lounged in the single unladen chair.

"Not exactly." He reached for a package of jelly wafers. It slipped out of his hand onto the yellow tile floor. One end burst, splotching a chair with purple confection.

From all others at Sentinel College, Korda had hidden his fantasies of power, biding his time. Then one day, by chance, he'd met Brennen Caldwell—already a fully vested Sentinel, at an age when Korda had only begun epsilon-turn training. The next day Korda had been called for reevaluation.

"Question of inappropriate ambition" had been the examiners' verdict, and Korda had been expelled, sentenced to report every ten-day Thyrian *dekia* to be treated with epsilon-blocking drugs, to keep him from misusing what skills he'd already learned.

Scorch Caldwell and his ninety-seven harmonics!

Temporary blocking drugs, fortunately. Only radical cerebral surgery could disable the ayin, the genetically engineered complex of brain regions where a starbred's power rose. After five years of intolerable drug treatment, he'd fled. They would cut him or kill him if they caught him now, but his abilities had returned. Korda lived without static shields. That kept him attuned to all that transpired around him and saved his energy for occasional bursts of shallow access (he'd never mastered voice-command), without distracting his spirit from the destiny he still pursued. It wasn't for nothing that common people shuddered at the fate of lost Ehret. Knowledge still equaled power.

Indolently Phoena peeled a pale green banam fruit. "It sounds as though you love him the way I respect my young sister. I wish there were a way to get to Tallis. I'd love to show her she can't escape her duty to the Electorate."

"Do you mean that?" Korda stopped midfloor and stared into Phoena's hard eyes. He felt her hatred, and yes, she would pay almost any price to see her sister obey her geis order. "Highness, I could get one of your agents offplanet easily, if you have a suggestible acquaintance on the Interplanetary Travel Committee."

"I have several men and women in key places." She wriggled her shoulders and gave him a sweet smile he read as very false. "You'd do it for me, Korda?"

"When the time comes, give me the name of your ITC contact. He'll see a face other than your agent's, no matter who he expects."

She pursed her lips. "You'd go too, of course. To Tallis."

Korda blinked. That had *not* been his idea. "Not to a Federate world," he said flatly. "Sentinels aren't kind to informers."

"You're not an informer." Phoena raised one eyebrow. "You're a turncoat."

He tried not to sneer. "In your service, Highness."

She laughed. "Good. Then you're now my agent. You could get to her, when others couldn't."

He considered. It would be delicious if he, a mere trainee, could slip past whatever Sentinel they'd told to guard Firebird. Surely they'd use a Sentinel.

But it would be terribly dangerous. "What about you, Highness? Don't you want to see it done? Correctly?" With a high-ranking escort like Phoena, it would be easier—safer—to slip through channels to his former student . . . and escape.

Phoena buffed her nails on one sleeve. "I do, but I cannot leave Netaia. I'll find another to keep an eye on you, someone with a particular . . ."

She was always doing that, trailing off before he could catch her thought. He dropped onto a hassock. "Grudge?" he prompted. "Against Firebird?"

"Actually, no." She smiled with one side of her mouth. "Perhaps it would shake your Sentinel compatriot in our lieutenant governor's office if we sent someone Caldwell thinks he's beaten. That could give us a psychological victory."

Korda frowned, shaking his head. "Caldwell has been bedimmed careful. He hasn't 'beaten' anyone yet that I've heard of."

"He'll have to, fairly soon," Phoena said placidly. "I have several men working quietly to get rid of that occupation base. The first time one of my men is caught, we'll move quickly. Can you get one more man offplanet?" she pressed.

"Highness," he said with a mock-deferential nod, "if you'll arrange my groundwork, yes. I can. I also want hazardous duty pay and privileges."

"Naturally." She glanced at the door. "You'd better leave. Leave the mess, too. His Excellency will probably come looking for you."

Korda swept out an arm and motioned her to precede him outside.

She strolled toward a servo instead. "No, I want to make calls without using a palace line. This suits me perfectly. Good-bye, Korda. We understand each other. I'll contact you at the house in Gorman when the time is right."

He dashed back outdoors and plunged the skimmer into traffic, steering toward the northerly highway.

Alone on her anteroom's tattered green lounger, Firebird grieved over a Federate newscan. Netaian networks weren't linked to any Tallan informational agency, so all her news came from this unsympathetic source.

Her own knowledge had helped engineer a disaster. A tear trickled toward her chin as she read the grim roster of destroyed facilities. She'd trained at Sitree, near the equator, vacationed at frozen Arctica, refueled at most of the other sites, and these very memories had given Brennen's forces their targets. Citangelo, Claighbro, Dunquin . . .

She stopped and read the long list again, frowning. Had she missed something?

No, it wasn't on the list: Hunter Height, just over 2,000K north by northwest of Citangelo, where the Aerie Mountains joined the Flenings, was one of her family's vacation homes and a fortified last-effort retreat. The ancient stone house sat over a tunnel complex on a granite mountainside, overlooking its own airstrip. It wasn't listed.

She sat upright, making the lounger creak. So her resistance hadn't been completely in vain. By focusing on other sites, she'd hidden one minor air base from Brennen.

Much good it had done.

Centered atop the glimmering page was a row of images: Brennen, Carradee, Siwann, a man named Lee Danton, and . . . Dorning Stele? She skimmed the account for his name. He'd been captured trying to sabotage the Federate command ship under the pretense of surrendering. Then, imprisoned and interrogated.

She thought she could guess who'd done the questioning.

The article credited Stele's extensive knowledge of Netaian facilities with providing the key for a quick victory.

Firebird threw back her head and laughed. Stele deserved this! The article didn't state where he'd been sent, but she found deep satisfaction in imagining him on board a Federate cruiser, locked into a tiny holding cell, wearing servitor's coveralls.

She touched Siwann's likeness more soberly, shaking her head. She'd never see her mother again. Siwann was dead by her own hand, killed by her own conscience, for the ruin she'd brought to her homeland. She ought to offer a prayer. *Powers grant you bliss, Majesty. Mother.*

Firebird rescrolled the newscan. Evidently Phoena, co-instigator of the invasion, hadn't suffered similar remorse.

But Carradee . . .

An odd thought struck Firebird. Staring out the window, she let it run its course. By tradition, Siwann should've eventually suicided once she judged her heiress fit to rule. Firebird had always suspected Siwann was expending little effort preparing Carradee. Siwann had intended to hold power for many more years. Now, gentle Carrie was thrust into a situation she couldn't control. Electors would be jockeying around her for the power the Federacy had already given back, in part.

Poor Carrie.

A week later, a lumpy packet arrived return-marked Citangelo. It had passed the censors unopened and was still slightly rolled from traveling in a message tube. A brown ID tape had been mounted on one corner. Below that, the packet was lettered, Personal. Security I.

Trembling, she carried it to her inner room, sat down on the edge of her narrow bed, and slit the seal. Inside she found three sheets of scribepaper and a scanbook cartridge. One paper was tightly folded and heatsealed, addressed in Phoena's flowery script. Another, unsealed, she recognized as Carradee's writing.

The other sheet was covered with an unfamiliar masculine hand. Though deeply surprised, she chuckled when she saw the formal letterhead atop the page. Brennen had learned quickly how to impress Netaians. It read:

Office of the Lieutenant Governor
Citangelo
Netaian Protectorate Systems

    Mari—
There is a lull in affairs today. Please believe that I've written at the first available moment. My title is "Lieutenant to Governor Danton"— actually, I am his bodyguard, chief of enforcement, and mentor. We are impressing people with our knowledge. Despite their isolationism, they're good people, and some are truly noble.

    We've met with hostility, but attitudes seem to be softening as Assembly elections approach (I've applied for transfer back to Tallis immediately afterward).

    I had words yesterday with both your sisters. The palace is full of your presence. I spoke briefly with an elderly butler or some such servant, who spoke of you as I walked through the portrait gallery. He gave the impression that you were respected on Netaia. Is that part of your problem with Phoena?

Firebird blinked at the gray inner wall. In fact, it was—particularly after the late Baron Parkai had commented within hearing of both of them that "it was a shame about the birth order in that family." Phoena had scarcely said a civil word to her since that day years ago.

    I may not be able to communicate again, and I didn't feel it was wise to prepare a personal recording. For the same reasons, don't answer this letter. Expense aside, I don't entirely trust the messenger service, even with an ID tape for security.

    The cartridge should answer most of your questions.
                      Yours,
                      B.

P.S. The portrait is lovely.

Carradee's message was warm, if officious. She asked after Firebird's treatment, warned her to maintain her dignity, and reminded her to avoid the low-born. She promised "appropriate" clothing to follow.

Phoena came directly to the point:

Firebird:
    So you have betrayed us all. If I ever see you again, I shall personally remove you from the succession.

                            Phoena Irina Eschelle Angelo

Another postscript had been added in Brennen's hand, despite the heat-seal on Phoena's paper:

Not if I have anything to say about it. I apologize for even including this, but it's important for you to know exactly how you stand with her. If it's any comfort, she would do the same for me.

                            B.

Shaking in her excitement, Firebird loaded the cartridge and scrolled down its table of contents. It contained dozens of news stories, all citing Netaian sources. They covered the Federate invasion and its aftermath, public reaction to occupation and other current topics . . . and she spotted a lengthy series on the Angelo family, with Siwann given a substantial tribute.

This should answer her questions, all right. She touched up the much shorter entry, "Captured at Veroh."

Her own commissioning portrait appeared on the viewer. She stared, wondering how she ever could've looked that self-assured. The entry itself was unemotional: the burned tagwing, the assumption of death, the Federate revelation. It didn't mention, didn't even suggest, her interrogation. After several readings, she decided that the entry's tone was mildly positive, which was more than she'd dared hope.

Exhaling with deep relief, she scrolled again and was amused to find an entry titled, "Reconsidering the Powers."

"Thank you, Brennen," she whispered up at her gridded window. This was truly a treasure.

She read and reread the personal letters as daylight faded, startled by the change in her feelings toward Brennen Caldwell. He'd stolen her destiny. He'd humiliated her and made her an exile, but only as his orders demanded. Since then, he'd acted with almost unconscionable mercy. He'd taken the trouble and expense to send news from her beloved home world, and he'd written, "They are good people." For that alone, she could almost call him a friend.

What had taken him to the palace? Had he advised Carradee, addressed the electors, or attended a social function?

Carradee's promised parcel arrived within a day, and in it a treasure: her clairsa, padded with clothing and detuned for travel. She caressed the intricate carvings in the leta-wood upper arch as though greeting a lost friend, and then set about restoring the tuning.

When Ellet brought the latest pocketful of aging Tallan newscans, Firebird offered a short concert. "I only play for enjoyment these days." She supported the long, thin, arched triangle in her lap with her left hand. "Not in public anymore."

Ellet smiled tolerantly. "I have a brother who plays a similar instrument."

Firebird ran her index finger along the strings, tweaked the tuning, then played a rolling arpeggio to warm her hands. A tinkling, resonant major chord climbed the ladder of strings in two swift strokes and hung in the air while metal strings rang out. She damped them before the chord faded away.

Crossing her ankles under the stool and leaning one corner of the small harp on her shoulder, she freed both hands and spun off a rollicking dance tune, the kind of music a young aristocrat learned as part of her well-rounded education.

"More," Ellet insisted. "Obviously you're not the casual player Labeth is."

Gratified, Firebird began the difficult etude she'd so recently memorized. *And Netaia*, she thought wryly, *is not the barbarian backwater you thought it was, Sentinel Kinsman.*

CHAPTER 13

ROGONIN

sotto voce
whispered, in an undertone

To Brennen, even the outbuildings of the Rogonin estate looked magnificent. Fronted with white marble, their corners and doorposts were carved with fruiting vines. The central residence was a monstrosity, rising three stories to a blackened metal roof and spreading long wings in each direction. As Electoral Ministers of Trade, the Rogonins had amassed an estate that would support some Federate space colonies.

It couldn't compare, though, with the Angelo fortune. Firebird had been raised with wealth that staggered him, in a palace larger and grander than this villa . . . almost as large as the Sentinel College, filled with more treasures than Tallis's Museum of Culture. Carradee had insisted, as they walked through the portrait gallery after an electoral meeting, that all Netaians owned that palace and its contents, just as they all took vicarious pride in Crown activities.

"*All?*" he'd asked cautiously.

For a moment, she'd hesitated. Then she'd repeated firmly, "All."

He eyed Rogonin's hedges for possible assailants. He'd brought two guards, one a tall woman in Tallan ash gray and the other a young Sentinel, but he led up the curving approach himself. A support craft hovered silently over the riverfront grounds.

An execution yesterday had done little to improve his mental state. One Federate ensign, kidnapping one Netaian girl, might've undone all the rapport Danton had worked to build these two weeks. As the "strong second," to appease an outraged high-common class, Brennen had been obliged to access the soldier, confirm his guilt, escort him into a public square, and witness his death. Brennen hadn't slept that night. Trained and experienced though he was, his nerves insisted that to execute in battle or self-defense was one thing, in cold blood another.

Vultor Korda, furthermore, had vanished from Citangelo. Brennen had run a complete data search and even checked public places for flickers of epsilon energy, but as he'd feared, both proved fruitless.

Four stairs rose to Rogonin's carved, ebony-framed door. He took them quickly and knocked. A girl's face appeared on a tri-D panel that had been invisible on the white background. "Yes?" she asked.

"I wish to speak with His Grace the Duke, miss."

"He is out, Your Excellency. Didn't the gate man tell you?"

Even in holo he could see she was lying, just as Rogonin lied when he'd claimed to be too ill to return to the occupation base for questioning. "This is government business, miss. Please ask His Grace to come to the door."

The image vanished. Behind Brennen, his guards watched the grounds. After a moment he extended a probe inside the door. He recalled the stale, musky savor of Rogonin's presence from his brief scan interview. When he felt it approach, he steadied himself for a struggle.

The screen lit again, this time with Rogonin's jowly face. "Your Excellency." The eyes widened—an attempt at surprised innocence. "How may I help you?"

"I must speak with you in person, sir, regarding a matter that concerns you closely."

"Excellency, that is out of the question. I am in my chamber. I do not feel well."

Brennen angled his hand and focused epsilon energy into the door's opening circuits. As it slid aside, he shifted his focus and caught Rogonin in command.

High ceilings rose above the unmoving nobleman, and ornate white-upholstered furniture stood along the broad entry hall. Two servants flanked the duke, staring in alarm.

"Take us where we can be alone, please, Your Grace," Brennen said.

His movement made awkward by the compulsion of voice-command, Rogonin shuffled toward a door on the hall's left. At Brennen's nod, the Tallan guard swept the room with her stare and then came to attention in the doorway.

Antique weapons hung on the study's walls over indigo leather furniture. Only one exit, only one window. Secure enough. Brennen waved Rogonin to a deep armchair and dropped his hand.

The duke hung back, clutching the wings of his chair. "Sir, this is the House of Claighbro and you have no right to force entry. I shall speak plainly with the governor about this intrusion."

"Governor Danton has issued me a warrant. Evidence has been given us that suggests this house conceals a store of weapons."

The duke glanced at several swords that hung on his study's walls. "If this is a problem," he said sarcastically—

"Tactical weapons," Brennen interrupted. "Please sit down, sir. My greatest desire at the moment is to see you cleared from suspicion, but I can do so only by searching either the grounds or your memory. Mind-access will take less of your time and demand fewer of your resources."

Rogonin remained standing.

Brennen motioned his Thyrian guard forward. Rogonin's fury exploded through Brennen's static shields. He countered by sending a calming frequency. "He won't harm you, and we have no desire for unpleasantness. Please."

Rogonin opened his mouth and took a deep breath. He meant to shout. Brennen caught him again in command. "Sit down," he directed. The duke complied. "Please don't force me to have you restrained in your own house, sir. I only want to clear you."

He let the command slip a little. Rogonin rose halfway out of the chair before Brennen could reestablish control.

He exhaled sharply. "I'm sorry, Your Grace. You leave me no choice." He nodded to the Sentinel guard. Carefully balancing his energy with the other's, he relinquished control. The moment transfer was accomplished, Brennen turned inward for his carrier, modulated it, and thrust it at Rogonin.

The duke's pain and rage sizzled, but Brennen held the carrier steady, probing quickly and hard for a flaw in the natural defenses of the nobleman's alpha matrix.

Rogonin had no idea how to resist. Brennen breached him in a second. His point of awareness plunged into heavy, distasteful pressure: strange voices, alien images, Rogonin's struggle to reassert his will, and a hatred as bitter as clemis root.

"We spoke of weapons," Brennen said softly.

Vision cleared. He seemed to stand in a dim room. Crates lined two walls, oblong cases of energy rifles and smaller, blocky metal boxes that might hide anything from handguns to photo-enhanced warheads. Filed with the image was its location below the villa's main floor. The interrogation lasted only a few seconds.

Brennen opened his eyes. Rogonin sprawled in the chair, almost convulsed in useless physical resistance. Brennen signaled his aide to let him go.

"Very well, sir," he said as the duke composed himself. He hated to arrest the man, which would scandalize the nobility, but inaction could mean violence. "I'm afraid you must come with us to the governor's office, to answer additional questions."

"You have no authority," the nobleman fumed. "I'll see you—"

Brennen angled a hand but did not command.

Rogonin shut his mouth and stood up. The guards stepped to his side. The Tallan woman caught one of his wrists in a restraint, touched his shoulder, and marched him out.

Unhappily, Brennen followed.

Three data desks, two secure interlinks, and a full-time recording apparatus had turned Princess Phoena Angelo's second parlor, in the palace's private wing, into the headquarters for a covert resistance operation. Soon it might threaten the Federacy, with or without Carradee's support. Burly House Guards watched her door in case the Federates suddenly altered their hands-off policy. Phoena might be gravely inconvenienced if they searched her rooms.

Phoena and her mother had often talked privately about the need for strong leadership, and of Carradee's reluctance. Those talks had led Phoena to hope that Siwann meant to quietly dispose of Carradee before stepping down from the throne.

Now Phoena must lead secretly, without recognition. *But only for Netaia and its rightful rulers*, she reflected, smiling with dignity. Deadly endeavors, she believed, were justified to focus power where it could be wielded. All her life Phoena had served that ideal—more sincerely, she felt, than any other member of her family. It grieved her to see Carradee display weakness.

Well. Her inconvenient older sister Lintess had met an untimely end. Her father Irion, who'd privately confronted her about Lintess's death, had been thrown from a startled hunting stallion.

Now—nearly midnight, two days after Muirnen Rogonin's arrest—a message light pulsed over Phoena's secure cross-town link screen. She glanced around the parlor before seating herself. She still lacked the equipment for disciplining her own people and any spies they caught: She wanted more monitoring devices, certain pharmaceuticals . . . and for emergencies, a restraint table.

She touched a key. Vultor Korda's pasty face appeared on the CT screen. "There you are," he said. "I got your roster. Did you find a ship?"

"Of course." She glanced over her shoulder. Earlier, she'd held a meeting of heirs. The suite had emptied, except for her private staff. One burly House Guard stood just inside her richly carved door. "Are you ready?" she demanded.

Korda nodded. "The diplomatic codes were hardest to get. You owe me for that one."

She shrugged. "You're sure we can get Rogonin out of lockup?"

"No trouble," he insisted. "His guards weren't any problem before." Yesterday, Korda had escorted her to Muirnen Rogonin's prison cell, at a midcity police facility occupied by the Federates. At three guard stations, she'd been ignored as if she wore a cloak of invisibility. Korda had used his powers to make the Feds look right past her. "You sure he's mad enough to cooperate?" Korda demanded.

"Oh yes." She'd only told Rogonin, "I've found a way to strike back." With his grounds violated, their weapons seized, and his brain made a Sentinel's picking grounds, Rogonin would've volunteered for almost any mission to embarrass the Federacy.

"False transponder for the ship?" she demanded.

Korda nodded again. "Ready to install."

"Diplomatic credentials?"

"We'll be as welcome on Tallis as Danton himself. With the transmission lag, by the time Tallis can double-check with Danton, we'll have struck. Now, you *promised*—"

Phoena stretched her long legs and signaled her personal girl to bring a cool drink. "Yes, I promise. If Tallis grabs you, I'll have you freed within weeks, or less." Unless that endangered her cause, of course. Korda was a unique and valuable servant, but to save her home world, she'd sacrifice him if necessary. "Enough money," she explained, "can buy almost anyone's loyalty for ten minutes . . . or ten years. Isn't that right?" she asked, lading her voice with sarcasm.

The Thyrian traitor touched his forehead and made a mocking half bow.

During three dull weeks, Firebird had rarely seen a smile wrinkle Ellet Kinsman's clear oval face. Gradually, Ellet had let their conversations—obviously manipulated to familiarize Firebird with the Federacy—touch on her own people.

Firebird leaned against the wall nearest her anteroom window, careful to avoid the security grid, simultaneously watching Ellet on the lounger and the free, outside world. Tiny clouds mottled the afternoon sky.

"What's the main difference between a Sentinel and a Master Sentinel, then?" she asked, continuing a piecemeal inquiry. "Is it a matter of degree, or a different set of skills?"

"Both." Ellet touched her four-rayed star without relaxing her tutorial stance. "The line of eligibility isn't drawn at any arbitrary point on the

Ehretan Scale. Some ordinary potentials also influence trainability. Focus, for example, is a function of any mind's power to concentrate. Other potentials are solely our own. I could levitate a fairly massive object if I could rest afterward. General Caldwell could control his own rate of fall, a more subtle and difficult skill."

A passenger shuttle swooped past Firebird's window. She ached to be outdoors. "Is it—a physical center in the brain, then? A—Ellet, this is an awkward question. I was taught that your people are genetically altered. Who created the epsilon abilities? And why? Didn't they know, didn't they guess, there could be trouble?" *A whole world, depopulated.*

"There is a physical region, involving several brain structures." Ellet's brows came together over her shapely but prominent nose. "As for our origins and history, you may read about those in the MaxSec library."

"I have," Firebird admitted, "but I think those chapters were written by non-Sentinels. I've studied some science. I'm amazed that the . . . chromosomal engineers achieved so much."

"And so," Ellet said stiffly, "you wonder if your own scientists might duplicate the feat?"

"Ours only work on plants and animals. Human research is considered immoral."

"That also was true on Ehret." Ellet's voice dropped, and she looked away. "We believe we were exiled for our ancestors' disobedience, in creating those gifts. But only the few, the obedient survived to reenter galactic society." She lifted her head. "There are reasons beyond ourselves."

Ellet's superior mannerisms made Brennen's kindness shine by comparison. Firebird folded her arms across her chest. "I'm only curious."

"You are too curious. Every people has racial secrets. You must learn to respect them."

"I do," Firebird insisted. "But tell me about those reasons beyond yourselves. Who do you serve . . . above the Federacy?" Ellet's absolute emotional control had started to irritate Firebird. It made Ellet aloof, untouchable—whereas Brennen's gave him a comfortable steadiness.

"We serve the Eternal Speaker, who created space and time."

Firebird straightened, bemused. These people didn't bother with small matters like Strength and Valor. "Space and time?" she echoed.

"Yes."

"Then this . . . Speaker would have to exist outside of both."

"Exactly."

Firebird frowned, unable to imagine so transcendent a being. Something Brennen had said sprang into her mind. *You intended to die for something you don't love?* She eyed Ellet. "Do you love that Speaker, Ellet?"

The Sentinel raised an eyebrow. "You are overstepping."

Yes, but it had seemed relevant. "Why are you so reluctant to display any feeling, Ellet?"

Ellet laughed, a puff of breath and no more. "Consider it yourself. Among telepaths, broadcasting emotion is boorish—performing private functions in public. We restrain ourselves because some of our colleagues can send well but shield poorly."

Evidently Ellet would rather discuss her people than her god. "Why?"

"Talents vary."

"Range, then. How far away can you sense a person's emotion or send the carrier wave?"

"That too varies with Ehretan Scale. There are exceptions under unusual circumstances, but generally, the width of a large room is the range of a solid epsilon carrier."

. . . Just as Brennen had probed her across Twinnich's war room. The experience had been an infuriating public humiliation, but actually, the sensation itself hadn't been as unpleasant as Korda had led her to believe—nor had the long personal sessions.

Her thoughts slipped out in words. "Between a starbred man and woman, are there . . . experiences others don't have?"

"Yes." Ellet drew up tall on the lounger and delivered the word like a slap.

Though startled by her vehemence, Firebird pressed, "Such as—"

"The subject is not your concern." Ellet flushed deeply. "I think I've talked long enough. I wish to listen to you now. Play your clairsa."

Well. She'd touched a nerve at last. Firebird knelt to pick up the narrow instrument, took a stool, and sat down.

The sonata she chose came mechanically at first because it took her a minute to erase Brennen's face from her mind, but as the composition moved from minor to modal, its chords swept her back toward the Netaian frame of reference. Her links with her past, with her deep sense of self, had weakened as she studied the Federacy. Netaian music made her strong again.

Ellet broke into her reverie. "I must go."

"Come soon," Firebird said absently. Ellet locked the massive door behind her. Firebird finished the sonata, then softly plucked out an old ballad, humming as the strings rang brightly. It was a servitor song, a plea for freedom.

Maybe this powerless sense of imprisonment was how servitors and low-commoners felt about their lives. She certainly could relate to the lyrics in a wholly new way.

You intended to die for something you don't love?

The words echoed in her memory.

Reconsider your deities.

There's a higher call on your life now.

We serve the Eternal Speaker, who created space and time.

Firebird held the silent clairsa against her chest. Compared with the Powers she'd barely even understood, that concept seemed unbearably grandiose. Could any mere human grasp it?

She tried for half a minute, shrugged, then replaced her hands on her clairsa strings and played an old love song.

Several days later, Ellet brought unsettling news. Preparatory to the Assembly elections, Netaia's reorganized Electorate had sent an embassy to the Regional council. They were petitioning for a gesture of cooperation.

"What are they asking for?" Firebird asked uneasily. She and Ellet sat on opposite ends of the green lounger.

"You tell me."

Guessing was no challenge. "They want to take me back."

"Correct. To quote, 'The surrender of First Major Lady Firebird Angelo, reportedly captured at the battle of Veroh.'"

Firebird considered. On Netaia, now officially governed by the Federacy, she might be legally safe . . . but it would take more than Federate law to change the heirs' deeply held convictions, and only one recalcitrant (or faithful) heir to kill her. "I suppose they're still waiting for news of my suicide. They'll never forgive me for surviving to be interrogated, and it wasn't my fault."

Ellet gave her a sharp glance, as intent as any of Brennen's.

"Not my fault," Firebird repeated. She stared through the wall, seeing Rendy Gellison before he died in his groundcar, killed by falling debris. Accidental death—maybe. "I don't want to go back," she admitted. "I've gotten used to the idea of living."

Ellet rose. "I'll convey your wishes to the council. They'll be considered along with the Netaians' petition."

"Why is the Federacy negotiating with them at all?" Firebird demanded.

Ellet raised an eyebrow. "Politics. Some highly placed people seem to think Netaia's resources will fall into Federate control if its rulers are treated . . . delicately."

"That's greedy," Firebird murmured. "If the Federacy wants to impress the Netaian people, it should show honor and patience and strength."

"Some forces in the Whorl would like to see the Federacy show weakness. They have agents on Tallis. SO exposes their spies when we find them."

"That sounds like an easy job . . . for you people."

Ellet hesitated, looking as if she wanted to speak, then strode out.

Later that evening, she returned with a startling escort: His Grace Muirnen Rogonin of Claighbro, and—incredibly—Vultor Korda, who looked pasty-faced in tight black shipboards. As the men preceded Ellet into the brown permastone anteroom, Firebird rose from her lounger, where she'd sat comfortably curled around her clairsa. Two burly Tallan guards followed Ellet. Firebird came to attention, glad she hadn't yet undressed for bed. Silently she berated Ellet. *You could've warned me!* Brennen would've shown that courtesy.

"Gentlemen." She tried to sound cordial. "Come in, sit down." She motioned them toward the lounger. One guard came to attention beside her door, the other at the room's opposite corner. It was good to see Tallis take "protective custody" seriously.

Rogonin settled his bulk on the lounger, hands on the knees of his black sateen breeches. Korda joined him. Ellet walked behind them to lean on the windowbar.

Rogonin's soft green eyes absorbed every detail of the bare little anteroom and rested finally on Firebird, who stood near the door, feet apart and hands clenched at her sides. "Suns, Firebird, this is no place for a lady of your house. Aren't you ready to go back?"

Rogonin had left the title off her name, which he never would've done back at home. Clearly, she was in disgrace among her own class. She sent Ellet a questioning glance.

"The council," Ellet informed her, "has tabled the Netaian request until your period of temporary asylum ends, in six weeks."

Firebird nodded.

"But they did allow us to speak with you personally," insisted Rogonin, "and to convey their assurance that if you chose to return with us, they would guarantee you safe passage to Netaia."

"I see." Firebird envisioned a return on their terms. She would step off a Federate ship, leaving behind a Federate guard who'd seen her safely home. The redjackets would wait below.

Beyond her glasteel window, streams of cars flowed along wide avenues to an arc of low hills, then climbed to the passes and vanished. A little higher, wing lights blinked on atmospheric craft. Higher still, the nearest stars looked brighter, noticeably colored, and shifted to new positions.

"No, Rogonin," she said quietly. "I've chosen to stay."

"Then you must settle matters here," he answered. "Yourself."

Her cheeks warmed.

"Your electoral colleagues sent a last gift. It was taken away." He glared at one big Tallan guard.

"What was it?" she demanded. She probably knew.

Ellet confirmed her guess. "Dagger. Very ornate. Poisoned," she added.

"A quick one," rumbled Rogonin. "In the hope you retain some sense of honor."

Korda leaned forward. In the presence of Ellet, who had completed training Korda had only begun, she doubted he would try any Ehretan tricks on the guards, but she watched him closely.

"I have a message from your sister." Korda's strident voice became sing-song. "Your people are shamed. The treachery you have dealt us will not be undone in many lifetimes. You would be wise to return and end the bitterness with which people speak your name."

He didn't say which sister had sent the message, but the words, calculated to sting a proud wastling soul, struck home. Where was her Valor, her Fidelity? She wavered. Could she go back?

As she glanced aside, she saw Ellet's eyes widen, focused on Korda. The Sentinel opened her mouth as if to speak, then shut it in a tight line.

What was this?

Firebird cleared her throat. "I want to go back," she said firmly, "but I don't feel this is the time. Thank you for calling on me, though."

"I think you're mistaken." Korda leaned forward, hands almost touching his feet.

Firebird tensed. That was an odd gesture. She shook her head and stepped backward. "It's not time," she repeated.

The quick probing of his fingers inside his boot top put her on full alert. It was the old game of stick tag, only this time, it was no game.

Ellet's jaw twitched. She blurted, "He's got a weapon!"

Korda whipped out a tiny rod. Firebird feinted left to draw his fire, then threw herself hard to the right.

Korda's first shot grazed her left shoulder. As she crouched to dodge again, she recognized the Vargan stinger, no longer than a stylus, but deadly if one of its energy bolts struck a vital area. Its little power cell could deliver four more shots.

But Korda toppled, stunned by a guard's shock pistol. Rogonin struggled to his feet. "How dare you?" he cried. "That man has diplomatic immunity."

"He just lost it." Ellet gripped her empty holster. "Or so I hope. Get up. I'll take you back to your quarters."

Rogonin thrust out a finger. "Your immunity is just as temporary, Firebird. Netaia will have you back, if the Federacy wants peace with us. No invader can hold our world for long."

One guard carried Korda, whose breath came in wheezes. Rogonin followed, and then the other guard.

"Are you hit?" Ellet asked.

Firebird fingered the scorched fabric. "Just grazed," she said, shaking her head. As blood rushed to the burn, it started to sting.

"I'll send a med." Frowning, Ellet strode out.

Firebird drooped on the lounger. *Ellet!* her mind cried. Ellet was her friend, her teacher!

But plainly, Ellet had realized—even before Firebird—that Korda had somehow brought a weapon past MaxSec scanners. And Ellet had hesitated to speak for several seconds, a lapse that could've proved deadly.

Why?

CHAPTER 14

ELLET

simile
as previously noted

Tel Tellai had visited Hunter Height before, when his father briefly had been a guest of the Angelo family, but never under these circumstances. This time, he came as Phoena's personal escort, leaving the concerns of his estate and holdings with his employees.

He shifted his ankles on the edge of a huge octagonal bed in the Height's uplevel master room. Occupying most of the top story, this room was oddly shaped, almost pentagonal, with windows curtained in drab brown. They commanded a 120-degree view to the north, east, and southeast of its mountainous environs. Although bare by his standards and devoid of fine art, the wood-floored room's spaciousness suggested grand possibilities—and the bed on which he sat had once been occupied by his royal granduncle and a previous queen.

Phoena, gowned tonight in brilliant green velvette, stood at the bed's foot, fists clenched in graceful strength on her narrow hips. In a high-backed wooden chair across from Tel, looking profoundly uncomfortable, sat a House Guard Tel didn't know by name. "Only their diplomatic immunity got them off Tallis," he finished explaining. "And a Federate account of the incident reached Citangelo on the same shuttle with them. Danton detained them on Base, this time."

At least they were back! Tel had been deeply relieved Phoena hadn't sent him to Tallis. He would've gone, as his duty to his class, but Federates terrified him, and particularly Sentinels.

"With Stele?" she demanded. "Same detention area?"

"Evidently not. And they've drugged Korda. Some kind of injection that keeps him powerless."

Coals of temper gleamed in Phoena's hot brown eyes. "So he can't even tell us which guards can be bribed."

"Not for eight to ten days, Your Highness."

"Then it's time to push Carradee." Phoena glared. "If she'll release them into my custody, I'll promise to keep them locked up. Here. Out of harm's way," she said bitterly. She swept the rustic master room with her gaze. "Actually," she muttered, "this is almost perfect."

"Beg pardon?" Tel asked.

"Do you know," Phoena said, "if—you," she snapped at the House Guard. "You're dismissed."

He made a full bow and hurried to the lift, which opened directly into the master room.

Phoena took up her thought again. "If we could move others of like mind here, quietly, we could expand our operation. The head maid insists no Federate has ever come here. I don't think they even know it exists. And downlevel, there would be room for a research laboratory. We could even restart our real work."

Tel pressed his palms together. "Brilliant, Highness. With the airfield and tunnels we could accommodate plenty of traffic. But would Carradee object?" He shifted his seat again, giving the rustic master room a more careful appraisal. "I can't see her giving permission without informing the Federates."

"She did suggest I come here. She wants me out of her way. I'll cut a deal with her. If she can convince Danton to send me Korda and Rogonin, I'll come back here and I'll stay."

Tel arched an eyebrow. "What about Stele?"

"I'll ask for all three, then back down on Stele. I don't trust him." Phoena sat down on the bed foot and arranged the folds of her gown with a slender, bare arm. "Hundreds of other naval officers were put out of work by demilitarization, and the Enforcement Corps is in turmoil." She scowled. "A select few could constitute a small defense force here. If any can bring military craft that survived the invasion, or weapons, we—"

"Yes," Tel exclaimed. "All the marshals, naturally, are absolutely loyal to Netaia. And nearly the entire upper echelon of our naval forces." At last, those tiresome military discussions seemed relevant.

Phoena pursed her full lips. "Tel, would you compose a message to be delivered quietly to—say, twenty of the best of them? Don't take them all off the top. They'd fight for the privilege of giving orders. Choose four marshals, then have them select their most loyal subordinates. A core, that's all we need for now. For now," she repeated, stroking her leaf green skirt. "After tomorrow's *elections*," she added, pronouncing the word with distaste, "we'll know better where we stand."

Tel rose and bowed. "I would be honored to serve you, Highness." He strolled toward the chair the House Guard had vacated. Stark and simple, it seemed almost lost on the wide wooden floor. "Of course, the master suite must be made over to suit you. So much could be done with carpeting, fine art pieces, flowering plants. It could be made a lovely place, and still efficient."

"Yes, and data desks . . . and there's room up here for a police operation."

Tel ran a hand over the unadorned chair's back. "If only we didn't need to hide our effort from the queen. If only . . ." He gazed at her glowing face. "Phoena, it should have been you."

She sat down in another chair. "Siwann thought so, too," she said earnestly. "It will be me, one day."

"Highness, I didn't mean . . ." Tel hated the tremble in his voice. "Carradee . . . and her little daughters? You wouldn't—"

"Never mind." She crossed her bare arms and shivered prettily. "It's cold here, Tel. I don't think they've adjusted the heat for autumn yet."

He stepped away, searching the nearest wall for a climate control board.

Phoena laughed softly and rose out of the chair. "I didn't mean that, Tel. Won't you serve my royal person and leave Carradee to her own fate?" Her voice faded to a whisper.

She couldn't mean what he hoped. "Phoena, I . . ."

Phoena stretched out both arms. "But you dishonor me if you refuse."

"Oh no, Phoena! Highness . . ." Tel's face flushed with scarlet heat as he stepped toward her. "I mean you no dishonor."

When Ellet returned to Firebird's cell several days later, the sky outside her gridded window was dark gray, as stormy and bleak as Firebird's feelings.

They pulled stools to the small servo table with a pot of kass Ellet had brought. Firebird drew a deep breath and steeled herself to ask questions that would probably alienate a woman who might have become her friend.

Ellet read her tension with the ease of natural ability and thorough training. "Go ahead, Firebird. You're in no danger from me."

Firebird wrapped both hands around her cup. "You spotted that stinger before I did."

"Yes."

That was a relief. At least Ellet would answer honestly. "Didn't you put them through a weapon scan?"

"I certainly did. It picked up Rogonin's dagger. It should've pinpointed the stinger, too. Korda must've fuddled the circuit. I certainly had no wish to access him."

"Explain."

"Vultor Korda is a traitor to my people. Worse, a partially trained traitor. You know how deeply people fear us."

"Oh yes."

"We found out too late that Korda's alleged diplomatic immunity was forged—as was Rogonin's. He was evidently under arrest and shouldn't have been allowed offplanet at all. The communications lag worked against us. Korda obviously abetted him."

"I see. But why didn't you speak sooner?"

Ellet gave her a wry look. "I had reasons for wanting to get Vultor Korda in custody. So long as he didn't commit certain crimes, I couldn't touch him. By our codes, he is the worst kind of criminal. He deserves death." Ellet studied her interlaced fingers. "Firebird, we police ourselves to keep the Federacy from turning on us. It fears us, as it should. The Sentinel who abuses epsilon skills sheathes a crystace in his or her heart. That's the first vow we take, even before training."

"So you wanted to catch him in an offense, but it had to be extremely serious. Such as . . . murdering a prisoner under protective custody."

"Or attempting it. You were anxious to die not long ago, in a good cause." Ellet looked up, eyes afire. "We've won the Federacy's trust. If we lose it by misusing our abilities, there'll be another war of annihilation. And this time, we will not survive." She shook her head. "But no, I couldn't let him attack you. I considered provoking him to attack me. In the end, I simply let the guards do their job. My responsibility is to protect you, under General Caldwell's orders, and I will do so."

"Until you decide to bait another trap."

"I did not bait a trap. I recognized the potential of that situation. It proved unusable."

Firebird kept her emotions bland, thinking only, *Maybe Sentinels really aren't worthy of trust.* But a person could try to stay within their good graces. Aloud, she said, "I don't intend to lodge a complaint. I just want to hear, from your mouth, what you have against me." There had to be more to this than Vultor Korda's past offenses.

Ellet refilled her kass cup, sipped, and then leaned back her chair. She exhaled deeply before she spoke. "Someone," she said, "had better warn you that Brennen Caldwell is interested in you, and I don't mean politically."

"What?" Firebird slid her elbows off the table. "What do you mean, not politically? He respects me, and I . . . respect him. Considering the circumstances, he has been almost a friend."

"He wants to be more."

Firebird stared. No decent man ever wanted a wastling for more than a friend. "General Caldwell? That's ridiculous."

"Is it?" Ellet paused. "Brennen has his eye on the High command at Elysia. He could make it too, one day, if he didn't get thrown off course by such as you."

He'd been decent and merciful. Nothing more.

But he thought she had a future. Even Corey had never dared to plan beyond their geis orders.

Still, she protested. "You're not talking about—"

"Don't worry, he'd never force a relationship on you. He's a gentleman." Ellet's lips crinkled. Obviously, she thought Firebird was vastly beneath Brennen's attentions. "But if you let him get close to you, you'll never get away. I'm giving you a chance to prepare yourself."

"What do you mean, never get away? Mind control?"

"Of course not," Ellet snapped. "If we were allowed to control others' emotions, I'd have altered yours long ago."

Nevertheless, Firebird envisioned a line of women eased out of Brennen's life by Ellet Kinsman, and suddenly, all Ellet's actions and hints seemed clear.

"I'm warning you," Ellet went on. "A man with Sentinel training will have found ways to please a woman without ever touching her, just as you guessed: ways that will leave her changed, unable to forget or go back. It's permissible if she has encouraged him. I don't think you'd be capable of resisting. So unless you're interested in marrying the officer who interrogated you, you'd better step carefully. We don't waste much time on courtship. And that leads to the subject of pair bonding."

"Pair bonding?" Firebird echoed. Changed . . . unable to forget?

"When a Sentinel marries, he—or she—enters a permanent mental-emotional link. You can't resist; you can't escape. It affects the deepest level of existence. Oh, you'd keep your identity, but you'd never be the same. It's tough on outsiders, which is one reason we starbred families have maintained our separation. Another is that we can't let our genes be diluted. There are other telepaths, too. Renegades. We are the Federacy's only defense against them. We have to keep the families strong."

Can't escape? Suddenly Firebird wanted to be alone. "I see," she declared. "You have plans for General Caldwell yourself. Don't change them."

Ellet silently arched one black eyebrow.

"I have no designs on your Master Sentinel, Ellet. None whatever." The very notion of a long-term relationship stunned her.

Ellet slipped off her stool, picked up the empty pot, and ambled toward the door. "Don't forget that I can read your emotions, Lady Angelo." She pronounced the name with a sneer.

Stung, Firebird balled a fist on one hip. "Do not mock my family, Ellet Kinsman."

Ellet hooted. "Your family? Compared to his, yours is—" She halted wide-eyed. "That," she growled, "was more than I should have said. You'll mention it to no one."

"Don't worry." Firebird glared back.

"Ask him about it, though. If you dare." Ellet paused with one hand over the lock panel. As she looked over her shoulder, her voice became polite again. "Though I didn't get Korda in custody, I am glad you weren't hurt. I am sorry we can't be friends. Perhaps it's better not to even try, until that other matter is settled."

Firebird stood up unsteadily. "Thank you. I'll think about what you said."

"Try to be objective. And think quickly. They've sent out his replacement." She left the room.

Firebird turned from her door, deflated. So these were the feelings Ellet had hidden from her, all these weeks!

Brennen Caldwell, lieutenant governor of her conquered people, thought of her in that way? What had Ellet seen or felt in him—and in her—to make her believe it? And was there no privacy with these Thyrians? Obviously, Ellet hoped Firebird would be so taken aback by her warning that now she'd avoid Brennen entirely.

And she might. Surely the Federacy had other minimum-security detention areas. She could ask to be moved. The notion of mental bonding—deeper than the level of thought?—of never emerging unscathed—made her shudder.

Yet something else Ellet had said made her suddenly wistful: the concept of an indissoluble link, where before she'd possessed nothing lasting. For all her self-reliance, she'd been denied so many ordinary attachments—a family's loving nurture, the honorable intentions of good men, even the friendship of all but the other wastlings. She'd never even kept a pet, fearing its torment at Phoena's hands after she died. Buried beneath her pride, she knew she hid a dark, aching loneliness.

But—mental bonding? She barely knew the man!

Oh, but he knew her. To the deepest depths of her memory.

And still respected her? Even, if she dared to think it . . . loved her?

Torn between dread and delight, Firebird walked to the tattered lounger. She mustn't take this as a profound compliment, but as a warning. More than ever, she understood why some Federates distrusted these telepaths, even though they were sworn to Federate service. Entangling herself in their personal affairs—accidentally!—had landed her in a precarious situation. She recalled how Brennen had told the Verohan guard, *"I apologize for deceiving you, but it was done in the best interests of the Federacy."* When juxtaposed with Ellet's actions and cautions, those words took on sinister overtones. Might Brennen deceive her, or sacrifice her, "in the best interests of the Federacy?" In the best interests, maybe, of a man seemingly destined for the Federate High command?

How could she extricate herself without offending or angering him, and so putting herself in new danger?

And who were those others . . . the renegades, who'd take the Federacy if they could?

Firebird seated herself on the lounger and picked up her clairsa, clutching its carved frame to steady her fingers. She tuned automatically and defiantly began with the Academy anthem, "Beyond Netaian Skies." But that reminded her sharply of Corey, who alone had given and received her wholehearted support. Despite her resolve, a quick mental jump took her from Netaia, and Corey, to the battle of Veroh and all that had happened after.

She stared out at the dull sky. If Ellet was correct—if she could dare to believe such a thing—at what point had Brennen Caldwell seen her as a woman he wanted? What had he found, deep in her mind, worth his . . . his love? Was that truly what Ellet had meant? Because she did . . . respect . . . no, like . . .

What did she feel toward that man?

She clung to the clairsa, letting her emotions tumble, and listened with her heart for the music they would bring. A melody came, and she shaped it. It rose in a steady, stable fourth and a fifth, fell scalewise, then turned upward with a questioning minor third. She laughed uncomfortably. How could so simple a phrase betray so much turmoil? A pair of descending scale arcs fell into the second phrase, ending on a leading tone that begged for resolution. But it wouldn't settle yet. That was all that came. She played it several times to set it in her memory.

Ask him, if you dare.

Her fingers fell limp. Did Brennen also come from a powerful family?

Laying aside her clairsa, she keyed up the MaxSec library.

An hour's search gave her no clue. None of his listed ancestors were politicians. None had won acclaim in any of the fields known as Sentinel strongholds: intelligence, medicine, diplomacy. It looked like a very small bloodline.

She drummed her fingers. There must be some person, some source, that could inform her before Brennen returned.

Special Operations? Two weeks ago, she'd sent a political query to that floor. They'd turned her down, "restricted to civilian resources."

Staring out the window, she combed through her memories of every dealing with Ellet.

Here was a thought. The Sentinel had left early one day, to attend a religious observance. The "chapter room," she'd said, was somewhere in the tower.

If that haven accepted visitors, maybe Firebird could convince a MaxSec staffer to take her there.

Think quickly, she reminded herself. *They've sent out his replacement.*

Abruptly, Firebird remembered the melody of her ballad for Queen Iarla, and a lyric started to flow for the stubborn second stanza. She seized her recall pad.

Stepping off a shuttle into the main-floor MaxSec garage, Brennen took a deep breath of warm wind. Home—the only home he'd known in ten years. He'd earned the month's leave, this time. He tossed his duffel to a porter, then headed for the Special Operations floor to check mail and messages.

Inside the broad, sunlit clearing room, a plump secretary bent over her data desk. Beside her, reading a governmental newscan, stood the very person he wanted to see first, Ellet Kinsman. He opened his shields to greet her.

She switched off the newscan. He caught a shielding blast of epsilon static. Through it, too strongly to hide, flickered a clear picture of Firebird and an alarming fight-or-flight reaction to his greeting.

Stricken, Brennen raised his own shields. What had he *not* been told about the Korda incident—or was this something else?

He glanced around the clearing room. The secretary ignored, or hadn't seen, their exchange. On her left, the door to a small conference room lay open. Brusquely he pointed toward it, then followed Ellet inside. Just short of the black conference table, he turned and leaned on its surface. The door slid shut automatically, closing them both into half-light.

Drop the shield, Ellet. You promised a full report.

She sank into a chair, glaring. "Brennen," she said, "you may have accessed Lady Firebird Angelo, but there are too many things you don't know—"

"Captain Kinsman," he said tightly. Dread grew in his mind.

Ellet shut her mouth and subvocalized. *There was an attempt on her life several days ago. I—*

He should've listened to his instincts. He should've sent someone else. Anyone. "Drop the shield, Ellet, or you are insubordinate."

"Very well." She tossed her head and stared up at him. "I have broken neither law nor custom, and you would do well to follow that example."

Her static cloud dissipated. Gingerly he swept across the outer emotional matrix of her mind. Jealousy, frustration, grim satisfaction: tasting her emotional state only whetted his shocked fury.

Fury? He'd lost affective control. He struggled to regain it, then bluntly requested memory access. She gave sullen permission. In the space of an instant, all her dealings with Firebird were transferred to his awareness.

. . . Looking through Ellet's eyes, he ushered Korda into Firebird's cell, felt Ellet's indignation at his coming, saw his inordinate attention to that left boot. Bringing a weapon into this cell wasn't the capital offense it would take to keep Korda in custody, but attempting to murder a prisoner would be! With one stroke, Ellet could rid the Sentinel kindred of traitorous Korda and a rival for the place beside Brennen in the exiles' perilous genealogy.

Ellet had held that thought for less than a second, then thrust it aside. Being tempted was no crime.

But only yesterday, she'd gone back to Firebird and deliberately poisoned any casual fondness she may have felt for the starbred—for himself— with fear, and entombed it in suspicion. Only yesterday.

He stopped the carrier flow roughly, deliberately shaking Ellet, wishing he were free to disrupt her epsilon center with a burst of his own power. "You'd better leave," he whispered. "I'll speak with you later, after I see just how much damage you have done."

"That woman," Ellet muttered, "serves false gods. In case you've forgotten."

Absorbed in misery, he didn't watch her go.

CHAPTER 15

BRENNEN

cantabile
as if singing

Leaving her MaxSec escort at the Sentinel chapter room's door, Firebird tiptoed inside. It had proved surprisingly easy to come here, but one glance spoiled her hopes. She didn't see a data terminal, a scan viewer, or even a historical tapestry.

Still, the silent peace drew her in. A hand-sized flame burned against the far wall, and an odd scent hung in the air. Incense? Overhead, a broad, bowl-shaped gold lamp hung from three metal chains that joined near the ceiling.

Under the flame lay a long, low table covered by brocade cloths of staggering beauty: red, blue, and green, with shimmering highlights and rough shadows. On the wall behind it hung a meter-high Sentinel star, with its sword-points haloed by countless fine gold wires. Two ornate, leather-bound books lay open on the cloths. Firebird glanced over her shoulder. Seeing no one but the MaxSec staffer, she stepped up to look. One book displayed an illuminated verse:

Lift up your heads, O people of light,
And rejoice before the cloths of the altar,
For He spoke His commandments that we might be led,
Holy is He.

The Eternal is One, His commandments are righteous,
From dust He made us to live with Him forever.
Lift up your heads, for your home will be with Him,
Holy is He.

Bless the Eternal One, people of light,
Confess your transgressions and receive His mercy,
For vast is His mercy, and it is forever,
Holy is He.

Distracted from her search, she glanced left at the other book. To her surprise, it was written in an unintelligible language.

She blinked. Almost every world in the Whorl, even Netaia, used Old Colonial. Curious, she leaned closer, then hesitated. Maybe she shouldn't touch it.

She called to her escort, "Would they care if I looked through this?"

The man shrugged. "This is a public place. If they didn't want it touched, they'd have put it under glasteel."

Still, she handled its supple pages carefully. She reopened at its beginning to find what looked like a table of headings: *Negiyah Zamahr, Cahal, Siach . . .*

Not one familiar word. These people had secrets, and they meant to keep them.

She stepped back to the right. That book's pages were also soft and heavy, but she found readable headings. *Confessions—History—The Prophecies and The Wisdom of Mattah—The Voices of Exile—Adorations.*

Carefully she paged back to the verse that had lain open, Adoration 29, and left the book as she'd found it. She didn't think she'd find Brennen's mysterious family in here. She sidestepped to a chair and sat down, disappointed. There wasn't even anyone in here to ask. Still, she didn't want to go back to her two-room prison, and this place didn't feel truly empty.

She'd been taught as a child to pray silently to the Powers for guidance. If telepaths claimed this Speaker, this Eternal One, then he shouldn't object to mental prayers. *Hello . . . Your Honor*, she thought into the eerie dimness. *Whoever you are, whatever. What was that about mercy?*

All the guilt she'd felt since Veroh oozed out of the hiding places where she'd contained it. She'd been torn loose from all she'd hoped to achieve. She'd accepted a treasonous asylum and refused to carry out her geis orders, both capital offenses, besides the matter of Alef and Jisha.

The Powers forgave nothing . . . if they even existed. They justified Netaian law, but also its oppression of nearly a quarter of Netaia's population by fewer than one percent.

Her chest ached bitterly. Was there actually some higher cause than the unfeeling state, some kinder authority than the holy Powers? A personal deity might have human feelings, maybe even a starbred empathy.

No, it would be even more cognizant than that.

She bowed her head. If there were a deity whose mercy was "vast" and "forever," what would it take to buy one guilty traitor free from her well-deserved retribution? She'd worn masks of courage and service for so long. Who was she, behind them?

Her next thought terrified her. Brennen Caldwell had probed the depth of her mind. Did he think she was a hero, a guilty traitor, or something utterly different from either?

Hearing a soft whoosh, she spun around. A gray-haired man wearing a Thyrian uniform walked in. Not wanting to explain her roiling confusion to a stranger who probably felt it, she stood to leave.

"You don't have to go," he murmured. "Stay, if you'd like. You won't bother me."

Years of social training brought her masks back up. As the intruder, she should offer a compliment. She gestured toward the low table. "Those altar cloths are lovely."

"Yes." He glanced down into her eyes. "You feel drawn," he observed. "I won't disturb your search. Please stay."

She flushed. This place had called strange thoughts out of her subconscious. She'd never guessed that she yearned for cosmic mercy.

"We're forbidden to seek proselytes," he continued, touching her shoulder with an open palm, "but you're being called. Otherwise you wouldn't be here."

Evidently he thought she'd come seeking spiritual truths. Flustered, she turned back toward the door.

In that moment, a surge of awareness flowed over her. Gone as quickly as it had begun, it carried the unmistakable tenor of Brennen's epsilon touch.

Was he near, or was this some other phenomenon? She stood still for a few more seconds, but the sensation wasn't repeated.

She glanced at the stranger. He seemed not to have sensed whatever she'd felt. "I need to get back," she murmured. "But thank you for making me welcome."

"Always," he said. "Come again." He took a seat and then faced forward, politely ignoring her.

She drew a deep breath. Brennen's arrival, and the untangling of feelings and events that it would bring, could be moments away. "I'm done," she told her staff escort.

Back in her quarters, she glanced nervously around the anteroom. Everything was tidily placed, except the answers she'd hoped would be tucked neatly into her mind before she ever saw him again. What would she do; what should she ask . . . or tell him?

Closing her eyes, she recalled the nuances of that surge of awareness, trying to make it flow again. It had suggested Brennen's strength, but not as she'd battled it over Veroh. She'd sensed a hesitancy this time, almost a tremble, as though he were afraid.

Of her?

An hour passed, but it felt like three or four, before her entry bell sounded. The MaxSec staff never rang before entering, and Ellet hadn't returned, but there wasn't the keen awareness she'd felt an hour earlier.

She walked to her door. "Yes?" she called, wishing she had a hall-monitor screen.

The door slid open. Dressed in ordinary civilian clothes, Brennen stood a long pace back. Field General, Master Sentinel, intelligence officer . . . and what else? She hardly knew him. He met her eyes from the distance. Undoubtedly, he was reading her feelings, but she felt no command, no pressure, no compulsion.

"Hello." His smile, too, seemed hesitant. "May I talk with you?"

"Of course." She stepped aside.

Brennen didn't move. "May I come in?" he asked.

What charming formality. "Come in," she answered, standing aside. "Welcome back."

He walked straight to her corner servo table and took a stool. Baffled by the change in him, she shut the door and then joined him.

He didn't look at her but at his hands, which lay open. Reminded sharply of the surge she'd felt, she blurted, "Was that you, about an hour ago?"

His startled expression delighted her. Whatever he was, he wasn't all-knowing. "Yes," he said when he'd recovered. "I was trying to read your emotional state before I came down. I thought I was being subtle. Few people can sense a quest pulse."

That felt wonderful. "I was several floors up," she admitted, "and I wasn't doing much, just thinking. You . . ." She groped for words that wouldn't say too much. "You seemed worried."

He pushed back from the table and stared. "I . . . the first person I met when I got to MaxSec, fortunately, was Ellet. My friend," he said bitterly, and the label became an accusation. "She showed me what she'd done. All of it. I could've choked her."

She could almost feel him seething. Thank the Powers, his anger wasn't directed at her. "As to the matter of Korda," she said, "I've almost forgiven her. I understand loyalty to a cause."

He gripped the table's edge, whitening his knuckles. "I'm going to find it harder to forgive. She'd have gladly seen you killed." His anger dimmed somewhat, and the hesitancy returned. "Then she tried to frighten you with concepts you must've found incomprehensible. She was brutal. I intended to explain, in the right time. Now I'm forced to begin with the end already known. Maybe it's better that way."

So he denied nothing. While she'd barely accepted his friendship, this fast-track Federate hero wanted her for his own. Thanks to Ellet, he feared he'd already lost. "Wait," she said. "Stop."

He paused, looking puzzled.

She'd be spaced in slip-state before she'd let Ellet Kinsman defeat him. "I have to be honest. I've . . . missed your company."

He set an arm on the table and brushed hair from his forehead, caught off guard again.

Staying one jump ahead of Brennen felt like playing stick tag with Corey, and winning: exhilarating!

"You've been at Citangelo with me," he said softly, "because my memory is vivid. If I'd had a clue, though, that Ellet would've treated you this way . . ."

Firebird shrugged. "I wasn't injured." That graze didn't count.

"Those offplanet clearances should've landed on my desk. I hope Korda is questioned. Then we'll get to the bottom of this."

"Yes," she murmured.

"Korda must be stopped, but not by risking your life. Our laws are strict, and harsh to traitors, but the intent is life, not death." He shook his head slightly. "I can only be glad Ellet didn't frighten you as badly as she intended."

"I don't scare easily." Firebird hesitated, remembering how plainly he would sense her feelings. "Well, she did scare me," she admitted, "but she could've misinterpreted. Exaggerated. I'd rather hear this from you."

"Shall I be plain?"

Powers help me now. She braced herself, then said, "Please."

He looked directly at her eyes. "I'll explain all you want to know, soon— as soon as possible—but first I have to tell you one thing." He extended a palm across the table.

Firebird slid only her fingers into it. Even as he curled his larger hand around them—a new sensation, warm and provocative—part of her still didn't believe.

"I do want you, very much," he said softly.

She sat motionless, struck dumb by those few simple words.

"I have," he went on, "since I first took you under access. Do you recall my saying how deeply I was impressed by your talents, and how I was angered by your wastling insistence on dying?"

She nodded, still unable to speak. She'd remembered those words during the hours since Ellet had spoken, but she'd invented other ways to explain them.

"Even earlier, I sensed our connaturality. Noticing that without specifically probing is unusual. But I couldn't tell you anything, back at Veroh. You considered yourself already dead."

"True," she admitted, finally finding her voice.

He still gripped her fingers, though gently. "You had a long turning ahead, even toward the decision to live. And you despised us—the Federacy, my people."

She nodded again.

"You needed to deal with your prejudices before you could face any personal feelings." He leaned toward her. "I never meant to deceive you, Mari. I've just gone slowly. Sentinels enter quickly and young into lifetime commitments because we can read one another. I haven't asked that of you."

"We don't waste much time on courtship," Ellet had said. "That's true," Firebird answered. "You haven't."

"You fear me, though."

Look what you are, she wanted to cry. Instantly, she realized she might as well have shouted. "Why should I believe you'll let me change my own mind?" she muttered. "If I even want to."

He sighed. "So Ellet succeeded. You dread the very ways I would've hoped to please you. Now I'm afraid to show my feelings."

"I'd be helpless, unable to back out, to . . ."

"To get away?" He echoed Ellet's phrase scornfully. "I'd never try to coerce you, overpower you, or trick you." Those glacial-ice blue eyes pleaded. "I want to be accepted for myself, not for my epsilon skills. If you fear them, I'll do nothing to please you that another man couldn't."

Irritation flashed through her, ignited by a fresh realization. She'd worn her masks for too long. She'd obeyed the Disciplines while aching to do other things—to show forbidden compassion, to sing illegal songs, to insist that she had a right to exist. She shifted her hand to grip his. "Don't you dare diminish yourself. Be what you are and I'll do the same." Then she pulled her hands away and clenched them in her lap.

Brennen rested an elbow on the table, leaned on it, and then straightened again. "That's more than I'd hoped for, Mari. I was prepared to be sent away. Thank you." He pulled in his feet and rocked forward, ready to stand. "You're upset. Shall I go?"

"No." Firebird drew a deep breath. "Tell me how things are in Citangelo."

Relaxing, he looked aside. "Not good," he said softly, "though it's not openly bad. Your government is frighteningly unstable."

She thought she could guess what he meant. "It's certainly not fair to everyone."

"More than that, Mari. If it's not reformed soon, Netaia is ripe for a major class revolution."

The words chilled her. How many ballads had she heard that pled for freedom? "Might your occupation government stabilize things for a while?"

"It's trying. The Assembly and the queen seem to be accepting many small changes in your legal system, but the Electorate holds too much judicial power. If we alter a sentencing protocol, the courts redefine the offense. We can't eliminate the electors without disrupting the entire system, so nothing goes smoothly."

"The electors," she snapped, "believe they were born with divine rights. But Carradee is a good person. We've always been friends." She flicked some hair behind her shoulder. "But can I assume Phoena is still. . . ?"

"Still what?" he asked gently.

"Agitating," Firebird suggested. "Making everything as difficult as possible."

"We suspect she's behind a number of problems. Probably even Korda and Rogonin's attempt on your life."

"That wouldn't surprise me," Firebird muttered.

"She has a new little moon-shadow. Count Tellai."

"Tel?" Firebird choked. "But he's a child."

"He's old enough, and he's willing enough to dive into deep trouble for that woman. They're on vacation now, together. Anywhere but Citangelo."

"Did you ever see . . ." She hesitated. It hurt to ask. "Daley Bowman or Delia Stele?"

"Daley hasn't contacted you?"

She blinked. "What?"

"He accepted asylum." Brennen shook his head. "The last I heard, he'd bought passage to Caroli. Advanced mechanical school."

She managed to say, "That's wonderful." Daley had lacked his twin's boldness. Given a chance to vanish, Daley must've seized it. Someday, maybe, he would feel safe enough to renew old acquaintance. "Good for him," she added mournfully. "He should do well. And Delia?"

"She died at Veroh. I am sorry."

Firebird slumped and shook her head.

Brennen walked to the window, checking the time on his wristband. She saw him catch a glint from inside the glasteel panel, lean close, and examine the honeycomb-patterned security grid. It cast odd shadows on his even features.

She sighed. Unlike Daley, she would never be able to vanish. But could she ever go home? And to what?

Brennen turned away from the window. "At least now I can take you out of this cage. I've had a Cirrus-class racing jet for four months, and I've been so busy since Veroh that I've had no chance to take it through its paces. I'd enjoy your company." He nodded toward her clairsa, which she'd propped in a corner below the windowbar. "If you'd bring that, I'd consider myself well repaid."

She straightened, brightening. "Oh, Brennen. You have no idea how much I'd like that. Or . . ." She shrugged. "I suppose you do know."

He frowned. "And I know you won't forget Ellet's intimidation. Can I give you some promise that I'll respect your will, give you room for your own decisions?"

Why should she believe any claim of restraint? She'd experienced what he could do, and the memory still stung. Unable to think of a stronger vow by which to bind him, she said, "Give me your word as a Sentinel."

He didn't hesitate. "You have it."

"Then I'd love to get out of here."

"Tomorrow? Early or late?"

"Early!" The thought thrilled her, but she felt oddly disappointed. After such a tumultuous meeting, they'd parted with respect on both sides. Now they had nothing but careful, distant talk for each other? She didn't dare drop her guard, but she was treating him as less than a friend. Surely he felt that tension too.

She stepped toward him and laid a hand on his shoulder. "Welcome back, Brenn." Pulling closer, she gathered her nerve and gave him a quick, awkward squeeze.

He drew away, eyes glinting. "Thank you," he whispered. "I said it before, and it's true—you have courage."

CHAPTER 16

AIRBORNE

ad libitum
at the performer's liberty

The deserted parking bay felt comfortably cool, full of swirling air currents, in the last hour before dawn. "There she is." Brennen pointed.

The small jet at the western end looked like a silver dagger. Gleaming, back-curved wings tapered to join a knife-edged chine that protruded from the fuselage, sweeping like a blade from its nose to twin atmospheric engines. The pilot in Firebird leaped for joy.

"It's pretty," she said as casually as she could. "What'll it do?"

"I mean to find out." He opened the passenger entry. Seating was side-by. On her seat Firebird found a combat type, five-point flight harness. The Cirrus racing class, whatever that specified, rose a notch in her expectations. She adjusted her harness as he laid a duffel bag and soft flask in the cargo area, then her clairsa case, and secured all with a heavy net. "I'll be just a few minutes," he said, then made a thorough walkaround.

"How many standard g's are you qualified for, without a gravity suit?" he asked as he climbed into the pilot's seat, so close that their legs almost touched. She laughed inwardly when she realized his flying leathers were the same kass-brown as the craft's interior. Both were trimmed in forest green.

"I don't know. Netaia doesn't use your standard g's. Two-thirty-seven pressure units, however that converts. Five-eighty with a life suit."

"And you don't scare easily." He ignited the engines, then handed her a headset.

She clipped it on before answering. "That's right."

Smiling, he got flight clearance and then slid a throttle rod forward. The Cirrus glided out over the city.

Out, she was out, she was out! Buildings and greenery changed angles every moment. Through a glare-shielded cockpit that afforded almost 360 degrees of vision, she feasted on the growing sky glow, the jagged skyline of the capital city, and its ring of green hills.

As soon as they left the outer city's slow-zone, Brennen maxed the accelerator and pointed the jet's sharp nose for the clouds. Thrust pressed Firebird back and down into her seat, and she reveled in the sweet, familiar feeling. She'd breakfasted lightly, hoping he didn't intend to fly conservatively. He climbed at battle speed until the sky started to darken. Surely he was relishing her feelings, if he sensed them at all.

He stalled over the top in thrilling weightlessness, and then set a lazy, downward spiral.

"She seems to handle well." He reversed the spiral. "But this really doesn't demand much maneuverability."

Firebird sighed. "This civilian racer climbs faster than our tagwings. No wonder we lost the war."

"This isn't entirely civilian-equipped." As if to prove that, he tightened the spiral, accelerated the dive, and they dropped like a spinning leaf, reversing again and again. His hand moved confidently on the rods and touch-panels, barely tightening, mostly relaxing. It was a tawny hand, fine boned—neither long fingered and slender like Phoena's, nor broad like her own, more typical of the Angelo line—but strong looking and—

Stop! she commanded herself. *He's reading your emotions!*

He turned to her, and though his voice stayed casual, tiny smile lines around his eyes confirmed that he'd read that emotional flicker. "Are you game for some fast low-level? That'll give me a chance to test her gravidics."

"Sure. You seem to know what you're doing."

"Then hang on."

The next few minutes were breathtaking. He dove into a black-stone badlands area of spires and canyons and skimmed the ground at near-attack velocity, barely clearing boulders, cornering at dizzying speed and doubling back with somersaulting accuracy. A natural arch loomed ahead. The Cirrus shot through before Firebird could check his setup vector.

They soared again. "No problems?" he asked as they burst through a cloud.

"That was great," she cried. This man could fly! All the same, she touched the snugging control on her harness.

"All right, then. One more thing."

He nosed down and pushed the throttle forward.

Acceleration squeezed her up into her seat. The rugged ground rushed closer. Suddenly her mouth went dry. She tried to swallow but couldn't. Her legs, as if possessed with minds of their own, braced against the fore bulkhead.

He leveled out. "Too much," he said gently.

"Wait," she cried. "No, don't abort. Do what you wanted."

"Too much like Veroh?"

He'd realized it before she had: That had felt exactly like her attempt to crash her tagwing. A bitter, metallic taste poisoned her memory.

She tore her stare away from the horizon, met his questioning look, and tilted her chin. "If you feel this ship can handle what you wanted to try, do it. I know you're not suicidal."

"You're sure?"

"Yes," she growled.

He hesitated only a second, then took the jet into a long climb. "If you want me to stop, just shout."

"I will," she said, then pressed her lips together.

He nosed over again. She forced her limbs to relax, averting her eyes from the upracing ground, watching the intensity on Brennen's face instead as he waited, waited for the right moment . . .

Trebled gravity drove her hips into the seat. He took the bottom of the turn through the stone arch and soared skyward again. She whooped. "I'd've thought that was impossible!"

"And I'd've thought," he answered, "I would never know a woman who would enjoy that." He straightened out and steered for a broad, striated mesa. "I think the compensators pass inspection. Let's give her a rest."

He made a casually perfect landing on dark stone and cut the engines. Firebird climbed out onto the silent plateau. Hot, dry wind whipped her hair around her face. She gloried in the lifting, falling feeling and stretched kinks from her limbs, gladly breathing the scent of unseen flowers and faraway thunderstorms.

Please, please don't take me back to MaxSec.

Brennen strolled to the rim of the tableland and peered over at a glimmering yellow desert. In civilian clothes, out of the cockpit, he seemed a different man. Not a telepath, nor an enemy officer, just a man who . . . who wanted her, who had her alone, kilometers from anywhere. Sensitive skin tightened at the back of her neck.

He pulled his hand from his coat pocket and pointed downward. A hunting bird soared far below, its markings almost the same as a red-tail kiel's. Seven to eight hundred years ago, the first colonists had used similar terraforming stock throughout the Whorl. By the time they reached Netaia, their science had blossomed into a high form of art. It had vanished during the Six-alpha catastrophe.

The bird swooped beyond a hillock. Brennen turned. "Would you like to fly it now?" He inclined his head toward the silver racing jet.

Delighted, she sprinted back across the tableland.

He caught up as she boarded. "The control panel is totally different from a Netaian display. I'll show you."

He adjusted the seat and footbars for her and went over the display several times. When she felt satisfied that she'd unscrambled the board, she fired up the engines and gently took it off the mesa. Concentrating hard, she dropped into the badlands at half Brennen's speed and cruised along their contours, mounting small ridges and dropping into adjacent watersheds. A half-eight through and over the looming black arch bolstered her confidence. Gradually she accelerated through twisted canyons, pulled into a climb over the mesa, and watched the badlands disappear behind. The mountains far ahead were shadowy green, rich with summer.

"Find a place to eat," Brennen suggested.

"It's not time yet, is it?"

He touched the panel. "If that's how closely you watch your instruments, I'm surprised you passed flight school."

She chuckled.

"Actually," he said, "you are a good pilot, for such a new one. The NPN was foolish to waste you."

"Despite the fact that I couldn't crash a fightercraft properly when I was supposed to?"

"That," he said bluntly, "was my fault."

The green mountains rose to jagged, tightly folded ridges. Firebird crested the first ridge, then decelerated. Her chest squeezed tightly again. Finally, she found the breath and the courage to ask, "It was you, that day. Wasn't it?"

His voice murmured in her headset, "You needed to know. Can you forgive me?"

She nodded, swallowing hard. War had risks. Wastlings died, and she couldn't grieve Corey continuously. Still, she spoke lightly with an effort. "Yes. How much landing room will we need?"

"I'll talk you through." Near the divide of the second range, they spotted a round lakelet nestled in a cirque amid old-growth forest. She set down below it in a long meadow. As she climbed out, Brennen pulled out the clairsa and lunch packet and swung them over one shoulder, then held out a hand to her. "Watch your step. Tripvine."

"Is that what's blooming?" Though she'd tried to thrust Corey out of her mind, she ignored Brennen's hand. She felt dirty, disloyal. She bent down to examine the tangled ground cover. From under a round leaf she picked a blossom with a shape like a tiny purple trumpet. She held it to her nose. "Yes, that's it."

"They export the extract for perfume, but the stems are as tough as docking cable. I'm not exaggerating." He offered his hand again. "I would bring him back if I could," he added. "I give you my word on that, too."

She looked up into kindly eyes. The electors, not Brennen, had sent her and Corey to die.

She took his hand. Carefully they walked up the vine-covered field to the lake, where water and leaves riffled in a fragrant breeze.

"Over by the water, on one of those rocks?" she suggested. He changed direction without comment, and they scrambled over fallen trees and stones to the tallest boulder, well over twice her height.

He boosted her to his shoulder level. She found a good toehold and scrambled the rest of the way up the lichen-mottled stone. Brennen tossed her the bags and then jumped to the top, holding her clairsa case.

She gulped air.

"Does that disturb you?"

"No," she lied firmly. It was about time he relaxed and let himself play. "Do something else."

Turning toward the shore, he lifted one hand. A glacier-smoothed boulder rolled into the air and landed with a slurping splash.

There it was. In or out of uniform, he was a gene-altered Ehretan.

"We don't flaunt our abilities." He sat down beside her and stared up at the rocky skyline. "They cost energy and wear us down. And," he added somberly, "we've survived by controlling ourselves. If the Federacy ever decided we were dangerous, we wouldn't last. There are too few of us."

She slid off the uncomfortable dress shoes Carradee had sent, then knelt and helped him spread out the lunch parcel. He'd packed dark bread, thinly sliced; a fish spread and a tub of soft, pale, sweetish cheese; and a bag of spiky green fruit. They ate silently for a while, discussing only the food. Finally, Firebird raised the obvious subject again. "I suppose it took a lot of work to learn those skills, though."

"It did. Sentinel College is grueling."

She poured clear red liquid from his flask into a pair of squared cups and offered him one. "Did they teach other things, too? Arts, science?"

"My education was slightly strange. They took me to college for Sentinel training before I'd finished junior school."

"Which did you finish first, then? Your master's training?"

"Yes. Then a year after that—"

"How old were you?"

"Seventeen," he admitted. She tried to imagine a seventeen-year-old youth, trained as a Master Sentinel. They must've utterly trusted him.

"After another year, I finally finished Academy," he said.

"Why did you pick the military?" She envied the choices he'd had.

"Desperate to fly," he admitted, "like you, but we weren't well off. This was the only way I could afford to get into a cockpit. By then, I was getting pressure to take a second degree, in politics. I ignored any courses that might've fit anyone else's plans. I wish I'd broadened. I would've had time."

She nodded. Graduating precociously, he'd have had plenty of time.

"What about your Academy?" he asked.

She sipped the tart, cool fruit juice. "It must be the same everywhere. Flight. Dynamics. Slip physiology. Weapons, navigation, strategies." She slowed, trying to recall what had kept her so busy for so long.

"Interrogation and resistance."

She glanced up sharply. He was smiling. Very well, she could make light of it if he could. "Not enough, though."

"Poor instruction." He offered a small yellow disk. "Have you ever had citrene?"

On her tongue, it melted to a puddle of sour sweetness. "Oh, that's good. Are there any more?"

He dropped several into her palm, then repacked his dishes and scattered the crumbs over the edge of the boulder. Firebird wrestled momentarily with an urge to tell him about Hunter Height and its airstrip.

Corey wouldn't have told him.

Stop, she commanded herself. *Corey's gone. You're alive, and you shouldn't be—wouldn't be, except for Brennen!*

She ate the last citrene and pulled her clairsa from its case. Hunter Height could wait a day.

She played several classical pieces. He sat close, knees pulled tightly to his chest. Encouraged by his unblinking attention, she closed with the theme and variations she'd just composed. She didn't introduce it, but his eyes closed as she began. She let her feelings melt into her music, and when she finished, he sat without moving.

"Did you write it?"

"Yes."

"How long ago?"

There'd be no deceiving him. "After I'd spoken with Ellet."

He took a long, deep breath. "Mari?"

"Hm?"

"May I touch your mind?"

Yes? No? What should she answer?

"Only a touch, Mari, only a feathering. As you've just touched me."

Her neck hairs prickled again. Ellet had warned that she would never be the same, never get away if she ever let him approach her. But she had good powers of resistance. He'd admitted that publicly. *And I played that suite to impress him. Maybe*, she conceded, *just this once, and I could still escape.*

But her voice trembled. "All right."

His eyes reflected the sky. He didn't move or speak.

Past the surface of her awareness blew a sensation of approval so deep, so complete, that she wanted to shout aloud for sheer joy. Someone knew her completely, all her strengths and her flaws, and was neither intimidated nor ashamed. Laughing at herself, for her fears that hadn't come true, she set the clairsa back into its padded case. "You know what I need most of all, don't you?"

"I could help fill that need in you, Mari, for as long as I live."

Only then did she appreciate Ellet's warning. A person who'd been loved in that way would never settle for anything less. Glowing inside, she leaned away from him and hastily changed the subject. "Could you really free-fall?"

He glanced down, and when he looked up again, his eyebrows had arched. "Yes," he said. "It's well within my grasp if I'm rested."

"And if I jumped?"

He shrugged slightly. "I could land you. Do you want to try it?"

What perverse impulse had made her choose that subject? *But I might never get another chance*, she told herself. "Yes, I do. If you're rested."

He grinned and pointed toward a high ridge. "We could launch from that ledge."

After a thirty-minute climb, they stood high on the broad, windy ridge. Far below lay dark forest and the silver Cirrus, dropped like a giant's dagger on shimmering green meadow. The gale made it seem ten degrees colder up here; it tugged her hair forward, whipping her face.

"Brennen," she said abruptly, "something's been bothering me."

"Yes?"

"It's crazy, it—seems like a contradiction. You Sentinels are trained in emotional control. You have to be, to face the barrage of others' feelings. Ellet explained that. But then how . . ." She scuffed a stone with one foot. "How can a Master Sentinel fall in love?"

"We have hopes," he answered, "as personal as anyone's. If we release our emotions, we love deeply, maybe more deeply than others. We don't forget the wonder of finding and winning."

Gazing into the hazy distance while trying to contain her hair with one hand, Firebird nodded. It was time. "Then what's pair bonding? You promised to explain."

He sat down on a large flat stone. She took one just downwind, slightly sheltered by his body from the hair-lashing blast. "I wouldn't think it was as 'rough on outsiders' as Ellet wants you to believe, though few of us marry out." He took a long breath. "It's a deep, permanent link that manifests in the emotions. Each feels with the other, anytime the other is near."

"The way you can read my feelings now?"

"No. Deeper, more certain, and eventually the awareness blends with the other senses. There's an adjustment period, but for my married friends, it wasn't long. I'd guess a few weeks for you—but less for me, because of my training."

"But an outsider wouldn't be taken over?"

"Absolutely not," he insisted. "Only . . . uncomfortable, for a time. A little confused."

She studied the rocks at her feet, flaked fragments of a disintegrating sedimentary layer. "I'd like to believe you. But it's easy for you to make that statement and impossible to prove."

"I've met nongifted people who married my kind," he argued. "They were distinct individuals, even decades later."

She shifted to a more comfortable position on her rocky seat and asked casually, "Your parents are pair bonded?"

"They were." He sounded wistful. "They were very happy. After my father died, it took my mother two years to recover enough to go back to her work. That's a powerful argument against your having me, by the way. In my profession, it's possible I'd leave you a young widow."

He hadn't bristled when she asked about his family. "They were both Sentinels?" she pressed.

"Not military. But both came from starbred families, and both trained."

"Then Ellet . . ." She hesitated. "Are you and Ellet connatural, Brenn?"

"Marginally, I think."

That confirmed Firebird's guesses. She plunged ahead. "She all but dared me to ask what's unique about your family."

His eyebrows came together for an instant. He covered his mouth with one hand. "I'll tell you what I can," he finally murmured, "if you'll let me make sure you tell no one else."

"You mean, do something to my mind?"

He nodded soberly.

Squill! She'd asked for it! But surely he couldn't do any worse than what she'd already experienced. "Go ahead," she insisted. "I want to know."

He touched her forehead with one finger, holding it there long enough that she almost wished she'd backed down. Then he drew his hand away. She'd felt nothing. "It's a very old family, Mari. It's always been small. But my brother and I, and his children, are the only heirs to an ancient . . . religious promise."

She'd heard the Ehretan survivors called "mendicants." "Yes? What is it?"

He flushed. "I'm sorry. That's all I can say, even now. I'm under command myself."

He'd compelled her to silence for that? She almost laughed, then guessed, "Is the secrecy meant to protect your family?" Ellet had mentioned renegade telepaths.

After a long hesitation, he said, "Yes. There's no wealth involved, no personal benefit. I'm sorry. I truly cannot say more about that."

Obviously, to him this was no casual matter. She picked up a smooth brown rock and hefted it, watching him, waiting to see what he'd say without prompting.

He said, "I would hope to have my own children someday. Soon, actually."

Children! He'd said it softly, and obviously, he meant it just as seriously as poor Corey had meant it. Admitting that hope made him vulnerable. But . . . children? Immediately?

"I was a wastling," she answered, stalling while she tried to picture herself as a parent. It was only slightly less difficult than trying to imagine an eternal being. "I wasn't supposed to have children, and I didn't try to want them." Her voice softened as their eyes met again. "The . . . altered genes don't make this impossible, do they?"

"No. We're all mixed blood now."

Yes. Korda had said that. "And you know that I come from a long line of daughters."

He frowned. "I saw that in the portrait gallery. Why?"

"There hasn't been a male born into the succession in over a hundred years. Not since the last time an Angelo prince married against the Powers' will, out of the noble families."

"I suspect that could be cured, whatever causes it. How has the surname survived?"

"Since Prince Avocin's time, the men who've married us have taken the name as a matter of rank and pride."

"I would not."

She opened her hands. "Of course not." A gust of wind caught her hair and tossed it wildly. She seized it again.

Brennen folded his hands around one knee. "Here is a secret I can tell you, Mari. The ayin—the complex of brain areas that gives us our abilities— ages slightly each time we use it. Over time, we lose our powers."

She didn't miss the fact that this time *he'd* changed the subject.

He stared at his lightweight boots. "Here's another. My people have lived as exiles for almost two hundred years. Everyone outside the kindred builds walls against us. They either give us more honor than we deserve, or fear and suspicion that we have to understand. We feel it. We do inspire fear.

"So you see, few people know me. If you did, the way I know you from access, you'd understand how well we complement one another."

But they were worlds different in blood and allegiance, right down to their little cultural habits. Her mind echoed with words he'd spoken in other places: "A matter of Federate security" . . . "I'm sorry to have deceived you" . . . "You could still be a great help to us" . . .

"Ellet said I could cost you the High command."

"That's true." Shrugging, he shifted his feet.

"Why?"

"My single-mindedness would be suspect," he said dryly. "You're not starbred. You're not even Federate."

With the rank he'd achieved at his age, he could have taken a shot at the top, where waning powers might matter less. "No, I'm not Federate. At this moment I have no home at all. At least you have Thyrica."

"And something even deeper. I hear that you visited our chapter room."

Cosmic mercy . . . "Do people from other backgrounds worship your god, Brenn?" she blurted.

He raised his head, and the light in his eyes became keener. "Yes. Many do. Grace and truth aren't limited by home worlds."

"On Thyrica, then?"

"And at Tallis, Caroli, Luxia. Wherever we've lived in numbers, we've drawn inquirers."

Firebird heard a note of utter confidence in his voice. She envied it. Whatever he believed, he gave it all his heart and mind. She hadn't felt that sure of the Powers in years. "But you don't push your beliefs on other people."

"That's forbidden."

"Why?" she demanded. "That's strange to me."

"I know," he said softly. "It's our greatest pain and our deepest regret. The powers our ancestors gave us came from their immoral experiments, on their own children. We live with the consequences, good and bad. Until we redeem ourselves by serving others, we've forfeited the spiritual rights we were promised, especially the right to proselytize. We're under divine discipline. Someday," he added wistfully, "that will change. But . . . because we tried to force ourselves on Ehret, we live as exiles."

A hereditary racial guilt?

"Someday," he repeated, "we'll be released to actively seek converts. That's another promise, another prophecy. But for now, it's a terrible irony. We have much to offer. We're in an era of collective penitence but individual mercy. At least we can point the way, when outsiders inquire."

Mercy . . . Again the ache pressed on her heart. Could a divine ruler demand utter obedience but stop short of punishing the guilty? And what did he mean, "redeem themselves"? Her head whirled with questions.

No, shrieked her conscience, *stop!* She stood close to committing fresh treason. For someone born to her position, acknowledging any authority higher than Netaia was deadly apostasy.

She mustn't ask. Tossing her stone over the side, she looked at Brennen steadily, knowing he would read her feelings all the more easily through her eyes. "Let me tell you how I feel, Brennen. I won't refuse you, but I can't commit myself, not yet. Not to any person, and certainly not to a strange religion."

His eyes flicked to each of hers in turn. "You'd like to," he murmured.

She felt her cheeks flush. "Who wouldn't?" If such a transcendent being could exist! She forced her gaze to stay on Brennen's. Her longing for understanding had momentarily overcome her need to keep a distance.

"But you still don't trust me," he said.

"I'm afraid to trust anyone."

"I understand," he said gently. "Because you're valuable to the Federacy, you suspect my intentions. You have that right." He took her hand and massaged it. "I don't know what I would do if I had to choose between you and my people. And I can't put you above my God. There must be one highest priority in your life for which you'll give everything—your possessions, your rank, your hopes, even your life—or you're not a full person."

"Don't I know it." She'd given everything for the Powers, the electors, and the Angelo family. She slid her hand out of his. "And what do you do when that highest priority fails you, Brenn?"

"You find a higher."

If only it were that quick and easy. Higher than the Angelo family, there'd always been Strength, Valor, and Excellence; Knowledge, Fidelity, and Resolve; Authority, Indomitability, and Pride. Higher even than those, in her heart: truth, justice, and love—not the sweet warmth of human affection, but her searing, self-sacrificial love for Netaia and its people.

Could Brennen's higher master return that to her?

He stood and brushed rock dust from his leathers. "Meanwhile, would you trust me enough to jump if I went first? It is the easier way down."

She snorted, appreciating the paradox he saw. She would trust him with her life in free-fall, because the worst that could happen would be a fast, fatal landing. But if she let him get too close, the worst that could happen might be . . .

Unfathomable.

Shivering, she scrambled to her feet. What if she bound herself to a Sentinel, and then one day he turned on her? How deep could that misery run?

But if they were truly bonded, heart and mind, could he ever do such a thing?

She stepped up to the cliff they'd climbed and peered over its side. The ridge was nearly as tall as the MaxSec tower, and here it was just as sheer. "I hate climbing downhill."

"Good. We'll jump." He eyed the cliff's distant foot as if picking a landing spot. "I'll go first. Once I'm down, give me a minute to rest. You'll feel it when I take a good kinetic grasp on you. Then don't wait too long, and be sure to jump outward."

"Like tower jumping." An Academy skill she'd enjoyed.

He walked to the other side of the ridge. She stared, still not quite sure he meant to do it without a parasail, an anchor line, or even a cushioned landing pit. Then he started to run. After six long strides, he leaped onto—nothing. Her heart pounded as she watched him drop. His shadow rushed to meet his feet. Seconds fled. . . .

With knees bent and arms outstretched, he alighted, absorbing the impact with loose-legged grace. He dropped to his knees, resting, then got up, turned and raised an arm. She felt something invisible take tingling hold of her.

Hesitating, she almost lost her nerve. That was ridiculous. She'd wanted to fly since she was four, and Ellet had insisted it was easier to control another falling object than one's own body. Brennen had just proved he could do that. She walked back ten steps from the edge, sprinted forward, and jumped.

Her hair whipped behind her shoulders and upward from her head. Chill mountain air tugged her outstretched arms. The hilly horizon lifted itself, and it was glorious—like the swell of an orchestra. When she blinked, the falling feeling went on, and on, like a dream. But she had to watch.

Brennen stood below. Time expanded, stretching every half second into a minute. Treetops clutched for her feet but couldn't catch her.

At last, Brennen's arms opened to receive her. She slowed almost to a stop, caught the glitter of his eyes, and then fell the last meter against his chest. She clung there and laughed herself breathless.

He held her close. One of his hands slipped up into her tangled hair and curled around the back of her head. Enraptured, she shut her eyes. A hesitant kiss warmed her temple. She tilted her head back, abandoning caution.

As he kissed her lips, her insides turned to fire. She'd never felt this kind of heat. She wanted to bathe in this warm, incense-filled sea . . . no, to drown in it.

Suddenly alarmed, she struggled for breath. His arms fell away, and a rueful expression clouded his eyes. "Don't be afraid," he whispered. "I'll never try to hurt you, or dominate you. And I'll never take advantage."

"I . . . I know," she stammered. She pressed her head against his shoulder, then pushed away and headed downhill toward the Cirrus jet. How could she explain that she was terrified, not by his feelings, but by her own?

CHAPTER 17

STEADFAST

mezza voce
in a subdued voice

When on leave, Brennen tried to stay as far from Special Operations as possible. He preferred to sort hard messages on the SO floor rather than having them sent up, though, so on this blustery morning, after a thorough thousand-K check of the Cirrus jet, he concluded with a stop at the clearing station.

The pileup was diminishing. After two scrolls of the main screen, he flipped through a stack of correspondence. There were routine messages, advertisements, and pleas addressed to him but which should be handled by Special Operations, and an innocuous-looking brown packet with a return marking that caught him by surprise: a private correspondence from his sponsoring master, Shamarr Lo Dickin. More than a Master Sentinel, Dickin was the spiritual hierarch of Thyrica. Brennen tucked it into a jacket pocket.

Several minutes later in his seventy-fourth-floor apartment, he pulled it back out.

Brennen:

In the power of the Word to Come I greet you, in our vows of service I join you, as my son of promise I embrace you. Stand firm in truth, for today's path determines eternity, and beware the subtle arrogance of self-sufficiency.

Is it true what Sentinel Kinsman has written, that your heart leans toward one outside our kindred? The thought gives me no joy, yet I can guess only one reason for it. Without absolute connaturality, any bonding would bring you pain, and because of your epsilon intensity it could be crippling. You need not protest that you've bonded no wife already for this reason. Life with an outsider, though, could be even more difficult. Hold steadfast. Be certain of the woman and yourself, and remain willing to refuse her.

Yet realize that you could bring her to salvation. More than that I will not say, except that you are in my awareness and surrounded by my hopes.

In steadfast love
Your father of ceremony
Dickin

A breath whistled between Brennen's lips. Ellet, interfering again! But hoping to draw the Shamarr's reprimand, she'd won him an expression of trust and support.

That sobered him. He understood what he was considering. His family was ancient, the promise sacred. His people's customs had kept the Ehretan genes from dissipating.

"Life with an outsider . . ." Yes. Just to start the questions, where would they live? Could Firebird make a home on Tallis, Thyrica, or—in time—Elysia? Would her epsilon inability wear on him, or could they work out their own ways of communicating?

And how would they resolve their spiritual differences? Even for her sake, he must never disobey the strict codes of exile. He hoped she'd understood that, when they talked on the high ridge. Fully accredited prophets, consecrated to speak for the Eternal Speaker himself, had delivered those codes. The clause she'd questioned stated that the starbred must never again force their will on other people, and so they couldn't even speak of their faith unless they were asked.

Brennen didn't fully understand the Holy One's reasoning, but because of that clause, he couldn't assuage Firebird's fear of eternal torment, of that terrible myth of the Dark that Cleanses. Not yet.

Intermarriage wasn't forbidden in the Exiles' holy books or by the Shamarrs. Their community was too small to survive without bringing in new genes. But with his heritage, could he join himself—heart, body, and mind—with a woman who wouldn't worship alongside him? *One highest priority*, he reminded himself. Setting down Dickin's letter, he stared out his window. He imagined how terribly his spirit might be torn if she tried to pull him away from the Holy One.

But if they were truly and deeply bonded, could she do such a thing? Any pain that she caused him would shred her own soul.

The prophecies added even more responsibility. If he might father the messenger, the Word to Come, could an unbelieving woman help raise Him?

Tarance has children, he protested. *He's the eldest. Let him fulfill the prophecies.*

That didn't wash. More was at stake than his personal desire.

Wasn't the universe's Creator capable of changing one woman's heart?

Of course. But He would not. He gave every soul the perilous freedom to choose, based on the information He led them to find.

Brennen covered his eyes with one hand. *Are you telling me I must wait until she chooses?* he asked, dreading the answer.

In a quiet corner of his heart, he felt a loving but firm touch, not an answer but an assurance. He was known; he was loved. He would find the right way.

Forgive my doubt, he prayed, and he knew he was instantly restored. He stood up and stretched stress out of his shoulders.

At least she'd started to question her assumptions—and to wonder what anchored him in eternity. *She'll ask again*, he told himself. *She has the inquisitive mind.*

Holy One, make it soon!

For the first time in her life, Phoena Angelo had worked a morning with her hands—and she'd found herself enjoying it because she labored for a great cause.

Swirling a conical flask with one hand, she added enrichment broth to a murky soup of dark green algae. Across the granite-walled laboratory, Dr. Nella Cleary stood hunched over her bluescreen. Cleary's laboratory coat was splotched with browned algae, front and back. Phoena glanced down. Her own coat was spotless.

Delicately, minding her freshly tinted fingernails, she filled her autopette with broth and started treating the next flask. The strain, developed by Cleary on Veroh, was safe to handle in this phase. When grown in a basium medium, though, it would produce deadly toxin. If exposed to hard radiation, it would bloom prodigiously. Three or four dozen *Chlamydiminas clearii*/basium warheads would fill a habitable world's oceans with poison within days.

A bell chimed beside Cleary's desk. The stoop-shouldered woman touched a button. "What?" she growled. Cleary often was cross. She'd hoped to tempt Netaia into buying out her family's basium mines, never guessing that the Electorate already meant to unify Netaia's social factions and spur its economy by annexing another buffer system. It wasn't Phoena's fault Dorning Stele had made Veroh open-air uninhabitable for the next three lifetimes. Cleary ought to be grateful. Despite Netaia's temporary embarrassment, Cleary now was wealthier than she'd ever dreamed.

From Cleary's desk came a voice. "Count Tellai to see Her Highness, Doctor. Is she available?"

"Tell him yes." Phoena set down the autopette and flask and wiped her hands on a towel. "This should be word from the Electorate."

Cleary tried to bow as Phoena shed her lab coat and dropped it on the floor. "Thank you for your assistance, Your Highness."

Phoena hurried up the stone accessway and stroked the palm lock of a huge metal door. This east branch of the tunnel system had been used in the past for medical projects, and Cleary seemed satisfied down here. She almost never came up into daylight, though Parkai and D'Stang had grumbled about working underground like burrowing tetters.

Phoena would sleep better after Carradee sent Korda and Rogonin to Hunter Height. She couldn't imagine why it was taking so long. *Soon*, Carradee had promised. *Any day now.*

Tel waited uplevel in the master room, pacing a deep new carpet in bright-eyed excitement. Phoena enjoyed being worshipped by such a sincere believer. She met his welcoming embrace and accepted a long kiss before pulling away. "Well? Tell me, how went the vote?"

His round young face crinkled with smile lines. "It passed, Phoena, despite Carradee's new electors. The mission will go ahead as we planned—through channels this time, as we should've tried before."

"Whatever works, Tel. Who will they send to get her?"

"This is the best part." He seized both her hands. "Captain Friel of the electoral police, to represent her class and her family, and Marshal Burkenhamn, the very officer who administered her commissioning oath. Everyone knows what that commission meant to her. I'm certain your sister will do the honorable thing if confronted honorably."

Phoena snorted. She sent a sidelong glance out the windows toward Hunter Mountain's towering triple peak. "The girl's utterly selfish, Tel, and I believe she has fallen to heresy. If I'm right, you'll see. She'll do everything she can to avoid the highest honor we could give her. She has no hope of bliss anymore."

He lowered his eyes, and his long, dark lashes fluttered. "I . . . I do feel sorry for her, Phoena, sometimes."

He admitted weakness! Phoena seized her opportunity. "Tel, your nature is noble, but in this case your sympathy is unbefitting a nobleman. Firebird was raised a willing wastling," she said patiently. "She is a traitor now, a Federate informer. She will not suicide. So to salvage her reputation, and for the sake of her eternal destiny, we must bring her back. The electoral police will take charge of her, as is their rightful office. They will honor her by doing so." Phoena stared past Tel's shoulder toward the portrait of Siwann they'd brought to dignify the Height. That last strong queen would have approved this mission.

For if Carradee were too weak to rule, Firebird had a perverse inner strength. Phoena had known all her life—or at least guessed—that this wastling was strong enough to seize power, to destroy the ways of the Charities and Disciplines, to tear the very fabric of Netaian society. In Firebird's position, Phoena wouldn't have gone willingly to a noble death!

"You won't see her imprisoned at the palace," Phoena declared, as much to the image of Siwann as to Tel. "The redjackets have detention quarters at their Sander Hill station. They'll hold her there—question her—until arrangements can be made for a proper, public trial, with all the pomp our House can afford. Not even the governor will interfere, if the Tallans bind her over." Phoena gave a long sigh and returned her gaze to little Tel. "As much as the notion pains me, they must punish her as an example. What would become of our ability to steer the economy if every wastling scattered his family's resources?"

Tel nodded sadly. "You're right, Phoena. You're absolutely right."

She shut her eyes. In her mind, the climax would occur at the Naval Academy's amphitheater, near that redjacket station. Just as when Liach was executed, there'd be a grand procession down the broad main aisle, a few final words, the fatal signal. Breathing a little quicker, Phoena decided to order a suitable dress for the occasion. She would observe from on stage. "The family will be shamed, of course, but it is for the good of our people, Tel. You must understand that."

"For Netaia," he whispered. "For our people."

When Firebird learned that Brennen had access to physical training facilities in the MaxSec tower, she jumped at his offer to take her there early in the morning. She'd had little exercise since leaving Netaia. For a week they politely ignored one another on training time. On the sixth morning, though, as she struggled to master one machine, Brennen abandoned his own station and paced toward her. "Stop and rest for a minute. Your effort is so loud in your mind that I can scarcely think."

She forced herself to relax and finish the set before looking his way again. He'd settled onto a nearby bench, breathing hard. His arms glistened, and his skin-thin white training suit clung to his muscular shoulders.

She managed not to stare. "It must be hard," she guessed, "for outsiders to maintain any privacy on Thyrica."

"No," he insisted. "The major part of our training is the Privacy and

Priority Codes. When we're allowed to use our skills, when we're not, and when we must. Memorization and then thousands of hypothetical cases, two hours a day for three years."

She wiped her forehead. "Three years?"

"The death penalty is enforced for 'capricious or selfish exercise of Ehretan skills.'"

She thought of Ellet and Vultor Korda. "So I gathered."

"The moral testing before acceptance for training protects us, as well as our society."

That made sense. "I'd suppose your religion creates a moral grounding for most of you."

His eyes came alive. "That's right. Not all those we train are walking the Path."

"That's what you call your religion?"

He virtually leaned into his smile. "What do you want to know about it, Mari? What can I tell you?"

"Only one god. Correct?"

"Absolutely."

"Then wouldn't you say that all 'Paths' lead people to Him?"

"No," he said flatly. "It's a Path, not a highway."

"Hm." All her life she'd attended state services in Citangelo—and, later, those electoral Obediences. She'd offered her life. But for what? "We serve the state," she said. "But we can see it. It's governed by written laws, by people we can look in the eye. How can you imagine a person who created time and space just by speaking?"

Brennen spread his hands. "Actually, in the original tongue the term means *sang*. One of our names for Him is Zamahr, the singer. 'He sang, and time began.'"

She liked that idea. A well-crafted song could have incredible power. "That sounds like a quote. Is it from one of those books in the chapter room?"

"It is. His Voice, His Word, and He himself are co-equal creators. He is *Shaliyah*, the Three . . . but the Holy One. Our Father, the Eternal Speaker."

Baffled by too many names, she flashed back to her attempts, as a determined three-year-old, to memorize all nine Holy Powers without knowing what most of them meant. "And you believe He exists outside space and time."

Brennen nodded solemnly.

She frowned. "I still can't grasp that, Brenn. If I don't, will that come between us?"

He dropped his small towel and clasped his hands. "Mari," he said gently, "you have a fine mind. I think that in time, you'll comprehend."

"I probably could." But did she want to?

"I shouldn't marry outside the faith," he finally answered, "and yet already I'm torn."

She felt stung, vaguely offended.

"I shouldn't, because of those promises to my family," he went on, speaking quickly before she could interrupt, "and because that is my highest priority. But I couldn't walk away from you now."

She refused to be manipulated. "I could respect your beliefs. Your . . . Path." She flicked a strand of drying hair off her forehead. "Couldn't you accept mine, for now?"

He raised his head, looking more deadly serious than in the war room at Veroh. Several seconds passed before he answered. "You told me yourself that you obeyed the Powers, but you didn't truly believe in them."

"Unfair," she mumbled. "You'd just been inside my memories."

"But it's true. You doubted them already."

She fell silent, too paralyzed to think any further. She saw herself standing at the edge of another cliff, almost . . . almost . . . ready to leap. But would anyone catch her this time, or would she destroy herself?

"Faith is foreign to you." Brennen spoke softly. "But sometimes it takes only a glimpse of His majesty. Eventually, true reverence—real worship—compels a seeker to learn more."

Majesty. One familiar word. She shook her head slowly. "That's too complicated. Perfect obedience was easier to understand." Even if it was impossible to give.

"If you truly believed, you'd want to obey."

"You know that from experience?"

"Yes."

She envied that. She had to know just one more thing, today. "What about . . . death? I died once," she said solemnly. "At least I thought I'd died. What do you people do to earn . . . bliss? Mercy?"

"It's not earned. We can only honor Him for all that He is."

"No obedience clauses?"

He smiled with arched eyebrows. "He's given us codes and commandments. But also mercy, in life and death."

"Brennen, it's too much to hope that eternal pleasure would come without your . . . Speaker demanding something. How do you qualify?"

This time he frowned and looked aside. He took several deep breaths before answering. "You're right," he admitted, speaking slowly. "There is a price."

"What?"

He bowed his head and looked up into her eyes. "A life."

"You mean a death, don't you?" she demanded. Not so different from what she'd owed the Powers, after all.

"Not in the way you think. Not at all."

But obviously, he didn't want to explain. Not yet. Confused and deeply troubled, she paced back to her machine.

Brennen picked up his towel and swatted his bench with it. He'd said both too much and too little, even after so many prayers for guidance. He should've simply asked her to declare herself an inquirer, before she so pointedly ended the conversation. Then he could've spoken freely from now on. But until she asked again, he'd have to show his respect for her and the One by keeping silent.

Ask soon, he pleaded silently toward her retreating back. Those shoulders had felt so good, so right, locked inside his arms in the high mountain cirque, but he ached for a far deeper union.

Even before leaving Veroh, he'd felt trapped by his memories of interrogating her. Now he'd given himself too deeply to back away unscathed.

Some fates will find you, Dickin had told him. Did the Holy One intend to refine him through Firebird's struggle toward faith?

He begged for wisdom, and mercy . . . for both of them.

CHAPTER 18

HERESY

risoluto
resolutely

One afternoon shortly after that troubling discussion, Brennen stopped by Firebird's rooms. He remained near the door, in uniform again. Had his month's leave ended already? "Mari," he said, "I must tell you something that you'll like as little as I do."

She'd given up wondering why he still called her that. It was simply something they shared with no one else. "Come in, then. Tell me."

Stepping forward, he said, "You have a day," then he halted. He started again. "Two ambassadors arrived yesterday from Netaia. They want to take you into custody."

She stared. She'd felt safe here. Protected. Now her worst fear sprang out of a corner where she'd half hoped it had quietly died. "They can't do that," she insisted. "There's a week left on my asylum."

"The council . . ." Anger lines formed on his forehead. "They're going to conduct a hearing."

"A trial? For what? They're not going to send me home . . . are they?" she protested, backing away. His silence frightened her. "Brenn?" she urged.

"Not a trial. But a hearing. Remember how badly the council wants Netaia to covenant."

"They have to show strength, Brenn—"

"I know. I agree. This wasn't a unanimous decision. There could be other forces at work, trying to weaken the Federacy. SO and Thyrica's Alert Forces are . . . concerned. But that won't help us tomorrow night in the council chamber. I can't use my abilities to influence anyone there, though I'll want to. That's our law. I must let events take their course."

Speechless, she nodded.

The line of his shoulders softened. "I'll do all I can, though. I've just come from recording a prehearing report—everything you've shown me about the Netaian mindset, and all I learned while I was there, that might be relevant. Three councilors want to renew your asylum. They'll be as prepared as they can be."

"Thank you."

He spread his hands. "But I must warn you. Even they are more concerned about maintaining order, and broadening their trade base, than . . ."

"Than with protecting me," she finished the thought. "That's not comforting."

"Don't give up." He stepped toward her. "I won't."

She slept poorly that night, and in her dreams, redjackets chased her through the back streets of a surreal Citangelo. The following evening her door slid away on schedule to reveal a pair of guards in flawless white. She'd dressed in a finely tailored blue tunic from Carradee's parcel. She took a deep breath to calm herself and then stepped out between them. Three councilors wanted to renew her asylum, three of seven. She must convince one more. Which three? Which one?

The guards took her back to the high-arched council chamber, cleared again of observers. Four other principals already stood at the other end, silent as she walked the long aisle. She recognized the tall Netaian delegates from behind. Captain Kelling Friel wore his red-jacketed police uniform, black cap tucked into his belt. Several steps from Friel, flanking a space evidently meant to receive her, waited an even larger man, First Marshal Burkenhamn. Knowing from his plain gray shipboards that Netaia was still demilitarized, and so he couldn't wear the cobalt blue, and remembering his fairness and sense of honor, she felt a traitor. What if these men could've read her recent thoughts?

She reached the stairs. One guard touched her arm. He nodded toward Brennen and Ellet, who waited opposite Friel and Burkenhamn at the right side of the wide steps. She wondered if Friel or Burkenhamn recognized Brennen as their former lieutenant governor. Probably!

"Stand with them," the guard directed.

She took the space between the Thyrians and glanced left. Captain Friel looked incongruous here in his finery, but the sight of that gold-edged crimson-and-black uniform reawakened an old, disquieting response: grudging but automatic submission to his authority. The electoral police represented everything she'd been raised to revere. What she thought, what she wondered didn't matter. She'd been trained to obey.

Brennen and Ellet seemed so alike in stature and their relaxed, easy bearing that she felt out of place between them. If they didn't dominate the chamber, they were comfortable here.

Tierna Coll's white robe rustled as she rose. Once all eyes had turned to her, she spoke. "We are assembled to consider the disposition of Lady Firebird Angelo of Netaia, which has become an issue of sufficient magnitude to warrant this council's attention."

Her amplified voice reverberated from stone walls and high ceiling. Firebird thought again how beautiful she looked in her dignity.

"The Netaian government shall speak first, as the body to which Lady Firebird is responsible. We then shall hear Field General Caldwell, the guarantor of her initial asylum, and Captain Kinsman, who served as temporary guardian under General Caldwell."

Ellet turned slightly to study Friel and Burkenhamn with her keen black eyes. Netaia had sent an imposing pair.

Tierna Coll went on. "Following the guarantors, any councilor who wishes to recommend shall speak. Then, as it is her own fate we decide today, Lady Firebird shall take the final position of influence and honor. Are there any objections to this order?"

No one commented.

"Very well. Which of you shall speak for Netaia?"

First Marshal Burkenhamn stepped forward as Captain Friel placed both hands on the hilts of his ceremonial sword. Firebird's breath quickened at the gesture that censured a defendant, though no one else in this chamber— except possibly Brennen—would recognize it.

"Your Honors," Burkenhamn began in his rich baritone, "the Crown and the electoral council request that Major Angelo surrender herself or be surrendered to the government which, by birth, she does represent, and which she serves under solemn oaths. She is called to appear in Citangelo and answer charges pertaining to her conduct as an officer of the Netaian Planetary Navy. As a sovereign government under the protectorship of this Federacy . . ." The marshal glared at Brennen. "We do insist that our internal laws be respected."

Then he did recognize Brennen. Firebird widened her stance to make sure she didn't sway. The Netaians' prudence worried her. They'd based their demand on the key Federate practice of self-government.

The dour General Voers stood to speak. "Marshal Burkenhamn, perhaps the Netaian delegation would postulate the whereabouts of a merchant vessel called the *Blue Rain*. It left Twinnich nine days ago with a shipment of basium concentrate and has not arrived at its destination, Ituri III."

Cleary, Firebird realized. *She's at it again!* Shock washed over her even as Burkenhamn's sharp intake of breath betrayed his surprise. He exchanged glances with Captain Friel before answering. "Your Honor, we have not been authorized to treat on any subject but the surrender of Major Angelo."

"I believe we were speaking of honoring internal law," Voers replied, but he sat down without saying more.

Tierna Coll motioned to Brennen. "General."

He stepped forward. "Your Honors, some time ago I offered a place among us to Lady Firebird, on behalf of the Federacy. I ask that the choice remain hers, to live among us if she so desires. We created the situation that makes it impossible for her to return to her home. For that, we owe her support and protection."

"General," called the head of the council, "do you make a recommendation as to her choice?"

One of Brennen's hands clenched down at his side. Firebird reminded herself that she still scarcely knew him. What was he thinking? "Let the Federacy remember that this is a person of talent and intelligence," he answered, "whose life should not be wasted. We owe her protection," he repeated.

"Then, do you recommend, General?"

Like a knot untied, his hand straightened. "The decision should be hers." Still looking forward, he stepped back into place.

She'd learned to respect that note in his voice. He couldn't say more. Perhaps his own highest priority stood on trial.

"Captain Kinsman?" Tierna Coll turned slightly. "Do you recommend?"

Brennen's head turned toward Ellet, and Firebird intercepted his cautioning glance. "No," Ellet answered blandly. "Let the council decide."

"The council," she'd said. Not "her." Very diplomatic.

"Colleagues?" Tierna Coll swept the arc with her gaze. Firebird searched for sympathetic faces.

Mister Lithib straightened on his deeply padded mobility chair. "Let the lady choose," he wheezed. "It is her destiny of which we speak."

Firebird smiled at him, although disappointed that he'd said no more. In the ensuing silence she heard a faint, rhythmic tapping. Captain Friel stood drumming his fingers against the red leather of his sword's sheath.

"Any others?"

General Voers stood. "My colleague speaks of destiny." He nodded toward Mister Lithib. "But one's destiny often lies in the hands of others. Furthermore, we follow a strict noninterference policy in local affairs. By trying to alter Netaian civil law, we may already have meddled in this situation more than is appropriate."

Firebird started. Were the Federate policy makers divided over Netaian reforms? Did those freedoms they enjoyed make it difficult to govern other peoples?

At the moment, that didn't matter. She must win one councilor, without losing any of the other three. "Any others?" Tierna Coll asked again. Firebird braced herself. It was her turn.

No, Madam Kernoweg had stood. "Colleagues, honorable delegates," she intoned. "The inequity among our worlds' resources has long been a source of contention for my people. We of Lenguad carry more than our share of levies to support other Federate citizens. We understand the Netaians' reluctance to involve themselves in federation, which they might perceive as a drain on their resources. We wish to assure them that they would be received by us as equals, perhaps by honoring their request today. At some junctures, my friends, practicality must take precedent over principle. One prisoner's fate must not outweigh the thousands who would benefit from Netaian covenance . . . on Netaia, as well as other worlds. We must not preempt Netaia's jurisdiction over a Netaian citizen." She sat down.

Captain Friel's fingers drummed a little faster. Dread knotted Firebird's stomach as she waited for Tierna Coll to motion her forward.

The white-robed woman beckoned graciously. Facing her and ignoring everyone else, Firebird stepped out from between the Sentinels. She spoke slowly, as she'd been trained to do. "Your Honor, General Voers speaks the truth when he says that my destiny lies in the hands of others. I am alive today because of words and actions of others here present. And while living here, I've learned that the rights of each individual citizen of a Federate system take precedence over all corporate rights." She glanced guiltily at Madam Kernoweg. Truly, thousands of Netaians would prosper if Netaia joined the Federacy. *Later*, she promised herself. *I'll do all I can for them—someday!* But first, she had to survive. "Therefore I ask to be heard as an individual, Your Honors. If I'm given the choice, I wish not to be sent back to stand trial."

Voers' dark baritone voice rang out, "But you are not an individual citizen of a Federate system, Lady Firebird. Consider, if you will, a hypothetical situation. Suppose we could not justify continuing this protective custody. If we could offer you only a dignified, private death rather than that public trial, what would be your preference?"

She started. Could the Federacy execute her, rather than continue her asylum against Netaia's wishes? Brennen had never hinted at that possibility!

"Hypothetical," he'd said. Maybe it was a rhetorical question, asked simply to establish every degree of preference . . . or convince one wavering councilor.

It did force her to declare herself. She couldn't choose to be publicly executed for treason. "Your Honor, if it came to that, without any other honorable choice, I would rather die here." She glanced down, then backed into her place.

"Well spoken, Lady Firebird." Madam Kernoweg lowered her prominent eyebrows.

Tierna Coll seated herself. "Colleagues, let us judge."

Now that it was too late, Firebird wished she'd said more. She watched the councilors confer in silent privacy, speaking via screens and touchboards. The chamber seemed cooler than it had been only a few minutes ago. They were taking considerable time with their decision. Whether that was a hopeful sign, she couldn't guess. General Voers looked more solemn by the moment. Madam Kernoweg ran a hand over her closely cut hair.

One councilor, she pleaded silently. *Just one.*

"General Caldwell?" Tierna Coll beckoned him to Admiral Madden's board. As he walked around the far end of the table, his hair—sun-bleached from weeks planetside—caught a stray gleam of light. He eyed the screen intently, glanced at Tierna Coll, then reached for the board. Firebird didn't think he looked pleased.

Not a trial. Not at home. A traitor's death wouldn't be as quick or as comfortable as Liach's firing squad. Netaia had grim ways to execute traitors.

General Voers stood. Firebird composed herself to stand steadily. "Lady Firebird. It is on record before this council that you would prefer to remain on Tallis, even if it means your death, and not return to Netaia. Please confirm that statement for our recording."

Powers that Rule! Had she lost?

No, no. They were following protocol. "If I returned to Netaia it would surely mean my death, Your Honor, in complete humiliation. Here, though I die, I've had a choice."

Voers returned to his touchboard. To Firebird's surprise, the seven councilors turned to Brennen.

He gave a slight nod and soberly touched a single panel.

Tierna Coll rose to her feet and beckoned regally. "Lady Firebird, come forward."

As Firebird slowly mounted the broad steps to stand at the center of the table's arch, Tierna Coll continued. "Worthy delegates, we now declare the following salient points. One, Lady Firebird has sought and been initially granted asylum among us. Two, Lady Firebird was taken by the Federacy as a prisoner of war, during an act of undeclared aggression initiated by the then-independent government of Netaia. Three, Lady Firebird is yet a Netaian subject."

As she emphasized those final words, Firebird's courage melted. She glanced at Brennen. He stood with his eyes closed.

"Legally, then, the Netaian delegation is entitled to demand her return. However, the attempt on her life here on Tallis has led us to believe that she will not be granted justice on Netaia. Honorable delegates, do you wish to respond?"

Firebird didn't turn aside, but she knew Burkenhamn's voice. "She will have a trial, Your Honor. Justice will be done."

"We assume that your verdict has already been delivered, Marshal Burkenhamn."

Only silence answered her.

"Very well. Lady Firebird, we wish a lasting relationship with your people. If that required your death, you would choose to meet it here?"

Again! Back at Veroh, it had seemed logical to ask for death. Now she choked on the words. Retreating into the role she'd played for so long, she raised her masks back into place and avoided looking at Madam Kernoweg. "Yes, Your Honor. If you so order, I will ask only for privacy and a well-sharpened blade."

"We do not order that, my lady." Tierna Coll nodded to Brennen.

Firebird kept her eyes on the council table but felt him walk slowly behind her. After an interminable moment she heard a high, keen note.

Aghast, she spun around to face him. He had drawn and activated his shimmering crystace. His eyes were clear, and his face determined, as he swept up the blade that was easier to hear than to see. He halted it a hand's breadth from her throat.

Had they ordered him to execute her, out of mercy—to keep her out of Netaia's hands?

"Face the council, Mari." Brennen's low voice allowed no objection. She remembered he'd said, *I question what I'd do if it came to a choice. . . .*

Obviously, he'd decided in favor of his people.

But he'd claimed that he cherished her!

She turned her back on him and on hope. Ellet's eyes shone. The chamber was as still as death, except for the singing crystace.

"Worthy delegates," said Tierna Coll, "you have witnessed the thrice-confirmed choice of this prisoner, to die on Tallis rather than return to Netaia for public trial. We request now that you acknowledge our authority to rule thus."

Kelling Friel sounded far away. "This is irregular, Your Honor. Lady Firebird's noble birth, and the offenses with which she stands charged, demand one of a few specific death protocols. If you will not give her over to custody, we demand that she be given the means to dispatch herself in a traditional manner."

Firebird breathed slowly, deeply, cherishing each lungful of air.

"We have been advised of Netaian suicide customs, Captain, but Lady Firebird does not stand on Netaian soil. Our decision hangs partially upon your answer. Marshal Burkenhamn, do you bow to our ruling?"

Firebird's ears rang as the sopranissimo blade hovered. How close?

Burkenhamn hesitated. To anyone raised outside the Netaian legal system, any death might suffice, but to a Netaian, ceremonial precision was almost half of justice. The Powers had decreed it so.

Powers? Firebird's mind raced. What were they? Dissociated attributes of gods who might never even have existed? Even if they had, even if they still did, what did they care for one young woman's fate? Or for anyone else, for that matter? Had they interfered at Veroh, when Dorning Stele slaugh tered civilians?

What claim did the Powers have on her life, after she'd tried to die for them? She had nothing else to offer.

"We abstain from voicing, Your Honor," Burkenhamn said at last. "Her fate should be decided by Netaian custom alone."

Firebird clenched her fists. Her heart pounded in her ears as she struggled to put words together. Before she died, she would give Kelling Friel something to remember.

But Tierna Coll called, "Then we declare our decision in full." Her ringing voice softened. "Lady Firebird, do not be afraid. You are free to die here, a Netaian subject—under *our* custom—or to return with these officers, if such is your choice. However, you need not choose either. This delegation refuses to acknowledge our right to give what they claim to want, which is your life. Therefore, we are not obliged to allow them to take it. You may remain on Tallis."

Firebird's mouth fell open. She snapped it shut.

"We will impose one condition, however. Would you indicate that one day, you might choose to become a Federate transnational citizen, as an example to your people? Under the duress of this moment, we cannot ask you to make any decision, but we do request some assurance that you could seriously consider transnationality."

Firebird blinked, forced her mind clear, and struggled to understand. The council had forced the Netaians' hand. Tierna Coll had made Burkenhamn refuse to endorse her execution, if it happened here. Then, surely Brennen wouldn't have . . .

Twisting her shoulders, she glanced back at him. Behind the

atom-edged blade, his lips remained firm but his eyes pleaded. Was he play-acting this role? Would he strike, if they ordered it?

It didn't matter. Her destiny had been given back to her, and this decision had nothing to do with Brennen Caldwell. Could she consider taking Federate transnationality?

Absolutely. As a priority, the government she'd been raised to worship had utterly failed her.

She flung off her masks. She wrenched free from the roles she'd tried so hard to play. Why, why, why die for a government that had deliberately corrupted its people's faith? . . . And how, knowing all she now knew, could she sacrifice her life for an electoral cartel that "protected" her people by oppressing them? Serving the Powers had created an insane dishonesty at the core of her being. She wouldn't serve them one minute longer. Not even if by dying in this chamber, she might have regained her chance at instant, eternal bliss.

As an example to your people . . .

Feeling almost light-headed, as if she'd shaken off a heavily armored helmet, she came to attention. She spoke the words that would damn her in her own family's eyes: "Your Honors, I will take Federate citizenship here and now, if that might bring our peoples closer together."

Tierna Coll's eyes widened for a moment, and then her cheeks twitched into a quick smile. "Lady Firebird, we demand no such commitment. In fact, we generally give citizenship candidates several weeks of instruction. But," she added, glancing at Friel and Burkenhamn, "we could make an exception in this issue. If you swear allegiance to us now, you will do so without duress and in full view of these Netaian representatives. Are you so willing?"

No second thoughts! Forget Friel, forget Burkenhamn—forget Brennen, too, if need be. This would be her first step toward finding a new, higher priority, a new set of truths. She would formally forsake her determination to die for a lie. "I am," she said.

Behind her, the crystace's hum snapped off.

Tierna Coll touched several panels and met Firebird's eyes again. "You will take this oath, then."

"Solemnly I swear this day," Firebird repeated after Tierna Coll, "my unwavering allegiance to the authority of this Federacy."

"I do acknowledge," intoned Tierna Coll, "that Federate transnationality supersedes any citizenship, affiliation, or rank that I hold under any local government."

Firebird glanced left. Captain Friel clenched his sword hilt. Marshal Burkenhamn shook his head, disbelieving, grieved.

She took a deep breath and tried to ignore him.

"Go on," Brennen encouraged softly.

But she struggled a moment longer. Besides her loyalty to Netaia and the Electorate, she had an aristocrat's pride in herself, in her own strengths. She'd hoped to win glory through utterly indomitable obedience.

But where had it brought her? The electors already believed she was of no further use to Netaia.

At last, she realized how badly that hurt. She'd have served her people with complete devotion, if only they'd let her. She steeled herself to step across an invisible line into an incomprehensible future. "Your Honor, would you repeat that clause?"

She finished the oath in a steady voice. Tierna Coll slipped a paper from her transcriber and turned it on the tabletop. Firebird picked up a stylus and firmly signed away her former life.

In her class's eyes now, she was worse than dead. An apostate, a heretic. Unable to look at either Friel or Burkenhamn, she rode with Brennen back to the minimum security floor.

Brennen stroked the palm lock. "Please let me come in," he said urgently.

"Come," she muttered.

As the door slid shut behind him, she flicked on the lights. "Shall I order kass?" she asked, taking refuge in meaningless hospitality.

"No." He stood close. "Talk to me."

"You talk to me!" She sank onto the raised end of her lounger. "Was that a trick, to trap them into letting me stay here? And why you, with the—the crystace?"

As she raised her hands to gesture, he grasped them. "It was Voers' idea, based on my prehearing report. We maneuvered them, but they made the critical choice."

"We? Did you know they were going to—"

"It was only a hope. You had to win one councilor. You convinced Admiral Baron Fiersson. Then I was ordered to go ahead. As guarantor of your asylum, I was the logical person for the role the council ordered me to take."

"But—"

"Voers and I were certain your people would demand to see things done their own way. And I was certain . . . enough . . . that you wouldn't choose to go back with them."

She pulled back her hands. "But it could've ended that way."

"If you'd asked to go home, the council would've sent you home, this time. You're dealing with a bureaucracy, Mari. An idealistic one, but a bureaucracy that includes Madam Kernoweg and many others like her."

"But if Marshal Burkenhamn had consented . . . to let you. . . ?"

"You don't think he could have. Neither did I."

"I don't know," she whispered. "He's gruff, but he's a good man. I probably broke his heart in there."

"Are you all right?" He peered down at her.

"I will be."

"You were magnificent, Mari. I'd never dared hope you would do that."

"I made an important decision," she said. "I should probably thank you." But she didn't want to. For all his explanations after the fact, he'd terrified her.

"I frightened you," he said, as if he'd read her thoughts.

"Brennen." She had to ask. "Would you have killed me?"

"How can you even ask?" he whispered, frowning. He held down both his hands to her. "I know exactly what it meant to you, taking that oath."

She shut her eyes, heartsick. He hadn't answered.

"Mari," he whispered from the distance. "Mari, I love you."

She squeezed her eyes even more tightly shut. "Sometimes," she said, "you have strange ways of showing it." Feeling him move closer, she looked up.

"I showed it," he said dispassionately, "by saving your life."

Truly, he had. Twice now. And she didn't doubt she'd made the right choice, swearing allegiance. "Sorry," she murmured, "but I'm too full of adrenaline to be rational."

Grasping her hands again, he drew her to her feet. She stared up into his eyes. She'd never felt such turmoil. "You never answered. What am I to think?"

His eyebrows lowered. "I would have died," he said flatly, "before striking you. Ellet would've had to execute us both."

She bowed her head and pressed her forehead to his chest. Salty puddles gathered in her eyes.

She felt his fingers lock behind her neck. She raised her chin, and as the puddles overflowed down her cheeks, he lightly kissed her lips. The smoky-sweet presence touched the edge of her mind again, warmer than before, and stronger.

Recalling the overpowering sensation of mind-access, she suddenly understood how much power he was holding back, and she glimpsed the magnitude of what pair bonding might involve. Appalled, she pressed her palms against his chest.

Once again, he instantly loosened his arms. She slapped the tears from her cheeks, pressed her head against his chest, and circled his waist with her arms, trying to release all thought and tension. She felt shattered inside.

"I'm sorry," he murmured. "I'm sorry. I'd hoped you would trust me. But how can you, when everyone else you've trusted has been destroyed . . . or else tried to destroy you?"

At any rate, now it was done. She no longer had any hope for eternity. This life, as long as it lasted, would be all she could hope to receive.

So be it.

"Oh, Mari," he whispered. He sounded as if he were close to tears himself.

She would have stood holding him that way for an hour, pressing her ear close to his beating heart, but abruptly she remembered Voers' words to Marshal Burkenhamn. "Brennen," she said. "That ship that vanished—the *Blue Rain*—I'm sure Netaia has it. They've got to be working on that basium project again."

She lifted her head and added, "And I think I know where."

RETURN

intermezzo con accelerando
interlude, becoming faster

He pulled a little farther away. She felt his scrutiny where a moment before there'd been only sympathy. "Go on."

"You probably don't believe me."

"Of course I do."

"I'll show you, if you'd like. Access, I mean."

"I think that would be wise." He motioned her back to the lounger. As he settled beside her, she reminded herself that this was the first duty of her new citizenship. She offered her eyes, then her memories of Hunter Height.

Brennen stood up before she'd completely refocused on her surroundings. "Come with me," he said. "We may be able to speak with Tierna Coll before she retires for the night."

The moment Firebird finished explaining to the tall woman in white, the outer office door slid open once more and admitted Ellet Kinsman. The Sentinel strode in without a word or glance to Firebird or Brennen, or even explaining why she'd come. "Your Honor, forgive me for intruding."

"I am glad you are here, Sentinel Kinsman." Tierna Coll motioned Ellet to take a seat. "Perhaps you can clarify an issue for me. Lady Firebird has just confessed to having concealed data from Master Brennen under interrogation, data which if genuine could require our immediate attention. In your opinion, is this possible?"

"Her?" Ellet sounded incredulous. "Your Honor, this woman is no match for Brennen—in any way!"

Firebird flushed.

"You've held her under access yourself?" Brennen glared at Ellet.

"I have not. But I know you, Brennen. I know your strength, and your training, and the heritage of your family. You seem to have forgotten who and what you are." Ellet turned back to Tierna Coll. "Your Honor, Firebird Angelo of Netaia could never have deceived Brennen under access, not then.

But maybe, now that she's had opportunity for learning to work around his abilities—"

"Your Honor, I would know deception." Brennen's face darkened. "And, Ellet, if you know my strength, you know that, too. There's a grave danger to the Federacy. I've offered my services to avert it."

Firebird bristled, too. "I'm not inventing this, Ellet. Access my memory, if you must." The notion made her cringe.

The head of the council conferred with her touchboard for a minute longer, then shut it down. "This is sobering, General. We must investigate, but without showing overt disrespect to the Netaian government at this delicate moment. Lady Firebird, thank you again for your transfer of citizenship. Still, a case could be made to support Sentinel Kinsman's suggestion. These weeks you have spent in General Caldwell's custody do suggest a possibility of truth."

"I'll give her access," Firebird said again, "if you feel she'd be more objective."

Tierna Coll glanced at Ellet, then Brennen, then smiled mildly. "That won't be necessary. In the morning, I will dispatch a message urging Governor Danton to investigate this locale. His staff should have answers for us within a few weeks, or immediately, should they feel the need to strike. We must walk a careful middle ground, without showing weakness. Thank you for your concern, Lady Firebird, and your counsel, Captain Kinsman. And, General, your offer is appreciated, but your services are needed here on Tallis. Please return Lady Firebird to her quarters."

Firebird's door closed behind them as she stumbled toward the table. "Kass now?" she offered wearily.

"Please." Brennen took a stool and stared at the table.

"At least she promised to investigate. Immediately." Firebird pulled a pair of filled cups from the servo's cubby and set one in front of him.

"Yes," he said slowly. "But you saw that she doubted my word. That has never—*never*—happened before."

"Maybe she doubts because you're a Sentinel."

"They do," he whispered. "They all do. Even those who respect us. I'm certain now." His misery showed in the set of his jaw and the lines between his eyes. "No wonder none of us ever reach the High command."

Firebird wanted to ease that misery, but she couldn't think of anything to say that might help. "Do you think," she said reluctantly, "that Danton will move quickly enough?"

He looked up. "No," he said. "Danton is first a diplomat." He bowed his head over folded hands and sat motionless, except for his shoulders' slow rise and fall.

Brennen's thoughts boiled. He must step out from this nexus. But in which direction?

Hunter Height, as Firebird had just recalled it for him, could support weapons research. Phoena Angelo, "on vacation" from Citangelo, was as determined as her distant ancestors to throw off "outsystem invaders," and just as likely to use violent means. The *Blue Rain* had carried basium, and the wealthy Angelos still owned ships that were capable of piracy.

Could he draw any other conclusion?

No. If the weapon were deployed before Lee Danton proved it existed— a small but disastrous possibility—millions, even billions, could die.

The Sentinels' Privacy and Priority Codes demanded that he step into danger when innocent others were at risk, "if he plainly possessed the resources to defuse that situation in a timely and appropriate manner." With Special Ops, he'd completed covert operations of exactly the sort he was considering.

But could he disobey a direct order? His people longed to put a Sentinel on the High command, where he might live out their codes and beliefs in plain view. Many sincere seekers might step onto the Path because of such an example. He had the abilities and the ethics to bring honor to the position.

But was some higher plan in motion? Maybe even his family's sacred hope?

Tonight, he must make only one correct decision.

If he went to Netaia covertly, against orders, he'd have to set aside his lofty military goal. Insubordination must carry severe consequences. He might be demoted, even forced to resign from Federate service, though he could hope that Regional would only reprimand him if the outcome justified his decision. But he'd never achieve the High command. Someone else would rise in his place.

He clasped his hands tightly. *Holy One, I need wisdom more than ever. Which way shall I turn, and how far must I leap?*

Then he silenced his mind and listened intently for the Holy Voice.

After a time, Brennen got himself another cup of kass, downed it standing, and tucked the cup into the sterilizer. "Get some sleep if you can, Firebird," he said firmly. She heard an odd, brave note in his voice. "I may be back, but don't wait up." He left without explaining.

She stumbled to the back room and fell fully clothed onto her bed. *"Firebird." How long has it been since he called me that?* Did it signify new respect, or rejection?

The next she knew, he was pulling her back to her feet and pushing another cup of kass at her. Trying to stand steady enough not to spill the bitter brew on herself woke her completely. He vanished into her freshing room. In a minute, she peered in. All her personal things had disappeared, and he was closing a small black duffel kit.

"What are you doing?" Blinking sleepily, she smoothed the wrinkled blue dress tunic she'd worn to face the council.

"I want to take you to Hunter Height. Will you help me?"

"Tierna Coll changed her mind? How did you do it?"

"She did not."

Firebird leaned against the doorway. "You mean to go without her orders?"

"Against them," he corrected calmly.

"Brennen!" She shook her sleep-fogged head. "What is it you want me to do?"

"Get us in. Identify Cleary and her collaborators. Help me stop the research. Then get us out, if you can."

"But Tierna Coll said—"

"If we go, if we're wrong, the Federacy can disclaim all responsibility." He handed her the kit. "But if we're right, your basium people have had too much time already since the *Blue Rain* disappeared. That gives them a head start."

"My basium people?"

He snorted softly. "Sorry. But we can't wait for Danton."

"Right. But the council—the High command . . ." Was he throwing away all hope of promotion?

Handing her the duffel, he spoke slowly, as though he were making sure he believed every word. "I must follow the vows I made when I was vested as a Sentinel. This woman Cleary is developing a way to foul an entire world, if you understand it right. It could be Caroli, Varga, Tallis."

There it was again, that highest priority. Those Sentinel vows, and his god. "Tallis," she suggested. "Phoena would like that."

"Knowing that Netaia will be eligible for full Federate covenance in three years?"

"There are Netaians who won't ever want that."

"That's true," he said. "Mari, if Phoena's project is finished and deployed, and if you're right, Tallis could be attacked in weeks, or less.

Danton wouldn't win any support for the Federacy by sending missiles into Hunter Height, even if he did investigate instantly. Two of us, though, might destroy the project without taking other lives. We have to keep Netaia from striking. For Netaia's sake, and others.'"

She straightened.

"Will you help me?"

"Of course." Firebird seized two extra pairs of gray shipboards from her open closet. "I'm ready."

In the gleaming Cirrus jet, they soared out to the Fleet's primary space-port, where she'd first stepped onto Tallan soil. An attendant took the Cir-rus into his charge at the gate of the massive clear dome, and Brennen watched apprehensively as the young lieutenant slid into the pilot's seat with undisguised glee.

Firebird watched Brennen's gaze follow the Cirrus to a storage hangar. She laughed silently in sympathy. If she owned a jet like that, she'd worry too. Then he led onto the base proper, past rows of parked atmospheric craft and streamlined dual-drive ships that were equally maneuverable in vacuum and atmosphere: interceptors, transports, gunships, shuttles. Her eyes wid-ened at the display of Federate striking power, gleaming under lights.

Inside a stuffy arms depot that smelled like institutional disinfectant, Brennen picked up a black drillcloth pack and gave her a peep inside at a load of miniature explosives—sonic, incendiary, and others she didn't rec-ognize and he didn't explain. Three stylus-shaped recharges for his blazer vanished into the pack's side pocket.

"I know the night sentry fairly well," he said softly as they zipped into high-g acceleration oversuits. "SO people often pick things up at odd hours. It's how I got a ship, too, and how we'll get offplanet."

Dozens of near stars shone through the arc of the dome, though the sky had started to brighten toward dawn. They stopped at a parking row near the dome's edge, and there she looked up at a thirty-meter craft with minor atmospheric adaptations. Its enormous stardrive engine dwarfed the slim, upper cabin compartment. "It's a DS–212, a Brumbee, designed for clan-destine message delivery." He examined its rounded surface and talked his way down its length. "They've pared it down to absolute essentials for long-distance slip. It'll maintain acceleration and deceleration at several g's past what normal translight drives will give you." He straightened and grinned. "In other words, it rides like a missile."

Firebird jumped for the security handle, got her balance on the door plate, and released the entry hatch. Brennen followed her in and secured the hatch behind him, plunging the cabin into darkness. Feeling her way, she slipped into the left chair. Brilliant blue striplights glimmered on above her. Brennen squeezed between seats and into the pilot's, then started rearranging controls on the slanting display. "Would you stow the pack?" he asked. "There's a bulkhead compartment behind you."

Atmospheric engines thrummed, responding to their lasers, as she closed down a magnetic seal. Returning to her seat as he finished his checkout, she slipped into her flight harness.

"If we should get into a scrap," he said, "you shoot, I'll fly. Here's the ordnance board." He touched a rectangular orange panel at the console's center. She studied it while he raised the ship and set it in motion.

A vast, wedge-shaped sky hatch loomed ahead, a pale slice of sapphire blue edged by luminous strips. He confirmed clearance for takeoff, flipped the last levers, then killed the striplights. The atmospheric drive roared to full power. Brennen released the ground brakes and they shot through the wedge.

The stars of the Whorl glowed brighter and more intensely colored, moment by moment. As Brennen had predicted, they weren't challenged, but she felt uneasy. She'd committed high treason, there in the chamber. Now she was helping Brennen flirt with insubordination.

His Sentinel vows, he'd declared, took precedence over the Federacy's orders. *As Ellet's interpretation of those vows took precedence over his orders*, she thought with a sudden chill. One Sentinel had betrayed her. What really, what now, were his intentions toward her—for this mission, and after? Uneasy, she wriggled in the deeply padded seat.

"Ten seconds to slip," he said.

"Ready." She snugged the harness, took a deep breath, and consciously relaxed every part of her body. First the odd vibration of the slip-shield took hold, and then the pressure hit. Even wearing a high-g suit, it was worse than she'd ever experienced. She pulled in a slow breath, and gradually, the messenger ship's gravidic compensators caught up with thrust.

Finally, she managed to lean forward and look around. The stars on their visual screen had vanished. Brennen seemed unaffected. "I checked the conversion factor for Netaian pressure units. That was six-seventy, perceptible. Almost twenty percent over your rating, but our suits are more efficient."

She took another deep breath, glad he hadn't slowed the mission to make it easy for her, but assumed command as a colleague.

Colleagues. She could accept that, for the moment. She released her harness and yawned.

"You're done in," Brennen observed. "It's been a long night." He brought the striplights back up and dropped one of a pair of broad shelves from the curved overhead compartments. "Here are bunks. Across the way—watch your head—is the galley servo. If I complain about the food, it's only overfamiliarity. I've been through the menu too many times."

She examined every part of the cabin. "How long do your psych people think a human can travel in a compartment this size and not go off balance?"

He let down the second bunk, little more than a black-blanketed pallet. "We have life support for two for just over a month."

"You're joking."

"No. These ships were designed to make the Tallis-Elysia run. The messenger service uses this model, and I've spent more time in one than I care to remember." He rolled his eyes at the recollection. They shone deep blue under the striplights.

Exhausted, she stared at those eyes a little too long. She could almost feel the power behind them.

She flushed. *Colleagues!* she rebuked herself. *He has proved he won't force himself on you.* Still, she couldn't bring herself to trust him entirely. He was a man, a stranger. Potentially dangerous.

Yes, and she was a traitor. Apostate. And if Phoena won the next round, soon they both would be dead.

Why did it still seem important to keep him at arm's length? He'd offered an honorable relationship.

What *would* it be like, to love him?

He leaned against a bulkhead, waiting for her to speak.

Her cheeks warmed. "Ellet admitted, that is—well, she said that you people had ways of . . ." Words stuck in her throat. She sat down carefully on the lower bunk.

He walked as far away as he could, to the pilot's chair.

Was he still trying to prove she could trust him? And was she being cruel, pushing him to answer such a personal question before she'd settled her mind about his faith?

But she had to know this. She found her voice. "Ellet said Sentinels could please one another in ways outsiders can't. Is it like—the way you touched me the day we took out your Cirrus?"

He nodded somberly.

His gentle-eyed respect seemed a priceless gift, particularly tonight, when she felt stripped of all honor. "Is it permitted to show me? Just a little," she added.

"As long as I don't touch you."

No wonder he'd retreated. "Please," she said. A tingle of apprehension heightened her longing. She could no longer pretend she didn't want this.

Brennen looked deeply into her eyes, and the tingle of access-beginning brushed through her. This time, though, he called up neither memory nor emotion, but sensation: a caress of the soul, like feathered wings beating against her heart.

She tried to look away. Immediately his strength flooded her, warm and reassuring. He would do nothing inappropriate. Gradually, the urge to struggle left her until she felt only Brennen's enfolding, accepting presence.

Then he drew back the tendril of epsilon energy, though she sensed a lingering glow. He'd relaxed sideways on the pilot's seat, and the beveled star on his shoulder caught the blue striplights, reflecting sparks that dazzled her eyes.

"Pair bonding," he said softly, "is created when two connatural minds join in a contact like that, only closer—to the total interweaving of emotional fiber. That seals the physical marriage. For life." He folded his hands. "Only the connatural can endure such a close approach. That's why only they can pair bond. But connaturality alone isn't enough to make a union. There must be love. Shared goals. And trust." He stressed the word a little sadly. "Each bond mate remains an individual. Each one can please or devastate the other."

"Brennen." This hurt her pride, but she had to say it. "You realize, don't you, that I'll never be able to do . . . what you just did . . . for you. Is that fair to either of us?"

He answered without hesitating, "Yes. I would feel your pleasure, and my enjoyment would pleasure you. It would echo between us. It wouldn't matter how it began."

An echo, a resonance of tenderness. "Do you still want that with me?" she asked.

"Yes," he murmured; then he added, "I've never asked anyone else."

She pressed her spine against the cold bulkhead. "First, we have a job to do. If it doesn't come off . . ."

When she didn't finish the sentence, he nodded. "Even if it does, the other masters could rule that I misjudged in disobeying orders."

Wouldn't that be amazing?—outcasts, both of them. "Better us in trouble than both our worlds."

He rose out of the pilot's seat, stepped onto the foot of her bunk, and climbed into the upper. "You're right." His voice came down to her, accompanied by rustling noises. "We'll talk about it later, when we're both awake again."

Awake? How could she sleep? Echoes of Brennen's touch ricocheted through her memory like laser fire.

Ellet had spoken truly. She would never forget.

Carradee Second stood alone in an ornately appointed sitting room that had been Firebird's. Only the furniture looked familiar. Servitors had archived Firebird's personal possessions when her death first was announced.

I will never bear a wastling. I could not take the anguish.

She'd talked with Danton for an hour today in her day office. He'd insisted—again—that Netaia was ripe for rebellion, and that the Federacy wanted to help the noble class prevent bloodshed by smoothing the change to a more equable system.

She couldn't concentrate on that, with Firebird in jeopardy again. What would happen if Friel and Burkenhamn succeeded and brought her back to Citangelo?

Sunlight streamed through high, white-curtained windows, giving marble walls a soft sheen and setting off dark wooden furnishings. More keenly, Carradee noticed things that no longer were there. Scanbooks full of pictures from distant worlds didn't clutter the dark fayya-wood end table. The coat-of-arms crested desk had been cleared of Academy trophies and ribbons. No flight jacket was flung over the brocade desk chair.

Burkenhamn would report to her, Friel to Phoena, whether their mission succeeded or failed. Soon, within days. They'd taken a fast craft.

She strolled into the adjoining study. This room had been stuffed with musical paraphernalia. Gone now. Sold, all but the clairsa, to pay those education debts. Firebird's portrait, removed from the gallery after Lieutenant Governor Caldwell drew her attention to it, hung on the inner wall.

Carradee touched its gold frame. She'd grieved for Firebird, really grieved, and storing this portrait in darkness would've been too much like consigning her to a mausoleum. Carradee had hung it here herself, in the music room where Firebird always had seemed happiest, if she were on the ground.

If they brought her back, must Carradee put her on trial? Even more terrible, must she arrange her execution and burial? Plainly Firebird wouldn't suicide, and with heir limitation outlawed, they couldn't touch her for geis refusal. No, it would be treason. A terrible death.

That was hard to imagine. Of all people, Firebird had kept the high laws so passionately. Her rebellions had centered on minor matters. Commoners' concerns, palace protocol . . .

Siwann had kept a healthy distance from the fire-haired imp, but not Carradee.

Surely, though, the Federacy would keep her on Tallis. Carradee stared at the diadem the girl in the portrait wore proudly—if a touch off center. Could the Federates let Firebird be punished for becoming the key to their victory? Perhaps it was hope, asking that. Phoena's hopes were different. Phoena's ideological retreat would be well under way now, free from Federate intrusion, as Carradee had promised.

Hunter Height—Carradee loved the place. She shut her eyes, basking in the pleasant sadness of her small martyrdom. She would stay in the bustling city, while Phoena and her friends enjoyed the majestic old Height. *At least Phoena will cherish it, and it won't stand empty. The lieutenant governor was right, though: The city is quieter without her.*

Carradee studied the portrait's impish smile, comparing it to the sad courage in her eyes. That artist had captured her sister's nature perfectly.

Could I attend Firebird's trial?

As queen, she must not only attend but preside. And she could not veto an execution order if the Electorate handed it down.

"Please!" she whispered to the unseen Powers. "Keep Firebird on Tallis!"

On their last day in slip, Firebird and Brennen finalized plans, talking through every level of tunnels under the Height, each spur, and the worrisome possibility of fumigation. He'd requisitioned oxygen sniffers and lightweight chem suits; he'd explained the different types of explosives. Finally she rose from her bunk, opened the galley servo, and stared at its contents. She'd stuffed her brain with plans and information. It wouldn't hold one more detail.

"Mari?"

Turning, she caught a wistful look in his eyes.

"What will they do with you if you're caught? Have you considered it?"

Why did he want to know? Could he intend to abandon her, use her as a distraction? "Kill me, of course," she answered, considering as abstractly as she could. "Any faithful Netaian would now. But I suspect—I think—they wouldn't shoot to kill on sight if they recognized me. Phoena has to be there. She sponsored Cleary's research from the beginning. If I know Phoena at all, she'd love to create a spectacle. Parade me around. Make it sting."

"And if they took me?"

"How could they?" she scoffed.

"It's possible. What might she do?"

Firebird leaned against the servo counter. It had never entered her mind that Brennen might falter, whatever he tried. The image of Brennen powerless in Phoena's hands appalled her. "That's hard. She'd want to hurt you, to punish you, but she'd want to make everything 'proper.' Are you—"

"Afraid?" he asked softly, completing her thought. "More than I have ever been. Afraid to have come this far but to lose what you and I could have had."

"You'll come through, Brenn. With your resources . . ."

"I'm not invulnerable."

"I suppose not." Only incomprehensible sometimes, such as in the council chamber with that eerie weapon—"Brennen," she said sharply. "May I look at your crystace?"

He flipped the bunk up out of sight, groped inside his left cuff, and drew the slim, dull gray dagger hilt. He laid it on his palm and held it toward her. Near the wide handguard she spotted a small, round stud. It was just as Korda had described.

Brennen shifted his grip, held the crystace at arm's length, and pressed the stud. Instantly, the piercing resonant frequency sang in her ears, and the blade appeared. It caught the monochromatic cabin light and reflected scarcely visible shades of green, blue, and violet. He swept it around to stand upright between them and eyed her through the shimmering crystal.

Korda had described the blade's edges as of one atom's width, and she finally believed him. Wonderingly, she reached out a hand.

Brennen gave it to her. She made a tentative swing in the air. It was lighter than it looked but exquisitely balanced. "What is ehrite?"

"I don't know. I'm no chemist."

She swept it side to side, across her midline and back, and traced a few tentative fencing parries she'd learned long ago in school. She was no swordswoman, though. Afraid she'd damage something, she handed it back.

He took it and pressed the stud. "Are you hungry?"

She chose the stew, variety number three, spicy and warming. Brennen ate without comment, preoccupied with a map he'd spread on her bunk.

Soon they sat at their stations, g-suited again, strapped to the acceleration chairs. The final seconds counted off on the break indicator, and then the little craft's engine reversed with a roar. Pushed painfully against the black webbing, Firebird glimpsed Netaia's majestic arc as Brennen leaned forward to correct their course. He'd assured her that the transponder codes he'd secured would take them past any Federate surveillance satellites. They approached from the south, over the vast polar ice, speeding toward the

South and North Deeps, as far as possible from any population center. One swirl of cloud frosted the Great Ocean.

The cabin heated with atmospheric friction as they crossed Arctica. She watched hungrily, more homesick than she'd ever felt. She could never call this beautiful white-frosted blue globe home again. Never. The thought made her chest ache, as when she'd lost Corey.

Still decelerating hard, Brennen dropped the craft to low-level and skimmed the flat, icy continent as predawn light began to glow. Then the Aeries raised their magnificent shoulders. Like a hovercraft on open sea, the ship rose and fell with high passes of that ice-locked range, running south.

"There it is." Firebird spotted two familiar peaks. League Mountain, separated by a short ridge from Hunter Mountain, filled the horizon. Both continued to grow as Brennen decelerated hard, dropping the ship on a snow field as near that ridge as the slope's pitch would allow. He cut the atmospheric engines. Silence rang loudly in Firebird's ears.

They unbuckled and stretched. Brennen moved aft, which was now downhill. From the cargo area, he pulled two dark gray suits and handed one up to Firebird. "Thermal controls on the left wrist."

She turned around, slipped out of her gravity suit and shipboards, and stepped into the heavy gray pants. After struggling with the shirt, she joined the pieces at her waist. The suit didn't hang too badly. The shirt collar fit high and snugly, and the sleeves ended in flexible gloves. She touched a wrist panel and immediately started to shiver. Obviously, that wasn't what she wanted. She touched a different corner. Warmth flowed through her hands, feet, and body.

"Have you figured it out?" Brennen came up beside her and eyed the wrist panel. "Comfortable?"

"A little too warm."

"Leave it that way."

She slipped back into her boots, then buckled on a gun belt. Brennen opened the outer hatch. Frigid air swirled into the cabin. They'd need no stepstand; the Brumbee's hot skin had melted a trench in the ice and snow. It still settled slowly.

She hoisted the drillcloth pack and jumped down, then waited in calf-deep surface snow as Brennen sealed the hatch, perching on the tilted door plate and clinging one-handed to the security handle. Gracefully he leaped down to her side and took the pack.

"I'll spell you carrying that," she offered.

"The best way to work as a team is for each of us to do what he—or she—does best. I'll haul."

He reminded her suddenly of a teacher she'd almost forgotten, one who'd urged her to study music and forget the military. "Go ahead. But I'm not along for the scenery."

He smiled. She headed upslope, trying not to break through a thin crust into deeper, older snow. It made for slow going, particularly for a man carrying a pack as heavy as that one.

"We're leaving tracks," she observed.

"We won't have to worry about it, going down the other side. Southern exposure."

"And what about the ship?"

"Danton's people aren't watching this area for anything so small."

True. They weren't watching this area at all.

He passed her and plodded ahead, breaking trail. Her heart pounded with the altitude and unaccustomed exercise, despite her recent weeks of training. They skirted the summit just west of the ridge, where the wind roared stiffly. Here, even the old snow had been blown away. They made faster progress on rocky ground. The view south into staggered lines of distant foothills raised her spirits, but they dropped down quickly to avoid presenting recognizable silhouettes to any watching eyes.

About ten meters below the ridge, Firebird stopped for a breath. Behind her, Brennen whistled softly.

Hunter Height lay below, on a stony knoll. The house, built of Hunter Mountain granite, was designed like a small hexagon atop a larger one. From the southern foothills, an ancient, winding road approached, and from the north a switchbacking lane led up from a box canyon, which ran east and west and concealed a sizable airstrip. The knoll was ringed by a venerable stone outwall—etched, as Firebird remembered it, by lichens and the wild mountain weather—and inside the wall lay informal grounds, often battered by blizzards, sheltered somewhat by Thunder Hill's forested shoulder.

"From orbit," he murmured, "it would look like part of the mountain."

Firebird smiled smugly. "That's why your recon flights haven't picked it up."

CHAPTER 20

HUNTER HEIGHT

crescendo poco a poco
gradually becoming louder

In MaxSec's bustling thirty-fifth-floor hallway, a man in Thyrian blue saluted Ellet Kinsman. Briefly puzzled, she returned the gesture. He looked familiar. He must've gone through college either before her (he was built older, tall, and well muscled) or after (but the face was so young).

"Captain Kinsman." He shone a cordial smile. "Air Master Damalcon Dardy, Thyrian Alert Forces. I'm looking for General Caldwell, and the secretary sent me to you. Is he on a security assignment?"

He was older, then, and he ranked her. Ellet kept her static shield thick. "Is there something I can help you with, sir?"

"I've just checked in from following up a Shuhr incident, and I'm only passing through. I wanted to introduce myself. However—" He touched her arm. Both pressed against a wall to allow a man steering a service cart to pass. "Since this obviously isn't a place for private discussion, would you join me for lunch in the officers' lounge?"

"Sir, the MaxSec lounge is expensive."

His even-toothed grin softened her reserve. "Then I'll take it out of my vital contacts budget."

He did precisely that, presenting his ID disk to the host and insisting on a private booth with a north view. For half the hour, while she savored a salad of genuine Thyrian shellfish, he asked only about her interpretive work, and she found herself warming to him.

"Caldwell, then." He spread garnerberry jam on his roll and switched to silent subvocalization. *I mentioned him at the SO office, and I was given the impression Regional has been overloading him, hoping he'll break or resign before they have to promote a Sentinel up to High command. What's wrong? Where is he?*

I don't know precisely, she responded tightly, and it was enough of the truth to pass. *He has gone with the Netaian woman, Firebird Angelo.*

Dardy set down his roll and leaned across the booth. "What do you mean?"

Ellet remained stoic. *When he turned up missing from duty, I put in for med leave to cover him and made a check at the depot. He took a ship, but they seem baffled too.*

Dardy tapped a finger on the tabletop and eyed the hilly horizon. *Well, they wouldn't have asked him any questions,* he sent back. *SO is SO. Have you reported him?*

"Not yet," she said aloud. She clenched her folded hands against the table.

"You're not telling me everything about this Netaian woman."

"No."

Ellet sensed a slight apprehension.

She's connatural with him? he asked privately.

For one moment Ellet wished for the long, slow period of making acquaintance that outsiders experienced. No one but another Sentinel would expect to be shown so much, so quickly and intimately—but that was their way. It had made the starbred a people who couldn't easily be divided or fooled. "Apparently so, sir."

"That's too bad." Dardy made a wry face.

She kept her response as stony as she knew how to make it. "This is not the end of the matter."

Dardy picked up his fork, speared a last mouthful of smoked fish, and chewed thoughtfully. The lounge quieted briefly as Mister Lithib rode in on his mobility chair.

"Tell me, then." Dardy laid down his fork and pushed back his plate, now entirely sympathetic. *How much do you know about where they've gone?*

She frowned. *Firebird's people aren't taking occupation well. She raised Brennen's suspicion that certain action needed to be taken there on Netaia, although Tierna Coll herself ordered otherwise. She played on his pride and won.* Ellet raised her head to meet the air master's eyes and sent the painful admission. *She won, sir.*

Counter to orders? Dardy looked—and felt—stricken. *Express or implied? Can the codes justify his action?*

Express orders. I saw them given. As to our codes, I can't say. That's for the masters to judge.

Dardy shifted his muscular shoulders to lean sideways in the booth. "It might not be too late to make him stand back and think the issue through. Could they be intercepted?—The woman apprehended for escaping custody and Brennen called back for questioning? Or . . . is there someone there on Netaia who respects our kindred but might hold the woman there at home, to pacify the regime?"

"Governor Danton." Pleased with the idea, Ellet sipped her kass. "He worked well with Brennen and wouldn't want to see him in trouble, but Danton's also close to the royal family. I'd assume that the queen wants her back." Ellet felt no compulsion to tell Dardy what that return might mean to Firebird.

"Perfect," he said. "Regional could alert Danton by the next messenger ship." *And we could maintain Thyrica's hopes to get a Sentinel on the High command*, he added silently.

Despite having found a genuine supporter, Ellet felt a pang of loss, for Brennen's actions had declared his choice: Firebird, unless she refused him. Holding her emotions under tight rein, Ellet raised her kass cup.

Firebird was glad for the thermal suit and stiff teknahide boots as they picked a way down slick, frosty rubble and scree toward the woods. Underfoot, little alpine plants clung to pockets of soil, turning red and brown with the onset of cold weather. Many glistened, edged leaf by leaf with delicate frost crystals.

Just above the evergreen forest, Brennen stopped and waited for her. She'd slowed her pace to scan the Height again before they entered the trees. "There." She pointed with a gray-gloved hand. "By the south wall. And another beyond the back gate."

He followed her gesture with his eyes.

"And there's another, walking along the west end of the grounds. See them?" she asked.

He nodded. "Three guards on morning duty."

"And infrared scanners we can't see. I think we'd better try that side tunnel first. It's farther to walk, but the house is well covered."

"Lead on."

Another hour's trudge took them up onto Thunder Hill, but at the entry site Firebird remembered, they found only a huge jumbled pile of stone.

"Squill," she exclaimed softly. "They've blocked it. Recently, too." She eyed the crushed vegetation, still green. "Can you . . ." She swept out her fingers as if levitating the rock pile aside.

High above her, Brennen peered down from the top of the pile. "That would take too much time and energy." He step-jumped down to join her.

"And we'd better save our explosives for the laboratory. Still want to try the kitchens?"

"Infrared alarms fail sometimes," he said. "If I can shoot one out over the service doors, we might have time to get in before they reactivate it."

"We'll have to get close. These are tiny ones."

He dug into the pack and handed her two energy cubes, and she chewed them dry. "Here." He dropped two more small, hard lumps into her hand.

Citrene! She popped both onto her tongue, then drank a gulp of water from his bottle. He shouldered the pack again and turned back down the hill.

They walked in silence, just to the right of a chute scoured bare of trees by avalanches. Woodsmoke faintly perfumed the air, and the afternoon sky over the treeless swath was purest autumn blue.

As she watched a hunting kiel soar on rising air currents, a roaring silver streak sliced the sky. She ducked into the trees.

Brennen joined her, hands on her shoulders. "It's an active place, all right." Peering back, she saw him smiling. His apprehension must've run its course. He looked almost eager.

In a copse of barren, prickly bushes they rested out the afternoon, and they moved down at dusk. The high wall, once worked elegantly smooth, now wore the cracks of antiquity, and here and there stones had fallen, affording Firebird all the footholds she needed after Brennen boosted her. Lying flat atop the wall for a few seconds, she spotted house lights through the trees, warm yellow in the lower windows and dim blue above. A scent of roasted meat made her mouth water. Convinced no one was near, she slipped down inside, rested her feet on the heavy iron handrail that circled the wall's inner surface—installed centuries ago by an elderly inhabitant— and then jumped backward down to the ground. Brennen followed.

When they reached the manicured tip of the forest, Firebird could see clearly into the kitchens. Lights still burned, and white-gowned cook staff hurried back and forth in front of southwest windows. She turned to Brennen, who stood in deep shadow behind another evergreen tree. He made no sign.

She looked up, startled by the almost starless twilit sky. Netaia was a splendid recluse at the Whorl's end. The brightest points of faint, familiar constellations winked down as she hid and waited. She spotted Tallis in the rising Whorl. Tallis looked somehow different now. She'd lived under that star as a sun.

The kitchen lights went out. Firebird shot Brennen a quizzical look.

He shook his head, and they waited in stillness a few minutes longer. Slow, even footsteps approached. A guard passed, vanishing around a broad corner.

Brennen flung himself prone and steadied his blazer on one hand. Firebird held her breath and averted her eyes from the energy pistol's muzzle.

He took a deep breath. Then another.

Then he touched the stud. A single flash fled out the corner of her eye. She waited a moment longer, until Brennen led out at a run.

She came close behind. As Brennen tried the handle, she flattened herself beside the kitchen door. The iron latch clicked as it released. He started to open the huge wooden slab, but before they could steal through, it ground on its hinges. Brennen froze.

Firebird bit her lip.

He pressed up and pulled the door outward a little farther, then motioned her inside.

The great kitchens stood empty, lit only by cracks below inner doors. Firebird followed the outside wall left a few meters to the kitchen store.

Brennen zipped the gloves off his suit, then knelt and pressed an open hand to the lockbox at waist level. Firebird watched, intrigued. In a moment, she heard another soft click inside the mechanism. Brennen pushed the door open. They squeezed into the pantry and closed the heavy panel behind them. A dim, pale green light sprang up beside her, Brennen's pocket luma. The tiny cube illuminated a ghostly green sphere around them as they threaded their way between shelves of foodstuffs and cooking equipment.

At the end of the pantry, a palm lock guarded the cellar stairs. Brennen dropped again to his knees.

"Wait," Firebird whispered. She pocketed her own gloves and pressed her bare right palm to the panel.

The door slid away.

Firebird smiled and murmured, "Well. They haven't changed the locks."

She led stealthily around the wedge-shaped stone steps that she remembered so well. They widened into the tunnel system, where cool air made her face tingle. After circling once, she could see an orange glow beneath. Brennen pocketed the little luma. She steadied herself with her fingertips on the left wall. In a few steps more she came out in an alcove that led to a cross tunnel. Its left branch passed eastward, toward the area they'd agreed to search first for Cleary's laboratory, but Firebird recalled a large chamber at the center of the system. It would have to be crossed if they traversed this level. Brennen motioned her to remain in the stairwell. He'd drawn his shock pistol. Stealthily he walked forward into what seemed an unnatural brightness, then disappeared left.

She edged along the right wall to the end of the shadow, drew her own pistol, and waited. Brennen returned, shaking his head. She pointed the other way. They scurried down the right branch, then made another quick right turn, down into darkness.

After they'd spiraled down another stone stair past the second level, he stopped. "She's here," he whispered.

"Phoena?"

"Yes. There were men in the main chamber, talking. They mentioned both her and Cleary."

"As if we had any doubt. That chamber would've been risky to cross anyway. Let's go without light, as long as we can still cover ground."

Edging downward in total darkness, Firebird found his firm handhold reassuring. The wall vanished beneath her skimming fingers. "Here," she said softly. "Eastbound."

Firebird led now. As they drew on, a yellow glow grew stronger.

At last Brennen whispered, "Stay here," and crept on alone. She watched in dim light, a little aggravated at being left behind. He paused, listening with some epsilon sense, then went on.

Straining her ears, Firebird heard footsteps from the west. "Brenn!" she called in a penetrating whisper. Before he could join her, she drew and aimed toward the steps. Her tiny red targeting beam showed movement. She fired. There came a surprised shout from up the corridor, and then silence. An afterimage of her weapon glowed faintly in her eyes.

"Quick!" he said. "There's a guard up ahead. He's sure to have heard." They sprinted back westward, as silently as two people wearing boots can run.

A north-branching corridor left the straight hall. "Here," breathed Firebird. She turned right in the dark and plunged downward only moments before laser fire lit the passage.

This tunnel's floor was more broken. Brennen tripped after only a few steps. She heard the scuffle as he caught himself, then the luma sprang back to life. Again she pushed herself to a run. The faint greenish glow made her bare hands look sickly and pale but sped their progress around the long curve east toward the main northbound tunnel. Several side passages led off into blackness. Their shadowy depths mocked the intrusion of light, faint though it was. Here and there, mineral crystals caught the emerald light and glittered eerily.

Once the curve had been put behind them, protecting them from following fire, they stopped to rest.

Panting, Firebird leaned against a smooth spot on the wall. "Unfortunately, now they know someone's here. If they split up they can have us like slinks up a tree."

Brennen was listening again. "No one's coming."

"He's reporting, then. Now we worry about fumigation."

"We have chem suits and sniffers."

"There's also that spur up under Thunder Hill. I was here once when they gassed for rodents, and I remember they talked about how heavy zistane vapor is, and how it sinks. The spur might be safe for a while. But it's a dead end."

"I do have an idea—" He killed his luma. "Get down."

Firebird dropped onto the hard stone and rolled against a wall, fumbling blind for her shock pistol. Nearby, a stealthy step broke the stillness. Then another, quieter yet. She held her breath. Then rocks, pistol, and Brennen gleamed crimson as he fired.

She heard him breathe deeply, and then the luma shone out again, held high in his left hand as he aimed his blazer steadily up the tunnel. Cautiously, she got back to her feet.

"I felt something alive back there," he whispered.

No sound flowed down the shaft toward them. Brennen slipped her the luma and backtracked warily up into blackness.

When he came back, he shook his head. "There's no body. But I don't feel it anymore."

"Something from down one of those side passages?" She shivered.

"Does anything live down there?"

"I don't think so. But the staff used to tell us monster stories that kept Carradee awake for nights on end." She moved a step closer, and he reached for her hand. "Let's go," she urged, stepping out.

"Wait a minute." He pulled her back.

"You said you had an idea."

"It's risky," he whispered.

"It couldn't be riskier than waiting to be fumigated. What is it?"

"To split up. I'd like you uplevel, out of the danger of gas. We have to find the researchers' main data base. You'll recognize the scientists."

"Yes. But—"

"If Phoena fumigates, the researchers should evacuate uplevel, especially if they have ground-floor offices. I'll suit up and keep working."

She stiffened, suspicious. "This is something you'd thought of already, isn't it?"

"Yes and no. It was always a possibility, but I hoped we wouldn't have to try it. You'll be in particular danger if we separate."

"I can take care of myself. I know Phoena pretty well, and the Height even better."

He drew her shock pistol and blazer from their belt holsters, checked both charges, then handed them back. "Can you kill, if you have to?"

"Not with this." She holstered the shock pistol on her right side, for an easier draw.

"They're deadly at point-blank range," he reminded her, "but the blazer is better. You could have to kill in self-defense. Can you?"

"Brenn, of course I—"

"Face-to-face?" He pressed her hand. "Even from a cockpit, you tried to put down the Verohan interceptors, not the pilots."

"I see your point. I—" She still dreamed sometimes about the pilots she'd shot down at Veroh. She did hope they'd survived. "To save my life . . . yes, Brenn. I think I could. If I'm careful, I won't have to." Finally, it hit home: "Phoena would kill me now, if I gave her the chance," she realized aloud.

"Remember that," he said.

"Yes." She wrested her mind back to their plan of attack. "The only real trick will be getting into the tubes."

Shipboard, they'd discussed the Height's hydraulic network, drilled through granite walls in a previous century to carry solar-heated water into freshing rooms, kitchens, and lower-level labs. As a child Firebird had found the abandoned hollow system, far wider than the pipes it held, and explored it over a series of summers. It had made an ideal hiding spot from Phoena, something she frequently needed. Painstakingly she'd cleared away obstructions until she could negotiate the entire system, and she'd kept it her own secret in this carefully guarded place. Assuming she hadn't changed shape too much as she matured, she should still be able to use it.

"Listen, then," he said. "If those researchers have data desks uplevel, destroy them. Any way you can. A shock pistol can fatally surge a main drive, too."

"I suppose it could." She wondered what kind of situation he'd survived to bring back that trick.

"Give me an hour to lay charges, then half an hour to get clear enough to detonate them. When I'm away, I'll send off a quest pulse homed on your feelings, as I did on Tallis."

She nodded.

"If you've destroyed the uplevel offices or confirmed there aren't any, and gotten off the height, concentrate on something strongly pleasing when you feel that probe. I'll touch off the charges."

"Off the height," she repeated. "Airstrip?"

"Perfect. Get a plane ready while I'm on my way. But if you're not clear when you feel me call, answer with fear. I'll feel it. I'll come for you." He opened a side pocket of the black pack while he spoke. "And here's one more thing." He handed her a palm-sized touch activator card. "I'll carry the explosives close to the lab and arm them before I do anything else. Blow them if I don't call."

She touched the card with one finger, shaken by his trust. He was putting himself at her mercy. "But you might be close. Surely it won't come to that, Brenn."

"It could. Could you do that, too?"

"I . . ." She swallowed. "No."

He slipped the card into her hip pocket. "I'd make it an order if I were your superior officer. Think. If it comes down to that, I want you to. The activation sequence is V-E-R-O-H."

"I won't forget that," she murmured.

"We can't let them devastate another world."

Abruptly she realized he carried his ancestors' world on his conscience, just as she carried Veroh. She nodded.

Within minutes, they cautiously approached the main tunnel north to the airstrip. Firebird peered out into its breadth. Everburners gleamed, imbedded in glossy black walls. Its floor recently had been scored by vehicular traffic. Even Brennen sensed no one nearby.

She met his eyes for one last time. "Thank you for everything, Brenn. I hope it works."

He took her in his arms. "Go with His protection, Mari." He kissed her, started to draw away, then reached for her again. She clutched him, wishing uselessly that their paths had crossed in peaceful, trustful times.

He stepped away. "Start timing now. An hour and a half."

He turned back down the side passage, and Firebird headed upward at a quiet jog. The paved lane was as still as a tomb, and she knew it could soon be hers, if something went wrong.

Where she reached the first level, the tunnel ended in a chamber just east of the main hall. She remembered a maintenance hatch in there, the nearest hydraulic access. Drawing her shock pistol, she stepped out into the chamber and listened hard. Elevators pulsing, a distant shout, her own heartbeat: She heard nothing immediately threatening, so she took half the ten meters to the opposite wall at a dead run.

Bootsteps clattered off to her right. She dropped, rolled, and came up shooting. A red-collared figure fell heavily. She dashed to the floor-level access panel, knelt down, and started popping out tracker bolts. The smooth rectangular slab loosened in her fingers. Meticulously she slid one edge outward, lifting as she moved it, leaving no mark on the black stone floor. Then she squeezed herself into the hollow beyond. Two white polymer pipes ran up and down along one side of a shaft that could've held eight—had been intended for eight, she guessed. It was snug, particularly at shoulders and hips, but she fit. As she pulled the panel home, voices echoed out in the chamber.

Extending her arms, she grabbed one pipe, wedged her feet against opposite sides, and shinnied upward in utter darkness.

Thick stone dampened all sound above her, below, and on all sides. Not even the occasional scuttering of small trapped creatures livened the hollow tonight. She wrenched herself upward another three arm-lengths, then rested a minute. Now that the first claustrophobic minute had passed, she felt safer in this dark sanctum than she'd felt since leaving Brennen.

Brenn. She twisted her arm and checked the time-lights on her wrist-band. She'd already used fifteen minutes. She had to hurry.

But the tube was slow going, particularly after she wriggled over into a horizontal cross passage. At one point it narrowed so tightly that she shimmied back a meter, eased out of the heavy thermal shirt and pants, and pushed them ahead of her, shivering and collecting scratches from the cold granite, until she passed the constriction. After that, she struggled back into the garments but left them unfastened, and soon she was glad she had. Three more times, she needed to shed every millimeter.

Finally, scraped and stinging, she judged that she'd nearly reached the safest place to pass into the house. Another five minutes' creep put her at the end of that hollow with an upward passage directly overhead. Once, it had held the feed tube to the collectors. Trying not to stir a deep pile of dust and small skeletons at the bottom of the drop, she worked herself up into a standing position, then patted the wall for a remembered crack between wood and stone.

After a minute's search she located it, and then the widest prying spot, two hands lower than she expected. She'd grown since first finding it. Cautiously she wedged two fingers inward. Gripping the wooden panel, she pushed it a centimeter. Then she waited. Watched. Listened. Just past this wall had been a walk-in wardrobe used primarily by staff. No light came through the opening. She pushed gently again and met squashy resistance. Linens, she hoped. She gave it another shove.

The wardrobe was silent, but shouting and heavy, running steps echoed in the halls. Cautiously she squeezed out of the hollow into a dark north bedroom.

Movement caught her eye, the hall door slowly opening. She dashed across the room toward the inner wall and pressed behind the door's path of swing. A shadow cast by the hall light appeared on the floor. Another House Guard slunk toward the open wardrobe.

She drew her shock pistol. One silent shot left him senseless and Firebird armed with another Netaian service blazer. She tucked it into her gun belt, then eyed the unconscious guard. She didn't think he'd seen her, but she didn't want to take the risk. She dragged him into the wardrobe and barricaded him in with the heaviest-looking chair in the room. Then she crept out into the yellow-lit hall.

The sound of footsteps sent her dashing for a utility room on the inner wall. Someone passed by and out of hearing. She tiptoed on, zigzagging between inner and outer rooms. What luck Phoena hadn't thought to reprogram the palm locks against her! Undoubtedly the House Guards thought they'd secured this hall already. Even Phoena hadn't expected her to come back.

Behind the fourth outer door she heard Dr. D'Stang and Baron Parkai, arguing loudly about having been dragged from their downlevel beds. She smiled grimly. If they'd gone to sleep without complaining, they would've been harder to find.

She pressed her palm to the slick black panel and heard the latch release. Then she secured her grip on her shock pistol and elbowed the door open wide.

agitato
agitated, excited

One shocked face turned to Firebird as she placed a silent stun burst. A man fell across a bed.

She sensed movement and whirled around. An older man stood behind the door, raising a blazer. Startled, she fired. He crumpled.

She secured the door and leaned against it, breathing hard. Then she dropped to her knees beside the man she'd stunned at close range: Elber Parkai, Baron of Sylva and DeTar. *Stunned?* she begged, checking his wrist and then his throat. No pulse. He wasn't breathing either.

He was dead, just as Brennen warned.

Struggling to inhale, Firebird pushed away from his body. *He meant to murder millions of Federates*, she reminded herself. Still she stared. She'd only meant to stun him. . . .

She stood up, hands trembling. Beyond the rumpled beds she spotted three windowpanels with their slatted filters closed, and a windowless out-side door. That, anyway, was perfect. No outdoor guard would peer in and see her.

A quick circuit of the room proved it was used only for sleeping, not research. She searched the nightrobed bodies and found no data chips, rods, or disks.

Disappointed, she muscled Dr. D'Stang into another large closet.

What about Baron Parkai?

She couldn't leave his body in plain sight. She felt like a butcher, drag-ging it into the closet and dumping it beside his stunned fellow-worker. This wardrobe had an ancient two-way lock. She unscrewed the inner knob and then secured it from the outside. Sighing, she steeled herself to slip back out into the hallway and search out Dr. Nella Cleary.

Wait. A voice from her training spoke up. *Never leave weapons behind enemy lines*. She spotted Parkai's dropped blazer near the inner door. *Can't leave Phoena's forces any additional arms*, she reminded herself. *Not that they seem to have any shortage of these.*

She stepped to the outer door, slipped through, and glanced around outside. All the outdoor lights burned fiercely, casting sharp grass shadows on the north leg of the outwall and obscuring the stars. Cold, still air stung her face. Judging from shouts echoing off stone, the hunt was up—far downhill and to the south. Someone must've spooked a brownbuck and mistaken it for a human intruder.

Near an untended flower bed, she spotted a pile of rotting grass clippings. She sprinted over, plunged Parkai's blazer deep into the decaying pile, then roughened its surface to hide the hole she'd left. Then she pulled the guard's blazer out of her belt and stuffed it too into the compost. She only had two hands. Better not to carry extra weapons that could be turned against her.

Now to look for Cleary.

She hurried back inside and cycled her shock pistol to a fresh charge.

Then she stole out into the hallway. Halfway to the next room she heard running feet, both ahead and behind. She sprinted toward the door, switching her pistol to her left hand so she could palm the panel quicker. The footsteps behind her pounded.

Someone grabbed her shoulders. She spun toward her assailant and instinctively kicked as hard as she could. A strangled cry and a thud sounded behind her. She wheeled away from the runner ahead and hit an inlaid wall, grinding her nose and cheek against it. Rebounding, she tripped on a flailing arm and fell.

Instantly there was a knee on her back and sharp pressure against the base of her skull. "Drop the gun," ordered a shaky voice above her. "Then take your hand away."

She could do nothing else. Reluctantly she let her shock pistol go and lay still, breathing quickly. The knee shifted. A well-kept, slender hand descended into her field of vision and removed her weapon, and then she felt it fumble at her holster. The weight lifted. Footsteps retreated across the passage, and then she heard the voice again. It sounded vaguely familiar.

"Now. Get up. Slowly."

She complied, facing the ornate wall.

"Hands on your head."

She locked her fingers and waited.

"Turn around."

She came slowly around to face him—them. Two men stood glowering at her. The smaller—young, dark-haired, and thin, wearing a noble's blue formal sash, held her own blazer trained on her. Beside him, the portly Duke of Claighbro, Muirnin Rogonin, stood shaking and seething, obviously in pain.

How had he gotten himself out of lockup?

Suddenly Rogonin's expression changed to utter confusion and supreme embarrassment. "Your Highness?" He shook his head. "I beg your pardon! Why are you—"

"No," his young partner interrupted. "That's not Phoena."

Then Firebird recognized him, too: Phoena's "little moon-shadow," Count Tel Tellai. She stood motionless, eyeing Tellai's firing finger, wondering if she'd have time to sprint for freedom while they stood baffled.

But Rogonin smiled. He wiped his palms on his white lace shirt front. "Well, Firebird. You came back after all. Call your friend uplevel, Tellai."

As Rogonin drew a shining blue-and-gold blazer, blatantly ornamental but just as deadly as the gunmetal gray service model Tel Tellai had taken from her, the young count hurried to the next room. She heard his voice. "Phoena, love, you'll never believe it. We've got her." Silence. "Well, someone you've been hoping to see. You're going to be—yes, it's she. Shall we— of course. Oh yes. Right away."

On a deeper level of awareness she felt Brennen's sudden, distant touch. He knew she was caught, then. She tried to assure him he didn't need to worry but should finish his job . . . quickly.

Tellai strolled back into view, beaming like a praised pet. Firebird glanced from Tellai to Rogonin, weighing her chances of escape—slight at the moment. She decided to play along. Brennen would need some time yet.

Tellai rocked on his heels. "Uplevel, Rogonin. Her Highness's room."

"One minute. I think we'd better spoil your sash first."

"Why?"

"Tie her."

"Surely you don't need to do that. This is a new one—a gift!" The slight young noble crossed his chest with one hand and smoothed the glowing fabric.

"I know this lady. Do you want Her Highness down our throats for losing a prize catch? She'll thank you for sacrificing that sash."

Tellai yanked it off. Rogonin improvised a tight wrist restraint, winding the excess up Firebird's forearms with an additional knot that strained her shoulders. Firebird submitted, willing herself to stay calm.

Her flash of fear had torn through Brennen. He dropped all shields, to be able to sense her—or the presence of guards. Leaning against rough stone, he sent off the quest pulse and let her feelings flood him. Defiance flamed through her emotions.

Caught, then. Recognized, but not yet threatened, and apparently not tempted to buy her life by betraying him to Phoena. Those had been his only earnest fears—that she'd be killed before they knew whom they'd taken, or that some old habit would revive her former loyalty, even though that would cost her life. She *had* hidden Hunter Height from him. Shouldering his pack, he headed up to search out the laboratory.

Five minutes later he reached the main lane and paused to quest-pulse again. Firebird remained fearful, but was even more controlled now. He drew his shock pistol and jogged up the lane, following the way she'd come. Where it ended in the bare chamber he turned left, hurried up a short passage, and stopped dead.

In front of him rose a three- by five-meter guardwall, its edges sealed to stone. Light from an everburner behind his shoulder reflected off a satiny surface that looked incongruously modern in these antique shafts. Above its locking panel, a sign warned: DANGER. No Unauthorized Entry.

He turned inward to focus a probe, then sent it on his epsilon wave behind the locking panel. Humming circuitry surrounded his point of awareness, a sensation that prickled like insects attacking. Up one course he found the resonating chamber of an alarm horn. A little farther on, a high-voltage conduit connected back into the palm panel's outer edges. It would deliver a killing shock were the wrong person to touch it.

Cautiously he traced the tangled circuitry into the confirmation box. At that point, a proper palm print would be recognized, an improper one rejected. He gave the point a nudge of energy.

The monstrous wall slid aside. Brennen stepped through the opening. Another pulse closed it behind him.

He looked around, gripping his pistol at loose ready. The corridor curved right, walled in old stone. Along the left waited several doors, all closed.

Brennen paused beside the first door, out of sight of anyone inside. Still feeling no warning presence, he opened it, then peered into darkness. Cautiously he slipped through. Using the tiny luma, he located a light switch.

A glass wall gleamed halfway across the stone chamber. Beyond robotic controls, claw fingered metal hands drooped in mechanical sleep. Past them lay a long, fat metal warhead. With a tendril of epsilon energy he probed its circuits. At its heart, it was one of the outmoded nuclear killers. What then made it such a reputedly formidable weapon . . . the basium?

Dull sheets of Verohan metal lay stacked alongside the half-plated bomb.

Inside the woefully inadequate protection of that hardened glasteel wall, a layer of basium could be wrapped around the warhead and sealed in place by mechanical arms. He didn't understand—neither the basium nor other changes in the warhead's circuitry, because this wasn't his expertise—but he would remember and report. The warhead itself was smaller than he might've expected. Undoubtedly, the key to the weapon's threat value lay in a sealed launching compartment near its nose. Something would be released with detonation.

Brennen slid off the backpack, thinking through an operation more delicate than he'd anticipated. Setting off the wrong explosives, too near, might detonate the monster and any of its kin in other rooms, atomizing the granite mountain and sending a radioactive cloud into the atmosphere.

In the second room he found an office setup, its bluescreen left on. From a safe distance he fiddled with its circuitry, but it wouldn't tell him any secrets in the little time he could spare. Using his shock pistol, he surged all its networking circuits. If he were caught and his work halted, that stroke alone would slow Cleary.

Then he moved on.

The third chamber held a stack of huge, shielded crates, a shelf lined with desiccator jars and several flasks of green liquid. The air smelled oddly marine, reminding him of Thyrica. He stepped back into the corridor and laid his pack on the ground.

At that moment the shriek of a whistle tore through the tunnel. An alarm—why so late? A signal to evacuate? Firebird's distress came through more urgently when he quested now. *Protect her until I can get there!* he prayed.

His empty pack lay like a rumpled black pillow at his feet. He shook out and donned the thin chemical suit, then turned back to his work. Deftly he armed every charge, as he'd promised Firebird. Then he distributed them: nothing into the rooms containing nuclear materials, an incendiary onto the office chair. In the hallway he eyed the stone supporting walls, and then, charge by slim charge, he created a hidden line in one natural crack that would bury the access under meters of blasted granite. He laid a second line up the other wall, securing each charge with a small lump of flexible adhesive. Applied dry, flexid would hold them almost indefinitely.

Firebird had stepped off the lift between her captors into the spacious master room on the Height's top floor. Loud, excited talking suddenly stopped.

The master room's odd shape had always fascinated her, but there'd been changes made. In contrast with the utilitarian tunnels, Phoena had made this room glitter, from springy red carpet to crystal-tiered chandelier. Even the black marble communications console and a long, bare metal table shone like mirrors. Below a row of formal portraits stood almost twenty people: older sons and daughters of the ten noble Houses, a few servitors, several House Guards and redjackets—and Vultor Korda, who stood under a long window, all but licking his lips with anticipation, tiny eyes narrowed to slits. Firebird's stomach curdled. Somehow, Phoena had freed both Korda and Rogonin. Was Dorning Stele here, too?

Phoena herself, in a flowing gown of brilliant yellow-orange, parted the line of people and walked regally toward her. Yes, Firebird admitted, that graceful, long-limbed (hateful, haughty) woman with the knot of chestnut hair was a beauty.

"You!" The scornful word rang in the room. "What are you doing here?"

Firebird stood silent, unmoving, eyeing the nearest redjacket, who gripped a twinbeam blazer.

Phoena glowered at Rogonin. "I just had a second report from down-level. Parkai is dead, D'Stang stunned."

Behind Firebird, a woman squealed, "No!" Firebird wondered if she looked as guilty as she felt.

Phoena folded her arms tightly against her chest. "Yes. Was she armed?" Tellai stepped up and handed Phoena the blazer and the shock pistol. "Ha," she said. "You searched her, of course?"

"No, Your Highness." Firebird heard a note of chagrin in Tellai's voice.

"Do it now," Phoena commanded icily. "Do it right. And if she moves, strip her!"

Grinning, Rogonin moved in. Firebird's flesh crawled as he started to pat down the thermal suit. She clutched the fabric tying her wrists, diverting her mind from Rogonin's examining fingers and the burning urge to kick him again. She knew Phoena well enough to believe in that threat.

Once Tellai and the nearest House Guards saw that she stood still, they approached too. Each groped into a pocket. Tellai found the touch card and showed Phoena. "What's this?"

"Explosives," she hissed. "I should've expected as much." Phoena seized the card. "You have a friend downlevel, I assume?"

Firebird didn't speak. Brennen could have armed those charges by now, though Phoena wouldn't risk destroying her precious laboratory by trying a touch pattern. Touch card, weapons, and her Federate-issue gun belt made a tidy evidence pile on the long metal table.

"It's time to carry out your geis, wastling. Loose her." A guard cut the sash from her wrists. Phoena smiled without warmth as Firebird straightened her thermal suit with all the dignity she could muster. "First, let's discuss your escort. I'll make it easier for you if you cooperate. Who brought you? Is he here now? Or is it a *she*?" she asked with a side glance at Korda. He must've told her about Ellet Kinsman.

Firebird stared back, not even tempted to answer, working warm blood back into her hands. Evidently Phoena hadn't yet heard what happened at the Regional council hearing. Firebird must have beaten Friel and Burkenhamn back to Netaia, but by how long?

Phoena slapped her face with furious strength. Firebird reeled away. Rogonin seized her shoulders and thrust her toward Phoena again.

"Who brought you? Where are they?" Phoena repeated.

"Don't you believe I could get here myself?" Firebird challenged her. Every minute she distracted Phoena was more time for Brennen to finish their real mission.

Phoena slapped her other cheek.

Vultor Korda spoke up. "Your Highness, would you like me to examine her? Her mind should be fertile ground by now. She and I have a score to settle over a certain encounter on Tallis." He took a step forward. "I would enjoy serving you, Highness."

Phoena sniffed. "I see no point in that, Thyrian." Firebird would've smiled if she'd dared. "This is obvious enough. She has always opposed me on this project, and she's here to destroy it. Guard—clear the tunnels. Get ready to gas them and run the new security unit. In one minute. I have no time to waste."

Firebird started, amazed that Phoena hadn't fumigated already. Was the basium project so close to completion that they were rushing toward deployment?

The guard hastened away as Phoena spoke on, running a fingernail along the inside of her own arm. "Do you know what this means to me, to be able to have you executed? We can even do it at first light." She stopped pacing. Rogonin's grip tightened on Firebird's shoulders. "This is for our family's sake, you know. In fact, just to show that the honor of the family comes first—to me—I'll give you a blade now . . . if you ask. But not poison. That would be too easy. And you'll have an audience.

"You see—" She turned again to Korda. "We offer poison and peace to those whose time has come honorably. A blade for penance or last resort. And for the criminal . . ." She drew back to include Firebird in her stare.

Criminal? Phoena didn't know the half of it!

"It may surprise you, Firebird, to hear that we brought a full complement of D-rifles to the Height. In such a delicate situation, I wanted to be prepared for treason in the ranks." Smirking, she pointed at Firebird. "And here you are."

Rogonin stroked her throat with a damp palm, clearly enjoying her predicament. Someone along the wall whispered.

Phoena turned to the nearest House Guard. "Charge the rifles." He too bowed and hurried out.

Firebird clenched her fists. The narrow-band D-wave originally had been developed for surgery, but it had to be used with heavy anesthesia because the field built slowly, disrupting nerve cells before disintegrating them, crazing a conscious patient with pain. Netaia had adopted the D-rifle for one of its public execution protocols, for which a victim would be stripped to the waist of any metallic object that might distort the wave. If a criminal's legs and feet remained to be buried, all the better.

Still, Firebird didn't panic. First light was hours away, and as she'd anticipated, Phoena wanted to wait until then—long after Brennen would be ready to come for her, if he truly meant to come. If he did—if he returned, risking himself for her sake—she must never doubt him again.

Had an hour and a half passed?

Phoena seated herself at the long marble desk below the southern window and touched a series of panels. Rogonin maneuvered Firebird along after her, keeping his grip tight on her shoulders. Others, whispering, formed half a circle a few paces behind them.

Above the desk, six visual screens lit. Each displayed a three-dimensional image of a stone corridor. Centered on the left screen were the double doors of the elevator shaft. As Firebird watched, they slid open. A yellow cloud started to spill out, driven by the lift's powerful fans.

Phoena gloated up at her. "Last chance, Firebird."

Firebird pressed her lips together. Brennen had insisted he could deal with the gas.

Movement on another screen caught her eye. As the cloud billowed downward, a man in House Guard red and black dashed into range of the wide-angle pickup, eyes down, running hard, a blazer clutched at his side.

"Phoena!" Firebird gasped. "Shut it down!"

The princess shrugged. "I signaled that there was no time to waste. I can sacrifice one guard to make the others realize they must obey my orders. And actually, this is perfect. There's something else I want you to see and hear."

The runner stopped, finally noticing the yellow cloud. Raising horrified eyes to the surveillance lens, he raised an arm in entreaty and waved the other arm back down the passage.

Phoena sniffed. Pale and wide-eyed, Tellai laid a hand on her shoulder. Rogonin grinned beside him.

"Now, then. We're fortunate to have a subject in view." Phoena reached forward, dragging her sleeve over the black marble tabletop. "I ordered this from offworld. 'Soniguard,' I think they call it. Federate technology. Watch." Her graceful finger stroked a small, glossy panel below the screens. Then a second, and a third. An eerie howl rose underfoot.

On screen, the guard's eyes bulged. He flung both hands to his ears.

Phoena sighed. "You'll appreciate this, Firebird, with your musical background. Those three notes induce what I'm told is a ringing in the brain, as if the entire skull were a bell. What is it, an overtone? At any rate, it's quite paralyzing. Fatal, eventually. All the cranial arteries rupture, one at a time."

Firebird's throat constricted. The guard retched, convulsed, and then collapsed onto the stone.

Brennen had just turned back to the massive guardwall when the first blast knocked him to his knees. It paralyzed his thoughts for two long seconds, while the second and third tones entered in deadly harmony. Invisible hands squeezed his brain. As his body curled into a fetal tuck, he struggled for recollection. He'd been trained to endure sonics, long ago. He must shut down blood flow to . . .

The pain bore deeper, making thought difficult. His epsilon carrier began to disrupt.

Phoena withdrew her hand from the panel and glared at Firebird. "You're wondering if your friend is far enough down the tunnel to be safe from this, I'm sure. We've installed relays clear to the airfield. I'd hoped to be able to test it."

As the guard's body vanished into bilious fog, Phoena turned fully around. "In fifteen minutes, the system will be flooded. But there isn't a gas suit in existence that can keep out sound waves. Who is it, wastling? Did Lord Corey turn traitor at Veroh, too?"

Firebird lunged for the glossy panels. She managed to touch one off before Rogonin heaved her away.

Phoena reactivated the tone. "That's enough. Guards. Restrain her." Five burly uniformed men moved in.

PHOENA

grand pause
a rest observed by the whole orchestra

Brennen blinked and pressed his temple through the chem suit's flexible mask. He knew he'd been stunned despite his effort. Silence blanketed the stone he lay on. His head pounded viciously. And the smell . . . foul . . .

He gasped. It made him retch.

Had he torn a leak as he fell?

Far above, he'd felt Firebird's fear mounting. He felt nothing there now. He didn't want to spend the energy for another quest pulse.

Poison gas! his own voice shouted, as from a distance. *You've been breathing it!* His fuzzed memory echoed, *tardema-sleep!*

It was a skill he'd learned for just such emergencies . . . but how deep should he send the cycle, to time his waking? How long until the gas cleared, and he could afford to breathe again? He turned inward and found his carrier. Another coughing spasm shook him.

Suddenly Firebird's emotions screamed, rousing all his instincts from a distance, just as she'd done at Veroh. Screamed—and then swiftly faded.

Horror-struck, Brennen opened one hand from the claw it had formed. He pushed it toward his pocket for the touch activator and worked out the first four letters of the detonation sequence. If he couldn't achieve tardema, then with his last effort—and one final touch—he would blow the lab.

They couldn't have killed her!

Yes, they could.

Battling the urge to breathe, Brennen turned inward for one more attempt to reach tardema.

Firebird had struggled frantically, but the guards caught her hands and dragged her to the metal table. One swept her gear onto the carpet and bent her backward over it. Another lunged for her feet and received a hard kick in the teeth in his mistress's service. The next seized both her knees and swung her around to lie flat.

An instant later she couldn't move, caught once again in a restraining field. She lay staring at the glittering white ceiling, her arms like immovable stone at her sides. The guards' hands pulled away. She lay panting, tears for Brennen streaming from her eyes.

"Nicely done," sang a female voice from somewhere she couldn't turn her head to see.

Close by, Phoena's voice held a note of deep satisfaction as she answered her friend, "This time she's ours, Liera." Then she spoke more softly. "Everything in one room, Firebird. Command post, secure sleeping quarters—and interrogation facility."

Something splashed into Firebird's face. It blinded her eyes and made her fight for breath. Brandy, she guessed from the piercing smell and the burning in her nose. She tried to spit, couldn't move even her head, and had to swallow. Phoena must've set the field on maximum range and strength. Only her eyelids responded, and her tongue, and she could slow her breath. Salty tears slowly washed away the stinging liquor.

When she could see again, a pink blur resolved into Vultor Korda's face. She averted her eyes.

"A toast!" shouted Rogonin's voice close by. "Netaia!"

"Wait," Phoena called. "Finn, bring glasses for everyone."

Firebird heard clinking and pouring as she blinked out the last of the fire in her eyes. Korda moved away.

"Netaia!" the shout echoed, followed by a wash of conversation.

Then Korda whined, "Highness . . . Your Highness, I sense a presence about your sister that I don't like."

The hubbub stilled. "Oh?" asked Phoena's voice, distant once more. "Explain yourself, Korda."

"I can't—quite—isolate the nuances. But, Highness, if she came with anyone at all, I think she did come with a Sentinel."

Cultured gasps and inhalations hissed on Firebird's left.

"You needn't be concerned if he—or she—was trapped in the tunnels," Korda explained, chilling Firebird. "But what if he hasn't yet entered the Height? They could be listening to us through her."

"They can do that?"

"Some can."

He was lying. He had to be.

"What do you recommend, Thyrian?" asked a low, menacing voice Firebird knew well. Rogonin.

"Kill her," Korda answered instantly. "Now. Or at least drug her. They can't touch or detect anyone who's unconscious."

"No, wait. Lock her up somewhere else," Tellai suggested. "Away from the command center. Alone, under guard."

Bless Tellai. Bless the little fop's cowardly heart.

"I don't want to move her." Light footsteps drew near, then Phoena's face. "Every second she isn't restrained, she could slip free."

"We could move the party," Tellai began, but another engine roar, flying low on approach, cut off his suggestion. Muttering voices clustered beyond Firebird's feet, probably near the communications console. She squeezed her eyes shut, trying to isolate the transmitted voice out of this commotion. Was it possible—had Governor Danton acted instantly on Tierna Coll's recommendation, after all, and sent Federate troops?

"No, no." Phoena's laugh sounded slightly giddy. "She's already here. I'm sorry you missed her at Tallis."

How could she laugh like that? She'd just killed at least one man. Maybe two . . . *Please, not two!*

The other voices finally quieted. Firebird faintly heard the static of an open line, then an answering voice. "We did not miss her, Your Highness."

Captain Friel!

"Explain yourself," Phoena snapped.

After a longish pause, Friel answered, "I'll be there momentarily. You say that you have her? Secure?"

"Absolutely."

"Alone?"

"So far."

"Do nothing until I arrive."

Whispers and muffled footsteps flowed away from the console. Phoena's face reappeared. "What's this, Firebird? You saw Captain Friel on Tallis? Perhaps there's something you would like to tell me?"

"Only this." Firebird's words came slurred. "You will not win."

Phoena hooted, reached aside, and seized a drinking glass from one of her friends. Firebird shut her eyes again, barely in time. More liquor splashed into her face.

A whooshing door admitted Friel several eternal minutes later. Bootsteps hurried to the restraining table. "This is amazing," Friel declared.

Firebird stared back at him.

Friel turned to address the gathering. "The hearing on Tallis went against us," he announced. "We were denied custody of Lady Firebird."

"But she was there?" Phoena strode to Friel's side.

"Absolutely."

"This makes no sense," Phoena argued. "They should have relinquished her without a murmur. Netaia's jurisdiction extends to all citizens, wher-ever—"

"But she's here, Captain Friel," Tel's voice interrupted. "Already."

"We were denied custody," Friel said evenly. "Has she told you why?"

"No," snapped Rogonin.

Firebird had never heard Captain Kelling Friel chuckle before. "Look at her," he directed Phoena's assembly. "First Major . . . Lady . . . Firebird Elsbeth Angelo. Wastling and traitor. Less than a week ago, standing in front of the Federacy's Regional council, First Marshal Burkenhamn, and myself, this woman swore allegiance to the Federacy."

"What?" Phoena's shout rose above the other shocked protests. "Don't taunt me, Friel. This is outrageous."

"Ask her."

"Firebird," Phoena cried. "Is this true?"

What could Phoena do worse than she already planned?

There were still hours before first light, Firebird realized, and Phoena—who knew all her worst fears—had just bragged about her interrogation facility.

"Korda," Phoena snapped. "Tell me. Did she do this thing?"

Firebird shut her eyes tightly. Footsteps approached once again. Prickly nausea touched the edge of her mind, but she thrust it away. She'd resisted a stronger Thyrian, and a better.

"Well?" Phoena demanded.

He probed again. Recalling his instructions, she envisioned her boot heels. She meant it as a taunt, and he would know it. But would he dare to admit failure to Phoena? *There's no mercy in your new mistress, Vultor Korda.*

"Your Highness." Korda oozed shock and sincerity. "Your Highness, it's . . . it's true."

Unbelievably, Phoena laughed—first lightly, then viciously.

Powers help me now, Firebird begged, and then she caught herself. There would be no more help from the nine Holy Powers.

All other voices fell silent. Phoena laughed on, and on, until her breath came in choking, hysterical gasps. The door whooshed. Voices murmured, fading, clustering, leaving in groups. Phoena's laughter grew desperate.

"Here," Tellai's voice soothed. "Take this. Wash it down with a little brandy. You'll need a good night's rest."

More helpless shrieking—then a momentary silence, the sound of chok-ing, and Phoena's frantic laughter subsided into a hoarse, hiccuping chuckle. "They're gone," she complained childishly. Whatever *take this* had been, it worked quickly. "Why did they leave? We could've had a good time."

"They'll be up very early, tomorrow." That was Rogonin, somewhere out of her field of vision. "Get your rest, Highness. The day will be glorious."

"Don't leave her alone," Phoena pleaded.

Tel's voice soothed. "There's a guard. Go to sleep, love. There. Shall I turn up the cover?"

Footsteps. The door whooshed again, and then silence fell like a curtain.

Firebird wrenched her eyes aside. A red-jacketed guard sat close by, studying a lap viewer. Phoena lay propped on a pile of gold-edged pillows, eyes closed, smiling even in sleep.

Sleep, Firebird reflected. She'd better rest. Phoena had guessed correctly: The moment they released her from the restraint field, she would spend every bit of energy she had left, trying to escape.

She couldn't shut her eyes, though. With Brennen almost certainly dead in the tunnels . . . or fled . . . the odds were enormous that she'd die at sunrise. Could she face an agonizing end bravely, confident that there would be no bliss, no Dark, no awareness at all beyond her execution?

If there wasn't, then her pain would end when the D-waves burned down to her major nerves. Then she'd simply cease to exist. Forever.

She shuddered. She couldn't summon enough faith to believe in an unending nothingness. Every instinct rebelled at the thought.

There had to be something beyond physical life, if only the echoes of death, fading into eternity. She couldn't expect help or mercy from the Powers. Her only hope must lie in something greater, much greater than even the Powers claimed to be. Something capable of forgiveness.

Had Brennen's people found the answer? A Speaker, a Singer . . . a composer-creator, a conductor of time's rhythms, who could punish her after her death for all her shortfalls and offenses . . . the life she'd just taken . . . or offer her mercy?

She desperately wanted that assurance, but she couldn't ask for it dishonestly. If she wanted death benefits, she felt she had to commit herself unconditionally, whether or not she lived past sunrise.

But I don't know enough to decide, she railed at the night. An answer came out of her memory: *Sometimes, it takes only a glimpse of His majesty.*

She lay still for several minutes, trying with all her might to imagine that kind of a person. She could picture huge, but not that huge. She could imagine old, but agelessness eluded her. And what about that hidden cost, that death Brennen had finally admitted as the final price?

She gave up. It was impossible. Unless . . .

Show me, she begged.

For an instant, nothing happened. Then an image flashed through her mind, of a vast, primal, and unending intelligence. It made a sudden music so incomprehensibly magnificent that the universe exploded into existence, every particle and energy wave singing praise at all frequencies, an exultant harmony that condensed into billions upon billions of brilliant stars and their attendant worlds. He was the ultimate otherness, the omniscience beyond any Sentinel's probing ability. He was the source of all life, and He was its goal, to which life would return enriched and ennobled. Strength and Authority were only the colors that robed Him, Valor and Fidelity His fingermarks on those who believed in His sovereignty.

Shocked by the image's richness, Firebird tried to seize and hold it, but it melted away like a symphony's last notes, too splendid for any recording to capture.

But even if she were too small to comprehend Him, He existed. He did!

Trembling inside, Firebird squeezed her eyes shut. She relaxed against the steely restraint table. *Take me, then. You are the one I have always wanted to know. Do what you will with my life and my death, even if that life can be measured in hours, and death comes hard. I'd rather die for you than the Powers.*

She listened, longing to hear an answer sung back, feeling tone-deaf compared to what she'd just heard. There was no voice, but her screeching fears had fallen silent, and now peace flooded her mind. If the Eternal Singer existed, who was Phoena to frighten her?

Exhausted, she plunged toward sleep.

Harsh human voices roused her to aching wakefulness and a terrible thirst, still constrained in a field that reeked of stale brandy. Footsteps hurried past. She opened her eyes and spotted several red-jacketed uniforms. The restraining field collapsed. Strong arms wrenched her up into a sitting position so suddenly that her vision dilated and almost winked out.

When it cleared, she saw four House Guards carrying weapons, standing close behind Captain Kelling Friel. It was Friel who gripped her shoulders.

This was no time to bolt. She'd have to wait for a better chance.

Phoena stepped through the line. "Ah," she cried, "you're awake." When Firebird saw what Phoena held in her hand, she changed her mind and flung caution away, springing up and aside. She almost slipped Friel's grasp before two others reinforced his hold.

Phoena laughed merrily. "Oh, you and needles. But I'm doing this for your sake. The more dearly you pay now, the better your chances of bliss . . . eventually." She drove a wicked silver spike through the thermal suit into

Firebird's shoulder, between Friel's fingers, then injected a stinging fluid. Firebird gasped. By the time she caught her breath, she recognized the sensory overload. Tactol again . . . and something more, this time. Her muscles tightened suddenly and firmly. She would've tried again to fling off the guards if they hadn't tightened their grip.

"Feel better?" Phoena tossed the medical nightmare onto the metal table. "Your color's better. Now you'll experience the full thrill of this hour, as I will."

Although Firebird's scraped hips and shoulders throbbed and burned, she felt as if she could climb Hunter Mountain in one leap, throttle all five guards at once (now she understood why Phoena had brought up so many of them), or tear the restraint table to pieces with her bare hands. But the injection had also intensified her emotions, and the sight of one guard's misshapen D-rifle, heavy chambered with a ceramic point at the barrel's end, aroused an adrenaline thrill of absolute terror. Another guard carried a massive tripod.

She would momentarily be reduced to a target, then to a victim dying in agony. She tried to relax, to control her fear and seize back the uncanny peace she'd found last night.

She glanced out the east window. "This hour," Phoena had said, and the faint glow beyond distant hills confirmed that less than an hour remained before sunrise. Her pulse beat in her ear like distant parade drums.

Where was Brennen? Had they found him, and was he dead or alive? Maybe he'd escaped. He must have, he must!

So these were her true feelings, sharpened by Phoena's drugs to pierce all her masks and defenses. She trusted and loved him. Completely. Even if they murdered her, even if he'd retreated to save himself, she'd die easier if somehow she knew he still lived.

But with morning arrived and their timetable long used up, then if he hadn't come for her, then he must be—he could be . . .

Brennen! she shrieked mentally. *Brenn, are you alive?*

Beneath the glowing chandelier, Phoena spoke under her breath to Tellai. Her dresser had robed her in another splendid gown, one that fit closely through the body and billowed out in a long dark skirt, looking like the legendary phoenix rising from its ashes. Tellai, in soft gray brocaded with silver, paled beside his regal mistress. A sweet spicy scent drifted from a pair of gilt cups on Phoena's bed.

Firebird bent forward and rested a little weight on her pressure-sensitive feet. "May I have a cup of cruinn?" she whispered to Captain Friel. "My mouth is full of dust."

He tightened his fingers. "I think not. You won't be thirsty for long."

Brennen, oh, Brenn. All the chances I wasted.

Phoena lifted something dark and limp off the bed, crossed the vast room again, and flung it at Firebird. A thin black jumpsuit with zipcloth closures landed at her feet, then a pair of flimsy night slippers. "Put them on," Phoena ordered. "And don't try anything, or I'll have you stunned and let you die out there naked."

The guards at her shoulders let go. Firebird turned her back and started to peel off her suit's bulky shirt. Her scraped shoulders, scabbed to its lining, felt as if they were being combed with knives.

Suddenly her spirit leaped. On the Height's north side, she'd hidden two blazers. If they hadn't been found . . . if she could stay free enough to dash toward them—

Another red-collared House Guard burst through the elevator door, saluting Phoena on the run. "We've caught the other one, Highness!"

Firebird gasped and went stiff. The guards grabbed her again.

Phoena splayed her fingers in the air. "Was Korda right? Is it one of *them?*"

The guard drew up even straighter. "Yes, Your Highness. His so-called Excellency, the former lieutenant governor."

"What? Not Caldwell," Phoena croaked. Tellai dashed to the lift.

"It is, Your Highness. And he's alive—barely. We took him in the east lab. But he's having trouble walking. I think he's harmless now. Korda should be able to tell us for sure. The rest of my detail is downlevel, disarming and collecting explosives."

"Ha!" Phoena breathed. "Someone tell Rogonin!"

Firebird's emotions whirled as she finished zipping into the execution jumpsuit. Harmless? Not Brennen. Never! But . . . if he wasn't, then how had they taken him?

Phoena hurried onto the lift and held a hand over its closing circuit. "Bring her. I don't want her out of my sight until it's over."

Yanked forward by her elbows and trying to exude meekness, Firebird boarded the lift.

In the living area, about forty people had gathered near the firebay, all wearing warm capes and coats except one. Brennen stood at an edge of the crowd, still wearing his boots and thick thermal pants but stripped of his thermal overshirt. Blinking as though barely awakened, he tottered from foot to foot. He didn't seem to see her.

Tellai bowed deeply and presented Phoena a priceless Ehretan crystace. She seized it and glared down her nose. "Good morning, Your Excellency.

Welcome to the Height. We've planned a brief ceremony in a few minutes, and I'd be pleased—delighted—to honor you beside my sister. Your fellow citizen," she growled.

"Let her go, Your Highness." Brennen's quavering voice horrified Firebird. Finally he glanced at her, with eyes that looked like dull gunmetal. "Send her to Danton. He'll take her offplanet. She'll never threaten you again."

Phoena snickered. "If you're trying one of those Sentinel command tricks, it's not working." She tucked his crystace into a pocket of the cape Tellai offered. "Someone check that skinshirt of his for metal. Where's Korda?"

"Here, Highness." The crowd parted to let the pale little man step through.

Firebird had never pictured their meeting this way. Korda advanced as Brennen looked away, trying to avoid the traitor's eyes.

"Do we really have him?" Phoena demanded. "Or is he shamming?"

Korda thrust a hand into Brennen's face. "There's no trace of shields on him," he gloated. "We have him."

No, no, Firebird pleaded. *Brennen, come back!*

"Prove it," Phoena demanded. "Tell us one of his secrets."

Brennen tried to back away from Korda. A House Guard shoved him forward again. Korda's eyes fell closed, and a rapt smile spread over his face. Firebird wondered what forbidden pleasures he was experiencing.

"Hoo," Korda crowed, "here's one for you, Phoena. Your mighty Master Sentinel really would rather die in your sister's place. He loves her!"

Hoots and suggestive glances answered Korda. Brennen glanced solemnly at Firebird, his eyes gray and yellow from the zistane gas he must've breathed. Then he dropped his chin and stared at the inlaid wood floor.

Captain Friel stepped forward. "Your Highness, that calls to mind something important. On Tallis, when Lady Firebird renounced Netaia, one of the Federates claimed she'd been living under Caldwell's guarantee of asylum. Furthermore—by the Nine, Your Highness—that oath of hers was taken at the tip of his sword!"

Phoena whirled around. "Yes," she crowed. "It all comes clear. I think we've found the *real* source of your intimate knowledge of Netaia, Your Excellency. Not poor Dorning Stele!" She stepped close to Brennen and slapped him, leaving crimson fingermarks on his pale cheek. "How dare you insult my house by trying to consort with its wastling?" She twisted her fingers into Brennen's hair and jerked up his head. "And you, Firebird. So this was the price of your treason. A lover. I should've guessed."

Firebird clenched her fists. Denying that charge would only remind Brennen how little she'd trusted him.

"The time!" Phoena exclaimed, swirling her cape onto her shoulders. "Tie her! Where's Rogonin? We can't wait."

One of the hallway guards moved in with a fat hempen rope. Brennen stared as the guard looped her wrists and then let her bound hands fall behind her back. The changing angle dug prickly fibers into her sensitized skin.

"Move," ordered Phoena. Firebird didn't dare try to bolt, leaving Brennen disabled in Phoena's hands.

Arm in arm, Phoena and Tellai led out the massive eastern doors, across the flagstones and left along the winding lane that descended to the airfield.

North, Firebird prayed. *Send them north.* She walked the paving beside Brennen and surrounded by guards. Her spirits sank further each time he stumbled, and every step jolted her tightly strung senses. Predawn cold flowed through her flimsy jumpsuit like ice water. She clenched and unclenched her hands to keep them warm as the road fell from the Height. Near the outwall, the procession turned left again onto the long northern field, where grassy, weedy terrain made slower going. Phoena and her friends dropped behind.

North. There still was hope. "Brenn?" she muttered.

He tripped once more, barely catching himself. "You woke me. Thank you."

Woke him? Had he heard her mental shriek, or her terror of Phoena's needle? How had he heard anything at all, if he was as helpless as Korda claimed?

Firebird glanced back over her shoulder. Phoena's people followed the guards by twos and threes, warmly bundled, few speaking. Two carried a long equipment locker between them. A rosy stripe glowed in pale gray clouds over the spot where the sun was about to rise. The glow hurt her eyes.

The guards had fallen back a few paces. "I hid two blazers," she whispered urgently, "in a pile of dead grass, near—"

She caught movement with one corner of her vision. The guards had caught up. Still, Brennen's quick side glance encouraged her.

Dew from the ankle-high grass soaked through her pant legs and flimsy black slippers. Side by side, they passed a stake driven into the ground. She guessed it at the customary thirty paces from the northern outwall. Four guards halted. She heard something clattering but refused to turn and look.

Her stomach twisted painfully. *The D-wave*, she heard again, *crazed a conscious patient with pain . . .*

Only Phoena would think to add Tactol to that misery.

At the outwall, two guards knotted the ends of the ropes binding her wrists to the freezing iron handrail. Two others placed Brennen a meter away.

"Your hands are behind the metal," one of Firebird's guards said smoothly. "Orders. 'Fingerprints are valuable proof of decease,' " he quoted, almost capturing Phoena's tone of voice. "But this isn't so tight that you can't shift them to the front of the rail, if you'd rather have it done cleanly."

Cleanly. Without leaving any part for Phoena to manhandle.

Another guard finished with Brennen and reached for his black neckscarf. "Do you want a blindfold, Lady Firebird?"

She shook her head steadily. If this was the end, she wanted to face it. If not . . . if they still had a chance . . .

The guards sauntered back to join the firing squad, who stood at attention behind four massive tripods, between Friel and Phoena. The princess's gown shone like orange flame among the guards' red berets and the others' more somber attire.

Now they stood alone, to die together. She never would've predicted this, back at Veroh. "Talk to me, Brenn," she pleaded.

"The knot is in reach of your right fingers."

She fumbled for it. Sure enough, a loop, fat and loose, lay inside her left palm. She picked at it with cold, swollen, supersensitive fingers. "I didn't think you were . . . done." Blessed freedom! She stretched enough slack from the loop to draw both hands through.

"Every minute they wait, I feel less sick. If I can get those blazers, are you up to shooting?"

The peak of Hunter Mountain gleamed suddenly orange, and slowly, the sunlit streak swept down toward the outwall. Firebird eyed the rifle squad . . . and Phoena, whose hatred and ambition had placed them here. "Yes," she murmured. "They've given me a stimulant. Are you really all right?"

"No," he admitted. He closed his eyes. She guessed he was focusing all the epsilon strength he'd regained. Couldn't she stall Phoena?

Not if that meant trying to hold off the dawn. Tellai strode out in front of the D-rifle line and called for quiet. Phoena would want to announce their offenses, and then invoke the Powers to witness this event. The "brief ceremony."

"Ready, Mari?" His voice was soft and steady.

"Brenn?" she whispered.

He glanced her way.

She had to tell him. "Brennen. I love you."

CHAPTER 23

FIREBIRD

allegro con fuoco
fast, with fire

"Loyal subjects of the Netaian queen," Phoena shouted. "At this dramatic moment—"

The ground shook with a low rumble.

Phoena froze before she finished her preamble.

The rumble echoed off League Mountain. Startled, Firebird slid her hands free of the loosened rope. Had Brennen even kept a touch card? Everyone had underestimated him, including her.

Phoena spun toward her intended victims. Firebird couldn't hold back a smile.

Phoena seemed to fill with hatred and purpose. "Present!" she shrilled to the execution detail.

Firebird glanced over Brennen's shoulder. Behind the house rose a dusky, billowing cloud.

"Sight!" Phoena screamed. The D-rifles swung on their tripods.

Firebird stared up two ceramic-tipped barrels into somber Netaian eyes. She shivered, and not from the cold. "Brenn," she muttered, clenching her fists. "Now or never."

He stretched out both arms to the compost heap. The handblazers flew toward his palms, trailing a litter of brown grass clippings. He tossed one weapon to Firebird.

Now she could fight back! She dropped to one knee on the frigid, wet grass and sighted up the nearest D-rifle, crouching as small as she could behind her metal blazer.

"Fire," Phoena shrieked, "fire!"

Firebird aimed for the House Guard, squeezed her firing stud . . . and missed. Phoena's drugs made her wrists and elbows quiver. Several of Phoena's friends bolted toward the house.

Brennen extended an arm again, reaching into the gesture with his whole body. As the D-rifles started to thrum, his crystace sailed from

Phoena's cloak pocket. Phoena grabbed for it, lost her balance on the uneven ground, and fell facedown in the weeds.

A weird, heatlike pain crept up Firebird's extended left foot. She yanked it closer to her body, behind that frighteningly small blazer, then fired again, aiming higher. She dropped the guard as Brennen caught and activated his crystace one-handed. To Firebird's amazement, he flung it away. It soared for the D-rifles. As Brennen, too, crouched to fire, it whirled through two rifle barrels, slicing off their ceramic points.

One of the disarmed D-riflemen lunged for a hand weapon the dead guard had dropped in the weeds. Firebird felled him as Brennen got the other man.

The horizon glowed. The light made her eyes water, but her clumsy-numb hands began to feel warm. She swept the scattering crowd with her sights for the ample silhouette of His Grace, Muirnen Rogonin. Had he drunk too much of Phoena's brandy to rise early?

So she happened to see Vultor Korda fall, twitching, and the satisfied expression on Brennen's face, and the crystace returning again to his hand.

A blazer bolt flashed past Brennen's shoulder. Forgetting Rogonin and Korda, Firebird returned fire. The redjacket swung his arm, and again she looked down a weapon's bore. Brennen's crystace swept in and deflected the shot. Firebird squeezed again. *Got him!*

With the last threats down or fleeing, Firebird relaxed her wrist. Then she spotted Count Tel Tellai across the tussocks of weeds, unarmed but bravely shielding Phoena with his body while she waved wildly at somebody else. The odds were still forty to two. Firebird's finger crept back toward the firing stud. *Should I?*

Down the shaft of her energy pistol Tellai drew up, stretched tall, and braced himself.

She hesitated. He *was* only a child. He'd been decent last night. She couldn't let herself become a cold-blooded killer.

She lowered the blazer.

Tellai gaped.

"Let's get out of here, Brenn!" Over the outwall, up the mountain . . . and then where? If Phoena kept her wits, she'd quickly lock down all vehicles, send Friel for infrared snoops, and hunt them down. How long could Brennen keep moving? Besides the gas, there'd been that hideous Soniguard attack. At least after an hour, when the Tactol wore off, she'd feel normal . . . if she were still alive.

The crystace's hum snapped off behind her.

Across the field, Phoena shouted to someone. Firebird caught the word "airstrip." Tellai and four others dashed down the field for the back gate.

"Brenn!" Firebird cried. "If they can put a fighter in the air, we're groundside targets!"

"Then we'll beat them."

She couldn't think of a better idea. Finally releasing her unnatural energy, she sprinted after Tellai. Each step jostled her spine. Before she'd taken ten painful steps, Brennen shouted from far to her left.

She stumbled to a halt. He'd headed for the northern outwall instead of the gate, running as if one leg hurt. She angled back to join him. The sun crept at last over the horizon, and she winced at the brilliance of . . . everything. At that moment he turned and shouted, "Drop!"

She plunged into prickly weeds that felt like small knives. A bolt of green light blew a stone from the wall, piercing the spot where she'd stood an instant before. Prone himself, Brennen fired once.

"This way!" He sprang back to his feet and started to climb hand over hand. "Hurry. I missed. It's Friel, in the trees."

He could've jumped that wall. His strength must be going. She hoisted a foot onto the handrail. As she did, she dropped her blazer. Another shot cracked a rock at her knee. She pushed up, caught the top of the wall, and peered back for her weapon.

"Leave it!"

She linked her hand around Brennen's wrist, clambered over the weathered gray top stones, and dropped with him onto the canyon's rim. Far to her right, five men sprinted in a group, halfway down the airstrip lane. Below on the apron lay four Netaian tagwings, golden darts glistening among shadowy private craft.

She bit her lip. If they couldn't get away, they'd have to hide here in the mountains. If only they could call Danton, for backup—

Brennen snatched her hand. He pulled her through rocks and bushes to the steepest point of the rim, directly over the tagwings. "Up!" he puffed. Before Firebird could protest that he was too weak, he swung her into his arms . . . and leaped.

She clung to his neck as the cliffs flew by. This time, the plunge made bile rise in her throat. "Can you fly . . . a second tagwing?" she demanded, gulping.

"If Burkenhamn can fit, we can. Barely."

Together?

The permastone apron rushed up. He released her at the last second. She landed hard, tumbling, then scrambled up, feeling as if she were covered with bruises. She glanced back. He was coming. Limping. She dashed up the apron for the nearest fightercraft.

The stepstand was gone, but she'd sprung onto a fore wing hundreds of times. She slapped the escape panel to raise the bubble, then jumped in. *Was* there room? She was small. Brennen wasn't large or tall.

He sprang for the cockpit and fell short. Firebird flung out a hand. She pulled him aboard as he leaned heavily on her arm.

"Ankle?" she asked, sliding the inclined seat to its maximum forward position, the way her crew chief usually set it.

"It's all right." He tried to struggle into the aft cargo bin.

"Too small back there," she realized. "Get up here on the seat. I'll sit in front of you." She stood up, leaned forward, and touched in a code sequence to ignite the laser-ion generator. Its roar rose to a hideous howl in her ears. Groaning, she covered them as Brennen settled onto her seat and locked it down at maximum-back.

"Can *you* fly?" he demanded.

She remembered the other time, and her all-Academy record. "If I'm angry enough," she answered, squeezing down onto the seat. It was tight. Too tight.

Brennen tried to pull the flight harness around both of them while she sealed the cockpit. "Too short," he gasped over the generators' roar. She looked for a helmet. Only a headset dangled beneath the display. Was she setting herself up for ear damage?

Better deaf than dead, she decided. She didn't want to talk to anyone here anyway. "I guess even Burkenhamn isn't this big around. Secure yourself and hold me." She hastily checked her controls. She'd done no walk-around. This could be a short, nasty flight.

"Wait." Brennen's right arm dug into her back, and then he handed her a lump of something sticky and gray. "Wet it," he instructed. "Wet it *well*, then put it in your ears."

She divided the lump, spit on both halves, then improvised a pair of ear plugs. When she sat back, Brennen's arms circled her waist. She barely had room to breathe.

Something moved away down the apron. The runners had reached the strip. One had raised the canopy of the far tagwing and was climbing aboard. Others had nearly reached the next ships. Firebird pivoted her fightercraft to starboard and fired its twin laser cannon down the row, enveloping the golden ships with scarlet lightning that made her wince and blink. Two men dove for cover. The nearest ship burst into thousands of metal shards. Then the second.

The third hull merely twinkled. "His slip-shield's up," Firebird cried. "I can't take him broadside now. But I don't think he'll oblige us by taking off first."

"We can't stay here." Brennen peered around her left ear. The other tagwing's engines glowed. "Get up fast if you want a good chance in a scrap. Do you know who that is?"

"No. But I hope he's a redjacket." *I am angry enough!* Firebird cut the brakes, raised shields, and careened off the apron onto the strip, accelerating at max before she hit the canyon straightaway. Seconds later, she pulled up. She banked hard starboard instantly to avoid being blasted from behind.

They skimmed Hunter Height, just clearing the outwall, where a large area of eastern slope had collapsed. Brennen had done it—enough charges had remained hidden and armed to bury the basium lab. But now her stern sensor board picked up her pursuer. The display showed that he'd dropped both shields, coaxing extra speed from his engines. Apparently the pilot was no amateur, and he meant to finish them quickly.

With double shields, she couldn't shake him. Spinning full starboard, she singled the shield. Projectile protection dropped away, and a surge of acceleration pressed her spine against Brennen's chest. *Let him leave those shields down*, she pleaded silently. *I wouldn't have to hit an engine port, I could take him with a side shot!* But his extra velocity kept him out of her sights, above and behind, closing fast to make the kill.

All right, then. We die trying. Save me a place in your choir, Mighty Singer. Simultaneously, she cut out her last shield, angled straight up, and laid into a fast roll. For a terrifying moment she passed directly in front of him. An energy burst caught the tip of her tail fin. The pitch threw her off her seat's edge. "Hold me, Brenn!"

His arms tightened.

Then inspiration struck. She wrenched the emergency blackout switch off her left-hand sideboard, cutting sensors and display to fly virtually blind, diverting the last erg of generator output into her engines. Totally inverted, her fighter looped back. The hillside spun crazily above the cockpit as she turned about, riding her instincts, pushing for the top of the tagwing's envelope.

Suddenly, incredibly, the other tagwing slid past the center of her cockpit bubble. She gripped a firing stud and reactivated her particle shield. A flash momentarily blinded her. Then the hull tinkled like singing metallic rain.

"We did it!" she cried, blinking. She righted the tagwing and cut speed to unload the generator. The horizon circled back down to where it belonged.

"Mari." Brennen exhaled the name like a sigh. "You are a Firebird. Well flown." His head fell on her shoulder.

"Well. With his shields down it was like hitting a radio dish. Easy." Wishing her voice had a little less shake, she wagged the damaged rudder. It seemed stiff.

Stiff, like Baron Parkai's body would be, by now . . . and she'd just disintegrated a Netaian pilot. . . .

Her eyes thickened.

"Easy," murmured Brennen. "You had to. You saved yourself. And me."

She drew a deep breath, and it calmed her slightly. *Phoena's drugs!* This was no time to grieve. "I don't suppose we'd better stay around."

"Probably not." She felt hair pulled back from her throat, and a warm kiss below her left ear.

"Don't," she begged. Nothing had ever felt so unbearably wonderful. "Citangelo, then?" She'd love to try that fast vertical roll again, with no one shooting. "Or should we pick up that messenger ship?"

"Citangelo. Danton can pick up the Brumbee before Phoena spots it. We should get offworld. Quickly."

"How?" Without that messenger ship . . .

"Citangelo," he repeated. "A drop-in with orders for Danton, and we'll pick up a ship with a little"—he flexed his left foot, sandwiched between hers and the hull—"more room."

One-fingering a long arc to port, she chuckled. "Orders? Who takes orders from whom, Brenn? You or Danton?"

"Call it news, then. Intelligence."

Laughing, she cried, "Hang on!" and sent the tagwing high into the morning sky, in the wildest victory roll ever negotiated over the craggy Aerie Mountains.

Then she soared southwest, staying low over the foothills of the Flenings, avoiding the central plain for as long as possible. Abruptly she pulled her hands off the controls. "Cleary!" she gasped.

"Dead, I assume." Brennen shifted one hand on the sideboard. "Just before they took me uplevel, I saw her in the chamber outside the basium lab, wearing a sniffer and hunting explosives—carrying several."

"Oh." She checked her altitude. She couldn't regret *that* woman's death. "Then here's one for Cleary!" She seized the stick. Again the horizon spun, but this time she didn't mind the dizziness. "What *was* she building?"

"Can you wait until I discuss it with my superiors?"

"Brenn?" She wriggled one cramped, slippered foot. "This time, I'd be glad to wait." She still felt supercharged, too full of emotion to speak rationally, to tell Brennen that she'd discovered how deeply she loved him.

He has to know, she reflected. *He must be choosing not to take unfair advantage.*

A softer kiss warmed the side of her throat. She leaned back her head and pressed it against his, ear to ear. "Thank you," she whispered. Again, his restraint seemed a priceless gift.

"Would you show me," he asked, "what happened after we separated?"

Access? Perfect. She felt awkward about trying to tell him what she'd seen and heard—and asked—lying on that restraint table. "Sure," she said lightly. "Go ahead. Just don't distract me from driving."

She relaxed into the warm, tingling sensation and watched memories speed past, as quickly as the foothills that slipped by below them.

They halted at the very moment when she'd imagined, and loved, One who'd sung in solitary magnificence; One who offered mercy and had given her peace, even such a small detail as a good night's rest.

"Mari," he exclaimed in a joyful whisper. His arms tightened around her middle.

"Maybe He helped us," she suggested. "Just now."

"Yes," he said hoarsely. She thought she heard his voice catch. "Yes," he repeated.

Half an hour farther south, as she crossed the Division River between the old town of Treya and metropolitan Kerrigy, a pair of elegant black Federate intercept fighters roared into escort position behind them and challenged over the interlink. Brennen reached for the dangling headset and answered in some kind of code. The other pilot sounded chagrined as he acknowledged Brennen's transmission. The pair peeled away as neatly as skin from a banam fruit.

She needed no warning to keep quiet herself. If anyone official found out she were here, she'd be instantly arrested, charged again with her crimes, and locked down.

The tagwing's roar slowly faded. Finally, she reached for one ear plug.

"Let me," said Brennen, and he carefully dug out both lumps.

She sighed and shook her head.

As she followed the Tiggaree into Citangelo, Brennen reached for the headset again. "Would you object to waiting in the tagwing while I talk to Danton? I'll hurry."

"No, that's all right." The familiar autumn colors of Citangelo's western outskirts swept beneath her. She was flying on visual and savoring the still-brilliant reds, golds, and browns. If her flight trainer had spoken over the interlink, she wouldn't have been surprised.

With another series of obscure-sounding transmissions, Brennen obtained landing clearance at the occupation base, then shut off the interlink and spoke softly against her ear. "You can still stay here if you want, Mari. This will always be your home world. I'm sure Danton would eventually untangle your legal status." He smoothed her hair over her shoulders. It made her tremble. "But you're welcome to go back with me to Tallis and face the consequences."

"Tallis," she said. "Of course. Do you think you're in trouble with Regional?"

"Danton will tell me. One way or the other." With words, she understood, or in ways only Brennen would notice.

She dropped the tagwing on an unfamiliar new breakaway strip and taxied, at Brennen's direction, toward an L-shaped stone and metal building with a tall viewing tower. As Brennen squeezed out, she stared at his face. It still was pale, but no longer yellow.

"I won't be long," he said. "You might want to keep your head down." He slid carefully to the ground and strode off, slowly, favoring his right ankle.

Tel steadied himself with one arm against a master room wall. He couldn't believe what he was hearing. Carradee jelly-bones was standing up to Phoena! After last night and this morning, he was almost glad.

"I told you," Phoena seethed into the tri-D pickup over her desk. "Caldwell was here—and with Firebird, like a mated pair! And of course it was a laboratory. You would've known that if you'd given it half a brain. Catch them! Don't let them offworld! She's sworn allegiance to the Federacy!"

"What were you building?" Carradee demanded. "You've played this secrecy game long enough."

Phoena clenched her fists. Her shoulders trembled.

"You'd better tell her," Tel whispered. "You may need her on your side."

"An ecological weapon." Phoena clipped each word. "Toxin-synthesizing algae, and a mechanism to make it bloom through an entire ocean system."

"To . . . to foul an entire living world, just as Cleary claimed."

"In days. The basium helps it along somehow. But they've destroyed the entire tunnel, my spore stock, the basium concentrate we just seized—"

"Enough!" Carradee's nightrobed likeness stood tall and imperious, and for one moment, Tel saw their mother instead of Carradee. "Phoena, as of this moment you are confined to your suite at the palace, and it will be thoroughly inspected before you walk in. We will send an escort for you, and if you value your safety, you will cooperate. We shall also send a team of engineers to see if the Height's understructure is reparable."

Phoena glared back. "The Federates should pay to rebuild it. They gave no fair warning, made no request—they just obliterated the east end. It'll take months to rebuild."

"If you rebuild that laboratory you will face sedition charges!" Carradee's passionate sincerity shocked Tel. Finally, Phoena had pushed too far. "You defiled the Height! You swore you were conducting a cultural retreat, and we trusted you. We—I took your word. I should have my head examined."

Tel glanced from sister to sister, alarmed. For the first time, he realized the Federates might take vengeance on Phoena, and—he swallowed—himself.

"Have you any more to say?" Carradee demanded.

"Don't let them get away, you incompetent! She's betrayed us completely!"

Carradee gulped air like a skitter. "If we find Firebird, we'll detain her. But if you break arrest, Phoena, then Powers help us, we'll send the redjackets after you, too!"

Brennen slipped into the governor's office without waiting for the secretary to announce him. Danton looked up from his bluescreen. He radiated alarm. "Caldwell! What in Six-alpha are you doing here? Tallis has asked me to detain you on sight." He set down his stylus. "So get out of my sight."

That was bad news, but Brennen couldn't bring himself to care. He walked forward as quickly as he could. His legs still felt weak, and his ankle throbbed despite his effort to numb it. He longed to lie down, to rest . . . preferably in Mari's arms.

"You had a tetters' nest up north, Lee," he said. "Hunter Height, a private estate—"

"Yes, I had that message yesterday from Tierna Coll, but we couldn't find the locale on any map. I put in a query to the queen's office."

Brennen reached for a map projection on the wall behind Danton's desk chair. "Here. They've kept it off maps, so I'm not surprised you couldn't find it. Phoena Angelo converted it into a nuclear laboratory. They were modifying bombs."

"That would be the height of stupidity," Danton objected.

"True. You'll want to send a mop-up crew, and a pilot to pick up a DS–212 Brumbee just over this ridge." He pointed again. "We left about fifty angry loyalists, probably armed. But they've no tagwings now, and no ordnance lab."

Danton rubbed his chin. "Bombs? But they signed a treaty."

"Dig it out if you want, sir. I'm leaving." He paused with one hand on a corner of Danton's desk. "What about Lady Firebird?"

"Caldwell, we have no idea where she is. None."

Brennen nodded thanks.

A small red light began to pulse beside a label on Danton's link board. It read "Angelo."

Brennen stepped backward. "If I were looking for me, knowing I might be in trouble, I'd try the Sentinels' sanctuary in the Procyel system." He offered a hand. As Danton clasped it, Brennen opened an unguarded corner of the governor's mind. *If that's Carradee, stall her.* Then he spun on his good foot and asked, "Would you clear an unidentified 721 for takeoff?"

"Consider it done." As the door closed, Brennen heard Danton's polite diplomat's voice ask, "Good morning, madam. May I help you?"

Brennen slipped out a side door toward the tagwing and glanced around. No one was in sight. Danton's doing, he guessed. He hurried toward Firebird.

She'd seen Him! And last night, she'd heard a music he'd never imagined in such heartbreakingly beautiful detail . . . and she'd watched it take effect. She'd been given a vision and a song by the Speaker himself, a glimpse—as Brennen had predicted—of His majesty.

He slowed his stride. Some of his people would say he still mustn't take her for his own until she'd formally joined their community.

But she'd received that image with childlike delight and offered herself as the sacrifice. He couldn't wait to see and feel her response when she learned that other blood had paid the price.

Holy One, I'm only a man. All that I am is your gift, including these desires . . . and this certainty that someday, we'll serve you together.

He'd reached the tagwing. His pulse quickened.

Firebird helped Brennen check the five-seat shuttle for liftoff. Her ears still rang from flying unhelmeted, despite the earplugs. Instead of programming the course for Tallis, though, Brennen gave the computer liftoff instructions only.

Then she felt his awareness touch her senses again, a deeper access than before, a long, tender stare at her moment of vision. She felt calmer now. Phoena's drugs were wearing off. As Brennen's probe re-created the instant she'd tried so hard to stretch out, her longings rose with it. She ached to rest in that peace, that mercy . . . that music . . . forever. In life and in death.

Brennen glanced aside. That broke the feathery sense of access, but he turned back to her. "Mari?"

Now she must face it: He also knew that she'd discovered how deeply she loved him. She sat erect in her flight seat, steadying both hands against the control panel. Ready-lights flashed across the board.

"We don't need to slip directly back to Tallis," he said. "The intelligence I took from that laboratory will keep, for now. I want to take you to Hesed House."

Firebird reached forward and released the flight brakes. "Where's that?" she asked, but she guessed his intention. Her hand trembled.

"Hesed is a sanctuary of my people." Thrust caught them, and they lifted. "A retreat, like Hunter Height but more pastoral. It is our traditional place for wedding. I can't offer you pomp." He touched her hand on the console. "You know what I offer."

Yes, she knew. Though the idea of bonding still frightened her, he offered it like a gift. She'd been a fool when she fought him for the right to die.

So what kept her from accepting him? Was it Netaian tradition, or cowardice? She didn't fully understand him. That might take a lifetime. But she knew enough, loved enough, to embrace his mysteries—and his certainty— and to step out on this path, too. Again she heard, or remembered, a timeless harmony.

She straightened. "Brenn, if you're willing to take a Netaian, I can face your pair bonding."

He gripped her hand. Instantly, she felt the same gust of approval that had blown through her mind in the high Tallan valley. This time, though, it carried an undercurrent of assurance and joyous anticipation. Brennen's eyes shone under blue striplights. He entered the destination coordinates for a south-spinward slip.

Stars sprang one by one from the blackness of space as Netaia's horizon curved far below. Unconsciously she started to hum, and then she almost laughed aloud. Another melody had sprung into her mind, her ballad of Iarla, the wastling queen who'd triumphed over her fate. Though still unfinished, it swelled in her heart like an anthem. She suspected she'd be able to write the other verses now.

Brennen smiled. "Ten seconds to slip," he said.

"Ready."

Like fire kissing water, the ship winked out of Netaian space.

AUTHOR'S NOTE

Most fiction, including most science fiction and fantasy, begins by asking, "What if. . . ?" In creating a spiritual struggle for Lady Firebird, I asked one of those questions: What if God had created a universe without Earth, and a chosen people with a vastly different history?

If the culture prepared to receive the Messiah had been obliged to wait two or three thousand years longer, then before He was born they might have developed space travel. They could've terraformed other worlds and experimented with genetic engineering, playing out Israel's cycles of sin and repentance under the Judges on a galactic scale. A few children might have escaped God's wrath in an arklike generation ship, and even in exile, a faithful remnant might await His birth. The Jews of Christ's time expected a military deliverer; these exiles might hold a similar hope.

Though their history would be different, they would know the same truth. God would have sent prophets to teach them that personal salvation rested on an atonement that was only symbolized by their ancient sacrifices. Their highest commandments would be to love the One God with all of their hearts, minds, and strength, and to love—to serve—their neighbors as themselves.

Our Lord's family tree includes people who were no more priestly than Lady Firebird Angelo, and at least one woman who wasn't born Jewish. Many, though—like Brennen Caldwell—knew the prophecies. I wonder how many men and women looked down into a cradle and wondered, "Could this be my King?"

Intriguing possibilities, but only speculation. The Firebird series isn't a spiritual allegory, but only an extended—slow-motion—parable of conversion. God actually sent our Messiah into a small Jewish household two thousand years ago, on an exquisite blue-and-white planet that He spoke into existence.

Kathy Tyers
Montana
September 1998

CHAPTER 1

NIGHT ATTACK

notturno minore
night piece in a minor key

Even rain on wet leaves can sound ominous after midnight.

Firebird stopped walking and listened intently. The dark hours were slipping away, but she'd awakened with both calves bound up in excruciating muscle cramps. Pausing on her third lap around a long, windowless training room, she felt positive she'd heard something—someone—out in the passway.

She would've known if that were Brennen.

Barefoot, she crept across the cushioned mat. Once a storage area, this room bristled with weapons, simulators, and exercise equipment. A home-security master board glimmered behind the flight simulator. She bent toward it.

One of her unborn sons kicked her ribs in protest.

Firebird straightened and pushed red-brown hair back from her face. She'd hoped to command a star cruiser someday . . . she never hoped to resemble one. Now, six and a half months pregnant with twins, she suspected she did.

She snugged the belt of her flimsy nightrobe. On the security board, an image of their two-story hillside home gleamed in pale yellow holo. Each entry and window shone red, fully covered by sensors and dispatch circuits. Brennen had invested his Federate severance pay in a lovely, defensible location near Thyrica's primary military base, then installed the best available home sec system. In ten years of intelligence work, he'd made enemies.

The board showed no sign of intrusion.

Firebird glanced over her shoulder. Blame pregnancy hormones, but she wasn't convinced. She despised this maternal jumpiness, this urge to protect herself at all cost. She'd been a military pilot, qualified on advanced fighter-craft and small rms.

Still, these days she must protect two other lives. She needed to be jumpy.

Brennen had merely rolled over when she slipped painfully out of bed. She wondered if she ought to go back and wake him now. She'd done that two nights ago, when she thought she heard noises. They found nothing wrong.

Deciding she didn't want her pride stung again, she opened a weapons cupboard. She bypassed several training knives, a broadsword, and two deadly service blazers. A bulky shock pistol—her weapon of choice, a gift from her husband—lay behind the blazers. Hefting it expertly, she thumbed a stud on one side of the grip and quickly checked its charge.

Husband. Unbelievably, she had a husband. Last year, she'd forsaken her home world, with its holy laws and traditions that demanded her death, and married Field General Brennen Caldwell. He'd been her enemy when they met. An expert telepath, he showed her how badly she wanted to live. He won her trust and introduced her to faith . . . and Firebird had never dreamed of love like Brennen gave her, day after night after day. Eight months ago, they had pair bonded in his people's way, linking their lives and their feelings in a marriage only death could end.

She reached for the door control, then hesitated again. She really would rather Brenn didn't find her prowling armed. If she stepped out into that passway quivering with nerves, her worry would wake him. The Ehretan pair bond sensitized each of them to the other's strong emotions, even though she was no trained telepath.

Quiet my heart, Mighty Singer . . . and help me, she prayed. Her determination, her jumpiness, and even her fond concern for her twins ebbed away. She touched the door control.

The steel panel silently slid aside. She braced against it until her eyes adjusted. Across the passway, diffuse city light filtered up Trinn Hill into their second bedroom. She peered out its glasteel window-wall. Rain had softened into thick fog. Two tiny red eyes shone out for a few seconds, then extinguished. Thyrica's planetary developers must've had a sense of humor, she guessed, to create those fist-sized, oozy night-slugs.

She steadied the shock pistol between her hands. Trying to move as serenely as the deep night, she shuffled toward a bend in the passway. She adjusted her grip on the pistol and then peered around the corner.

Her breath caught. Silhouetted by a floor-level luma, a wiry stranger stood facing into the master room. He braced against the doorway with his left arm. She couldn't see his right hand.

She squeezed her pistol's grip.

The stranger whirled, brandishing a black energy blazer in one blackened hand. He thrust his other hand toward her too, palm outward.

Firebird knew that gesture too well. "Brenn!" she shouted. She shot a wild burst—

Then toppled sideways, dropping her pistol with suddenly limp fingers. The intruder had a telepath's power of voice-command. Her right shoulder hit the wall, and she pitched toward the floor. She mustn't fall hard—must not miscarry—but her arms turned to jelly. She couldn't catch herself.

As she flopped on the carpet, barely missing her pistol, she felt Brennen come fully awake. His confusion burst into the back of her mind. Less than a second later, the hall flashed blood red with blazer fire. The prowler's attention shifted to Brennen. Freed from command, Firebird groped for her pistol.

"Mari!" Brennen shouted. "Stay down!"

She raised her head. A four-armed silhouette danced wildly atop their bed, grappling and kicking. She crawled forward on her elbows and knees. If she could get into the room quickly, she might stun both men with one burst and hit the house alarm.

Too late! Deadly red lighning flashed again. Half the silhouette flew toward the bedroom window-wall, and then—unbelievably—glasteel exploded. "Brenn!" she cried, pushing up on her knees just outside the door, struggling for balance. An alarm klaxon blared. Flood lamps activated outdoors.

"Stay there," he called again from the bed. His combat focus throbbed in her awareness, but his voice sounded steady. "He's gone. Don't come in, though. There's glasteel everywhere."

Warm light flooded the master room. Her husband perched on the foot of their bed, dressed in drawstring trousers and aiming a blazer out into the night through a gulf that had been their security window-wall. Middle-sized, muscular without any extra bulk, he stared down the blazer's sights as if he'd been welded to the weapon.

Firebird lumbered to her bare feet and backed into the extra bedroom to look outdoors. Under the flood lamps, fog dripped from fragrant, ever-green kirka-tree limbs onto soggy undergrowth. The night-slug had left a gleaming slime trail, but she saw no footprints. Damp, resin-scented air drifted into the house. The klaxon's tritonal wailing shut off.

A warm hand touched her shoulder. Brennen's concern wrapped around her, warming her much better than her flimsy nightrobe could do. His pale russet hair drooped over one ear, flattened by six hours of sleep, but his cheeks looked flushed, and his intensely blue eyes showed no drowsiness. He still gripped a blazer down at his side. "Are you all right?" he asked.

"I'm fine," she said, catching her breath. "Just a little bounced around. But are you?"

"Yes. Stay out of the bedroom. I'm calling Alert Forces."

Stepping back, she clenched a fist. Thyrica's Alert Forces tracked the lawless Shuhr, renegade cousins of Brennen's telepathic kindred. She had wondered if someday those enemies might attack Brennen just because he was the strongest Sentinel of his generation. "I'm coming with you," she declared.

"Well—yes. You could lie down in the study." He paced up the hall, comforting her with his presence but keeping both hands free, on the chance the intruder might come back.

Firebird followed. She hated feeling vulnerable. At any other time, she might've gone out the window chasing that prowler.

Brennen jabbed the com console near the steel door, then raised one eyebrow. "No contractions?" he murmured. "You're sure you're all right?"

Sensing his worry, actually feeling it secondhand on the pair bond, she let him feel her own concern . . . and spotted a reddening streak on his right forearm. "He grazed you!"

A male voice blared through room speakers, reverberating off durahcrete walls. "General Caldwell, your alert's lit up. False alarm?"

Brennen turned away, hiding his scorched arm, but now she spotted blood trickling down his left shoulder and side. "Real thing. We're all right, but we'd appreciate backup."

"On its way. Your location?"

"Downlevel. Secure room. Intruder's gone, we think."

"Stay there."

Brennen paced back to the half-open steel door, still gripping that blazer. Misty air seeped along the floor.

Shivering, Firebird crossed to the weapons cupboard. She was too full of adrenaline to sit down, and only starting to realize they'd survived a murder attempt. Had the intruder wanted Brennen, or her . . . or both? "What happened to your shoulder? Your side?"

He craned his neck. "Oh? Glasteel, probably. Not serious." He'd taken life-threatening injuries in intelligence work. He'd also saved her life. Twice—no, three times. "I'll get you to College," he said. "Master Spieth can watch you for complications."

"Good idea." She bent over to seize one of the other blazers and a half-used spool of medical biotape and was soundly punched again.

All right, then, I don't resemble a star cruiser. A cruiser-carrier. "I guess our secret's about to come out," she complained. She'd gone into hiding as soon as her pregnancy showed, hoping to shock her family with the news just before their twins arrived . . . and Netaia's nobles would be deeply shocked. Brennen, blessed with a knack for avoiding danger, had agreed she should vanish for a while.

"You stayed out of the public eye long enough, Ex-princess," he said tenderly, raising an eyebrow as he cupped one hand over his forearm.

"I never was a princess," she insisted through gritted teeth. "Let's tape that burn."

He swept her long hair back over her shoulder. "Well . . . no. It probably needs more than biotape. I'll let Master Spieth treat it."

"That was close."

He nodded.

"Hurting?"

"It's blocked." Among other Sentinel skills, he could cancel nerve impulses. "I'm more worried about you."

"Let me clean your shoulder, Brenn."

He craned his neck. "Still bleeding?"

"A little."

"It doesn't hurt. Just leave it."

"Did you pick up any clue to who that was?"

"No." He strolled back to the door—standing guard, she assumed, but wanting not to worry her.

Good try, Brenn.

"What woke you up?" he asked.

"Leg cramps. Again," she groaned, massaging her left calf.

He peered out. "I never thought I would thank the Holy One for your leg cramps."

Neither had she. But if she'd been asleep a few minutes ago, they might both be dead.

She shivered again and snatched a high-protein bar off a shelf. Medical Master Spieth supplied these nourishing snacks by the crate.

Two of his Sentinel colleagues arrived four minutes later. "Mistress Firebird," one exclaimed.

"Hello, Dardy." She extended a palm to Air Master Damalcon Dardy, whose massive frame belied a boyish face. Hoping he wouldn't feel her hand shake as he clasped it, she said, "Haven't talked to you in months."

"Are you all right?" he asked. Then he took a second look. "Oh my," he said softly. "Are you *sure* you're all right?"

"So far as I know. Thanks for coming."

Dardy and his partner walked them around the house. Built by a retired star captain who'd spent too much time between Federate systems in a tiny messenger ship, the hillside home had a rambling upper story and a long deck that overlooked central Soldane and distant Kyrren Fjord, and a double rooftop landing port. Dardy's partner's instrument scan plainly showed large shoe prints leading up to—and through—its airlock-type main entry.

Firebird shuddered. So much for advanced security.

As she reentered her home, Soldane city police arrived. The officers took statements, low-light images of the intruder's entry and getaway, and more scans. Though they addressed Brennen respectfully, Firebird noticed they never stood close to any of the three Sentinels. It had taken her, too, a long time to trust these hereditary telepaths, Brennen's kindred.

Standing at the foot of the bed, she tapped one foot, now booted. "How did he get through that window? It was reinforced glasteel."

"This was etched in advance." Sentinel Dardy pointed at a rim of glasteel that protruded bladelike from the windowbar.

"Squill!" she exclaimed. "He was here before, setting us up." She must've heard him two nights ago. She felt like a target. These days, she'd be hard to miss.

Brennen stepped out of the freshing room. He carried a medium-sized duffel. "Anything else you want, Mari?"

No one else called Firebird by that name. Brennen had given it to her last year, helping her hide from a hostile regime. When they married, she made it part of her legal identity. "Mari" meant her new life.

She shook her head. Finally, she felt safe enough to realize she was terrified. "I don't need anything but you," she insisted. "Nothing."

Inland beyond the craggy Dracken Range, at the small town of Arown, the Sentinel College maintained one of the Federacy's best medical facilities. Master Sentinel Aldana Spieth laid her soft sonoscope on an examining room counter. "You'll be fine," she said, "all three of you, but I'd like you off your feet for a day."

Relieved for her twins, and glad Spieth didn't need to give her any injections, Firebird swung around to sit up on the table. Master Spieth's lovely, laugh-lined face was framed by silver hair, and a gold star adorned her white tunic. Its eight rays proclaimed her a Master Sentinel like Brennen—one of Thyrica's most powerful telepathic refugees.

"How's Brenn?" Firebird clutched the internally warmed table's yielding edge. "Where's he gone?"

Master Spieth scribbled on a recall pad with one fingernail. "Kyrie probed out the glasteel shards, and that flash burn's not dangerously deep.

He's all right. He's busy for a while, though. You get to finish your night's rest."

"It's morning." Firebird glanced out the window. Beyond three rounded, red stone buildings, a new band of clouds turned orange-maroon. Dawn was racing the next eastbound storm inland. "There's a murderer out there—"

"You will rest," Spieth said flatly. "For two more months, you have a higher priority than chasing—"

"I can't lie down and let Brennen take all the risks—"

"Yes, you can." Spieth laid down her recall pad and narrowed her iron gray eyes. "Your balance is completely out of whack. You could take a dangerous fall just by stepping down wrong. Couldn't you?"

Firebird barely got her mouth open.

"Yes, you could," Spieth snapped. "If you won't promise to cooperate, I'll either put you under voice-command or else lock you in. Which will it be?"

Firebird shook her head. She had no intention of risking her babies' lives. She was determined to keep them safe too—but she hated acting timid. "I can at least help Brenn. He won't rest."

"He'd do almost anything for you, but he can't carry a baby until you deliver." The master touched a call button. "You're young, Firebird. You're strong and healthy, but a twin pregnancy has extra risks. You've just been stressed. You will rest. I'm ordering you an early breakfast as well. Eat it all."

Firebird folded both arms round her belly and those unborn sons, barely resisting the temptation to roll her eyes. She was eating six times a day and napping twice—ridiculous, but . . . but Spieth was right. She needed both. She felt like a cruiser, but she couldn't seem to gain enough weight to suit the medical master or her staff.

She tired quickly too. So far she didn't think much of motherhood, even if her children-to-be carried the genes of a tremendously gifted family. "Find me a bed," she said curtly. "I'll rest."

Brennen eyed a newscan screen in the med center's third-floor lounge. As soon as Spieth had treated his cuts and his burn, he called his mother, wakening her to explain what had happened before she heard it from some other source—and sure enough, here it came over the net:

Master Sentinel Brennen Caldwell, new General Coordinator of Thyrian Forces, was attacked last night in his home by an unknown assailant. Neither he nor his wife, née Lady Firebird Angelo of the occupied Netaia Protetorate Systems, was seriously injured. Alert Forces and Soldane Police are investigating.

Brennen's mother would've spotted the message and worried.

Her parting words were "Please call your brother." He nodded, though he and Tarance didn't get along.

He cleared the connection and touched in a call code. He hated to wake Tarance's family. Once Destia bounced out of bed, Tarance and Asea might never get back to sleep. That would lay one more small grudge in the weighty basket Brennen's older brother carried so proudly.

Still, he didn't want Asea worrying.

The call light flashed for several seconds, then repeated. Brennen frowned. Normally Tarance jumped on night calls. They could be medical emergencies, and Tarance zealously guarded Asea's sleep. Tarance's medical practice, subsidized by the College, earned him general respect among even the nongifted.

Brennen canceled his call, hustled up the passway's blue shortweave carpet to Firebird's room, and stepped in. Beneath a battery of deactivated sensors, she lay curled away from the door. Sensor deactivation was a good sign. Spieth didn't think she or either of his sons was in danger.

They would both be relieved when she delivered those twins. He endured most of her discomfort and frustration right along with her, especially the mood swings. He laid a hand on her shoulder.

Her eyes opened. "Hm?" Then, instantly, "Brenn!" She pushed up onto her elbows. "What's happening?"

Muting his concern, he kissed her forehead. "I just contacted Mother. She wants me to check on Tarance."

She wrinkled her forehead. For an instant, she looked almost childlike.

Brennen knew her toughness, though. This small woman had nearly beaten a deep mind-access interrogation and faced a firing squad. Scarred though she was by her cruel upbringing, she was literally part of him now, as he was part of her. "I know you're frustrated," he said, "staying here like this. It won't last forever. I'll give you an oil rub when I get back. Fair enough?"

Smiling, she shut her eyes, and as she sighed once more, her alert state faded in his senses. In less than a minute, she slept again.

She did need the rest, with her body changing so quickly. Six months ago, neither of them had known about a twin pregnancy's physical demands. Brennen caressed her shoulder, then returned to the lounge and tried Tarance's personal-carry line. Tarance kept that close, even when traveling.

Air Master Dardy poked his head through the door and eyed the com screen. "Everything all right?"

Brennen nodded. Dardy's aggressive deference made Brennen feel like an icon, instead of a talented human who was as guilty as the rest of the starbred—including the renegade Shuhr—of carrying artificially altered genes. Their ancestors had been created by scientists who hoped telepathy would create lasting peace on Ehret, their original home world. Instead, the first telepathic Ehretan starbred matured into normal, selfish young men and women whose power cravings touched off a devastating civil war.

"I'm just trying to reach Tarance," Brennen answered, "and let him know we weren't hurt."

"Heavy sleeper?"

"No. He could be on vacation." Or . . .

Holy One, is he all right?

Brennen and Dardy hurried across Dr. Tarance Caldwell's rooftop landing pad. The coastal drizzle soaked moss-hung trees far below, down on the avenue. Early commuters guided streamlined groundcars through puddles. Their headlamps made glittery streaks in the rain.

Eleven years ago, after eight years of college and medical training, Dr. Tarance Caldwell had bought a compact home in this area, one of Soldane's pleasant urban neighborhoods, settling into a life as comfortable and secure as Brennen's had been unpredictable.

No one answered Tarance's entry bell.

Dardy frowned.

Brennen turned inward for his epsilon-energy carrier and sent a quest pulse indoors. The home felt eerily empty.

They could all be asleep, he reminded himself. A quest pulse would only locate alert minds.

"Could they be on vacation?" Dardy asked.

If Dardy sensed Brennen's unease, he must've diffused his epsilon shields. Sentinels normally surrounded themselves with mental-frequency static so they wouldn't sense the constant assault of others' emotions. "He would've taken his personal-carry," Brennen objected. Tarance hated it when he let himself in, but he felt he had no choice. He keyed up the unlock sequence.

Dim gray daylight filtered onto Tarance's longweave carpet and the overstuffed furniture down below on his main floor. Cushions lay everywhere. Tarance and Asea's three children often stayed up late. Brennen paused at the foot of the stairs and dropped his own epsilon shields.

He still felt no one awake but Dardy. "Hello?" he called. "Tarance? Asea?"

Dardy paced into the kitchen to open the cold cabinet. His concern rose to answer Brennen's, and now—without epsilon shields—Brennen felt it with excruciating accuracy. "Full of perishables," Dardy said, shaking his head. "They haven't gone far."

Disquieted, Brennen strode up the hall. He turned left, into the master room.

On the bed in half darkness, plush covers draped two forms. "Tarance," Brennen called. He repeated, louder, "Tarance." Neither body moved.

Brennen waved on the room light. Tarance lay on his back, Asea on her side. Their eyes remained shut, their faces peaceful, but neither breathed. Brennen froze, as helpless as if he'd been caught in voice-command. "No," he croaked.

Dardy hustled around the bed. Brennen reached toward his older brother's throat to check for a pulse, then saw the scorched left ear. Blazer, point-blank range. Death would have been sudden and silent.

Dardy laid down Asea's wrist, shook his head, then pulled up the bed sheet to cover both faces. "Get out of here, Caldwell. Go sit down."

"I've seen death before," he said, but his hands felt numb. "Let me help." Then he exclaimed, "The children!" and flung himself across the passway.

The boys, Brit and Kether, lay on narrow beds across a smaller room from each other, two gangling teenaged bodies that showed no sign of pain, struggle, or life.

Dardy met him in the hallway. "Destia?" Brennen cried, wheeling toward the third bedroom.

Dardy shook his head. "The girl's . . . dead too. Go sit down. I just called Soldane police."

Brennen sank onto a lounger and pressed both trembling hands over his eyes. Twice in eighty years, someone had tried to wipe out his ancient bloodline. Did this make a third attempt, or had Tarance's family fallen to someone's private vendetta?

He slumped. His breath came in puffs. He was trained in emotional control, but he couldn't squelch this sudden storm of grief.

No, not grief. Guilt.

Stop, reason insisted. *You aren't responsible. You merely survived—because Mari was awake.*

Then who struck here? The Shuhr?

According to Alert Force reports, none of their renegade cousins cared about the Sentinels' ancient faith. Surely the Shuhr scoffed at prophecies about the Carabohd-Caldwell family, although—as a precaution—the Sentinel kindred tried to keep most of those prophecies secret.

Who else would've done this?

Tarance's dim living room seemed light-years away from Brennen's point of consciousness. *You're going into shock*, reason observed. *Lie down. Get your feet up.*

He obeyed. *Tarance*, he groaned again, this time into the invisible realm. *O Holy One, welcome him. Make him content, as Asea and I never could do in this lifetime.*

Another memory stabbed deep. Only two dekia ago, twenty all-too-short days back, they celebrated Destia's spiritual coming of age by consecrating her into the faith community.

Twice before, one . . . only one . . . adult male in his line had survived.

But Destia was only twelve! And what about Asea? They had never killed women before!

Or was this someone else's work?

Agony choked him. He was too numb to weep.

CHAPTER 2

ECHOES

morendo
dying away

Two days later, Firebird stared out a barred, trapezoidal window. Five stories down, pounding rain soaked an enclosed lawn of jujink, a primitive blue-green ground cover. Red stone walls dotted with other windows surrounded the courtyard. These high-security campus apartments housed medical patients' families from all over the Federacy, including—now—four of the five surviving members of Brennen's extended family. The Caldwell murders that scandalized Soldane had landed her back in protective custody, just as when she'd been a Federate war prisoner. Brennen could still commute to work, but last night, even he had stayed indoors. They'd packed yesterday, escorted by half a dozen hurrying College staffers and Alert Forces Sentinels. Today, the first home she and Brennen made together would go back on the market—and a killer walked free.

Unspeakably frustrated, she turned away from the window. This apartment was too small for a full cooking unit. It had a servo table linked to the building's provision facility, a small living space, and two even smaller bedrooms. Last night, she'd unpacked only a few clothes and her clairsa, then stayed up past midnight, playing her sorrow and frustration on the Netaian small harp. She knew an enormous repertoire of traditional ballads, plus a dozen of her own.

Brennen squeezed out of the inner bedroom, threading a path around boxes and moving crates while he adjusted the cuffs on his midnight-blue uniform. He'd taken only one day of bereavement leave. As his first shock of grieving faded, she felt more of the pain squeezing his heart and mind, keen and sharp on the pair bond.

The preliminary police report stunned her too. Tarance, Asea, and the boys died without waking up, but Destia had been bound and forced to kneel for her execution. The only blessing was that Dardy—not Brennen—found her body. What had that black-handed stranger planned for her and Brennen?

"I don't understand," she murmured. The empathetic pair bond was helping her and Brennen learn to communicate, despite vastly different upbringings. Her grief and outrage should be all the clues he needed to catch her meaning. "It isn't right," she added.

He halted in the narrow hall. His hair looked damp, with fair dry wisps over his forehead and ears. She caught a whiff of herbed soap. "I agree," he said. "Destia didn't deserve that. No more than any wastling on your world deserved to die horribly and young."

Firebird tilted her chin. "But that's different. They serve the Powers." Raised to sacrifice herself for those merciless Netaian demigods, though even as a child she doubted they existed, Firebird had finally forsaken them. "Reverence for the Powers holds our government together," she said, "but that's Netaia. Why would the Holy One let this happen to one of His young people, unless He's powerless—too?"

Brennen's forehead furrowed. "Terrible crimes happen every day, throughout the Whorl. Flawed humans are free to commit them."

"That seems wrong." She shook her head. She'd learned so much since leaving Netaia. "Our God is vast, He's . . . infinite, ancient, and wise."

"You want to know," Brennen said slowly, "why evil and pain can exist."

"Yes," she exclaimed. Someday, the galaxies' Creator would mend the evil and injustice she hated so deeply. His books made that promise. She hoped to play a part in its fulfillment. "How could Netaian noble families order their own children's deaths?" she demanded. "Why is there pain and terror, why are there Shuhr, and why, why are they doing this to your family?" A tear spilled down her cheek. That poor child . . .

Brennen caressed the teardrop away. "Even pain can be a blessing if it wakes us up to danger."

Yes, her leg cramps had saved her, and Brennen, and both their unborn sons. But that hadn't helped Destia.

He shook his head. "As for evil—it exists, and we've all partaken."

Now he was quoting. They'd argued about this, one night after her Path instruction session. Sensing his feelings didn't mean she always agreed. How could Brenn's people believe even the best of them were tainted? She didn't feel evil. She'd found mercy and peace in the Eternal Speaker. She never would've murdered a twelve-year-old girl.

"The existence of evil isn't a question anyone should have to settle before work." Brennen quirked an eyebrow. "Can you wait for this evening?"

"Of course. But Brenn, answer one question. Why Tarance's whole family? It wasn't to punish you, because he came to kill us next. Do you think it's the prophecies?"

"Yes." Brennen had been voice-commanded not to explain those predictions to anyone who hadn't formally joined the faith community. She only knew that he and Tarance were the last heirs to important promises.

Intrigued, and enthralled by the One who replaced her guilt with mercy, Firebird had finished Path instruction. Whether or not she felt soul-tainted, his people demanded a formal consecration for full membership. She'd set a date. The rite would be private, since she wanted to avoid publicity. Only Brennen's family would attend.

Yesterday, she canceled. She couldn't put Brennen's widowed mother through another consecration ceremony less than three weeks after Destia's. "If the Shuhr are attacking your family," she murmured, "then they know what you won't tell me."

"I can't," he reminded her. He walked to the barred window. "Unfortunately, one of the minor promises is fairly well known. Evidently, some descendant of my ancestors will destroy a so-called nest of evil that sounds— in one of the prophecies—like it's probably their world."

"Oh," she said softly, "oh." If the renegades thought they were threatened, that was reason enough to kill Caldwells. Some descendant . . . maybe Brennen himself, avenging this quintuple murder? "That's a minor promise?"

He nodded, turning back to stare with those startling blue eyes. She guessed that he wanted to read her thoughts. Like all military Sentinels, he swore to respect others' privacy unless security was at stake.

Should she offer him mind-access?

Later, maybe. For now, she just hoped he'd keep talking. "Do they follow some rival god?" she pressed.

"As far as we know, they serve no one but themselves. But that selfish attitude does honor the Adversary. He has strong servants. We must be stronger."

Firebird crossed her arms, which wasn't easy these days. "Absolutely." Still, if Tarance had died for those prophecies, she and Brennen were in danger. She glanced at the locked entry.

"College has a Class-One security net. You're safer here than in Base housing."

"I know," she said.

He caught her in an embrace, kissed her gently, then strode out.

"You be careful," she muttered.

A queer little contraction rippled across her taut belly. "Good morning, princeling." She stroked the spot. She felt like a dance hall these days, with all those little limbs kicking and punching.

It had been more than a century since her dynasty produced a male child. Hoping to give Brennen the son he obviously wanted, Firebird had visited this medical center even before they tried to conceive. She'd thought the Sentinels might diagnose some reason for her family's odd history. Master Spieth found—and treated—Mazo syndrome, a hereditary disorder that sometimes arose among Thyrica's small Ehret-descended enclave.

The notion sent Firebird spinning. She was no Ehretan descendant! She was of royal blood . . . pure Netaian . . .

Bending over Spieth's data desk together, she and the Medical master had accessed Netaian historical records. The last Angelo male, Prince Avocin, had married outside the ten noble families. His wife, Sharah Casvah, was allegedly born in Denford, on Netaia's southerly continent.

Master Spieth had craned her neck to look up at Firebird. Her iron gray eyes shone out of their net of creases. "Casvah is an Ehretan name," she announced. "If this woman was a full-blooded Ehretan refugee, she could've easily inserted a birth record into the Netaian register. She had none of our Privacy and Priority Codes to keep her from manipulating data. As soon as she set her eye on Prince Avocin, nothing stood between her and the palace."

Firebird laughed shortly. "We were taught that this sudden lack of male heirs was the Powers' lasting judgment on Prince Avocin for marrying out of the noble families."

One more blow to Strength, Valor, and Excellence; Knowledge, Fidelity, and Resolve; Authority, Indomitability, and Pride—the nine holy Powers, who weren't gods after all.

Two days after that visit with Spieth, Firebird had come out of shock and asked Brennen if she could attempt Sentinel training, if she carried even a few altered Ehretan genes. Even before she conceived, she had vowed to learn to protect her children.

Truth to tell, she was already a little afraid of raising them.

Brennen tried gamely to dissuade her, calling Sentinel powers a mixed blessing, the result of illicit research—and a burden besides. *No sensible person would want them*, he claimed.

She passed two qualifying tests immediately. First, Master Spieth confirmed epsilon potential in her midbrain. Then, character examiners awarded her a passing score (though not without warning her of her faults).

She'd barely started studying for her final qualifying test, a memorization exam over the Privacy and Priority Codes' first volume, when—to her delight and chagrin—she found herself pregnant. She couldn't travel daily from Soldane to Arown for training and keep her pregnancy secret, so she took up other studies and pursued them at home on Trinn Hill, overlooking Soldane.

Suddenly, she lived at College. She'd suspected, ever since Spieth diagnosed twins, that she would end up living here. The best medical care in the Federacy was moments away . . . and so was the best training.

Eyeing the packing crates, she tried to remember where she'd buried that Code book.

CHAPTER 3

TALAS OIL

legato
smoothly

Before leaving for Base One in Soldane, Brennen spent an hour with six members of the special Alert Forces, closeted in an office under the College's administration building. He sat at midtable, surrounded by supportive colleagues.

It was hard to leave Mari alone. He couldn't shake the sense that he ought to be home defending her and their sons. His wife, trained by the Netaian Planetary Navy, could probably fight off most assailants—even pregnant—but if the Shuhr had decided to wipe out his family at last, she was in danger.

"About one-seventy centimeters," he answered Dardy's first question after they'd offered condolences . . . and sincere congratulations. These six were all consecrants. With Tarance and his sons gone into eternity, these men and women had been relieved—delighted—to learn that the Caldwell family had twins on the way.

Brennen strengthened his affective control and continued, "Wiry. Short, curly hair. Cleft chin."

"Black hair?"

"He'd blackened his face and hands," Brennen reminded the other Sentinels. "His hair looked black."

"Epsilon strength?"

"I didn't have time to test. But he was strong. He tried to put me under voice-command." Without any outsiders present, the codes would have allowed this group to subvocalize—speak mind to mind, sending and receiving words on epsilon waves. That wasn't commonly done, though. Whenever a Sentinel used the epsilon-energy-producing region of his or her brain—the ayin complex—it aged slightly.

"Good." The woman next to him poised her hands over a specialized recall pad. "Now that he's firmly in your mind, let me see." Her fingers swept the pad. Brennen felt her access probe study the mental image. By the time she'd finished, a portrait gleamed on the pad's surface.

"Yes," said Brennen. "That's him."

She touched the SEND key. Alert Forces would post the image at all locations.

In the eighty years since the Shuhr colony was discovered, all attempts to negotiate with that other major Ehretan remnant had ended in one-sided massacre. *Shuhr* meant "enemy" in the holy Ehretan tongue.

"I've studied the records," said Dardy. Seated across from Brennen, watching him on behalf of a concerned medical master, Dardy rested muscular forearms on the table. "If they've really committed most of the unsolved piracies, they have everything from metals to museum pieces on that world of theirs. And who knows how many murders we could trace to them."

"I'd guess," an ethics instructor said slowly, "most of us who've vanished."

"All right." Dardy stared at Brennen, who felt a gentle emotional probe follow the stare. "Then why are they killing the Caldwells so doggedly? The Shuhr have never walked the Path. Why would they try to thwart prophecy?"

"Exactly," said the artist.

Brennen spoke up. "I have a theory." He'd scarcely slept, thinking this through.

"You have the floor." Dardy opened a hand on the table. "You're the one in danger. We'll back you, whatever it takes."

Brennen thanked Dardy subvocally, then spoke aloud. "Wealthy, secure people crave excitement."

Dardy raised an eyebrow.

"It's as you said," Brennen pressed. "They don't care about prophecies. So out of boredom, or maybe on a dare," he added bitterly, "someone has taken up a devilish challenge."

"Three times in seventy-eight years?"

"This time," Brennen reminded Dardy, "it was different."

"He tried to kill all of you, including the women."

Brennen's emotions escaped control again. Destia had been the lively young flower of Tarance's family. Why *had* the Holy Speaker let that happen? It was one of the most difficult issues that honest, thoughtful worshipers faced. How could the Eternal Sovereign allow suffering and death? It had caught Mari square on, and she lacked his twenty years in the faith.

Guide her, Holy One. Give me words to explain. Your ways are perfect and your wisdom is eternal, but I hear you so faintly sometimes.

Dardy rubbed his chin. Brennen sensed that Dardy had raised his epsilon shields, probably to block out Brennen's private feelings.

"If you're still targeted," Dardy said, "our best hope is to lure him out again, then bring him down. But that will have to be done carefully."

"Lure him out," echoed the ethics instructor, who had also shielded to let Brennen grieve. "Yes, but how?"

Brennen rejoined the conversation. "For myself, I'm willing to risk setting a trap. And Firebird is a fighter. But the children must be protected." He'd never felt so exposed, so easy to attack. "They would only be truly safe back at sanctuary, at Hesed House."

"Then go," urged a woman down the table. "Leave today. If you hadn't left Hesed after your wedding, maybe this wouldn't have happened."

"Unless we'd come here," Brennen reminded her, "unless Spieth had treated her Mazo syndrome, we couldn't have conceived them."

She nodded somberly. These unborn lives, heirs to so many prophecies, were now even more precious to this kindred than before—if that was possible. "We'd be vulnerable between takeoff and slip if we tried to get back there," said Brennen.

"We can't risk them," the instructor agreed. "Not unless it's a last resort."

The woman added, "With unlimited wealth, the Shuhr could chase you across the Whorl."

Dardy's eyes narrowed. Again Brennen felt him probe. *I'll be all right*, he insisted subvocally.

Silence fell. In his mind's eye, Brennen saw Tarance as he crowned Destia with a beribboned garland of yellow and white flowers, only two dekia before. He clung to the image for a moment, reaching into his belt pocket to touch a small bird-of-prey medallion Tarance had given him twenty years ago. He'd carried it all over the Federacy. He never would part with it now. It still seemed impossible that he would not spar with Tarance or laugh with Asea again. Not in this lifetime.

"One Shuhr agent," the instructor murmured, "masquerading as one of us, could turn the Federacy against us. Then we would all have to run for Hesed, or else be annihilated."

"We're the Federacy's best defense against them," said Dardy. "As long as the Shuhr pose a threat, the Federacy needs us."

"So we hope." Brennen too had faced fear and jealousy from nongifted individuals. If the Federates ever turned on the Sentinel kindred, his people would not survive. "Then we must set that trap. Make it look as if I'm fleeing offworld. . . ."

Four hours later, Brennen stood on an observation deck and peered down at ocean breakers nibbling a long, stony beach. No matter how many planets he visited, the vast Thyrian ocean always filled him with awe. Less than a sixth of this planet's surface was dry land; the rest was ocean and ice. Clouds swirled against the Base's clear zone. Here, Thyrian Forces tenuously controlled the weather systems this huge ocean flung onto a peninsula between two deep fjords.

The onshore wind stung his face. Northward, to his right, sea-beaten cliffs bent westward into an inlet and then faded into haze.

Midafternoon, his spiritual father had arrived on Base and suggested they speak alone, outdoors. Shamarr Lo Dickin's snowy hair and ministerial tunic whipped in the wind. Gray-blue eyes glimmered beneath his furrowed forehead. A direct heir of Mattah Dickin, the Ehretan Shamarr whose family saved fifty-one starbred orphans from planetary destruction, Dickin was the spiritual leader of Thyrica's starbred community. He'd taken Brennen as a protégé during Brenn's Sentinel training, and they'd grown closer during the seven years since Brennen's father died.

"Show me," Dickin said simply.

Brennen dispersed all epsilon static. He glanced aside just long enough to welcome another access probe, then relaxed against the glassite railing, clenching his hands while his mentor looked into his mind.

The Shamarr's epsilon touch rested on the tragic murders and their discovery. He paused to spread comforting warmth over Brennen's grief, then lingered to examine this morning's exchange with Firebird Mari. Then his warm presence withdrew. "Tell me your fears," he said. "Speak and release them to Him."

Brennen hadn't seen Destia's body, but he had read the report. "I'm afraid they could catch Mari," he said, grappling with his emotions. "That they would be cruel, for sport. That they'd watch her terror from inside her own mind, while they . . . killed our sons. And then destroyed her."

When Brennen fell silent, Dickin frowned. A seascape of parallel waves formed on his forehead. "Go on," he said.

Brennen exhaled. Really, he hadn't expected Dickin to let him escape without voicing this too. "Father, she knows enough now to ask the deep questions. She was raised in a false faith that molded her thinking. She might find satisfying answers in her own mind instead of the Speaker's words. She might step off the Path." A detour could be agonizing for the wanderer and everyone close to her.

"Now," said the Shamarr, "let Him take those burdens, as He promised."

Brennen squinted out to sea. "I can objectively. But can I sincerely?"

"Are you the only one watching over her soul, Brennen Caldwell?"

He exhaled. "No."

"Be careful, Brennen. Your tremendous accomplishments tempt you to rely too much on yourself. In His will, Firebird Mari and your sons are safer than you or I could keep them. Of course," he added, raising his head, "that doesn't mean we'll let down our guard."

"I won't," Brennen murmured, "believe me."

"And the Word to Come," Dickin added, "remains in the One's mighty care. Don't confuse yourself with fear. That would be wasted effort. Fulfill your duties to Thyrica. You are still in the heart of His will."

"Truly, Father?"

"As you said this morning, if you hadn't left the Procyel system, they couldn't have been conceived. Your presence here is part of a plan."

The plan. Centuries before Ehret's destruction, believers were promised that one day, a Caldwell—Carabohd, in the old language—would father a king with the power to destroy and renew the universe, who would replace the symbolic covering of ancient sacrifices with soul-deep purification, and finally bring peace to guilty humanity. That holy messenger would have been born on Ehret, but when the Ehretans genetically altered their children, they delayed His advent. This Word to Come, King of the New Universe, would wait until they requalified themselves by serving unaltered human-kind. The Sentinel community now realized that even their fall had been prophesied in their older holy book, *Dabar*.

Dark gray rain slanted down from a cloud bank out at sea. At the corner of Brennen's vision, Dickin drew a blue-green vial from a tunic pocket.

Brennen straightened, surprised. He'd seen this vial before, when Dickin commissioned a teacher to lead the faith community on Caroli. It held the purified oil of a spice called *talas*, once grown on Ehret.

Dickin poured his left palm full of oil and corked the vial one-handed. Then he laid both hands on Brennen's head and looked toward the gray clouds. "For the trials ahead, Mighty One, strengthen this man, your servant. Give him wisdom and courage and mercy. Speak clearly to him, the eldest of your holy lineage. Let him carry that burden honorably. So let it be."

In that moment, Brennen realized Dickin came not just to counsel, but to anoint him as the eldest surviving heir of his family. He hadn't known there was such a rite. Some of these heirs experienced sacred dreams, even waking visions, in dangerous times. He squeezed his eyes shut and added a heartfelt prayer to Dickin's. "I'm no perfect servant, Holy One. Carry my fears, as you promised. Let me hear and obey you in all things. So let it be.''

He stared into Dickin's eyes for a few more seconds, drawing strength and peace. Despite the sea wind, he caught the sweet fragrance of talas oil. *Soon*, he prayed silently, *let me tell her what one of our sons might become. What one of our descendants will be.* That, he guessed, would be all she'd ever need to walk the Path steadily, until death took her Across to His kingdom.

Firebird sat at their new apartment's small data desk, which was also their servo and dining table. Brilliant blue letters gleamed on a darker blue field. She sipped a cup of bland herbal tea Master Spieth had prescribed.

MIN OF JUDIC, she keyed in, scowling. REDUCE FREEDOM COEFF TO 20%.

As the program returned a result, her spirits sank again. This simulation was her link with Soldane University. For four months, hiding behind a pseudonym, she'd studied governmental analysis. Her home world was repressed by a noble class that claimed to represent the nine holy Powers, deified attributes from an ancient mythology. Netaia now was subdued and occupied by the vast Federacy, but those electors refused to step down. They believed ruling was their ordained right . . . whether or not they were capable, Firebird reflected bitterly, whether or not they cared squill for any of the people they claimed to protect.

Netaia's class system, and its steel-fisted electoral monopolies, denied almost a quarter of its populace basic rights that most Federates took for granted. Even before Firebird left Netaia, she'd sat in back rooms where her sisters never dared to go, listening to illegal ballads. Her clairsa had been her entrée to those clubs and warehouses, her deep love for her people's songs her shield. No one had ever assaulted her. She'd heard songs and seen crowd reactions that should've made other electors tremble, but she guessed no other elector had ever heard them.

Now Soldane University's analysis program confirmed her fears. The Netaian low-common and servitor classes had suffered too many harsh judgments, too much hopelessness and inequity. They wanted to participate in the vast wealth and culture Netaia's nobles and high-commoners took for granted.

Could change come peacefully? Occupation Governor Lee Danton had implemented reforms, but Firebird hadn't simulated one reform program that eased interclass tensions in time to prevent a greater than eighty percent chance of civil war breaking out on her beloved home world. Netaia's noble and generous populace might never recover from that catastrophe. Its high culture might become easy prey for others who wanted its wealth.

Not the Shuhr! she begged. *Have mercy on my homeland!* She bowed her head, remembering how she'd plunged with her oldest sister Carradee through feathery snowfields outside the winter palace. At tropical Sitree that same week, she nearly drowned proving she could swim farther underwater than their middle sister, Phoena.

The next year their father died on a hunting trip. Without Prince Irion, their mother led no more family vacations. All Firebird's later memories were of Citangelo. She recalled sitting in an ornate balcony at the Conservatory's symphony hall, savoring every note of a viol concerto's premiere performance . . . and sitting before the Electorate, performing an original ballad at all of eleven years old.

> Netaia, Netaia,
> Green mountains and blue oceans,
> Mighty Tiggaree, roll, roll along . . .

The main entry whooshed. Wholeness and union, contentment and strength washed away her homesickness. She looked up, gladly welcoming her partner in the pair bond. Brennen stepped around moving crates between the main door and servo table. Outside the trapezoidal windows, daylight faded.

"Long day," he said softly.

"Long," she agreed.

He sank down beside her. Instead of reaching out, he kept both hands in his lap, comforting with waves of tender assurance. She didn't need to be touched. She felt whole again now that he'd entered the room. Already, the sweet emotional stereo of feeling his emotions along with her own seemed completely natural. Once, she'd been as fiercely independent as Netaia itself. Now she knew the downside of pair bonding. She never would feel complete, as long as she lived, unless Brennen was with her.

"I should apologize," she said slowly. "You didn't need a dose of my doubts this morning on top of your grieving."

"I'm glad you're honest. Now let me be honest with you too."

She shut down the bluescreen.

"I'm deathly afraid that the Shuhr will attack us again," he said.

She didn't like to think that Brennen could be afraid, but she had to understand. Even a crack shot could be surprised and murdered. He'd ordered a voice-activated, supplemental security system for this apartment, which should be delivered tomorrow.

"I worry that this time," he went on, "they'll target you before me."

She laid a hand on her stomach. "Because they've found out."

"Yes. But now that I've said it, I have to tell you I've been reprimanded for worrying." He smiled sidelong.

"Reprimanded?"

"Shamarr Dickin came to the Base today," he said. "He counseled me, prayed for me."

"I am in awe of that man," she admitted. "Has he always been your spiritual father?" That relationship must've been a little like calling the queen her mother.

Brennen shook his head. "You know how young I was when I won my master's star. Too young for that much responsibility."

Seventeen, she recalled, catching a whiff of something sweet.

He stared at the nearest wall. "When they vested me in the Word, I got the shock of my life. Shamarr Dickin himself stood to declare himself my sponsoring master. I almost burst with pride. Then he explained at great length, before all the masters who were attending—and my family," he added, putting more love and regret into that word than Firebird would've thought possible, "that this was no honor but a strict discipline. I would answer to Dickin for any misconduct. That raid without orders, at Gemina, earned a penance to go with the Federate Service Crest."

He turned his head. One side of his hair looked oddly dark, as if wet. "What did you lean against?" she asked.

"Nothing. That's oil, from when Shamarr Dickin prayed. Smell it."

She stretched her neck and sniffed. Slightly sweet, slightly . . . green. Not what she smelled a minute ago.

"Do you still want to talk about why evil exists?" he asked, and she felt his willingness.

"Not really." She squared her shoulders. "At the moment, I just want to fight back."

"I thought you would. I brought you something," he added, raising his hands. Now she realized he held them cupped around something.

"A new weapon?" she wished out loud.

Laughing, he opened his fingers. His hands cradled a blossom. Eight intensely blue-green petals framed its yellow center, and its heady, honey-rich odor made her blink.

"Oh!" She leaned her head against his shoulder. "What's it called?"

"Mira lily. They grow at Hesed."

Her memories of Hesed House, on Procyel II where they married, were splendid but vague. After she recovered from bonding shock, they hadn't stayed long. At Hesed, Brennen received a fateful communiqué. Regional command, reprimanding him for disobeying a direct order, dismissed him from Federate service. Intoxicated by finally touching the depths of his strength, and sustained by his supreme, careful tenderness, Firebird hadn't cared a skitter's fin for the Federacy's rebuke. She now guessed that her attitude helped him cope with the setback.

He was ambitious, though he hid it well.

"It'll stay fresh indefinitely in this damp climate," he said, "if you give it enough light. It only needs air and a little moisture." He tipped the lily off his hands onto hers.

"Thank you," she whispered. Gingerly, she examined the delicate blossom. Behind the bloom curled a short pale green root covered with netlike brown lines.

"If we're careful, you can wear it in your hair." He reached into a pocket of his wide belt and pulled out a silver clip, took back the lily, and wove its succulent root through half the clip. Firebird held her breath while he pinned the bloom over her left ear. "There." He arranged her long hair about her shoulders.

She felt his wash of approval and returned fervent gratitude. He knew . . . he felt . . . how it roused her when he toyed with her hair. For a moment he pressed into her mind, caressing her with his very existence, and she felt as if she were floating on a tropical sea flooded with sweet incense.

Then he reached into a deep tunic pocket and handed her a thin parcel. "And this was delivered just before Dickin arrived."

Firebird lifted its pressboard lid. Inside, a spiraling ebony handgrip protruded from a supple black sheath. "Ah!" she exclaimed. She tipped the dagger out of its box, caressed the beaded pommel, and exclaimed again, "Brenn!" The grip felt so comfortable that she guessed he'd ordered it for her small, broad hand. She drew the blade. It too was finished in flat black, to be invisible at night, tapering gracefully from narrow waist to symmetrical point, with a wicked double edge.

"It'll split hair." He smiled down the blade. "I tried it. I reserved a training room for this evening. I'd like to see if you remember what I taught you. A dagger's easier to conceal than a shock pistol—or a blazer."

Truly, she never should go unarmed now, not even at home. Maybe especially not at home.

". . . And then maybe a foot rub?" he offered.

That was incentive!

"I remember," she insisted. Exercise, and then a massage . . . glory, that would feel good! She sheathed the dagger and carried it into their crate-crowded bedroom. "I'm just not sure I can still do it. I'll show you after dinner," she called, laying the dagger beneath her dressing mirror under a small, square pendant she'd hung on a fine gold chain. Mounted inside that pendant was Brennen's first gift, a microcopied document that had guaranteed her Federate asylum.

He appeared in the doorway. "What?" he teased. "Not this instant? You're not hungry, are you?"

To think that she tried to refuse that asylum!

Gently she slapped his cheek. "We, sir, are starving."

CHAPTER 4

SHUHR

allargando
slowing down and growing louder

At the heart of an underground colony known to its population as the Golden City, Eshdeth Shirak's black-haired grandson approached on dragging feet. Beneath a ceiling fused *in situ* from space-black obsidian, Shirak had displayed a massive Kellian tapestry, once worked in brilliant colors but faded by six and a half centuries; three fused-silica artworks by a deceased Elysian master; and his new favorite, a three-dimensional curtain of mist that was six meters long and three high. Inside, icicles of light and stalagmites of darkness thrust and parried, battling for mastery. His desk was another masterwork, laser sculpted by one of his uncles from the City's native obsidian. On this Ehretan colony of Three Zed, every settlement had been blasted, tunneled, or fused from a tube-riddled surface of lava, obsidian, and dusty gray pumice.

Shirak's grandson, Micahel—now twenty—was a favorite among City girls for his curly hair and that impish face with its cleft chin and high cheekbones. Today, though, Micahel walked with his head down, emanating disgust and faint dread. He held his right arm against his side.

Shirak tapped a stylus against his desk's gleaming surface. Micahel halted several meters away—maintaining his epsilon shields moderately well, Shirak observed, despite the leakage. Youth made him strong.

At Shirak's right shoulder, his Testing Director waited at relaxed attention. Tall, slim, and muscular, wearing his silky black hair long over a red collar, Dru Polar stood surrounded by the dense epsilon cloud of his own shields. Shirak could almost see them, they deflected so strongly. Dru Polar looked thirty. He was sixty-eight.

Ninety-six himself, Eshdeth Shirak had ruled the Golden City for seventeen years. Before he died, the unbound starbred would finally conquer the Federacy. Millions of Federates would die in that war, but to Shirak, their lives were worth precisely nothing. When Ehretan bioscientists finally tapped the Federacy's resources, all projections showed that the

Ehretan unbound would achieve immortality. A genetically superior race deserved deathlessness—and with unlimited wealth, who would ever grow tired of living?

Also, without the nongifted competing for resources, Shirak's people finally could multiply freely. The cost would be sterilizing settled worlds, one at a time, of inferior human life. Eshdeth Shirak was prepared to exact that cost, and he had the means to do it. He'd built up this colony through long-range planning.

Dru Polar kept it strong by eliminating weakness. Polar had spent two years training Eshdeth's grandson—and others. Micahel's final training mission should have sounded a death knell for the Federacy's dominance of the Whorl and its Sentinels' oh-so-smug complacency.

Flicking his thumb, Shirak signaled his grandson to diffuse shields. "You failed?" He spoke aloud, partly out of disdain, partly to rest his epsilon centers. His carrier had started to falter, despite hundreds of ayin treatments. The injectable hormone was harvested from his own cloned offspring, by extracting their undifferentiated embryonic brain tissue. Postponing the dreaded epsilon waning was Three Zed's second greatest medical accomplishment after life extension.

An epsilon torrent of information scrambled with anger coursed out of the boy.

"Sit down," Shirak ordered, ignoring Polar's subtly projected approval of the way he spoke aloud. On many occasions, vocal speech did convey insult. "You're babbling. Organize your thoughts."

Micahel folded his body into a hard black chair. He kept that right arm close.

"Hurt yourself?" Polar asked, also disdainfully vocal.

Micahel addressed his grandfather by title. *Yes, Eldest, I failed*, he subvocalized to them both. *I missed one of the pair.*

Testing Director Polar stepped around Micahel. His black eyes—lashless, top and bottom—narrowed in his long face. *The arm. What happened?*

Micahel touched his elbow with his left hand. *Shattered*, he grumbled. *Went through a glasteel window. They just fused it down on Second South.*

Pity, Polar sent blandly. *Ending that line would've made a dramatic opening statement.*

Micahel glared up at his trainer, then frowned across the desk at his grandfather.

Eighty years ago, Eshdeth Shirak's father had made a critical discovery. Though most of the Ehretan Sentinels still called themselves a chosen people, they'd altered their names when they agreed to use the Whorl's trade language. The ancient Carabohd family became Caldwell. Hiding, probably, but the unbound starbred found them. Their mythical significance made them splendid targets.

I matched your record, at least, Micahel sent. *And raised you two female bystanders.*

"How?" asked Shirak.

Four out of five, with clean head shots in their sleep. Micahel's cheek twitched.

Dull, Polar agreed, *but permanent. And the fifth?*

Micahel smiled sidelong at Polar. *Young, unbreached, and alone with her family dead. I had time to force her mind open and show her what I'd done. How I intended to finish.*

An answering smile spread across Polar's long face. *Ah,* he sent appreciatively. *Lend me the memory someday. Especially how she reacted.*

Steepling his fingers, Eshdeth Shirak frowned. "Never forget," he said, "that this family doesn't really threaten us. Striking there simply impresses the faithful."

But someday, Polar answered, *when the last of that family lies cold in his grave, that won't simply end their idiot hope for a messiah. It will prove that their so-called god never existed.*

Micahel squeezed his left hand into a fist.

Polar's determination to disprove old theology puzzled Eshdeth Shirak. He couldn't bring himself to care about Ehretan religion, with its blood memories and unintelligible prophecies.

On the other hand, they'd sent Micahel to Thyrica to prove himself, not to enjoy himself. "May we assume you missed the younger one?" he asked. "The Master Sentinel?"

Of course. The one who's trained in self-defense.

Ah well, Polar projected mockingly. *Did you muddy your tracks?*

Micahel managed a smile. *Remember Paxon, who was thinking about defecting to their camp?*

Shirak frowned. *That's not something we forget.*

I left him under deep command, to wait a week and then attack the College.

That, at least, met Shirak's approval. The Sentinels' College at Arown had the largest number of Sentinels anywhere, except for their impenetrable sanctuary. Every Sentinel dead left the Whorl safer for Shirak's immortal, unborn great-grandchildren.

And if Paxon survives, Micahel added, *he has my memories of that night. Then if they catch and access him, they'll think the murderer's in custody.*

Polar quirked an eyebrow. *This with a shattered elbow?*

Micahel squared his shoulders.

"With that," said Shirak, "your family is pleased."

But I have news. Micahel's epsilon sense darkened. *Master Caldwell's mistress is already pregnant. With twins. And I missed her.*

Shirak groaned. "Then you could've left them three males, not one."

What happened at his house? Polar demanded. *What went wrong?*

Micahel rested his chin on his left hand and shook his head. Plainly he wished Polar hadn't asked. *The mistress was awake and out of their room,* he sent at last. *She roused him before I could get him under command.*

Polar stroked his long face and taunted, *Undone by a pregnant woman. Shame, Micahel.*

Micahel glared.

Polar raised his head and stared sideways, up at the ceiling. *Wasn't she Netaian royalty?* he asked, seemingly out of nowhere.

"Why would that matter?" asked Shirak.

Netaia, Polar projected. *Recite, Micahel.*

Their student turned toward a transparent tank near Shirak's desk. Inside, an arch of shimmering stars mapped the local Whorl, which trailed its arm of the galaxy in slow rotation around the hub. Without gesturing, showing off a new epsilon skill, Micahel swept a blue indicator dot off their own golden pinpoint. He drove it counterspinward toward a pale yellow star near the Whorl's end. *Netaian system,* he projected. *Absorbed by the Federacy only last year. Twelve planets, two colonized, with three deep-space modules in orbit nine. Two subjugate "buffer" systems,* he added, flicking the dot side to side. *And yes, Director. Mistress Firebird is one of Netaia's ruling matriarchy. One of three sisters, all named for native birds.*

Shirak smirked. "Provincial fancy-bred."

Polar stopped stroking his face. *That wasn't my point. Weren't we in touch, decades back, with one of our own who made planetfall on Netaia and was stranded there? I think she was Casvah family. I know she wanted medical attention for her daughters.*

Shirak shrugged. He worked with the long plan—with the future, not the past. Non-Federate worlds didn't interest him.

Polar switched to vocal speech. "We offered treatment if she would come here, but her last communication said one of her daughters had married royalty, and they decided to stay. We lost touch with the line."

"A lost Ehretan family?" Shirak pursed his lips. "Adiyn will want to discuss this." The City's chief geneticist had mapped all known Ehretan chromosomal lines. Could they be sure, though, that the Casvah genes survived, still mingled with royalty? Shirak made a note to alert his Thyrian agents and the newer ones on Netaia.

Micahel half closed his black eyes. Wounded pride throbbed in him. *I won't disappoint you again.*

"You nearly succeeded," Polar said with unusual generosity. "And you survived the attempt. You'll get another chance."

"Don't fixate on a superstition," Shirak warned Micahel, adding an epsilon nudge for Polar's sake.

"Meanwhile," Polar said, "Caldwell has a new weakness, a pregnant bond mate. We could exploit this and bring in new genes with a simple kidnapping."

Director, Micahel interrupted boldly, *Grandfather, stop thinking like old men. For decades, you've held back, just because there are few of us.*

For good reasons. Polar glowered.

Shirak glared too. They tended to distrust their strong-willed young people. Maybe Micahel would benefit from a year's exile to the settlements.

Micahel stood up. He walked to the star tank and stretched out his uninjured arm, as if seizing the Whorl. "Let me hit their college," he said. "Hard. If we started a real fight with the Sentinels, most Federates would trip themselves backing away. They'd abandon the Sentinels like plague carriers. They only half trust them anyway." He held up one finger. "Give me one real attack ship. I'd turn it into a dozen, and those into more. Paxon's feint won't close the College. Every Sentinel trained is one more fighting us." It was the inverse of Shirak's dictum, of course.

Polar eyed his student. *He's fixated, all right. But why not let him try? Tallis might abandon the Sentinels. If it turned on them, that could clear our road straight to Regional command.*

"It's not impossible," Shirak admitted. Breaking up the Federacy would end its ability to defend single worlds. Shirak's son Modabah, administering one of the City's outlying settlements, would enjoy creating several plans of attack.

Polar gripped Micahel's left shoulder. *All we have to lose is Micahel, a few ships, and a few—you weren't thinking of recruiting from the City, were you, Micahel?*

No. The young man's epsilon sense turned sullen. *Settlements.*

We'll talk. Polar gave him a friendly shake.

"Dismissed." Shirak waved a hand. "Congratulations."

Micahel hurried out.

Dru Polar sat down on Shirak's desk, hung a leg over its side, and sent the indicator spark spinning around a remote star system, high over the galactic plane: Ehret, the devastated world where their forbears created genetic telepathy.

Shirak secured his epsilon carrier and wrenched away the spark. Under his direction it whizzed back down into the Whorl, past Thyrica and the Sentinels' sanctuary in the Procyel system, to circle Tallis. "Don't let him strike too hard, too soon," he reminded young Polar. "The armory team isn't ready, and neither are our people on Tallis. Our fathers—your grandfathers—lost their chance to take Ehret because we weren't yet invulnerable—"

"We lost it," Polar interrupted, "because the unaltered cretins resisted. They destroyed it."

"Anger and revenge are fine in your students, but control them," said Shirak. "Don't let Micahel waste too many lives. Not even from the settlements." Until the armory team created impenetrable personal wear, few City adults would venture off Three Zed. No sane, mature person would waste two potential centuries of life on a hazardous mission.

But Shirak remembered his impetuous twenties. He'd tasted a helpless victim's terror. His pass at the Carabohd family eliminated Master Brennen's granduncle.

Casvah, rejoined with the Thyrian remnant. Juddis Adiyn would be ecstatic. He often ordered heredity lines recombined by his reproductive technicians, hoping to produce new abilities in the next generation. A "lost" line could contain untapped gene sequences, more precious than jewels. One skin cell, one drop of blood, would give him a gene sample. An intact specimen would yield better data.

Mistress Caldwell, or a relative . . .

"We can spare a few out there." Polar gestured toward the nearest settlement. Any truly promising youngsters would've left the settlements to be trained in the City. "I'll keep Micahel reined in. He deserves another chance to launch this campaign. He's my top student and your grandson."

Shirak activated the sonic massage unit built into his chair. "Very good. Send him to the settlements, send him offworld, and stand back. But don't interfere with our long goals, friend. It's certainly vital to take the Federacy, but not to thwart the birth of some mythical future messiah."

Brennen followed Damalcon Dardy into Corporal Claggett's underground office at the Base One complex. Claggett and Cristod Harris, a military instructor from the College, were pouring hot cups of kass when Brennen entered.

Seven days had passed since the murders.

Harris was a small man of cocksure stance. He laid a hand on Brennen's arm. "I'm terribly sorry about Tarance and his family. How's your mother?"

"She left yesterday for Kyrrenham." Brennen frowned. He'd passed through shock and anger into a new stage of grieving. Whenever he thought of her, his heart and mind silently challenged the Holy One. She'd mourned his father for years. He felt she deserved better.

"That spiritual retreat south of Peak?"

"Her cousin works there."

"And how are you?"

Instead of answering aloud, Brennen diffused his outer shields and looked into Claggett's eyes, then Harris's, again offering full access to his emotional state.

"True," Claggett murmured. "Those four simply awakened on the other side. What an easy way to make the Crossing. And Destia is past all pain now."

But his mother was not. Did she need so much refining?

He restored his shields. "We should begin. Thank you for including me."

"It was time you joined us." Dardy rolled out a wide sheet of scribe-paper on Claggett's desk. "If you're going to try setting a trap, you'll need this. It's an experimental technology we've named RIA," he said, pronouncing it Ree-a, "Remote Individual Amplification. It's not on record, except for this sheet, because it mustn't be tapped by the Shuhr under any circumstances. So far as we know, they haven't discovered that this feedback cycle can be operated by a single individual."

At the Federacy's Regional command center on Tallis, before his dismissal, Brennen had been a respected Special Operations intelligence officer. Now he coordinated procurement and training, serving as a liaison among Base, College, and Federate-service Sentinels. Dull work, especially after Special Ops, but he embraced it. Now his punishment for disobeying an order kept him near Firebird—and soon, his children.

He eyed the schematic. Generally, a Sentinel working alone could sustain an epsilon wave no farther than a room's width away. Brennen could achieve twice that, but he would love to extend his range.

"Harris discovered it," said Claggett. Harris smiled slightly at the acknowledgment.

Brennen reviewed the P and P Codes, which he constantly refreshed in his trained memory. He couldn't find any clause that banned extending their working range. "But it's not on any file? Have you kept this secret from the Federacy?"

Harris and Claggett exchanged dubious glances. Claggett frowned slightly. "For now," Harris explained, plainly uncomfortable.

Then they disagreed. "Is that wise?" Brennen asked.

"I'm surprised to hear you say that." Dardy raised one eyebrow. "After they expelled you."

Brennen clasped his hands. "I disobeyed an order. Even though I did that to follow my vesting vows, I expected to be disciplined." When he did that, he dashed Dardy's hopes—his own too—to see a Sentinel rise to the Federate High command at Elysia. After ten years on the fast track, he'd had a legitimate chance.

Claggett thrust one hand into a hip pocket. "We're determined to keep this from the Shuhr. That's all."

"I would think so," Brennen murmured. "This has weapons potential." He leaned closer to the schematic. "Show me how it should work."

At that instant, something touched the back of his mind. He whirled away from the schematic and seized the distant quest pulse before it extinguished, then rolled it in his memory, examining its nuances, trying to identify the source. He knew every Sentinel on Thyrica.

This had come from none of them.

He turned back around. Dardy still studied his diagram.

Did any of you feel that? Brennen demanded subvocally. *Quest pulse.*

Dardy raised his head. Claggett and Harris exchanged alarmed glances. "No," Dardy exclaimed.

"Then he wasn't looking for information," said Brennen.

"No." Dardy pointed at Brennen. "He was looking for you."

Brennen touched a control on Claggett's data desk. "Central," answered a bland voice.

"Security alert," Brennen ordered. "We may have a Shuhr agent on Base."

CHAPTER 5

DAY STRIKE

rinforzando
sudden, short crescendo

Brennen keyed Claggett's com over to College Security. He knew the woman who answered. "Carola. Possible Shuhr intruder on Base One. Is my apartment secure?"

"I'll post a guard" came the crisp reply.

"Two, if you have them."

"I'll see if I do."

Harris strode out the door as Claggett secured his documents. Dardy stood glancing from the door to Brennen, hesitating until Brennen sprinted after Harris. A feminine voice droned through the passway speaker. "Stage One alert. Possible intruder. Secure classified data. Stage One alert . . ."

Harris stood holding the lift. Brennen beat Dardy and Claggett inside it and pushed the emergency switch. The door almost caught Harris's foot as it shut, then the cubicle plunged upward at knee-straining speed toward the ground-level command center. When the doors shot open, Brennen hurried across the clearing area. A smoked glasteel roof curved overhead.

Command and Control, a cliffside room, was walled in the same smoky glasteel. Barely glancing at the awe-inspiring sea view, Brennen strode to the main wall of projection screens and controllers' stations. The Base commander, Major General Stieg Moro—a small, florid Thyrian in his fifties—frowned over a controller's shoulder.

A slender young man with a sparse but neatly trimmed beard sat at the number one controller's station. He looked puzzled. "No intruder in this structure," he said.

General Moro wore a row of service and honor ribbons down his left sleeve, the "thread tracks" of a distinguished career. Brennen's thread tracks would have been just as long, but military Sentinels wore no decorations or rank insignia. "I'm having security double check," Moro greeted him. Unlike some nongifted Thyrians, Moro worked well with Sentinels. "Why did you give the alert?"

"Quest pulse," Brennen began.

An angry voice from the main speaker panel interrupted him. "Com One, this is Hangar Two. I've got two MPs down, apparently dead, and an unauthorized startup of one of the FI–2s. Send backup."

A hijacker, inside a hangar full of deadly intercept fighters?

As the bearded controller answered into his collar mike, General Moro scanned the main screen for local air activity. "Scramble the MPs. Have we got a flight up?"

"No drills scheduled until fifteen hundred, sir." A second controller fingered his touchpanels. "Flight Six is in ready room."

Brennen's wartime instincts awoke as if he'd never left Veroh, his first major command. Launching a fighter element would take twelve minutes. By then, that FI–2 could threaten the city of Soldane.

Moro scrambled Six anyway. Brennen stepped back and tried to outthink the intruder. The immediate risk: that he would double back and attack the Base and anything they scrambled to pursue him. Evidently Moro thought so too, because his next order raised the alert level, along with full particle shielding. The intercept fighter still could escape, but nothing incoming would penetrate. No missile, no suicide pass.

Now. Try stopping him inside the hangar.

As if he and Brennen were thinking in tandem, Moro turned to his second controller. "Stage Three," he ordered. "Lock us down." Then he leaned on the console. "Status, Hangar Two?"

The controller relayed. Brennen stayed at the second controller's shoulder. "Give me a visual for Hangar Two."

An interior image appeared at eye level. Ten night black intercept fighters stood side by side. Nine cockpits hung open, already prepped for afternoon drill. The third FI–2 from the right had been closed down. Heat rippled from its laser-ion engines, and Brennen spotted a dark helmet moving inside its cockpit. Near the hardened hangar's main entry, two military policemen lay motionless.

He grimaced. The intruder had penetrated the Base—not difficult—but he'd also breached a guarded hangar and keyed in the ignition code sequence for an FI–2's generators. Those codes were classified.

His next thought made his neck hairs stand up. Besides the hijacker, there could be a traitor among Base Security.

Sunlight shone through the hangar's massive main door. Brennen leaned over the controller's shoulder. "Shut down," he ordered. "Contain him."

"Can't" came the answer over the com. "Circuit's disrupted or something."

"Try manual," Moro barked.

The FI–2 rolled forward. A man's figure dashed toward the fighter, drawing his service blazer. He couldn't beat that ship to the main door. Instead, he dropped to a firing crouch behind a power cart and targeted the landing gear.

The FI–2 kept rolling. The second controller caught Brennen's eye. "Flight Six on its way to Hangar Four, sir. Should be airborne in nine minutes."

Firebird glanced up from her data screen, surprised by a midday knock. It would feel good to stretch, she decided. She walked to the main door and checked its passway monitor. A surprisingly tall, broad-shouldered young man stood just outside, brandishing an ID disk labeled "College Security, Benj Rasey" in his outstretched palm.

As promised, Brennen had installed the secondary security system as soon as its hardware arrived. That door wouldn't open unless she or Brennen touched a control and simultaneously spoke up. The master room had an additional security layer. "Yes?" she asked, keeping her hands at her sides.

The young man raised both eyebrows. "Mistress Caldwell, there's an alert out at Soldane, at Base One. Possible intruder. Nothing's happening here, but I've been asked to stay at your door until I'm given the all-clear. Just didn't want you worrying if you looked out and spotted me."

"Oh." She glanced back at the table. She'd been deep in sociopolitical-economic machinations, surprised to find herself starting to grasp several key concepts. She'd always despised bureaucracy, but every time she ran another simulation, she hoped to find something that might save her people from a bloodbath. College and Base security were light-years from her mind. "Thank you, Benj," she muttered. She switched off the passway monitor, turned away from the door, and plodded back to the servo table.

Curious, she canceled her connection with Soldane University and punched up the Base's public activity channel. Instead of its usual welcoming animation, a geometric pattern filled the inset screen. Three lines of text announced a Stage Three alert in progress.

Firebird's pulse quickened. *What in Six-alpha?* Stage Three was battle status!

Brennen watched the largest screen, which displayed an aerial grid of the Soldane quadrant. A threat-red speck swooped out over Kyrren Fjord, north of the base. The bogey's long turn took it back toward populous Soldane.

Moro's florid face paled. This was a Base commander's nightmare. He'd just alerted public-defense authorities.

Hangar Two reported again: the hijacked fighter carried no missiles, but its laser cannons were half charged. Moro tried to communicate with the unknown pilot. He got no response.

Brennen glared at the screen. If a threat carried bombs or missiles, an intercept anywhere—even over a population center—would be top priority. In this case, he would try not to intercept over a city. The fighter, not its weapons, posed the greatest risk.

The red speck overflew Soldane, still accelerating. Someone behind Brennen said, "Soldane's safe." It headed inland, aiming for the cleft in the tall, jagged Dracken Range, where air and ground traffic passed through.

Inland. Arown. The College!

Brennen turned back to General Moro. "Sir, I need an inland line."

General Moro gestured him to the vacant third controller's station. As Moro alerted other land and ice bases, Brennen keyed for College Security again. The same operator answered. "Carola," he said, "there's a hijacked intercept fighter on its way toward you. Get the particle and energy shields up. Can you evacuate?"

"ETA?" she asked.

He eyed the map screen and took his best guess. "Thirteen minutes."

Her voice rose. "No. Can't evacuate that fast. We'll call shelter drill."

"Good." Double shields should keep the civilians safe, even from a suicide dive by this size ship, and the underground shelters would provide extra protection. But if Security had a traitor, the College's shielding couldn't be trusted. Base and College shared Security staff.

"Carola," he said, "one more thing. Extra security around the shielding generators."

"On its way, General."

Firebird's bluescreen went red. Out in the passway, an eerie klaxon started to whine. Moments later, black letters filled her screen. SHELTER DRILL. REPORT TO UNDERGROUND SECURE AREA. DO NOT DELAY. USE STAIRWELLS, NOT LIFTS.

Someone pounded on her apartment door. "Just a minute," she shouted. She pressed to her feet, crossed the small living area in four steps, and seized her clairsa from alongside the lounger. If anything happened to that handmade instrument, she could never replace it. She shoved it into its long, triangular hard case.

Then she had a second thought. Benj Rasey, College Security, could be a Shuhr agent. They were here, and they had no mercy. She buckled on her dagger's new forearm sheath and tugged her sleeve down to cover it. Then she hurried to the door, pressed its entry control, and said, "Open." The Security man stood with one hand on his shock pistol. "All right," she said, "I'm coming. Are the other apartments alerted?"

"That's what the siren's for. I'm supposed to get you downlevel."

"We can take ten seconds and beat on some doors," she exclaimed.

Another door slid open. A tall, nightrobed woman with craggy features blinked down at her. "Shelter drill," Firebird called. "We have to go down-level. Use the stairs. Anyone else in there?"

"No. My husband's at the med center."

"Good. They'll get him to a secure area. Come on," said Firebird.

Young Benj opened the stairwell's manual door. Firebird glanced at the time lights on her wristband. Two minutes had passed.

Is that new RIA unit operational? Brennen shot the thought at Corporal Claggett.

Claggett stood several paces back, with Dardy. He shook his head. Behind them, the deck had started to fill with Base staff on extended kass breaks.

Moro snapped at his controller. "Full speed, then. Get it into range. We can't shoot down over traffic."

Brennen followed Moro's glance. On the worldwide forces map, one heavy cruiser orbited far south and slightly east, out over the ocean. The cruiser, *Lance*, had electromagnetic catchfield capability. Its normal orbit would've taken it far west of Soldane, but it had shifted course. If they could get it in range, it might snag the hijacker out of midair, no matter how thick the cloud cover or how low he flew.

He? Brennen canceled that assumption. The last time he called for a catchfield, the enemy's young suicide pilot had been female, Netaian, and of royal blood. Shuhr too came in both sexes.

The controller called over his shoulder at General Moro, "Intercept range, eight minutes, forty seconds."

Brennen's shoulders sagged. With the hijacked ship still accelerating, its ETA at College had dropped below six minutes.

Firebird's breath came in gasps by the time she lumbered down two flights of stairs, but she kept going. Benj caught up at the third floor above ground. Leaning on his arm, she hurried through a dark blue blast door and looked around, panting. He pulled her toward the nearest bench and tapped a man on one shoulder. The stranger looked up and instantly offered his seat.

"Thanks," Firebird mumbled. Twin pregnancy was humbling—she looked helpless, and she knew it. She'd rather be out there in the danger zone, fighting at Brennen's side. "Here," she said to Benj. "Give me that."

He handed down her clairsa and stayed close. Firebird concentrated for half a minute on breathing deeply. Meanwhile, her mind raced. Why had the College been sent underground, and why weren't they being told why? Something had happened at Base One. A missile launch botched, a satellite malfunctioning?

An attack from space?

Brennen. *Protect him, Mighty Singer! He's your faithful servant, and Thyrica needs him. I need him!*

The brightly lit duracrete shelter looked to be a quarter-klick long, with a double row of benches up its center and bunks along both sides. Its ceiling curved in a strong-looking half cylinder. It felt hot, and close . . . or maybe that was just her.

The nightrobed woman stood nearby, crossing her arms and glaring around. Firebird spoke up. "I'm sure he's as safe as we are," she said, taking a guess.

"Where's yours?" demanded the woman, making a good guess of her own.

"Soldane."

"This isn't a drill, is it? Something's wrong."

"It's a strange time for a drill," Firebird agreed. She drew a slow, deep breath. If this were another attack on her family, she'd unwittingly endangered hundreds of people by moving to College. Base housing had been considered safer from heavy attack; College, safer from infiltration. They'd chosen with both administrators' blessings.

Mistakenly?

This would be her last pregnancy, she vowed. She hated feeling helpless and defensive and responsible.

She looked around the shelter, abruptly realizing she was somewhat responsible for these people too. A year ago, at Federate Veroh, she'd waited groundside for an attack from space. But that had been a military base, defended by Federate squadrons. These were civilians.

Somewhere close, a child wailed. Firebird leaned forward and poked Benj's broad shoulder. She motioned him out between the benches, beckoned him to bend down, then murmured in his ear, "All right. What's going on? I want a report. Why isn't anyone talking to us? Don't we have inter-link?"

His eyes widened, then his smile crinkled sideways. "That's right, you were military."

"Yes, and my husband's on Base." She said it softly but firmly. Spotting a little local-band interlink on his belt, she reached for it. "Come on," she urged. "Get us a report."

He drew it, thumbed it on, and spoke softly. "Rasey in Unit Five. What's up?" Then he held it to his ear. His eyebrows pulled together, then down. His arm dropped. "College just lost particle shielding," he whispered, "and there's a hijacked intercept fighter on its way in. ETA four minutes."

Appalled, Firebird stepped away from him. She glanced around. No particle shielding?

Maybe the hijacker wasn't headed here.

And maybe skitters will sprout finny wings and fly.

A baby kicked. Hard.

Brennen held his breath as he tracked bogey and cruiser.

"*Lance* can't make it," the controller muttered. He'd done the calculations three times.

Brennen clenched a fist. A cruiser might exceed theoretical max speed, but only with enough advance time to shut down nonessential systems and gradually accelerate. Over his head, the scrambled Thyrian fighters finally roared above the dome and banked eastward. They couldn't catch up, either.

Three minutes, twenty seconds. He'd been decorated for creative thinking under pressure. *Help me now*, he prayed in deadly earnest.

"Don't let me fall," Firebird snapped at Benj. Seizing his shoulder with one hand, she hoisted her right foot up onto the bench.

"Wait," he protested, "you can't—"

She pulled hard against his shoulder and lunged forward, then up onto the bench. Her momentum almost carried her over its other side. Benj grabbed her hand and steadied her. She waved her other arm, shouting, "Listen! Hey, listen to me." A few voices quieted.

A piercing whistle shrieked near her feet. Startled, she glanced down. The nightrobed woman lowered her looped thumb and forefinger.

Firebird shouted into instant silence, "Listen! This isn't a drill. Take cover. Get back under those reinforced bunks along the walls. That's one reason they're here. They're the strongest points in any shelter. Don't hurt each other, but don't waste time. And don't argue," she added. "I've had some emergency experience."

Firebird hadn't given orders since Veroh. To her relief, the shelter's mur-muring occupants parted down its center and moved toward its sloping sides.

"Now," Benj growled. "You get down. Carefully."

Firebird's legs wobbled. Ten flights of stairs, carrying this load! Master Spieth was right about one thing . . . her sense of balance. She let Benj and the woman steady her down, then snatched her clairsa case and hurried to an empty stretch along one rounded wall. Feeling as awkward as a fighter carrier in atmosphere, she sank to her hands and knees, then eased down onto the cold duracrete. She wormed sideways under a bunk, dragging her instrument behind her.

Then she had time to imagine herself lying there, buried under tons of rubble, breathing dust.

She spotted an interlink speaker. Why hadn't topside broadcast to them? Had a line shorted, or did topside have worse problems?

Her forehead felt sweaty again. Her ribs itched. One of the twins shifted gear from slow punches to flutter kicking. *Mighty Singer, protect my children!* Not far away, another child whimpered. Firebird guessed this would be an awful memory for that youngster.

Benj Rasey rolled in alongside.

"You're safer along the wall," she said. "Isn't there room back there?"

"Yes. But if this thing collapses, you're safer if I can help hold up the slab."

"Thanks." She grimaced at the notion.

She hated her next thought, but she couldn't afford to reject it. Benj had acted kindly, even aggressively protective, but he still could be a Shuhr agent.

She loosened her dagger in its new sheath and pushed her back against the rough wall. *Brenn, whatever you're doing, do it fast!*

"Base One to *Lance*," Brennen transmitted. General Moro had just authorized an experimental tactic. "Catchfield on narrow beam, max range. Tug that bogey off course."

"Roger. Narrow beam."

Brennen stared at the Dracken Pass screen.

"Look!" The second controller pointed. "He's drifted."

Lance's catchfield had pulled the hijacker south, barely off course.

"He's correcting, though," Brennen observed. This seemed to be an experienced pilot . . . but maybe—he hoped—not quite experienced enough.

"*Lance* to Base One," said the distant voice. "We have low-grade intercept. Bogey's pulling north and groundward to maintain vector."

"Right," Brennen murmured. He'd pulled against catchfields, flying combat. It felt like compensating for a strong crosswind . . . but crosswinds rarely died as suddenly as a catchfield could be switched off. Let the pilot assume *Lance* really was trying to haul him in. . . . Raising his voice, Brennen directed, "Hold intercept until I signal. Then cut catchfield. Stand by."

"Roger that."

"Good idea," Dardy said softly. Brennen hadn't realized he stood so close.

"What?" a junior officer whispered loudly. "What's he doing?"

Dardy stepped back. "The bogey's trying to maintain his course by steering hard against *Lance*'s catchfield. The field's pulling him up and south, toward *Lance*. He's got to steer north and down to hold his course. But if they suddenly shut off the field—"

"Now," ordered Brennen.

On screen, the red blip bumped north . . . and vanished.

"*Lance!*" called General Moro. "Bogey down?"

"Confirm," said the distant voice. "Bogey down. Getting a smoke plume."

Thank you. Brennen's shoulders sagged with relief. He covered his face with one hand. Someone gripped his shoulder. Someone else cheered.

"Any sign of a chute?" Moro asked.

"Negative, chute," the voice answered. "No sign of evacuation. Looks like a kill."

CHAPTER 6

CONDEMNED

mezzo forte
moderately loudly

Firebird waited behind their apartment door as Brennen strode up the passway late that afternoon. Spotting him on the monitor, she hit the door control and exclaimed, "Brenn!" He lunged through, caught her in both arms, and held tightly.

Benj had gotten the all-clear after five minutes under those bunks. Firebird helped reassure scared children and their anxious parents before taking her turn in the crowded lift. Master Spieth sent a courier ten minutes later with a new prescription, some foul-tasting syrup to prevent early labor.

She and Brennen stumbled together into the apartment, still holding each other. He hit the door control. Then he kissed her fervently, pressing hard against her body. Little limbs pushed back.

After a minute she relaxed, and they fell away from each other. She headed for the servo table, pushed aside the snack she'd been munching, and touched in a triple order.

"The pilot's name was Paxon." Brennen followed her. "Emil Paxon. Recent arrival, allegedly from Tallis."

"How in the Whorl did he get an FI–2 into the air?" Firebird knew about security checks, military police, and generator code sequences. This implied a terrible security breach.

"We don't know." Brennen sank into the opposite chair and pushed hair out of his face. Sweat stains marked his tunic. "I stayed long enough to supervise deep-access questioning of every security tech on Base. Everyone there came up clean. There are still two to check, but they're off duty today."

"Will they check College people too?"

Brennen pursed his lips. "Same crew. That was beyond coincidence when you lost shielding here. Both Base and College have gone to heightened alert. They'll stay that way until further notice." He rested his arms on the table, then laid his head on them. "There's one thing I don't understand," he mumbled. "It takes six days for a messenger ship to reach Three Zed. Their leaders couldn't have found out that the original attack failed, in order to command Paxon to try again—not for five more days."

An exquisite smell drifted out of the warmer slot, distracting her. "Go back to that access questioning," she said. "Remember, I hid things from you under access, back at Veroh."

"Possible." He pushed up off the table. "But only if a subject's extremely strong. There's usually some sense of resistance."

He talked casually about advanced interrogation techniques. . . . *And I still haven't even started learning!* she grumbled silently. It was high time she took that last qualifying test. "Aren't Shuhr supposed to breed for epsilon talent?"

"That's only a rumor."

She stared at the digital timer over the warming slot. Ninety-three seconds until dinner. Ninety-two. Ninety-one. "Maybe," she said, "you just proved it. Who's our sec tech for this building?"

"Harcourt Terrell. He was the first one suspected, but the first to volunteer for access. I checked him myself."

Brennen had been the Federacy's top access interrogation specialist. If he hadn't found deception, no one else possibly could.

But just as she'd felt Benj Rasey was no threat, she doubted this Harcourt Terrell. He made such a logical suspect. "Please don't count him out. Keep an eye on him."

"We will."

"Do you suppose," she asked, "that Paxon was our . . . the murderer?"

As Brennen's eyebrows lowered, she felt the deep rumble of his anger. He too must've stared at the newsnet image of an FI–2 burning on a boulder-strewn slope, inky smoke turning white as the first flames subsided. "I hope so," he said. "If he was, he's no threat now."

Firebird plunged back into both sets of studies the following day, and the next. On the third, she reported to a tiny, bare cubicle across campus and recited into a monitor for two hours.

The College didn't keep her waiting for the results. Immediately, the test administrator sent her to an office in the same building.

A woman answered the entry alarm. Thin, arched eyebrows almost vanished under her wispy bangs. *What a lovely woman*, Firebird observed. Was she fifty? On second thought, she must be younger . . . possibly by quite a bit. Sentinels couldn't use youth-implant capsules, which most Federate citizens carried under their skins from early adulthood. An implant released synthetic hormones that forced aging and mutating somatic cells to replace themselves, but by bitter coincidence, that process attacked the genetically altered ayin complex. As a wastling, Firebird had never needed an implant.

"Mistress Caldwell," said the woman, "come in. I'm Janesca Harris."

Firebird followed the Sentinel inside. She reached up out of habit to flick hair over her shoulder, but she'd tied it back today, like she used to do when training for battle. "Good morning, Sentinel Harris."

"You may call me Janesca, Firebird. Congratulations on passing your first memo exam. First of many, I'm afraid—if you're sure you want to proceed." Beneath slightly drooped eyelids, Janesca Harris's clear brown eyes pierced with a brilliance like Brennen's.

"I'm sure." Firebird glanced all around. The office looked out on the College quadrangle, where knife-edged shadows scuttled across the wet jujink lawn. On an interior wall, in Janesca's meter-square aquarium, primitive green proto-fish slithered between pink and yellow creatures that looked like pompon flowers.

Her stare caught in one corner, where a triangular stringed instrument sat on a wooden stand. "Oh," she exclaimed, "is that a kinnora?" She'd heard of the Thyrian small harp, but hadn't hunted one down. She'd been sightseeing while she could, studying what she must, and turning the beautiful house on Trinn Hill into a home.

She missed it already.

Sentinel Harris picked up the dark instrument. "Most visitors ask if I play or if it's just for decoration." She strummed the colorful strings with one fingernail. They rang together in a sweet, sustained pentatonic sweep, with no jarring minor seconds. "I understand you're a harper too."

"I've played since I was eight. It's the only thing I owned on Netaia that I still have. I play for the boys when they kick." Firebird stroked her loose skyff.

Janesca motioned her toward a simple kirka-wood chair, then pulled a dark blue bound volume off her shelf. No common scanbook cartridge, it matched the Code book Firebird had studied. "Before I issue this," said Janesca, "I must administer a sekiyr's first oath. Our abilities carry grave responsibility. Are you ready to hold yourself accountable to the College and its masters?"

"Of course."

"You understand the consequences if you ever use these skills selfishly? This is your last chance to back down without consequences."

"I understand," Firebird said soberly. "Brennen and Ellet Kinsman both explained that misuse is a capital offense."

"Very well." From a closed compartment, Janesca drew a dull gray object that looked like a dagger hilt. Firebird recognized an Ehretan crystace, the Sentinels' ceremonial weapon. One touch on its activating stud, and sonic waves would bombard the ehrite-shard blade inside that hilt. Two of the blade's axes would elongate, stretching it to arm's length.

"Place your hand over mine on the crystace," said Janesca.

Grinning, Firebird grasped the older woman's hand. She loved ceremony. Most Netaians did. Still, she didn't lean too far forward.

"It's a simple vow," said Janesca. "Repeat as I do. 'This is my vow, to use only in the service of others, in obedience to the holy Word, any skills that I learn in this training.'"

Firebird followed phrase by phrase.

"'This is the crystace with which I shall keep my vesting vows, if my skills and compliance satisfy my masters.'"

Firebird felt her eyes widen. Her own crystace? She'd seen Brennen's, even held it and swung it. But her own!

"'This is the crystace . . .'" Janesca spoke on, her eyes more solemn. Firebird repeated the words.

"'. . . they shall sheathe in my heart, if ever, defying this oath, I use Sentinel skills for capricious or selfish purposes.'"

Firebird's hand tingled as she echoed the final clause. That was a risk she felt willing to take.

Janesca returned the weapon to her wall compartment. "Congratulations," she murmured. "Never take that oath lightly. It has been done."

"I understand." If Brennen could keep these codes, she could too.

"Well!" Janesca handed her the midnight blue book. "Read the first subheading."

Firebird took it with trembling fingers. Inside, her new name—Firebird Mari Caldwell—already had been scribed on the coverleaf in a flowing, feminine script. Seeing that, she warmed even more to Janesca Harris.

One. P'nah, The Turn.

The release of mental energy onto a modulated epsilon carrier presupposes an ability to identify and locate epsilon energy and to separate it from background sensory imagery. Turning inward to sense one's self at the primal level was originally considered the best way to begin. Beyond oneself, though, other powers exist, some good and some evil. Proceed with prayerful caution.

At the moment before falling asleep, when thought is stilled, there occurs an inward-chasing of the mind's natural pattern that will lead in sleep to dreams. To consciously follow that chase inward, to sense the

energy arising in one's own ayin complex, has proved a practical beginning for this course of study.

"Ready to try?" asked Janesca.

Firebird didn't quite understand. "What exactly is turning?"

"It is a preparatory mental posture. The epsilon energy we use is already
present in certain locations in your nervous system. You must learn to sense
it before you can use it."

"I see."

"You'll learn to take this listening, or turning, or grasping stance quickly
and smoothly. Then, once you can maintain the turn, you'll learn to control,
then project, the wave of epsilon energy."

"Right." Firebird closed her eyes. Determined to succeed, she relaxed
toward sleep—or tried to.

The next hour surpassed any day spent with her sister Phoena for sheer
hellish frustration. Though Janesca encouraged and offered suggestions, the
simple act of mindfully listening inward seemed utterly impossible.
Thoughts of food—she'd forgotten to eat while studying (she couldn't face
the traditional Thyrian fish breakfast these days, anyway)—new concepts
she'd studied, and even the sun playing hide-and-search outdoors all took
turns distracting her, though once she thought, almost . . .

Her leap toward the odd momentary sensation brought her alert and
drowned out the faint touch with a chorus of mental comments.

Exhaling, she let her head droop.

"Relax," said Janesca. "Rest."

Firebird pulled the soft tie out of her hair. This was unbelievable. The
simplest, most basic mental gesture—and she couldn't make it. This would
go on her record. She longed to conceal her failure. *Not in this enclave, you
won't!* . . . And she'd have to tell Brennen first, when he came home tonight.
That would dent her thickheaded pride. The College's character examiners
had warned that she faced a lifelong battle against willfulness, impatience,
and pride. She'd gone home that day feeling branded. Tattooed. Brennen
hadn't comforted her when he confessed that he too had been warned . . .
of ambition and overconfidence in his abilities.

Pride, one of the Powers, had been drilled into her as a virtue! It still
drove her to always, always excel. "Was any of that even close?"

"No," said Janesca. "Like mind-access, it's a specific sensation."

She compressed her lips. "How will I know when I get it?"

"I'll tell you."

"I can't study, can't practice at home."

"Not until you can do this. If you have time at home, start studying the second Code book."

"I'll try again," Firebird insisted. "Once more."

Janesca spread her hands. "I'm sorry, but we've gone past your time. Come tomorrow at eight hundred. Bring your . . . clairsa," she suggested. She must've found the instrument's name in Firebird's vita. "I've worked several girls through their first turn with music."

Firebird had barely stumbled back into the apartment when its entry alarm rang again. Startled, she set down Code book Two and took a deep breath. This didn't necessarily mean another attack. Actually, with her thoughts looping around and around, inventing excuses for her failure, she would appreciate a distraction.

On the passway monitor screen appeared a woman wearing quicksilver gray.

Federate messenger service! College Security would've scanned both the messenger and her parcel. Firebird sent the door open.

"For you, Mistress Caldwell." The woman handed her a short metal tube. "Prepaid."

For decades, faster-than-light ships had provided the fastest communication over interstellar distances. Firebird laid the roll on an end table and read the source, then shook her head, disbelieving. It had come from Citangelo, her home city. Had another Netaian month passed already? This should be her monthly summons to return and answer charges of high treason, heresy, and sedition.

She leaned against the windowbar and stared out at another Thyrian rain shower. She stood charged with high treason because—very much against her will—she survived her first and only military mission . . . and interrogation.

Heresy? Essentially, Netaians worshiped their government as the Powers' elect presence. Captured during Netaia's attack on Federate Veroh, she had watched her navy slaughter civilians and in her grief, accepted asylum. Later she took Federate transnational citizenship . . . and by defecting, betrayed the Powers.

They added "sedition" to her charges when she and Brennen—acting against Federate orders—thwarted her sister Phoena's deadly plot to restore Netaian independence. She killed a researcher . . . accidentally, but who on Netaia believed that? Instead of charging her with simple murder, they included that in the grave sedition charge.

She was guilty of all these "crimes." What charge would they add when they learned she was pregnant? That news would arrive on Netaia momentarily, because of the Shuhr attack and the police report.

Angry—that simply by living, she became a high criminal—she curled up with her new Code book and the first half of lunch. Netaia's electors might've discreetly celebrated if Emil Paxon had killed her and dozens of others.

Electors deserved to be overthrown. She would just ignore that message roll. . . .

But she couldn't. As minutes passed, she stole one glance at it, then another. In Citangelo, where it originated, formal gardens along the palace's white marble facade would be bursting with early summer's white, scarlet, and gold blossoms.

In back, the private lawns would lie like sun-washed carpets. She'd taken dry weather for granted there! She had loved to run barefoot downslope toward the reflecting ponds, flipping somersaults whenever no electoral red-jacket followed to make sure she maintained her dignity.

Lady Firebird Angelo, queen's wastling, had tried passionately to serve Netaia, to contribute by life and by death to its glory.

And she'd killed a man. A nobleman, whose wastling children she'd known, and whose father publicly praised her . . .

Tears blurred her vision. She glanced out the window, upward this time. Shredded gray clouds raced overhead. A hundred klicks north, it was probably snowing. Brennen's soaking wet world was lovely and lush, but it would never be her home.

Pregnancy hormones! Aching, she seized the message roll and twisted its seal.

A bound bundle of hard copy dropped out. Its heavy cover displayed her own scarlet-and-gold family crest, a shield with three stars, above the gold electoral seal. This was no summons, but a legal transcript. The electors had finally tried her *in absentia.*

What was the verdict? she wondered, though she guessed. She flipped past pages of legal exposition to the summation.

Charge of high treason: guilty as charged.
Charge of heresy: guilty.
Charge of sedition: guilty.

Surprise, she sighed silently. No elector would defend a royal wastling for obeying her conscience . . . and by their terms, she was unquestionably guilty. She'd even committed one more crime, which they never proved: She helped a fellow wastling escape offworld.

She paged backward. Her sister Phoena's name appeared at several places, testifying against her and even suggesting they reopen the old investigation of Lord Alef Drake's disappearance. Her oldest sister, Carradee—married to Alef's brother—had presided but said little.

Firebird turned to the end, oddly nervous. Had they sentenced her?

To death, of course. By a sadistically tidy execution protocol known as lustration, in the largest available public venue, should she ever reenter Netaian space.

She swallowed hard. *No chance of that, noble electors!*

Lustration was an old word meaning "purification," and the sentence was reserved for the apostate. Beginning at fingers and toes, the condemned prisoner's extremities—and, eventually, torso—were compressed by slowly moving metal plates superheated to vaporize flesh and bone. Lustration could last for hours, giving the prisoner ample time to atone for her heinous crime . . . and maybe to recant.

Nauseated by the thought, she spotted a loose sheet of scribepaper and held it up to the rainy daylight. Occupation Governor Danton had exercised his prerogative and granted a full pardon, though he recommended that she not return until the noble electors rescinded her sentence.

Thank you, Governor. Sadly she rerolled the papers. Her fellow electors would never do that.

She whacked the windowbar with the bundle, slapped tears off her cheeks, then compulsively reopened and reread the sentence against her. It carried the official seals of both Crown and Electorate. They'd even forced Carradee to sign it.

She must learn to belong among Brennen's people or else belong nowhere for the rest of her days. Why should this hurt so much? As a wastling, she had lived under a death sentence all her life.

But in only a few days, Netaia would celebrate Carradee's official birthday, on the same date when all queens had been honored. Last year the palace's first-floor ballroom had rung far into the night with music and giddy gaiety. She and her fellow wastling, Lord Corey Bowman, had whirled in each other's arms until neither could stand upright.

Corey died when Netaia invaded Veroh—turned instantly with his tagwing fighter to fusion fire.

Firebird straightened her weary back. She wouldn't cry anymore. Her past died with Corey, and she lived for a future that would include her sons. Someday—soon!—she would master that epsilon turn. Seizing the codebook, she opened it back to chapter one and read, *Shielding in the Presence of the Nongifted. In Service . . .*

CHAPTER 7

PHOENA'S CHOICE

quasi maestoso
almost majestically

For Phoena Irina Eschelle Angelo, the final hours of the queen's birthday always had been the highest point of her year. Tonight, the main palace ballroom—floored in black marble shot with gold—was curtained with Angelo-crimson velvette swaths. Bas-relief portraits representing all nine holy Powers observed from the gilt-crusted ceiling, while life-sized gilded statues of historical electors watched over furniture groups from their periods. Phoena had dressed in her finest. Tonight she would dance with every nobleman on Netaia, young and old, from all ten noble families, receiving their homage. This year the Queen's Ball honored Phoena's sister instead of their mother, but that changed nothing important. Nor did the slightly jealous new husband who hovered nearby with friendly words for her other dancing partners.

She and Count Tel Tellai had married in splendor two months ago. Tel was an elegant little husband, well dressed and well mannered, with a passion for Netaia that almost matched her own, but beauty must be shared, or it would wither. Phoena's honeyed complexion made men blink and stare. She could unnerve the most noble duke with a flicker of hot brown eyes.

She shook out her gold-toned sleeves and took the thin arm of Baron Reshn Parkai. At the far end of the ballroom, below triple ranks of jeweled chandeliers, a fine orchestra filled the dais. Tonight, the Netaian aristocracy ruled a crowd sprinkled with only the best-connected commoners, and not one uniformed Federate was in evidence. Tonight this did not look like an occupied world.

The orchestra played superbly. A pity Firebird couldn't hear it, Phoena observed as she took the baron's half-gloved hand. Music affected her wastling sister in baffling ways. It altered her moods and brought out a perverse inner strength. No rightful heir or heiress had been safe from scornful glances when Firebird lived on Netaia. Obviously, Firebird had hoped to displace Phoena in the succession. She would have tried if she dared, but that crime carried terrible consequences.

How satisfying to know she wouldn't return. With the grim sentence passed, Phoena finally could put Firebird out of her mind. Though she would willingly witness the lustration, she'd voted for lethal injection. Firebird was positively terrorized by needles.

Traitors' executions weren't horrendous just for deterrent value. The more a criminal suffered while dying, the shorter her agonies would be in the horrific Dark that Cleanses, where all evil was purged from offenders' souls before passage was granted to eternal bliss.

Phoena and Parkai bowed correctly to one another. A line of trumpeters strode forward through the orchestra and assembled on the dais steps. Their fanfare called the crowd to assemble and toast Carradee Second.

Phoena summoned her dainty-faced prince with a crooked finger. They joined Carradee and Prince Daithi on a platform near the conductor's podium. Servitors in scarlet livery circulated hastily, balancing goblets on gold trays. As tradition decreed, the queen's future would be saluted by nine people, and then Carradee would answer. Phoena, asked to toast, had declined. She explained to Carradee that any woman would rather be praised by a man than another woman!

And Carradee believed her. "Carradee the Good" and "Carradee the Kind," Phoena had heard her called.

Carradee the Federate Toady, Phoena pronounced to herself. She loathed insincerity. She couldn't have wished Carradee a long reign.

First Lord Bualin Erwin knelt at the foot of the dais. "It is my sublime privilege . . ."

Phoena gave her nails a quick buff on her sleeves and displayed her public smile. She knew how to feign gracious interest. Beside her, Tel straightened the fringed formal sash of his new rank by marriage. After the debacle up north eight months ago, Phoena had been forced to arrange repairs to Hunter Height and pay costs from her personal accounts. Then she'd been threatened with a further investigation, as Occupation Governor Danton pressured Carradee for details of Phoena's research. Phoena had needed to distract Carradee. Tel obliged by proposing the wedding.

She eyed her sister. Carradee, tallest of the three Angelo sisters, looked radiant, though Carradee wasn't known for her beauty. Why tonight? It couldn't be the simple blue gown, though that set off her pale gray eyes and camouflaged her tendency to carry an extra kilo or two (or five). Nor her conservative sweep of blond curls. Even with a full staff of servitors, Carradee showed no imagination in clothing or hair. But tonight she wore the delicate Iarla crown, a confection of goldstone and ruby-set arches, and she looked glowingly happy.

It would be lovely to be queen at the Queen's Ball, standard bearer for holy Authority and the three Netaian systems. Phoena kept smiling, but she ached with jealousy. Last year, she'd reached for power and missed. Pacified by Phoena's insistence that she never meant to take the throne—only to help liberate Netaia from the Federacy, which they both wanted—Carradee had apparently forgiven her. But another chance might come, so Phoena had endured her month of house arrest with Tel's devoted help, paid her fines, and then turned back to guiding the secret loyalist movement. One day they would throw the Federates off Netaia.

Carradee rose in her turn, elaborately thanked each person who had toasted her, and drained her glass. Then she raised a hand and signaled the orchestra to wait. "One other thing," she announced.

This is it, Phoena observed. Whatever had Carradee so tickled, it was about to come out. Phoena shook her shoulder-length chestnut hair, which tonight she wore in perfect waves, each lock beaded at the end with a cluster of emeralds. Tel flicked imaginary dust from his black sateen jacket. He too understood the importance of appearances. He had the makings of a very decent portrait painter, and he'd landscaped exquisite gardens at the Tellai estate before she moved him into the palace.

"We have the privilege," Carradee continued, clasping her short-fingered hands, "of making an announcement no other queen in the history of our great people has made. We do singularly feel the honor, the delight, and the hope that this is only a foretaste of years ahead, as Netaia takes its rightful place among great systems of the Whorl."

Hmm. Well put, for Carradee.

Carradee's gold-jacketed Prince Daithi remained at attention, with his brown curls for once slicked smooth, as Carradee slow-stepped along the dais's edge. "In recent weeks," she continued, "we have been forced into difficult, even impossible decisions."

At the reference to Firebird's death sentence, Phoena narrowed her eyes. She regained her composure, but now she listened suspiciously.

"Yet our great world has entered a new age of great thoughts, great deeds, and great hearts," Carradee insisted. "And so, noble electors, gentlemen and ladies, we rejoice to tell you this. We have received news from Thyrica, where our youngest sister, Lady Firebird, now lives in enforced exile. Although we have decreed that she may not return, we ask you—our good guests—to rejoice with us on this festive night. Lady Firebird expects a child in less than two months."

For five seconds, if a greenfly had landed somewhere in the ballroom, every partygoer would have heard it. Never had a wastling gone so far. Sacred Disciplines barred even Phoena, as the second-born, from bearing children unless Carradee died without issue . . . and she had two young daughters.

Other faces showed shock, or disbelief, or delight that quickly was concealed, but Carradee beamed. Then a wave of sound splashed banner-hung walls. Everyone started to speak at once.

Except Phoena. Scandalized by Firebird's new crime against the heritage that should have meant more to her than life itself—should've ended her wretched life almost a year ago—she stood motionless until Carradee reached her and spoke softly over the clamor. "Phoena, I tried to reach you alone, earlier, but you were at the tresser."

Phoena crossed her arms and frowned severely. Tel kept still, as he should. This was an Angelo concern.

"She can't come back, Phoena. You saw to that. Evidently they were trying to keep this a secret, but—"

"I should think so."

"It came out in a newscan. She and General Caldwell were attacked in their home."

"But?" Phoena leaped to the disappointing conclusion. If they'd come to grief, Carradee would have made a graver announcement.

"No, no. They weren't hurt."

"I'm sorry to hear that."

"Yes! One should be safe in one's home." Carradee seemed, or pretended, not to understand. "Phoena, listen to me. Insofar as the Crown is concerned, you and Tel are welcome to have children of your own too. If you and I stood together, I am sure we could persuade the other electors to establish a kindlier law of succession. No other culture practices heir limitation. No estate is worth preserving at such a cost to our beloved children. I truly believe that. Don't you?"

Phoena wanted to shriek, but commoners would hear. Carradee Second, this monarch, this head of the Electoral Council—this Federate puppet!—approved Firebird's apostasies. She offered a chance to commit similar crimes with impunity. Had she too lost all honor? All sense of Strength, Valor, and Excellence . . . and how about Fidelity? Resolve?

Authority! Those Powers, and all the others, glared down from the ceiling.

Once again, Carradee proved that she didn't deserve to wear that arching, jeweled circlet—with the extra chins it gave her—nor any other crown.

"You'll see what I believe," Phoena answered in a low voice like poison.

Carradee backstepped, wide-eyed, and finally signaled the orchestral conductor. As he directed the opening chords of another dance medley, Phoena gathered her skirts. She whirled from the dais, trailing Prince Tel behind her. Dancers dodged as she strode across the marble floor.

She had almost reached the crimson-curtained doors when a tall man stepped into her path. She glared into his eyes for an instant.

Bowing apology, he ducked aside. She swept out the doors.

At three hundred that morning Phoena lay awake, irritated to the core by Tel's soft, regular breathing. In privacy, he'd admitted he felt glad for Firebird.

Glad! The little slink!

How could this be happening? Power was slipping away from Netaia's rightfully ordained nobility, the only rulers who could govern with justice and far-future vision. Three centuries ago, outworld invaders devastated Netaia. Only the noble class, undergirded by a dying religion they altered and revived for this purpose, had restored order and prosperity. Bound to obedience at all social strata, Netaia achieved cultural glory.

Now, under the Federates, commoners lusted for rights that could undercut long-range justice, even for their own descendants. The Federates surrounded Carradee, poisoning her with low influences. Carradee had even appointed four business leaders—commoners!—to her Electorate.

Carradee had no backbone. If Phoena sat on the throne, by this date she might've thrown off Governor Danton and his minions . . . but Phoena couldn't challenge the militarily powerful Federates alone.

No, but by Ishma and Delaira and the littlest moon Menarri, she knew who could!

Shocked by the thought, she sat upright in her octagonal bed. Brennen Caldwell's colleagues supposedly had relatives who had never bowed to the Federacy. She'd never considered asking their help for the loyalist movement . . . until tonight. Why now?

Why not? Phoena wrapped long, bare arms around her knees and stared into the dismal future Carradee was creating. Prosperity, culture, and security would vanish from Netaia, unless someone made a bold throw to save it all, to dare—and risk losing—everything that made life satisfying.

She must not leave Citangelo without taking precautions, of course. A pair of loyal House Guards, a Vargan stinger—deadly, but easy to conceal— no, two stingers.

She threw off her silken bedcovers. Maybe no one else had the courage to do this, but in future years, Netaia's nobility would recall Phoena's choice and salute her with reverence.

In her private freshing room, she slipped into an unostentatious traveling suit, then gathered a few bits of feminine trivia for her shoulder bag.

Tel stirred on the bed, snorting as he flailed toward the warm spot she'd left empty.

She froze and waited for him to speak, but he rolled over again and sank deeper into sleep. She found a black coat. Somehow she knew exactly where she ought to go. Should she leave Tel a message with her personal girl?

No. He'd try to stop her, and she didn't want to be followed. He would realize soon enough that she'd left him.

And by all nine of the Powers, and for their sake—halting in the doorway, Phoena pressed one hand to the marble wall and vowed it—she would not return until she came home to be crowned.

By stealth and luck, Phoena left the palace grounds unobserved by her other House Guards, by the Federates, and even by a team of Sentinel aides, whose watch was focused at that critical moment on partygoers leaving through the front gate. Two escorts followed her across the parklike lower grounds to a minor gate, unguarded but keyed to family members' palm prints. Without hurrying, she proceeded down a darkened, increasingly dangerous street into a neighborhood between landed estates. Footsore and shivering, she tapped on the tinny door of a ground-level apartment built from graying duracrete blocks, then glanced back up the narrow street. Neither Federates nor criminals had trailed them. Finding the entry alarm, she pressed it and held it down.

The door slid partway aside. "Yes?" asked an unfamiliar voice.

"My name is Phoena Angelo," she muttered. "Let me in."

As the door slid aside, Phoena stepped into a world she rarely visited, the realm of the low-common class. Two meters ahead, up a narrow hallway, shone a blinding yellow lamp. She caught a whiff of old grease and musty perfume and hoped her sense of smell would fatigue quickly.

She beckoned her guards to follow. One drew a shock pistol. The other kept both hands free.

Following this stranger up a worn shortweave carpet, Phoena saw a table and several padded sling chairs. One was occupied.

Penn Baker, a flabby-figured man whose eyes never stopped watering, finally introduced himself and then the lanky man with dark hair and bony cheeks as "My host Ard Talumah, a traveling merchant." She recognized the long-faced man, a commoner. How was that possible?

On Baker's ceiling, she spotted the compulsory receiving grid, a hand-sized panel installed in one room of every low-commoner or servitor's dwelling. There always was a slim chance Enforcement was watching or listening. For the first time, it worried her.

"Forget that." Penn Baker waved toward a tiny pyramid on his scarred tabletop. "Compliments of Talumah," he explained.

Phoena eyed the device. "Scrambler?" she asked. "If this room ever comes up for inspection, and there's no image—"

"There'll be an image," Baker interrupted. "Sound, too, with the sonic signatures of people who might actually be in the room. But repeating whatever was programmed ahead of time."

Impressed, Phoena frowned at the device. For now, she would use it. But when she returned as queen, she would eliminate such technology.

The floor rattled for several seconds, startling her. "Maglev train," Baker explained. "We're over the tunnel."

Talumah's stare amplified her unease. "You're offworld?" she demanded. "Here on business?"

"Call it that." Talumah's dark smile was almost a sneer. She decided to ignore him and deal with Baker. It took only a few words to explain what she wanted.

"Of course, I'll represent you to them." Baker rubbed his eyes with a pale hand. "I'd be honored. Who else knows you came to me?"

"No one. That is the only way to keep secrets."

"Well done, Highness." Talumah applauded insincerely with his fingertips.

"These men will come along." She gestured back at her House Guards. "I would also appreciate your concealing my presence until I take a few further precautions."

"Naturally, Your Highness." Talumah unfolded himself out of his sling chair. To her surprise, he bowed reasonably well. "I would be honored," he said. "Deeply honored." As he stared, just longer than she would call polite, strange new thoughts tickled her mind. Really, why bother with extra precautions? The unbound starbred would value her as one of their own. She was welcome to bring honor guards, but the Shuhr would not merely respect her. They would revere her.

He smiled. Finally, she recognized him. He'd stepped into her path near the crimson-hung doors as she led Tel from the ballroom, shortly before she decided to go to the Shuhr.

Talumah left before sunrise. For four days, Phoena showed Penn Baker her public smile, wore borrowed clothing, and paced that stale-smelling hallway. Its duracrete-block walls were so poorly cured that flakes and even gouges had fallen, leaving holes that some previous occupant, amusing himself, had painted the precise shade of orange that represented Excellence—her personal favorite of the Powers—in Netaia's noble-class heraldry. She could've purchased her own ship ten times in four days, but Baker kept claiming he needed more time.

So she tracked the newsnets, none of which carried any word of her disappearance. Carradee undoubtedly was frantic, but afraid to advertise Phoena's disappearance. Not even the cheap channel, which had sunk to new lows of scandal and rumor under Federate governance, mentioned Phoena. Carradee wouldn't go to Federate Governor Danton until it was much too late. She never would know Phoena had hidden within a stone's throw of prestigious River Way, less than three klicks from the palace.

On the fourth evening, Phoena sat in one of Baker's sling chairs, idly watching an evening newsnet broadcast. Danton's spokeswoman claimed that the Federacy was paying fifty percent of the costs to rebuild Netaia's shattered planetary defenses. "Less than that," Phoena fumed. "My friends are selling off resources to pay his new taxes. This is a Federate ploy to disfranchise the noble class."

Baker snorted. "Selling off resources? I'd like to see you try to buy anything technical on my wages, with so many factories blasted away."

She sniffed. "No one's trying to rob you of your heritage. Your very identity—"

"You electors," he interrupted, "gave us the Veroh War. You brought the Federacy down on us. If the Feds only make you pay half to rebuild, that's generous."

"Shut up," she snapped. With one crosstown call, she could send him and all his family to Hinnana Prison.

"You'll see." He glared at the wall screen. "Someday, you nobles will see what your people really think of you."

Her cheeks heated. "Shut up!" she repeated through clenched teeth.

The next morning, when Baker slipped back into his apartment, he seemed properly subservient again. "Are you ready to leave, Your Highness? I've found a ship."

"Good." She sniffed. "I have made my arrangements. It's time we were gone."

She never thought to wonder where her House Guards had gone, and she forgot the Vargan stingers.

CHAPTER 8

GOLDEN CITY

energico
with energy

Phoena could hardly wait to debark from Penn Baker's six-person shuttle. Years before, Firebird had scornfully labeled her a "groundhog," and on this ten-day slip there were miserable, claustrophobic moments when she wished she too had adjusted to space travel. She hated the constant vibration in her body while the ship and every molecule aboard remained at right angles toward normal space—turned that way by the slip-shield so they could exceed light speed. Worse, she gasped a little every time she remembered that light-years of vacuum sucked at the ship's shining hull. At any moment, something—some infinitesimal something—could end her mission, and no one would ever know where she had gone or why.

But here they were. She didn't spot her final destination until the last few seconds before landing, when with a pudgy hand Baker pointed to several incongruously smooth strips around an old volcano on this airless lump of a planet. "Shielded entries," he explained. "Not every lava tube on Three Zed is settled, but wait until you see this one." Then he busied himself at his controls. She couldn't understand the splatter of glowing panels on his display, nor did she care to. As inhospitable as that lava field looked, she would prefer solid rock to this flimsy, cluttered lifeboat.

An entry cracked open. They glided through. Penn Baker grounded the shuttle at the center of a small hangar with pocked black walls and said, "We'll pass through into the main bay when we have air."

The hangar darkened abruptly. She seized a grab bar. A second pair of smooth metal doors swept open beyond the shuttle's nose, and Baker followed a stream of light into the cavern.

A minute later, as Phoena walked down the landing ramp, she felt her first qualm about coming to these people. Her suit smelled musty. Their first impression would not be as Excellent as she wished. But never mind; they shared a goal. Resolutely wrapping long fingers around her shoulder bag, she watched ten men approach between rows of service machinery under an irregular metal ceiling. Two of them stopped short of her. The rest, evidently service personnel, passed toward Baker's ship.

Phoena eyed the greeters. Both had wavy dark hair and cold, distant brown eyes in nicely masculine faces.

"Your Highness?" The one on the right barely bowed. He wore an edging of gold on the collar of his deep gray-green jumpsuit. It looked like a uniform insignia.

"Yes," she said. "I'd like to speak with someone in authority."

"Those are my orders." He gestured toward a metal door. Baker offered Phoena his arm. As she stepped out, the other greeter paced a few steps behind.

The door slid open. Phoena felt her eyes widen. Beyond the landing bay opened a long, straight tunnel that was roofed, walled, and floored in brilliant, nugget-textured gold. Delighted, she clutched Baker's arm.

He covered her hand. "Welcome to the Golden City," he said. A smile dimpled his pale cheeks.

Phoena tilted her chin, raised her chest, and strode forward.

The gleaming corridor branched several times, sometimes at right angles and sometimes into side passages that curved like tetter tunnels. At last they passed through a golden sliding door into a major chamber. Overhead, the ceiling vanished into an unlit distance. Beneath her feet opened a chasm whose depth she couldn't guess, but over it, a transparent floor of gray volcanic glass had been laid. Inset here and there on faceted walls of gleaming gold, gems and metal filigree sparkled in artful arrangements. A flowering vine clung to trellised supports nearby.

Phoena smiled. She could learn to be comfortable here.

Near a group of chairs, three men stood to acknowledge her. One, stocky and stubby legged, had puffy eyes and a crooked smile. The man who stood centrally was a head taller, broad shouldered, gray at his temples but otherwise impeccably blessed with stunning black hair. He gripped his wide belt with lightly furred hands.

The third man appeared closest to her age. As tall as the one in command, he'd grown his hair to a stunning shoulder length, and from collar to cuffs he wore brilliant sapphire blue, with a black sash belt. His eyes were black, and as she stepped close she saw that he had no eyelashes, top or bottom. Manly confidence streamed from him like a corona. She couldn't imagine a more stunning contrast to her spineless little prince of convenience.

"Your Highness, welcome." The man at center spoke with a heavy, unidentifiable accent. "I am Eshdeth Shirak, director and Eldest of the

Golden City. My colleagues, Juddis Adiyn, whose research continues to extend both our youth and our old age." The stubby man inclined his head, grinning as if she'd brought him a wonderful gift. "Testing Director Dru Polar," Shirak continued, glancing toward the one in sapphire blue. "Director Polar and his staff train our young people in what you would call starbred abilities."

Polar reached toward the vine and snapped off a fantastic bloom. Ribbonlike petals of pink, white, and gold cascaded from its furred purple throat. "Welcome, Highness," he said, offering the flower.

She took it graciously. In Lieutenant Governor Caldwell and his colleagues, those starbred abilities repelled her. In Polar, they drew her like a heady fragrance.

"Your presence on Three Zed honors us." Polar flicked one hand. Footsteps rattled behind her. Turning, she saw Penn Baker—whom she'd already forgotten—and the two greeters exit the cavern through a sliding door.

To business, then! Gripping the flower's stiff stem, Phoena spoke. "Gentlemen, let me introduce my mission without unnecessary formalities. I believe that we face a situation as intolerable to you as it is to me. My home world has been invaded."

"That would be intolerable," said Shirak. "Please, let us be seated."

Polar motioned her to the tallest straight-backed chair. Flattered, she glanced around as they all sat down. What a splendid use for jewels . . . always displayed, instead of hidden in dark treasure vaults.

Testing Director Polar addressed her. "But I fail to see why you think we would find your position intolerable."

She leaned toward him. "On Netaia, I lead a movement to restore independence, the same freedom your people obviously cherish, and with the same zealous spirit."

"And?" Polar prompted.

"There is more. But first, gentlemen, let me state clearly that I am no friend of the Federacy. Nor of Thyrica."

Director Polar smiled darkly. "You probably mean a fairly small Thyrian population."

"Not small enough," she said, clipping her words. "My youngest sister has married an ambitious man, who obviously means to use our royal heritage for his own gain."

Polar and Shirak shared an oddly intense glance.

"In doing so," she continued, "she has despised her nation and her family. She stands convicted on several capital counts, but we are unable to execute her sentence because of that man and the Federacy.

"Yet we hear that his family was just attacked. Reportedly, some of your people were responsible."

"I won't deny that," said Shirak. "I won't confirm it, either."

Excellent! "I've come to offer assistance."

Polar raised an eyebrow. "Oh?"

"Why do you hate her, Highness?" asked Adiyn.

Phoena tilted her chin. "I hate no one. But she only pretends to revere our ways." Merely thinking about Firebird put an edge on Phoena's voice. "She is a rebellious, power-greedy child. She always thought she should've been born first, that she should be queen."

"Did she say so?" Adiyn's grin faded to a bland smile.

Phoena felt flushed. "I believe she did. Worse, she convinced others to say so."

Polar looked appropriately pained.

"We gave her everything." Phoena raised the bloom and sniffed its rich, royal purple throat, and then lowered it, disappointed. It gave off a putrid fragrance. "Comforts, the finest education, and best of all, the promise of eternal honor . . . but even that didn't satisfy her.

"She murdered one of my friends. A researcher," she added, glancing sidelong at the scientist Adiyn, "who was working to give Netaia a future, a weapon that might have restored our independence."

Polar cocked an eyebrow. "Murdered? Personally?"

"Shot him dead at close range," Phoena growled. "She is vile, gentlemen. Greedy, and faithless, and . . . and spiteful."

Shirak crossed his long legs. Soberly he stroked his chin. "Surely you would expect some favor in exchange."

His prompting made her bold. "Wouldn't eliminating her and her husband be its own reward?"

Shirak shrugged. "You have other desires."

"I mentioned the loyalist movement," she said, "and our desperate hope. But another sister stands between me and the throne. The Federacy has made Carradee a collaborator of the worst stripe. She must be removed from power. And her daughters—"

"How old?" asked Adiyn.

"Four and one. Innocent of any crime. Perhaps they could be assimilated into your culture. They are lovely girls. They would look good in this magnificent city." Gesturing with the blossom so that its streamers caressed her wrist, she spotted a constellation of brilliant-cut diamonds—no, a galaxy!—set over Polar's shoulder in the golden wall. She tore her stare away. "I could give you information that would help you accomplish that too."

"Then we put you on that throne?" Polar asked dryly.

"I have no lust for power, gentlemen, but I am the only remaining confirmed heiress. I am both capable of ruling and truly loyal. In fact, our mother, Siwann, wanted to make me her heiress." Siwann never said so in words, but she'd admitted Carradee did not have the stern will of a monarch. "I am no murderer," Phoena added delicately, "but Carradee is gravely misguided. Something must be done. Quickly."

Dru Polar turned back to Shirak. Again she saw them stare into each other's eyes, and she abruptly realized they must be speaking mind to mind, excluding her. Shirak turned next to Adiyn. The frumpy man's grin broadened.

She frowned at the snub. "I have, of course, left messages." She detected a hint of slouch in her posture and corrected it. "If I should fail to return or send word within this month, Netaian calendar, the Federacy will be notified as to my whereabouts. They consider themselves obligated to guard my family."

Dru Polar stood and offered his right hand. She clasped it and rose, pleased that he didn't let go immediately. "We don't fault your measures for your own defense, of course," he said. "Unquestionably, we can reach an agreement."

She glanced at Shirak for confirmation. He dipped his chin, then said, "Let us discuss your offer and return word to you."

"Meanwhile," added Polar, "you must consider yourself my guest." She brightened, warming to him as he continued, "I shall have you shown to our best visitors' rooms, where you may rest while we discuss your proposal. And . . ." At last he dropped her hand. As his lashless eyes looked down into hers, she felt a sharp, compelling sensation she couldn't identify. He smiled with one side of his lips. "Thank you for coming, Your Highness," he said.

Phoena followed the gold-collared greeter down two levels to a suite that seemed small and stark after that high golden chamber. Its walls looked like silver, not gold, with a common, low white ceiling and gray shortweave carpet. Still, the narrow receiving room had such basic appointments as a comfortable lounger, and the inner bedroom seemed spacious. The lack of windows disturbed her, but compared with Penn Baker's ship, this was a palace suite. Obviously, her road to restoring Netaia's noble heritage lay through this golden city.

She wanted to bathe, but she had no fresh clothing. She searched a wall compartment in the back room but found nothing.

Surely the city had magnificent shops. She was Director Polar's personal guest. His hospitality would extend to discretionary credit.

As she crossed the silver sitting room, its door opened. A woman stepped inside—no, a girl. Brazenly voluptuous, she had a sullen face and long, straight hair that hung below her waspish waist. Phoena gaped at the hair. It was black at its roots, then yellow blond, and then red, in a repeating reptilian pattern. She carried her head with extraordinary poise for someone so young. "You'd like clean clothes," she said blandly. She signaled behind her with a hand controller. A service cart glided in. "Penn Baker says you brought nothing along. That was wise, if you wanted to vanish mysteriously. You are about my size." She looked Phoena up and down. "Director Polar asked me to lend you some things."

"Thank you." Phoena stood her ground for a moment, then realized the girl expected her to unload the cart. She reached for it casually, as though she'd anticipated no more. The first armload of formless blouses smelled faintly of strange sachet.

"Are you related to Director Polar?" Phoena asked between loads, when the silence became uncomfortable.

"We're all cousins of some degree. Why do you ask?"

"I noticed a resemblance." Phoena was so glad to find dresses in the second compartment that she said nothing about the striped-haired girl's impertinent familiarity.

"You look like your sister too." That tone of voice conveyed no open insult, but the girl's stare suggested she knew it would be received as no compliment. "My name is Cassia Talumah. I was born in Cahal, an outlying settlement near here. Those of us who show particular talent are brought here to the Golden City to train. Why live anywhere else? We have the youth lab, the ayin extractors . . . and we set policies for all of this world."

Then this was a common power-grabber who must've learned Phoena was born to authority. Moving regally, Phoena transferred the last items onto the lounger. "You've already finished your schooling?"

"By your calendar, I graduated twenty-three years ago."

Phoena narrowed her eyes. "I think not."

Cassia slid both hands up her shapely hips. "Your mistake," she said, smirking. "I'll be seeing you."

Phoena chose a likely ensemble of pale yellow lace and then treated herself to a long, delicious vaporbath in the tiny freshing room. Once dressed, she decided to explore while the men finished talking. There must be other halls as exquisite as the one where they met her.

And had Cassia mentioned a youth lab? Could that girl possibly be in her thirties, or even older? Not even the finest implants would keep anyone so youthful.

Her receiving room's outer door had no handle, no visible control panel. Puzzled, she pushed it. It wouldn't budge.

She stepped backward, bumped into the lounger, and then sat down, fighting sudden alarm with reason. No doubt they soon would finish their council. They'd want to be able to reach her immediately. Meanwhile, in the absence of servitors, she would put away her borrowed clothing.

A few minutes later, she heard footsteps and returned to the outer room. Testing Director Polar had entered. His loose blue shirt shone against the silvery walls.

"Well?" she asked, but his smile told her all she needed to know.

"We've accepted your offer," he said. "I am certain we'll value your help, as you value ours. We want everything you can show us concerning Lady Firebird, her personality, habits, and history. We need to be able to predict her most likely responses to several possible attacks. Then we'll evaluate Netaia and our approach to Carradee. You know Citangelo—the palace layout, the travel routes she and her children usually take."

"When I'm queen, you'll be able to keep a close eye on me as well, won't you?"

"We're not worried about keeping eyes on you. We'll have other concerns."

Mollified, Phoena took a seat on the long brown lounger. It felt harder than it looked.

Polar pulled over the smaller of two mock wooden chairs and sat down almost knee to knee with her. "Have you experienced mind-access before?" he asked. His smile looked faintly sensual.

Disgusted, Phoena slid away. "Director Polar, I have every intention of answering your questions. There's no need to make this an interrogation."

"I believe that, Your Highness." He reached for her hand. She drew it away, but he lunged forward and seized it. From the heat of his fingers, she realized that hers had gone cold. "But I can do a quicker, more thorough job this way, and it won't hurt . . . badly."

She snatched her hand free and sprang to her feet, yellow lace fluttering around her. "This is unnecessary. I demand to speak with Eldest Shirak."

"Sit down," he said with a queer quiet tone in his voice. Phoena found herself obeying.

"How dare you," she breathed. He was enjoying this!

"I'm told your sister wasn't eager to be accessed when Caldwell first breached her. Cooperate, Phoena. Those are Shirak's terms. Do as we say, and we'll see you well rewarded."

The throne, she reminded herself. The Crown, the Federates banished from her home world, and that Fire-brat settled forever.

Gathering her courage, she raised her eyes to meet his.

Phoena came to herself lying on the hard brown lounger with a painfully empty stomach and odd twinges on her scalp and arms, but her awakening impressions were of peace and safety. She'd never known such contentment.

Cassia Talumah brought warm fruit-scented pastries, a hot cup of kass, and another exotic flower in a crystal chalice. Without even rising from the lounger, Phoena grabbed a pastry.

"Oh, Your Highness, one thing." Cassia reached around her striped hair to lay paper and a stylus on Phoena's end table. "Your husband must be worried sick about you. You should let him know you're safe."

The busty little snake was right. Poor loyal Tel would be frantic by now. "Thanks," Phoena said, lounging and eating without the slightest care for propriety. "I'll get around to it."

"Now," said Cassia.

Phoena sat up and reached for the stylus.

Carrying a recall pad and a full cold-case of tissue samples, Juddis Adiyn walked with Polar toward their apartments. "I think you were right," said Adiyn. "The preliminary scan is mixed-Ehretan."

"Congratulations." Polar kept walking.

"She's positively slavering to believe that we owe her a throne," Adiyn observed. "I never saw a mind more amenable to suggestion."

"Shef'th," Polar swore, "those Netaian implants have devastated her ayin. Of course she can't resist."

Adiyn smiled. Already, royal Netaia was Three Zed's new treasure trove. Baker's shuttle carried crates full of trinkets from its museums and vaults, procured by Ard Talumah. Adiyn had claimed a tiny necklace and bracelet set in graduated emeralds and flawless sapphires, crafted for some long-grown countess or duchess.

Evidently, Talumah had needed only one moment's encounter in a ball-room to set the hook of mind-manipulation deep in his royal prey. "I'll have Terza map her cell samples today," Adiyn announced. "Mitochondrial first, since that should be our Casvah line. Nuclear material will differ in the sister. Carabohd and Casvah," he mused aloud. "The good name has married the vessel."

"Sounds ominous."

"I'm sure they would like us to think so. Evidently the new mistress isn't helpless, even pregnant."

"She murdered a researcher." Polar mocked Phoena's words in a fluttering falsetto.

"Does this affect Micahel's plans for the College?"

"Not at all." Polar shrugged. "I only wish I could be there to watch."

"He's eliminating the unfit for you?"

Polar smiled darkly.

"What if," Adiyn said slowly, "General Caldwell comes here?"

Polar glowered. "Have you foreseen that?"

Adiyn adjusted his hold on his sample case. "So long as Netaia is under Federate protection, so is the royal family. They wouldn't dare assign anyone but a Sentinel to try to rescue her. I can see them sending him."

"Possibly," said Polar. "He's been overconfident before."

"It's on two branches of the shebiyl," Adiyn declared. He had a special talent, exceptional clarity in glimpsing the elusive shebiyl, which was a set of branching, alternate paths that the future might take. This was an epsilon skill their Sentinel counterparts swore not to use. They called it *keshef*, sorcery.

Their loss.

Polar transferred his recall pad from one hand to the other. "If he comes, don't waste him on Micahel."

"You want him . . . for your antipodal fusion work?" As always, Adiyn considered the colony's research programs before endorsing anyone's license to kill.

"Yes." Polar drew out the word's sibilance. "Absolutely."

CHAPTER 9

DABAR

vivace
lively

With only a month left before her due date, Firebird's energy level dropped daily. She'd been in excellent shape eight months ago. Now, young and strong though she might be, simply staying mobile took most of her strength.

At least she wasn't confined to bed. This morning, on one of Brennen's days off work, he joined her downlevel for exercise. She missed their training sessions with her new dagger, but she couldn't change directions quickly anymore. Now she had to settle for a long, slow daily walk.

Since it was pouring—again—she trudged around the housing complex's training room, doggedly counting laps by opening her fingers one by one on Brennen's arm, reminiscing. . . .

Brennen had circled to his right on the springy blue training mat, blanking all expression from his face. Even matching her slower reaction time, he executed the footwork of Carolinian dagger play with a classical dancer's grace. She would've loved to sit down and just watch him.

Playing along usually raised her spirits, even on legs that ached from carrying too much weight, but this time, she stepped out of stance. "Oh, Brenn, maybe not today. Somehow I can't bear the thought of blood." She didn't even like eating meat these days.

"Mari." He crouched. "There won't always be a shock pistol handy. You'd get no second chance in a confrontation. Trust me, if I'm in danger . . ." He gave her a one-sided smile. "I'll react."

He lunged. Automatically she dodged, surprised by her body's quick reaction to his dulled training dagger, even now. She swiped for his arm but missed. Instantly he spun and cracked her forearm with his handgrip. "Come in *short*." He glared. "That Netaian sword thrust will get you killed."

Sighing, she sank down onto a bench and puffed out a breath. "I'm a barge," she muttered. "A tanker."

"You are my beautiful bond mate. And Spieth says you're still too small."

"I'm trying to gain weight, Brennen. She says the babies are big enough—I'm just small."

"You want to be able to nurse them," he reminded her.

"Yes," she grunted. "I do." She rocked forward, preparing to stand up.

"Caldwell?" called a husky, disembodied voice.

Brennen hustled toward the door, peered at the passway monitor, then reached up. As the door slid open, Damalcon Dardy stepped through. "Hello," Firebird cried, unashamedly glad to have company.

Then she caught Brennen's unease. Evidently Dardy had already shown him that this was no social call. She leaned back again and unweighted her legs.

Brennen snatched his sweater off the floor. "Should we go uplevel?" he asked Dardy.

The big man shrugged. "You're not in danger. It's just bad news." He strode toward Firebird, lifted another bench, and pulled it out into the room. He sat down facing her. Brennen joined them.

"How bad?" she asked. Her arms felt clammy.

"Your sister Phoena's missing again."

Firebird relaxed slightly, relieved it wasn't worse. "Has Governor Danton checked Hunter Height?" Absently scratching her breastbone, she gave Brennen a wry look. Phoena might be conducting weapons research again. Danton would have to rein her in without their help this time.

Dardy frowned. "He found traces right there in Citangelo. We're afraid the Shuhr are involved."

She drew up straighter.

"Evidence?" Brennen asked.

Dardy shrugged. "She wasn't declared missing until eight days after she vanished. Two House Guards disappeared about the same time, and at first they were suspected. Danton's people, working with your Enforcement Corps, finally picked up several hairs in a dust tracing outside a recently abandoned apartment."

Leaning forward over clasped hands, Brennen frowned. "Whose apartment?"

"Recently reregistered to Penn Baker." Dardy eyed Firebird as he spoke the name.

She shrugged. She'd never heard it.

"Netaian born. Low-common class. Took up offworld trading early this year—and then moved in with a roommate," he said. "A trader we've watched with concern."

Shuhr, she understood. But why—

"Mazo syndrome," she exclaimed softly. That condition Master Spieth diagnosed, which robbed her family of male heirs, occurred only in Ehretan descendants. "Could they have gone after Phoena once they knew about our Ehretan genes?"

Brennen shrugged.

Dardy crossed his muscular arms. "Possibly. Or they could want ransom. For now, we're assuming she was abducted. They found no trace of the guards."

"There are thousands of ways to hide a corpse," Firebird muttered. A voice at the back of her mind taunted, *If they're trying to hurt us by harming Phoena, they've got a surprise coming!* Still, she shivered. So many had died: Corey, Baron Parkai, Destia . . .

"No evidence she was injured?" Brennen actually sounded concerned.

"No blood. Debris analysis said she'd lived there for several days."

Brennen exhaled sharply. "What's been done to protect Carradee?"

"Everything short of putting her under protective custody, like you two. At least until we confirm some kind of motive."

Firebird stared at her aching, sandaled feet. Protective custody? She'd never guessed how desperately she loved open spaces.

Later that night, she lay staring at the ceiling over their bed. If Phoena were dead, she'd be immensely relieved. All personal torment aside, Phoena would've killed millions, even billions of innocent civilians with the fruits of her secret armament research.

But what if she wasn't dead? What if they made her cooperate with the attempt to wipe out Brennen's family?

Why was that woman even born? she challenged the Singer. She had no trouble believing Phoena's soul was tainted!

Brennen rolled over. "Want help getting to sleep?"

"Sorry." Firebird sighed. With a telepathic husband, she couldn't lie there and brood. "No. I'm finished. Good night."

Phoena's hosts showed her their spotless armory center, squired her out to the weapons testing facility, and let her tour the tunnels devoted to biological research . . . and several bioformed zones with ecosystems that were so stunningly complex she almost forgot they lay underground . . . but she never grew tired of her gray-walled rooms. Meals arrived on schedule, and intriguing visitors came to call. This morning, two stepped through her door.

"Welcome!" Juddis Adiyn, the frumpy geneticist, she already knew. He'd visited several times. Who, though, was this tall young man with the strongly cleft chin? He virtually radiated the holy Powers of Strength and Indomitability. She motioned both men toward her lounger and remained standing on the shortweave carpet, showing respect.

"Micahel asked to meet you," Adiyn explained. "Princess Phoena Angelo of Netaia, this is the Eldest's grandson, Micahel Shirak."

The Eldest's grandson? No wonder! And he'd asked to meet her. . . . Wouldn't Dru be jealous?

"Will you be Eldest someday?" For an instant, Phoena wished Adiyn would get up so she could sit down beside this comely Shuhr prince. Then she remembered her new manners.

"In a century, maybe." Micahel ran a hand over short black curls that she ached to touch. "We never wish death on our Elders."

"I should think that you . . ."

How odd. Her mind had blanked.

Micahel crossed his long legs. Stretching out both arms, he sprawled on her brown lounger. "I had a close call with your sister," he announced. "Recently."

Phoena felt her eyes widen. Had Micahel already eliminated Carradee? Was it time to start planning her coronation? "How splendid—"

"Your younger sister. Vastly pregnant." Micahel pantomimed a huge belly with both arms.

Deflated, she demanded, "Where?" She didn't want to even think about Firebird. Thinking about her *pregnant* was almost pornographic.

"On Thyrica. Briefly. I'd just come from visiting her brother-in-law."

"Caldwell has a brother?" That hadn't occurred to her, but surely even a monster could be related to someone. Some of the Powers admittedly showed in his actions. It had taken Strength to escape her at Hunter Height—but now she had allies. And yes, she'd heard something about an assault.

"He had a brother." Micahel half smiled.

"Oh?"

Adiyn clasped both hands around his knees. "Micahel made a productive visit to Thyrica. General Caldwell lost his only brother, his sister-in-law, two nephews, and a niece."

"Micahel!" she exclaimed. "I must introduce you to Carradee." Phoena stepped forward, intending to offer her hand for a kiss. Halfway to the lounger, she realized they wouldn't want that. And she must please them.

But she'd learned that they felt her delight. They must've come just to give pleasure . . . and feel it. "How did you deal with this brother of his?" she asked eagerly. "And why did you bother?"

Micahel laced his long fingers, straightened his arms, and stretched his hands. She imagined him holding a weapon and liked the idea. Wouldn't Dru be jealous? "My family and Caldwell's have a history that might surprise you," he said. "My grandfather killed all but one male in his line. My father took his three uncles. This was my turn."

Phoena sighed. "Pity," she said. "You didn't quite finish the . . ."

Blank.

She tried again. "I wish you success in finishing, sir." She inclined her head in respect. "Have you ever considered visiting Citangelo, Micahel? I'll return, one day—"

Blank again. Longer this time, and deeper. For several seconds, she stood flicking her borrowed skirt, trying to recall what she and Adiyn had been discussing.

She only remembered the favor she'd asked him the last time he came. "You promised to read my future," she prompted. "I'll pay for your services when you take me back to Citangelo."

He blinked his odd little eyes. "Highness, I'll tell you what I've seen gratis, because it amuses me. Of course, what I read might not happen. We see possibilities branching in all directions."

He'd tried to explain the shebiyl concept. She found it tiring. One future, that's all she asked. A grand one. "But you saw a destiny? For me?"

"Oh yes."

His nameless young escort, already forgotten, uncrossed his long legs and stared at him.

Phoena clasped her hands behind her back. "Long life?" she asked, smiling expectantly.

Adiyn answered in a flat voice. Simply, "No."

Phoena cocked an eyebrow, wishing she hadn't asked . . . yet this future-possible might not be all bad.

"Neither will you be happy," Adiyn added, staring up into her eyes, measuring her reaction. Evidently she didn't look frightened enough to amuse him, because he pressed the point. "Never again, unless we choose to deceive you. Would you like to know how you will die?"

"I think not." Rattled despite her Resolve, she glanced toward the door that led to her private bedroom. A strategic retreat . . . "Thank you for the information," she said firmly. "I'll use it wisely . . ."

Blank.

"Of course, Princess," Adiyn exclaimed, spreading his hands. "You may expect to live long and well. Haven't we begun your longevity treatments?" Beside him, the young man winked.

She didn't remember any such treatments, but with her mind blanking so often here, she must take Adiyn's word for it. She inclined her head graciously. If only she could remember the younger man's name! She'd like to see him again. Judging from the wink and the way he stared, the feeling might be returned.

Wouldn't Dru be jealous?

"I also foresaw plans for your coronation," said Adiyn. "Grand plans. Very grand."

"Ah," she exclaimed, smiling down at . . . Micahel. That was the name. "I'll make sure you're invited," she told him. "And you." She glanced at Adiyn.

"Imagine how long you'll reign," Micahel suggested. "We live two hundred years, and you are still young—"

"And a glorious death," said Adiyn, "in the name of the greatest cause possible."

Phoena tilted her chin and smiled at Micahel. "I am not ready," she answered, "to speak about dying."

Benj Rasey escorted Firebird back across campus from another fruitless, frustrating, virtually pointless session with Janesca Harris. She flung her rain cloak over the lounger, stomped to the kitchen's servo unit, and programmed one of its few lunch options that didn't include wretched Thyrian fish. After washing it down with Spieth's foul syrup, she shoved her dishes into the washer, cleaned up in the tiny freshing room, and then dug into a moving crate she still hadn't unpacked.

Phoena could rot in the Shuhr's deepest dungeon for all she cared . . . and today's second nap could wait. She had a dream to chase.

She'd tried last week to reschedule her formal consecration, but Brennen's mother begged another few dekia's reprieve. Firebird had honored that plea. It moved her to belong to a family that cared for one another.

But as of today, she'd finished waiting to hear those Caldwell prophecies. In Path instruction, she'd learned a little of Ehret's ancient language and how to use a tutorial scanbook.

Willful, she reminded herself. *And impatient.*

Deep in the crate, she found the scan cartridge. She loaded the cube into her bedside scanbook. Then, clutching the flat viewer, she marched back out to the servo table.

Brennen's unadorned copy of *Dabar* stood on a shelf close-by. She often stumbled out of bed to find him already dressed, sipping a cup of kass and reading this. Last week he'd said, "Listen to this, Mari," and translated a long lament, a plea that the Speaker might explain why evil men flourish . . . then destroy them. Some nights, he read to her in bed and then settled in to pray. She was learning almost as much about the Singer from Brennen's prayers as from his books. Once, she'd rolled over at midnight to find him still praying.

Mattah, the newer holy book, had been translated into Colonial. She'd studied it with her Path instructor. Path instruction only outlined *Dabar*, though. Publishing that volume or any part of it in any other language was forbidden. She still didn't understand why.

She sighed, then yawned. *So much to learn, so many questions.* At least now she felt confident that answers existed. As an inquisitive child, she'd pored over Netaia's written Disciplines. She had found little she could grasp, except that the government must be obeyed. The rest seemed like double-talk.

The difference, she realized, was that this God truly existed. He touched everything, unlike the distant Netaian Powers. His mercy had washed away her guilt over betraying their false, legalistic religious system.

She opened Brennen's light-bound volume and laid it beside her scanbook. *Dabar* contained twenty-two books of prophecies, some with over thirty chapters.

Setting her chin on one hand, she paged backward and forward. At several places, Brennen had made faint marginal notes in Ehretan.

She selected a marked passage, switched on the tutorial's memory option, then painstakingly started keying in phrases.

Several minutes later, these words gleamed on her scanbook's square screen:

Send out your light, lead me to your open door,
To your altar, and there make me clean.
Wash me, strip from me
The ashes (note: scum, residue) that fill my dark heart.
At the altar, I shall know
As you always have known.

Firebird frowned. She had mixed feelings about approaching that altar. The consecration service she'd been promised would include a transfer of memory, handed down from generation to generation, of the last sacrifice offered in Ehret's great temple. She'd been appalled—and nauseated—when her Path instructor told her that only shed blood assured divine mercy, and only faith in its efficacy bought her salvation. In time, she began to grasp the concept of atonement, of a covering for all past offenses.

That didn't mean she looked forward to seeing it happen, even second- or fourth- or tenth-hand from Shamarr Dickin. But she would prove she was willing to join Brennen's community.

And she wanted to know those prophecies. They foretold *her* future now too.

Without bothering to translate Brennen's neat marginal note, she flipped to another marked passage.

I will be with that remnant.
I will refine and test them as meteor steel
And make them a sword in my hand.
Word to Come, Mighty One, Holy King of the New Universe,
Refine all the worlds and their peoples.
Wield your children in justice, the suns in your truth.

Better! Word for word, she keyed in Brennen's note. Seconds later, she read, *Loose sword = useless. Effective only in His hand.*

She scratched her ribs, puzzling over the passage. "That remnant" obviously referred to the Sentinels. "Refine and test them . . ." Their exile, their vows to serve others? "A sword in my hand" she liked. Meteoric iron made tough, splendid blades. She'd seen one in a museum, at Citangelo. She hated killing, but she did love the understated, deadly elegance of a ceremonial sword.

Brennen had also underlined all three titles for his God but made no note beside them. "Word to Come" had always intrigued her. At first, she'd thought it odd to refer to God in future tense. But an eternal Person had to exist in the past, present, and future. The second aspect of Ehret's Shaliyah, the Three, they generally called the Word. Speaker, Word, Voice—three manifestations of the Holy One. She would always think of Him, though, as the Mighty Singer in a dimension beyond space and time. He'd shown himself to her that way one night on Netaia. Facing a lonely death by Phoena's order, she'd seen a brief, compelling vision of His primal music launching time and space on their courses. Instantly, she'd turned from her guilt and doubts to worship Him.

She saved both passages to memory and paged on. Some time later, she was keying in a short verse when a sweet inrush of sensation swept over her.

As Brennen walked in, she rocked back from the servo table and watched for a reaction. "Anything new about Phoena?" she asked.

"No." His presence swept deeper into her emotions. "New frustration," he observed gently. "Did things go poorly with Janesca again?"

"No worse than usual." She didn't want to explain until he saw—

He glanced at her scanbook and his open *Dabar*. She felt a surge of delight before he tempered it. "What are you doing?" he asked, smiling wryly. He knew, of course, that she felt his real reaction.

"Research," she said. "I know you're under voice-command, and I don't like to nag. I thought I'd see what I could find for myself."

He sat down beside her and tucked an arm around the small of her back, kneading her perpetually sore muscles. "As long as you don't save to memory," he murmured close to her ear. "That's publishing."

"Oops," she said. "I'll dump the passages I saved. I don't think I found any family secrets," she added.

"They're only clear in the canonical context." He stood again, and joy shone through his eyes. She'd first seen that glow months before, when she asked about his faith—and again at Hesed, as they stood at the waterside making their vows. "But you're enjoying yourself," he observed.

"Actually, I am." She pushed the scanbook aside and steeled herself. "Anyway, you were right. Janesca tried a different approach today. A visualization, based on a passage in *Mattah*. It was one more disaster."

He encouraged her with his sympathetic silence.

"I tried for an hour. Nothing."

"Give it time," he said. "You've had years to develop thought habits. You can still learn new ones."

"After a month of complete failure? How long did it take you to master the turn?"

"That's not relevant. I was twelve and extremely gifted."

She refused to be sidetracked. "How long? At least let me enjoy your success vicariously."

He looked aside. "I read the section with Master Keeson. He explained, and I tried it. We went on."

He'd turned on his first attempt, as a twelve-year-old. Her shoulders sagged. What should she expect from a boy who won a master's star at seventeen?

Once again, a child kicked her, rudely reminding her to sit tall, no matter how weary she felt.

Brennen glanced at her black clairsa case, propped against a wall near the nondescript lounger. "How long did it take you to learn to play a chord?"

"I was eight and a good learner, and . . . all right, Brenn, I had an excellent ear. We have different gifts."

He smiled, obviously still pleased at finding her knee-deep in *Dabar* and not worried about her failings. "You'll learn to turn."

"I'll turn," she said through gritted teeth, "or die trying."

He raised an eyebrow.

"Just an expression," she muttered.

Later, as she undressed for bed while Brennen finished in the freshing room, a jab of pain and regret caught her from nowhere, like a blow to her solar plexus. Was this grief for Phoena?

Then she realized it came on the pair bond from Brennen. She dropped her day clothes down the chute and closed the window's security slats. That switched on a small, intensely white luma below the bottom slat. By its light, Brennen emerged. He stepped around the bed.

"What?" she asked softly. "Tell me."

"I . . . no." As he lay down, the anguish ebbed away, but she suspected he'd only shielded it from her.

Emotional shielding—one more ability she would never learn, at this rate.

She climbed in beside him, settled in on her side, and stared across her pillow at his straight-nosed silhouette. "Brenn, you can't do all your grieving alone." She stroked his shoulder. "Let me at least listen. It'll help." He was so strong, so capable—and in desperate pain. Having a family that cared also made him vulnerable.

He stared at the institutional white ceiling.

"What were you remembering?" she urged. "I felt it. All of a sudden."

His eyes fell shut, and the dull ache gripped her chest again. "I missed their wedding," he said. "I was in College, on Sanctuary rotation, and they decided to marry here. At my next holiday, I came home at my own expense, but Tarance turned me away at their door. I could've gotten family leave, he said. I hadn't known. He said Asea was crushed. I could tell she felt hurt," he added, "but Mari, she was too happy with Tarance to be really upset. They were nineteen."

"So you were fourteen?" Firebird vividly remembered the first intimate days of pair bonding. Lacking Brennen's training, she'd been plunged by their union of body and mind into a joyous shock state so deep she would've forgotten to eat if Brennen hadn't shared his meals. Nothing mattered, nothing had even existed, except keeping Brennen close, and the exquisite new pleasures he gave her. If Asea had experienced that, she'd have easily forgiven a tardy young brother-in-law. The public ceremony really only entitled them to seal the pair bond privately.

Tarance had simply been spiteful. Nineteen and full of himself. "You were just a child, Brenn. You didn't know you could get . . . family leave."

"No," he said, "but I didn't ask, either."

"Your parents didn't tell you to ask? Your teachers?"

"It happened quickly. They married about three weeks after a friend introduced them."

That was normal. Telepaths could tell quickly if they found a connatural mate. Brennen, still single in his late twenties—past thirty on the Federate calendar—had almost given up when they met.

"I . . . wish I'd taken the trouble to apologize, later."

"Seems to me," she said, "he should've apologized to you."

"I could've made the first move. He was always jealous of my abilities, especially since he was five years older. I passed him by at College."

"I see. I understand."

"I don't think you do. We loved each other as boys. Losing his love was my first deep pain. It would be easy to hate the man who killed him. I mustn't."

"Why not?" Self-sacrificing love might be a virtue, but so was justice. "Glory, Brenn. I hate him."

"It's forbidden." She watched his silhouetted lips move as he whispered, "Anger's allowed, but not hatred. We all need mercy. Eleven million Ehretans died for each one who survived."

"That's ridiculous. You didn't kill those people."

"I've killed others. My squadron killed your dearest friend. Freedom is a terrible gift, and so is power. Especially yours. What if we tried to take the Federacy?"

He'd resisted her mood swings, but she couldn't fight his grief. "You wouldn't," she said bitterly. "Evil people started the Ehretan war. And how," she wondered aloud, "why, did the Speaker let that happen? Fifty million deaths?" Those numbers suggested an enormous weight of suffering.

"Evil exists," he said, "and we've all partaken. We've all broken our fellowship with the Holy One. We need atonement—"

Abruptly the twins tried to rearrange themselves, pushing and kicking in all directions at once. There no longer was room for that. She carried the stronger kicker high, on her right. The less active twin now rode low, left. "Oof!" She groaned, arching her back. "Oh, Brenn. Carradee used to complain, and I never gave her any sympathy. I wish I could talk to her. I wish I could get out of this apartment. Between babies and walls, I can hardly breathe."

Brennen pressed his body against hers, as he loved to do when the babies moved. She sensed a dim light of hope dispelling his grief. "It will end, Mari. Probably sooner than Master Spieth is predicting. And maybe," he murmured, "they'll get along better than Tarance and I did—or you and Phoena."

CHAPTER 10

TELLAI

risoluto assai
very resolutely

Janesca Harris didn't give up. Two days later, Firebird sat with her eyes closed, trying again to concentrate on a visualization that might enable her to turn. Simply listening for the epsilon energy hadn't worked, so Janesca and Medical Master Spieth had conferred.

"Try this," Master Spieth had said. "It may sound strange, but all this has to happen at the mental level. Try to imagine a wall. A wall standing between what you once were and what you are in our community. Loved and secure in the Speaker's will and fully qualified to tap into significant power. 'You are no longer the Adversary's prisoner, for I have purchased you,'" she quoted. She extended both hands, palms out. "Push through that prison wall, where you waited for death, into your new life."

Janesca added, "This might also help fine-tune your ability to concentrate on a distraction image. You'll want that for childbirth."

It had sounded good, but it wasn't working. Again Firebird sat in Janesca's office. Again she vividly remembered the outwall at Hunter Height, on Netaia . . . where she truly had waited for death. Maintaining the image, and closing out all memory of Phoena's firing squad, should help her ignore all distractions.

Weathered but solid, the wall's granite surface had crusty, irregular splotches of green and orange lichen. She recalled its roughness and the iron handrail icy cold in the moments before dawn. Instead of an execution site, she tried picturing it as Master Spieth had suggested, as a final barrier separating her from the glorious life, the depth and strength she hoped to achieve.

She imagined the wall crumbling to gray gravel. She tried pushing it down. She recalled scrambling over the top, escaping with Brennen. She prayed over and over for guidance.

Nothing happened.

She opened her eyes. "I'm sorry, Janesca. I still can't see the energy . . . or hear it."

Today they sat alone. The dark-haired woman reached toward her instrument stand. "That's not bad, but you still focus more tightly on your music. Let's play."

Relieved to escape Hunter Height once again, Firebird picked up her own small harp. Beside Janesca's lyrelike equilateral kinnora, Firebird's Netaian clairsa looked as if it had been stretched almost to breaking. Its longer strings were spun from brass-toned metal alloy, its curving upper arch hand carved from a rare russet-colored Netaian wood with a design of intertwined knots. She steadied it against her shoulder and belly, placed her hands, and then spun off a cartwheeling arpeggio.

Janesca struck up a stately Thyrian melody. Firebird listened once through, resting her forehead against her instrument's soundboard. As the melody repeated, she placed her fingertips, then joined in. Instinctively she twined cascades of chords and high, tinkling appoggiaturi around the pentatonic folk tune. One verse of this melody suggested green Thyrian hills that rolled toward a rain-blurred horizon. Another, the broad Tiggaree River that flowed over multicolored stone through Citangelo.

A weird little contraction gripped and released, then grabbed her again. Distracted, Firebird let her hands fall from the strings. Mister High-and-Right started kicking.

"You're getting close," Janesca observed. "They'll be early."

"Twins often are." Firebird wasn't ready, not really. The longer she managed to carry them, the healthier they'd be.

Janesca laid a hand on Firebird's clairsa, smiling. "If they're early, they may be small. You might have an easy delivery. And our neonate facility is excellent."

Firebird frowned. She would be glad to shed all this weight, to escape leg cramps and short breath and indigestion, but she dreaded labor—unmedicated, to prevent damage to the infants' fragile ayina, their epsilon centers. She'd been taught all kinds of distraction techniques too. But once the babies arrived, these training sessions would end. She'd be much too busy with infant care.

Sighing, she leaned her head against her clairsa's top arch. "Am I your most difficult student ever?"

"Pride, Firebird."

Oh, Janesca, I'm pregnant and irritable. Don't scold me.

"Inverted pride can be as dangerous as exaltation. Most of the time, you'll fall somewhere between top and bottom. Be content with that."

Firebird gripped both edges of her clairsa's sound box, willing herself not to react. She would always aim for the top rank in everything she attempted. "Are you sorry you agreed to train me?"

"Never."

Firebird laid her clairsa back in its case, yawning mightily. It was high time for her morning nap. "Shall I come back tomorrow, or shall we end this . . . until after?"

Janesca's eyebrows lifted. "Which do you want?"

Firebird flicked two closures, then hoisted the case onto her left shoulder, cramping her ankles and calves one more time. "To come back," she said. "Who knows? Tomorrow could be my last chance for months."

Brennen found a disturbing report in the midday intelligence summary.

He framed the report, keyed for hard copy, then leaned back on his desk chair to commit it to memory. Overhead, clouds whisked inland above his smoked glasteel ceiling. As General Coordinator of Thyrian Forces, he had a ground-floor suite, more prestigious than Claggett's underground office. Heightened Base security meant an extra ten to fifteen minutes' wait at the landing area each morning while MPs checked each arrival's credentials and vehicle. It was a small price to pay for the confidence that no more FI–2s would be hijacked.

But according to this report, a Second Division training flight had vanished from maneuvers with the Federate fleet. Twelve one-year-old ships, deadly even when carrying dummy missiles, were gone without a trace.

Brennen fingered his cuff. Another hijacking . . . and this one succeeded. Back on Tallis, Special Ops would be comparing reports from all over the Whorl and assigning Sentinels to investigate.

That was no longer his job, but it was his grave concern. The Shuhr were raiding again.

Tarance. Phoena. Now this.

The vanished craft were Narkin Flightworks 316 Fighters. From another well of memory he dredged up specs: Dual-drive and maneuverable in vacuum or atmosphere, they could be flown against space convoys or used to attack planetside facilities. To his knowledge, their only weakness was what his fellow intercept-fighter pilots called "stodginess." A little slow and not particularly maneuverable.

Holy One, not the College again.

He blinked. He still had stunned moments when all thoughts seemed unclear except his memories of Tarance, Asea, his nephews, or Destia—and moments when he couldn't remember their faces at all. He'd served the Federacy for ten satisfying years, but now he wondered if anything he'd done had lasting value. What did military intelligence matter, with eternity one heartbeat away? He must protect Firebird and their sons from an Adversary that waited to devour them.

The Speaker did allow suffering, to refine and strengthen His people, but evil was strong. So was hatred. Brennen could've found targets, if hating were allowed. Destia's murderer. Firebird's family . . .

A light pulsed on the communications panel recessed into his glass-and-leather-surfaced desk. A message from Captain Frenwick, who sat beyond the near wall at her station, followed in five seconds. "Man to see you," vocalized the desk's circuitry. "No appointment, claims urgent."

Brennen pressed an ACKNOWLEDGE panel. With a flicker of epsilon energy aimed through one hand, he cleared away several papers, some into a scribebook and some, memorized or rejected, into a sonic shredder. The desk's leather matched the coppery ironbark wood that lined his interior walls, and like his office, it was almost embarrassingly expansive. He didn't need opulence to do his job well.

A transport roared over on low approach. Distracted, he thought back to the unsettling news. For thirty years, the Shuhr had successfully attacked convoys with old-line interceptors.

Absently, he pressed another series of panels to answer Captain Frenwick. "Name, business, query?" He stared again at the transport, now parting Thyrian fighter groups on afternoon drill. Thyrica's Home Forces didn't fly NF–316s yet. The Shuhr could attack here with devastating consequences. With new Narkin VI slip-shields, NF–316s could travel short distances at faster-than-light speeds. They were also hard to destroy with a shot to the shields' critical point, aft of the engines—

"Tellai-Angelo, Tel," Captain Frenwick answered. "Home world Netaia. Won't state business. Shall I spell the name?"

Speaking of Firebird's family! Brennen lunged toward the touchboard. He had last seen Count Tel, now Phoena's husband at all of twenty-two, eyeing Firebird over the muzzle of a deadly D-rifle at Hunter Height. *You may not hate!* he reminded himself. In Tellai's case, pity was more appropriate. "Audiovisual confirmation, query?"

Captain Frenwick's husky voice filtered through the com console's speaker. "Look this way, sir, for an identity check."

A screen lit in the desk's near corner. On it, a slight human silhouette stood under the smoky dome's curve. The stranger stepped into indoor lighting and appeared as an individual, small nosed and almost girlish in his face, with large, soft eyes as dark as his hair.

This was Tellai, all right. Disbelieving, Brennen pressed his TRANSMIT key and said, "Send him in."

He heard a clatter as Captain Frenwick replaced her remote lens in its slot, and then, "The door on the right, sir."

Brennen had cleared his desk by the time Tellai stepped through. "Sit down, Your Highness," he said, dispersing his epsilon static to read Tellai's emotions quickly and clearly.

The new Prince Tel took a deep chair. Brennen caught fear and hostility, but not the determination there would've been in an assassin's emotional state. Tellai eyed the curved ceiling of smoked glasteel, the ironbark walls, and memfiles that held most of the Federacy's historical, industrial, and intelligence records. His long-lashed eyes stared up at a mounted pair of silver dress daggers, surrounded by a squadron of training certificates with the framed Federate Service Crest flying lead, then down at the massive desk. When Tel finally faced him, Brennen grudgingly thanked his office's extravagant designers. The young popinjay had been taken down several levels before he even spoke, and by then Brennen had made a chilling guess.

"Have you heard from Princess Phoena?"

Tellai groped into a breast pocket and drew out a folded paper, but he held it tightly. "General . . ." He cleared his throat. "I read this to Governor Danton, who sent me to you. It is from Phoena, in her scribing, but something's wrong." Brennen read disdain beneath Tellai's judiciously arched eyebrows. "Danton said if anyone in the Whorl could help me, you could." He shrugged. "So. I've come to you professionally, knowing you have no personal reason to help me. I suppose I owe an apology, if I mean to seek your help."

Help? Brennen would've liked to refuse before even hearing Tellai's request. He would like to call two MPs to escort him off the Base. But he respected Netaia's occupation governor, Lee Danton, who had helped him and Firebird finish that unauthorized mission to Netaia. "All right," he said quietly. "For the present, I'll forget your politics and what happened at Hunter Height. But I must demand one condition before we discuss anything." He met and held the stare of the proud brown eyes. "I can't trust you blindly, Tellai. You're Phoena Angelo's husband. I have to make sure you aren't here to murder me, nor Lady Firebird."

Tellai smoothed a black velvette sleeve. "I expected that."

"Then you'll allow me access to confirm your motives."

Tellai blanched.

"Didn't you assume I would want that?"

"I hoped you had better manners than to ask. What guarantee do I have that you won't do more than look around once you get inside my mind?"

"What are you hiding?"

Tellai turned away. Brennen waited silently. Another flight of intercept fighters buzzed the dome, and Brennen wished he were flying one, instead of interviewing a spineless aristocrat. He fingered the edge of his desk top.

The prince probably had plenty to hide. Count Tel had supported Phoena's plots even before Netaia fell to the Federacy.

Finally, Brennen spoke again. "You're free to leave, Your Highness."

"I can't," Tellai mumbled. "What must I do?"

"Only look this way. Then don't fight me."

Brennen caught him, held, and probed gingerly at the surface emotional layer of Tellai's alpha matrix. He confirmed the hostility and terror of himself, dominant in a web of plans and dreams that was utterly tangled and uncontrolled. Tellai didn't know his own heart any better now than when Brennen had first read him, back in the lieutenant governor's office at Citangelo. Something in Tellai's misplaced pride also recalled the labyrinth that once had been Firebird's emotional state. Even now, sometimes she baffled him by clinging to vestiges of that graceless Netaian mind-set.

He couldn't hate this man, and for the moment he didn't need to fear him. Withdrawing the probe, he brushed delicately at Prince Tel's suspicion. With Tellai slightly calmed, they could get through this business with less anger on both sides.

The prince shook his head. He probably hadn't liked the sensation of access. "That's all the time it takes you?"

Brennen closed his eyes for a few seconds, resting, then said, "I know your motives, but little else in that time. Now tell me why you came."

As Tellai exhaled, the supercilious arch of his eyebrows softened. "I never thought I'd be glad of your abilities, but they've saved me a long convincing speech. Here." He handed Phoena's letter across the black scribing pad.

Brennen unfolded it to book-page size and flattened it against a glass inset. "I'd like to duplicate this for my records."

"Granted," Tellai said stiffly.

Brennen turned the sheet over, pressed a concealed panel with his knee, then picked up the letter again.

Darling Tel,
    I'm safe and can write you now. We have friends at Three Zed with the power we need to reach all our goals. Keep C. calm. Don't let her go rushing off to Danton. She needn't.

Phoena was alive, then, but confirmed in Shuhr hands. Disturbed, Brennen read on.

They're treating me respectfully, so you needn't worry. Soon we'll be together, and Netaia will be put to rights.

> Till then,
> Your love,
> P.

Brennen rested his chin on one hand. He knew Phoena well enough to agree with her husband: This letter's tone was odd. "Do you have anything else that she scribed?" he asked. "Something older?"

Tellai blushed vividly. "I do, sir, but it's extremely personal."

"I won't copy it, then. But I need to see it."

Brennen stared up into Tellai's soft brown eyes. Having just held him under access, he could read his emotions easily. Tellai struggled transparently between hope and indignation. Brennen waited. One man would walk away from this meeting as the acknowledged dominant.

Finally, the nobleman drew a tri-D from his pocket and slid it across the desk. Brennen accepted it in both hands. It was a head-and-shoulders portrait of Phoena in goldstone tiara and orange velvette robe, scribed with a message that accepted his marriage proposal and promised revenge together on the Federacy and other enemies, including Firebird. Ignoring the texts, Brennen placed them side by side to compare scripts.

He frowned. "Come around, Tellai. Let me show you something."

Tel hurried up to stand by his shoulder.

Brennen pointed out several short words that occurred in both texts. "Look at the difference in the rhythm of her strokes. The hand is the same, but its cadence has changed."

"Didn't she write this, then?" Tel touched the new missive.

"I think she did. If it's a forgery it's excellent, but I think we can believe she is alive."

Tellai rested a trembling hand on the desk. "Have they done something to her mind, Caldwell?"

"I'm afraid it's likely." He couldn't deceive a frightened husband, not even this one. "That would account for the changed cadence and for the tone of the text, which reads 'not Phoena' to both of us."

"What?" Tel demanded. "What could they do?"

How much to tell him? Watch-link, memory blocks, subvocal seduction—even implanting false memories—all were possible. The Shuhr had no Privacy and Priority Codes. "I'd guess," he said slowly, "that they've simply lulled her to keep her under control."

Tellai swallowed hard. He pocketed the portrait. "Then I'll tell you what

I think, Caldwell. I think she went to them out of anger, when we thought it was rather nice that Firebird was having a baby."

Brennen started. "Who did?"

"Carradee and Daithi and I."

Brennen studied Tellai through narrowed eyes. Incredibly, he sensed no sign of evasion. Tellai told the truth. Despite Netaia's vile wastling traditions, Tellai was happy for Firebird. He liked her.

Oblivious to the sea change he'd just caused, Tellai went on. "Phoena could intend to help these people kill Firebird and . . . maybe Carradee. That's what I'm really afraid of," he admitted. "Carradee and her girls stand between Phoena and the throne. I tried talking to her, but she wouldn't listen. And she has a bad habit of underestimating other people. These Shuhr . . ." Shrinking from his speculation, Tellai walked away.

As Brennen waited, he formed his own theory. A Shuhr agent could've found the vindictive princess easy prey. One offer of illicit power could have brought her down.

Tellai spun around. "Once they take what they want from her, will they keep her alive and leave her . . ." His hands trembled. "Leave her . . . herself?"

"They might, if they think she could be of use to them."

"Make her a puppet queen?"

"Possibly." But even as he said it, Brennen guessed the Shuhr needed no symbolic ruler for Netaia—or any other world.

Tellai squared his narrow shoulders. "Danton thought you might be able to help."

"I can't promise anything," Brennen returned carefully. "What did you hope I could do?"

"That you'd help me try to get her away from these people."

Brennen resisted the impulse to laugh.

"Rescue her," Tel plunged ahead. "I have resources. The cost of fuel would be no problem—"

"Why did you come to me?" Stung by this flaunting of wealth, Brennen pressed both forearms against his desk. "You could've joined Phoena at Three Zed. Why do you think now that they're dangerous and we could help? What changed your mind?"

Tellai addressed the sturdy memfiles across the room. "That's not easy to answer, Caldwell. It's more a matter of what you haven't done than anything you have. I know more about you Sentinels now, and you in particular, than I did before. All I can say is that you've played very discreetly, compared with what you could've done. I can't side with you, but I respect you as an opponent." He wheeled suddenly. "Powers, Caldwell, isn't it enough that I've swallowed my guts and come to you? They'll probably destroy my wife if you won't help me!"

Rescue Phoena Angelo? The idea turned Brennen's stomach. "Your Highness, I'll do nothing for Phoena that endangers Firebird. Maybe you're aware that we're at risk ourselves."

"I heard that." Tellai slumped back into his chair. "Please accept my condolences . . . on your brother and his family. How is Lady Firebird?"

"She's quite sick of being pregnant."

"How long now?"

"Under three dekia, if she carries full term." He felt Tellai's spirits sink.

"I suppose you'll wait here for that."

"What do you mean?"

"That you won't go anywhere until the baby comes."

New information: Nctaia didn't know Firebird carried twins. "That's right," Brennen answered. "Naturally. There will be other factors to consider, as well. Professional commitments." He drew a deep breath. "If I were to leave Thyrica, it would take time to decide how to move, and whom to leave with Firebird when she was vulnerable, with . . . a newborn. Others might assist you." *And what about those missing fighters?*

Tellai folded his elegant hands. "I'm sorry I must ask this, but I know nothing about Thyrica—can you find me a place to stay? I shall certainly repay your services."

This time Brennen ignored the subtle snub. "It's more to the point that you'll have to be guarded, and that I'll need to know where you are. But I don't want to have you locked up." As Brennen considered housing Tellai on Base, down in Soldane, or inland at College, he realized that this day's other news made him even more nervous about leaving Firebird alone in their apartment.

He eyed Tellai, startled by a new thought. The prince did have cars and eyes. And if he could be absolutely sure of the man . . . maybe put him under voice-command . . . "I'll make an offer with a price," he said cautiously.

"Offer away. I can probably afford it."

Then buy yourself a planet. The retort flitted across Brennen's mind. Instead of venting it, he eyed Tellai over folded hands. "The price is a deeper access, Your Highness. I want to know precisely how you stand in this intrigue with Phoena, and why."

Tellai's face lost all color.

"I wouldn't ask for deep-access lightly. If you can convince me you're not a danger to us, that will alter our relationship—permanently. Prove that your concern is genuine, and I'll try to find an apartment in the complex where Firebird and I have taken a suite—if she approves. If she doesn't, or if I suspect you when I have finished, I can offer protective custody here on the Base or send you hotel hunting. But I warn you, you might not be safe in public housing."

Tellai clenched a fist in his lap. "I can't waste days looking for secure rooms. I begrudge hours." He laid his head against the back of his chair and stared at the ceiling. "I need you," he admitted. "It would be more than I expected, if you would allow me that close. What do you prefer?"

Brennen walked to a chair beside the abashed young prince, then sat down. "I want the truth, Tellai. I know how to keep secrets, and a strict code of law controls my use of anything I learn. I don't abuse what I learn in deep-access. But that is what I want."

Tel's eyebrows lifted again, pleadingly this time. "No brainsetting. No—what did you call it, 'lulling.'"

"None. And I give you my word that if I feel it's necessary to use voice-command, I will tell you in advance."

Tellai covered his face with his hands.

CHAPTER 11

ULTIMATUM

con sordino
muted

"They've been in there for over an hour, Damalcon," said Ellet Kinsman.

She was taking her kass break in Air Master Dardy's office, hoping to get news from one of Brennen's closer friends. Ellet was a classical Thyrian beauty, tall and slender with a long face and slim, slightly prominent nose, and she'd worked with Brennen at Special Operations on Tallis.

Air Master Damalcon Dardy had a small Base office with room for a desk and two reasonably comfortable chairs, and a small cliffside window. He plunked one booted foot on his desktop and shrugged, smiling. "I saw His Highness arrive. Quite the little fop."

Leaning back in Dardy's extra chair, Ellet examined her fingers. "Of all the complications we don't need," she muttered. *Another Angelo*, she thought behind her static shields. *I would to the holy Word they'd all been smothered in their gilded cradles.*

She felt an answering sweep of comforting frequency, and she glanced back at the tall man behind the desk. Physically, Damalcon Dardy out-muscled Brennen Caldwell, but in rank and epsilon rating no one began to compare . . . and now a faithless outworlder had conceived the next heirs to the Carabohd prophecies. Personally, Ellet believed that Netaia, not the Shuhr, was responsible for Dr. Caldwell's murder.

I tried to save you, she reprimanded Brennen in a shielded corner of her mind, where his friend Dardy wouldn't sense it. Brennen was reaping a harvest he sowed back at Veroh, where he lost his affective control during an intelligence-class interrogation. Tellai's flight to Thyrica proved that Brennen hadn't simply pair-bonded First Major Lady Firebird Angelo. He had wed into a turbulent, powerful dynasty.

Pair bonding might last until death, but Ellet guessed Firebird Angelo wasn't the kind of woman to enjoy a long life. She'd take the wrong risk someday. Hopefully, someday soon.

Dardy levitated a stylus and passed it from one hand to the other. "They may have to run for Hesed House," he speculated.

"Are they planning to go? What do you know about it?"

Dardy touched the stylus to his forehead. "If they were actually planning, and if I knew anything, it'd be confidential. But I'm not in on all Caldwell's confidences. There's deep water in that sea."

"I understand." *He feels too cordial*, she realized inside that quiet, shielded corner. Was Dardy building toward a connaturality probe, wondering if she might make a suitable mate? He was just enough older to have missed meeting her in College. He'd introduced himself only a few months ago.

Connatural with Dardy? Ellet shrank from the notion. For one man only, she was prepared to wait half a lifetime.

Not Damalcon Dardy.

Another Sentinel in the Base One complex had Damalcon Dardy on his mind. Staff Officer Harcourt Terrell's office was on the first floor below ground. Though he lacked the status to get a cliff-face window, the designers had installed a realtime receiver on the top half of his inner wall. He could've watched surf lap the cliff while shrieking sea-gliders rode updrafts, diving now and again for helpless fish in the shoals.

Terrell wasn't watching the realtime. He had just checked Air Master Dardy's location with a subtle quest pulse.

Harcourt Terrell had been a restless youth, barely accepted into Sentinel College, slow to win promotions. Three years ago, a stranger made him an incredible offer: youth-restoring cocktails and biennial injections of a substance that wouldn't just put off his waning, but—unbeknownst to his colleagues—increase his epsilon output. The stranger only asked him to provide a tissue sample and then stand ready for a further assignment.

Who could've refused?

Four dekia ago, they contacted him again. They gave him a fresh ayin treatment, the strongest he'd ever had, and explained his assignments. Whether he succeeded or failed, they would then transport him to the Golden City. He looked forward to learning new skills at Three Zed. He'd started here with the watch-link that gave him an eerie, occasional sense that someone was looking over his shoulder. A team of them could see through his eyes, move his hands, even put ideas into his mind and read his uppermost thoughts, from considerable distance.

As assigned, he had switched off the College security grid for Emil

Paxon's hijacking attempt. A bold effort, but in Terrell's opinion doomed to fail. Too public, too slow.

Since then, he'd maintained a mental list of Alert Forces by location. General Coordinator Caldwell posed the greatest danger and naturally took the top spot on that list—but even after Terrell defeated Caldwell's access probe, he knew better than to use quest pulses to track a Master Sentinel. That mistake cost Paxon his life, by Caldwell's own admission.

Last week, Micahel Shirak himself reappeared. He'd admitted that he set up Paxon as a diversion and boasted that it worked. After Paxon's death in the crash, Soldane police stopped looking for the new Caldwell assassin.

Now Micahel would hit Thyrica. He'd timed the strike to follow Mistress Caldwell's impending childbirth. His new force waited a two-day slip outsystem. The moment Terrell heard she'd gone into labor, he would alert a particular messenger. Then, while Micahel distracted Caldwell and the Home Forces, Terrell would switch off the College grid once more and clean out the nest like an egg snake, mother bird and all.

Even before Caldwell probed Terrell, he'd disliked the Master Sentinel. Years ago, Terrell's personality examiners had warned him to beware of jealousy. He'd fought it with a whole heart, until one day he realized he simply acknowledged a genuine injustice. Since the access, he deeply resented Caldwell. Terrell had seen his arrogant side—

He did pity Mistress Caldwell. By all accounts, she'd been an outcast. She'd lived with injustice too.

Still, for a chance at personal greatness—and he'd never guessed that he would learn to beat access interrogation!—he would fulfill his orders.

The next step puzzled him, for Micahel had assured him that he would escape. They intended to destroy the College and Caldwell in one strike. Terrell didn't understand the timing, or how he would get away. Sometimes, he suspected he'd been subliminally manipulated.

But they wouldn't do that to a loyal recruit.

In the apartment complex's downlevel lounge, a whistle interrupted Firebird's best session yet on a blazer-simulation game. This was one way she could still train . . . sitting down. Gripping a mock Federate-issue service blazer, she plodded across the empty lounge and keyed its comscreen console onto "answer" mode. She didn't even count off the ID rhythm. The only person who called here was—

Brennen's face appeared. "Mari?"

She laid the sim blazer on a kass machine. "Brenn. What is it? Someone for dinner?"

Brennen looked slightly aside. "Maybe. Prince Tel is on Thyrica."

"Here?" She shoved hair back from her face. "On Base?" Then she made a guess. "He's heard from Phoena."

"Yes. He came to ask my help."

Oh no. No, Brennen. Don't do it. "Any confirmation on where she is?"

"The good news is, she's alive. But she is with the Shuhr. She seems to have gone to them of her own accord."

Well done, dear sister. Firebird groaned. "Then Tel can't be serious."

"I took him under access, and he means us no harm. He loves that woman with a selflessness that borders on idolatry. He's in the waiting area. Would you be willing to let him take the spare living unit on our floor until I decide whether I can give him any assistance?"

"Say that again?"

He did.

She shook her head. "Do you mean to let him stay that close to us? Is that wise?"

"He actually seems rather devoted to you, Mari. But he's terrified for Phoena's sake."

"Of course." Sweet-face Tellai, Firebird snorted silently. The noble who'd been fool enough to propose to her bloodsucking sister. At least he had more sense than to charge off toward the Shuhr.

So did Brennen—didn't he?

"Are you all right, Mari?"

She glanced back up to the screen, glad that Brennen sat too far away to pick up her uneasy scorn. "You offered him a place?"

"I did, but it's contingent on your approval. He'd be company for you. And backup. But you don't have to agree. There are protective custody rooms on base." His lips twitched into a smile. "If you can endure that, he can."

That would only be fair. Still, Tel wasn't the guiltiest party. He hadn't gone to the Shuhr. And what would it be like, married to Phoena? She winced. "If you offered a place, I can't turn him away. I'm as much a Tellai as he is. His grandfather was my father's older brother. Look at Tel. Small boned and long waisted. Just like me."

"We can reprogram the security alarms if he'd worry you."

Tel? That was a joke. "You said you accessed him."

"I did."

"Then I trust your judgment." —Though it was hard to believe Brennen's generosity extended to that young idiot. "And your ability to command him, if necessary. Tell him he can come."

"Thank you, Mari."

"Brenn."

"Yes?"

"Don't do anything rash." She touched off the screen and rode the lift uplevel.

Firebird breakfasted with two men the next morning, and when she finally sent Brennen off to his Advisory Board briefing, it was with a touch of irritation. He'd never hovered before. Finally, she took him aside and showed him the shock pistol she'd belted beneath her skyff and the dagger up her sleeve.

Brennen also demonstrated the voice-activated auxiliary locks. He explained how Firebird could secure herself in the master room if necessary, and Tel seemed completely cooperative.

Then he stepped off down the hall. Firebird returned to the servo table and sat down across from her young second cousin, now also her brother-in-law—this heir of his house, who'd never associated with wastlings—and folded her hands. "All right, he's gone," she said severely. All wastlings hated and envied heirs, who had the power of life and death over them. "You have other questions, don't you?"

Tellai brushed a speck of dust from his blue sateen knickers. He'd come to them without a tailor or a dresser, poor thing, and he'd nearly fainted when he first saw the size of her. "Well, yes, I do. Especially about him."

His Netaian accent sounded so melodious, though. She wondered if she'd started to speak like a Thyrian. "I probably asked the same questions," she admitted.

"Has he—has he twisted you, Firebird? Forced your mind—changed you? Would you even know if he had?"

She took a deep breath and stretched her weary back muscles. "He wouldn't. He waited for months while I settled my own mind about the Federacy. The Sentinels can't impose their convictions on other people. They face the death penalty if they're caught meddling." Now she'd taken that sobering vow too. She wrapped her hands around a steamy cup of cruinn and drew a long, grateful whiff. Tel had produced half a kilo of the spicy Netaian beverage from his luggage. "Brennen gave me reference materials, and he answered questions, but he never, never forced me."

"But he trapped you." Tellai's voice trembled. "We all know that. He met you, and *zzt*, he wanted you. That's not natural, Firebird."

How had Tel known that? She sighed. "They call it 'connaturality,' when two individuals' minds follow the same thought patterns, but their personalities balance each other's strengths and needs. They're trained to stay alert for connatural individuals simply because they can't marry anyone else. Only the highly connatural can pair bond, and Brennen's nature isn't like most of the starbred. He hadn't been able to find a mate near his own age among them."

"What did you think of all that?" Tel raised a narrow eyebrow.

"He frightened me. But he offered something tempting."

"Oh?"

"Life." Firebird stared between window slats at a red stone wall that constituted her outdoor view. It suggested one more visualization—if ever she returned to Netaia, the redjackets would bolt her to a wall like that one, and . . .

She steered the thought aside and gently hugged her twins. "Life with honor," she added, "and a cause that I found I could believe in. And now, an enemy to fight together."

Tellai pulled his hands into his lap at the mention of that enemy. When his hands vanished, Firebird's crept toward her shock pistol. She didn't think he meant to attack, but she mustn't drop her guard. "These Shuhr," he said in a soft voice. "Who are they really?"

"Gene-altered Ehretans like Brennen," she answered, "with mental abilities like his, but who don't follow their laws." *And, Singer, why don't you blast them out of existence?* "The little I know isn't pleasant. Are you sure you want to hear it from me?" She brushed the servo table's surface with one hand. "We can access the Federate Register from this terminal."

"Would you?"

She refilled their cruinn cups and then punched up the database.

"All right," she said. "Shuhr."

A coded message headed Brennen's queue when he arrived. He reached for his touchboard and frowned. A familiar row of letters and numerals indicated its source—and Regional command, Tallis had little reason to contact him since forcing his resignation. Brennen touched up the decoding sequence. A golden consular crest flared on his screen.

He read the message that followed.

General Coordinator Caldwell, Greetings.

Regarding: The disappearance of Her Highness Princess Phoena Angelo of the Netaia Protectorate System.

The Veroh scout station has confirmed the passage of a subspace wake matching that of a missing craft posted to us by Governor Danton of Netaia, and its course toward the Zed system of the Shuhr.

If Her Highness has indeed been abducted by that people, or even if she went freely to them, repercussions among other Federate-protectorate peoples could be disturbing. "Protectorate" status implies enforced safety for a people under our shield.

Because of your intimate knowledge of the Netaian aristocracy, the Regional council requests that you assist Special Operations in the matter of Princess Phoena, as an independent on-site operator. Our reciprocation would include your restoration to full Security I privileges, and also to eligibility for use of Federate facilities, even should you remain in Thyrian service.

Lady Firebird's own status remains dubious with the Netaian government. Measures have been proposed in some quarters to petition the Federacy again for revocation of her transnational citizenship. Technically she remains under our protective custody, as you know, as surety for her conduct.

> Honorable Madam
> Kudennou Kernoweg
> On behalf, F.R.C.

Brennen resisted a sinking, angry sensation. *You can't mean this, Kernoweg.* That councilor had made a personal crusade of currying Netaian favor, and this wasn't the first time her policies threatened Firebird. Revoking Firebird's transnational citizenship would leave her wide open to the execution of that death sentence. Chilled despite his emotional control, Brennen reviewed the message.

". . . as an independent, on-site operator."

The Council, not just Kernoweg, was asking him to go to Three Zed.

But they couldn't order him, after asking him to resign. They could only hold Firebird's status over his head, and that tenuously.

Lee Danton carried a heavy burden. Brennen had found flaws in several Federate policies toward Netaia. Economic conciliation only encouraged the wealthy Netaian separatists.

He glanced back at the screen. So Phoena's whereabouts were public now. Her defection did point a finger at a real problem. No ordinary Netaian would believe she'd gone willingly to the Shuhr. They would think she had been kidnapped, or else brainwashed . . . which was not the seduction he suspected. A seduced individual still was responsible.

Regional, then, was scrambling to prove it could protect subjected citizens without causing conflict with the Shuhr.

Especially with those new fighters missing, he realized. Since Regional didn't want to provoke Three Zed, they hoped he would go on his own.

Scanning the third full paragraph, he confirmed its unwritten ultimatum: If ever he hoped to return to Federate service, requisition a Federate ship, or use Security channels, he must attempt this mission.

It was the last thing he wanted to try.

Alert Forces could possibly pull off a rescue, though. He'd already talked to Claggett and Dardy about the need to run a reconnaissance ship past Three Zed.

Even alone, he'd attempted clandestine missions. Sometimes a lone agent could accomplish more than a large, visible force. To get back on track for the High command, his life goal, the risk might be worth taking—

No! This was insane. *Ambition*, he warned himself, *overconfidence. Be careful!*

If, and only if, AF would assist him?

He could ask Dardy.

He eyed the message's coding sequence, hoping to find reply passage prepaid. It was not. They didn't want any reply extant in their file. If he failed in the effort, Mari would have only this message to prove that Regional requested his action. He'd seen Federate pensions granted on such evidence to widows and widowers with dependents.

He keyed for a hard copy and watched letters appear on a sheet cradled by his print unit, snatched up the page, and then hesitated. Pursing his lips, he watched another transport soar over his slice of the glasteel dome.

Actually, he had no intention of complying. The reward—his questionable chance at the High command—wasn't worth the risk with those babies due. Firebird, too, had been stung by Regional's request for his resignation. Why was he even considering pension issues? She would accept no pittance from Tallis, with that pride of hers.

Deeply relieved, he decided not to mention the message to Firebird or Dardy, unless further developments made it important to speak.

But he wouldn't answer Regional, either. If he told Madam Kernoweg he would not comply, the High command was gone for good. There must be some way to revive that hope without taking insane risks.

He shifted his hand over the touchboard and saved Regional's message. Then, turning to his schedule, he dropped the printout into his sonic shredder.

CHAPTER 12

THE DARK

stringendo
pressing, becoming faster

Particles of scribepaper were settling in Brennen's wastebin when Firebird straightened and took a long, deep breath. Something like a strong hand gripped her taut belly and squeezed hard enough to hurt.

She set her third cup of cruinn on the servo table. She'd sent Tel back to his own apartment and settled in to her work. She had almost finished composing a final essay for her home course, on behalf of the imaginary Mari Tomma. Mari would soon have one more credit toward an upper-level degree in governmental analysis.

She stared out into a steady rain. *Is that you?* she asked the twins. *Can't you wait just two more weeks?* In case it would help, she choked down another dose of Spieth's vile syrup.

Before noon, she had no doubt. Syrup or no syrup, they were coming. She'd delayed this as long as she could. She touched the SEND button to submit her essay and then called Brennen.

Weeks ago, Master Spieth had warned Firebird that childbirth pains would start slowly and accelerate—and that Brennen wouldn't be allowed to block them, except at certain stages. Pacing a secluded walkway near the medical tower, gripping his arm, Firebird started to sense the acceleration. Rain drummed on the walkway's awning, a mezzo-soprano drone she found pleasantly hypnotic.

Before night fell, her labor established in earnest. A pattern emerged: Each contraction started like a jab in her low back, then her muscles tightened around her sides, ending with the girdling stricture. Each grew just slightly harder and longer.

"All right, love?" he whispered, pausing near a tall kirka tree.

The pressure eased. "Still fine." He knew that, of course. But he also knew that it comforted her when he asked.

"It's almost too dark to see. Let's go in."

"One more. Please. It may be a while before I'm out in the fresh air again."

An hour later, he insisted. Then, she walked with him inside the medical tower's misty atrium, skirting a shallow reflecting pool edged with more moss-hung trees. Controlling sensation with the focusing skills Master Spieth had taught her, she also concentrated on closing out a series of amazingly strong emotional surges. Brennen would need to shield himself from those. *Breathe*, she reminded herself. *Focus—relax* . . .

She clenched Brennen's arm and felt his concern. "That one almost got away from me," she admitted.

"You've done enough alone. I'll send for Spieth."

She rested her head on his shoulder. "I'll be all right a little longer. Let her sleep."

"Too late." He touched her hand. "She's awake now."

"The contractions begin . . . how?" White hair neatly combed as if she always rose just after midnight, Master Spieth laid a fluffy blanket across the second tiny cot in a white-walled birthing room.

"Here." Firebird sat astride a complicated, angle-adjustable chair. Brennen rubbed the small of her back as the precious minutes passed between contractions. *If this doesn't get too much worse*, she reflected, *I wouldn't mind*. At the edge of her vision, Brennen reached for his kass cup and stole a sip.

Spieth folded her wrinkled hands. "These little ones are both head-down," she said. "They should come easily."

"I wasn't supposed to have children at all." Firebird winced as tender muscles tightened again. She glanced at Brennen. To her surprise, the discomfort faded. Perversely, she tried to shake off his help. She ought to face the contraction, ride through it. Clutching the chair's back, she rocked back and forth. The pressure became pain as she lost control. "The redjackets execute wastlings who become pregnant—or abort them—"

"Breathe—focus—breathe, Firebird!" Startled by Spieth's voice-command, Firebird obeyed.

"That's better," Spieth said when the contraction let go. She strode around Firebird to glance at numerals that glowed on the room's side wall. "Be reasonable. He was only showing you how he can close out the worst of it, when it comes. —You're doing perfectly," she told him aside as she took a turn massaging Firebird's lower back.

"Has Tel been sent for?" Firebird gasped. Yes, she was being unreasonable. She didn't care. "Brenn, send for Tel. The Electorate will demand a witness to their parentage."

Brennen grasped her shoulder. "He's down a level from here, reading, under guard. Be quiet, now. Review the calming patterns you studied. . . .''

Firebird shut her eyes and concentrated, as Spieth and Janesca had taught her, on that granite wall, stout and strong and impenetrable. That last part—the impenetrability—seemed real enough. Concentrating on the image did keep her out of pain's reach, forcing her to focus her mental effort elsewhere instead of fighting every contraction. She rode through one spasm without feeling truly uncomfortable. Opening her eyes at its end, she grinned her triumph at Brennen.

As hours passed, though, as morning-shift workers came on duty and then vanished for lunch, her exultation faded. Evidently the twins hadn't heard Spieth's prediction of a short, easy labor. *Enough of this! I want to see my babies.* Firebird knew she must maintain focus—not mindlessly, but with mindful attention—but her strength was fading, her concentration starting to wander. The contractions became more painful, though Brennen eased them whenever Spieth let him.

Night fell again, according to the wall chrono. Master Spieth helped Firebird back up to the kneeling position she found most comfortable. Firebird draped her arms across Brennen's shoulders, feeling vaguely disoriented.

"Transition phase," Spieth announced. "Thank you, Brennen. You must let her go on alone for a while."

At last! But this would be the hardest part, even harder than delivering. Now Firebird must concentrate her mind on the calming patterns, letting her body use these waves of physical power to speed delivery along.

Whether from stress or exhaustion, all her senses seemed to blur. Had she lapsed into a link with these frightened twins who would have Brennen's epsilon strength? Was that possible? If they were conscious, what were they going through?

Brennen's voice, though close against her ear, sounded faint. Spieth's lined face faded. Only this unbearable pressure seemed real. Again she envisioned the granite wall surrounding Hunter Height. In this variation, it separated her from pain.

A thought struck her. How could both visualizations be valid? If she wanted to turn, maybe she was doing this wrong, trying to break out to a new perspective. She actually needed to locate mental energy that already was close at hand. Her birthright.

She blinked. As Brennen stroked her back, she closed her eyes and envisioned the same wall, but from outside. Was this the right way after all? She pressed harder. *Mighty Singer . . . help me . . . push . . .*

Rough granite gave way. She plunged through and found . . . not Hunter Height, but terror.

So black that it absorbed all light, this darkness rippled and flamed in phantasmagorical patterns, an ebony void torn by hungry black energies. Like black flames, they nibbled and gnawed even at the abyssal darkness around them. They reached out to seize and consume her. One tongue blasted right through her.

Scalded, her very soul shuddered.

What was this? She tried to flee outward but couldn't find the wall. Another contraction mounted. Heat and pain drove her back into the darkness, one powerless presence in a vast, flaming emptiness.

An instant later, she recognized the imagery. For years of nights, lying alone in her palace suite, she'd forced herself to imagine the afterlife Netaians feared most: the purgatorial Dark that Cleanses, grim fate of the disobedient. She imagined the Dark in vivid detail—searing heat, utter blackness—so that lesser terrors wouldn't frighten her when she must die bravely, sacrificing a brief life to win everlasting bliss. Months ago, she threw off all hope of achieving bliss that way . . . and supposedly, all fear of the Dark . . . yet deep in her mind, this hideous vision remained.

What did this mean? Did the Dark exist after all, and the scorned Powers too? Were they showing her where justice awaited her? —Or was this only a phantasmal memory, a truer glimpse than ever of the old life she'd escaped?

Battling the pain of yet another contraction and pursued by a blast of black flame, she fled back toward where the wall must be . . . found it . . . and couldn't thrust through. Trapped in her own visualization, she spun and pressed her back to the wall. The flame licked like a beast eager to devour her.

She must have died and passed into the Darkness. Why else would she feel herself vanishing . . . fading . . . disintegrating . . .

She would never see her sons.

Help! she begged the Singer. *If you're real, if you're listening! Help me!*

Sudden anguish assured her that she was alive. Another contraction gripped her. Voices muttered. Brennen urged, close to her ear, "Mari! Firebird! *Breathe!*" He turned away. "Spieth! She's . . ."

She struggled to focus on reality and Brennen's cue. Master Spieth's voice approached. ". . . blood oxygen is dipping dangerously, and the upper twin is trying to go breech. Keep her awake, or we'll have a crisis. . . . No! You must still stay out!"

Awake.

The word jogged Firebird's memory to a phrase from Janesca's instruction book: "The inward-chasing of the mind's natural pattern that will lead in sleep . . ."

Dear Singer, had she finally turned? Was this terrible Dark neither a hallucination nor a memory, but the inner energy she'd tried to find?

"No!" she shrieked. "Brennen!"

Another clench of pain began. Someone seized her hands. Clutching back, she moaned, unable to regain control.

When it passed, she saw Brennen's ear and Master Spieth's head and shoulders and Tel hanging back across the room. The time was close. Another pair of ashen-faced Sentinels stood against the far wall. Unfamiliar medical equipment had been moved into the room.

"Don't let that happen again." Spieth's cheeks looked pale. "You have only a few moments before the next contraction begins. Prepare yourself."

Brennen slipped a chip of ice into her mouth. "You can't lose control like that, Mari. I can keep you conscious if you stay in control."

She swallowed the precious drops of melted ice. She must've been panting for hours. "But, Brenn! During that last contraction, I—"

"No time!" He motioned toward a monitor that gleamed green on a smooth black wall panel. "Focus, Mari. Relax. They're moving."

Despairing, guessing one more would finish her, she closed her eyes and obeyed. Again her senses faded. Again, before her mind's eye, the wall arose. She hesitated.

But if this were some bizarre visualization of the epsilon turn, then beyond that wall, inside that blistering blackness, there must lie an epsilon carrier. Medical tests had confirmed its existence.

I will turn, she'd said, *or die trying.*

She flung herself through.

A fresh tongue of black flame blinded her inner vision. Another shot around her, tightening, pinning her in place while a third threaded straight through that spiral and burned through her soul's very center.

She'd believed, all those wasting years, that imagining purgatory would help her die with such courage that the Powers wouldn't send her there. Shielding herself with thin, flammable rags of courage—and a new faith that was barely a hope—she broke free. She dove deeper into the darkness's heart.

Something flickered down there, a faint nebula of blue-white energy. Around it the darkness flamed hotter, licking and hissing as if it craved this too. Maybe this gleaming center anchored the Dark inside her subconscious.

Maybe it kept the black flames from haunting her adult dreams, the way they had during her childhood. Could that flickering center be her epsilon carrier?

What else could it be?

Pain and exhaustion suffocated her now, within sight of fulfilling her quest. If she lost sight of the glimmering nebula, she might never see it again—but if she touched it, she might finally learn to turn, to access other minds . . . to be a Sentinel mother to a Sentinel's sons.

She pressed even deeper, farther from consciousness. A new flame roared to life. It seared into her lungs, burning her from the inside out. Coughing and choking, she closed her airways against it, certain that if she inhaled that fiery miasma once more, it would consume her.

From another dimension of existence, a blast of pain exploded in her face. Brennen's voice shouted, commanding her to do something she couldn't comprehend.

Flaming darkness ripped away one edge of the glowing nebula. She would fail—she was too late! Anguish tripled her strength. With lungs all but bursting, she groped through dark flames, stretching toward one faint blue-white line of illusory force.

She seized it. It pulsed under her touch, icy cool, growing and shrinking at the same time like something from some unimaginable dimension.

Again pain burned her face, then pressure of the fires forcing into her lungs. She choked and struggled not to breathe. Gripping that knotted line of force, she tried to wrench it free of the darkness, back toward the rugged wall. She must pull it through, outside, away from the horrors and into the outside light—or else the Dark would destroy it. Longer than she could've believed possible, she held her breath. Like a last, tickling touch of coolness and light, the thread energized her.

But her strength faded. Something stabbed deep down her airway. A new pain came on, a tearing pain she'd never felt before. Like thousands of cruel hands, it seized her, squeezing, tearing her open. . . .

Master Spieth's lined face focused in front of her eyes, over the clear lump of a breath mask. The keen otherness of the medical master's epsilon probe drove into her consciousness. All shreds of illusion fled. "Hold there, Firebird!" Spieth shouted. "Push! Brennen, now!"

Firebird tried to shake Brennen's arm off her shoulder. He mustn't see the imagined horror. She would die of shame—

He grasped her chin and turned her to face him. "Mari." He held her stare with full epsilon force. "You're in my strength now. Yours is gone. Hold on! Only a few minutes more . . ."

Pain! Firebird gave a last startled cry and then surrendered to Brennen, unable to move or struggle or even think. She saw only his eyes, blue and unblinking, felt only the command that held her. Longer, longer . . . she was turning inside out. . . .

Without warning, he released her. She gave a little hiccuping gasp, saw the startled look on his face—and then saw nothing.

Firebird awoke to see Spieth's iron gray eyes hovering where Brennen's had been.

She lay on her back. She hadn't done that for weeks. She recoiled as memory returned. What had she seen inside her soul?

"You fear me?" the master asked quietly. A delicate probe flicked the fringes of memory.

Firebird choked. "Master, are the twins—"

"Be still." Spieth drove her epsilon probe deeper. Afraid to do anything else, Firebird held down her defenses, though the deep touch brought up waves of queasiness. She waited out the access open eyed.

Movement at the corner of vision caught her glance. Spieth's blue-skirted apprentice approached with both arms laden. The oblong mass on the girl's left arm yelled vigorously, but Firebird couldn't focus on it. Spieth's otherness felt too strong.

After a minute Spieth averted her stare and withdrew the probe. For several seconds she sat silent and erect at the edge of Firebird's bed while Firebird fought back tears of lingering embarrassment. "Please," she mumbled. "Give me my babies."

"In a moment," Spieth said at last. "Now I see why you struggled so. I wouldn't have thought such a thing was possible. If you'd been alone, we would've lost you—and both your sons."

Both? An awful fear gripped Firebird. Apparently the master sensed it. "They live," she answered before Firebird could ask. "Both are healthy, in the nineties on their physical response tests."

She glanced at the student-apprentice sekiyr's squalling burden, then whispered, "Where's Brennen?"

"Gone to rest. I put him down myself. He was distraught. You'll see him soon." Spieth pressed a hand against Firebird's forehead. The touch felt cool and satiny.

"Give me . . ."

Spieth beckoned and touched a control, raising the head of Firebird's bed.

Firebird turned to the sekiyr and reached for the source of the wailing that'd gone on at the edge of her attention.

The sekiyr laid an infant in Firebird's crooked elbow. Firebird tugged back a fuzzy warming blanket and found a tiny sloped head, wrinkled from forehead to chin in fury. "This is the second-born," the girl whispered.

This is mine? "What's wrong?" Firebird clutched the tiny, shaking damp thing. It smelled of disinfectant. "Is it . . . is he all right?"

"Hungry, I'd guess."

Though the baby shrieked on, beneath Firebird's bewilderment surged a deep, awestruck joy. For once, she felt sure that she'd done something absolutely, inarguably right.

She peered at her firstborn, who lay quietly on the girl's other arm. The sekiyr fingered his blanket away from his face. This head wore a faint sheen of light brown hair. Glancing down to confirm a surprising comparison, Firebird ran a finger across the second-born's wispy curls. As they dried, they showed plainly auburn. "Kinnor," she murmured. "Little kicker. You have my hair, but it's curly."

"Kinnor—kinnora. That's lovely." Spieth stepped behind the sekiyr and reached onto a service cart for something Firebird couldn't see.

"And this one?" The sekiyr sat down on the bedside. Firebird couldn't look away from her firstborn's gently squared, fine-featured face.

"Kiel. Brennen and I chose the names months ago, to follow my family tradition. 'Kiel' is a Netaian hunting bird. Kiel Labbah, after Brennen's father. And Kinnor Irion, for mine." She felt her chin quiver. She still couldn't look away. "Oh, Master Spieth. Kiel looks so like . . ." She gulped. "*So* like . . ." She struggled to finish the sentence. "So much like Brennen."

Then she wept without hope of controlling herself, clutching Kinnor to her breast. *What is Brenn going to think of me?*

An hour later, after Firebird tried to feed both twins and then, exhausted, surrendered them to the sekiyr's care, Brennen came down. He stood motionless in the doorway for several seconds. She sensed his emotional state firing off in all directions, like his disheveled hair. Letting the door slide shut behind him, he came in and sat down beside her on a chair.

"Have you spoken with Spieth?" she asked.

He leaned toward her. "Briefly. I won't stay long. You're exhausted, physically and emotionally. But, Mari . . ." He leaned away. "She confirms . . ." He lifted his chin and looked into her eyes. "Mari."

"I turned."

"I felt it."

To her surprise, the door swung open. Spieth stepped in. Firebird felt

Brennen's irritation rise, and then all foreign emotion cut off. Which Sentinel was shielding her perceptions?

Brennen gripped his knees with both hands and cleared his throat. "We'll have to speak to Shamarr Dickin," he said in a louder voice. "He needs to know what happened, and he'll want to see how your established alpha patterns are reorienting. It could drive you mad if you tried to continue. You must believe me. But, Aldana—"

Firebird opened her tired eyes wide. She'd never heard him call the medical master by her first name.

"Dickin could order . . . what happens to Mari?"

What was he talking about?

"No," Spieth said calmly. "Not yet. She's been weakened too badly. She can't face an evaluation access during maternal bonding. I'll approach Shamarr Dickin. Brennen, congratulate your wife." Spieth pointed at him. "She made her first turn under extremely difficult circumstances."

"I do," he said softly, and Firebird thought she saw sincerity in his gaze, though she couldn't feel it. "I knew she could do this. Mari is the strongest woman I've ever known."

Spieth gave Firebird a tiny, triumphant smile. "It's good to hear him say that, isn't it? Now, Firebird." Spieth's lips curved down again. "You *will* do nothing about turning again until we speak with the Shamarr. You haven't got the strength for it, and at any rate, Brennen is right. There is a significant risk of madness. You're suffering an intense upheaval in your alpha and epsilon matrices. You will not speak of what happened."

"Gladly." Firebird rubbed her fingers against her palms.

"I'm glad you consent, but you may as well know you didn't have a choice. I've put you under command for a full day. And Tellai, and the sekiyr Linna too, until I release them, Brennen. They won't tell anyone she turned—if they even realize it. For now, it is our secret." She took a step backward. "Keep it so, Brennen. You're the only one who is free to talk besides myself."

She hurried out. Once again, Firebird sensed Brennen's disquiet. He took her hand and threaded his fingers between hers. "Tell me what you saw," he said, "if you can. No one wants to access your memory for it, but we all felt your terror release when you fainted at the end. We thought it was only birthing pain, but it seemed exceptionally intense even to Spieth."

In a faltering voice, she told him about the nights she had spent, years ago, scalding her mind with a hellish fear, hoping it would empower her to face glorious death.

"Willfulness, impatience, pride," he murmured.

Firebird glowered. "That's not fair!"

He clung to her hand. "Mari, you thought that on your own you could face down your mightiest enemy, death itself. Isn't that pride? And," he pressed, "you insisted on willfully doing it yourself, long before you truly needed to do it, as if you couldn't even wait until they gave your geis orders. . . ." His voice trailed away.

She couldn't argue. "I don't think I have much to be proud of in this."

Brennen kneaded her wrist and hand. "Oh, Mari. Mari, I am proud of you. Proud as I've ever been. But I'm afraid for you too."

"Is there really that great a risk of madness?"

It pained him to speak—she felt it—but he met her stare. He spoke softly, almost in a whisper. "All I know is this. With your epsilon carrier so firmly anchored inward, behind imagery like that . . . if you ever tried to use it, what would it do to you? How could anyone control it, even with training?" He shook his head. "Not even Janesca will know how to train you, because no one has ever . . . ever . . . experienced this kind of a turn before."

"Pray for me, then," she whispered. "Please. Right now. I'm too tired to even try."

He bowed his head over her hand, brushed her knuckles with his lips, and then squeezed his eyes shut, furrowing his forehead.

CHAPTER 13

SECURITY BREACH

forte, marcato
loudly, stressing each note

Brennen tried to ignore a persistent shriek from the apartment's servo table, but the rhythm chirped on. After one day's rest in the medical center, they had moved back to the secured apartment. Firebird slept with the twins in the master room for the present, while he took the entry room lounger, on night guard. She seemed less emotionally brittle now, but her uncontrollable epsilon turn had plunged them both into postpartum depression.

What had she really seen behind that wall? Was it only a memory or something more ominous? He prayed those questions again and again, listening intently for the Holy Voice. This time, the Speaker's first answer was silence.

Bleary-eyed, he sat up and paid attention to the rhythmic signal. Five. Pause. Two. Longer pause.

Base One, Priority Two. No social call.

He stumbled to the small servo table, touched for a cup of kass, then hit the ACKNOWLEDGE key.

The abominable shrieking, more discordant than Kinnor's cries to be fed, finally stopped. "Call-up, General Caldwell," said a synthesized voice.

He stared at the servo cubby where his kass cup would appear. Frowned at its glowing chrono. He'd slept less than six hours.

He stabbed three digits with his index finger and got a human answer. "General Caldwell," clipped a mature voice, "are you confirming your call up?"

"Y—no. I'm sorry, but my wife delivered our twins yesterday. No, the day before. I should be on the med-leave list."

"You are," the voice agreed. "This is an AF call. We've got a three-flight of NF–316s coming in. They won't ID."

The stolen fighters! But where were the rest of them? "Point of origin?" Brennen gathered the rest of his wits.

"We've read an anomaly out near Shesta that could be a carrier. You'll be briefed when you arrive, sir." Shesta, one of Thyrica's companion planets, was at its closest orbital approach, almost in conjunction.

He left the kass cup steaming in the cubby.

Firebird woke with the uncanny feeling of being under surveillance. Not quite half an hour earlier, Brennen had checked in on his way to the Base, apologizing for his AF call-up. Feeling too tired and defeated to tease about his poor timing, she dismissed his apology with all the false cheer she could summon and then fell back asleep. The College was providing meals and housekeeping service, and with Brennen's help, she'd spent two days simply feeding, cleaning . . . caressing . . . trying to forge a mother-child bond that she'd never experienced and wasn't sure she would recognize. She felt dull with exhaustion, oddly distant from these precious children. They awakened her seven times last night. Kiel slept through Kinnor's feedings, but every time Kiel woke first, Kin wriggled awake and squalled too.

Had she sensed another unfriendly sound? She sat up.

"Mistress?" called a pleasant male voice outside her bedroom door. She heard a soft *rap-rap*. "Med center."

"Just a minute." She glanced down into the cribs. Her sons, once only dreamlike images, now had faces—one so Brenn-like that he startled visitors, and the other an elfin intermingling of Brennen's fine cheekbones and firm mouth with her delicate nose and large eyes. Each boy had his own beauty.

She swung her legs over the bedside toward the security panel and wrapped her nightrobe over a belly that still looked too round and felt too soft. It hurt her to sit, even on the soft bedside. As she reached for the lock panel, programmed to confirm her index-finger print, something inside her woke up.

The main entry alarm hadn't sounded.

No one should be inside the front room. Not even another Sentinel, whom locks rarely stopped. Not with this new security unit!

"I have medicine for Kinnor," came the smooth voice. Underlying the words she felt the powerful compulsion of voice-command: Let him in!

Firebird froze. College Security had gone down again. An enemy had breached the net and even released their apartment's entry lock. If not for their layered auxiliary system, she would have wakened to find him beside her . . . if she'd wakened at all!

She rolled across her bed, away from the cribs and security unit. *Mighty Singer . . . help!*

"Lady Firebird," said the voice. "Unlock, please."

Relaxing, she stretched toward the console again.

Then she yanked back her arm, resisting the kindly voice. Without epsilon shields, she couldn't withstand this subliminal urging for long.

But she must! If she touched that confirm panel and spoke to deactivate the voice lock, she'd die . . . and so would beautiful Kiel . . . and Kinnor, her red-haired reactionary.

"It's all right," urged the mellifluous voice. This time, she plainly heard the Ehretan modulation. It would be simple to hold down the tab, she realized. To speak just a word. Then all her struggles would end. She'd have real peace.

No! Sentinels never, never used their powers this way. She shoved a finger into each ear, fighting the impulse. Could Tel help her?

How? She'd locked him out. Anyway, his mind was as shieldless as hers against epsilon attack.

Keeping those fingers jammed in, she slipped off the bed's foot toward her dressing table. A gleaming shock pistol lay between her mira lily and the night black dagger.

Halfway there, her feet stopped as if tethered. She heard nothing this time. Evidently the intruder altered his attack when she changed her resistance.

Perspiration beaded on her forehead. She had to take three more steps to reach that pistol.

She couldn't.

A glance aside at Kinnor, serene in his sleep, gave her the will to step once. The invader didn't want just her. Someone meant to wipe out Brennen's family. Their hopes, their destiny. She couldn't let him win.

Her legs stiffened. The room seemed to rock. How was he doing this? If she fainted, would he take control of her body?

He's a friend. Let him in. The silent urging was almost irresistible.

She fought anyway. "Tel!" she managed to shout at the wall between apartment units. Instantly, she regretted it. Tel could never get in through the entry, and her shout wakened Kinnor. A choking wail started in his crib.

"Be quiet," oozed the intruder. To Firebird's alarm, Kinnor's cry cut off. She sprang toward his crib. He lay on his back, wide-eyed and breathing shallowly.

She pulled a deep breath and shouted again, "Tel?"

"Are you all right?" Tel cried.

"No," she moaned.

The voice: "Be quiet."

She couldn't hold out much longer. And could the invader read her intentions as easily as he could voice-command?

A door rattled. Terrified, she eyed hers. It didn't move. That had been Tel, trying the entry . . . but it was fail-safed. Brenn had checked it.

So how had this man—

Tel shouted, "Let me in, Firebird!"

"I . . ." she squeaked.

"Be quiet." So calm, so reasonable. "Unlock your door."

No!

Was this the same man who murdered Destia? Tarance, Asea, and those polite, spirited boys?

". . . can't!" she squeaked again, stretching toward the dressing table, trying to reach her shock pistol.

"What is it?" cried Tel.

As she struggled in too many directions, her mental control slipped. She rounded the bed and strode past the cribs. Before she could stop it, her arm reached for the console. She watched her own finger press the confirm panel and hold it down.

"Now speak."

One word, one inarticulate grunt, would complete the voice-print circuit and open the door. She bit her tongue. She tried to wrench her finger away. It stuck as if cemented.

The voice rose. "I'm coming," it called.

No! she wanted to scream.

"Speak!"

She spotted an alarm key. Before the invader could sense her inspiration, she hit it with her thumb. Even if someone put down the College's entire security net, Brennen's personal-carry would alert him. But Base One was seventeen minutes away.

Was he there yet, or delayed en route?

Seventeen minutes. Almost forever.

"Speak!"

Tel pounded on the entry.

Recon satellites had picked up those intruders coming in at startling speed. By the time Brennen reached Base One, Thyrica knew that they didn't intend to decelerate. This was a suicide dive from beyond orbit. At all five major bases, surface-air defenses tracked the plummeting bogeys. Base One had already dispatched a messenger ship to Regional command. Orbiting ships were diverting to try an intercept.

But by the main computer's calculation, the hijacked ships would burn up at precisely ground zero. Brennen caught his first glimpse of the tactical display as he sprinted into the cliffside com center.

Base Commander Moro bent over the tac board. "Sunton," he exclaimed. "Get shields up at Sunton!"

A synthesized voice confirmed Moro's pronouncement: "Impact at two three south, four six point two west. ETI two minutes." Simultaneously, a light flashed on the far coast of Thyrica's single continent. In two minutes, the ships would smash into ground at that point.

"Negative, shields for Sunton," said the controller in front of Moro. The town supported no military presence, so it needed no shielding dome. "Evacuate outlying areas?"

"No," Moro shouted. "No time. Send them to shelters!"

Brennen stared, appalled. This attack was insane. Sunton was an arts and retirement center, one of the loveliest cities on this world, and utterly vulnerable.

Moro shouted into his collar mike again, evidently at a civilian defense commander, "Yes, I'm serious. We're going to lose Sunton. If they try a second hit, it'll be too late to confirm a second trajectory and evacuate. Get all population centers into shelters. Repeat, all! Evacuate outlying areas. Scatter whatever you can without killing people in the air or on the roads. Move, move!"

On screen, the flight plummeted. ETI forty-six seconds.

Brennen felt a hand seize his shoulder. He glanced up into Damalcon Dardy's grimace. "Sunton is almost as far from the College as you can get," said Dardy.

Suddenly a high tone sounded from Brennen's personal-carry com. "Firebird," he exclaimed. She wouldn't use that alarm lightly. Firebird . . . and their sons.

"Wait," Dardy exclaimed. "If the College is targeted, that's the last place we want you. I'll send College Security."

Brennen gaped. How could Dardy say that? "Sir?" He whirled toward General Moro.

"Go," Moro barked.

Brennen spun on his heel. "Call Security anyway," he ordered Dardy.

Two minutes later, he yanked his little jet's hatch closed and fired its engines. "Caldwell," he snapped into its transceiver. "Takeoff clearance. Expedite."

Rapid engine check, control check. He'd do them no good if he crashed halfway home due to an equipment malfunction. "Clearance granted, General Caldwell," crooned the controller.

He took the eastbound breakway strip at max. After that, he could only set his controls for automatic. Below him, air and ground traffic scattered out of Soldane, north up the fjord and east into the Dracken Range. Everyone who could leave quickly was evacuating.

He touched up a secure channel. "Caldwell to Base One. Command Center." Even full particle and energy domes, even deep underground shelters, couldn't have protected Sunton's population. The mass and speed of three ships gave them horrendous momentum. Outside Sunton's impact zone, though, there might be survivors in underground bunkers. *Holy One, help them!*

"Caldwell?" answered a voice on his interlink. "Dardy here."

"Sunton?" Brennen held his stick and throttle in a death grip.

He heard a moment's hesitation. Then, "No damage reports yet, Brenn. Just a fireball. Get her—get them out of Arown."

"Any more threats out there?"

"We've confirmed a carrier, near Shesta. Moro's diverting *Lance* to intercept."

"Nothing inbound?" Brennen glanced down at his console chrono, out at landmarks. Twelve minutes to College. *Save her!*

"Not yet—" Dardy's voice broke off. "Yes," he exclaimed. "Confirm launch from that carrier. It's time, Caldwell."

Weeks ago, they created a plan. He'd hoped to try to trap the Shuhr attackers alone.

But now, if he escaped College alone, that would mean . . . tragedy.

He'd always been able to quest-pulse to Mari over surprising distances. He focused his strength and reached toward her, but felt nothing.

Firebird stood her ground, silently sweating. She thought she heard a familiar klaxon out in the hall and someone pounding on something.

Abruptly the voice changed again. "End this, then, Mistress."

On the stranger's epsilon carrier came a self-destructive convulsion. Firebird's own hands rose to squeeze her windpipe. Ducking her chin and struggling for breath, she collapsed on the carpet.

"Firebird!" Tel pounded as he shouted. "Tell me what to do!"

"Quiet in there!"

Tel's pounding stopped. Firebird dug in her chin and gasped down a deep breath.

Then the invisible assailant flung back her head to expose her throat again.

She had no epsilon shields yet, and her turn was a powerless agony—but it was all she could think to try. *Only in service to others . . .* was this. . . ?

Surely self-defense was allowed! She dove inward, imagined the wall, and swept through.

The intruder followed into her mind, a second presence that held on to hers like a limpet. Something else, something evil, seemed to be staring over his shoulder. She felt the intruder's surprise, his terror, then his determination to use the flaming agony that he saw through her mind's eye. He drove her deeper. Darkness licked up to welcome them both with a fatal embrace.

As her brain ran out of oxygen, Firebird stretched toward her distorted core of epsilon strength, that glimmering visualized nebula. Deeper— deeper—

With her last strength, she touched it.

The darkness exploded.

Brennen held two fingertips against Firebird's throat, tracking the faint pulse in her carotid artery. She lay unconscious on the bed, much too pale. Her hair looked like tangled dark flames over the pillow and her nightrobe. He'd arrived to find College Security cutting down the bedroom door, stymied by his supplemental locks. Bursting through, he found Mari lying half dead on the floor, her nervous system failing.

Nothing he tried revived her. Tel couldn't explain, either. There'd been a voice. Firebird had panicked. There'd been a thump, as of someone falling . . . and then silence.

No silence now. Tellai had steered the warming cribs into the other bedroom while Brennen called for help, but Kinnor wailed on, and on . . .

Tel sat opposite him on the bed's other side. "Pulse still steady," Brennen told him.

"She's too tough to fade on us, Caldwell."

Brennen managed to smile.

The entry alarm chimed. He sprang up. "Stay with her," he ordered.

Tel nodded.

Brennen dashed toward the entry. In the main room, two security men huddled over a blanket-covered form near the master room's door. From the media unit, a voice tolled the destruction at Sunton and repeated orders to evacuate all population centers.

Master Spieth burst through, and with her came someone Brennen hadn't called: Shamarr Dickin. "Come in," Brennen exclaimed. "Tel's with her."

Dickin swept toward the master room, then paused to glance down at the shrouded corpse.

"Harcourt Terrell," Brennen explained. "Staff officer on Base. Security tech." Mari had been right, suspecting Terrell. But how had Terrell defeated interrogation? He lay dead, with no mark on him except for his bulging, terrified eyes. Sprinting to Firebird's side, Brennen had almost tripped on him. Tel had covered him with the blanket.

Dickin frowned, then plunged into the master room.

Firebird still lay motionless. To Brennen's surprise, Tel stood and bowed to the Shamarr.

Dickin walked briskly to the bedside. "No brain activity at all," he murmured as he threw off his cloak. "Spieth. Caldwell. Assist me."

"Tel, see to Kinnor." Brennen sank onto the bed.

Blue.

Blue everywhere, a vast firmament, a wide sea.

Could she be swimming underwater?

No, she felt solid warmth under her. She blinked hard.

Blue again. Blue eyes. Brennen's eyes.

She lay on her back. Brennen held her in his stare. Her arms ached, stretched taut by his weight as he leaned over her and gripped both her wrists.

"There," he said, and she felt an intense inner tension release. "That's done it. Tel, get her a glass of water."

Firebird shivered, euphoric. She was alive!

Brennen let go of her arms and sat back, still staring from beneath lowered eyebrows. Her wrists hurt. She rubbed them. Had she been struggling to hurt Brennen, or herself? Memory rushed back like a nightmare. "Brenn, I—"

Master Spieth seized her right wrist and held a medical scanner against it. One second later, Firebird recognized the Shamarr. Not a large man, nor handsome by her world's standard, Thyrica's spiritual hierarch still had such a potent presence that Firebird knew she should stand and salute—or curtsy. His snowy hair and white tunic drew attention to the only ornament on his clothing, his Sentinel's star. Eight-pointed like Brennen's and Spieth's, it was set with a single large sapphire and circled in silver.

Her next reaction was to try not to think about the darkness behind her turn, or the way her own hands tried to strangle her. "Brenn?" Her voice still squeaked. "What happened?"

He stretched forward and touched her lips. "Lie still, Mari. Don't ask questions. We'll tell you what we can."

Tellai came back with the water. Barely rising on her pillow, Firebird took the glass left-handed and drank deeply. Tel walked to the foot of her bed and sat down with Brennen, pale cheeked but determined.

Firebird gave Spieth the empty glass and braced for a humiliation. Pride, impatience, willfulness—the Dark . . . a horror lived inside her.

Brennen hunched over the bedside, speaking gently. "Mari, your alpha matrix was just manipulated. We're not sure what else happened, but as of this moment, we must assume that everything you see, hear, or verbalize is telegraphed straight to the Shuhr. Shamarr Dickin brought you out of deep shock."

Telegraphed? To her attacker?

She glanced up at the white-haired Shamarr. Dickin stared solemnly, as if examining her soul without needing mental access. "How could I be telegraphing?" she asked. "I don't feel anything."

"This isn't access," replied the Shamarr. "It's called a watch-link. We don't use it, but we know it can be done."

"It's not permanent," Brennen assured her, "but the range is considerable. Comparable to planetary fielding."

She shut her eyes and shook her head. Why had they ever left Hesed? Why try to have sons if they'd only be murdered?

At least Kinnor's cries meant that he too had survived. "Is Kinnor all right? Is Kiel?"

"Yes. We must assume you're watch-linked," Brennen said softly, "but it might not be so." He stroked her cheek. "Rest for a minute. It's all we can afford. I have to speak with Shamarr Dickin."

"All right, Brenn." Watch-link? The Shuhr had trapped her from inside her own mind, mocking her hopes that once the twins arrived, she would be her old, independent self again. *Singer, I'm grateful to be breathing . . . but I'm sick of helplessness!*

Brennen strode from the room, followed by the older man. Master Spieth dropped her monitor beside Firebird's pillow. "You're coming up," she said, "but not quickly enough to suit me." Frowning, she strode to the door and poked her head out. Firebird faintly heard a media voice out there. She guessed someone had turned on a newsnet station.

All right, Firebird thought, deliberately shaping angry words, *if anyone's listening:* She told the Shuhr what she thought of them, with a vicious string of vituperation she'd learned in the Planetary Naval Academy and never spoken aloud.

Spieth returned to the bedside. "Sit up if you can," she said. "Tel, help her."

Firebird let them pull her upright.

Spieth pressed the monitor against Firebird's wrist again. "You have to be able to walk. We're evacuating College."

"What else is happening?"

"Sunton was just attacked." Spieth studied the monitor, then looked hard at Firebird's eyes. Evidently she didn't like what she saw. She reached back down into her kit bag.

"What do you mean, attacked?" Firebird asked.

"Shuhr. Suicide flight." The medical Master rummaged in her kit. "Three fighters, probably with pilots under voice-command."

Firebird didn't like the way Spieth kept her hands hidden. "Anyone hurt?" she asked, stalling. What was Spieth doing in there. . . ?

"Look away," Spieth ordered. "Tel, talk to her. Distract her."

Out of the corner of her eye, Firebird saw Spieth moving in with a swab and a venous injector.

Tel nodded grimly. "Firebird, it's bad. They came in from space without really decelerating. A whole city was destroyed. To ground level, and deeper . . ."

To Firebird's shame, she couldn't concentrate on the tragedy, only on the foreign object that pierced skin and muscle, then injected cold, stinging fluid. She'd tried so hard to conquer this wretched phobia. She could barely breathe until Spieth let her go.

As she lay back on the pillow, Brennen stepped into the bedroom again. Firebird had never felt him so dismayed. Dickin didn't reappear.

Evacuation? Had she heard right?

She kneaded her arm as Brennen and Spieth exchanged a long glance that was probably full of information. "We have to leave. Now," said Brennen.

Already she felt stronger. Embarrassed, she turned to Spieth. "Thank you. I apologize. That was childish."

Spieth dropped the injector back into her kit. "Brennen, I want to check her again. Call as soon as you're back."

Brennen nodded once. Now Firebird realized that he carried a small, blanketed bundle. He handed it to Tel, who took the swathed infant as Spieth hurried out.

Firebird resisted the urge to grab her baby from Tel. "Tel," she said as she rocked to her feet, "thank you for trying to help. I never expected that."

"Oh. Ah." Tel's childish eyebrows arched. "Heavens around, Firebird, how could I have done any less? I won't forget looking down your gun sights at Hunter Height . . . and that you didn't fire."

She flushed, ashamed that she'd even considered touching the trigger. Tel couldn't have hurt her.

He hurried out. With Brenn's help, she pulled on the first clothes she could find, a rumpled red skyff and loose blue pants. "I'll get Kiel," he said. "Grab what you can. We may not be back."

Her dagger lay on the clothes chest. More determined than ever to protect Kiel and Kinnor, she strapped the sheath onto her left forearm and pulled down the skyff's loose sleeve to cover it. From now on, she would learn to sleep wearing it. She pocketed her precious pendant too, then hastily clipped the lily to the front of her skyff.

Brennen came back, carrying the other tightly swathed bundle.

"You'll smother him," Firebird cried.

"I've put them in t-sleep."

"Oh. Good idea." Many Sentinels could induce tardema, a deep unconsciousness that was barely alive. Any Sentinel could waken them later, when they arrived . . . wherever on Thyrica they were going.

She didn't dare ask. Watch-link! Numb and silent, she stretched out her arms.

"I'll carry him," said Brennen.

"Please!"

Brennen gave her the bundle. She fingered white fabric away from its small end. Kiel's dark blond baby fuzz was only a shimmer against a birth-pointed skull. Tel laid her rain cloak over her shoulders. She pulled it forward and draped it over Kiel too.

"Hurry, Mari," Brennen said shortly. Her clairsa case hung over Brennen's arm. Steadying her shoulder, he walked her out the entry.

The College was eerily deserted for this time of morning. As they strode between buildings, Firebird spotted activity in a security blockhouse. She glanced up. Something shimmered between ground and the gray sky, probably the College's particle shield. That would explain why it didn't seem to be raining. Not at ground level, anyway. The shimmer was probably water streaming down the shield's surface.

What had Tel said about an attack at Sunton? She was finally starting to wake up.

"Brenn," she said as they hurried toward the small airstrip, "who just attacked me? Have they caught him?" As she spoke, she suddenly wondered if the Shuhr had shot that thought into her mind, using the watch-link to see how far afield the investigation had already gone.

Brennen kept one hand on her shoulder and practically pushed her forward. Tel came behind. "You honestly don't know." Brennen sounded concerned, but she could barely sense his feelings. He must have forced them down deep, under affective control.

"Know what?"

He shook his head. "Please. Don't ask questions. I'll tell you all I can."

What had she done? Her mind buzzed with questions she mustn't ask.

To her surprise, Brennen bypassed their parking row at the dark break-way strip. He gripped her arm. "I don't think it will surprise your Shuhr listeners to know," he said, still propelling her forward, "that we're going to take something that can shoot back."

CHAPTER 14

FUGITIVES

tremolo
fast pulses on one tone

"AC–128." Brennen identified the craft, an armed courier with rounded lines. He stepped once around, running a hand across its surfaces. Tel steadied the stepstand as Firebird groped up it, cradling Kiel. Her cloak flapped at her ankles. Nearby, beneath an undulating rain screen, she spotted a single deeper shadow: one intercept fighter, the Federacy's primary front-line attack and defense craft. She'd flown against those intercept fighters, in a Netaian tagwing.

She'd lost.

This courier had a significantly larger cockpit than either of those fighters. She ducked through its hatch and eased between its padded rear and front seats, then over—between—down onto the wonderfully padded first officer's chair, side by side with the pilot's seat. She found and touched the striplight control on the bulkhead beside the hatch, then carefully laid Kiel—so limp and quiet!—on her lap. Brennen secured the entry as Tel dropped onto the backseat behind her. A sucking whoosh thrust into her ears, and the sealed cockpit started to shimmer with blue light.

"The controls are set up just like on the sim we had at Trinn Hill," she observed, fervently wishing they could've stayed there. She suddenly envied people who lived dull, peaceful lives. "Except . . ." She waved a hand over one end of the silvery console that curled around both forward chairs, a dotted patchwork of screens, panels, and gauges.

"That's an advanced energy-layering system." Brennen reached for a cargo net between seats. By searching out mirror-image controls, she found the other. In half a minute, netted securely with a blue lily between them, Kiel and Kinnor slept unmindful of their strange bedroom.

Tellai peered over her shoulder at the display. Firebird wondered if they could trust him on board.

Yes, she realized, they could. He'd let Brennen perform a deep mind-access, just as deep as he took Firebird's memories at Veroh. Tel was no

Shuhr agent. He was exactly what he seemed, a pitiable aristocrat. They couldn't leave him behind, and there was no time to send him elsewhere.

Brennen activated the generators. "The AC–128 is the best-shielded courier in the inventory."

"You should know." As she pulled off her cloak and folded it, she felt his emotional blocking slide away.

He lit the navigational computer screen and charged the ordnance banks, then put on a headset. "Two-Alpha coming up." She felt him poised and determined, precisely as if he were headed into battle.

Firebird straightened on her seat. For nine months she'd done practically nothing but eat and sleep and grow. "How can I help?" she demanded.

Six external sensor screens took up a pale blue-gray glow. "Just strap in and help Tel." Brennen glanced over his shoulder. "Tellai, how do you do with high speed?"

Tel netted the long clairsa's hard-sided travel case at his feet. His face looked pale beneath the blue striplights. "Poorly. Motion sickness."

"Then strap in tight," Brennen ordered. "Your helmet's in your side-board. Keep your hands off the controls. I'm sorry, but this will be rough."

"But we have nothing with us!" Tellai clutched Brennen's seat back.

Firebird twisted around and helped Tel pull black harness webbing across his blue velvette shirt. "We have rations in the compartments and clothes on our backs," she declared. Though her eyes were adjusting to the odd light, he looked green inside his helmet. "Brenn, do we have any tri-sec?"

"Under your seat." He slipped into his own helmet, a close-fitting black cap. He slid a lever back. The ship rose smoothly and started to glide for-ward.

Bending double, which felt glorious, she stretched her arm to reach a little shelf between metal struts. She eased out several strips of wafers in clear cellopaper. "Here, Tel. Chew two of them." She sorted out a sheet of tri-angular green tabs and tossed it over her shoulder. "And the rest if you need them. They'll keep breakfast in you, if you got any." Her stomach growled at the thought. She peeled two trisec tabs off another sheet and chewed them.

"Thanks," Tel said weakly.

She tipped her head into her own helmet. "But if they're watch-linking with me—"

"This isn't what I wanted," Brennen said tightly. "No one at College or Base even wants you on board. Or them," he added, glancing down at the twins. "I'd blindfold you, but I need you. The simplest infrared detector would spot a flight of this size, anyway."

Blindfold? She shivered, but she understood. The watch-link made her an unwilling Shuhr spy.

"They've brought a carrier behind Shesta. Maybe if we leave Thyrica they'll stop pounding it." She felt his fury, but he mastered it quickly. "They're probably waiting for us to do exactly this. They don't know our ships, though. Nor our pilots. We may surprise them."

This ship was taking forever to taxi! "But, Brenn—"

"They could be catching your *vocalized* thoughts." He touched another panel, and the engine's pitch rose. "Those uppermost in your mind, the ones you slow down and think in words, are all they can track. Try to stay calm. Try to just react."

"All right," she mumbled, adjusting the webbing on her seat.

"Mari," Brennen added softly, "this is an order. Pray."

She shot off a request without hesitating. *Mighty Singer, don't punish Brenn or the twins for my willfulness. Protect Tel, even. Help us, and save the College. Show your huge mercy—*

The interlink interrupted. "Flight Two, stand by. We're on approach. You're covered."

Brennen flicked a switch. "Two-Alpha, on taxi." Other voices echoed from the transceiver. "I'd hoped we five could go alone if we had to escape, but they're watching for us. And now they sense your location, because of the watch-link."

She nodded and eyed the readouts in front of her, then wondered if she ought to even look at the board. She'd spent hours in a simulator at Trinn Hill, reprogramming her reactions from familiar Netaian fightercraft to standard Federate controls. Maybe she could help Brenn with her eyes closed.

Movement on the sensor display over their weapons board caught her attention. Their ship had skimmed to one end of the breakaway strip, but she hadn't realized they were being followed. Now she saw five heavy fighters arrayed behind them in a long, narrow wedge with Brennen's armed courier flying lead. She was glad she hadn't known Brennen had an escape plan. She would've revealed it to the enemy.

Brennen diverted full generator power into propulsion. All across the board, lights came on. The engines roared. "Go limp, Tel," he warned.

Suddenly the sensor screens flooded with blips. A mass of ships swept in from behind, perfectly aligned to destroy them. Firebird choked back a cry.

Acceleration smashed her into her seat. The pursuers appeared on the curving visual screen overhead, and as the ship went airborne, she realized they were Thyrian too . . . a larger group of gray heavy fighters, flying escort in mass delta formation. The rumbling shock wave passed over. She flexed her hands in relief.

Brennen pulled in below and behind the upper group's second echelon. The flight shifted, going three-dimensional as it swept high over the sea and eased into a thick cloud bank. Above her, the curving visual screen glowed eerily, a ghost cloud illuminated by other crafts' lights. Like a flock of kiel hunting along Netaian cliffs, the flight banked again, broke through the storm, and soared over atmospheric blueline.

Brennen frowned. Finally, he explained, "We think the strike at Sunton was either a feint or a test run. I'm sure we were their real target. The College's governor asked us to leave."

That was no surprise. "What happened at Sunton?"

"Three ships they stole from the Federacy were piloted from space down to ground. No deceleration. The city's a crater. In a small way, that could work to our advantage. The Shuhr commander just sent three of their pilots, probably voice-commanded, to their deaths. I doubt they trust him at the moment."

Firebird seized the thought and repeated it silently, aiming it in fury at those unseen listeners. Surely they didn't prepare from early childhood to commit noble suicide.

She pressed a resolution panel and extended her beyond-visual sensors' range a hundredfold. On BV, the Thyrian squadron shrank from a majestic flight to a small blunted cone, dashing into a wide exposed field of space.

Her conscience raised a protest. Those other pilots were flying with them straight into a trap, offering more lives to save her family.

"They're all Sentinels in the other ships," Brennen answered before she spoke. "AF chose them out of the Home Forces because they could keep this plan shielded away secret and defend themselves against Shuhr. All had the option of staying back. It's prophecy they're defending, not us."

Did the Shuhr believe, after all, that Brenn—or Kiel or Kinnor, some-day—might destroy their headquarters? And if that was a minor part of that prophecy, what was the rest of it?

She'd come so close to finding out!

Her seat vibrated. A ventilator hissed. She looked down at the little passengers webbed snugly into cargo cradles. *Tardema-sleep*. She shook her head. He'd planned well.

But how soon could he wake them? Her body wasn't feeding them well, but . . . hours? Days?

No time to worry about discomfort. Breathing deeply to control her adrenaline, she glanced at the sensor display. A Thyrian cruiser and six support ships hung in high orbit, already deployed to prevent another suicide attack.

Wait . . . should she be looking?

"I'm going to need you," Brennen said tightly, and she guessed he'd struggled with the same thought. "Cover the ordnance board, but if you find yourself acting irrationally, stop shooting. Instantly."

She examined the orange weapons console near centerline. Controls protruded for six energy guns, twenty heatseekers, and two Nova-class drones. More adrenaline gusted into her bloodstream, focusing her concentration and shortening her breath. Shutting her eyes, she flicked the guns' tuning slides randomly to cover several slip-shield wavelengths.

"There they are!" Tellai cried.

She opened her eyes. An ominous, threat-red oval shape and an insect-like flurry of fighter-sized speckles emerged on the port BV screen from behind the red-brown ball of rocky Shesta. The bogeys fanned out in all directions. "Trying to trap us inside a globe formation," Firebird muttered. "Classic strategy." *Because it tends to work*, she remembered Marshal Burkenhamn's explanation.

Brennen called a series of numbers. Firebird eyed the screens. Their own formation didn't seem to change. "Laying in a slip course will be tricky," she said. To escape this horde, they must clear Thyrica's magnetic field, then jump into slip space beyond light speed.

"That's why they're close." Brennen nodded. "They want to take us before we can slip."

Firebird bit a fingernail. It split, leaving a ragged edge. They'd reached only point-one *c*. The heavy courier accelerated far slower than the little Federate messenger ship she'd ridden before.

"Brenn!" she cried. Three enemy ships appeared high on the starboard screen, diving into that half-globe net. An instant later, she spotted another enemy attack wedge on port ventral.

"Target vector one, one-two-zero, mark," Brennen called. "Vector two, six-zero, mark."

And another wedge! Firebird rubbed the ragged fingernail against her seat cover and stared. Besides englobing, the Shuhr were threatening from three points of an equilateral triangle. The globe would prevent their escape while the wedge-formation pilots attacked.

This is what you wanted, she reminded herself as she steadied shaking hands against the ordnance board. *You're out of the apartment, fighting at his side in a Federate ship!*

Ellet Kinsman sat twelve levels below ground in Base One's command complex, playing and replaying a satellite image. The Shuhr suicide flight plummeted almost wing tip to wing tip, overheating as it decelerated, holding together until less than a kilometer over Sunton.

Then for a second, the flight turned into a small sun. Ellet keyed for slow motion and stared. For two images, the beautiful vacation community remained as she remembered it, lit dazzlingly from above.

Then every flammable object—green trees, grassy lawn, wooden buildings—burst into flame. Impact: a shock wave blasted two kilometers into bedrock. The satellite image vanished, obscured by flying debris.

Ellet decreased the image's resolution. Even at orbital distance, by daylight, the flash showed plainly. This was a terrible blow to the Federacy. It could happen again. Anywhere. The fleet must strike back, she vowed. Three Zed mustn't get away with this.

A message alarm whistled from one corner of this small data desk. Ellet slapped the blinking light that appeared with it, then read her message.

SENTINEL EYES ONLY, FROM SHAMARR DICKIN. ANOTHER ATTACK HAS TAKEN PLACE ON THE CALDWELL FAMILY. MISTRESS FIREBIRD CALDWELL IS NOW ON *AVOID* STATUS. DO NOT APPROACH. MAINTAIN EPSILON SHIELDING IN HER VICINITY.

A-status? What in Six-alpha happened? Ellet stared at the message for a full minute, trying to reconcile those sentences. Who attacked whom? Had Firebird proven to be a Shuhr spy? What else could make her a deadly threat and put her on A-status?

And what about Brennen's new twin sons? Ellet would defend them with her life, if allowed. It was even possible he'd named one for her. Kinnor might be a fanciful nickname for Kinsman.

Dardy! She snapped her long fingers. Damalcon Dardy would know what happened. Leaning over the touchboard, she punched up his call code. *Not only would he know*, she reflected while waiting for relay, *but he'd want me to know quickly*.

Two minutes crept by. Ellet glanced around the emergency center. The scurrying and shouting died away, leaving a stunned calm. Dardy didn't answer. *He's involved, then.*

Sudden memory swept her back . . .

. . . to his office. Tellai had just arrived. She'd asked if the Caldwells might leave Thyrica. Dardy touched a stylus to his forehead. "If I know anything, it's confidential, Ellet." She felt again the tingle of his epsilon static, something he didn't normally use in her presence.

Dardy. He was involved. He was gone.

He was closer to Brennen than she'd realized.

Surely they were fleeing to Hesed House, the Sentinel sanctuary. *How can I get to the Procyel system?* she wondered.

And if Firebird had been placed on avoid-status, what was Brennen going through? Was there a chance of . . . freeing him from that woman, now that she was on A-status?

The alarm pulse rang again. Quickly, she touched a key.

OUTSYSTEM MESSAGE RECEIVED AND PROCESSED FOR CAPTAIN ELLET KINSMAN.

She touched in her code sequence.
One more line appeared.

REPORT MAXSEC, TALLIS.

No explanation followed, no further order: Regional command had called for her days before this attack force arrived.

Ellet grimaced. She wanted to go to the Procyel system, not Tallis!

But at Tallis, she might help steer a Federate response to this strike. She might be the first Thyrian witness reporting to the Regional council.

If she hurried.

Firebird glanced from screen to screen. Like heatseekers locked on a target, those three attack flights closed on the Thyrian heavy-fighters. Beyond them, the incoming net kept closing, catchfield ranges overlapping, cannon lighting even from beyond ranging distance. Didn't they know their own weapons? Firebird slid into the familiar, almost hypnotic accord with her sensor screens, translating two-dimensional readouts into a three-dimensional battle. She poised both hands over her orange weapons board.

"Ready, Tellai?" Brennen accelerated.

Tel groaned.

"Ree-a," Brennen ordered into his headset. "Six-zero. At will."

"Confirm." That was Dardy's voice. Firebird was glad to realize she had another friend out there.

Three Thyrian ships broke formation. They veered to high starboard and charged one attacking wedge. Stars shifted on the visual monitor as Brennen vectored low, port, toward the slightest gap in the net.

He kept calling orders that were so much gibberish to Firebird . . . to her relief.

Could the Shuhr read strategy from her mind anyway? No time to worry about it. They swooped into targeting range. Firebird raised slip-shields. Brennen steered toward that slight gap.

Scarcely aware of the familiar quivering in her body as their slip-shield took hold, Firebird felt the ship reel with unevenly absorbed energies. Brennen fought the armed courier stable to give her a clear shot. She targeted the closest enemy with her port gun, fired twice, then sent a heatseeker down the beams.

Brennen's glance flitted from fore to visual screens as he pushed the ship toward escape velocity.

"Blast," Firebird muttered. The enemy caught her heatseeker in mid-flight and sent a missile flurry in return. She clipped one an instant before it passed on her starboard wingman's side.

"Thanks, Alpha," came a deep male voice on the interlink.

"Anytime." Enthusiastically, she picked away the rest of the missile swarm with the port laser cannon. They could've been deflected with particle shields, but that would drain the generators. Brennen needed their output for speed.

The ship lurched sideways. Firebird glanced at the screen and saw only empty space where that wingman had been. Her insides sank.

"What was that?" Tellai's voice quivered.

"They got Gamma from the other side," Brennen said tightly. He rotated upper-starboard and gave Firebird a clear shot at the ship that destroyed their wingman. Betting that the enemy pilot would also avoid using particle shielding, she sent him a missile and counted three. One bogey on the screen vanished.

As the metal hail swept by, she doubled her particle shields, which briefly arrested their acceleration. A brilliant light charge passed before their noses, atomizing a candescent trail through debris and momentarily blinding her through the visual screen. Firebird bit the tip of her tongue. If they'd been just quicker, just farther along, they would've been overloaded—and dead.

Which we still could be at any moment. We lost shield overlap! She glanced down at Kinnor and Kiel. Surely the Singer would spare them. Surely!

Stars spun on the visual monitor. To her dismay, Brennen pulled away from the net, unable to pierce it here.

They dove back toward its empty center. Firebird searched her screens. One Shuhr attack flight was engaged, but the other two closed rapidly.

"Max shields," Brennen ordered. "We're outgunned."

CHAPTER 15

OUTFLANKED

martellato
with "hammered" strokes of the bow

As the ship decelerated, Brennen spoke again. "Flight One, maneuver echo. Course two-three-zero."

Firebird engaged every shield on the board. On screen, half the friendly pips peeled away. She gasped. What did Brenn think he was doing, splitting this flight, with three enemy fighters dead ahead?

"Hold fire, Mari. I need power."

She clenched her hands. Her shield board flashed as slip and particle protection deflected fire. This moment was meant for a massacre. Yet stars spun and slipped sideways as Brennen jerked his throttle and stick. The pips that were his remaining wingmen followed through every maneuver. She stared, awed. Maybe they were outgunned, but they weren't out-trained.

Abruptly, a wave of hostility washed into Firebird from nowhere she could see. "Brenn!" she cried.

"I felt it. Sit back," he snapped. "They could make you shoot our own ships."

The ventral screen flashed. The enemy's attack wedge passed so close she could count its guns.

"Mari!" Brennen shouted.

Startled, Firebird pulled away from the console . . . and the ordnance board.

"Sit on your hands. I can't help you."

"But can't I—"

A massive firebolt grazed their shields. The ship lurched. Brennen's anger flooded the bonding resonance for the first time in Firebird's experience. "Tel" he shouted, "grab her hands. Mari, give them."

Abashed, she stretched her arms to both sides and bent her elbows. Clammy hands seized her wrists. "I could do some shooting for you, Caldwell," Tel offered. Firebird heard an edge of determination in his voice.

"Only if you hold her too."

Tel's grip shifted as he tried to grapple both her hands in one of his own. She'd seen a side-hand ordnance board back there.

"Can't do it," said Tellai. "Sorry."

"Then hold her."

Pinned to her seat, Firebird watched the screens. The net closed inexorably. Slowly, the Shuhr attack wedge that had passed them decelerated and turned about. Within minutes, it came back, accelerating. Ships out in the net started to spew missiles again.

"Arm Nova One," Brennen ordered his pilots. He reached for the orange ordnance panel. He touched a prominent button. It turned brilliant red. "Fire!" He punched it flat against the board.

The ship gave a coughing groan.

Brennen followed the huge missile for a few seconds. "Tighten up," he called, then he banked hard to port.

The drones Brennen and his pilots had launched sped forward. The fighters banked aside. On enemy screens, the clusters of blips would look alike until targeting computers reprogrammed. That would take less than a minute.

A Shuhr attack flight split. Two ships closed in on the Novas. One followed Brennen.

Seconds later, the drones and attackers connected. The visual panel splashed with white light. Attuned to six pale screens, Firebird felt the flight ride broadside along a wave of debris that had been two top-line Federate ships—now Shuhr contraband—and several Nova missiles. Brennen accelerated toward the net again, gripping his stick while he checked his navigational computer. "I'm afraid it'll be worse than this trying to get down at Hesed. If they could send DeepScan signals over that range, we'd never make it."

Hesed, of course. They'd be safe at the sanctuary! "Can we jump for Hesed on this heading?"

"No. Have to make an intermediate jump."

Her eye caught movement on the ventral screen. The second attack wedge, reduced by one, left the other Thyrian flight behind and accelerated toward Brennen. The other Thyrians pursued.

Suddenly Firebird had an idea, so crazy she almost dismissed it—or was it a plant? She decided to speak anyway. "Brenn, do we have power and life support enough to hit their base at Three Zed and still get to Procyel, or could that be a trap?"

"What?" He lifted one hand off the sideboard.

"You're afraid they've got ships at Hesed waiting for us. Could we draw some off by hitting their home base? At least these ships would follow us there instead of attacking the sanctuary. At best, we could do some serious damage." The prophecy . . .

He scarcely moved. "Yes!—but . . . yes, that may be one thing they wouldn't expect us to try. They've probably pulled their defense force to gather this fleet." He bent back to the computer. "We can do it," he said, "and it's in this slip quadrant. If we can get clear to jump."

She hadn't missed that pause. "But," what? Chilled, she squelched the thought. Who else was listening?

Brennen jinked wildly, closing the distance to the remaining hostile ship. Obviously he meant to take it before two others joined it. "Gemina maneuver," he called suddenly. A signal?

Yes! He'd been decorated—and rebuked—for that battle at nonaligned Gemina.

Tel released Firebird's hands, probably to wipe his forehead. Immediately she found herself reaching for the ordnance board. Disgusted, she twined her fingers into a double fist and clenched it between her knees, then crossed her legs. In her tagwing, that wouldn't have been possible. *Got you!*

Brennen accelerated the armed courier, then pulled straight back on the stick, looping vertically. Firebird pressed deeper into her seat. She tightened her legs on her weirdly rebellious hands. The attacking pair shot off low, to port.

"Arm Nova Two." He touched the second button. "Fire! . . . and . . . mark one."

To Firebird's disbelief, he retrofired, plunging her forward against her harness straps. He would be rammed by his own pilots!

No, they braked too. The drones sped toward the net.

"Mark two." He shoved the stick forward. The ship accelerated again, chasing his own drone.

Firebird held her breath. Chasing missiles to targets was suicide . . . or was it, if this ship had the best shields in Thyrica's courier inventory?

Again Brennen maxed the particle shields. "Hang on, Tel."

The fore screen flashed. "Pull in," Brennen ordered.

The ship tossed wildly, thrusting into waves of debris that expanded in concentric globes. Firebird clenched her hands as turbulence buffeted them from all directions. An alarm light pulsed on the shielding monitor. "Doubling's down," she cried.

Brennen stared straight ahead, pushing the stick left, down, up, right.

Firebird stared at the visual screen. Along the outer shock wave of destroyed Shuhr ships, their less massive fighters—whose shields couldn't turn the metal storm—came apart to form waves of wild, brilliant chaos.

Suddenly the fore screen blanked. That was deep space. They were through! Brennen swatted off the particle shields. Acceleration mashed Firebird against her seat. "Three Zed heading," he ordered. "Jump in fifteen seconds. Who else is clear?"

Ten pilots responded. He touched ten panels in rapid succession, then hit a bar to cross-program the other navigating computers.

The jump light pulsed. One kick and they'd be free.

"Be ready for anything when we break at Three Zed," he called to his escort.

It didn't matter if the enemy heard him. Clearly that was his intention. Firebird whooped. "Hang on, Tel!"

Brennen poised both hands over the board. "Mari! Shut your eyes!"

Startled, she obeyed. She felt the ship buck as she faded into her seat, and then a scarcely tangible touch slipping away, as if she'd stepped out of polluted water. She was finally free of the watch-link.

All six external screens shimmered with the blue chaos of quasi-orthogonal space. Firebird yanked off her helmet and let out the breath she'd been holding.

Brennen too set his helmet aside. He presented his right hand, smiling faintly. "Very professional, Major."

She pushed her back deep into the seat. "Where are we really headed?" Her heart still pounded.

He brushed sweat-soaked hair from his forehead. "Hesed," he said. "They wanted to lure us to Three Zed. That told us they couldn't be blockading Hesed."

"Why not?"

"Numbers. There just aren't that many Shuhr. Actually, you saved us twice. That 'Gemina' command was a decoy signal too."

She pulled him close and kissed him so hard her teeth hurt. It hadn't gone anything like she planned, but they'd fought together at last. She must thank . . .

Mighty Singer, you showed yourself. Thank you. For their sake. She glanced down at their infant passengers.

Finally she remembered Tellai. Massaging her scalp, she twisted around.

His eyes shone as big and round as Triona's twin moons. Focused as though hypnotized on the sensor display, they glimmered with tears and the reflection of sensor lights.

"Are you hurt?" she asked, pressing a control to recline her high-backed seat.

"I guess not." He cleared the gravel from his voice. "I was . . . thinking about Phoena. Those are the people who have her. Was that a major battle? That is, compared with . . . you've both done that sort of thing before."

Brennen rubbed his palms on his thighs. "If our shields had gone we'd be dead, just as if it'd been a full-scale war. Actually," he said soberly, "this might be exactly that. War."

Tellai groaned. "I'll never make a soldier."

Firebird dried her own palms, and the ragged fingernail scraped her skyff. "Will you have to go back to Thyrica?" she asked Brennen. He wouldn't take them to Hesed and leave, would he?

"Not for the moment. General Moro ordered me to Hesed. Once there, I'm under Master Dabarrah." He pulled a packet of gray concentrate cubes from below the console and shared them around. Firebird crunched and swallowed, stretched, and pushed her seat back farther down. She ached with exhaustion, but her blood was so full of adrenaline that her hands shook. Not to mention Master Spieth's injection. Surely it wasn't normal for a new mother to do what she'd just done, without medical assistance.

"You should sleep, Mari."

"You're right." She glanced down. This time, the babies wouldn't wake her up. And she felt too comfortable. Maybe she wouldn't be able to nurse them after today. "But I won't sleep without your help."

Brennen reached over and touched her forehead. Instantly, drowsiness wrapped her like a thick bedcover.

"Whatever she is now, she was born an Angelo."

Carradee Second stressed that last word. On the handwoven carpet of her sitting room, erect in a row of gilt chairs, sat three members of her Electorate: the Aquaculture Minister Count Wellan Bowman, Baroness Kierann Parkai of the Judiciary, and His Grace the Duke of Claighbro—and Trade Minister—Muirnen Rogonin. As she reached his end of her course, Rogonin shifted on his slender-legged chair and lowered his manicured brows. Carradee ignored the implied criticism. She needn't be cowed by Rogonin. She might not be a strong queen, she might be drifting away from the Powers' ways of ruling, but she was queen.

"Born an Angelo," she repeated. "We will not move that she be restored to the succession, nor the Electorate, but that she be given back her citizenship, noble electors. The Assembly's review of her conduct at Hunter Height was conclusive and final." If only the Assembly had acted sooner, before that terrible electoral trial! "Lady Firebird took no unnecessary action, spared life when possible—from the standpoint of self-protection, and her mission objectives—in short, she defended herself and her . . ." It still felt strange to say this, glad though she was for Firebird's happiness: ". . . and her husband, from harm. Whatever our views regarding the Federate presence, Princess Phoena's motives and actions at Hunter Height must be called dubious at best."

Carradee eyed Muirnen Rogonin as sternly as she could, with the steely glance she'd inherited from Queen Siwann and practiced in front of her boudoir mirror. She had been furious—furious!—to learn Phoena had established an illegal weaponry lab at the family's lovely old vacation home, and now she knew Rogonin had been another prime instigator. She had stood back and let Occupation Governor Danton levy a stiff fine against Rogonin's estate. Not that Rogonin missed several million Federate gilds . . . and with Carradee's approval, that money had gone straight into Federate programs to repair selected war damages.

Phoena's secessionist movement had not died at Hunter Height. Nor did Carradee imagine Phoena left it leaderless when she went . . . wherever she was in hiding. Surely its new leader sat here, opening a tin of after-dinner mints, with his sateen-swathed bulk resting uneasily on a delicate chair. Carradee didn't entirely disapprove of the movement. She too wanted Netaia to be independent again, but some of Danton's reforms clearly were benefiting her most impoverished subjects. If Netaia joined the Federacy as a full covenanting member, the general good might outweigh the loss of full independence.

"She took Federate transnationality, Majesty." Rogonin flicked a mint under his tongue, pocketed the tin, and then folded both hands across his middle. "Renounced her citizenship, the Powers, and all hope of eternal bliss. You would rewrite her name on the rolls of the righteous?"

"Who knows how deeply her conscience is aching?" Though her Electorate daily took back more of its dominance over planetary affairs, Carradee vowed she wouldn't back down on this issue. Firebird plainly had been determined to fulfill her martyrdom and earn glory in Netaia's electoral pantheon at Veroh. Carradee couldn't imagine that Firebird was comfortable or content out in the Federacy.

She pulled a white notum blossom from a bouquet on the end table beside Rogonin and rolled its stem between her fingers. Personally, she held nothing against Governor Danton anymore. He was a better administrator than she'd been led to believe, ordered to believe, at Siwann's deathbed. To appease the Powers, though, and their other noble representatives, she would keep challenging Federate reforms. She still needed Strength, Valor, and Excellence . . . and the other Powers . . . to help her rule.

"Madame." Count Wellan Bowman tapped his brass-tipped walking stick against the leg of his chair. Bowman was a tall man, with the full but softening shoulders of a former athlete. Frowning, Carradee held the notum bloom to her nose and peered at the nobleman over its petals. "Madame, if Lady Firebird's survival confuses the succession, how much worse now that she carries the heir of an offworlder? A Federate, a—Sentinel? She may have already given birth. What status must we grant her children? Will they be noble wastlings? Or common, like their father?"

"We have considered that, Bowman. If the Electorate and the Assembly chose to restore Lady Firebird even to the succession, then we would consider her offspring. But for what circumstance would she be restored to the succession?" She lowered her voice. "There's no need. Our elder princess is nearly of an age to be confirmed." Four-year-old Iarlet could be ceremonially declared an heiress to the throne as soon as she memorized a short electoral litany, and Iarlet was a brilliant child. For that matter, Iarlet could be crowned if Carradee died before naming an heiress.

Carradee strode up the center of the long, high-curtained sitting room. At the end of the chamber nearest the dark fayya-wood door, she laid the blossom on a butler's tray. "Noble electors, we shall make the motion tomorrow. We would be pleased to count on your support." *Not that I expect it from any of you*, she thought, but she would not say that aloud. "I'll ask only for her citizenship—as a token, my friends. If she had meant to harm us, to damage Hunter Height—" Carradee collected their stares and held them a moment. "Escaping in a tagwing fightercraft, she could've done serious damage. She is a fine pilot and a skilled markswoman."

She tapped the door twice. A servitor opened it from outside. Parkai and Bowman left silently.

Carradee paced to the near window and gazed out. This room faced the palace's public gardens. Beyond those, a bluff fell south toward the serene Tiggaree River. Two long white groundcars pulled slowly toward the curb to receive Baroness Parkai and Count Bowman.

She frowned. Only the four commoners she had personally appointed supported her in the Electorate. Phoena's poor, lonely husband, Prince Tel, would vote with Rogonin when he returned. The other young nobles followed similar patterns, shadowing their elders.

That wasn't the way Mother's Electorate voted. The Crown was a figure-head once again, ruling on behalf of mighty Authority.

Did she really believe her coronation had made her a priestess, even a demigoddess?

Fingering a yellow curtain—she despised jeweled window-filters and had replaced them all with antique sheers—Carradee sighed, then turned.

Rogonin still sat.

"Majesty." His eyes narrowed beneath plucked brows. "What do you intend to do if she turns on us again?"

"She won't." Carradee stopped in a warm shaft of lamplight. "She never did, Rogonin. She protected herself and exposed an illegal operation."

The Duke sniffed and strode out.

Carradee waved off her servitors and retreated through the chamber's east door into her private apartments. Prince Daithi sat in his own room, propped against several pillows, reading a scan cartridge on a viewer that made his face glow. "Daithi?" she asked softly.

His eyes were soft and dark like a brownbuck's, and brown curls formed a cap on his head. Though eight years her senior, he looked up to her. Sometimes he seemed like the younger brother she never had—the brother no Angelo had had in over a century.

"Would you sleep in my room tonight?" she asked.

He laid the viewer on his brown velvette coverlet. "Of course, 'Dee." She rested one hand on his shoulder and touched his smooth throat, and he reached up to grasp her hand. She smelled leta-wood soap. He'd bathed a second time today, as usual, in case she made that very request.

She walked through his room into the adjoining double boudoir and changed into her nightgown. A chambermaid followed Daithi through, carrying cool drinks on a tray. Carradee sighed contentment. Daithi would help her relegate Rogonin to the zone of forgetfulness.

Hours later, she woke perspiring. Muirnen Rogonin had stalked her dreams, challenging and belittling her. Rogonin wasn't really like that. She stumbled out to the boudoir. Examining her scalp, she thought it looked oily. A hundred strokes would do it good and wake her out of this daze.

She found her pulse brush and set it for low speed, held its vibrating bristles to the crown of her head, and shut her eyes. Then she set to brushing.

At the ninetieth stroke, terror seized her. She dropped her brush. The powerful, irrational sensation almost paralyzed her—

It's coming from another mind. The thought flashed into her consciousness.

Sentinel? she answered with a thought of her own. She thought she felt distant, scornful laughter.

Shuhr? Firebird had sent warnings. Now the thought rang so loudly in her mind that her lips formed the word.

A sharp *crack* echoed behind her. Walls groaned. The world flew to pieces. Screaming, she flung up her arms to protect her face. Something struck her from behind. She tumbled off her stool, clutching long tufts of carpet. The floor heaved. Rattling noises trailed off into silence and absolute darkness.

She tried to get up and run. Something pinned her down, making her shoulders and legs throb with pain. "Daithi?" she cried. The explosion had come from behind her, where Daithi lay sleeping!

CHAPTER 16

SANCTUARY

lucernarium
song for Vespers, evening worship; its texts often
refer to light

Carradee thrust down harder with her arms and pushed up with both
shoulders. Her head smacked something.

"Daithi," she moaned. "Are you there?"

For some time, she drifted in and out of a faint. Crashing and crunching
sounds roused her. Perhaps someone called her name, perhaps not. *Shuhr?
No*, she thought. *Sentinels?*

What if they're in league?

Holy Powers, she pleaded, *help us!*

The weight shifted, slicing into her legs. "Hello," she gasped. "Hello,
I'm here."

"Majesty." It was a male voice, breathy as if he were frantic. "Majesty,
keep talking."

"I'm at the dresser," she shouted. "It's dark. I think my legs are hurt,
and maybe my back—"

Light flashed on a slab of rubble above her. "You can stop, Majesty."
She saw two faces, one familiar and comfortable. "Doctor Zoagrem," she
cried. The weight on her legs lifted. She grappled forward, trying to crawl
out of the debris. "Daithi was in my bed. Find Daithi."

The doctor pressed something cold against her arm. "We will, madame.
Lie still."

Governor Danton was good to come to her hospital room.

Carradee shifted on the bed, and its contours shifted underneath her.
Doctor Zoagrem assured her that the fractures would heal, and with regen
therapy she soon would walk without limping. But Daithi . . .

He'll live, she reminded herself. *Be grateful for that, and wait to see what
else the doctors can do.* She had sent her servitors away. She gulped back an

urge to weep on the shoulder of this professional diplomat who'd always been kind. With whom she never had to fight, the way she constantly battled her electors. But she mustn't weep with him. She was queen, though every instinct screamed her anguish.

"If," she said steadily, "you can get Iarla and Kessaree to a safe locale, do it. Please. Do it quickly." Then her reserve crumbled. The electors would not approve, and she had to make someone understand. "Up until now, Lee, whenever we've talked I have spoken as queen. Now I'm only a mother. I cannot explain these instincts, only obey them. I'll answer for my own safety, but I could never live with myself if there were anything I could've done for my daughters, and through my not having done it, they were harmed. Do you understand?"

He nodded. Fading afternoon light gleamed in his blond hair. "I do, Majesty. I had three children of my own. Lost one. Only between us, madame, I've dreamed of her—monthly, sometimes. I do understand. Now, there are several possib—"

"No." Shutting her eyes, Carradee pressed her head into the pillow. Her mouth tasted queer from some medicine they'd given her. "I don't want to know where, Governor. If your suspicions are correct—if what I felt before the explosion was some sort of psychic taunt, meant to trumpet my killers' identity—if they come here again, and they can read my mind—I want no knowledge of where my daughters are sent into hiding." Grief tugged at her. "At least, not yet. You can tell me later, but you cannot unsay anything you say now."

She opened her eyes and saw Danton nodding.

"Do they want us all dead?" she whispered.

The governor swung one leg over the other. "You are well watched, madame. We've enlarged a special guard for you and your daughters from the Special Operations branch of Federate forces, including five Sentinels to cover all watches. Any Shuhr agents on Netaia will have to be very careful. I don't think they'll try anything against you for some time."

"But you'll see to the other matter?" she asked. "Please?"

"I will, madame."

Muirnen Rogonin took two steps along the north colonnade and stopped to run a fleshy hand up and down the smooth white marble of a supportive pillar. Fortunate that the ancient palace still stood. Only one wall had collapsed. Danton was wrong to credit precision explosives: The virtue lay in Netaian architects, who designed for strength. They built a strong palace, a strong Electorate . . . a strong Crown, backed by Powers the Federacy could not call on.

Fortunate too, in a way, that Carradee had been brought down before she could press for the wastling's citizenship. Carradee Second tended to forget that her sister Firebird still stood under a well-earned death sentence for treason, sedition, and heresy.

"She will be disabled for some time," he told Count Wellan Bowman. A breeze fluttered his collar. Irked, he smoothed it. "Emotionally, she'll be unable to govern for several weeks at the inside."

"According to. . . ?" asked Bowman.

"Her own physician. Zoagrem."

"She is distraught over the prince's injuries," Bowman suggested. "She mustn't be given authority until his condition stabilizes."

Rogonin shook his head. "The Electorate is authorized to designate an interim regent, with Crown authority to act at electoral meetings. Emergency powers only, of course," he added, "but there is no need to set a limit on his term of service."

Wellan Bowman rapped the column with his walking stick. "'Iarla's accession, at her majority' would make a logical phrase, should any of the new faction press for a limitation," he said smoothly.

That would give him fourteen years or more. In fourteen years, a regent might throw off the outworlders. He could assemble his own Electorate and establish his own family in the palace. "Yes." Calmly, Muirnen Rogonin drew out his tin of mints. "Yes, it would."

When hunger woke Firebird, the autopilot chronometer read eighty hours and both men slept. Tel curled toward the aft bulkhead. Asleep, he looked even more childlike. Brennen lay beside her, resting his head lightly against the back of his seat, as if the slightest change in attitude would wake him.

Firebird crossed her arms, pressed hard against her chest, then exhaled heavily. One more small defeat. For better or worse, she would not be nursing those infants. She located her cache of flavorless gray concentrates and washed down a double handful with a packet of vaguely tart electrolyte drink, wondering if she should awaken either of the men. The break indicator showed over two days remaining on their jump to sanctuary. She glanced down at Kiel and Kinnor, who still lay like small duffels stowed between seats.

They were safe. Nothing else mattered, not even the blue mira lily that had slid loose. Two of its long, curved petals hung limp, crushed and mangled.

Brennen had been so happy to give her that blossom. *If that's our only casualty, I have to be grateful.* Sighing, she loosened her harness, pulled up her cape, and tucked it around her, for comfort more than warmth. Her thoughts wandered. . . .

This retreat would end her College training, probably for good. The thought struck hard, and then a humbling response: She would miss Janesca, but what little she accomplished, training at College, had been a disaster.

That raised another disquieting thought. The Shuhr had unilaterally attacked Thyrica. How could the renegades hope to survive with the Federacy's might turned against them? . . . Unless, she reflected, the Federates balked, more afraid of the Shuhr than they were of the Sentinels who served them.

But why, if Three Zed meant to kill Sentinels, had they attacked Sunton instead of Arown? A feint, as Brennen suggested, or a test run? To her, it sounded like incompetent leadership. Or maybe they meant to turn Thyrica against its small starbred communities. Thyrian mobs might do Three Zed's dirty work, sending Sentinel families fleeing to Hesed House.

Hesed, in the Procyel system, lay off the trade routes. Procyel II was marginally developed during the first human expansion, then abandoned during the Six-alpha catastrophe. Four centuries ago, Sabba Six-alpha—a binary near the Whorl's midpoint—started to spurt ionized particles and deadly radiation in unpredictable, decades-long bursts. Intersystem travel ended and civilizations declined all over the Whorl. That storm lasted two hundred years.

Between its last bursts, Brennen's people made Procyel's most fertile mountain valley their refuge. They dug out an underground complex.

Firebird would never forget her first glimpse of the sanctuary commons, almost a year ago—

She'd stepped through golden double doors, and a vast white hall opened ahead of her. Ahead shimmered a shallow artificial lake surrounded by a latticed rail. Paths of square stepping stones connected islands of greenery, and sunlight streamed down from countless skylights, dancing and reflecting on the water. From somewhere she could hear more water rushing and splashing.

The Master Sentinel that Brennen had introduced as Jenner Dabarrah stepped around from behind them, tall and thin, with blue-gray eyes as pale as his golden hair. Dressed all in white with an eight-rayed star, he wore his age well: forty, perhaps? Or fifty?

"Have you eaten?" He touched a bell.

"Enough." Brennen squeezed Firebird's hand as she stood in motionless wonder. Escaping Phoena's forces at Hunter Height only days before, they'd exchanged their Netaian fightercraft for a Federate shuttle—with Governor Danton's help—and then, at last, Brennen had asked the question she longed but dreaded to hear. Somehow, she'd summoned the courage to accept a telepath's marriage proposal.

Later that night of their arrival, she walked with Master Dabarrah and Brennen—who looked like a lord in his Federate dress whites—out onto the stepping stones. Skylights dimmed. A band of pale light gleamed around the edge of the waters, reflecting blue and green off the stone walls and ceiling and Brennen's white tunic. Firebird wore a pale blue gown lent by a student-apprentice sekiyr.

They halted on a paved island beneath a spreading evergreen tree. Firebird faced Dabarrah, and Brennen drew close beside her.

"You have no doubts?" Dabarrah asked softly. "You will hold this bond before all other loyalties, Firebird. And you, Brennen? Your path may not be easy." He must've known their life together would never be simple.

Brennen nodded slightly. She did the same.

Master Dabarrah placed his hands on their shoulders, speaking softly and musically in a tongue she heard then for the first time, the Ehretans' ceremonial language. A blessing, she guessed, or an invocation. Brennen answered briefly in the same language.

Then Dabarrah dropped his right hand, leaving one on her left shoulder. "Firebird Mari," he said gently, "you have chosen a Sentinel. Your culture has done nothing to prepare you for this."

Firebird met the steady gaze of those pale blue eyes. "That's true, Master, but Brennen has explained pair bonding. I've accepted it—and him."

"Then, I ask to touch your spirits."

She felt Brennen step close behind her. He circled her waist with one arm and pressed into her mind, far deeper than he'd ever gone before. For a sweet moment she held steady, but the inrush to union became a hurricane inside her, tearing her from her moorings even as it filled her with the presence she'd come to love more than flight, more than freedom, more than life.

She remembered little of the next few days. They spent most of it inside a skylit stone room, with one wall veiled from end to end by falling water. Here and there, a meal stuck out in her memory, home-grown foods like she'd never tasted . . . and one morning Brennen had taken her swimming in a river draped with fragrant trees.

In less than a day, she would see Hesed again.

Curling toward the starboard hull, she let the superlight engine's thrum and the slip vibration lull her into a deep, contented sleep.

No Shuhr ships challenged as they entered the Procyel system. Under falling darkness, ten heavy fighters and an armed courier settled on Hesed's grassy landing strip.

Firebird stepped out, feeling grimy and salty, clutching Kiel against her shoulder. She couldn't wait to see him awake again. She felt vaguely guilty for letting them bring him so far in tardema-sleep.

Near a boarding ladder that hung from the lead craft, two familiar figures stood waiting. Jenner Dabarrah, Sanctuary Master, was as tall, lean, and poised as she remembered, with pale yellow hair and a white tunic that almost shone in fading daylight. His mistress Anna wore her dark hair long enough to touch her green belt. She smiled warmly, holding out both arms. Abruptly Firebird remembered that Anna was childless.

Feeling a new kind of pity, Firebird carefully gave Kiel to her. "He's in tardema," she said, then wondered if she needed to explain that to the Sentinel woman.

Cradling him tenderly, Anna pushed the blanket away from his face. "He's beautiful," she said, and Firebird felt warmer despite a chill sunset breeze. She glanced up at the mountains that surrounded Hesed House.

Tellai followed down the stepstand, carrying her clairsa case, and then came Brennen with Kinnor. Tel strode forward. "Tel Tellai, sir." He bowed to Master Dabarrah. "Actually, it's Tellai-Angelo, Your Honor."

"You are welcome at Hesed House, Your Highness," said Master Dabarrah, "as a member of Mistress Caldwell's family." He extended an arm and presented, "My wife, Mistress Anna."

Anna Dabarrah inclined her head toward Tellai. Deep brown hair touched with silver slipped over her shoulder, covering Kiel. She swept it back.

"Master Dabarrah?" Firebird caught his eye and mouthed a thank-you for allowing Tel to pass the security perimeter at Procyel II. Under other circumstances, he would've been turned away like any other non-Sentinel.

"Mistress Firebird." Anna Dabarrah rocked Kiel from side to side. "Are you and the children well?"

"Yes." Firebird inhaled free air as several other pilots passed by on their way indoors. This evergreen scent brought back a whirl of tender memories, with one image of Brennen, all in white, shining at its center. "But I still could sleep away a dekia."

"Come in." Dabarrah gestured toward the House's main groundside lift. "Please."

"Let me take the children while you bathe and eat," Anna offered. "Firebird, you surely remember the way to your rooms. Brennen, why don't you freshen in our suite?"

They rode the lift downlevel to the vast underground chamber. As before, Firebird followed a young student-apprentice sekiyr. Beyond the white latticework railing, the huge reflecting pool's blue-green underwater lights still reflected asymmetric patterns off a high ceiling and dozens of darkening skylights. Paths of stepping stones dotted the bright water like floating square shadows.

She sighed. Breathing room!

In the skylit bedchamber where she had spent most of her previous stay, she gladly peeled out of her musty red skyff and blue trousers. She bathed without hurrying and almost fell asleep in a warm, deep pool in the freshing room. Then she slipped into a blue gown she found laid out on the bed—just as before—near the watery wall that cascaded down the room's south side. She studied its outflow, below floor level at the bottom of a finger-deep pool. Someday, she decided, she would simply stand in the flow and bathe here. Water flowed almost everywhere at Hesed. *Of course*, she mused as she smoothed the long, damp waves of her hair. *People from watery Thyrica built this sanctuary*. Had Ehret been a wet world too?

As her thirsty ears drank the sounds, she caught a whiff of the Trinn Hill woods. *So those are kirka trees on the islands*, she reflected. The depth of her relief to have reached sanctuary awed her. Had the hormones of pregnancy and motherhood done this? Had she lost her hunger for adventure, or had her brief honeymoon in this place so enthralled her that she would never be a callow warrior again?

Her children were safe. For now, that was enough.

Brennen waited on the walkway with Tel, who wore a plain gray jumpsuit that lent him a new air of understated maturity. "You look more comfortable," said Brennen, extending an arm.

"I feel a world better." Deeply relaxed, she took his arm. Then she sensed his reserved mood. "Where are the babies?"

He stepped out down the walkway. "We're expected in Dabarrah's office."

The Sanctuary Master waited inside like a white-and-gold statue, but she saw no sign of Kiel or Kinnor. "Prince Tel," said Master Dabarrah, "forgive me a moment's necessary rudeness. May I speak alone with the Caldwells for ten minutes? Then please rejoin us."

"Certainly. I would enjoy a closer look at your landscaping." Tel retreated out the arch toward the pool.

Dabarrah nodded to Brennen, who looked serious and now felt troubled. "You have to know, Mari. This won't wait."

As she sat down on a white stone bench, she had the odd sensation that a shadow was blowing toward Hesed House's rippling serenity.

"Before we left College," Brennen said, "Shamarr Dickin put two prohibitions on us. First, I'm not to touch your mind. No Sentinel can. I cannot now, nor . . . when I come to bed."

"Brenn!" she whispered, aghast. Not in loving her? Clearly that was the gist of Dickin's prohibition. Not to touch Brennen's depths . . . she would wither, starve, after months of feasting on intimate pleasure.

Had the Shamarr somehow discovered the darkness behind her turn? Had Spieth told him?

She glanced aside. Master Dabarrah sat across the room on another white bench, casually drawing one long leg up beside him. His sad eyes and open palms suggested compassion.

"Why?" she demanded.

Brennen cleared his throat. He sat down beside her and took her hand. "Mari, somehow—and this is the danger, we're not sure how—you killed Harcourt Terrell."

Firebird blinked. "Terrell, the security tech?"

Brennen nodded, frowning. "He's the one who attacked you at College. He put you under the watch-link."

"I killed him? I didn't even see him."

He held her hand tighter. "We found his body outside the master room door. No injury, no sign of suicide drugs. No other explanation."

Firebird looked at Dabarrah again. The elder Master Sentinel pressed his palms together and stared down.

She'd killed before. In memory, she dragged Baron Parkai's corpse into a wardrobe. She'd meant to stun him.

"Do you remember what you did to Terrell?" Brennen asked.

"I didn't do anyth—wait. The last I remember, I tried to turn." She frowned, remembering. "You don't think I scared him to death?"

Brennen didn't answer directly. "When I arrived, your mental strength was completely spent. You were dying. I had to strengthen your beta energies to keep your autonomic nervous system functioning while your strength built again. It's called psychic shock." Shifting his feet, he fingered his cuff tab. "Tell Master Dabarrah about the dark images. I explained as well as I could, but he should hear this from you."

Though it brought back all her misery, she carefully described the flaming darkness and its precedent in Netaian mythology.

Master Dabarrah inclined his head when she finished. "Thank you. I see you dislike speaking of this."

Brennen touched her hand. "If your carrier is bound to that imagery, then maybe your epsilon strength is unalterably joined to the images. Maybe, just by turning, you did somehow kill him—and his death at such proximity sent you into shock. But we don't know, and even Shamarr Dickin doesn't know what to do, except to protect others from you. He put you on what's called avoid-status."

She stared.

"You only turned?"

"That's all I remember."

Brennen frowned. "Any trained Sentinel has substantial control over his own beta centers. It's possible Terrell shut them down involuntarily in response to your imagery and epsilon turn. If that's the case," he said, furrowing his forehead, "you could only harm the starbred. Especially those of higher potential. It would take the mental strength of two, at least, to kill this way. Yours, plus the attacker's—"

"Or so we believe," Dabarrah interjected.

"No Sentinel has ever been able to do this," Brennen went on. "You have no control, no training. I think you see the potential danger . . ."

"To you! And . . ." Firebird paused, silenced by a horrible new thought. "The babies?" she whispered, turning to Dabarrah. "Could they be strong enough to—no, Master, Brennen wouldn't attack me, and neither would an infant. I was only trying to protect myself, and that nearly killed me. I can't turn accidentally. It's a battle to turn at all."

"That is all true," said Dabarrah, "but there are psychic reflexes no one can control. You did not counterattack. You merely turned. Under Shamarr Dickin's order, you must be kept from your children until we are absolutely certain you won't harm them . . . merely by turning."

Firebird gulped air. Heat rose to her cheeks. "You're not listening. I'd never go after them. They wouldn't try to hurt me. Give me my boys."

"You did not kill Harcourt Terrell deliberately," Dabarrah murmured.

Nor Baron Parkai. But—"This isn't right!" she cried. "Brennen, tell him not to do this!"

Brennen seized her hand and held tightly.

"He is as angry and confused as you are." Dabarrah shifted on the white bench. "Still, the injunction is temporary. My degrees are in psi medicine, Firebird. I may approach you safely. I have developed special defenses. The infants' minds are unformed," he stressed. "They're utterly at the mercy of others."

Firebird clenched her free hand behind her back. *Blessed Singer, did Brennen put Kiel and Kinnor in tardema-sleep, clear back at College, to protect them from me?* Had Brenn known? She tried to pull back her other hand. Brennen held on.

Footsteps approached on the waterside walkway. A young sekiyr entered, followed by a gliding cart crowded with earthenware dishes. The sekiyr extended the cart's legs and carefully set out dinner. Master Dabarrah slid four stools to a wooden sideboard.

Tellai stepped into the arch. "May I join you?"

Brennen and Dabarrah turned to Firebird.

"Come," she said numbly.

Firebird accepted the thick stew Brennen served her, filled with chunks of vegetables so bright they must've been carried on the run from garden to kettle, coarse brown bread with a seductive aroma, and plump berries—colored and faceted like garnets, they were the size of eggs but smelled like melons.

They tasted like dust.

She'd killed a man. Again. Again, it was self-defense . . . but this time, she'd used only the darkness inside her. What if she did harm Kiel or Kinnor—or Brennen? Had a miraculous string of failures kept her from killing Janesca?

But if her turn killed people, then why was Medical Master Spieth alive? Spieth was there when she turned the first time . . . and Brennen, and Tel . . . and at least one sekiyr . . .

Brennen and Tel ate quickly, relating the battle at Thyrica to Dabarrah, though Firebird saw and sensed several inquiring, empathizing glances from Brennen. She did feel his hurt now, and his anger with Dickin. No wonder he'd shielded his feelings as they left the medical complex. He had known that the avoid-status barred her from contact with Kiel and Kinnor.

Once, only once, she'd tried desperately to stop Kinnor's wailing. But never by harming him! She couldn't hurt a vulnerable child, the union of her very life with Brennen's.

"There's a chance we may be blockaded," Dabarrah was speculating, "since they can't hope to attack through our fielding net. So we've run messengers everywhere our people live in numbers. Tallis will pass news to the High council at Elysia. No action is being taken yet, and we're fully self-sufficient, but plans of several sorts are being discussed—as is your RIA work, although only among ourselves."

Numbly shredding a chunk of brown bread, Firebird glanced up. What was RIA work? Immediately she felt a cautionary surge from Brennen. Tel, examining a four-bite garnetberry, seemed not to hear.

She dropped the bread chunk. Suddenly she wanted to be alone.

Brennen rose. "I'll see you back to the room, Mari. Then I want to talk to Tel a little longer."

Her anger had faded. The numbness was passing, and tears could come next . . . and then, maybe, a plan. She pushed back her stool. "Thank you, Brenn, but I can find my way." She caught his glance and thought hard at him, *Leave me alone for a while. Please.* "Good night, gentlemen." She slipped out.

Halfway to her room, she broke into a run.

CHAPTER **17**

CALLED

appassionato
impassioned

After they finished eating, Brennen led Tel onto the waterside pavement. Overhead, the turquoise ceiling rippled with dusky blue shadows.

He'd returned, but neither at peace nor in triumph. He had known what Jenner must tell Firebird about Kinnor and Kiel. Shamarr Dickin had forbidden him to tell her himself. *She must see you stand with her*, Dickin explained.

You tell her, he wanted to retort. Sometimes, years ago, he'd resented his father. Now he knew Dickin too could be peremptory.

But Dickin was right. Until Dabarrah finished evaluating her, he could only comfort her. "I've loved and trusted Master Dabarrah," he told Tel, "since I served as a sekiyr under him. He shows the power of gentleness clearly." He stopped at the water's edge and rested both forearms on the lattice railing. An hour ago, he'd wakened Kinnor and Kiel while Firebird bathed. He held them tightly before relinquishing them to Mistress Anna.

"I see what you mean." Tel stepped up beside him. "It's not Dabarrah's authority that gives him such strength of spirit, but the other way around."

Brennen nodded, surprised. "You're stronger yourself than anyone realized. Until you came up against real adversity, you had no chance to show it."

"Thank you." Tel raised his head and stared out over the bright pool. "This is an impressive place, Caldwell."

"It's a far cry from the Angelo palace."

"It's quieter. But there's a deeper power at work. Even I can feel it."

"Hesed is probably the most heavily protected enclave in this region of the Whorl."

"Then Firebird and the babies finally are out of danger," Tel observed.

Yes. Out of danger, he thought, surprised to recognize another source of bitterness. *From the Shuhr, and the Federacy's threats.*

Holy One, help us to take these separations as kindly as Dickin surely means them. He'd never felt less kindly toward Shamarr Lo Dickin.

And how would the Sunton attack affect his people's standing with the Federacy? He stirred, unable to shake a heavy new dread. "I almost wish we hadn't left this place," he murmured, bowing his head. Would the Shuhr have blasted Sunton if he'd stayed here? What was the final death toll?

"If you hadn't gone to Thyrica," Tel asked, "would I have been able to contact you?"

"No."

"Then I'm glad you did."

And Kinnor and Kiel had been conceived because he and Mari went to the College for her diagnosis and treatment. He mustn't blame himself for the devastation on Thyrica. Others would do that for him.

Water lapped at the pool's edge near Brennen's feet. After a time, he spoke again. "We live close to the soil here. We do without weather control, we grow food the old ways, and keep animals—to refresh the spirit, and remind us of our kinship with the rest of creation."

"Then this is your . . . monastery?"

Brennen shifted his elbows onto the lattice and rested his chin on his hands. "Not quite. Everyone at College spends a rotation here, studying the commandments and our duty to carry them wherever we serve. And how to add beauty where necessity has been satisfied." He gestured toward the stepping-stone islands. Far out on the water, those trees seemed to ripple with waving reflections. "Many of our elderly come back when their epsilon abilities wane. They spend their last active years in defensive fielding service, protecting the Procyel system. The sekiyrra do most of our manual labor, but everyone must work to maintain the retreat." There'd soon be an influx, he guessed: Sentinels with small children, fleeing before the Shuhr struck Thyrica again. Dabarrah was ready. For decades, they'd known Hesed would be their last haven. "Firebird probably will be excused from the heaviest labor because she's still recovering from childbirth," he went on, "but we'll join the task rotation tomorrow morning, you and I."

Tel flexed his slender arms, almost smiling. "That's where you built the shoulders, Caldwell?"

"It's a good life," Brennen admitted. "It serves a profound need in the Ehretan starbred. On Thyrica we've always been a people apart. You'll be content here."

Tel straightened his back. "No," he said. "Never content. Phoena is a prisoner." He drummed long fingers on the railing. "I came for your help. I don't know that I'd have the audacity to ask again, now that I understand your situation. But every day she's there, I can't help thinking she will be in more danger."

Brennen sensed Tellai's fear and his hope. He glanced toward his own door and guessed Firebird would want a few more minutes alone. "If I stay here for Firebird's sake, will you try to go to Three Zed yourself?"

The dark eyes caught his glance, welcoming scrutiny. "Yes."

Brennen tried to relax his taut jaw muscles. "You haven't a chance against those people."

"I know."

Numbly he rubbed his face. Phoena had become a focal point, regardless of her personality. The Federate summons rose in his memory, and Regional's offer, and the veiled threat against Firebird.

Would that summons change? His mind worked backward, counting days, wondering . . .

Yes. The attack on Thyrica could've been launched after Phoena arrived at Three Zed. What had she shown them that helped precipitate it?

And what were the Shuhr doing to her? Questioning her, tormenting her? Altering her mind?

He cringed to remember that he'd personally cleared Harcourt Terrell from suspicion. For decades, the Sentinels thought they held back the Shuhr threat. Maybe the Shuhr had just been marking time.

Hesed, at least, could not be attacked the way they struck Sunton. It was fully protected from any piloted strike or unpiloted drone.

"The two of us might succeed. She'd come away for me." Tellai broke into Brennen's thoughts, then faltered. "I think."

"I don't mean to be unkind," Brennen said, "but for the moment, no one's going anywhere. Even if you tried, they have powers you can't resist. If I had to protect you, I wouldn't be able to work against their surveillance."

Tel tilted his chin up, though his eyes looked thick. "I understand."

"I'll contact the Alert Forces from here," Brennen said gruffly. "I'll help if I can, but first we need to see how they respond to the strike at Sunton."

"That could take weeks."

"I'm sorry, Tel. That's the way it has to be." Brennen glanced at the door again. *Now*, he guessed. *She needs me now.*

He slept badly that night. Well after midnight, he slipped into a familiar dream.

He gripped the controls of his intercept fighter, patrolling an unfamiliar world, with no idea why he'd been sent there. No objective glowed on his onboard computer, no route/risk data on his display. The console seemed realistic, but below him, landforms varied from the normal to the bizarre.

He flew over a river that flowed preposterously up and down a line of rolling blue hills, then a city that looked like a two-dimensional grid map, with human icons traveling dashed-line streets. A huge golden cube stood at the grid's center, seemingly dropped from the sky.

He banked north toward a line of purple mountains. His atmospheric sensor showed well within the green range, so there must be breathable air outside. Still, his cockpit smelled stuffy. He couldn't stay airborne much longer.

"Brennen," said a voice in his headset.

This was new. So was the mountain that stood alone, surrounded by cloud wisps and dusted with snow. A wreath of broad white waterfalls obscured its feet. "Caldwell here," he answered.

Landing data appeared on his display. "Come. We will speak."

He activated an automatic landing cycle. A duracrete breakway strip appeared halfway up one waterfall, on a ledge that broadened as he approached. The strip had no support buildings, no hangar or parking area, no refueling dock. He circled once and touched down. His craft rolled to a stop at the waterfall's edge. He popped the canopy, then pulled off his helmet.

"Brennen," said the voice again.

He looked around. He saw no one. Disquieted, he reached for his blazer—

And then realized he knew that Voice. Sometimes it whispered at the back of his mind.

He sprang out of the cockpit and dropped to his knees on the duracrete. "I am here, Holy One."

Cool air flowed down from snowfields high on the mountain. On both sides of the breakway strip, blue flowers nodded on long, leafy stems. The voice seemed to flow from that near waterfall, in a deep, mellow timbre without accent. "Your enemy plans to destroy Hesed," it said, "and most of your brethren. Stop him."

How could he feel so calm, conversing with the King of the Universe? Yet he knew how to answer, as if he'd been given a protocol briefing. "Thank you," he murmured. "This is the highest honor I can imagine."

"Go to Three Zed, for Phoena. Leave in two days."

"Three Zed? Alone, Holy One?"

"You are never alone." The voice didn't shame him for asking, but reassured him, heart-deep. If he were ordered to go there, he'd be empowered. Equipped.

He looked up at the waterfall, half expecting to see an ancient face in the spray.

He saw a faint rainbow instead, with waterdrops flowing through it like diamonds. "Thank you," he repeated. He bowed his head . . .

And found himself sitting upright in bed. Mari lay at his side, breathing peacefully. At the other side of his bed, the watery wall cascaded on.

The next morning broke fresh. Bursts of autumn wind cooled sekiyrra who labored in Hesed's gardens, east of the hillside.

Firebird picked her way down a gentle slope. She and Brennen had walked up here after morning prayer service. Her pale blue gown trailed the last summer flowers, and tears chilled her cheeks. Last night, she'd cried bitterly in his arms over Shamarr Dickin's isolation order. And now, he'd had a dream. A mountain, a waterfall . . . a voice . . .

"But it makes no sense." Firebird pushed out the words as evenly as she could. "You can't—"

"Mari," he interrupted. His eyes seemed to focus on something infinitely remote, and his voice sounded distant. "I'm the oldest heir to the promises. Sometimes, at critical moments, the eldest is given a vision. Like the Shamarr. I never doubted, but I never imagined it could be so vivid. So plain."

He couldn't mean this. Only last night, he promised to stay here unless Alert Forces backed him up.

But she felt his utter confidence, his serenity, even a new strength. When they first met at Veroh, he'd seemed this remote and full of power. Now he claimed that if he stayed here, the Shuhr would destroy Hesed. "Think it through," she urged. "At least wait until Master Dabarrah finds out if Terrell did further damage. Dabarrah might want help with my dark visions too. And Kiel and Kinnor need us, not Mistress Anna."

"Dabarrah estimates several weeks to help you. I must go in two days, Mari. Supposedly, Hesed's fielding will turn back any attack, but can we be sure now?"

"Nothing has changed," she insisted. Halting, she reached toward him.

He stepped into her arms. "I've made a career of military intelligence," he reminded her. "I've been prepared for this. I don't want to do it, but I must."

Stunned, she pressed her cheek to his shoulder. One week ago, she'd had a family. She'd been a mother, a wife.

She still was both! "You're not being overconfident?"

"He wouldn't send me," Brennen answered, "if He didn't know I was capable, with His help." He curled one hand around the back of her head. "Dabarrah's equipped for his work too. The children have him, and Mistress Anna, and every teacher and sekiyr and elder here to care for them, until Dabarrah feels certain you can . . . control that wild talent."

"But it's a trap, Brenn! It's not Phoena the Shuhr want, it's you! Listen." She pulled away. "The Federacy won the Veroh War quickly because you took two prisoners. Me, and then Dorning Stele. What would the Shuhr do with all you know? They've opened a war against the Federacy. You could betray it." She remembered that guilt and shame too well.

"No," he said. They walked on down the grassy hill. "My situation is different from yours. Special Operations trains its agents in selective amnesia techniques. Those cannot be broken. I'm not just equipped to resist mind-access. I can defeat any interrogation."

She sensed, though, that the thought finally broke his serenity. She felt him cringe.

"If you don't find Phoena there, they'll kill you. And for what?"

"For the Sanctuary. This call is an honor, an expression of the Speaker's trust in me."

Firebird lengthened her steps in pursuit. "But not even Danton wants Phoena around!"

"No." He turned his head so she could hear his answer. "There, you're wrong. The Federacy contacted me shortly after she disappeared."

"And?" Shocked, she halted in midstride.

"For them, it's political. Apparently they've realized how badly they want Netaia as part of the Federacy. Madam Kernoweg herself asked me to consider going to Three Zed."

Firebird gaped. She'd squared off against Councilor Kernoweg's greed . . . and seen recent stats. Even after demilitarization, Netaia's resources were estimated at almost a quarter of the Federacy's.

"They urgently want to show Netaia they can protect their own. Even though she probably went to them, Mari."

"But—"

"I know, Kernoweg only makes marginal sense to me too. But the Council has declared that trying to save your sister is a security matter. That frees me to use all my abilities without breaking the Codes, even if I have to take her against her will. And if I succeed, the Federacy wants me back. Probably at Tallis."

"They need you now," she muttered. "More than ever, after Sunton. They're idiots to risk you like this." She stared out over the river into a red stone valley. At the corner of her eye she saw him take several more steps down the meadow, then turn back.

"All right." She balled a fist on one hip. "Then I'm going with you."

"You mustn't. The dream was clear about that too. The Speaker wants you here, for the moment."

He wouldn't thwart her that easily. "Is Phoena worth it, Brenn? Is . . . is the Federacy?"

He looked up at her, and she devoured the sight of him standing square-shouldered with the wind in his hair. "I'd never leave you for Phoena, nor for the Federacy. Only for one Person anywhere." He shook his head, and his eyes wandered again. "I never thought to be called like this." She felt his heart deeply at peace. Not even terrible danger could turn him from this resolve.

Nor could she! *Your fame's assured*, she wanted to cry. *Do you have to be a hero ten times over?*

He reached out and closed his fingers around her hand, and they walked down toward the house. "Remember why Tel came to us, and what I promised him. It's been as hard for him to change his thinking as it was for you."

"Harder, probably." She stepped over the burrow of some small creature and lengthened her stride to match Brennen's. On the ground, leaves were reddening on red stones. "Tel has a secure position on Netaia. He still could go back. I had nothing left to live for."

"I'm glad you see that." He stopped again. "Now that your sister has seen the enemy, maybe she's even found enough wisdom to realize what they are."

"Brennen." Her eyes filled with stinging tears.

He drew her into his arms. It was on the tip of her tongue to beg him: not to go alone to Three Zed, not to risk himself when she needed his support. Or at least to bring her along, now that she could move and act and fight without endangering Kiel and Kinnor.

But they agreed that a person needed one highest priority, something to serve above everything else. He was called. Firebird had been ready to die for much less over the red sands of Veroh. *But how can you do this now, Mighty Singer?*

"Please," Brennen said softly, "send me with your blessing. I've never saved my life by sheltering it. If I don't go, Hesed will fall, and we all could die. You, me . . . most of the kindred. It was clear, Mari. There was nothing eerie or questionable about it."

And now she knew how it might happen. "But it's the wrong time. And Phoena's the wrong reason." And he would not go alone. Maybe he'd feel less responsible if she stowed away. She could do it . . .

But could she hide her intention? He'd sense even a stranger's dishonesty, unless that stranger were a powerful impostor like Harcourt Terrell. Her chin drooped.

His arms tightened their circle. He didn't answer, but she read a new emotion in him. He ached beneath his confidence, for her and for the timing. She also felt his growing paternal pride.

And did he fear her mysterious killing ability?

Surely he must. She did. "I can't bless you," she said at last. "I don't know how. But you know I won't forbid you. Don't ever diminish yourself for me."

He nearly crushed her against himself. "Your strength," he whispered beside her ear, "has always been greater than your fear. Be strong for Tel when I'm gone."

Gone. It sounded so final.

She drew on his calmness to gather herself. When she mastered her grief, she tangled her fingers with his. They walked on down.

He led her to a musty underground hangar. At the hilltop fielding station, he'd shown her a defense system that protected Hesed. A fielding team of Sentinels could project subtronically coordinated mental energies over a distance, just as a Shuhr team kept her under watch-link during the Thyrica battle.

In the hangar, she saw that most of their escorts had shipped out, leaving one heavy fighter. It lay partially gutted. Busy crewers transferred portions of its electronic heart onto a smaller craft. She watched a thin sekiyr walk across the hangar, carrying a large cylindrical object several inches *above* his outspread hands, practicing epsilon skills as he helped.

Brennen beckoned her outside. On the grassy breakaway strip, new growth glistened in the scars of recent landings.

"Back at Thyrica," he explained, "several of us were working on a device that would let one Sentinel extend his or her skills much farther than across a room. Ship to ship, actually."

She thought that through. "Was that what got us past the englobement?"

"Yes. Dardy tested it there. We call it Ree-a, Remote Individual Amplification."

She formed a small "o" with her lips.

"We progressed with it far enough to mount two systems into HF–108s before the emergency arose, and we brought one along," Brennen said as he walked. "The power's still low, but it should give a Sentinel the remote capability to pass through a fielding net undetected. We know the Shuhr use fielding technology to defend Three Zed.”

She sighed. “So you’ll take that smaller ship. The one they’re modifying now.”

“Exactly. Mari, I know what you want. I’d bring you if I could. Your skills would be invaluable. But you must stay and work with Jenner. It’s urgent to get our children back.”

She didn’t look up. “You can’t wait? You’re certain?”

He shook his head. “The Shuhr are as unbalanced as they’ve ever been. We’ve disabled their fleet. Now is the time to go, before they recover.”

“Brenn.” She halted at one end of the landing strip. “If you have one day here, could I be consecrated? Will they still have me?” she added, feeling dubious. “On avoid-status?”

His grip tightened on her hand. “I was just trying to decide how to ask if you’d want that. Yes. Master Jenner is a psi healer. Even with A-status, he can access you to give you the ritual memories.”

Had he thought of it for the same reason? she wondered. If he didn’t come back, then she wanted to remember standing beside him, fully accepted as one of his community. If it was the last gift they gave each other, she would hear those mysterious prophecies explained in his own tenor voice.

“I only wish,” she muttered, “you weren’t doing this for Phoena.”

“Not Phoena, Mari. This is for you. For Kinnor and Kiel, and for Hesed.”

“Two hundred ships!” thundered the Eldest, Eshdeth Shirak. “Nearly all that we had!”

Phoena covered her ears.

Eldest Shirak wore black, as did forty other men and women who stood between his Kellian tapestry and that misty battle curtain. He’d declared a day of mourning. Before him, side by side under scrutiny, stood his grandson Micahel and a smaller man with arrogant pale green eyes.

“And Caldwell had how many?” purred Dru Polar. He sat near Phoena on one end of Shirak’s obsidian desk top. Polar’s satiny orange sash was the brightest flash of color in the room, outshining the star tank’s tiny jewels. Phoena liked Polar’s sash belts, though she distrusted his lingering glances at Cassia Talumah, who looked ripe and supple in black shipboards.

“Thirty-two, Mine Eldest,” said the smaller man.

“Shef’th,” Polar swore.

Lumpy little Juddis Adiyn sat near a gold-sprayed wall. Mockingly, he touched one ear. "What was that, Arac? I couldn't have heard correctly."

Micahel glared at his comrade, his fury obvious even to Phoena.

The other's—Arac's—pale green eyes hardened, as if he foresaw his fate. He'd failed the Shirak family. He'd pay with nothing less than his life. "Thirty-two ships," he repeated distinctly. "They rendezvoused at the Sentinel College and took off from that point. Heavy-fighter class, trained to fight as a unit, and solidly led. And something else too, some disruptor field we've never encountered before. We had more guns, Eldest, it's true, but many of our pilots hadn't flown warships before last month."

"We still would've taken that one vital ship," growled Micahel, "if you'd paid closer attention."

"How so?" Eldest Shirak rose from his chair. He strolled around the projection tank.

"Before we lost touch with Harcourt Terrell," Micahel snapped, "he brought the Caldwell woman inside his watch-link. Arac supervised. We should've been able to anticipate their every maneuver. We should be celebrating an overdue victory."

Shirak turned on his grandson. "And if you had attacked the College first, instead of testing your equipment somewhere else, they wouldn't have had time to run. If you were any kind of commander, you'd have hit the target we want. You could've taken out a hundred Sentinels with one strike. Half of them, Micahel. Half!"

"But the Federacy would've defended the rest of them." Micahel set his chin. "This way, Thyrica lost more nonaltered than starbred. They're the ones we need to frighten."

Phoena only understood this: Caldwell's squadron had delayed Micahel's force long enough for Thyrica's Home Forces to launch more ships. The Thyrian force smashed Micahel's battle group, taking revenge for that cratered town. His fifty-ship command flight fled back here. Other pilots—settlement recruits, voice-commanded to fight to the last missile—covered his retreat.

The Federacy wouldn't dare to try striking back here. A fielding team could disrupt and destroy approaching minds and divert falling objects.

"Do you have any idea," growled Micahel's grandfather, "how much work went into collecting that fleet?"

Phoena compressed her lips as the graying Eldest paced before the two young men. The idiots. She couldn't believe it herself. First, the Netaian strike team missed Carradee. Now all those young Shuhr had died, while Firebird eluded them again. They might've eliminated not only her but two illegally conceived male—male!—by-blows of the Netaian nobility.

She lowered her eyebrows at Arac. He, at least, would pay.

"I do know, Eldest," Arac said quietly. "I went on the Narkin raid."

"Do you think that excuses you?" Shirak's pacing brought him close to Phoena and Dru Polar, where he turned again. "We can live two hundred years. If we risk ourselves in battle, we expect to return safely. Your surveillance team was our guarantee. You betrayed us."

Phoena glanced sidelong at Dru Polar. Dru stood with his arms crossed low, over his sash.

"Eldest," said Micahel, "this is no defeat. We know exactly where the Carabohds are now. All of them. We can take them out. Let me try this again, at Procyel."

"Hesed has epsilon fielding! How many ships do you think we can throw away?" Shirak lowered himself into his desk chair. "Adiyn, have you seen my grandson die in this room?"

Juddis Adiyn stood close to the tapestry. He looked hard at Phoena. "Not Micahel," he said, "but Arac." The green-eyed man flinched. "I have foreseen a lost Ehretan family stretching out a hand of execution. Casvah, the vessel, a cup full of death."

Phoena frowned. She was no Ehretan half-breed! Dru accused her of carrying Sentinel genes, though. She'd given up arguing. He was a titillating companion. Fascinating, frightening. Thrilling.

"Good," said Shirak. "Polar, show Her Highness how to operate the striker."

Polar slid a weapon from his sash. Arac raised his head, and his green eyes widened fearfully.

Phoena leaned closer, examining the weapon as Polar rolled it between his strong hands. It had the look of a baron's baton of office, a silver rod with several buttons within finger's reach of its knurled handle. Dru touched one. A needlelike probe sprang from its far end.

She reached out a hand.

"If you'd like to see what it can do, use a low charge and avoid the nervous system. You'll have to be careful if you don't want to kill him." He slid a black stud toward the pommel. "The farther up the shaft you set this, the more power to the probe. Activate here." He stroked an orange button below the thumb cradle.

Phoena snatched the baton. She'd never personally killed anyone, not even a wastling, and she didn't want Polar or the others to know that. If one counted the hundreds of cloned embryos whose brains they'd pulverized, she was the only person in this room without that distinction.

For a minute she merely retracted and extended the probe, getting the feel of holding it. Then she stepped out beside the desk, faced Adiyn, and inclined her head. "Sir, I am no Casvah, but the house of Angelo honors those who assist it. Shall I demonstrate the consequences of failing us?"

Benignly, Adiyn smiled. "Please."

Phoena considered Arac, who outweighed her by half.

"You. And you." She flicked a graceful finger at two of Shirak's staff. "Hold him for me."

Arac flinched but didn't cry out when she touched the probe to his elbow at very low power. She crossed behind him, considering, then pierced the back of his knee. When again she pressed the orange stud, his weight shifted. His involuntary back kick missed her by centimeters, and then his leg hung twitching.

Intrigued, Phoena started to experiment in earnest.

Later, Dru escorted her to her rooms. "What was your hurry?" he asked. Arm in arm, they rounded a corner of the steely inner corridor. "We were enjoying ourselves."

"I didn't expect the highest power level to kill him from a finger touch. That's a long way from the brain."

"Effective use is complex," he confessed. "At that power, if you even approached a major nerve, he'd have gone almost instantly. As it was, he took several minutes to die."

"He did." Phoena stepped regally, savoring the sensation of having ended a life. She felt almost omnipotent. Later, she would look up "Arac's" life story and find out whom she'd executed.

This striker would make a fine deterrent for Netaian criminals. She would order a production plant built to furnish her Enforcement Corps.

At her door, they stopped. She turned toward Dru, though not too close, and lowered her eyes seductively. "If I ever get a chance at Firebird, Dru, will you lend that to me again?"

"If it can be arranged."

"What's the absolute worst you could do with it? I'd want to know I was giving her the very hardest way out."

"Lowest power, throat pressure point." His eyes seemed to crackle as he reached for the side of her neck. He caressed the smooth skin at the hinge of her jaw, below her ear. "Here," he breathed. "Not as slow, but excruciating."

She pulled away in fright. "No," she said firmly. "Not me."

"You deserve no better, Phoena Angelo. You're a traitor to your own kind. Your own sisters."

Phoena tried to struggle out of his arms. She'd wondered, she even suspected that the Shuhr never meant to make her queen. She had one moment of ghastly lucidity—

Blank.

Fully relaxed, she pressed against his hard, muscular body. No man had ever drawn her as intensely as Testing Commander Dru Polar.

"Will you come in?" she whispered.

Dru dropped his arms and stepped away. "I'm tired. I've had enough pleasure for one day."

Phoena pressed an open palm against her door's lock panel, then slipped inside, giving Polar a kittenish farewell smile. Content again in her lovely gray little rooms, she sealed the door she could open so easily from the passway—but not from inside.

CHAPTER 18

CONSECRATED

moderato
moderately

Firebird stood in the broad entry to Hesed's chapter room, shifting from one bare foot to the other. The flagstones felt cool underfoot. Inside, voices sang softly.

Finally, she could put this behind her. No more covert looks or whispers, no regretful subvocalizations on Brennen's behalf.

She flexed one foot and toed a crack in the stone.

Years ago on Ehret, Brennen's ancestors had welcomed each new consecrant with a blood sacrifice, to illustrate the Speaker's covering for her transgressions. With Ehret desolate, those temple sacrifices could no longer be practiced, but the faith community still insisted that every child inherited the taint of evil . . . and that until the Speaker himself made perfect atonement, a believer should confirm true faith by attending a sacrifice. Now, instead of bloodying their hands, they passed down an excruciatingly vivid memory.

Brennen stood close by, waiting with her for the door to swing open. He wore military dress whites. She'd borrowed another simple sekiyr's gown—white, this time. Traditionally, a consecrant came unshod. "You're all right barefoot?" Brennen had asked, washing up after his morning's fieldwork. He'd volunteered for the task rotation, no matter how briefly he would be here.

"I don't mind." She liked her toes free, especially now that her feet weren't swollen. Still, she felt uneasy. Remembering her catechismal answers didn't worry her at all, but she didn't look forward to what would come after, when Master Dabarrah transferred that last sacrifice into her memory. From Path instruction, she mostly understood the concept of substitutionary sacrifice, but she still didn't like it. Even after finding that Darkness inside her, she didn't feel evil . . . and the Singer had already brought her to himself, accepting her with all her flaws.

Still, the faith community felt it necessary to prove how seriously the

One took a believer's shortcomings. The memory transfer was considered a teaching tool, to stress that even now, covering was only bought with a death.

In that case, she'd demanded, *how could the deathless Singer ever finish a perfect atonement?*

A mystery, as yet unrevealed, her Path instructor said.

We aren't told exactly, Brennen explained later, but she felt a suppressed tingling in him. He had a guess, or at least a suspicion.

Fine, she reflected, toeing another rough spot. *I'll do this, but they still won't convince me I'm tainted. I know what evil is. Phoena is mostly evil. Shuhr are totally evil—aren't they?*

What about their children? she wondered.

The soft singing stopped. She glanced up.

Brennen took her hand and kissed it, and she felt his assurance. "Just don't try to turn," he reminded her.

"Not a chance." She didn't want that flaming darkness to ruin this occasion. From all she'd heard, the sacrifice was awful enough.

But she'd seen death. She was as well prepared as anyone. Better than most.

One door swung open, held by a smiling young sekiyr gowned, like Firebird, in white. "We're ready," she said.

Firebird stepped into the long room. On benches at both sides of its carpeted aisle, about fifty Sentinels and sekiyrra stared back. She hesitated on the threshold and glanced around. Most of Hesed's transient population must have gathered. This would be no private rite, the way she'd originally planned it. Holding Brennen's hand, she paced forward.

Master Dabarrah waited under a skylight, near the center of a curved platform. Behind him stood an altar like the ones in other chapter rooms, its length draped with brocade cloths of pure red, blue, and green. An oil lamp burned on the blue cloth between open copies of *Dabar* and *Mattah*. Behind, on a wall built of red Hesedan stone, a large gold Sentinel's star hung seemingly suspended in space. Faint light also came from tall blue candles burning on gold sconces along both walls.

On the altar's right side, a tall youth sat on a chair, playing a kinnora like Janesca's. The congregation sang with him in that strange, throaty Ehretan language.

A kneeling bench, cushioned in red with a smooth wooden rail, had been moved to the center of the dais, in front of the altar.

She approached it.

Brennen gripped her hand. He'd longed for this day, never guessing it would come here, but the Speaker's timing was always perfect.

He glanced at the young kinnora player and smiled. Someday—probably soon, since Mari would be anxious to meet him—she would find out that this solemn sekiyr was Ellet Kinsman's brother.

Fill her heart, Holy One. Her eternal standing was already assured, but this rite never left a consecrant unchanged. Besides, ceremony meant the world to Netaians, especially to Mari.

Dabarrah had also made him a special promise, for afterward.

Firebird looked up as they reached the aisle's end. Master Dabarrah's eyes shone with the solemn joy she'd seen in Brennen on other holy occasions.

"Come," he said, beckoning them up the three steps. As they stepped onto the dais, he said, "Brennen, take off your shoes, for this is now holy ground."

Brennen left them on the steps. Firebird peered forward. Sure enough, Master Jenner and the musician also stood barefoot.

She smiled slightly. They probably didn't kick off their shoes as often as she did.

Standing before the small bench, she reviewed all she'd studied with her Path instructor. Fortunately, Dabarrah asked, and she could answer, in familiar Old Colonial. Brennen's consecration had been done in the High mode, entirely in Ehretan.

Not long ago, she had sat on a chapter-room bench on Thyrica, listening while Destia Caldwell answered the same questions. She would never forget patting a handful of tear-dampened soil onto Destia's grave. She blinked and swallowed. Surely Destia was safe in the Singer's strong arms.

Master Dabarrah led her through the main tenets of her new faith: the Singer's oneness, His infinite holiness, wisdom, and power, His sovereignty over history. And His merciful love, so different from the unfeeling Powers.

She'd made the right choice.

She made it through her questions without major stumbles. Finally, Dabarrah looked deep into her eyes and her mind and asked, "For what purpose have you come, Firebird Mari Caldwell?"

She answered firmly, as she'd memorized, "To see the sacrifice for my covering."

"Then come and see." Dabarrah laid his hands on the kneeling bench's raised rail.

She stepped away from Brennen, rested her hands between Master

Dabarrah's, and sank onto her knees. *Take a few seconds to get comfortable*, Brennen had warned her. *You'll be there for a while. You don't want your legs to fall asleep.*

The soft harp music started again. She braced herself, then looked up at Dabarrah's gray-blue eyes. *Do your worst*, she thought at him.

He half smiled. "What you will experience," he said, "actually happened to Timarah Gall, a young person of Modabah city, on a morning 190 years ago." The Sentinels sang on, but as Dabarrah's epsilon presence entered her mind, her vision shifted. The chapter room darkened. It grew, stretching into a huge arena . . . no, an auditorium . . . a temple, six-sided, almost totally blacked out. Timarah Gall wore loose, lightweight clothing, as if for a warm summer morning.

Firebird could barely see Dabarrah or the altar. She shut her eyes. Timarah seemed to be tiptoeing behind two men in their twenties, one of whom waved her abruptly to halt.

She listened hard with her epsilon sense . . . and Firebird plunged willingly into the vision. *So this is how turning should feel!* she realized just before she lost all sense of separation from young Timarah.

She pulled hard on a rope wrapped around her left hand. Gently she curled her right fingers around the soft muzzle of a knee-high animal, black-headed with tall, hairless ears, but otherwise covered with an exquisitely soft, curling beige pelt.

It was a kipret, a sacrificial yearling. After searching for a week, she found this one wandering the hills, driven from its pen by raiders.

Ehret lay bleeding, gripped by a war between generations. Her own father had murdered her brother in bed. He'd been reaching for her when she leaped out a window. Her friends had all died. She'd found these two young men, former temple acolytes, by accident—or divine help. The newest peril was plague, a hideous disease created by *her* side.

The young Altereds had sacked the Elders' temple, slaughtering kipreta out of scorn for the ancient faith. Only a few of the new Altereds still bowed to the Speaker, as she did. If Elder forces caught this trio today, they would die gruesomely, with special measures taken to destroy the brain centers the Elders bred into them.

She listened again, questing cautiously outside each door as she stroked the kipret's furry head. It licked her forearm, then butted her leg. Unfortunately, she'd grown fond of the moronic creature. They came here before dawn, hoping to finish and escape undetected.

She'd put off this appointment for too many months. Then the war erupted. Surprisingly, she found herself clinging to faith as friends died around her. The Speaker couldn't look on imperfection, though, and she was full of old lies, selfishness . . . and now hatred too. She stood condemned by her conscience and by the repentant but deadly determined Elders who once worshiped here. Coming here might cost her life, but if she made it down these steps, she could die with every possible assurance.

The others crept forward. *Hurry*, one urged subvocally.

Releasing the kipret's muzzle and tugging its rope, she followed. *This won't hurt*, she tried to assure it. *They'll be quick*. Still, she wanted to drop the rope, slap its rump, and drive it away—to save its life, rescue it.

Instead, she led it down, down the long stairstepped aisle to the platform at center. Two high altars shared that platform. She hurried the stiff-legged beast up three steps. A cold breeze blew through shattered black windows.

The men pushed her into position between the altars. She knelt with her arms around the furry kipret's neck, repelled by what she had to do, comforted only by the sweet, blank-faced idiocy that had been bred into kipreta. "I've come," she murmured. "I'm here, Eternal Speaker, to see the sacrifice for my covering. Thank you for purifying my heart, for joining me with you in eternal communion. When my death comes," she added, glancing up at one of the six huge doors, praying no Elder forces waited outside, "take me to yourself. Accept my faith, small though it is. So let it be."

One of the men brought up a large wooden bowl. He set it on the rubble-strewn floor in front of the kipret, who started to nibble a ripped curl of carpet.

The other moved close, gripping a gleaming knife. Bone handled, that blade was almost as long as her forearm. "Hold its head up," he ordered.

She swallowed hard and tugged on the rope. Bile rose in her own throat. She squeezed her eyes shut.

She heard one gargling bleat, and then the rope wrenched her arm straight. She let go.

The kipret had collapsed over the bowl. The older man dropped his knife, wiped his hands on the twitching creature's back, and curled his fingers around her head, reciting the Scriptures that promised her full acceptance.

Moving quickly, they worked as a team to haul the kipret by its legs onto the higher altar. Tears thickened her eyes as she carefully bent its still-warm limbs. Blood stained its chest and back.

The younger man knelt beside the bowl. Shuddering, she crouched beside him. The creature's blood smelled more like metal than meat.

Now she must identify, symbolically, with the kipret's death. She could finish her part with a drop . . . or by immersion. Considering the price she might pay for it, she wanted the full experience. She pulled a deep breath, eyeing the bowl that now looked in dim light to be full of blackness. *That's the kipret's very life*, she thought, staring at it. *Now it's death . . . a bowl full of death . . . because I needed covering.* Everyone who ever lived had fallen into disobedience. . . .

Blackness flamed at the depth of that bowl. Suddenly Firebird felt herself flung out of the ritual. The blackness licked up as it had done at the depth of her mind, luring her down, drawing her in. It called to her, singing of power and mastery and death. Consecration? A ludicrous hope. Eternal music? Only the black silence was real. *Turn*, it sang. *Turn, turn to me, instead. . . .*

Master Jenner! she thought frantically. *Help!*

Dabarrah's epsilon presence folded around her. The vision refocused. No more flames roiled in the bloody bowl—symbol of life, and then death, and finally the most sacred atonement promised for all her transgressions. She only needed to take a drop on one finger and touch the skin over her heart.

She hesitated, appalled by its gruesome, sticky-looking reality and feeling—for once—completely separate from every offense she'd ever committed.

Firebird identified utterly with Timarah. She'd hated, she'd lied, she'd broken her own promises. She still served Excellence and Pride instead of the Speaker's will. *I've bloodied my hands, even though they look clean.*

She made it her confession and plunged both hands to the bottom of the bowl.

The elder acolyte pushed a soft cloth at Timarah. She wiped her hands and wrists, pausing to touch one finger to her chest, knowing that would stain her best pleated tunic. Now she was marked. If they caught her before she could bathe and change, they would know why she had come and would punish her for desecrating the altar. Altereds were no longer eligible to offer sacrifice. Elders decapitated her kind for a bounty.

One man raised the bowl to the high altar and draped the cloth over it. The poor kipret lay with its eyes and mouth open, its thick pink tongue clearly visible. Firebird shuddered at the contrast between the living beast and this stiffening corpse. She hated herself for luring it into her arms with honey flowers, when it could've gone on grazing wild in the hills.

Her offenses had turned its life into death. Only One could restore life. . . .

The other man hurried to the low altar. He fingered open a hidden panel and reached for a control. *Ready?* he subvocalized.

As her hands dried, they tingled and itched. She dropped to a runner's crouch and faced one aisle. The other acolyte's footsteps pounded off in another direction.

Ready, she sent back. She must stand on the dais as he fired the altar. . . .

A whoosh filled the temple. Orange light illuminated all six walls as flames consumed corpse, bowl, and blood, and she ran for her life. . . .

Disoriented, Firebird clutched the kneeling rail. Master Dabarrah was speaking again, but she didn't understand him. Her hands felt wet. Cringing, she opened her eyes and looked down at them.

Not blood but her own tears glistened there. Relieved, but more repelled than ever, she wiped her eyes, mortified that the Ehretans had been told animal sacrifice was necessary. And yet . . . yet, as a teaching tool, it worked. Her insides roiled, whipped by revulsion, both of the ritual killing and of the darkness in her own heart and mind. Darkness like a deep, black bowl full of blood, like consuming dark flames. She'd never despised evil so deeply before.

She'd just recited to Dabarrah that the Speaker could not be approached by uncovered imperfection. Now she felt it at gut level. Before giving her life to the Mighty Singer, she was repulsive to His holiness, every bit as offensive as a bloody-handed killer, despite all the goodness she could claim. Somehow He'd placed her under His own protection, loving her because she reflected His image—not for her accomplishments. The Adversary could not snatch her away.

A large hand pressed down on her head. Still struggling for self-control, she took several breaths. She'd sensed, she'd shared, Timarah Gall's sympathy for the innocent kipret. She'd never had a pet of her own, but she adored the small animals Carradee brought home. *Was this truly necessary?* she begged the Singer.

"Draw comfort from this assurance," Master Jenner announced to her and the congregation. He lifted his hand from her head and touched the underside of her chin. She looked up. In his other hand, he cradled a copy of *Dabar*. He read several sentences in Ehretan.

Close behind her, just as he promised he'd be, Brennen translated. "You are my beloved; you are mine. Your transgressions lie beyond the sacrifice, separated from you as far as the galaxy's hub from the outermost worlds. Be not afraid, but comforted."

The congregation kept singing. Firebird realized she'd heard music continue throughout the grim vision, beneath her consciousness . . . amplifying her emotions, making her even more solemn and sad.

She blinked, still slightly nauseated. She reminded herself that she knelt at Hesed. No one waited outside those double doors to lop off her loathsome head. She wouldn't have to pick out a herd beast to die on this altar. She checked her fingernails anyway, making sure they weren't crusted with blood.

The sekiyr who'd opened the door walked forward, carrying a circlet of white ribbons and flowers. She gave it to Brennen. He laid it over Firebird's hair like a crown. She tried to smile back at him, but she still felt more stunned than satisfied. Now she knew why Destia had risen white-faced from that kneeling bench.

Brennen steadied her as she stood, then took both her hands and faced her, keeping his back to the altar, so that she looked up over his shoulder at the beveled star that seemed to float over the altar flame. She would never see that flame again without remembering one poor beast whose body burned on a much older altar.

Master Jenner still held the book. "We depart now from the usual rite, Firebird Mari." He raised a hand and spoke in a strong baritone, using the unintelligible Ehretan.

Weren't they finished? Firebird wanted only to relax, to rest, to think about what she'd just seen.

"Hear the words of the prophet Melauk." Brennen translated Dabarrah's quotation, but she paid little attention. She could almost feel the planet spinning under her soles, but she couldn't focus on Brennen's voice until he nearly finished speaking. She caught only the last few words, ". . . who shall rule over all worlds and peoples."

She raised her head, wanting to ask him to repeat what he had said.

Dabarrah reached up and spoke again.

Brennen's hands tightened momentarily on hers. He must've felt her senses start to return. "Hear the words of the prophet Renonna," he said, looking into her eyes. "From you shall spring the Mighty One, Word to Come, king of all nations and tongues, eternal and merciful."

Suddenly she realized what she was hearing. These were the prophecies she wanted to hear, and he'd longed to explain.

Dabarrah spoke again.

Then Brennen, solemn-faced: "Hear the words of the prophet Amar. You are few but precious, and My hand shall be on you forever. . . ."

". . . In Him shall perfect peace, true atonement, be fully accomplished. In Him is your covering swept away, made unnecessary, and drowned with your offenses in the depths of forgiveness. . . ."

"Out of you, Carabohd, shall come this mighty One, and all the worlds shall worship . . ."

". . . and in His hand shall be power to unmake all that His hand once made; unmake the universe and form it again, perfectly, as in the beginning. A new song you shall sing. . . ."

Brennen spoke firmly, without hesitating on any of the Scriptures, and she realized he wasn't even translating. He'd committed these verses to memory.

Her eyes dried as she stared, stunned a second time. *Our child?* she thought at him. *This could be our child?*

Still reciting, he finally smiled. He laid his hand on her arm and turned back toward the holy flame.

The Sanctuary Master laid a hand on her forehead. She heard the Ehretan voice modulation as he solemnly commanded her never to speak thoughtlessly of what she'd just heard, and not to reveal it at all to a non-consecrant.

Brennen had been under this very command, all along. Now she joined him in this too.

Our child? No wonder Alert Forces defended Kiel and Kinnor!

The musician steadied his harp again. The congregation started a hymn. Firebird recognized it, but she couldn't find her voice. Dabarrah laid his book on the altar, then gripped her shoulder and Brennen's, murmuring, "May He bless you both." Then he stepped away.

He could have formed inside my body?

Brennen looked deeply into her eyes, and she felt another steadying caress before he turned his head toward the door. Feeling deeply self-conscious, Firebird faced a hundred eager eyes. The other Sentinels kept singing, but now she knew why Brennen and Dabarrah had conspired to tell her these things here. This let the faith community see and sense the awe she felt as she finally learned what was promised to Brennen's lineage—and now hers. They would pass down this memory, honoring her as one of themselves, sharing and remembering her awe.

She wanted to smile at them, but she seemed to have lost control of her face, as well as her voice. Walking in step with Brennen, she hurried toward the double door. As she stepped off carpet onto flagstones, she exclaimed, "Your shoes!"

Brennen laughed, and the strong set of his shoulders softened. "I'll go back for them another time." He steered her along the stone wall, out of sight of anyone inside. Then he seized her and held her close, murmuring against her ear, "Yes, Mari. Our child. Or one of our descendants. Word to

Come, Holy Messenger, King of the New Universe. All the might of the Speaker, in human form."

She held tightly, still trying to imagine such a person even existing, let alone calling her one of His ancestors.

And she'd grown up forbidden to even consider having children!

"Brenn," she mumbled, "could we be alone for a while?" She still had a head full of glistening fog.

Brennen nodded. "We don't have to stay."

They hurried back to their room, found shoes, and then walked up the stony hillside once more. At a large flat rock, they sat in the mountain valley's vast silence, staring up at snowy peaks and speaking in whispers.

At one point, it occurred to her, *Now I know why Ellet wanted him.* Irked with herself for even thinking such a thing, she thrust it away. *Kiel?* she wondered. *Could He be . . . my Kiel?* Or did Kinnor's struggle for comfort with physical life mean that he came from a better existence?

Undoubtedly, Brennen's mother had wondered this about him and Tarance.

Brennen's deep peace eventually brought her back to the valley, comforting her even as he remembered—vividly, she knew—being given that ritual memory. "It's said," he told her, "that everyone sees something different, deep in that bowl. Don't worry," he added quickly. "I won't ask. That's between you and the Holy One."

She nodded. "I won't ask, either." White ribbons fluttered around her face as she curled forward, closing her eyes. *Thank you, Holy Singer,* she prayed, *that Kiel and Kinnor are safe here. Give them back to me soon.*

And while she was at it . . .

Singer, there isn't much time, but you're so good at mercy. Change Brennen's mind. Hurry, she begged as she clutched both hands into fists. *Give him another dream tonight, a better one. Keep him here, if you love him as much as I do.* What renegade would bloody his evil hands by taking Brennen's life?

No, she begged, doubling over. Brennen seized her shoulders and tried to flood her with comfort, but nothing could touch this grief, because she hadn't yet suffered the loss.

CHAPTER 19

FOR HESED

offertorium
presentation of the offering

Carradee limped into her dusky sitting room. Regeneration treatments and three lightweight braces had her back on her feet, but a servitor waited just outside with a mobility chair.

Sandy-haired Governor Danton rose to greet her. She extended a hand. "Excellency," she said in a soft voice. "You wished to bring news personally and not through our acting Regent. Are our girls safely hidden away?" She seated herself beneath a dark window.

He took his own wing-back chair again. "Madame, we could not hear of their safe arrival for several days yet. There is a long communication lag. But official news has arrived from Thyrica regarding Lady Firebird."

"Ah! Do we have a niece?"

Danton's lips twitched as if he wanted to smile. "Your sister delivered twins, Madame."

"Twins!" Carradee laced her fingers. "There's no twinning in *our* family."

"Fraternal brothers." Danton crossed his legs and leaned back. "Kiel Labbah and Kinnor Irion."

Carradee's hands fell limp on her lap. Brothers?

He beamed. "She sent us messages some months ago that her medical practitioner had discovered a distinctly Ehretan syndrome. Remember?"

Carradee rose off her chair. Scarcely noticing that Danton stood too, out of protocol, she took a few tentative steps down the patterned carpet. "She was treated. I do remember. We discussed that. Phoena nearly died of rage at the suggestion."

"Yes, Madame." He stepped to her side and offered his arm.

"When Daithi is . . . better," she said, remembering her beloved lying paralyzed on his bed, "perhaps I, too, should be . . . treated. Quietly." She faced him. "Can your medics hold their tongues?"

"Of course, Majesty."

"I cannot decide now. Later. Thank you for coming, Governor. Is there any other message you wish to give me?"

"No, Majesty."

"Is there no . . ." She would prefer to sound queenly, but she was deeply afraid. "No more sign of Shuhr activity here?"

"None," he answered.

"I—we hear you won a great victory yesterday." She limped to a chair and sat down. She'd been warned not to walk too much yet. "In the Assembly."

"That was not my victory. It belongs to your people. The first three ministerial monopolies have fallen."

The Ministries of Agriculture and Aquaculture had been under pressure from the low-common class for decades. Science had lost all real power when information started to flow from the Federacy. "So the door has cracked open." She frowned up at him. "Where will it end, Danton? Will you destroy the noble class?"

He crossed his arms high on his chest. "No! Its grandeur, and much of its wealth, can be maintained even if some riches are reinvested to benefit more people."

"Reinvested?" she asked wryly. "Sir, your new taxes will wipe us out."

"No," he exclaimed again. "Majesty, the Federacy cannot bear the whole cost of upgrading your world's defenses—"

"Though your battle group destroyed them?"

He spread his hands. "Madame, your predemilitarization defenses wouldn't have turned an attack like the one at Sunton. Your class is now fulfilling a role it always claimed—that of protectors. You wouldn't run to the countryside while the Shuhr attacked Citangelo. The Powers honor charity," he reminded her.

"And Discipline." Sunton images from the newsnets haunted her. "You've made no move toward reforming our penal system. We have watched closely."

"Why, madame?"

Her cheek twitched. "Lee, I don't want to watch Firebird die by millimeters. I think I know something, now, of what other Netaians suffered when their loved ones were sentenced to execution. My class shows little sympathy for the commoner or the servitor. Yet they too love their children," she said, faltering. Where were Iarlet and Kessie bound, and how soon would she see them again? Gathering her poise, she folded her hands. "Daithi's condition is showing me something that disturbs me, Governor."

"Majesty?"

She shook her head. "Swear silence, Danton."

He raised both eyebrows. "I do."

She glanced all around. Her most loyal servitors kept this sitting room secure, but that naturally made it a target for Rogonin and the electoral police. The Electorate, not the Crown, was Netaia's highest governing body. Breaking protocol, she beckoned Danton closer. He bent toward her. "That penal system is founded in our worship of the Powers, Governor."

His eyes widened. "Majesty?" he whispered.

Carradee bit her lip. She'd said too much, hinted too plainly at her painful doubts. Since her accession, she'd signed over twenty execution orders, including Firebird's . . . and twice that many reductions to servitor status. Although the holy Powers required their priestly electoral representatives to practice charity, their laws—their penal system—offered none. Each time Carradee signed one of those orders, her heart cried, *This is wrong! Electors aren't omniscient. We've made mistakes, but we're never allowed to forgive.* . . .

Straightening, she extended a hand in dismissal. He touched his lips to it and stood, then left the chamber with one glance over his shoulder.

Carradee rang for her servitor. A middle-aged woman hurried into the chamber, steering a sleek mobility chair. Carradee sank into it gratefully.

My children . . . She'd made it a point to spend time with Iarlet and Kessie, far more than she'd been given by Queen Siwann. She missed their adoring faces, their soul-tickling laughter.

And her husband . . .

She guided the chair toward a slender pole lamp. Danton didn't know—couldn't be told—that the finest medics on Netaia barely kept Daithi alive. He lay in their temporary apartment, a wastling's suite, sedated as heavily as they dared keep him. Quietly, with Rogonin—whose work as her temporary Regent, until she could settle her familial concerns, had been irreproachable—she had finally agreed that they must try to conceive another child, a wastling. The electors demanded that assurance that a noble line would continue if anything unforeseen happened. She hated the idea, but for the sake of stability in unstable times, she must make the sacrifice.

But the act proved impossible, and electoral law would automatically disbar any heir medically conceived.

Daithi did have moments of painful lucidity, granted by the doctors who felt even the safest sedatives couldn't be administered continually. Daithi understood the situation. If anything happened to Iarlet and Kessie, he would feel it his duty . . .

No. He mustn't, she wailed to herself.

. . . to suicide, leaving her free to marry again as her own proper service to the Electorate.

Phoena too was an heiress of this house. Appalled by Phoena's defection, Carradee intended to quietly and privately eliminate Phoena from her list of personal heirs. Officially, she couldn't afford to do so (*not in front of Rogonin!*). That would leave only—

Carradee sat upright. Did Firebird truly have sons? If they were confirmed as heirs . . . even only one . . . that might buy Daithi time. By Netaian tradition, the second-born was considered to be first conceived and was therefore the true elder. That would be . . . Kinnor Irion?

Her servitor hung back by the door. A huge, glowering portrait hung between two high windows, and Carradee raised her hand to touch its ornate frame. *Could I have Kinnor Irion named a reserve heir?*

Rogonin would oppose it, of course. But what about the others? *There are more male than female electors. They might support the possibility of naming a prince.* If they could be made to understand that the Angelo line was part . . . Ehretan . . . already and had served Netaia for three centuries, then maybe the electors couldn't consider Brennen Caldwell's heritage alien.

Glancing up at the glaring, long-dead grand duke, she snatched her hand away from the portrait's frame. *Oh yes, they could!* They could even strip the throne from the Angelo dynasty. The Electorate had that right.

Her sense of heritage rebelled. She gazed out over the lights of Citangelo, broken only by the Tiggaree River's sluggish swath. Even the city carried her name. There would be no new taxation, no costly particle-shield generators under construction, if Netaia weren't now a Federate protectorate—if Siwann hadn't attacked Veroh.

Painfully she recalled her mother's masterful way with her electors. The queen was a legal figurehead, but Siwann had been a real ruler, adored by her electors. Only once in Carradee's memory had an elector dared to countervote Siwann on a unanimity order. That stubborn young honorary elector had been Firebird, on the occasion of initiating the tragic Veroh War.

Firebird had been right to oppose that conflict. It changed Netaian history forever.

Carradee drew herself erect. *I'll be strong. I must.*

Brennen let no one but Firebird see him leave.

They stood on the scarred, grassy breakaway strip beside his RIA-modified craft, clinging to each other.

"No regrets." He kissed her cheek. "This is my calling. You knew my work when you married me. I'd take you again if you'd have me."

She felt one of his legs press against her own, smelled his warm breath, gripped his fingers. "You'd do it again, knowing that in bonding with me, you got a willful, proud woman who had to learn to turn—and Phoena in the bargain?"

"Yes." Tenderly he pressed his lips to her other cheek. "Be patient. Grow in faith."

"I love you," she answered. "I'll always love you. Go and fulfill your part of the prophecies."

His surge of love and gratitude burned as he covered her lips with his own, held tight, then pulled reluctantly away. From the pocket of his belt he drew his bird-of-prey medallion on its gold chain. "Keep this." Her hand closed on the memento of his childhood. "Stay close to Dabarrah until you're healed. I'd serve Shamarr Dickin by living or dying, but Master Jenner I trust out of love. He and Mistress Anna will do everything for you that can be done."

"You'll be back," she insisted. "And on track for the High command."

Smiling gently, he swung up into the cockpit with the briefest glance over his shoulder. Firebird clutched the golden bird and backed away. The dawn sky was thickening to rain, as on the spring morning when they had lain in a stone shelter just upriver from here, with all the worlds and the future in their hands.

The hatch swung shut. Firebird felt his anguish, tangibly distinguishable from her own, gradually disappear under attention to procedure as the generators' howl modulated into purring sublight engines. She knew she should cover her ears, but she couldn't. That roar meant Brennen was still here. The silvery craft rose, seemed to hover a moment, and then streaked skyward. She clung to the awareness of his presence as it slipped from her. Farther . . . fainter . . .

It flickered and went out. The roar faded.

Incredibly, the sun rose over the Hesed Valley, even though Brennen had left it. Firebird sat through a lengthy *Dabar* reading in the commons, then went at Master Jenner's request to his private study. Motioning her to take a wooden chair near his desk, the lanky blond master seated himself. "Are you all right, Mistress Firebird?"

Firebird crossed her ankles under her chair. "Not really," she muttered. Her chest ached as if someone had kicked her. She wanted to lie down and sleep until Brennen came back.

Dabarrah extended a hand across the desk. "It's normal for the pair bonded to grieve when separated. We learn to deal with the depression.

Unquestionably, Brennen is feeling the same."

You're trained, she protested silently. *And so is he.*

"He warned you to expect this?"

She clenched her fingers. "Master, everything that matters except my faith has been taken away from me. How would you react?"

He drew back his hand, but the compassionate arch of his eyebrows didn't relax. "Then, are you prepared to see what can be done? It's possible that you had less to do with Harcourt Terrell's death than we've had to assume."

"For Kiel and Kinnor's safety. That's the only reason I can stand this isolation."

"I'd like you to turn again now. I'll observe from a distance, well shielded."

"All right." Could she even do it, feeling this way? If she succeeded, she wondered how he would react. To rally for the effort, she would have to forget the Dark's fiery, seductive pain.

"I'm here for you, my lady."

She steeled herself and pressed inward. No sense of a probe followed, so Dabarrah had to be shielding heavily. Twice she called up her vision of the stone wall and recoiled. Forcing herself to focus, she pressed through.

The searing darkness engulfed her. Burning in every nerve, she groped toward the glimmering cords of energy. She took a deep breath, dove toward one cord, and grabbed it. It stabbed, it strangled, it scalded, its energy steeped in the anguish that had surrounded it so long. Humbled by this scar of her wastling years, she let go of the turn and opened her eyes.

Dabarrah paced rapidly from wall to wall, clear across the room. It was so unlike him—unlike any Sentinel—to show such agitation that Firebird stared, speechless. Had she done something peculiar to him too?

At last he sank back into his desk chair, furrowing his forehead. "Now," he said, "now I understand." Firebird wondered if he realized how rapidly he was speaking. "I must think this through. How—I'm sorry, Firebird, I'm not feeling myself. Let me think. . . . Thank you. Oh," he added as she stood, embarrassed and frustrated. "Well done. Your turn. A remarkable feat for one of your age and background."

"Thank you," Firebird mumbled. She started to hurry away, but paused just short of the archway. "Master? What is that, inside my mind?"

He raised his head and drew a deep breath. "Come back in, Lady Firebird. I didn't mean to send you away."

She dragged back to her chair and sat down. "Please," she said. "Tell me what you think it is."

He moved his chair closer. "Hear me through. Don't take offense before I finish."

Not an auspicious beginning. "All right," she said slowly.

"I believe you've been given a terrible gift. You've been shown the evil, the Adversary's own foothold, inside your heart. We're all touched by darkness, but few truly know it."

Firebird's head came up. She'd entertained that thought, but only under the duress of childbirth. Since then she'd had time to reconsider. "But I'm accepted now. I'm covered."

"Let me finish," Dabarrah insisted. "I'm not singling you out."

She nodded cautiously. *We deserve death*, she heard in her mind. *We're not holy enough to survive in the Holy One's presence.*

"You admitted before the altar that He can't tolerate imperfection, and that you aren't perfect. Firebird, when we merely say that we're flawed, the necessity of atonement seems barbaric."

"Yes," she murmured, still sorry that poor beast had been slaughtered.

"But if we feel the reality behind those words, we'll do anything He asks, anything, for His assurance that we can be freed from evil."

Firebird frowned. Her motive for seeking consecration hadn't been that pure. She'd also wanted to hear Brennen explain the prophecies. "Those aren't my shortcomings behind that wall. Master, I'm willing to fight evil to the death, but . . . that Darkness isn't my character." —Despite the Electorate's death sentence! Incongruously, her one unconfessed crime sprang to mind. Alef Drake, Prince Daithi's younger brother, would have been executed for geis refusal if she hadn't helped fake his death while he escaped Netaian space.

She shoved the memory aside. It was irrelevant here.

Dabarrah rested his chin on one hand. "We are exalted creatures, made in an immaculate image and likeness, but born with tainted souls. Our very nature is a paradox. Even at our best, our thoughts and our actions are . . . less than perfect."

Firebird straightened her pale blue skirt. "If everyone's evil inside, then how can you explain the fact that others—outside this community—have been loving and serving each other, even dying for people they never met, for hundreds and thousands of years?"

"That is the original image. The way we were sung into existence," he said. She'd shown him her beautiful vision, opening her memory to him, shortly after they met. "In the end," he added, "it isn't a sacrifice that makes us His willing servants. It is our own dying to personal ambition and fully accepting His life in us."

Dying? Firebird snorted. "Master, I sacrificed myself once for a religion. I'll really die, eventually, but I'm not in a hurry anymore."

"I'm not speaking of physical death. Dying to willfulness would release you from your final bondage to self. It would let you serve a higher purpose—and be at peace."

Willfulness. Wouldn't they ever let her forget that wretched character screening? She crossed her arms and steered the conversation aside. "I know what I see when I try to turn. When I was little, I believed that the Powers punish disobedience after our death. I created a mental image to scare myself into submission. That image is exactly what I see. It's only an image, a memory—not evil itself."

"It was not memory I just accessed. I know how to identify memories on an alpha matrix."

She stared straight ahead. "Master, why has the Singer let evil exist? Real evil, like Brennen has gone into?" —though she couldn't dwell on that if she hoped to carry on a rational conversation.

"That," said Dabarrah, "is the strangest and deepest miracle. He made us independent from His infinitude. Think of it. We're even capable of acting against Him and deliberately working evil."

Independent from infinitude, which was everywhere. . . . For an instant, she grasped the incomprehensible. "Yes!" Then she wilted. "But it isn't turn-darkness that's keeping me away from Kiel and Kinnor," she reminded him.

He shook his head slowly. "No. It's the fear that you would harm them accidentally."

If she had killed a grown man, what could she do to an infant? "I'm willing to cooperate, Master. Tell me what to do."

Dabarrah smiled gently. "Give me two or three days to create a strategy. I promise, we won't rest until those children are back in your arms."

Two or three days? How would she fill all those empty hours?

"Master," she said suddenly, "I started a degree through Soldane University. Could I do course work here?"

"Excellent idea. Tomorrow, I'll set you up with one of the sekiyrra's tutorials."

She spent the rest of that day working outdoors with two sekiyrra, pulling spent garnetberry canes. Fine brown thorns dug through her gloves and pierced her hands, but she hardly noticed.

Singer, how could you do this to Brennen and me? Don't you love him . . . like I do?

Startled by the thought, she dropped a handful of spent canes. Was this heartaching flicker jealousy? How could she be jealous of the Eternal Singer?

But surely, even He couldn't love Brennen as deeply as she did.

Ashamed, she blanked the notion. Only Phoena could be that petty.

Yet why should it surprise her if sometimes she could act very much like both of her sisters?

Be with Carradee, she prayed. *Strengthen and guide her. And . . . and Phoena . . .*

Her hesitation stretched into a numb silence. She couldn't pray for Phoena, not even now. For Phoena, Brennen was preparing to offer himself like a kipret led unknowingly to the high altar.

But unlike a kipret, Brennen knew what could happen there.

Ellet Kinsman flung down a pile of hard copies and addressed the ceiling of her close little cubicle. "Any deadbrain with the Second Division could've done this!" Brennen had taken his sons to Hesed, and here she sat, on the Special Operations floor of the MaxSec Tower, at Regional headquarters on Tallis. Stuck on a dimwit's job. She'd expected important liaison work.

Sighing, she sent a flicker of epsilon energy at her desktop to sweep papers together. Daylight streamed through the window on her left. Through her open door drifted other workers' voices.

Regional command had just sent a full military division and a fact-finding team to Thyrica. To Three Zed went a strenuous warning to expect retaliation . . . not nearly enough, in Ellet's opinion. Retaliation should be swift, unannounced, and irresistible. Regional command didn't have the technology to break Three Zed's fielding, though. The Shuhr were as invulnerable as Hesed itself, behind the same kind of fielding-satellite web.

Except that now, Thyrica's Alert Forces were developing RIA. She wondered how long that secret would last if the Shuhr struck again. She'd filed a supplemental report with the SO office, recommending a general security upgrade on all Federate worlds.

Meanwhile, she found another compensation in being on Tallis. She undoubtedly knew more than Firebird herself about the current Netaian situation, about the secessionist element's attempt to set up a long-term regency, and the underlying movement to dethrone Carradee. Carradee's weakness and "alien blood" were both factors. Losing her royal connections would cure Firebird's pride.

Ellet scanned the top page of her official business again. It was a policy review, regarding the status of the Carolinian mining colony, Veroh. Brennen had watched the Netaian invasion of Veroh, witnessed the horror of weapons that sterilized air and ground for centuries. Apparently, the last colonists were struggling to keep Veroh's basium mines open—a skeleton crew, men without families, only enough of them to maintain the mining robots. But the Netaian attack left deadly radiation in the atmosphere. Regional was drafting a recommendation that Caroli evacuate Veroh permanently. No dome, no matter how well shielded, would block all radiation. No wonder the use of flash weapons was forbidden by so many treaties.

Scorch those Netaians! All of them!

Ellet pulled the review board hard copy from its slot, reconsidered it, then dropped it in again. She wanted lunch. Another day, and she'd be sent back to Soldane.

She rested her head and arms on her desktop. Could she get to Hesed instead?—and once there, could she convince Firebird to rescue her sister? She'd conceived a plan, playing on Firebird's pride, impatience, and willfulness, but she would have to set it in motion herself, there at Hesed.

Ellet wasn't due for fielding rotation for years, though. She wasn't sick, needing sanctuary. The only legitimate excuse that would justify a trip to sanctuary would be pair bonding, and despite Damalcon Dardy's hints and meaningful epsilon touches, she was not a candidate for that state.

Not while Mistress Firebird lived.

Ellet pressed a control surface on her desk top, darkening her window glass. Then she shut her eyes to think.

CHAPTER **20**

THREE ZED

pianissimo
extremely softly

The Shuhr had settled a planetary system deep inside the Whorl, above the galactic plane. Its single temperate planet lay just outside a dense asteroid belt. Over decades, to supplement their fielding net, they had dragged many of those asteroids into orbits so skewed from their world's that no pilot could carelessly approach the inner system. Common sense suggested leaving slip-state in its outer reach.

Brennen ignored common sense, trusted his call, and used full particle shields at drop point. He reentered normal space to find himself thousands of kilometers from any danger.

His long-range heavy fighter had two narrow seats that could generously be said to "recline for sleep," a cache of emergency rations, and onboard water recycling. It had been a comfortless trip.

Just outside Three Zed's fielding net, he eased into a long orbit matching the planet's and activated the new RIA unit. He relaxed in his chair and tentatively extended his awareness forward. As in practice on Base One, the sensations that reached him through the experimental RIA relays became slightly blurred. He sifted space above the planet's surface for satellites and orbiting ships. That took several hours.

En route, he'd called up in mnemonic sequence all his dealings with Phoena and searched each encounter for a clue that might win her trust. Unfortunately, he'd never needed to access her thoughts. The puzzle plagued him. If he hadn't already solved it, it might have no answer.

Finally, satisfied that he'd located each fielding satellite, he asked his computer to correlate data. A pattern sprang up on the six screens. Portions of the local fielding net double-covered the planet, but over some areas only a single satellite projected his enemies' epsilon energy. He chose the single-covered area nearest the major colony and turned RIA toward its satellite, shielding himself from a barrage of destructive energies. Against that out-welling he felt inward, into the physical form of the satellite itself. Tracing its circuitry, he found similarities with Hesed's fielding design: resonal circuits, a toroidal juncture. Once he understood the differences, he nudged the energy in one line across a gap to another line, simulating a disruptive meteor pass. The satellite's main power shorted dead.

Quickly, knowing the groundside fielding team's checks could reset the malfunctioning circuit at any moment, he pulled off the RIA headset, engaged steering thrusters, and slid a throttle rod forward, alert for any challenge.

He could've used Firebird's help. She should be in that empty seat, with her alert eyes and keen intuition. She'd been more help than she knew against the Shuhr trap at Thyrica, even despite her watch-link. And he already missed Kinnor and Kiel—with a burst of epsilon static, he cut off his longing to rejoin them. He'd come here because of that family, his love sprouting into the future.

I'll be back, he promised them. *As soon as I finish here*—if the Holy One brought him through the attempt.

And he needed that seat for Phoena.

He dropped through the breach, slipped again into the RIA system, and probed ahead for Three Zed's mass detector. He was still untracked. He set an autopilot course, then again took up the RIA accord. With finely focused attention, he brought the ship closer. He sensed the mass detector's outer field as it started to echo with his craft's presence. His extended consciousness rode a wave down to the main complex. The part of his mind that remained free of RIA directed his left hand to slip-shields. Power to the mass detector dipped as groundside energy guns fired automatically on the threatening object. He might still be unnoticed, though, since bits of meteor debris occasionally passed any fielding satellite, and this system was rich with debris. At the moment that his slip-shields deflected energy, he nudged the mass detector's circuits. On the ground display, his blip vanished.

Once again he turned his attention to guiding the ship toward a toothlike volcanic crag near the major settlement his sensors had detected. On minimal power, with occasional checks through the RIA unit to see if his presence was monitored, he glided between black boulders to a small clear space, fired braking rockets to set down, then secured the ship. He wished he could camouflage it. On this black surface, its silver hull wouldn't go undetected for long.

He checked his uniform and belt pockets. From a hollow in the RIA bank he slid a small metal ring that was actually two rings joined around their circumference. This was a detonator mechanism for the ship's inbuilt explosive system, easier to conceal than a touch card. Now that RIA had proved it could penetrate a fielding net, its value to each side tripled. The Shuhr must not capture the RIA secrets, neither from the ship nor from him. If they took him, he must destroy the RIA craft . . . and take another step he dreaded. Special Ops memory blocks left an agent functional but mentally injured. A psi healer could release the block, but this left scars—memory gaps, personality shifts.

The ring felt cold on his finger and a little too large. He wriggled into an emergency vacuum suit and helmet, sealed and pressurized them, and then activated another security cycle. This one would stun anyone else who tried to gain entry. On his left side, opposite his blazer, he hooked a shock pistol. He wanted both options, the humane and the deadly.

He breathed a prayer as he swung off the ship onto a volcanic landscape. *I am here, as you called. Guide me now.*

A short dash took him to the entry, a panel four meters tall and five wide. It slid open as he approached, designed to admit small craft. He stepped softly through a pitch dark pressurization chamber toward a faint, pulsating blue luma.

Interesting. The outer door might open automatically, but this little side hatch had an epsilon lock, hardened against mental tampering. Fortunately, it wasn't activated. Brennen wanted to study it, but he couldn't take the time. He unsuited, hiding his gear behind bulky machinery. Then he crept out into the lava-tube corridor, surrounding his very presence with a shielding cloud of epsilon static. He remembered Phoena's aura vividly, but he didn't dare extend a quest pulse through any door.

He now walked where no Sentinel had gone and returned alive. He found a lift shaft and plunged to a lower level, looking for an unattended life-support relay, where he might access the complex's main database and find out where Phoena was being kept.

Catching a whiff of greenery, he followed its scent to an unlocked door arch and slipped inside. A vast lava chamber opened in front of him. Meter-wide shelves rose toward its ceiling, each shelf thick with plant growth. Water dripped between planted levels. Dazzling lights glared off the chamber's whitened ceiling and walls.

He stepped to one shelf, intrigued despite his hurry. Something grew on it, plantlike but fleshy and brown.

They cloned edible plant parts. Many Federate worlds used the technology. It seemed so ordinary that he felt encouraged.

He turned a full circle to make sure he was alone, then found a terminal close to the arch, against the fused stone wall. Its main display showed that this was the deepest part of the colony's night cycle—and he saw something else that made his neck hairs stand up. The touchboard's guide keys were labeled in the holy Ehretan language.

These were his kinsmen.

Several minutes of guessing and fiddling with the touchboard finally brought up a record of recent in-out traffic. He keyed cautiously, watching its circuits with care, alert for any alarm mechanism.

Finally he found a power-use map. Here and there on the grid, active circuits showed that some residents of this colony had not gone to sleep.

Then he spotted what he wanted. In a cluster of temporary quarters close to this entry, only one air-circulation system drew power.

Phoena. As the Voice said in his dream, he was never alone.

He tried to access Security next, to plan a route that wouldn't take him past checkpoints. Just as his finger hovered over the final key to break into the security net, he sensed an alarm he'd primed with his previous touch.

He canceled the query, drew his blazer, and edged back out into the corridor.

He heard nothing.

Steel corridors connected the round-roofed lava tubes in this part of the complex. He crept along, wondering if against all expectations he might reach Phoena and escape without a fight. At one point he heard footsteps and sensed a human presence. He backstepped up the corridor and waited until the sound faded away.

He found the door he wanted at the midpoint of another long passway. Carefully he evaluated the palm lock. It seemed unalarmed. He touched it experimentally. A door slid open.

Behind it he found a stark room, furnished with two chairs and a lounger, dimly lit by a freshing-room luma. He started to wave the door shut, then changed his mind. He couldn't cut off his escape route. He must do this quietly.

He tiptoed deeper inside, fully alert but fully shielded, and still holding his blazer ready. This could be someone else's quarters.

But he found Phoena lying on a narrow bed. She wore yellow, a gown of more color than substance. In her sleep she looked helpless, even frightened, and her resemblance to Firebird stirred his pity. He holstered his blazer, stepped to her bedside, and touched her shoulder almost tenderly. If only he could convince her to come away, without fighting him . . .

She rolled over and murmured, "Dru?"

Then her eyes focused. She sprang off the bed like a cat, headed toward the outer room.

Brennen caught her in voice-command just short of the arch.

Watching her dark eyes, he touched her alpha matrix, barely stroking, gently reassuring her. "Phoena," he whispered, using his voice to send calming overtones. "Don't fear me." Her will resisted his as powerfully as Firebird once had done, but Firebird had meant to sacrifice herself, and Phoena's will was unswervingly selfish. He counted to ten slowly before dropping his hand.

"I'm sorry, Your Highness. I'd rather not have done that."

Phoena turned fully around to face him, clenching both hands at her sides, her hot brown eyes narrow and defiant. "Brennen Caldwell," she seethed, fighting the voice-command that kept her whispering. "This time, you two have gone too far." She glared around the bedroom. "Where is she?"

" 'She,' Phoena?"

"Firebird." Phoena took a step backward. "Do you think you can destroy Three Zed the way you took Hunter Height? Are you letting her lay the explosives this time? Only this time it won't work. You'll never leave this place alive, either of you."

"She's not here, Phoena," he answered levelly, stroking again to calm her. "I've come alone. But not to destroy this facility, Your Highness. I've come for you."

"To do what, Caldwell?"

"To save you from the Shuhr before they murder you."

Her body relaxed, and she wheezed out a laugh. "Me? Sentinel, you've created a flattering little fantasy. I am the personal guest of Testing Director Dru Polar—whom, I assure you, is ten times your equal. I have been accepted among these people. I will leave their colony as Queen of Netaia."

As she boasted, he probed. He found an emotional discontinuity at her mind's surface, a scar that could only be caused by repeated, careless breaching and manipulation. Just as he feared, she was not herself—hadn't been for weeks.

He projected more understanding and respect into her subconscious, focusing his energies in a narrow pattern. "I came on behalf of your husband, Phoena. Prince Tel asked for my help, hoping to rescue you himself. I wouldn't let him try."

"For your information," she snarled, "I only married Tel to get Carradee off my elbow." She sat down on the other side of the narrow bed. "Carradee is a simpering idiot with no feel for the dignity of the throne. And Tel—"

"The Shuhr have lulled your defenses," he interrupted. "I would show you what they've done to your mind, but there's no time. You're in terrible danger. They're not letting you see it."

She met his stare, resisting him with unembarrassed hatred. "You were stupid to come," she whispered. "I'm not leaving. And the second you're gone, I intend to call Dru. And Micahel," she added cheerfully.

He didn't see an interlink in either of these rooms. The poor, deluded fool couldn't call anyone. "Then for the sake of your family, I must take you unwilling." He angled one hand slightly and modulated his voice to command again. "Come with me. Keep silent."

She opened her mouth to protest, but now no sound came at all. He slowly lowered the hand. Still she didn't move. Satisfied with his hold on her, he stepped toward the outer door.

"Come," he ordered.

Her fury flamed beneath the compliant exterior, and for an instant he wondered how in the Whorl Tellai would win her back.

That, he told himself, *is Tel's problem. Mine is to get her to the ship.* "Your Highness, if we're caught they'll destroy us both. You must believe me. Even Testing Director Dru Polar has no affection for you. Give me your help." He searched her eyes for warmth but found none. Even after all his subtle stroking, he expected none.

He stole out the door and sensed Phoena's surprise. Couldn't she have opened it? He amplified her sudden fear. A chance—maybe a last chance to win her. "Yes, Phoena," he whispered. "You came on your own, but they made you a prisoner. I want to free you."

The escape route he planned took them down one more level, through a darkened maintenance area, toward the hatchway where he'd entered.

The inner door had been shut.

He pressed the palm panel, then probed the locking circuits. Nothing happened.

They have to keep their children indoors, he told himself firmly. *Particularly if they do breed for talent.* "Where did you come in?" he asked Phoena, then forced the knowledge from her memory. There was a magnificent chamber, a golden-walled tube. Impressed, he nudged her. "Show me." He turned her toward a corridor that bypassed the heart of the facility and made her run.

Shuhr. Ahead. He felt the flickering energy of their epsilon matrices, heard audible voices. He shielded himself.

The muttering stopped. Brennen edged closer to Phoena, drew his blazer, and modulated his carrier for access, to command a breach deep into her alpha matrix. He could hide her if he acted quickly.

Leaning against a sparkling wall, gasping and panting, she shook her head and squeezed her eyes shut.

He pulled out his shock pistol left-handed, backed out of the deadly point-blank range, and fired. Phoena crumpled to the floor, unconscious and undetectable—now. As he hoisted her onto his shoulders, measured footsteps drew closer. They halted, then retreated again.

Maybe they hadn't felt her presence. They might know of some poorly guarded exit. If he quested skillfully, they might not sense him—

A foreign quest pulse brushed past him. Instantly he withdrew his own. Balancing Phoena over one shoulder to keep his blazer arm free, he ran back toward the rim of the colony, down a long duracrete ramp. From his trained memory he called up the map he'd seen at that terminal. He could try several ways out. Surely not all routes were guarded. He paused and risked another probe.

The counterblow nearly stunned him.

Down another side tunnel he pelted at a dead run. At every corner he raised his arm to fire, then let it fall and pump. Phoena wasn't light. How long would it take them to seal the complex?

Abruptly he felt a powerful presence close behind. He shielded himself with all the static he could raise.

It wasn't enough. He'd never felt such energy. It drew closer, suffused with the assurance that he could not escape. He blocked fatigue from his awareness and ran on with Phoena bumping on his shoulder. The presence followed without tiring. He passed a dozen doors, all closed. Around one bend farther, out of sight, he sensed other Shuhr in front of him.

Trapped! Breathing heavily, he dropped Phoena into a doorway, then pressed in to stand over her.

Footsteps echoed off to his right. He felt it again: the pursuer, the power. One figure rounded the bend on the left, then another. Which was it?—or were all Shuhr this strong? He stepped without hesitation across the hall and fired. An epsilon howl ripped through his subconscious. More figures appeared ahead.

He fired left, then right, trying to keep the Shuhr at each end of the straightaway. He didn't have time to draw his crystace.

Something lashed his left shoulder. Shock waves whipped through him. He fell senseless.

CHAPTER 21

WELL REWARDED

straziante
anguished

He woke curled on a glassy floor. His left shoulder ached where the shock pistol connected, and his left cheek stung. He blocked the sensations. Multiple presences, foreign and strong, pulsed nearby. He shielded himself from their probing as he ran his right hand down his numb left forearm. They'd already taken his crystace, but his ring remained. Could he still get to the ship?

He stood—slowly, searching the tapestried office with his inner eye for weak spots in the strength that surrounded him, hoping to find one mind open enough to voice-command.

He found only Phoena. She glowed with triumph. Beside a massive black desk, she stood between two men with tangible darkness in their eyes. *Dru Polar and Eshdeth Shirak*, he understood without spoken word.

Dru. Her personal host, whose name she murmured as she awoke. Brennen saw confidence in that dark-browed face and magnetism in his lashless eyes. Beside Polar, Eshdeth Shirak seemed shadowy, though Shirak wore his authority like a broadsword. Subdued resentment sparked between them. If the circle had a weakness, it was that rivalry.

Brennen pulled his heels together and straightened his back. Phoena sidled closer to Polar. "Oh no," she exclaimed in a theatrical soprano. "The Federate revenge for our strike at Sunton. What shall we do?"

"Phoena," Brennen said sternly.

"Brennen," she mocked, warbling his name. She extended an arm with a twisting motion, as if flinging away dirt. "You'll never kidnap me again. Do you believe me now?" She pressed her palms together and struck a graceful pose. "Gentlemen? I would love to see him crawl."

"Naturally." Polar slowly raised a hand. Brennen felt another quest pulse, a foreign mind savoring his dread. As Brennen waited under absolute affective control, the epsilon entity condensed before him that had chased him down Three Zed's halls.

Dru Polar's epsilon presence staggered him.

Command pressure fell on him like invisible wires that circled his limbs and then possessed them, slithering into his bones to move them at another's will. "Crawl to her, Caldwell," Polar sneered.

Brennen didn't waste energy resisting. His body buckled to the glassy floor, and then his arms dragged him to Phoena's feet. She wore shoes now, with small sparkling decorations. As he edged toward them, he realized what he must do. He twisted the halves of his ring, joining the contacts that would blast his escape ship apart. Then he focused deep inside himself. Using a skill that required epsilon power but no turning ability, he cued the Special Operations amnesia block. As it fell like a curtain over his military past, his arms trembled. Bile rose in his throat.

The world blurred for an instant. Then Phoena kicked him full in the face, knocking him over. He sprawled at the circle's center, automatically blocking excruciating pain in his cheek, counting rapidly to clear the haze from his mind. Eleven of them stood there. He remembered who they were, focusing probes and shields against him and waiting—for something specific, but he couldn't catch it. Should he have known?

He knew who he was, where he lay, and that he had hoped to take Phoena Angelo away from this place. He also remembered how to use his abilities, so he kept his static shield dispersed. He recognized one man, but didn't recall why.

And Dru Polar. He'd just learned that name. He rolled onto his stomach, scrutinizing the long-faced Shuhr with silky black hair. How could he resist Dru Polar? If Brennen were the strongest Master Sentinel of his generation, what chance did any of his people have against adversaries like these? Why didn't the Shuhr already own the Whorl?

His left shoulder throbbed as the shock pistol's pulse wore off. Pressing to his feet, he wiped warm blood from his cheek. Steadily he walked back toward the desk, halting three meters from Phoena. She stood like a queen, flushed with satisfaction and the pride that was her heritage.

Eshdeth Shirak grasped her hand. She smiled coyly as Shirak raised her fingers to his lips. "Highness, you have served us well."

She curtsied.

Brennen felt the circle of minds tighten with expectancy. He wiped his cheek again.

Shirak dropped Phoena's hand and bowed. "You may take that knowledge with you," he said, "to the bliss you so righteously expect. Or maybe into the Dark that Cleanses. Polar?"

Dru Polar reached into the folds of his sash and drew out an arm-length rod, its glossy silver surface momentarily reflecting orange fabric. A thumb-cradle and several control buttons interrupted the length between its pommel and distal end.

Phoena saw it a second later. "Dru!" Outrage heated her voice, but she stared at Polar's hand, the whites of her eyes showing all around her brown irises. "He doesn't mean it! Dru. . . !"

Brennen guessed he should recognize the weapon. Obviously Phoena did, with her body stiff, her alpha matrix humming with terror.

"Don't toy with her." Stepping toward a holo tank full of stars, Shirak wiped one corner of his mouth. "It's too early in the morning. Just file her away."

Phoena took a mincing step backward. Her chestnut hair glistened under warm office lights.

"Ordinarily, I'd agree. She has been helpful, Eldest." Polar seized Phoena's hand. As she shrank toward the tapestry, he coiled his fingers around her wrist. "But she wanted to know about this. For her sister's sake, Caldwell. What were your words, little Phoena? Tell Master Brennen." His dark brows barely lowered. Brennen sensed a controlling thrust of epsilon energy travel from Polar to Phoena.

"If I—" Phoena squeaked to a halt. Polar barely strengthened his effort, and her voice dropped a sultry half-octave. "If I ever get a chance at Firebird, Dru, will you lend that to me again?"

Polar's hand slid up Phoena's arm. His control over her never flickered. "If it can be arranged," he said quietly, as if repeating old lines of his own.

Phoena blinked in lazy contentment. "What's the absolute worst you could do with it?" she murmured, oblivious to her leering audience. "I'd want to know I was giving her the very hardest way out."

Brennen pressed his lips together and calculated the distance to Phoena and Polar.

"Lowest power." With a long finger, Polar slid a control all the way into his palm. "Throat pressure point." He stroked the angle of Phoena's jaw with the weapon's needlelike probe, and slowly, he relinquished control. "Here. Not as slow, but excruciating."

He jabbed the contact into the side of her neck.

Phoena croaked a tiny protest. Her hands crept up toward the silvery rod.

Polar shook his head sharply. "Put them down."

Phoena obeyed, drawing a long, husky breath. "I am, Dru. I did."

Brennen's trained instinct urged him to jump before Polar could trigger the weapon. He could beat most of these enemies to Phoena's side. But before he did, Polar would finish her.

He cautiously modulated his carrier. Maybe, even through those monstrous shields, Polar could be commanded.

Polar slid his hand around her shoulder, pressing his body against hers. "Poor little Phoena. I haven't done a thing, though. Maybe I won't. You know how we play."

His thumb shifted to poise over the orange stud.

"You don't need to do this, Dru. I—" Her voice took a new note, one Brennen never thought to hear. She begged. "Please, Dru . . . please? Don't kill me." She glanced toward Brennen. From her stricken eyes, all hope vanished—but though her dignity disappeared, those eyes glittered defiance.

He saw Firebird in those eyes. Infuriated by Polar's hands on that vision, he flung a disruptive burst of epsilon energy at Polar.

Polar flung it back. "Down!" cracked his voice.

Again Brennen tumbled to the floor. He lay still, dazed again, while his carrier rebuilt. Polar caressed the small of Phoena's back.

"Even now Caldwell would save you if he could." Shirak leaned against the glossy surface of the holo tank. "Isn't that touching, considering what you really are . . . lovely traitor?"

Polar's epsilon aura flickered, and he eased a lulling, deep-level discontinuity off Phoena's consciousness. Brennen felt it happen. He sensed her moment of confusion—of hesitancy—and then her mental shriek as finally, she fully understood that she had never used Dru Polar. Polar used her from beginning to end, letting her live only long enough to trap Brennen, and he was about to use her for the last time. Brennen also guessed Polar's reason for removing all of his anesthetic tampering: to let her recall all their abuses, feeding her terror so he and his comrades could enjoy it.

Brennen struggled to his feet. "Phoena," he whispered as he stepped toward the desk. He knew now that he couldn't save her life. He sent calm instead, peace for the Crossing. As to what awaited her on the other side . . . that was not his responsibility.

Phoena turned ferocious, like a cornered animal done with cowering. "You were going to make me queen!" she shrieked. She flexed her hand into a claw, pulled it back to strike Polar's face—

And Polar's hand tightened on the silver rod.

Phoena shuddered as if she were jolted . . . and then collapsed, wailing in a voice that sounded only half human. Polar followed her down, holding the rod at her jaw's angle until her head thumped the carpeted floor. A wave of neural overload spread down her arms, her writhing torso, her legs . . .

upward, across her face . . . until in Brennen's epsilon sense there burned an explosion of pain, a glimpse at one of the damned.

He shifted his weight to spring.

"Hold him!" Shirak stepped away from the tank. Four Shuhr seized Brennen by his shoulders and arms, too engrossed in the spectacle of Phoena's agony to divert epsilon energy into commanding him. Polar stood motionless, hands pressed together around his weapon, eyes fixed and unseeing, mouth barely open, his tongue touched to his upper lip.

Revolted, Brennen leaned hard forward. His captors held on. Phoena's limbs flailed on the dark carpet.

Could he at least shorten this?

Another Shuhr, standing close to Brennen, sent laughter into his awareness. *Put her out of her misery? No, Caldwell. By your standards, her misery's only beginning.*

Brennen thickened his shields. Phoena moaned, gasped, and then moaned again. A third wave built, rippling back down her body, but this time no flailing went with it.

His hands tightened to fists. He glanced from the black-haired young Shuhr beside him to Polar and then away, repelled by Polar's rapture.

Phoena pulled into a fetal curl. A slow minute later, she gave a single gasp. Like claws, her twitching fingers reached toward Polar. A trickle of blood stained her cheek where she'd bitten her lip. She could no longer move, but Brennen felt her agony. Fully conscious, she had no doubt she was dying. She fought for another breath.

He dropped both his epsilon cloud and his inner shielding. If he could do nothing for Phoena, at least he could force the engrossed Shuhr to feel how deeply he pitied her. It might be the only compassion any of them ever experienced. *Mercy, Holy One! Show her your eternal lovingkindness. None of us deserve that.*

Polar's lashless eyes lost their glazed look. They focused on Brennen. "Release him," he rasped.

The gripping hands dropped his arms and shoulders. Brennen sprang forward and gathered Phoena into his arms, questing with a last pitying, calming touch for her awareness. But as he held her, it ebbed. One drop of blood from his stinging cheek fell like a tear onto hers. Her eyelids fluttered. Then the echoes of her agony faded with the pulse in her wrist.

Brennen knelt helplessly, cradling her yellow-gowned body against his own. What incredible irony, he groaned. He was her only mourner.

At least Tel hadn't seen this.

Shirak flicked a finger. Brennen's captors stepped forward again. Before they took Phoena from him, he gently closed her eyes and uncurled her long, clenched fingers.

Then he wiped his cheek, stood, and turned to face the colony's Eldest. Four young Shuhr carried Phoena out of the chamber.

Very chivalrous. Shirak folded his hands across his middle. His "voice" rumbled through Brennen's alpha matrix, using the ancient language Brennen's kindred reserved for worship. *But you're a fool. You face a similar fate.*

That's not in my hands, Brennen answered in the same way. He'd been called. He'd come. But what would happen to Kiel and Kinnor if he did not come back?

True, Polar projected, walking closer. A sated smile gave his eyes a sleepy gleam. *It's in our hands. We've had time to plan for your arrival. Read me and see.* He dropped all shields.

Instead of probing as invited, Brennen shielded himself and took two steps backward.

Polar laughed. *Coward.* He adjusted a power control on the silvery rod. Then he raised his left hand. "Come here."

This time, Brennen planted his feet. The compulsion to move battered him, growing steadily as other Shuhr joined Polar to pound his resistance. Step by slow step he approached the Testing Director.

The contact bit his forearm. Agony lashed his body and crippled his senses. He felt eager probes lick forward, wanting information that he couldn't remember. Too distracted by pain to shield himself, he turned to his last defense. He disrupted his own beta centers, willed himself unconscious, and crumpled to the glassy floor.

He came to his senses lying in a cell that made no pretense of being a guest suite. The black ceiling rose far over his cot, which was a narrow slab without padding. A bare luminescent strip near his head shed little light, but he saw rough black walls. Ghost echoes of neural pain flickered through his body. His shoulder throbbed, his cheek burned. Gingerly he touched it, and his hand came away blood streaked.

He hadn't been unconscious long, if that wound hadn't scabbed.

Over him stood Dru Polar, with Shirak, and a buxom young woman with grotesquely striped hair. *Cassia Talumah,* she silently told him, and how she would love to rip him apart for destroying her brothers at Mazar.

Mazar? He no longer had any memory of that place, or any mission there. But as he dropped his feet over the cot's edge to sit up, he glanced at her hands. With those nails, she could do it.

Then he started. When she stopped sending he no longer felt her presence, nor the others, only pain that did not fade when he tried to will it away.

Turning with deliberate care to link with his carrier, he felt nothing.

They'd dosed him with blocking drugs. For eight days at least, he would have no epsilon abilities at all. He was helpless.

"As I was saying," Polar began aloud as though the conversation had barely been interrupted, "we've made our plans. They're half fulfilled, Caldwell. We've already sampled your genes. That precious bloodline of yours will mingle with ours now. We'll be the Kings of the Universe," he said, leering. "And here's a generous promise. We won't kill you. At least—not until we've taken at least one other victim. Your wife, and hopefully your freeborn children."

Then they knew the prophecies. *You cannot break the perimeter at Hesed*, Brennen subvocalized, then realized he couldn't send, couldn't even turn. He glanced around again and concentrated on the single factor working in his favor: They meant to hold him alive, conscious, and out of medical stasis. "You cannot break the perimeter at Hesed," he repeated aloud. They could have taken Hesed only if he refused this call. He clung to that knowledge.

"That's true." Shirak's head bobbed. "We can't, any more than your Special Operations agents can break ours. But we won't need to attack Hesed to take Lady Firebird. She'll come to us."

"No."

"You know she will, Caldwell. We know her too, you're forgetting. We know her . . . like a sister."

Phoena. They'd taken that knowledge from Phoena. Mari would try. Would Jenner hold her back, out of mercy? Or would he—in mercy—let her make the attempt?

"When she dies here," said Shirak, "your bereavement shock will weaken you to the point where we can break you."

Infuriated by his shieldless transparency, Brennen tried not to think, to only feel. But his mind plunged ahead. He had to believe Mari would be protected. Even if the Shuhr killed them both, the children would be safe.

"Those children won't be able to threaten us for years, Caldwell. By then . . . oh, but you didn't know. By then, we'll take the Federacy. With your help."

Alert Forces had always suspected that intent, but this was a plain confession. It made escaping even more critical. Meanwhile, he must find out how they meant to do it.

"One more thing," Shirak went on. "We'll not actually kill your Netaian lady."

Brennen resisted Shirak's baiting until an image sprang into his mind, projected by one of the Shuhr. He shrank against the coarse wall. The image showed him with Firebird, and . . .

Cassia Talumah threw back her head and laughed enthusiastically. "Oh, that was classical!" Then, apparently catching an undercurrent Brennen no longer could touch, she stepped away from Polar. She looked fearful—and if Polar fed on fear, what did Cassia expect from him?

Polar reached into his sash. "That's right, Sentinel. The Eldest believes that the best use of her is putting you in bereavement shock. So you'll kill her yourself."

He flourished his weapon. "Phoena's way."

CHAPTER 22

DEPOSED

ritenuto
holding back

Carradee gripped both arms of her ceremonial chair and stared down the right and left branches of her U-shaped electoral table, unable to internalize the debate going on around her, only sure that the Powers were about to deliver a blow even crueler than the blast that injured her and Daithi.

Close on her left, Wellan Bowman stood. Formerly the Minister of Aquaculture, he cut a fine figure in black, tall and white faced, leaning on a diamond-crusted walking stick. ". . . but with Danton feeding this legislation to the Assembly," he continued, "it is seizing more power. Before the Electorate loses all authority, before these new taxes beggar us all, we must consolidate behind a strong ruler. I do support the Duke of Claighbro's motion."

Carradee kept her eyes open, her back straight. That made seven of them. Seven of her highest-ranking nobles, asking with a single voice that she leave the throne. Seven electors out of twenty-six. Not a majority, but enough to tear the Electorate apart and maybe destroy its ability to govern, if she resisted. Queens suicided for less.

Beside her, Rogonin shuffled his legs under his bulk and stood ponderously. "Madame." With a sateen-swathed arm, he made a sweeping motion that took in all the table. "Your service to Netaia in this trying time shall always be honored, whatever course we take from this juncture. Perhaps you alone could have led us through the Federates' temporary overlordship. Yet the situation is changing." He crossed his arms. "We must resist the Federacy with unified strength, or every minister here will lose his or her jurisdiction."

This was *her* Electorate. Months ago, she chose some of these men and women because they seemed to respect the Federates. She hoped to ease the inevitable transition from occupation to Federate covenance. Yet to most electors, covenance was anything but inevitable. One high commoner, a professor wearing his dignified scarlet robe, nodded solemnly at Rogonin.

How long did he think he'd last at this table if she stepped down?

Rogonin leaned on the table, knitting his sculpted eyebrows as if he felt compassion. "Madame, we sympathize with you. We know your concern for His Highness, and that you would prefer to stay with him." Rogonin glanced at the empty chair at Carradee's right side. "And, madame, you cannot keep his condition secret much longer."

Carradee blinked. Truly, she'd give up everything she owned if it meant having Daithi whole again.

"Majesty, you should not have sent your heiresses away." Rogonin smoothed the ends of his blue nobleman's sash. "Netaia must have a strong confident ruler—even if only a regent-designate, acting on behalf of the Crown. There is a precedent, at the end of the first century of Angelo rule . . ."

Carradee let him expound. She knew the story of Grand Duke Tarrega Erwin. Everyone in the room should know it. Regent for the infant Queen Bobri, "Bloody Erwin" steered Netaia through the Coper Rebellion.

Her left leg ached, but she didn't move to ease it. That would look weak.

They were speaking of a long-term regency. Unlike her mother, Carradee never had enjoyed power. This meeting was forcing her to admit it—to herself, at least. Would it be best for Netaia if she followed Siwann's example and stepped down?

Surely not for the common classes!

Her stiff skirt rustled as she straightened under the Chamber's high dome, leaning into her leg braces. "Should a regency prove desirable," she said, "there is the matter of rank. First Lord Baron Erwin. Baron Parkai. Consider your positions. Have you weighed the responsibility that would be thrust upon you should one of you serve as regent for our daughter, Iarla?"

As she sat down, whispers passed around the table. These men and women obviously assumed that Rogonin, temporary regent while she cared for Daithi, would take any quasi-permanent regency. Suggesting these higher-ranking alternates should slow the proceedings to a fuddbug's crawl, giving her time to consider her options and plan a strategy.

Bualin Erwin stood on her left. A stooped man in his seventies, implant-young otherwise in his appearance, Erwin cocked one eyebrow. "Madame, my father's removal from this body after the Veroh War left somewhat of a stain on our family. At present, if called upon to serve as regent, I should decline for the sake of maintaining good relations with the governor, until his departure . . . or overthrow."

"Oh," Carradee murmured, surprised to hear Erwin pass by the honor so quickly.

Beside Rogonin, young Reshn Parkai rose. "For the same reason, madame, my father's death at the Hunter Height debacle precludes my accepting the scepter."

And that left Muirnen Rogonin, Duke of Claighbro, who sat beside her with smug decorum. She wondered if the barons truly stood down out of honor, or if Muirnen Rogonin had made offers.

Carradee felt lightheaded, as if she were floating away from the world she knew. By sacred tradition, if she had a daughter ready to rule, her next task would be simple: Procure two doses of gentle, deadly Somnus, one for Daithi and one for herself. But four-year-old Iarlet could not ascend the throne for almost a decade and a half. Rogonin meant to have a long rule.

Still, noble suicide was an honored practice. Rogonin obviously felt ready to govern. Carradee jerked to her feet. "Noble electors, this body is recessed, to meet tomorrow morning at nine hundred. At that time, we . . . there shall be laid before you certain documents. That is all."

Her touch deactivated a transcriber at her place on the table. She stepped back from her chair and walked toward the gilded doors, followed by her personal servitor. Slowly—the electors could wait. She still was queen. The heels of her leather pumps clicked on the chamber's gold-shot black marble floor. Its high white ceiling echoed back the soft clicks. She imagined she could feel Rogonin's soft green stare follow her around the table.

He didn't expect to see her alive again. He would probably shed real tears at her state funeral.

Was this fearful bewilderment how Firebird felt when the electors issued her geis orders? She'd looked courageous, calmly kneeling at the foot of that table.

Two red-jacketed guards stood beside the gilt doors. They reached simultaneously for handles and pushed outward, letting Carradee through. The doors shut behind her: *boom*.

Numbly she stood listening to the faint scrape of chairs and a sudden rise in voices. She looked up and down both grand corridors of the palace she called her home. This building where queens lived, worked, and died.

Clutching a handful of stiff skirt, she limped up the long curving stairs to Daithi's room. There, she lifted his arm that once seemed so strong. She lay down beneath it and let it fall across her back. "Daithi," she mumbled, "what shall I do?"

Heavily sedated, he could not answer.

Solicitor Merriam, whose forefathers had been legal counsel to queens for two centuries, came to her an hour later, carrying the tools of a time-honored trade in his papercase: recall pad, vellum sheets, long black calligraphy pens. He spread them on a spiral-legged table and pulled up a chair.

"I wish two documents made." Carradee sat stiffly on the other side of an antique table in the secure sitting room. After a long mental struggle with the cruel, fickle Powers under Daithi's limp arm, she'd bathed, put on fresh clothes, and made up her mind.

Truly, she wasn't strong-willed enough to rule effectively—because she didn't even have the courage to commit honorable suicide. Rogonin meant to break with the Powers by seizing the throne? Then she would break with them in her own way. Something else waited for her. She wasn't sure how she knew it, but she knew. She would carry Daithi to Danton on her back, if need be, and beg the governor to transport them to a Federate medical center, or maybe to Firebird. Then she would send for Iarlet and Kessie. They could all live together elsewhere—humbly, without palace servitors—and Muirnen Rogonin could manage Netaia without the Angelo fortune. That belonged to her blood relations, not the Electorate.

"Two documents," she repeated. "A new will, and a document of abdication."

Merriam laid down his pen. "I have no standard form for an abdication, Majesty."

"I know," she said firmly. She folded her hands. "We will create one together."

Eleven days dragged by after Brennen left Hesed. Dabarrah examined Firebird's turn several more times, always shielded, but they made no progress toward controlling it. Between sessions with Master Dabarrah and quiet hours practicing and composing on her clairsa, she started another new course, a detailed comparison of Federate regimes. That, and a review for credit of the *Transnational Government* text she'd studied in protective custody, kept her mind busy while her body ached for those absent babies.

This morning, she stood at the waterside edge of Hesed's commons. A white-haired couple lingered at one of the tables, sharing ching tea. Something loaded with sugar and yeast was baking in the kitchens, but Firebird had no appetite. In Dabarrah's study, a meeting was under way—an evaluation of that new RIA technology, she guessed.

Anna Dabarrah stood close by, so Kiel and Kinnor must be with a sekiyr. Only Jenner and Anna at Hesed knew that Firebird was on A-status for deadly reasons. The others simply knew that she mustn't be accessed. The sekiyrra didn't seem afraid. They coached her with essential Ehretan vocabulary, words such as garnetberries, thorns, and leather-palmed gloves.

Firebird reached up to her throat and touched Brennen's medallion. She wore it, a small comfort in her solitude. Anna had just reported that earlier this morning Kinnor had changed from an alert, if difficult, baby to the very embodiment of tension. Suddenly he couldn't keep still, except in sleep. He demanded constant touching, comforting, stroking. "I believe he's picking up your anxiety, Firebird," Anna said. "It hurts him. For his sake, stop fighting the Holy One. You cannot bring Brennen back by worrying."

She might as well have asked Firebird to stop breathing. By her calculation, Brennen could've arrived only hours ago at Three Zed.

"Kinnor needs his father." Firebird glanced over her shoulder at the retirees sitting peacefully at tea. "Brennen understood Kin's moods from the first day. Brennen could help him. If he were here."

Anna stroked the white rail, and Firebird studied her profile. Hesed's mistress, mother to five sekiyrra at any time of year, had deep, intelligent eyes and a nose almost jewel-like in symmetry, a little too long for beauty, but Anna's real beauty was internal. One sekiyr called her "the holy woman."

"Master Dabarrah," Anna said, "will help Kinnor. You can help too, by submitting your will to the Speaker. By learning to trust Him. Besides," she added, softening, "many small crises come and go for every child. Most problems vanish with time and tenderness."

But Firebird feared deeply for Brennen. Had he arrived . . . and survived that? Would Phoena cooperate? *Help them, Mighty Singer!*

Anna flicked silvered brown hair behind her shoulder and gazed up at the skylights. "Babies of strong epsilon potential can be difficult," she said, "because they have no way of telling you what's disturbing them. I was ten when your Brennen was born. I remember the rumors."

What made Anna an authority on babies?

And if Firebird lost Brennen, how could she ever guide Kinnor and Kiel through their boyhood? She never even had a brother. . . .

Anna bowed her head. "Firebird Mari, you're not listening. As soon as my husband finishes with this meeting, you must go to him again. Tell him I asked him to address your tension."

"I'd rather go back out to the garden. I won't disturb Kin up there." Finally, she had license to wander.

Anna reached for her hand.

Firebird pulled it back. "Don't touch me, Anna. I'll crack." Silently she prayed, *He can't die there! Singer, you wouldn't call him there just to let them kill him, would you?*

Anna lifted her hand. "You are disrupting the sanctuary. Brennen was sent to Three Zed, and following a sacred call is the safest place in the Whorl. Our Holy Speaker cares for His own."

Firebird backed away. "Don't comfort me with platitudes." Her wistful depression turned to anger, and she didn't care if the elderly couple sensed it. Every day she felt more of a misfit here, even after her consecration.

Anna's voice took on the subtle tone of command. "Firebird, calm yourself."

Firebird resisted. "Brennen has taken a virtually untested craft against an enemy that represents all we despise. He is the finest man Thyrica could've sent against the Shuhr, and he was probably the best intelligence officer the Federacy ever had." Her voice kept rising. "If he succeeds it won't be because of dreams or platitudes, but because of skill—and hard training—and perseverance—and prayers, including mine."

Her peripheral vision caught a lanky form striding along the waterside. She recognized Master Jenner and stopped speaking. Her cheeks felt hot, her throat tight. Compressing her lips, she stared at the water.

Anna's light footsteps hurried away.

Wonderful. Now she'd face the psi healer. What was the treatment for anguish and anger?

He touched her shoulder. "Firebird," he said softly.

"I'm sorry," she muttered. "I shouted at Mistress Anna."

"She understands better than you know." The Sanctuary Master smiled ruefully. "She loves you, Firebird."

Love? Anna had peculiar ways of showing it.

Then again, she once thought that of Brennen. "How are my children, Master Jenner?"

"Kiel is thriving," he said. "Healthy, contented. Gaining weight. Kinnor is just as strong, but restless."

"So I hear. Master Jenner, every day I'm without them, they feel less real to me, as if I only dreamed them. This can't be right. What kind of mother are you . . . is this making out of me?"

"Firebird," he said softly, "be patient. They will be yours again. They will claim your heart. You will have a bond with them almost as deep, and just as real, as your bond with their father."

She stared at the water, feeling hollow. "I'm going uplevel for a while," she said. "Tell Anna I apologize."

She strode up the pavement to the golden double-doors of the groundside lift. When she stepped off onto the broad lawn she halted, hearing music.

At least music still moved her. She followed the haunting melody up onto the hillside. It sounded like a kinnora, beautifully played.

Kinnor, she moaned silently, imagining the warm weight of her child in her arms. *What's wrong, little Kin? I'm sorry. I don't mean to hurt you.*

Halfway to the hilltop, she found the sekiyr. He sat cross-legged, with black hair falling into his face—the same youth who played for her consecration service. This angle of his face gave her another heart-wrenching flash of memory. Lord Corey Bowman, her dearest wastling friend, had waved jauntily from the stepstand of his Netaian fightercraft the last time she ever saw him. Black hair had tumbled into his eyes, too, before he tipped head into helmet for the battle where he died. Her more-than-brother, black eyed and rebellious, wildest of the wastlings . . .

She stepped slowly, trying not to disturb the sekiyr and shatter the dear illusion. Everything had ended, everything changed.

Corey too . . . soul-tainted?

Brennen! Singer, protect him! If she couldn't do anything else, she could pray constantly.

The young man laid down his instrument and looked up with solemn blue eyes that dispelled all imagery of Corey Bowman. "Hello, Mistress Caldwell."

"Hello. You're. . . ?" Firebird winced. "Forgive me."

"Labeth Kinsman." He swept one finger up the strings.

Wonderful, a relative of Ellet's. A cumulus cloud passed in front of the sun, but that wasn't what raised prickles on her arm. "Please finish, Labeth. That was lovely."

As he plucked another melody, she sank onto the soft, cropped grass and kicked off her shoes.

When he finished the piece, he lifted the instrument from his lap. "You play, don't you?"

"A similar instrument. And I dabbled a little with a kinnora." She wished Janesca were here. Or Carradee! She was unutterably lonely.

"I thought so, from the kind of attention you pay." He held it out to her.

Her clairsa was back at her room. On kinnora, she'd make an amateurish fool of herself. . . .

Firebird, she told herself, *forget your pride. It's friendship he's offering!*

She took the little harp, balanced its sound box on her thigh, and picked out a tune she often heard at chapter.

He smiled. "Self-taught?"

"On kinnora, yes."

He reached for the upper arch. "Let me show you the proper position."

"Please!"

For an hour she listened, watched, and tried to emulate Labeth. That afternoon, when Labeth reported for work, they harvested the first snow-apples together, Firebird at ground level and Labeth in the treetops.

The round white fruit felt heavy in her hands, and the rapidly filling basket promised food for months to come. *The Sentinels are right; it's good for the spirit here . . . whoops!* She bent to retrieve a dropped fruit, but before her fingers closed it flew to the basket, apparently of its own accord.

"I'm sorry," Labeth called down. "I should've seen that fall."

"It's all right." Gazing out over the valley, she leaned against the rough trunk and finally asked, "Labeth? How are you related to Ellet Kinsman?"

Autumn brown leaves fluttered as he laughed, rising from tenor to coun-tertenor. With a rattle of branches, he dropped down to land beside her. "I'm her brother." He regained the mature timbre. "Not her favorite, I'm afraid. It's not easy, being the youngest in the shadow of such a grand lady."

Firebird thought of Carradee and Phoena. "Believe me, I know."

He flicked a net-winged insect off the basket. "But we correspond, and I heard about you a year ago. She never mentioned the clairsa, only General Caldwell. Ellet's a raptor on the hunt. She'll do well." Hefting a snow-apple, he bit into it noisily and grinned around the sweet mouthful.

"Labeth," she asked, abruptly curious. "Why do *you* think evil can exist? Why does the Speaker allow suffering?"

He shook his head. "I don't know why, but I see His wisdom and power and creativity." He gestured toward the garden, then up to the peaks, with his white snow-apple. "I've felt His love, and I know He is molding me to serve Him forever. When things go wrong, that's all I can cling to. I may not know why, but I know *Him*."

That, she understood. "I have so much to learn." She scuffed her feet in the leaf-strewn grass.

"Don't we all?" Labeth rose back up the trunk.

Firebird closed her eyes, letting her heart cry in longing and anguish. *Brennen! Mighty Singer, help him!*

Brennen walked up a golden corridor in a fog of epsilon silence. With his inner sense chemically blocked and much of his memory gone, he felt disoriented. Seventeen-year habits kept tripping him. He kept trying to shield but couldn't. He couldn't measure his captors' emotions or tell when they lied. But he mustn't stop trying. His memory wouldn't come back without outside help, but blocking drugs wore off. He must stay poised to escape.

A nameless escort walked ahead of him, Testing Director Polar behind. Two golden doors parted as he approached. The three men passed into a volcanic chamber filled with head-high, transparent museum cases. "Slow down," Polar ordered in the holy Ehretan tongue. "You'll want to see this."

Brennen couldn't get used to hearing that language spoken casually, sometimes even profanely. How naive his people seemed now. They forbade translating *Dabar*, hoping to hide prophecies from a people who still spoke Ehretan as their primary language.

He glanced into the nearest case. Inside, on a golden tripod, perched the mounted body of a long bird with pale blue breast and green back. He stared. On its wings, outstretched to fill the transparent cubicle, the colors intensified to brilliant indigo and emerald. Its wing tips splayed in two downy proto-paws. At College, in a class scorned by many older classmates, he'd studied Ehretan zoology as part of his heritage. That memory hadn't fallen behind the curtain. "That's genuine," he murmured.

"Of course."

The Ehretan creature had been perfectly preserved. Thyrica had no such relics. "Was it a pet?"

"Hunting trophy," said Polar. "Three of the Six took their favorite possessions shipboard before it became necessary to flee."

"The Six?"

"You aren't taught your own history?"

Brennen drew a blank. "Please explain," he said. Should he remember?

"The first group of babies to survive Altering. The first who could function as normally human, so weren't humanely killed. They were in their fifties when the war broke out. They led the Altered revolution. You aren't told?"

He hadn't forgotten. He'd never known. His forebears hadn't honored the war makers by naming them. "I suspect you know what we're told," he answered. He stepped to the next case, which contained six torso mannequins. Each wore clothing and jewelry he'd seen in the historical record: knee-length vests with formal headdresses, pleated tunics, gloves trimmed with the fur of animals that hadn't survived Ehret's destruction . . . or had they, in Three Zed's bioformed zones?

Slowly he turned a full circle. Three aisles were lined with enough cases to spend days standing and studying.

"It's our ancestors' hall." Polar rested a hand on his holster, casually reminding Brennen of their captive-captor relationship. "I'll bring you back shortly, if you'll answer my questions."

Then they'd only paused here on their way to an interrogation. Brennen had wondered how soon that would start. "What kind of questions?"

Polar smiled coldly.

Brennen barely shook his head.

"I'm glad," Polar whispered. "I like a good fight. Walk on."

Brennen had been assured that Special Ops memory blocks couldn't fail. That guaranteed him a harrowing time.

The next double door led into a darker corridor, round-walled with an evenly poured duracrete floor. Three turns later, they approached several men and women waiting in a wider passway. All of them stopped speaking and stared as Brennen approached. One swept a hand toward an open door. The Shuhr guard led inside. Brennen's stomach churned. *You are never alone*, he heard, but his palms turned cold.

At the room's center waited a heavy black chair. Behind it stood a cart with resuscitation equipment and a life-signs monitor, and on its side he saw adjustments for a restraining field.

The others filed into the room behind him. Polar came last. Brennen parked himself just inside the door and let the others pass by. He wouldn't move toward that chair until they forced him. Polar halted too, watching him.

"Sit down." Polar raised a hand as if to command, then smiled narrow eyed and waved at an observer's chair.

Brennen guessed he should recognize the technique: Frighten the prisoner, then accommodate him. Suggest you could show mercy.

Recognizing the technique didn't keep him from responding to it. As he took the small chair, tensed muscles relaxed with his immense relief. They wouldn't begin, not yet.

Most of the others sat down with heads tilted toward him, though three women carried on a silent conversation betrayed by their glances at one another.

He felt utterly alone. Even if Polar were the only one armed, anyone here could command him.

"General," Polar exclaimed aloud. "Welcome. Meet your eager students." Instead of introducing them, he gestured aside. On the wall behind him appeared an image of a Thyrian city. Another picture sprang up next to it, then another, until all four walls glowed with cityscapes or aerial maps. He knew them all.

Polar touched the near wall. On it, two gray cloud banks and a white-capped ocean framed cliffside Base One in Soldane. "Thyrica, naturally."

He tapped the image twice. Brennen recognized the remote orbital image that appeared next, a complex of croplands and pastures surrounded by snowy peaks. "Hesed interests us, in the long term." He swept out an arm. "But first we want to discuss Tallis." Images flashed around the room: ground and orbital bases, Regional command headquarters in the MaxSec Tower, satellite nets that surrounded the Federacy's Regional capital world. One diagram he didn't recognize at all.

The amnesia block was worth what it had cost him, then.

Polar extended a hand, offering Brennen a chance to speak willingly.

Brennen crossed his legs, laced his fingers around one knee, and leaned back. They would discover the block soon enough. Meanwhile, he would enjoy what physical comfort was left to him.

Polar took a vacant seat across the circle, toying with him again, pretending he posed no threat. From that position, he could menace more effectively later. "There is an alternative, of course, to infiltration." He waved a hand in the air.

The room went dark. One new image appeared on the wall directly in front of Brennen. On Thyrica's western coast, between foothills and sea, a crater rimmed by fire-blackened ruins slowly filled with ground water. Brennen leaned forward, examining the image, grieving. This was more recent than any he'd seen.

"We could strike Tallis that way." Polar waved the image away and brought up the lights. "We have agents there, of course. I don't imagine that surprises you."

"No," said Brennen. He didn't try to recall his co-workers. He guessed at this technique too: Polar wanted to know who might be under suspicion. In his mind's eye, resisting Polar with a more edifying image, Brennen studied an exquisitely illustrated page of liturgy often sung in Hesed's underground chapter room.

Polar crossed his knees and swung one leg. "Answer one question, Caldwell, and we will send you on your way home."

Brennen raised an eyebrow. He didn't dare hope Polar was serious.

Polar's casual posture couldn't hide the deadly intensity in his voice. "How did you get into this city? Our force at Thyrica reported a new kind of disruptor field. Your arrival confirmed it. What is it?"

Brennen couldn't remember, but now he knew what Polar wanted most. "I am sorry," he said softly. "That information is classified."

Polar raised one eyebrow and nodded across the circle.

A thin, strong-looking young man rocked onto his feet. He sauntered toward the empty chair next to Brennen, staring all the while into Brennen's eyes. Feature by feature, Brennen catalogued the resemblance to a blackened-faced intruder who had leaped onto his bed at Trinn Hill.

Previously motionless observers uncrossed their legs and rocked forward. The wiry young man stared down at him for several seconds, then sank into the empty seat.

"My name's Shirak, Caldwell. Micahel Shirak. I'm the Eldest's grandson. I work in enforcement. Today's my last chance to speak with you. I've been assigned to an outlying area. A settlement," he growled, "while I study basic military tactics. But I helped plan a special reception for your mistress. I hope they use it."

Brennen stared at Micahel's full lips, cleft chin, and high cheekbones.

"They'll call me when she comes. I only hope I can get back in time. I don't want to miss the celebration."

Brennen wrested his mind to the liturgy.

"Give up, Carabohd." Micahel Shirak's nostrils flared. He stretched one fingertip toward Brennen's forehead and thrust an image into Brennen's mind. Brennen saw through Micahel's eyes, in Micahel's memory . . .

. . . a dim doorway, where he gripped its frame to listen cautiously. The hall was almost dark, but in less than a second, Brennen recognized his brother's home. His own right hand gripped a blazer, thumb covering the safety. One glance over his shoulder . . . he still was undetected.

Brennen struggled to break Shirak's control, to raise shields, to fight free of Shirak's memory.

. . . Under rumpled covers, a small form sprawled on the bed. Tousled blond hair hid most of a sweet, feminine face.

Destia.

He shuffled closer.

"Stop." Brennen flung out both hands, and the image blurred into a rage-red mist. Micahel Shirak's leering face reappeared, framed with black curls.

Brennen's hands, seemingly possessed, seized his own knees and dug in. In his mind, though, he was choking this Shuhr who had terrorized his beloved niece. His cheeks flamed. He'd controlled his anger, his temptation to hate, since Tarance's death. He couldn't hold back now. It didn't matter that he was titillating his audience. He didn't even feel rational.

"It didn't start there, Carabohd." Micahel brushed his hand on one pant leg, as if he'd soiled it by touching Brennen. "My father killed your uncles. My grandfather, your great-uncle. Your family and mine have intertwined for years, and you didn't even know it."

So that was the explanation. "Why?" he demanded.

Shirak shrugged. "I think you can guess."

Brennen's thoughts fled for one uncontrolled instant to Hesed.

Micahel shook his head. "We know where your sons are. Give us one boy," he suggested, "and we might spare the other."

Brennen forced himself to breathe slowly, to ignore the taunt. It was nothing more.

"Maybe." Dru Polar's voice startled Brennen. "But maybe not forever." Standing at Brennen's elbow, he glanced toward the heavy chair and life-signs monitor.

Did Brennen remember enough to betray Hesed's defenses?

Polar's prisoner crumpled forward, willfully unconscious, as before. Micahel glanced up and sent, *Let me stay on. Let me help.* He glared toward the interrogation chair. *That family is mine.*

You know your assignment, Polar reminded him. *Study your tactics. You're not ready for this one.*

When Brennen awoke in his stony cell, his shoulders and backside ached as if he'd been dragged back down the black-and-gold corridors. The room light had been dimmed. Around the massive black door, an arch of red strip-lights pulsed dully.

He clenched his hands, longing to crush Micahel Shirak's throat . . . or better, to thrust with epsilon might into the other man's beta centers, as the Codes absolutely forbade . . . to stir Micahel's physical energies into a vortex, creating heat, pressure, pain. Brennen would have paid for that attack with his life, whether he tried it here or on Thyrica, but what was that life worth here?

Amnesia blocks could cause personality changes. Brennen recognized despair, hatred's fellow destroyer. He rolled onto his stomach, clenched his hands, then begged a silent heaven to let him live long enough to avenge Tarance's family. *Why did you call me here?* he cried silently. *I've accomplished nothing!*

Again, the first answer was silence.

CHAPTER 23

DEATH STROKE

con timpani sordi
with muffled kettledrums

Six days later, he lay in his stone cell, too exhausted to sleep. All week, Polar worked at breaking his amnesia block, digging for information that was still stored in his synapses. Now Brennen knew the misery of interrogation without epsilon shields.

Faintly lit by the slowly pulsing red arch, this cell never was truly dark. He rolled over on his cot, which was as narrow and hard as a chapter room's altar. Seventeen years had passed since he'd endured pain without the ability to block it. When he willed himself unconscious, Polar shot him full of stimulants and kept probing.

At least he retained affective control, and he could forget the tortures after they ended. He shifted again and called up other thoughts. Micahel Shirak's face rose to mind. Heartsick with hatred, he thrust it aside.

Holy One, was I mistaken? Did I follow a false vision here?

Not necessarily. Even holy men suffered. He remembered an Adoration—

My mortal enemies surround me;
I am caught, they have tracked me down.
They watch with sharp eyes,
They fling me to the ground, their teeth tear me.
I am their prey.
O Holy One, save me by your hand.
Come down, rescue me. . . .

Rescue me, he repeated. Unless he could prevent Mari's coming, her death seemed as certain as his own. But he couldn't think of a way to warn her off. If she came, what kind of "research" would she endure? How would they use her if they found out she could kill . . . had killed?

He shut his eyes against the pulsing red lights and a buzzing headache. The blocking drug was wearing off early, and he must hide that fact from his captors. They'd underestimated their dosage.

My mortal enemies . . .

Micahel appeared again in his mind, leering as he forced the rest of his cruel recollections into Brennen's memory. Hatred boiled in Brennen's spirit. Unless he subdued that emotion, it would grow like malignant cancer. Micahel Shirak had deliberately poisoned him, and not just with memories. Brennen couldn't retain this lust for revenge and still live by faith, not here, not anywhere.

His black door slid open. Cassia Talumah stepped through. At each shoulder of her sleeveless jumpsuit fluttered a white streamer scarf, setting off her weirdly striped hair. He rose warily off his cot and greeted her. She'd come once already, with repellent suggestions.

"I'm not staying this time," she answered, "though I still could develop a taste for your kind. But if you want to eat tonight, I'd suggest you come with me to Polar's quarters. He's asked us to dinner."

"Us?"

She turned half away from him, displaying her provocative silhouette, brown beneath white gauze. "He asked me. But I'd rather not go alone. I'm choosing to bring you."

He backstepped. "No. But thank you."

Instantly, fire crawled over his skin like a hundred tiny demons. He gasped and hunched forward.

Cassia smirked. The burning sensation ceased without leaving even a sense of warmth.

He shivered. "What was that?"

"My wild talent. Synthesizing a heat response at nerve endings. Shall I call it up again?"

"No," he said.

"Then come." She reached toward his face. "General, I believe you're going to have a scar."

He touched his cheek, still tender where Phoena kicked him.

"I like it," she observed. "Very rakish."

He rubbed the roughening cuff of his tunic, fingers still twitching. "Polar," he said. "You fear him, Cassia. What has he done to you?" He remembered how Polar leered, watching Phoena die. Cassia had probably seen worse. He trained the children. What did he do to those who failed?

"Nothing yet. And he'll do nothing tonight." Cassia drew a shock pistol. "After you."

She directed him down golden passways. As he stepped into Polar's apartment with Cassia's hand arched on his arm, he blinked, visually hammered by riots of color. Each chair and lounger seemed to have been chosen to clash with its nearest neighbor, the floor underneath, or the walls behind. Above a long mirrored cabinet hung the trophy head of a huge cat, lips curled back to show six upper fangs. The room's opulence appealed to him after seven days in a tiny cell, but it crowded him with brightness. Could Polar be color-blind, or was this his taste?

Polar wore a shimmering long shirt of magenta belted in black and formfitting black pants. His hair, set in tight waves, glistened with matching magenta flecks. *Not color-blind, then, unless someone dresses him.*

Cassia caressed Brennen's arm. "A change of scenery could stimulate the prisoner's memory."

Polar's glance returned to Brennen. "Certainly, Cassia, if it will entertain you." He poured a glass of ruby-colored liquor. "Steen, my friends?"

"Naturally." Cassia took the cordial.

Polar raised one eyebrow toward Brennen as he handed Cassia her drink. Brennen shook his head.

The entry opened soundlessly. As Brennen took a fan-backed chair beside Cassia in the dining alcove, a hurrying youth set down a dinner that looked and smelled very different from the subsistence food Brennen had eaten on six previous nights. He dispatched the delicately spiced dishes quickly, without trying to hide his enjoyment. Cassia watched him, amused, but he refused to notice. Even if kindness wasn't her motive, tonight he moved unfettered among the Shuhr. If he escaped, he'd carry out knowledge no one else had reported.

As he sipped excellent kass, a second training-age youth removed platters. Even stripped of probing ability, Brennen could see that the young man radiated fear in Polar's presence, almost dropping a goblet in his haste to be gone.

Brennen thanked the Holy One that this man didn't train Sentinel children. He wondered if Dabarrah had given Kiel and Kinnor back to Firebird. That might keep her at Hesed.

Polar pushed back his chair, strolled to a wall unit, and opened a cabinet. "A fascinating thing." He twisted his hand. Brennen heard the familiar singing note of his crystace as Polar turned around. He rose from the table. His first unshieldable impulse was to wrest it from Polar's hands. Cassia laughed at Polar's vacant smile while Polar swung the shimmering, virtually invisible blade of the Sentinels' ceremonial weapon. "I tested it on a few substances: permastone, duracrete, sub-adults. I haven't been able to shatter it, but I suppose I haven't really tried. I'd rather keep it for my collection." Fingering off the sonic activator to return the ehrite crystal's molecular bonds to their stable length, Polar tucked it into tonight's black sash, then smiled.

Brennen sidestepped toward another pair of loungers. When he committed himself to one, Cassia pointedly joined him.

Polar crossed his arms. "Caldwell, your surface memory is cluttered with knife-fighting drills. Have you been studying recently?"

"Not recently."

"Of course." Polar opened one hand and conceded, "It's more likely that you've been teaching someone."

"Not recently . . ."

"Cassia has been tutoring my son Jerric." Polar glanced from Brennen to Cassia. "Here we are with an hour to spare and a chance to try something novel. If the two of you held a practice match, I'd find that entertaining."

Unlimited wealth, uncanny power . . . and the man was bored.

"Not him, Dru. This kind wants to hold back. I would waste too much effort," Cassia said, but as she spoke, she plucked the streamer scarves from her shoulders as if trimming for battle.

Polar flexed his arms. "Then I'll take you, Cassia, if you're willing. Too long without practice leaves even a knife edge rusty. Our pet Sentinel can referee."

Cassia and Dru reached for their boots. Each came up with a triangle-bladed dirk half the length of a Carolinian dagger. Observing no preliminaries, Polar sprang toward the lounger. Before Cassia had fully risen, Polar's blade flickered. Startled, Brennen stared. Cassia's bare arm bled below the elbow.

"Well?" She glared at Brennen. "That counts."

"Score," he murmured. "Polar."

Polar led Cassia to the cabinet and drew out a medical kit. In a minute, they returned to center floor.

"We'll try that again." Polar poured and drained another cordial. He had drunk freely during dinner. "There. Now we're more evenly matched."

"Ready." Cassia's tone defied him. This time they both looked at Brennen.

"Begin," he said.

Now Cassia slashed fiercely. Polar hung back in a casual stance, all his weight on one foot. Suddenly she stepped in close, tripped him, and swung her dirk. He twisted as he fell. The blade sliced only shirt and skin, but it was a near-miss of a major artery.

"Score," Brennen said softly, sensing Polar's freely broadcast anger and surprise. "Talumah."

Cassia nursed Polar this time and then ignored him, walking instead to

Brennen's lounger. Polar stayed behind, leaning against the cabinet with yet another goblet. He sipped delicately.

"Now, Sentinel?" she asked, flicking her dagger's edge. "Now that you know I can hold my own?"

He rose uneasily, suspecting he'd better not refuse. "All right, Cassia. Polar, will you lend me a blade? Mine is elsewhere." He glanced at the sash and his crystace.

Polar chose two more knives from his cabinet, another slender dirk and a long fighting blade. He extended the dirk to Brennen, grip first. In the moment both men held it their eyes met, and Brennen glimpsed hatred flickering there, not the least blunted by liquor. "That one's a handicap design." A corner of Polar's mouth twitched. "Watch your hold."

Brennen followed Cassia to the center of the room. Polar clenched his blazer in his right hand and the longer knife in his left, on guard.

Cassia crouched, eyeing Brennen hungrily. Brennen adjusted his hand around the unfamiliar grip. Its hold was perpendicular to what he considered normal, and he'd swat with the flat unless he paid as careful attention to his hold as to Cassia. He didn't dare harm her, he didn't even want to bloody her, but he could see by the spark in her eyes that she would enjoy slicing him.

She sprang. He ducked and dodged but didn't counterattack.

"Wake up." She planted her fists on her hips, reptile-striped hair draping her shoulders. "If you're not going to cooperate, give the knife back to Dru."

He nodded and stepped out clockwise to lead with a glaring feint, then parried her counterstroke with the flat of his blade. Metal rang.

She pulled back, wringing her hand. "What are you trying to do, disarm me? We don't play that way."

"You won't fight, Sentinel?" Brennen spun in time to see Polar drop his blazer, shift the long knife to his right hand, and lunge.

Hastily Brennen backed out of the Shuhr's reach. "Wait, Polar."

"You'd best defend yourself. You could serve our purposes just as well with one less—arm!"

Polar lunged again, closer this time. Brennen sprang away, watching for the slightest opening. Polar offered none but crouched closer yet, steady on his feet: barely, dangerously liquor-relaxed.

Brennen prepared to leap in any direction as he turned, seeking his carrier across the gap that kept narrowing as the drug wore off.

There! The turn felt tenuous, but he could tap resources Polar expected him to lack.

Polar's attention flashed to Cassia for approval. Brennen unleashed his hatred and attacked.

Polar responded with astonishing reflexes. Fire bloomed on Brennen's chest. Automatically blocking the pain with familiar epsilon energy, he aimed a cut at Polar's withdrawing knife arm. Polar laughed as he sprang away. Brennen's hold on the grip had shifted, and what might've been an effective slice was a comical swipe.

The black-haired Shuhr returned to his crouch, gloating through lashless black eyes. "We'll tape you later. Say it, Cassia. Score. Polar. And here's a better." He charged again.

"Dru!" Cassia shouted. Brennen saw the knife homing for his shoulder. "Cool down!" He twisted aside. "Shirak will have your head if you maim him!"

Polar spun. He stabbed again from well within Brennen's guard, aiming for his chest. A death stroke.

Brennen's backward leap both saved and betrayed him.

Polar straightened. He stood breathing heavily, eyeing Brennen. Brennen felt Polar's probe touch his epsilon matrix. He relinquished the turn too late.

"My mistake," Polar said icily. "I shouldn't have tried that. You're too valuable to kill." He turned aside. "Cassia, our guest needs his medication. Would you be so kind as to administer ten mils of DME–6?"

Cassia stopped circling. Her face clouded for an instant, then she tossed her head. "Oh. I'd enjoy that. Of course, Dru. I don't suppose you keep any in here?"

He gestured toward a black carryall on the floor.

As Cassia knelt to sort ampules, Brennen tensed, wondering if he dared to resist.

"I wouldn't," Polar said quietly, very sober now. "I'm growing tired of your conceit."

Brennen fingered the thumb guard of his dirk and turned again. The carrier flickered. He hadn't regained solid enough linkage to depend on it.

Cassia snapped a cartridge of clear blue fluid into a long-needled venous syringe, tightened the barrel, and then flicked it almost casually. Brennen could feel her crowing as she stood up. *Hold him, Dru.*

Polar lifted a hand in casual command stance, strode forward, and took the odd knife from Brennen.

"I'm ready." Cassia stepped up. "Kneel."

Kneel? Brennen sent, hoping only to gain time.

There are other positions. But this is best for the spinal fluid.

Brennen swallowed hard. *Nonsense.* Even a dart-pistol dose, injected into muscle, could disable.

On your knees, Caldwell. Polar's hand shifted, and Brennen's legs buckled. Cassia's talons tilted his head. A UV beamer kissed the hairline at the base of his skull. Then cold pain mocked his hope of escape, he grew dizzy, and Polar let him go.

He scrambled to his feet, fighting to retain contact with the carrier, though they watched and laughed. The pain of his chest slash intensified as his control slipped. He wiped salt water from his eyes.

Cassia flicked a fingernail across his shoulder. "I'll tape you. But you'd better get back to your room first. You'll be asleep in five minutes."

CHAPTER 24

FUSION THEORY

attacca
continue from previous section without pausing

Firebird sat beside Tel on a bench under a sweeping kirka tree. Around their small square island, the underground reflecting pool lapped quietly. As on the past four nights, they'd reminisced and shared hopes. Brennen and Phoena could conceivably return in as little as four more days. But Firebird's sense of disaster hadn't diminished, and tonight, when Tel mentioned Kinnor and Kiel—a month old today—she broke into long, racking sobs.

Unexpectedly Tel reached out and pulled her head to his shoulder. Sitting, he was barely taller than Firebird . . . but the gesture was comforting, his arms warm, and his shoulder already becoming too solid for a noble's. When she stopped shaking, he kept one arm tucked loosely around her waist.

At least she had a waist again. She'd lost all her pregnancy weight and then some.

"I should be shot, Firebird." He whispered so softly that she almost couldn't hear him. "I wish I had never left Netaia. Caldwell would still be here, if not for me."

On another small island, one she could see from this stone bench, they'd spoken their vows. She sighed, then saw the guilt contorting Tel's delicate features. "Don't talk that way," she said. "We made our choices, and not in ignorance."

"Firebird . . ."

She smiled at him fondly, but her tears gathered again.

"If neither of them comes back—I mean, if Phoena is . . . gone—then you're no wastling anymore. And if you ever wanted to go home—"

"It'll be a very long time before I stop hoping he'll be back."

"Let me finish." Tel laid his other hand on her arm, clutching with his long fingers. "Please. I couldn't bear to see you left a widow because of me. I'd owe you—well, anything I could give. If you wanted it."

Firebird saw that he too wavered near tears. "Thank you, Tel. I'll remember that."

The next day, a trio of Sentinels arrived at Hesed with messages. Firebird heard most of the news over lunch from young Labeth, but Dabarrah called her into his private office to deliver another message.

"We had more bad news from Netaia," he said solemnly.

"Another attack? Is Carradee all right?" If one more thing went wrong, she might pack a duffel, snatch back her babies, and run off into the mountains.

"Not harmed, but deposed. The Electorate forced her to abdicate."

Firebird could've sworn her heart stopped for a moment. "She didn't suicide?"

"No. No, I'm sorry I didn't make that clear. She drove Prince Daithi to Governor Danton. His condition is more serious than we were originally told."

But she hadn't taken the Powers' way out. *Bravo, Carradee!* "Will Daithi live?" Again she thought of his brother Alef, alive somewhere in the Federacy. Daithi still thought Alef was dead.

Dabarrah eyed her closely. She wondered if he sensed the old deception, even though she hadn't lied out loud. "With care," he answered.

"Will Danton send them to Tallis? Or—"

"I would allow them at Hesed."

"Yes," Firebird urged, glad to help save two more lives. "Thank you." Then she had to ask, "Who rules?"

"The Duke of Claighbro. Not as regent for Carradee, but for a new queen, Iarla Second."

Carradee had named her first daughter for their great-great-grandmother, Firebird's heroine—a wastling who survived to be crowned Queen of Netaia. Firebird's own ballad for Iarla now took on a new layer of meaning. Its chorus flitted through her memory: *Iarla the compassionate, Iarla the queen—Iarla, doomed to die young.* "Is there any news on Carradee's daughters? Do we know little Iarlet is safe?"

"Governor Danton sent them to Inisi, one of Ituri's protectorate worlds. There has never been Shuhr activity there. We should have word within days of their safe arrival."

That would be a relief. But . . . "Rogonin." Firebird mouthed the hated name, and her throat tightened. Rogonin would undo everything Danton and Carradee had accomplished. Where would that lead Netaia? "Master," she said urgently, "there's a simulation I worked with back at Thyrica. Can you call up what I left at Soldane University?" She had to know how this power shift would affect her home world, by the best Federate projection.

"I believe I can." He turned to his touchboard. She walked closer and watched over his shoulder as he routed a query. "We're updated by Soldane University whenever a messenger arrives from Thyrica."

"Don't look under my name," she warned him. "I took the course as Mari Tomma."

He touched in that name. A page appeared, written in academic jargon. She couldn't find even her name. Squinting, she leaned closer. "I turned in my final essay the day I went into labor. Did I pass?"

He touched a key, then smiled up at her. "Honorably. Congratulations. You were selected for University publication." Then he touched another series. The first page of her simulation appeared on the screen.

"That's it," she exclaimed.

"I'm transferring this," he said, still tapping keys, "to your data desk. Done. You're wise to follow events this way. It's a good use of your time."

"I can't leave it alone. But I'd rather have Kiel and Kinnor back. And Brennen. How can I stand this?" she begged. "I'm not simply half a person now. I'm less. I . . . can you tell," she blurted, "has he died?"

"He's definitely alive. I can tell by watching you that the pair bond remains intact."

Relieved, she pressed on. "You've accessed me ten times now. I haven't hurt you. I won't hurt Kiel or Kinnor. Please give them back."

"Firebird Mari." He steepled his fingers and raised both eyebrows compassionately. "There is too much at stake. We haven't solved your mystery, and you still cannot use that turn in any practical, controllable way. You must learn patience."

"I've stretched my patience to its end. It's gone."

His eyes softened. He pushed back his chair. "Then pray for strength and the will to go on for one more day. Our Speaker doesn't exempt His people from pain. He only enables us to bear it and be strengthened."

Firebird worked her fingers together. "I suppose you define impatience as a lack of faith."

Jenner Dabarrah held her stare with kind blue-gray eyes. "Your insight is excellent, Firebird Mari," he said, and she felt an assuring access-touch. "Faith and patience are closely linked."

Comforted, she found the courage to say, "Master, I have to get something off my conscience." She told him about Alef Drake and the lovely common-class woman who went into exile with him, and the wreckage she and Corey strewed in outer-system space, faking Alef's death. Her reluctance slowly turned to relief. "I don't know," she finished, "if it would do any good to confess this on Netaia. The electors would've killed Alef for no purpose. And I'd only be charged with another capital crime."

"I would advise keeping the secret a little longer." The master stood. "For now, confess it to the One."

From Him, Firebird could expect forgiveness.

"And write a song for them," Jenner suggested. "You have a gift for melody. You should use it more."

Tel leaned against the waterside railing and watched Firebird hurry away from Dabarrah's office.

He'd changed here. Like his muscles, his spirit had hardened. He actually enjoyed taskwork. The stable master claimed he showed a real talent with breeding animals. That work heightened his sense of identity, of a human dignity that came without aristocratic titles or pseudo-godhood.

But Phoena had left him.

She'd acted as if she needed him, as if she treasured what he could give her. . . .

But now he knew better.

After Firebird vanished under an arch into her room, Tel stepped out across the stones. Firebird hadn't noticed his agitation. Other concerns consumed her, and this matter hurt his pride. This wasn't something to share with another woman.

He rapped at the master's door. Dabarrah called softly, "Come in, Your Highness."

The master sat on the long white stone bench carved into his left wall. Tel sank into a still-warm wooden chair.

He dreaded that Dabarrah would ask, "What can I do for you?"

How would he say it? How would he humble himself again to a Sentinel, as he'd done by asking Brennen Caldwell's help? He stared back at the serene master, whose hair shone white-gold under the skylight. On another occasion, he might have suggested painting the man's portrait.

"Good afternoon," the master said simply. "Welcome."

Tel nodded slightly. "Thank you."

"You've been abandoned." Dabarrah spread his hands. "I will not—I cannot—eliminate your hurt. That would diminish you as a feeling person. But if you came for healing, I could escort you back through some of your memories of Princess Phoena. You need to recall her accurately, knowing now what she has done. In doing that, you may gain a deeper understanding of her motives and your own. It would help prepare you for her return. That's a kind of access healing," he said. "Is it something you feel can help you?"

"I think I already understand my motives."

Dabarrah raised an eyebrow.

Tel reached for his sash ends, but he wore no sash now, only simple gray shipboards. "Muirnen Rogonin and I were friends before the Veroh invasion, before Hunter Height. I know you just told Lady Firebird that he's trying to take power on Netaia."

"How?"

"The sekiyrra are buzzing with it," Tel explained. "And I knew weeks ago that he meant to try to talk Carradee off the throne. I . . . encouraged him, especially when he spoke about Phoena's natural nobility and about her sacrifices as our leader in the loyalist cause. I dreamed once of sitting beside Phoena as prince consort." The image promenaded through his mind one last time. "Now I know what Rogonin really wants. The crown. Just as Phoena did. Does," he corrected himself. He would not give up hope.

In the silence that followed, Tel heard water running beyond the arch. He shifted on the hardwood chair.

Dabarrah shook his head slowly. "Yes, Prince Tel. I agree with you about Rogonin, and so does Lady Firebird. I'll be contacting Governor Danton. Her Majesty and the prince should join you here in safety."

"Oh." Tel stared, considering. "Absolutely," he decided. "But Carradee will need to feel she has discharged her duty to Netaia, done her utmost, before she leaves. She would seek to fulfill that responsibility first. Yet . . ." He pushed upright in his seat. "Master, either Phoena or Firebird would have made a stronger queen."

Dabarrah stood. "You would be more comfortable in the inner room, if you still want the healing."

Tel pushed up out of his chair. "I'm ready," he said. "My conscience is clean."

An entry bell sent Three Zed's geneticist, Juddis Adiyn, hurrying past a terminal where his young technician sat keying in chromosomal data. Many of the unbound raised their own children, but the best and most gifted came from this laboratory. Rows of softly humming cylinders nourished embryos and fetuses destined for birth. Another wall held shorter-term incubation tubes, one row for each Golden City resident, their cloned embryos awaiting harvest and ayin extraction.

Ard Talumah, trader in unusual commodities, stood outside the main door. He pulled a pair of sample cases out from under one arm and looked down his long nose at Adiyn. "Yours."

"Any trouble?" Adiyn took the small cold-cases. He'd filled identical boxes with tissue specimens from Phoena Angelo. Until these new cases received alphanumeric designations, their labels were neatly printed

Casvah/Angelo, Iarla; and Casvah/Angelo, Kessaree.

"Think about it." Talumah lounged against the doorway. "Blasting a shuttle is easy. Leaving the passengers intact enough to get samples takes a little more effort."

"I would've preferred them intact. Alive." Adiyn sent a hint of displeasure on his epsilon wave. He'd looked forward to introducing two little girls to Three Zed's ways.

Talumah shrugged. "Hard vacuum isn't kind to the body. I pieced together what you wanted. Blood, deep tissue. All five types of nerve."

"Ayin?" Deep in the brain, those regions were difficult to harvest after a skull hardened. He hadn't taken Phoena's ayin sample until after her "execution," when they carried her down to be stased.

"I said all five."

Adiyn set the cases next to his tech. "Terza, designate and map these. Nuclear and mitochondrial. Priority. This is our new chromosome line."

Brennen struggled apprehensively to consciousness, fearing at any moment to feel the probe Polar had flung repeatedly through his alpha matrix. The lights had been brought up, and—he cautiously raised one arm—he'd been released from Polar's restraining field.

Then Polar had finished again.

It was the eighth day of interrogation. Yesterday, Polar claimed he'd broken the amnesia block, and flaunted a sheet of data. But Brennen saw nothing on it that Shirak's agents couldn't have learned from Harcourt Terrell's cohorts on Thyrica. Polar must have noted that thought, because this time he said nothing. That was a different kind of torment. Exhaustion and hatred weakened Brennen as Polar experimented with interrogation drugs that left him shaky and babbling.

The more power He gives us to wield, he heard in his own voice, *the more He must purify us.*

Have mercy . . .

Only footsteps, no sense of approaching mind, alerted him to Polar's return.

He opened his eyes, then sat up on the edge of the steely slab, gripping its rim with both hands. That last defense, willing himself unconscious, had returned to his control when he discovered a way to counter Polar's stimulants. It weakened him, though. So did the fear of what Polar might do to his body while his mind was elsewhere.

Polar stepped close. "Come," he ordered. "I have something to show you."

In a second laboratory lay a recently opened stasis crypt, a coffinlike apparatus designed to hold one severely injured patient almost indefinitely, until revival for treatment or permanent disposal. Beside the crypt, on a metal table that radiated warmth, lay a thin, dark-haired boy with a terrible head wound, inadequately bandaged. Brennen took a stool, double-guarded like the boy.

The boy groaned.

"Quiet." Polar rolled his own stool close. "I'll ease this for you if I can. And remember. There's a Caldwell watching. Carabohd. Do you understand?"

The boy turned dark eyes on Brennen, who saw mingled with his fear an awful hatred.

"Better." Polar reached for the boy's chest and let his hand lie there. "My real hopes are built on this, Caldwell. Today you'll see how fortuitous your arrival has been.

"This boy suffered massive brain injuries several years ago, fighting an age mate. We stabilized his condition, but he can't recover." Brennen glanced at the stasis crypt. Its pressurization mask dangled over one edge, and a super-cooling net lay limp in its depth. "He knew when we stased him that he'd serve our long plan by helping with research, instead of draining resources."

"I see he's no volunteer." Brennen clenched his stool.

"Watch your manners, Caldwell. He's unhappy enough. Now, let me explain. I place electromagnetic disruption probes here . . ." He slipped a hand under the small of the boy's back and taped on a wire. ". . . and here." He repeated the act at a pale, sweaty temple near the boy's wound. "Using a standard power source, I'll create a momentary reversal of his epsilon wave's electrical polarity. That will mirror-image its wave forms. Can you understand, brain damaged as you are?"

Brennen considered. Standing epsilon waves stabilized in uniform patterns, any of which was polarized in a particular direction, relative to the spine and ayin. Yes, he could understand.

Polar went on. "Any starbred subject reacts to the reversal with an involuntary turn. If at that instant I can access-link, that will superimpose my normal epsilon wave over his reversed-polarity wave. My theory is that this fusion should release a surge of wave-synchronous energy. I should be able to hold that energy as long as I can hold my own turn. The experimental evidence points that way, anyway. I do know it'll leave him little more than a husk."

"For certain?" Brennen asked dully.

"Yes. We've been unable to proceed past this point. You'll see why."

Brennen guessed Polar's "research" had proved more successful than he would acknowledge. "You're anxious to have me observe, then," he said, to mask another awful suspicion.

"Oh yes."

So this was his intended fate. If he didn't escape, he would be the next experimental subject, or the next. "But, Polar, this boy couldn't have begun to exercise his potential. And the injury—"

"Does age affect potential?" Polar reached aside. "And his ayin was undamaged." He brandished a syringe filled with pale pink fluid. "From my clones," he explained. "Undifferentiated brain-tissue suspension."

Brennen's heart wrenched. "You kill your own children."

"We 'harvest'—we do not 'kill.' Embryos have no sentience." He stepped behind a fabric screen. Brennen reached toward the doomed boy's shoulder, but a guard stepped between them.

Polar returned with his head tossed back and his eyes gleaming. "You must try it someday," he said. "The most breathtaking sensation I know."

"Never," Brennen whispered. But they'd surely extracted genes from his own cells. Were reproductive technicians culturing his cloned embryos?

Polar settled back onto the wheeled stool. "Hold him." Guards seized the boy's wrists and ankles. Polar leaned over the boy's body. "Now," he barked.

For one moment, Brennen felt a secondhand surge of epsilon energy thrust through him . . . and then fade into familiar silence. The boy lay without breathing, his face gray and contorted.

Polar sighed deeply, straightened, and then whirled his stool. "So you see. None of my subjects have survived the reversal. I think they simply weren't strong enough to maintain mental function while I tried for fusion. I need a stronger subject. Just one." Polar smiled, showing a row of perfect yellow-cream teeth. He snapped his fingers at Brennen's guards, then pointed up the passway. "Take him back."

Keeping all thought silenced, Brennen walked with the Shuhr guards to his cell. The door shut behind him soundlessly, and this time Brennen was grateful to be left alone. He dropped onto his cot.

What really happened in that laboratory? Did Polar devour the boy's potential, as Brennen suspected? Or had the demonstration failed, as Polar claimed?

Polar thought he could create a surge of incredible power simply by accessing a subject whose epsilon carrier wave was forced to reorient itself in a mirror image.

Brennen's thoughts sprinted on. The isolated Casvah-Angelo line had picked up at least one hereditary disorder, the one that caused Mazo syndrome. Could there have been a mutation too? Had Firebird Mari inherited a naturally reversed-polarity epsilon wave?

Could that have empowered her, when Harcourt Terrell forced access, to draw him into those horrific images? He stared at the black floor. Terrell's native abilities shouldn't have destroyed his beta centers. . . .

But if Terrell were in the Shuhr's pay, they might've given him ayin-extract treatments. Brennen imagined too much power to control . . . power enough to beat an access interrogation . . . then doubled, tripled, amplified enough to destroy himself as Firebird's dark images drew him in. Also, Terrell meant to murder her. Maybe she turned his own intention back on him.

The data fit perfectly, but that didn't mean his theory was correct.

Oh, Mari . . .

He sat up straight, imagining it again, picturing Firebird's vivid vision of darkness linked to Polar's notion of fusion power. If it really could be created, and if Terrell and Firebird both were turning at the moment he tried to destroy her, without any shielding static between them, then Terrell's accentuated epsilon strength—and the wave-fusion—might have blasted back through his mind, which was focused on death—and killed him.

He rubbed his stubbled chin. Or maybe that energy surge always killed the weaker partner in link. Polar destroyed all his subjects, though he tried to keep them alive.

All theories, just theories. He actually understood only one thing. Polar meant to use him, too, for a research subject, after trapping Firebird and forcing him to kill her. In bereavement shock, he'd be truly undone.

Not if he escaped! But his captors kept him locked down and guarded. This cell was as secure as any at MaxSec.

Knowing the worst possible fate gave him an odd sense of calm. Yes, they would suffer if Mari came here . . . but that would end. Even Destia hadn't suffered long, compared with the peace she now enjoyed. And maybe Mari would stay at Hesed, after all.

He had broken despair's stranglehold. Now for his hatred: He drew a deep breath and called up the final image Micahel Shirak had poured into his wounded memory—Destia's gentle blue eyes, terror wide in a last silent scream.

He imagined, then, those eyes as they widened farther with wonder, opening again beyond the Crossing, seeing first all her family—together—and then One who had brought them safely Across.

Any pain we endure as we die, he had read, *is the last we will suffer forever*. He sighed deeply.

Another thought shattered his momentary peace. If Dru Polar achieved this fusion, how would he use it?

CHAPTER 25
FOR BRENNEN

con molto affetto
with deep feeling

Late that afternoon, two Special Operations ships reached Hesed's perimeter. After watching them glide in on the grassy strip, Firebird seated herself in the commons for dinner with Tel. He listened, frowning, while she explained the Federate simulation's projections for Netaia under Rogonin's regency. Barring unforeseen circumstances—outside attacks, natural disasters, significant scientific discoveries—their home world might slip back toward stability for a few years. "But at what cost," she exclaimed, punctuating the sentence with her soup spoon. Behind Tel's shoulder, two uniformed Sentinels strode across the stepping stones toward the commons. "You know Rogonin. He'll strip the low classes of everything Danton gave them. When they finally stand up and resist him, when they've stockpiled weapons and recruited disgruntled military people, the uprising will be much worse than if—"

She fell silent. The uniformed Sentinels reached the waterside commons—bulky young Air Master Dardy, followed by a tall black-haired woman with proud eyes, a shapely but prominent nose, and slightly concave cheeks. Could that be—?

Tel craned his neck around, following her stare.

Firebird scrambled to her feet. "Ellet!" What brought her here? Firebird reluctantly thrust out a hand. "Hello, Dardy. Join us."

"Mistress Caldwell," Ellet Kinsman returned smoothly. Her face looked pale, her eyes red.

Tel stood too. Firebird laid a hand on his shoulder. "This is my sister's husband, Ellet: Prince Tel Tellai-Angelo. Tel, this is Captain Ellet Kinsman of the Federate forces and Air Master Damalcon Dardy of Thyrica."

"We know of you, Prince Tel," said Ellet. "We've come from Master Dabarrah's rooms."

Firebird sat back down. Dardy seated Ellet, then walked off to find a sekiyr to bring two more bowls. Firebird's stomach clenched so tightly that she hoped her soup would stay down.

"I've had the news," Ellet said quietly, "from Master Dabarrah. I'm sorry. For all of us."

Of course she was sorry. And had Ellet asked him why Sentinels were told to shun Firebird?

Tel checked the silvery pitcher. "I'll get more kass." He hurried toward the servo, leaving Firebird and Ellet alone.

Firebird took a deep breath. She ought to tell Ellet it was good to see her, or make some other insincere small talk. She'd never been good at that.

Ellet glanced darkly at Tel as he bowed gracefully to a sekiyr and then turned back to the table. "Tonight," Ellet muttered. "We need to talk."

Firebird sat on her bedside, clenching a slick red-and-blue audio rod in frustration.

"He's alive, then," Ellet remarked as confidently as Master Dabarrah had done. "And since he hasn't come back empty-handed, we can assume his RIA unit took him past their fielding."

"Then he's been taken prisoner." The constant cascade poured down the wall, and beside Firebird and Brennen's bed a luma globe shone dimly. "I can't do nothing, Ellet," said Firebird. "If I thought I could break out of Hesed's perimeter and pass the fielding at Three Zed, nothing could keep me here. You've seen Mistress Anna, and everyone else, with the twins. Even if I failed, Kiel and Kin would be raised as lords—or princes." Her chest no longer ached when she thought of them. Only numbness remained.

"Never doubt that."

Firebird raised her head. "Yes. I've been to the altar now. I know."

Ellet mumbled, "Congratulations."

Firebird sighed. "What can you tell me about the Three Zed situation? They attacked Thyrica. Does the Federacy intend to do anything?"

"Oh yes. They sent the Fleet to Soldane."

"That's not what I meant." . . . *and you know it, Captain Kinsman. Will they give Three Zed what it deserves? What they did to Netaia?*

Ellet compressed her lips. "There's been debate, but several representatives are stalling. They're afraid. They want to stand back and let us settle the problem."

"So now we're a liability to other Thyrians. If the Shuhr attack us again, they'll get in the way." Firebird bowed her head. "Regional command . . . are they still angry with Brennen?"

"They never were," Ellet said dryly. "They simply enforced regs."

"What about the Special Ops agents who came with you?"

"They're headed out. Covert."

Surprised to get so much information, Firebird absently tapped the audio rod against her bedside table and stared around the room. "What kind of ship do you have?"

"Dardy and I brought a four-seat J46 transport with a RIA system."

Firebird's breath caught. She felt as if Ellet had handed her an armed missile. "You have RIA?"

Ellet barely smiled. "So you know about that too."

"Brennen showed me. Here."

"Claggett found a way to make RIA catch a carrier," Ellet explained, "to spare effort for finer work. There are five RIA ships now, still concealed from the Federacy. As we were coming to Hesed, we were allowed one."

If a RIA unit could *catch* an epsilon carrier, whatever that meant technically, she might not even have to hold a turn. "Why did . . ." No. Firebird shouldn't ask that. Ellet's business here was her own.

But Ellet answered, holding one hand near her mouth. "Damalcon has asked for my hand, and he wants Master Dabarrah to bless our bonding ceremony. I haven't consented, but I agreed to consider it. For the master's advice, and for news of . . . you and Brennen, the run to Hesed was worth applying for."

A detached part of Firebird's mind understood Ellet's machinations. "Might I look at your RIA ship?" She didn't turn to meet the tall Sentinel's eyes.

"I would have been surprised if you hadn't asked. You've undoubtedly been wanting to get back into flying."

Firebird spun to see Ellet's face, solemn and knowing.

So. Ellet meant to give her a chance to slip to Three Zed. Ellet also knew it would probably kill her—in a worthy cause, as before: this time, a chance Brennen might escape alone. A long shot, but Ellet would risk anything to free Brennen from the Shuhr . . . and from Firebird.

Firebird slid a finger up and down the audio rod's gleaming surface, and for one moment, she sympathized with her rival. Undoubtedly Ellet also suffered from visions of Brennen in Shuhr hands. Brenn imprisoned, abused.

Ellet's cheek barely twitched. "I wouldn't even be surprised to find Damalcon willing to check you out in it tomorrow. There'll be time before we meet with Master Dabarrah."

Ellet strode out across the stepping stones, deeply satisfied. Although untrainable and unstable, Firebird now was determined to go—and would unquestionably fail at Three Zed.

But she might get a RIA ship to Brennen before they killed her.

Dardy had brought the J46 from Thyrica to Regional HQ at Tallis, never suspecting Ellet hoped to send Firebird after Phoena. Today's news, that Brennen had already left Hesed for Three Zed, nearly crushed Ellet.

So she would send Firebird after Brennen instead of for Phoena. Obviously Firebird wanted that. *I would want it too*, Ellet admitted.

Tomorrow, Firebird would commandeer that transport. To keep a RIA craft from falling into Shuhr hands, she and Dardy would be justified in taking a fast Brumbee messenger ship and chasing her—before they had time to forge a pair bond! Dardy was a good man, attractive and certainly connatural, but he wasn't Brennen Caldwell.

They'd never be able to intercept her in slip, but in a Brumbee they could beat her to Three Zed. The two trained Sentinels then would free Brennen. Assisting another Sentinel in danger was allowed by the Privacy and Priority Codes, regardless of risk or expense. Ellet and Brennen—and hopefully, Dardy—would return with both ships. That was how she'd justify it to Dabarrah.

They'd save Firebird too, if they could.

But if Firebird and her ship were destroyed there . . .

Brennen would need comforting.

Firebird did find Dardy willing to check her out in the new transport ship, though she had to wait for the next evening, and her cautious attempt to run up the RIA unit was less than encouraging.

But when she returned to her chamber, she found not Ellet but Jenner and Anna Dabarrah standing at the foot of her bed . . . with her babies. Master Jenner cradled Kinnor over his shoulder. Anna held fair little Kiel in front of her like a shield.

"Firebird," Master Jenner murmured, his voice heavy with concern. "I can think of only one reason you would've gone out with Sentinel Dardy."

Firebird stepped closer. A force more powerful than gravity drew her to those blanketed bundles.

"This is your son," Anna said hoarsely. "The image of your husband and the promised of your God. How dare you consider leaving him? How dare you, Firebird?"

She ached to touch him, hold him. Would Anna let her?

Let her? She was his mother! "You've already taken him from me, Anna." Firebird's voice shook. "And you, Master Jenner."

"Do you consider yourself more of a match to the Shuhr than Brennen, who was called there?" asked Anna. "Do you wish these children orphaned? Never to know mother or father?"

Firebird crossed to the cascade. She parted the watery curtain with one finger, but she couldn't take her eyes off the child Anna held. Image of his father . . . yes! Gently squared chin, even beneath his baby-round cheeks—sapphire eyes—and Kinnor slept so peacefully, curled around Master Dabarrah's shoulder. "Never to know the horror their mother found inside herself?" she reminded them.

"It lies in everyone, Firebird." Mistress Anna caressed Kiel's plump cheek with her nose, then looked up, softening. "We simply can't see it. But, Firebird, you're so frightened. That's why you anger so easily nowadays." Anna appeared to relax, though Firebird never felt certain of most Sentinels' real emotions. They controlled so Powers-blessed well. "Don't leave them. You cannot. You must not."

Firebird sank onto the bedside and looked up into Master Jenner's compassionate eyes. "Will you make me a prisoner again, then? That's what it would take to keep me here."

"No," said Jenner.

Startled, she looked from Jenner to Anna. Anna pursed her lips and clung to Kiel.

"Firebird," said Jenner, "if you mean to go, we have no right to contain you. I ask only that you let me know your decision. Let me send help with you."

"I . . . will," she said shakily. This gracious capitulation was the last thing she expected. "Thank you." Then she stretched toward Mistress Anna. "Give him to me. Please. Let me hold him."

"I cannot. Shamarr Dickin—"

"You can. I'm his mother. I've never broken your unnatural prohibition. I'd never harm him." After fourteen uneventful sessions with Master Jenner, she believed it was true. Terrell's death must've been coincidental. "Give him to me."

Frowning, Anna stepped to the bedside. She laid the wriggling child in Firebird's arms.

A familiar warmth pulled Firebird's shoulders forward and her head down, curling her body womblike around an infant she'd longed to hold again. He felt heavier than she remembered, with a faint, milky smell. "Kiel," she whispered. "Precious one." She clutched tightly.

Squirming, he gave a short cry. Firebird stiffened. She'd forgotten what to do. Her very instincts seemed to have died.

Anna arched her eyebrows. She reached down again. Kiel started to whimper.

"I am not hurting him." Firebird sat motionless for a moment longer, then raised her child back up to Anna.

Anna seized him, pressed him possessively to her shoulder, and rocked from side to side. Kiel quieted instantly.

Firebird felt as if she'd been stabbed. She stood and tiptoed around Master Jenner to look into Kinnor's elfin face. He scowled in his sleep.

She backed away, not wanting to wake him. "Thank you," she whispered dully.

As the Sentinels carried the twins out her door, she sank onto her knees on white flagstones. They wouldn't keep her here, after all! She could leave freely—

Then she shuddered. Leave her children? What was she thinking about, going to that place? Clenching her hands, she curled forward. *Holy One, help me. Show me. They've given me the choice. What shall I do?*

For several minutes, she prayed. Then she listened. She prayed again, focusing this time on His nature, His love, His will, and the song she had heard in her vision—the primal music of creation. *Show me*, she begged again.

An incredibly strong urge hit her. She must leave. She must leave *now*. Without delay. She felt no fear, only an unshakable conviction.

She sprang to her feet.

Master Dabarrah entered his office. Mistress Anna followed him, bowing her head.

"She still means to go," Anna murmured. Her tightly guarded tone and facial expression said nothing, but on the resonance of the pair bond Dabarrah felt shock and reproof. "Even knowing all she now knows. I thought her heart would change when she saw the children again."

Closing the outer door and dimming his office lights, Dabarrah shook his head mournfully. "Anna, remember. Firebird was raised by servants, not her mother. Her own mother ordered her death. She never experienced the mother-child bond we take for granted."

Anna folded her hands against the skirt of her long blue gown. "Reconsider, Jenner. Send a sekiyr to watch her rooms. Guard her. Keep her here, under gentle restraint."

"No. I gave my word."

Dabarrah felt her disappointment. Immediately it turned to waiting steadiness. How he loved this godly woman!

"Yes, we could keep Firebird here," he said. "She is welcome."

"But she unsettles the Sanctuary with her misery," Anna admitted. "That would only grow worse."

"Maybe she too is called there. Kiel and Kinnor have been given life. They are safe, and the line will continue. Imagine her pain, giving them birth and then having them wrenched away."

Sadness, sympathy, and pain flooded the bonding resonance. He laid an arm across Anna's shoulder. "I know two full Sentinels here who would willingly join Firebird in her mission. Tomorrow morning I'll speak to them, choose one, and send Firebird with our help and blessings." He sank with Anna onto the stone bench, careful not to sit on her long straight hair.

"You know her willfulness," Anna answered. "She'll bring him back or die."

He wrapped her in his presence, comforting her. "There is the matter of Sentinel Kinsman," he added.

Anna's eyes clouded. "How does that follow? Does she guess what Firebird means to do with her ship?"

"Ellet came to Hesed precisely for that purpose. To lure Firebird to her death and launch a rescue effort for Phoena . . . and then Brennen." Dabarrah visualized, for his bond mate, the sum of Ellet's actions that led him to this conclusion.

Anna tilted her head, indignant. "So thanks to Ellet, we must send at least one more Sentinel into the trap at Three Zed, to protect the RIA secret." He nodded. "I wouldn't have thought it of Ellet," said Anna. "She's the responsible one, Mistress Firebird the volatile one."

"Neither is so simple as that." He knew them both too well. "Firebird has shown me moments of surprising wisdom. Ellet's sense of responsibility vanishes where the Caldwell family is concerned."

"Is she still chasing Brennen?"

"She has made herself ill with jealousy."

"Why did she come here with Sentinel Dardy? Is she deceiving him as to their compatibility?"

"No, they're deeply connatural. In denying him, Ellet is probably resisting her only chance for bonded happiness."

Anna slipped out from under his arm. "You must discipline her, then, Master Dabarrah. 'Reproof is painful, but love requires it,'" she quoted. "Ellet is a wonderful woman with many talents."

"Yes, and she can be cured. Restored to useful service. Would you bring her—and Air Master Dardy—to the office, my love?"

Anna stood silently for a few seconds, fingering her skirt. Then she squared her shoulders. "Ah," she said. Smiling, she nodded. "Indeed." She turned toward the door.

Two minutes later, Anna Dabarrah stood outside that same doorway. Inside, Ellet Kinsman and Damalcon Dardy occupied all her husband's attention and half of hers. Ellet's voice rose, arguing vehemently.

Anna wanted to call a sekiyr to attend Kinnor and Kiel. Yet she'd just checked their alpha rhythms, and those infant heirs to the prophecies slept deeply. For half an hour, they wouldn't need her.

Only half an hour. That much time, I can give Ellet and Damalcon. She opened the office door and went in.

Firebird halted outside that office door and raised a hand to knock. She heard voices through the door and hesitated. The conversation sounded low and intense. *Don't interrupt.* It felt like the same Voice, and it roused not fear but a deep, holy awe. *Don't delay.* If she waited for Dabarrah's help, that might take hours.

One minute, she begged the Voice. *Just one.*

She whirled toward the next door. For the only time since the prohibition had been laid on her, she stole into Dabarrah's private rooms.

By the dim light of a round ceiling luma, she found two tiny warming cots. She bent and kissed each child, her heart aching under a load of guilt. *Little sons of destiny*, she crooned silently. *Forgive me for going.* If she didn't come back, they wouldn't even remember her. One tear splattered on a tiny cheek, but fortunately it was Kiel's. He wriggled but didn't cry out.

Oh, Singer, she pleaded, *watch over them. Keep them safe, help them grow, let them know that I . . . loved them. I loved them as well as I could.*

Firebird wrenched away from her sons' cribs, crept along the pool, and rapped quickly on Tel's door.

It took less than a minute to explain her intentions. "Meet me at the hangar in five minutes," she finished, "or I'll be gone."

"Fuel banks are charged? And there's room for four to make our escape?" He jumped toward his bureau.

She nodded. "The question is whether I can learn to control that projection module well enough to matter before we reach Three Zed. It's only a twelve-day slip, and I have no RIA training. I can't even turn every time I try. I'll have to do it mostly on instinct."

"I have every confidence in your instincts, Firebird." Tel threw a handful of clothing onto his bed. "I can practice piloting in slip on the override sims, so I'll be able to help if you need it."

"We do have to leave quickly. I . . . prayed about it," she said self-consciously, "and that's the answer I heard. Master Jenner actually offered to help us."

"He did?" Tel stood up straight.

"Yes, but he's busy, and I don't dare wait for him to finish."

"That would make a difference?"

"Probably hours." Hours, she mourned, that she could've spent with Kinnor and Kiel. *Singer, I really could use Master Dabarrah's help. . . .*

Go now.

Tel tossed a duffel onto his pile. "I'll be ready in two minutes," he said. "Go pack."

"I'll fly it out." Firebird slip-sealed the craft and harnessed in. A four-seater with bunks aft, this light transport smelled of damp soil and kirka trees. At the edge of her peripheral vision, Tel stowed and secured their satchels. She worked through the preflight check, sinking her maternal depression deep down. "We're going to alert someone no matter what we do, so we'll make this fast. It's a straight shot out the hollow. I'll accelerate the second we hit the bay's main aisle. Ready?"

Tel swung into the other front seat and secured himself. "Ready." On his face she saw hard determination, and though she despised the object of his affections, in that moment she knew she'd learned to love Tel.

They blasted into a starry sky. Firebird punched in the fielding drop code she'd seen Dardy use and set a vertical course, and the speedy little ship responded as designed. By now, she guessed, Jenner and Anna had found the message she left, thanking them for their offer of help, explaining the urgency she felt, begging their forgiveness . . . and asking that if she didn't return, the twins would be raised together. Soon the transport passed out of Procyel II's gravitational interference. Firebird fed her computer the celestial coordinates she'd researched from Hesed's database. The onboard translation program turned those into a slip heading. Firebird took a confirming readout, shot off one more prayer—for the only help that really mattered—and then pressed the jump bar. The slip-shield activated, the translight drive pressed her spine against the seat's frame, and they were away.

"Just like that?" Tel asked.

Firebird smiled down the console, wishing she could give him a friendly kiss but not daring to offend his sensibilities. She sighed and stretched, then sat fingering Brennen's medallion on its chain. "Just like that. Now the work begins. Unless I can learn to ride this RIA unit in twelve days, we'll do just as well ringing the bell and asking the Shuhr to take us in."

CHAPTER 26

ONE CROSSING

allegro sussurando
quickly, whispering

On his bed in an emerald-encrusted chamber, Juddis Adiyn lay staring at his obsidian ceiling. A bedside field generator projected threads of light—blues and purples, yellow and pale red—onto the glimmering blackness. Their hypnotic flickering helped him reach a trance state, in which he could call the elusive shebiyl to mind and glimpse the future.

. . . The young woman he knew from tri-D images to be Firebird Caldwell, sleeping in a spacecraft bunk near an effeminate young man sprawled on a flight seat . . .

Then she was on her way, or shortly would be! Sentinels were fools not to use the shebiyl. Perhaps they thought it caused pride. But he'd seen his own death too many times, in too many ways, to grow proud of this work. He used all his skills to serve his people. He was as committed to their purposes as any Sentinel was to the Federacy. Unfortunately, only one group could win the long war.

He closed his eyes again.

The path branched. He pressed his awareness down one stream of possible events—

. . . She lay at his feet. That striking auburn hair masked her face as she writhed out the last breaths of her life. Caldwell clutched the dendric striker in shaking hands. Anguish and shock hammered him to his knees. . . .

Excellent! And from the clarity of this branch, highly probable. Polar would want to see this. Smug despite his self-warning, Adiyn pressed his point of consciousness across the gap between branches, toward another gleaming vision—

. . . An explosion filled his brain, fire and blinding light . . . and then darkness. . . .

Another possible death! Hastily he probed backward up that stream to see what had gone wrong. He'd evaded deadly danger three times that way.

The branch vanished before he could manipulate it. He rolled on his bed, cursing the shebiyl that afforded such clear glimpses but would not always yield to skilled handling. What event had opened that branch? Where was the nexus point? How to prevent disaster?

He forcibly slowed his own pulse. Once, he'd foreseen his death as a high probability, at Dru Polar's hands. He avoided the confrontation and still managed to get his own way. Now he sent epsilon signals throughout his body, gradually calming its shaking and perspiring. Then, though the shebiyl faded, he pressed his point of focus across emptiness toward another strong branch.

. . . There, too, she lay at his feet, writhing. . . .

She was an attractive woman, in agony. Very much like her sister.

And just as they could keep using Phoena Angelo's ruined body for genetic research, they would take Firebird Caldwell's . . . though in Firebird's case, they would allow full, irreversible brain death. Phoena's stasis crypt would preserve the princess for decades, irreparably crippled but medically alive, available for sampling or further experiments. Adiyn's tech also had gene preps well under way for both dead child-princesses. Adiyn owned the Casvah chromosomal line now. It was one more step in his people's self-evolution.

Smiling, he waved off the ceiling lights. The shebiyl faded as he drifted toward sleep.

Brennen lay restrained on the contoured couch. Today it felt ominously comfortable. In his cell last night, Polar had mounted a device that screeched every few minutes to keep him awake. He couldn't guess what Polar meant to try. He blinked his aching eyes as the long-haired Shuhr steered a cart toward the head of his couch. On it rode a device that was roughly cubical and vented, with a conical protrusion.

"Yesterday evening," Polar said, "I remembered that natural amnesia can result from an alpha-matrix discontinuity. One of our researchers worked on that topic several years ago. He developed this to restore alpha function."

A hard point pressed against the top of Brennen's skull. Caught in the restraining field, he couldn't move away.

"First, we'll read your alpha frequencies. Scan the matrix to produce a map."

The device hummed. Polar stood over him, looking first at his face, then past him, then at his face again. After several minutes, he reached toward the device. "Yes," he said softly. "There's the gap. It looks as if something cut a scoop right through your associational grid. Want to see?"

"Why not?" Brennen muttered. Maybe Polar would release the restraining field for a few seconds. If Polar watched the grid instead of his victim's thoughts, Brennen might catch him off guard . . .

A red image appeared on the ceiling, shaped like half a melon and crisscrossed inside and out with yellow lines. One area flickered even as he watched, while another faded. Brennen recognized the standard College visualization of the complex alpha matrix.

"See it?" Polar asked.

Deep inside the hemisphere, an asymmetrical slash disrupted a major area, separating it from every line in the main grid. It did look like a dark scoop. No lines crossed that terrible disruption. Inside it, the alpha grid had turned a grayed, inactive shade.

That was his conscious mind, the resource that made him a Sentinel— made him human. He'd done the damage himself. But as long as that area held his most sensitive memories, keeping them isolated from the surface of his mind, no interrogator could access them.

"All I need," Polar said, "is to restore one link, one crossing. Amused, Caldwell? Today, I hope to cure you."

"You can't." Only an access healer like Dabarrah could restore amnesia blocks.

"I think that this time, I'll prove you wrong." Polar shut off the projection, fiddled with the device, and then stepped away. "Feel anything? Warm spot?"

"No."

Polar shrugged. "According to my records, this device worked best during natural sleep. So relax," he murmured. "Pleasant dreams, Caldwell. Pleasant, healing dreams."

He strode out, pausing only to wave off the room light, leaving one guard on watch.

Brennen struggled briefly and uselessly against the restraint field, then blinked up into drowsy darkness. It would be easy to sleep. If he just shut his eyes and surrendered, he'd sleep deeply.

Hoping only to stay awake, he prayed.

Father and Speaker of the Eternal Word . . . Creator . . . Sustainer . . . you fill the universe with glory, and all time bows to you. Thank you for calling me your servant. Holy One, I have nothing left to give you but my life. If there is no other escape from this place, lift me into your presence. Keep me from betraying my people and the family you promised to honor.

"Mari," he whispered. *Mighty One, mercy! She thinks she found complete love in me, and I let her think it. Forgive me! Don't hold my arrogance against her. If you have to remove me to bring her close to yourself, I am your willing servant.*

Let her die to pride . . . as I should've done. I depended too much on my abilities, too little on you, he confessed.

Had he rushed into this trap? No . . . he'd come as the Speaker called, motivated by mercy and faith, but believing that the call confirmed the Holy One's faith in him. *She knew, Lord. She saw my pride because she is proud herself. Spare her. Show us both, willful as we are, how to obey you.*

Shamarr Dickin told him, long ago, that any place the Speaker called a believer was a place for an altar. Now the truth of that statement shattered the last of his pride.

And finally, he heard the Voice. *I have asked all that you are. Are you ready to give it?*

"Yes," he whispered. "Take me. Only spare Mari. Please, Holy One." Her image rushed into his mind, as when he first saw her . . . her delicate chin and soft red cheeks, that sweat-soaked auburn hair clinging to her forehead . . . dying by poison, by her own hand, as ordered . . .

. . . the image shifted to a dusty sky, and his mission to defend Veroh. He had to be dreaming. Mari flew as his wingman, and their wing tips almost touched. Her voice sang over his headset interlink, a song he didn't remember.

Wing to wing,
O my love,
Touch me, take me—

A hot light blasted him awake. Dru Polar settled into his usual seat near the couch's right shoulder. The silvery rod protruded from his sash belt. *Dendric striker,* Brennen realized. No world calling itself civilized participated in that weapon's manufacture. It scanned a victim's reflex-arc frequencies, then launched a cascade of motor-nerve firings. Poor Phoena!

"Welcome back," purred Polar. "One thread. One crossing. I told you that's all it would take."

He recognized the weapon! What was this treatment device? Special Ops needed to know it existed . . . but he wouldn't be the one to bring back that information. He must cue another amnesia block. He drew a deep, shaking breath. The alpha matrix wouldn't tear as cleanly as before. He would cause worse damage—deeper, and more likely to prove permanent. Polar would restore one more thread, and Brennen would be forced to create another block. After only a few cycles, he'd be truly helpless.

But useless to Polar as an intelligence source. And, maybe, as an experimental subject.

I will ask all that you are. Now he understood. This, too, was an altar.

At least he'd awakened refreshed enough to remember the Voice. Polar couldn't make him sleep, not naturally, for several hours. He might not break today. After tomorrow, though, there might be little left of his mind. *If this is your tempering for eternity, Holy One, strengthen me to face it. If not, guide my fight!*

"Don't do it, Caldwell," said Polar. An image flashed onto the ceiling: the tall, angular MaxSec Tower, the Federacy's stronghold on Tallis IV, headquarters of Regional command. "You're finished, and you know it. We'll start here."

"No," Brennen whispered. "You won't." He winced as he cued the second block.

A red stone valley carpeted with brown grass and graceful animals cantering on low hills: These, and a cold sky veiled by wisps of cloud, framed Carradee's first glimpse of the Hesed Valley.

A lanky Master Sentinel introduced himself as Jenner Dabarrah. He escorted her underground and showed her the vast pool rippling under its skylights, then they saw Daithi revived from travel sedation in a warm, impressively modern special-care cubicle. This underground hall felt oddly familiar, as if she'd dreamed it.

Dabarrah took her into his office and offered a simple wooden chair, then apologized that he must deliver unsettling news.

Carradee crossed her ankles under the chair and gripped her hands in her lap. "Very well," she said. "Tell us, Master Dabarrah."

His voice conveyed real pain. "To our best knowledge, the shuttle carrying your daughters has not arrived in the Inisi system. We should have had word five days ago. A search has been mounted, madame."

The edges of Carradee's vision darkened. Her throat tightened. "Master Dabarrah, do you think they are alive?"

"We have no way of knowing," he said gently. "Accidents in slip-state are extremely rare but not impossible."

"Abduction?" she asked, pressing a hand to her chest. "Murder?"

"Majesty, our people are checking all sensor records of arrivals and departures in Inisi space. It could be some time until we receive word." He extended a hand. "I can at least ease your worry. In our terms, let me place a site block in the alpha matrix that carries your thoughts and emotions. You will accomplish nothing by suffering. May I help you this way, while others help by searching?''

When she shut her eyes, she saw a small, trusting face rimmed with curls bent over her bedside to kiss her good-bye. Exhausted from travel and from worrying about Daithi, Carradee gulped tears down the back of her throat. Truly, her misery wouldn't solve the mystery, heal Daithi, nor bring back Firebird, General Caldwell, or Prince Tel.

You are weak! she berated herself, but she nodded. "Yes, Master Dabarrah. Please help me."

Dabarrah rose from his chair, stood over her, and laid both hands on her head.

An hour later, after stopping briefly in a room that adjoined the medical suite and had been assigned to her, she joined Master Dabarrah and his wife at a circular table near the waterside. Young men and women ladled out bowls full of fragrant stew as a young couple sat down next to Master and Mistress Dabarrah. The master introduced them as Sentinel Dardy and his bride, Ellet. Ellet's dazed, joyous stare never left the Sentinel's boyish face, and he waited on her with tender deference.

"Bonding shock." Dabarrah leaned toward Carradee, his smile full of compassion. "It lasts only a few days. It's good for the Sanctuary to have them here. All of us feel their love and wonder, and they don't mind our company. They scarcely notice us."

Carradee stared a little longer at the oval-faced woman. She certainly seemed happy. Was this what happened to Firebird?

Dabarrah had dulled her grief from a frantic, serrated knife edge to this calm sadness. These truly were good, kindly people. Governor Danton hadn't deliberately sent Iarlet and Kessie into oblivion, either. If they were alive anywhere in Federate space, Federate searchers would find them. If not—

O Mighty Powers, receive them into bliss. And comfort me. But the Powers never comforted. She had defied them, refusing to suicide—sending her daughters offworld—coming here.

"After dinner," said Anna Dabarrah, "please join us at a vespers service. We will offer thanks for your safe arrival and prayers for your daughters."

Had the woman read her mind? "Thank you. You surely know that I've worshiped other gods all my life. I betrayed them by coming here."

"You are welcome to join us at service," said Master Dabarrah. "At Hesed, we speak a language of grace."

Carradee spooned the last drops of brown broth from her bowl. *A language of grace.* That sounded so comforting. "I . . . want to know more,

Master . . . Mistress. But first, please, may I meet my nephews?"

Firebird's onboard computer brought her out of slip-state near Three Zed. As she anticipated, it seemed all too soon. Tel had helped her experiment with the RIA apparatus. A Sentinel probably wouldn't have let him try, fearing a loss of secrecy, but she couldn't have done this alone.

It took hours to navigate through the unexpected asteroid debris, using only touches on steering thrusters, but finally she approached the planet. Then, grasping Tel's hand in unspeaking understanding, she gave him control of the ship.

She slid on the splayed-finger RIA headset. Edging inward to turn, she felt strangely composed. The flaming terror no longer frightened or called to her. It was only a pseudomythical memory . . . she hoped. She passed through its familiar horror storm, secured her carrier, and then reached back out for the RIA harmonic. The new technology snatched and held her crippled epsilon carrier.

Instantaneously, her senses extended outward, passing through the ship's bulkheads into space. Using the RIA unit, she found she could focus them in any direction. She exhaled in relief and listened toward Three Zed, while watching for motion in high orbit.

"There," she murmured to Tel. "I found their fielding net. But don't go in yet."

To her altered perception, the fielding satellites felt like dozens of disembodied intelligences glaring into space, poised to destroy an approaching mind.

How to blind one of those satellite eyes? She could rely only on instinct, on her barely adequate control of the RIA unit, and a remark made long ago by her traitorous old instructor at the Planetary Naval Academy. Vultor Korda had heaped scorn on a Sentinel who could only "push a few electrons along." If phase control was a simple skill, then maybe in concert with the powerful RIA unit she could kill a satellite.

She'd also experienced, kneeling in front of Master Dabarrah, how it should feel to listen with her epsilon sense. She extended her probe a little farther and touched one solar-sailed cylinder. Passing inside its metal walls, her amplified senses heard a cacophony of electrical activity, hissing and buzzing in staccato rhythms.

Like the visualization that let her turn, this sparked an idea. Maybe if she had learned to hear this way, she also could sing.

Imagining a note at utter tritonal disharmony from the satellite's fundamental pitch, she willed that note to sound, using the satellite's circuitry as her instrument. It vibrated at the frequency she commanded. The satellite howled around her, every surface a sounding board. A series of harmonics built, tone on shattering tone, that made her cringe and almost flee. Then it fell absolutely silent.

She wrenched her awareness back across kilometers of vacuum into the pilot's seat, and the universe seemed to shrink. "I got one, Tel," she gasped. At last she appreciated how exhausting the outlay of mental energy could be. "There." With the computer's light wand she set a spark onto the fore screen and covered one smoothly moving point of light.

"It's too far ahead of us now." He pulled one hand off the controls. "We've fallen back in orbit."

"Chase it! I don't want to do that again!"

The transport shuddered as he accelerated, pursuing the corridor of marginal safety. Firebird snugged her harness, leaned back with her eyes closed, and forced herself again into accord with RIA. Pressing the RIA sense forward, she scouted for the weird music of those satellite eyes. She waited seemingly forever for the ship to drop, all the while trying to hold blinders over the darkness that rose with her carrier. To distract herself, she hummed the melody she'd written for Iarla, her niece's namesake. That tune made her feel brave.

"We're through their orbital altitude," Tel whispered loudly. "Where do we set down?"

She too wanted to whisper as she eyed the sensor screens. "Squill," she exclaimed softly, "I don't know." Extending the RIA probe one more time, she scrutinized the black sphere for "sounds" of life. "Take us as low as you can," she mumbled, and she swept her point of awareness along the planet's distant surface. "We don't know if those fielding satellites see downward as well as up." Had Jenner's? She hadn't paid attention. She'd lost all her old training habits. "This could take a while."

Finally, she spotted the largest colony by its cackle of enharmonic voices. "That peak. There. Don't get too close."

He cut speed and dropped lower yet, into the shadow of a volcanic crag. "Here, Firebird?"

"Good."

He set down with a jolt that Firebird ignored. Gladly she pulled off the headset and shook out her hair, shaking free, too, of a sickening dread at the pit of her stomach. For a while she'd be glad to avoid contact with that tainted epsilon carrier.

Tel unharnessed first. "Hurry, Firebird. Powers go with you."

"Do you still—"

"Go. I'll guard the ship."

"You're sure?"

"I'd only trip you up." He looked away, and she knew how badly he wanted to storm the citadel. "Can we keep in touch?"

"If I transmitted back to you by interlink, they'd find us both. I don't dare."

"Well, then . . . go."

She unclasped her flight harness and stood. Working quickly but deliberately, she checked the gear she'd scavenged from the ship's emergency supplies: food concentrates and painkiller jellies, a little electronic tap circuit, two doorbreaker charges that would send their pulse to a panel's edge and detonate there, and two recharges for the Federate-issue blazer she brought from Hesed.

No shock pistol this time.

She unclasped her web belt and slid the pouch around to ride on her left hip, then made sure the dagger Brennen gave her was bedded securely in its forearm sheath. *Doesn't look like much*, she observed. She hoped, though, to depend not on gear but the bond link to find Brennen, and then on his abilities to escape.

Just before she debarked, she embraced Tel awkwardly through her gawky pressure suit. "Give me one day," she warned as she opened its helmet clasps. "I probably won't survive even that long if I don't find Brennen, but give me a standard day. If I'm not back, or if you see any sign they've found you, get offworld fast. I can find another ship." *I hope*.

"Firebird." He sniggered, a most ungentlemanly sound. "Do you think I could do that?"

"Tel," she growled, knowing they couldn't threaten each other anymore.

He shrugged.

Raising one eyebrow, she smiled. "You're right. I can't order you away. Be careful, then, if you come in. Chances are, Brenn and I will be dead together."

He bent and kissed her cheek. Firebird stood a moment bowing her head, searching for words to apologize for the hatred she once nurtured for him and his kind. She couldn't. She could only turn back and salute him ten minutes later when she neared the edge of the craft's visual range.

Struggling against the too-large vacuum suit, she crossed a boulder field under a starry firmament in sense-deafening silence. She needed to enter without being seen or setting off an alarm.

But why would their airlocks be alarmed? As far as they knew, no one could pass their fielding net. RIA changed everything. She bypassed two sizable airlocks, circling the obviously inhabited area, flitting between boulders that provided good cover, and finally found a minor entry that appeared unguarded.

She stole nearer, keeping to shadows, until she felt sure she'd spotted the external monitor. She steadied her blazer on a rough boulder and fired once. The monitor didn't spark, sputter, or give off any other sign of damage. *Go?* she asked the Voice she was learning to trust.

When she heard no other leading, she walked straight to the small side lock, stepped inside, and brought its air pressure up. No audible alarm went off. Once inside the entry bay, she stripped off her suit.

The bay looked volcanic, and it vibrated with the sound of air-cycling machinery. Firebird tiptoed across. Then she peered down a long inbound corridor, twitching at the safety stud on her blazer. At her first sight of the golden passway, she blinked, awestruck. Then she ignored it. Gold had no value now.

It wasn't difficult to sense the colony's layout. Like the tunnels under Hunter Height on Netaia, curving passages ran parallel to the outside, straight ones led in or changed level. She halted at the first junction. Now where? And how to stay hidden?

A powerful hunch, vaguely like the bonding resonance, told her Brennen would be nearer if she took the left straightaway.

But was it a trap? A psychic defense invented by the Shuhr, luring a careless intruder to her death?

Again, why would they bother? They thought their fielding defense was impenetrable.

Resolutely, she turned left and followed the hunch inward, straining to hear footsteps. The corridors remained uncannily quiet. At every junction and lift shaft the sensation repeated, until after several minutes she stood before a blackened, forbidding metal door sealed to solid stone. Its lock panel was arrayed with colored tabs and an alphanumerical coder. It looked fit to contain a powerful, valuable prisoner.

She hesitated, fighting the panicky sense of being one minute too late. Every beat of her heart sounded like approaching bootsteps.

Flattening a hand on the door, she tried to relax. After her panic faded, she kicked the door three times with a metal-tipped boot, then waited— then did it again. After another second she felt a faint, thrilling surge of awareness as if she'd awakened—

Brennen?

Was this him? Something felt wrong, something fundamental and deep.

She felt . . . otherness. It could be a pretender, keeping her here with some mockery of Brennen's presence.

His first instant's welcome turned to utter confusion. Firebird gasped as if he'd sliced her. Tempted to turn and run, she begged, *Singer, where—*

Before she finished framing the prayer, an answer rang in her mind: *Stay*.

She forced herself to relax into the pair bond, loosening her right hand to let it rise in Brennen's epsilon control. Surely he'd observed the unlocking sequence on that panel . . . if this was Brennen.

Nothing happened. Fear seeped into her soul. Only deadly determination kept her moving. From the gear pocket at her belt she pulled one of the little explosives and pressed it to the door. It seized hold with a soft *chunk* she hoped Brennen recognized. Then she set the delay for four seconds.

She stepped up the corridor as far as she dared to go, drew her blazer, and trained it on the door. If this were a Shuhr impostor, she must kill without hesitating.

A wild crackling noise made her flinch. The panel fell outward, clanging like a gong, and she steadied her blazer arm again.

A man leaped through the frame, over the fallen door. He looked right—and she felt whole again! Though the otherness baffled her, she let his presence flow over and through her, penetrating and completing her—

Something inside the cell screeched. Brennen seized her hand and pulled her up the corridor, heels pounding. At the first corner he palmed a panel and pushed her into a tiny service room. He pressed in after her, palmed the uncoded closing panel . . . and then shrank away.

"Brenn," she gasped. Hastily she holstered the blazer. "What's wrong?"

In dim orange half-light, he shook his head, arching his dark eyebrows. "Forgive me," he murmured. "Forgive me. I feel who you are, and what you are to me . . .

"But I don't remember you."

CHAPTER **27**

FUSION FIRE

stretto
climactic section in faster tempo

Firebird gasped. She wanted to kiss and caress Brennen, despite the desperate need to escape and the certainty that others had heard that door fall. But finally she recognized the new sensation as a deep irrational terror. Like her phobia of needles and injectors, it was far stronger than his affective control. "What have they done to you?" she demanded.

"They didn't. It's a . . ." He firmed his lips. "An amnesia block. I've had to induce it twice, at least." He eyed the bird-of-prey medallion hanging over her shirtfront, furrowing his forehead as if he knew it but couldn't guess why she wore it.

"Is phobia a side effect?" she asked.

"I don't know. I don't r-remember."

Heart-wrung, she circled his waist with both of her arms and laid her head against his chest. He returned the embrace hesitantly. His hands trembled against her shoulders. *Hurry*, urged a voice in her mind. *Hurry!*

Was that wisdom or impatience? She needed Brenn's help. She had to bring his memory back. Otherwise, how could they escape? She looked up. His face looked thin—he'd lost more weight than she had, worrying about him. A dark scar marked his left cheek where some injury had gone untreated. They'd stolen his master's star, and he wore ill-fitting blue shipboards. But under the tiny orange luma, amid deep lines of pain, fear, and exhaustion, she saw gleaming blue eyes that still were windows to the soul she loved.

He was in there somewhere. Their bonding resonance still pulsed faintly at the depth of her mind. "Do you remember that you're a . . . Sentinel?"

He nodded grimly. "Master. I haven't lost everything. But they've been drugging me. I can't touch my carrier."

That alone would explain his anxiety.

"You know I'm your bond mate."

He nodded.

"My name's Firebird. You call me Mari."

"Why?"

"It's . . . an endearment." *Reason enough.*

"Mari," he repeated. "You're one of us, aren't you?"

Mighty Singer, has he forgotten me completely? "Not . . . no," she admitted. There was no time for posturing. What could she say that might bring back his memory, his Special Ops skills? "I've just started turn training."

"How in the Whorl did you get here?"

"In a RIA ship. With Tel. Prince Tel. Do you remember RIA?"

His eyebrows arched, and she felt a fresh spasm of fear. "Forgive me, Mari. No."

"New technology. Projects an epsilon carrier. Like fielding."

"F-fielding," he muttered. "I remember that. Vaguely."

"That's something." She wished she could sense his emotions more plainly . . . or did she? He'd tried to help her fight her own phobia. If only she'd persisted! "Tel, Phoena's husband, is guarding the RIA ship. Let me tell you where it is, in case you get out but I don't."

"I doubt that'll happen," he said bitterly. Still, he listened closely as she described the way back.

Then he drew a ragged breath, and her worst doubt fled. With that breath came intense, uncompromising gratitude. Even now, without the full bonding resonance and half of his memory, she could read that. And he'd helped her through terrorized moments. Surely she could distract him, reassure him.

"You can turn?" he asked. A light seem to come back on in his eyes, despite the service room's dimness.

She was on the right track!—she hoped. "Sometimes. It's intermittent."

At least now he seemed focused. "I've been blocked," he explained, "but if you could turn and open completely to me, your carrier and the bonding resonance might take me across the chemical blocking to my own. I might be able to function for as long as I could hold a turn."

That might bring back his memory too. "Good." Firebird tried to feel confident. "Here." She took several deep breaths and shut her eyes.

Did she really believe she wouldn't hurt him, even kill him, as they thought she killed Harcourt Terrell?

She hadn't harmed Jenner. Both their lives—and Phoena's and Tel's—depended on this one turn. She was relaxing against his shoulder, envisioning the wall, when approaching footsteps brought her alert.

"Easy," Brennen whispered. He slipped her blazer from its holster and trained it on the door's edge.

That was the Brennen she knew . . . except that his hand shook.

The footfalls passed.

"Try again. It's worth the delay." He closed his arms around her, one hand at her waist and the other arm crossing her shoulders. The quavering blazer tickled her spine.

A minute later, tears streaked her cheeks. "You're trying too hard," he whispered, and she felt his fear rise again. "It should be like falling asleep."

"I know. I just can't do it that easily." If only she could! "Where's Phoena? We've got to find her. Do you remember—"

"Dead," he murmured. "The Shuhr executed her the day I arrived. I've forgotten her, but they love to remind me why I came, and that I failed."

She felt kicked in the chest. "Poor Tel!" Faintly, like an echo of the resonance they'd known, she felt his anger. It didn't seem possible for Phoena to be dead. She'd always been there. "Well," she said, "we need a way out, and a distraction—some way to keep them from hunting us down."

He shuddered. She had to steel herself against his fears again. This was like facing a battery of immunizations! "I do have a f-feel for this part of the city," he told her. "As for distraction, my instinct is to sabotage their nearest power source. It's night shift here. The best time to try." His face darkened. "I wish we had another blazer."

"Keep mine." He would feel less helpless that way. His marksmanship had been just better than hers. "Generator, then. That'll kill their fielding and energy guns too, so we can take off." Airlocks also used power, but she'd never seen a lock without emergency reserves.

She shook off her fears. Brennen needed her . . . and more. *Help us, Singer*, she pleaded. *We can't do this alone. Give us back what he was. What he still should be.*

With two fingers he pried open the sliding door. He peered through and then motioned her into the passway ahead of him. "There's a drop shaft," he whispered. "End of this hall, turn right. It'll be on the left. I'll cover behind."

She stretched back to plant a kiss on his stubbled neck, then sprinted down the gleaming corridor. Her heart started pounding again. As her blood flowed harder, she began to believe they'd escape.

Careening around a tiled corner, she flew practically into the arms of a tall stranger in black. She recoiled, flailing for balance. This was a Shuhr, a renegade! His hand angled upward into command stance. He hissed one unintelligible word. Her body froze wide-armed.

He smiled with his mouth, but his dark eyes narrowed. "Mistress!" he greeted her with an odd, throaty accent. "Mistress Caldwell! Oh, don't be afraid, not of me." He took a step forward. "I won't harm you. Shirak's standing orders are 'alive and unhurt.' Have you found him?"

Brennen rounded the corner. The Shuhr's glance darted away, his hand changed angle, and just as at Trinn Hill and at College, Firebird felt her assailant's command shift away from her. Her arms and legs came back under control.

Brennen sprawled on a slick tile floor. Galvanized, she pulled her black dagger from its hidden sheath and lunged.

The stranger seized her arm. She twisted away. She wished she could kill again, deliberately this time, the way she killed Harcourt Terrell. If she'd killed him!

Come in short! she admonished herself, remembering that bruise Brennen gave her in training. The Shuhr struck her elbow aside. Insistently, he kept his free hand at a peculiar angle, holding Brennen under command.

Firebird tightened her hold on her dagger. He grabbed for her. She wriggled out of a half headlock, but he dove forward to pin her. Brennen had beaten her that way several times, in training—but Brennen had never fallen with all his weight, and she'd never done this with a real blade. She spun, clenched her dagger two-fisted over her ribs, and let him come down on her.

He seemed not to see it, intent on driving her to the ground hard enough to stun her. She felt the dagger slide home. His shriek tore at her ears. Her spine hit the floor, and they rolled sideways together. Skull ringing, she pushed away two-handed and then pressed to her feet. Her ribs hurt, her head still rang . . . and her dagger protruded between the Shuhr's clutching hands. She shuddered violently.

Released from command as his captor lost consciousness, Brennen hurried up and drew out her dagger. From point to hilt the black blade shone wetly red. Firebird retched, surprised—after all she'd been through—to find herself sickened by a bloody knife. She had a sudden flash of memory: her hands, plunged wrist-deep into an innocent creature's lifeblood . . . but this man was no innocent. In the next instant, she realized that her nausea came secondhand, from Brennen. He stared at the blade, eyes fixed, exactly the way she'd stared at Master Spieth's injectors.

Enclosed spaces. Blades. What else terrified him?

She wrested the dagger out of his grip, then wiped it on the stranger's stained tunic.

Recovering in an instant, Brennen murmured, "Well done, Mari. You're quick with a d-dagger."

She fumbled it back into its sheath, turning away to hide it from him. "I had a good teacher," she answered, trying to sound confident. "You."

Brennen's eyebrows arched, and she felt a low rumble of worry as he tried searching his memory.

"Forget it," she said. "Go."

He gave back her blazer. "I can't use this." Then he broke into a run again, leading up the passway toward that drop shaft.

Firebird came close behind, running hard to smother her shock and fear. Shouldn't she feel guilty too? But she didn't—only worried that Brennen might not remember the way.

She jumped down the shaft after him. Knees bent, she landed. Then, sprinting like racers, they pounded along a lower-level passage.

Brennen vanished around a blasted-out corner. Firebird felt his sudden surge of terror, and . . . was this hatred? She skidded to a halt barely around the bend.

In the wide access to an obsidian chamber, two men and a woman stood as if they expected her, each holding one hand at the angle to voice-command. She knew she was caught, even before she felt the invisible cords draw tight on her body.

They looked ordinarily human, and yet—yet—their eyes betrayed them. Quick-moving and suspicious, those eyes trusted no one.

She didn't dare try her epsilon turn, didn't dare even to hope she might use it against them. These were no Sentinels to respect her mind's privacy. They watched her like hunting kiel.

First one stepped closer, then another. Then the third. They all wore battle gray, except for the younger man's wide sulfur yellow sash belt. That one grinned at Brennen, triumph lighting his lashless eyes. Brennen stared back. Loathing contorted his features.

"Good evening, Caldwell. Couldn't sleep?" The older man's voice echoed with a weird twang off shining black walls and a mass of humming machinery. He took another step on long legs.

The woman paced closer to Firebird, separating her from Brennen. Firebird stood panting and didn't try to flee, staring instead at the woman's bizarre striped hair.

"Mistress Caldwell." The elder's voice flowed like honey. He was a handsome man, silver haired at his temples, with a broad mouth and a strongly cleft chin. "We heard you'd arrived. We've been expecting you."

The younger man stood with his head high, as arrogant as any Netaian nobleman. He chuckled. "My lady, you're surprised? Certainly you didn't think you arrived unnoticed. Your strike at our satellite was charmingly original, but I would have thought the woman of Brennen Caldwell's choosing would remember to deal with our mass detectors."

Mass detectors? *Oh, squill* . . .

He folded his arms. "I had to call a special training session to keep the security division from interfering with the drama we're about to play. We'll recall it for them." He glanced at the older man, back to Brennen, then smiled wickedly and said, "Poor Micahel. He can't get in from Cahal for at least an hour—"

"We're not waiting," interrupted the other man.

Firebird's hand tightened convulsively on the grip of her blazer, but her arm hung useless down at her side. Her finger rested far from the firing stud.

"Oh. Forgive our lack of manners." The handsome older man stepped back. "I'm Eldest Eshdeth Shirak, director of this outpost. My colleagues, Testing Director Dru Polar and Cassia Talumah. Polar, in particular, has looked forward to meeting you. He and your sister were close."

"Very close." Polar touched a hand to his forehead and bowed. "To the depths of her subconscious mind, to the very moment . . . when she died. So you see, I know you well, as she knew you."

Firebird shuddered. What little pity she'd felt for Phoena died right along with her uneasiness over knifing that Shuhr. Phoena had come willingly to Three Zed. She started this deadly bait-and-switch.

Cassia Talumah stepped closer, her fluid movements unhampered by military-cut shipboards and framed by ripples in her snake-striped hair. She raised a finger and laid it at the bridge of Firebird's nose. "Mistress of the faithful master," she mocked, turning the fingernail and then drawing it down, scratching deeply. "What do you think of him now?"

Still caught in command, Firebird couldn't pull away. Her eyes teared with pain. She glanced at Brennen. He took long, slow breaths, his expression closed, his eyes hostile.

Polar strode to him, drawing from his yellow sash a rod as long as her forearm. "Take it!" he barked. Brennen's hand jerked out. Firebird trembled at the sight of her Master Sentinel voice-commanded. "You remember this, don't you? Throat pressure point . . ."

Brennen seized the haft an inch from the weapon's orange thumb stud. Polar's hand slipped along its surface, touching and sliding controls. A long needle thrust from the other end.

Firebird's throat closed. She gasped.

"Ooh," breathed Cassia. "She's phobic too!"

"So I see." The corners of Polar's mouth twitched.

Eldest Shirak hitched his thumbs into the side pockets of his elegantly tailored shipboards. He glowered at Brennen. "Wait. You're surprised. How could you not know Lady Firebird was already phobic?"

"Ha! It's his amnesia block again." Polar batted Brennen's ear. "You don't remember her, Caldwell. Do you?" he taunted. "You pitiful slink. You've spoiled this for us."

"Not entirely," said Shirak. "He'd have to know what she is. That can't be disguised." He turned back to Firebird. "And we have no real use for you alive, milady. So let me explain precisely what Master Caldwell will do with that dendric striker . . . for your education."

The scar along Brennen's cheek darkened as his fair skin grew pale. The silvery rod shook with his hand. She stared at it as Shirak spoke. "It causes all the central motor neurons to fire. Every muscle contracts, every synapse sparks as if it were insane. It will tear your muscles from the bones, and eventually stop your breathing . . . but it leaves sensory nerves intact to the very end. Enjoy this honor, Lady Firebird. When your breathing stops, we'll take our guest back to his quarters."

"He won't last long." Polar's smile broadened. "We'll crack the amnesia block now—enough of it to pick out some threads of what he used to be. He's done too much damage, though. You never would've gotten him back. Not the way you knew him. You understand that now, don't you?"

Horrified, Firebird finally tried to break command. She couldn't.

"So I suggest we enjoy the pleasure at hand." Smiling, Dru Polar tapped Brennen's shoulder with the weapon. "Even with amnesia, when you die he'll experience—good, you've heard of bereavement shock. I think that will work in our favor. I'll help him to sense the pain of your dying too, since he's less than fully able."

Now Firebird understood why Brennen hated Polar. She gritted her teeth, trying to project to Brennen—through her fear and defiance—trust, and complete forgiveness, and the hope he'd escape. The Singer would want it that way.

"Acch," Cassia hissed. "That's vulgar! You can do better than that. Don't you believe Polar? Give this murdering master the end of your blazer!"

Firebird's right hand jerked up, still holding the weapon. Automatically, her forefinger slid off the safety circuit and took up the slack on its firing stud. Three meters down her sights were the glacial-ice blue of Brennen's eyes.

She fought to swing it. If only she could sight on Dru Polar instead! *Singer*, she pleaded, *distract them! Please—just for a moment—let me try to turn.*

"Maybe I'll let you do it," Cassia blurted. "Save your true lover from watching you die, and from Polar's experiments. He'd rather die now. We could bargain. Maybe you'd like to hear what happened to your nieces."

Iarlet and Kessie? But Governor Danton sent them to safety! Firebird gasped. "No, I would not."

"Cassia," growled Polar, "he's not yours to kill."

Cassia paid no attention. "But my brother Ard brought in the tissue samples. He said they were such pretty little girls."

"No!" Firebird cried. She would trust nothing the Shuhr woman told her.

Cassia shrugged and stepped away. "Fine." Tossing her head, she made her hair ripple again. "You're as ungrateful as the rest of them."

"Caldwell," said Polar. "Go to her."

Firebird felt Brennen resist, but he couldn't fight Polar's command. He approached step by reluctant step, holding the rod low with a quivery arm, while her blazer—Cassia's toy—followed his eyes. When he'd crossed the distance, it touched the bridge of his nose. Still Cassia left Firebird's forefinger free to move. *Please*, she begged. *Help us!*

"Cassia!" Polar called again. "No! I have research to finish." The two young-looking Shuhr glowered at each other.

It was the distraction she'd prayed for.

"Can you turn?"·she read on Brennen's lips.

Drawing a deep, shaking breath, Firebird tried to blank out her surroundings: the humming generator, the Shuhr hungering for her agony, and the promise of death in Brenn's trembling hand. She tried to picture the granite wall, hoping the bickering Shuhr wouldn't sense her effort.

Brennen's nearness distracted her. She could ignore everything except the presence she'd missed so desperately. Everything but Brennen, though he stood there disabled. She would've loved him if he'd always been as powerless as Tel Tellai.

Tel! Had they found him too?

Gasping, she let her eyelids fly open. Her blazer still rested on Brennen's nose. Down at her side, he brandished the silvery horror.

She mouthed, "I can't."

"Try again." She felt no anger from him, no impatience, only hope . . . and a faith deeper than his terror.

Polar gestured angrily, turned away from Cassia, and stepped closer. "Now," he ordered, and Firebird lost her chance. Brennen's arm lifted and jabbed the contact into the angle of her throat. Panic seized her. She already couldn't move. Now she could scarcely think.

"Do it, woman," Cassia urged from her other side. "Kill him! Kill him before he can kill you! He'd thank you for doing it."

"Cassia!" shouted Polar. "Follow orders or you will be breathing vacuum!"

"You low-blooded—empty-headed—half-watt!" Cassia shrieked, and Firebird still could've fired. "You don't rule the Talumahs!"

"And you have no right to kill a Caldwell!" bellowed Shirak. His hand twisted violently. Cassia fell away from Firebird and crashed against a corner of the volcanic corridor.

Firebird gasped, released from command but held helpless by the terror piercing the skin at her throat. Brennen's quivering hand made the needle shake.

Polar laid one hand on Brennen's shoulder, one on hers, and shut his eyes, smiling.

Firebird narrowed her focus and clung to Brennen's love, still pressing into her mind. He knew why she'd come. If he remembered only that, he loved her for trying. *Strengthen my will, Mighty Singer*, she prayed.

No, not my will! Do yours! I don't know why . . . but I know you. Labeth's words flushed her with strange excitement. She bowed her head and murmured, "Mighty Singer, take us to you."

—And turned.

A flicker of terrorized strength licked through her. Back on it flowed an indescribable surge of energy. It had to be Brennen's carrier, resonating with her own—

Her throat skin tore as he flung the striker away. Roused by pain, she let go of her turn, wheeled, and fired. She wanted Polar—ferociously—but Shirak was there. He fell backward, eyes wide in disbelief.

Something landed on her back. Strong hands seized her head and twisted her neck, gouging her scalp with long, cutting nails.

"Brennen!" she choked, falling hard. Where had he gone? Had she killed him?

Cassia's voice seethed unintelligible words into her ear. Flaming anguish erupted all over her body, from no visible source. Every nerve insisted she was burning, her skin turning crisp! Hatred and nauseating otherness throttled her mind. Pinned to her enemy, Firebird flailed for her turn. Cassia clung snakelike to her point of awareness, tightening her arms, painting deeper patterns of crippling heat onto and into Firebird's body.

Firebird fled inward through the ancient wall. Black spouts of flame, the deepest heart of the Dark that Cleanses—flames just as black as this evil chamber—illuminated the greedy darkness inside her. Smoke filled her lungs.

Evil, evil!

In that instant, she knew the truth. Dabarrah was right . . . this was evil, not memory! It had held her prisoner to the unholy Powers. It tried to destroy Kiel and Kinnor as they were born, and even reached out to seduce her during her consecration.

Cassia's psychic coils loosened. Firebird sensed the other woman's startled terror.

Despairing, Firebird dove toward a black depth. Ravenous flames thickened as she plummeted. She drew a last cool breath. Cassia's fear flooded her senses. She thought she heard a long, quavering scream. *Save Brennen!*—She shot away the prayer and then called up one truly evil memory. In a Netaian tagwing fighter, she accelerated toward death on a black Verohan pinnacle. This time, she took Cassia with her.

But could she really choose to die?

At the last possible instant, she wrenched the EJECT lever . . . punched out . . . and then seized her carrier. She felt Cassia ride the plunge clear down to her destruction.

Impact! The pain of disintegration lasted less than a heartbeat. The fireball caught Firebird from behind.

Then she felt nothing at all.

As Firebird seized her epsilon carrier, Brennen grabbed the spark, a desperate strength that shocked him with its intensity. He drove that spark across the drug-induced chasm between control and his own carrier—and found it! Shouting triumph, he turned. The stuffy chamber seemed to broaden as he mastered the terrors. He could breathe deeply again! Access-linked with Firebird across a doubled carrier, he glimpsed her blazing core of white energy and black anguish, like nothing he could remember.

Then a swell of power rose through him, shock waves blasting through trained checks and controls, so much energy that he couldn't direct it—or had he forgotten how?—but he didn't dare stop its flow and return to his blocked state. Throwing both hands wide in bewilderment, he sent the hideous striker flying and stood stupefied.

Polar tackled him to the ground. Energized by adrenaline, Brennen rolled away from the Shuhr, breaking his fall while he struggled to bring this inward explosion under control. From too little epsilon strength he'd passed suddenly to far, far too much!

Polar sprang up and flung out a hand. From Shirak's lifeless palm, a blazer flew to him.

Brennen forced back the energy storm to keep it from paralyzing him, the way the phobias had weakened him until he turned. He willed a wisp of power into his voice and pressed up from the floor. He stretched out a hand. "Down!" he commanded Polar.

The Shuhr fell sideways. His blazer glanced against stone and fell loose. Still minimizing the frenzy of power, Brennen directed the excess inward on itself, holding energy with energy, and let free a kinetic burst to call that blazer.

It slid past him, out of control.

Polar staggered to his feet and reached into the air to gather and focus power. Around the black-haired Shuhr condensed a massive epsilon shield. Brennen loosed the energy storm in a desperate strike at Polar's mental centers, but even against this, Polar's shield held unbreached.

Brennen gasped, fighting despair. Against such an adversary no mental attack had any hope. Its only weakness was Polar's human body. He must strike Polar physically, cut him down, but he had no weapon.

From his sash, Polar pulled and activated a crystace that had to be Brennen's own. Its whine filled the chamber. "You can't escape," Polar roared. "You're finished." He held his arm high over his head, poised to fling the crystace. "You, and your Speaker!"

Roused by fury, Brennen sent a last word of command. The torrent of energy burst its gates, and he flung it—not at Polar, invulnerable behind that shield, but at his own weapon. "Down!" he commanded it. Power flowed up, and through him, and was gone. He couldn't hold his turn one second longer.

Polar vanished with a crash. The chamber seemed to shrink. Crushed by the weight of returning fears, Brennen fought to keep breathing. The suffocating silence was eased only by the piercing note of a crystace and the generators' steady bass hum.

Brennen lurched to the spot where Polar had stood. An impact crater half a meter deep and wide, bisected by a slender trench almost a meter long, had been blown into stone. His crystace lay in the trench. Burying most of the terrible blade's length . . .

Turning away, Brennen swallowed hard. He'd glimpsed a width of gray sleeve darkening with moisture. Under that, in the crater's depths, lay an unrecognizable mass of crushed flesh and bone.

His crystace, powered by the incredible force of fusion energy, had crushed pommel first through Dru Polar's body, creating a shock wave so powerful that bone and muscle were reduced to jelly. Only the stony floor stopped its travel. The crystace lay across Polar's remains, intact, humming softly.

That's got to be a new use for a crystace. Brennen gasped down another breath.

Then he saw Firebird and Cassia lying near the chamber's black wall, auburn hair and striped hair twisted like silken rope around both their throats.

No! he cried silently, stumbling forward. This small, beautiful stranger was his bond mate, his beloved for life. He dropped to his knees, then rolled her onto her back while he quested for echoes of her consciousness.

He felt nothing. He inhaled to shout his fury, not caring who would hear. Let them come! He'd bury her body under corpses—

Realization slapped down his anguish. He was chemically blocked. Of course he felt nothing! Cradling Firebird's head, he fumbled at her throat and searched for a pulse.

At the carotid it throbbed, weak but steady. Relieved but more confused than ever, he searched her body for other injuries. He found only scratches and the crusting cut at her throat, where the striker's probe had torn free.

He stretched a shaking hand toward Cassia. At no angle could he find a pulse, either in wrist or throat.

Had Firebird killed her?

Their enemies were dead. They must flee.

Generator first. Then ... outside ... someone waited in a RIA ship. She'd tried to explain RIA.

The thought of squeezing into an even smaller enclosure stopped his breath again. He would almost rather die here than attempt space flight. But for her sake, he had to try.

She couldn't turn for him now. He must do this phobic and powerless.

He fumbled in the narrow trench that his crystace had blasted in the stone floor, crossing Polar's crater like a grave marker. He plucked out his weapon, deactivating it while he looked elsewhere. Polar's "training session" might keep other Shuhr away until he reached that ship. But if they'd seen her coming, had they impounded it? They wouldn't have known about its special features. They might have left it alone for the moment.

Tel straightened in the pilot's seat, blasted upright by the sense that someone had found him. He examined his external screens. Sweat broke out on his forehead. None of the glimmering forms outside had changed position. This had to be—

Welcome to Three Zed, visitor, boomed a voice.

He sprang off the seat and grabbed his belt holster. They'd found him. But how?

We're nowhere near you, visitor. There are three of us watching, the voice taunted, and sure enough, he sensed a kind of echo. *We would have greeted you sooner, but all fielding teams were detained in a training session.*

He drew his blazer.

They laughed inside his brain. *Put it down, visitor. We can destroy your mind or send you screaming out the hatch into vacuum—but we'll just put you to sleep for a while, until it's convenient to come out and take you and your ship. It must be a remarkable ship, visitor.*

He shrank against the galley servo. "Cowards," he cried. The longer he distracted them, the better chance Firebird might have to save Brennen and

Phoena. "Cowards and bullies. I've known people like you. I've had friends like you," he added, bitterly remembering his faithful service to Muirnen Rogonin. "Come out here. I'll lay down my weapon if you'll switch off your—"

Again he felt laughter. *We're so frightened. Sleep well, visitor.*

Limp and blind, he collapsed.

Brennen spotted a control board high on the generator. He wanted to jump to its metal-grate service platform. Instead he pulled himself up a long ladder with shaking arms. He glared at a glasteel cover bolted over rows of relays, then reactivated his crystace. Again the sight of a blade made his throat constrict. Averting his eyes, he sliced the cover away. Then he cut again, deeper. The chamber plunged into blackness.

That would put down their weapons, their scanning capability, even the fielding team. He hastily touched off the humming crystace.

Tormented by silent darkness, toeing gingerly for each rung, he descended to the floor, then dropped to his knees. He groped cautiously back across the chamber, not wanting to pitch headlong into Polar's remains.

Another minute's creeping brought him to the soft, labored wheeze of Firebird's breathing.

Had Shirak called her *Lady* Firebird?

What should he remember?

Gently he lifted her over his shoulder, but when he tried to step, his legs buckled. He let her fall, cushioning her impact as well as he could. Infuriated by his weakness, he gripped both of her slender shoulders and shook her, first cautiously and then harder. "Mari," he pressed. "Mari."

She didn't rouse. "Mari," he whispered. "Get up!" He couldn't believe no one had heard the commotion in here. Sliding his hands down her arms, he found her wrists and dragged her up the space-black passway.

EMBERS

rallentando
gradually slowing

Tel groaned. He lay on the deck near the galley servo. Someone was shaking him—

Caldwell! Suited for vacuum, the Sentinel let a smaller suited figure slump on the transport's deck. *Phoena?*

No, Tel realized. Through the faceplate he saw Firebird's darker eyes, open but blank. He sprang up. "Where's Phoena?" He lunged toward the remaining vacuum suit.

"Stop!" Caldwell wrenched off his helmet. "I couldn't save her. We have to take off. Now."

Pressing the heels of his hands into his eyes, Tel folded forward. She was dead after all—his Phoena, gone forever . . .

"H-help Firebird," gasped Caldwell. "Secure her, please, hurry. We're dead, too, if we don't move fast."

Shaking, Tel knelt. He fumbled an unfamiliar helmet off Firebird's head, then wrestled her onto one of the aft bunks and belted her down.

Caldwell fell against the airlock, slip-sealing it with one hand, then flinched away from a bulkhead. Dark lines and circles surrounded his eyes.

Tel sprang to his feet. "But how long has Phoena been. . . ?" He couldn't say it.

"I—I can't count days," Caldwell stammered. "I tried to save her. Forgive me. Please."

Tel glanced at the airlock. Caldwell couldn't stop him from going back, from trying to claim her body—

And what would that accomplish? "Then take off," he said, slumping again.

Caldwell passed a hand over his eyes. "I've forgotten how to pilot. I've forgotten your name, I've forgotten . . . almost everything."

What had they done to him? Tel finally realized that Caldwell kept glancing at bulkheads as if he expected them to collapse. "What about the RIA unit?" he cried, springing forward onto the pilot's seat. "Can you use that?"

Caldwell sank down beside him. "Does it take epsilon skills?"

Tel punched up the generator. "Just the turn, and not even a strong one. That's all Firebird can do, anyway."

Caldwell shook his head. "Then I can't use it. They've blocked my turn too."

Tel gaped.

"Lift off," Brennen pleaded. "Hurry, before the fielding team gets its power back!"

Juddis Adiyn backed against the star tank and eyed the Golden City's new Eldest, Modabah Shirak. Modabah was a taller, more glamorous, but oddly stooped version of his father Eshdeth. Moments before the generator-room fiasco, Adiyn had spotted disaster on the shebiyl. He'd summoned Modabah to the Eldest's office even as Eshdeth Shirak's body stiffened.

Modabah slammed a hand onto his new obsidian desk top. Some tech in the waste-processing facility was taking the brunt of his fury. "If that generator isn't running in five minutes, your corpse will be waste too! Am I understood?"

An organic odor filtered from Shirak's air vent. Most of the City's auxiliary life-support stations had come on line when main power winked out, but not at waste processing. The Golden City was filling with a foul, choking stench.

Modabah waved off the circuit and barked at his com unit, "Give me main generator."

Adiyn stepped closer to listen.

"Update," Modabah ordered.

Seconds later, someone answered. "They're installing the new panel now. We expect switchover in six minutes."

Adiyn glanced at a surveillance image on Modabah's data desk. In six minutes, the tiny spark fleeing Three Zed would be out of range, both of groundside guns and of the fielding satellites. "What happened in there?" Modabah demanded.

Yes, what? Even Adiyn hadn't guessed until the last instant that they stood at the brink of disaster. Eshdeth, gone. Polar, gone too! Even young Cassia. Unavoidable. Why, though?

Maybe the Sentinels' god gave explanations. The shebiyl never did. "We don't know," said the downside voice.

"I never trusted Polar's research," Modabah declared, turning aside. "I warned him he'd destroy himself someday."

Adiyn eyed his new Eldest through narrowed eyes, careful to keep his thoughts shielded by epsilon static. Polar might have created an epsilon-power mishap and destroyed his own body, but plainly—from the profound satisfaction in Modabah's alpha matrix—the new Eldest also suspected that Polar had meant to seize leadership. Maybe Modabah Shirak was paranoid, or maybe he was right—but who would train the young people now?

A gilded door slid open. Micahel Shirak charged toward his father, tight-lipped, clenching both fists. Spotting Adiyn, he spun aside. *Did you foresee this?* he demanded. *Didn't you warn Security? Why didn't you delay them until I got here?*

"Not even you," Adiyn said evenly, "could've saved this situation." His imagination now filled in the blanks from his glimpse of the shebiyl. Polar's self-destruction could've distracted Eshdeth Shirak and Cassia Talumah long enough for their prisoners to strike, reach the generator, then escape.

They're gone, aren't they? Micahel glared with wide eyes. His jaw twitched.

Modabah Shirak pointed at the surveillance screen. "There they are. But we're weaponless for five and a half more minutes. The fielding team can't even put Mistress Caldwell's backup pilot back into tardema. Fielding's without power."

Give me a ship, Micahel pressed. *I'll pursue.*

Adiyn eyed Micahel and Modabah. Eshdeth Shirak, a sensible leader and a stable strategist, had always followed his own brilliant father's long plan. Eshdeth would be missed. The Ehretan unbound had suffered a staggering blow.

At least their genetics would stay in competent hands.

"Adiyn?" Modabah caught his attention. "I need a shebiyl reading. Now. How can we use what's left of the Angelo princesses to settle this? What about Caldwell's gene samples? Or our agents in Citangelo?"

Father! Micahel's epsilon sense seethed like a boiling pot. *I said give me a ship.*

Modabah turned aside, glaring. "You will follow my orders," he shouted, "or you will be executed."

Adiyn guessed that at this moment, Modabah would love to see some-one die. Micahel must've understood too. He stood clenching his fists for two seconds, then stomped out. Adiyn watched him go, wondering behind his deepest shields if it would be best for his people if *he* stepped in and took over, wresting power away from Modabah Shirak.

Perhaps later.

He sat down in a chair near the star tank. Staring into its depth, he searched his mind for the elusive shebiyl, hoping to glimpse what the future might hold for the Golden City under Modabah . . . or himself.

Tel stepped out the RIA transport's hatch into a predawn wind. Under the lights of Hesed's grassy landing strip, beyond Master Dabarrah, a tall woman waited. Master Dabarrah had warned them over the interlink to anticipate Carradee. He'd told them about her new grief for the missing princesses.

Tel glanced back into the ship's darkness.

"Go ahead," said Brennen's voice. "I won't drop her."

Squaring his shoulders, Tel stepped down the ladder. Hesitantly, the woman waved.

He hurried toward her. "Carradee. Majesty." Kneeling on damp grass, he took her hand and kissed it.

"Prince Tel. It is you. You look different in shipboards." Beneath loose blond curls, her forehead wrinkled. "Are you all right, Tel? Phoena . . . they tell me . . ."

He sighed relief. The Sentinels had spared both of them from having to inform each other. "I will be all right. Caldwell and I have . . . talked. At least I know, Carradee. I can hardly imagine your pain, wondering—"

Carradee gave a little gasp. Tel sprang to his feet. Brennen emerged from the transport, carrying Firebird. She lay in his arms, legs dangling, hair hanging over his elbow. Carradee shivered and pulled her woolen coat close.

Nodding a somber greeting to Carradee, Brennen passed them. Dabarrah hurried toward him.

As Tel stepped out behind Brennen, Carradee took his arm. An image of Phoena exploded into his mind: Phoena as he'd known her, the paragon of all nine Powers: Strength, Valor, and Excellence . . . Knowledge . . .

He faltered.

The fifth Power was Fidelity.

No, he realized, humbled by his sorrow. No, that virtuous image was Phoena as he imagined her, and she had never existed.

A sekiyr strode toward them, carrying a warm jacket. Tel slipped into it. "At least Firebird's condition didn't deteriorate en route," he told Carradee. "Since she survived this long, Dabarrah will surely heal her." He stared at Brennen's back. Caldwell, the invulnerable, implacable Master Sentinel, had also existed only as a facade, a controlled image that concealed a good man. They'd talked for hours, returning together. Tel helped set up the shipboard blood-cleansing equipment that filtered the blocking drugs from his system and brought back most of his epsilon powers. As long as Caldwell could hold a turn, he could hold down his crippling new phobias. But he could not sleep, and his memory survived in tatters.

Tel pressed Carradee's hand. "I'm glad you came, Majesty. This is a good place." He stared up at the shadowed red rock of the Hesed Valley. "Was Rogonin unkind to you?"

"Yes," she murmured, but to his surprise, she smiled with sad eyes. As they walked toward the downside lift, she related the electoral mutiny. Procyel's sky lightened over her head, and curls blew into her face. Carradee Angelo Second, whom he'd rarely seen happy since she acceded to the throne, looked rested . . . ready to lead the search. "It's peaceful here," she said, glancing around. "And Daithi is so much better. The first time he saw Firebird's babies, something inside him came back to life. Come with me, Tel. Come see him. Would you?"

What a courageous woman. "Of course, Majesty. It will be good to see Prince Daithi again."

Master Dabarrah laid down his recall pad. "This is encouraging," he said.

Brennen tried to sit up. His arms still shook, and he couldn't pull a deep breath.

"No," Dabarrah insisted, "lie still. I'm going to put you back down in just a few minutes. But first, I want to assure you there's been no shift in sensory, critical, or moral judgment." He touched the recall pad. "Your personality profile still fits the imprint when you tested for training, if I adjust it for age."

At that news, Brennen's skylit bed seemed to grow softer. "Brain damage?" he asked.

"Physically, none. Alpha matrix . . ." Brennen heard calming overtones in Dabarrah's voice now. "Yes. Memory patterns, associational ability, and especially recall. I can help you with those, to a certain extent."

"I haven't just lost old memories. Tellai had to tell me his name twice." The realization had devastated him.

"Your trained powers of recall are damaged. With retraining, we can probably improve what you still have."

"You're saying it won't come back?"

Dabarrah laid a hand on his shoulder. "All things are possible."

That was scant comfort. Brennen squeezed his eyes shut. "And th-the fears? The stammer," he added, disgusted by his own voice. "What am I so afraid of?"

Dabarrah's forehead furrowed. "Most of your terrors seem related to

Three Zed. Darkness, solitude, locked or enclosed places.''

"Sleep," Brennen suggested.

"Yes, loss of consciousness. Certain weapons. I found odd fears too. Red lights, and anything made of gold."

The suggestions made Brennen choke.

Dabarrah's access touch lightened the sudden weight on his chest. "What do you remember of *Dabar*?" asked the Sanctuary Master. "Of *Mattah*?"

Brennen shut his eyes and concentrated. Isolated phrases sprang to mind, chapters and verses that ended in blank spaces—

"Stop. The problem is there, Brennen. The Holy One has not forsaken you, but you've forgotten much of what you knew about His commandments. Including those against fear."

Brennen groaned. "At least I know where to start studying." *Be my courage until then, Holy One.* He stared at the stone ceiling. This still was worth all it had cost him, if he'd saved the sanctuary. Using deep access, Dabarrah had refreshed his memory of that dream, of the call he followed so confidently. Evidently Dru Polar's colleagues had meant to strike Hesed House. Apparently they would have succeeded. He would've died here. He, Mari, Kiel, and Kinnor . . .

But had the amnesia block held at Three Zed, or had he betrayed secrets he no longer remembered? He must've broken at least once, to need a second block. How had Dru Polar pierced his amnesia?

"Without perfect recall," Dabarrah said, "you must learn as others do, with study and repetition. It will be slower than you're accustomed to, but you'll still have unusual advantages. I urge you to access people who've held key positions in your life, to regain your own past. I will gladly serve you. I would also suggest accessing Sentinel Dardy. And Lady Firebird, when I awaken her."

"How soon will that be?" He dreaded the deep, healing sleep he'd been promised. He feared lying alone, even here where nothing could harm him.

"Her psychic shock demands total rest, so I'll keep her down several more days. But I'll move her in here," Dabarrah told him. "You won't be alone."

"Jenner," Brennen whispered, "is it possible they've tricked me, that Phoena isn't really dead? I . . . don't remember what happened."

Dabarrah pursed his lips. "I probed first for that, Brennen. You have a deep, unaltered memory. You saw her die. Be at peace about this. You did not betray Tel."

One more thing—"I've lost carrier strength too. I can feel it, right now. I'm not as strong as I was."

"That may not be permanent."

Brennen shut his eyes. The ayin complex, and epsilon power, had been created by their ancestors in disobedience. Over the decades, it had caused more evil than good . . . on war-blasted Ehret, and now stretching out from Three Zed. Someday it might be a relief to lay down that power.

But not yet, if he could help it! Tomorrow he would step out on a wholly new branch of the Path.

There had been pain . . . and terror. They haunted the region between dreaming and dozing, but Firebird felt strong again. Strong enough to wake.

Something warm lay on her chest. She raised a hand to touch it and felt silky hair on a firm skull. Longingly, she threaded her fingers into that hair.

An even warmer sensation invaded her inner awareness, the essence of a tropical sea that smelled of incense. . . .

"Brenn," she whispered.

Then she came fully awake. Should he be inside her mind? They must escape! She struggled to sit upright.

"Rest, Mari," he said softly. "I remember you. We're safe."

She exhaled and relaxed on the bed. The Shuhr, the chamber, her horrible revelation—that Dabarrah's claim had been true and her inner darkness was essentially evil—all seemed irrelevant.

Brennen was back.

"Not completely," he said. His smoky-sweet access probe shifted at the back of her mind. "Dabarrah did all he could for my memory, but I still have gaps. I'm filling them in. Studying. Accessing others."

She rolled her head, looking around. White stone shone above her. Beyond one wall she heard water whispering and splashing. A skylight glowed with the soft orange-red of sunset or dawn.

She'd been carried from horror to Hesed. She caught a breath of damp kirka trees as Brennen's delicate epsilon touch danced through her memories. It paused here, lingered there, to relearn what they'd shared, and as it did, some of the strangeness in him faded away. "The blocking drugs they gave you at Three Zed. You beat them!" she exclaimed.

"There's medical equipment aboard all our craft," he murmured. "Blood cleansing. I see that we did it once to you, at Veroh."

"You'd forgotten?"

She felt his sadness. "I had," he admitted.

Should he be doing this? Wasn't she still on avoid-status? "Where are Kiel and Kinnor? Are they all right?"

Distracted, he opened his eyes, though she felt his probe linger on the moment when she'd told him of her pregnancy. "They're close, and better than all right." He arranged her long hair around her shoulders. "Master Jenner has promised to take you off A-status and give them back to us as soon as I finish this." He raised her chin with one finger, leaned close, and brushed his lips against hers. The touch at the back of her mind shifted again, stroking as it comforted.

Firebird savored the pleasure she'd missed so intensely. "Be careful, Brenn," she whispered. "There's evil inside me."

He hesitated, then answered, "And in me. But, Mari, the darkness is only a taint on us. Years ago, the Speaker covered that taint. I came to Him, needy. To faith. He met my need, just as He met yours."

Master Jenner had tried to explain all this. Perfect holiness couldn't even look at evil, not the slightest taint. But the Holy One had found a way to let offenders stand in His presence. Not by the ancient sacrifice, but by her faith in it . . . no, in Him . . . He could lay a covering over her, like a garment.

"I think," she said softly, "I'm starting to understand."

"And someday there'll be no need for covering. He'll take the evil from us and sweep it away."

She relaxed completely. If Brennen remembered that much of his faith, everything else would fall into place eventually. Sweet sensation rose in every niche of her body and mind.

"You once asked," he said, "why He allows suffering and evil. Now you'll ask why He called me to Three Zed and nearly let me be destroyed."

She looked deep into weary blue eyes. "Yes."

"I don't know why He let the Shuhr kill Tarance and Destia, but for myself . . . answering the call is everything. We're forbidden to tell others about the obedient life, so we must show them."

"That's all?" she whispered.

He took her hand. The skylight over his head glowed brighter.

"What did you change?" she murmured. "What saved Hesed?"

"We unbalanced the Shuhr, Mari. We killed two of their strongest leaders. And . . . there was more. Let me try to remember. . . ."

She'd never seen him struggle for memory before. It felt almost like pain.

His head drooped, and a strand of hair fell toward his face. "For a while, they were moving toward confrontation. I think we've won a respite. The

One who called me there is sovereign, and He accomplished His purpose. Mari, I had to trust your help at Three Zed, in the same kind of faith—I only knew what you are to me. I know what He is, in a greater, deeper way. So I trust Him."

She pressed his hand against her cheek. "Finish what you're doing for Master Dabarrah."

He nodded. "Don't turn, Mari. I'm going to go deep."

His warning cued up an image of the rough, cold granite wall, but the epsilon power deep inside no longer held any allure. She had nearly died at that wall . . . again.

Suddenly Brennen straightened, exclaiming, "Polar's research!"

"What?"

His eyes lit with smile lines, and the tension smoothed out around his mouth. "Polar would've created his own version of RIA. Then there would be no stopping him, here or anywhere. The Shuhr would have taken the Federacy."

Firebird nodded. Brennen had saved the Federacy . . . and Regional command would never even know! Unfair—yet even more vitally, he'd filled in a memory gap without any help. Maybe more of his past would return.

He laid a hand on her shoulder. "Mari, when I stop turning now, my fears will come back. I have so much to relearn. Until I do, you'll feel them."

She covered his hand and squeezed. "Thank you for warning me." She braced herself.

Slowly, gradually, he pulled his probe away. As he did, she felt an eerie change come over Hesed House. The room seemed to shrink, the light dimmed. Brennen's hand trembled. She gripped it harder.

His eyebrows lowered. "Are you all right? Can you deal with this?"

"As long as you're here," she said firmly. *Don't you dare avoid me just to spare me from sharing your pain!*

He smiled again. Straightening, he leaned toward a wall panel and switched on an interlink. "Done, Jenner," he said. "She controls her response beautifully." He rubbed the dark mark on his cheek with his free hand.

Had that been some kind of test? If so, she'd obviously passed. She eyed his left cheek. Maybe every victory left scars, visible and invisible.

"I had a message yesterday from Regional command." He turned away from the link panel.

"They want you back," she guessed.

"Yes. An offer of full reinstatement. I wouldn't even have to return my severance pay—"

The door opened silently. Anna Dabarrah glided through, followed by a slender sekiyr. A kicking blond baby gazed toward Firebird, held around his waist by Anna's arm. "Kiel!" Firebird exclaimed, and she would've leaped off the bed if she felt stronger.

Anna gave Kiel to Firebird, who took him as carefully as crystal. His warmth, his musky smell, his tiny curled fingers . . . all seemed as familiar and right as her own face in the mirror, or Brenn's.

The sekiyr laid auburn-headed Kin on her lap. To her shock, Kin worked his jaw and plump cheeks in his sleep. "He's been so content since you came back," Anna admitted. Firebird fingered his fist, marveling at its smoothness. "Somehow, he made peace with the world. Your worry disturbed him, but now your presence comforts him."

In her arms, the blond twin hiccuped, stared a little longer, and then broke into a broad smile.

Firebird tightened her arms, drawing that pink-gummed grin even closer. "Kiel!" she exclaimed. "Do you know me?"

"Ghh," said her son. He tangled her hair in flailing fingers and dragged it toward his mouth.

Helpless to do anything else, Firebird pressed her cheek to Kiel's. The sanctuary women left the room, and Brennen's arms tightened, folding Firebird, Kiel, and Kinnor together. "I suppose," she mumbled, "I'm in trouble with Thyrica over taking that RIA ship." She didn't even care. Kin arched and wriggled, and she rolled him toward her shoulder. There had to be some way to cradle them both. . . .

Brennen shook his head. "The transport was Jenner's to send, from the time Ellet brought it here."

"Ellet," she muttered. If only she could forget that woman, or make Ellet forget Brennen! *Just one touch of amnesia* . . .

Brennen carefully pulled Kiel out from under his brother. At last, his eyes came alive with mischief. "Mari," he said, "I have something to tell you about Ellet—and Damalcon Dardy."

AUTHOR'S NOTE

The FIREBIRD series isn't a spiritual allegory, but an extended parable of conversion. In *Fusion Fire* I used the science-fiction idea of psychic abilities as a plot device and placed those "powers" in an alternate universe—a universe without Earth, where Messiah's time had not yet fully come, and in a chosen people with a vastly different history.

In our universe, the greatest power we can experience is the Holy Spirit's work in our lives. All metaphors or allegories pale by comparison with the moment when He finally breaks through our innermost wall and makes us His own.

On the other hand, the Sentinels' abilities aren't meant to represent God's presence in their lives, but an imagined privilege (and responsibility) that they must bring into obedience, or else misuse and face the consequences.

These pre-atonement believers are taught that their personal salvation rests on a future event that is only symbolized by their ancient rituals. I suspect that the concept wouldn't be easy to grasp, whether at Hesed House or in Israel B.C.

Firebird's attempt to develop her latent Ehretan abilities gave me the chance to address several issues. In *Firebird* I touched on God's existence and His mercy. In *Fusion Fire* I tried to deal with the existence of evil and our separation from God.

It's dangerous to focus on evil, because it pollutes our hearts and minds. Equally wrong (though tempting to the kindhearted) is the attempt to excuse genuine evil as "mistakes" or "bad choices." In Psalm 17, David prays in desperation: "Keep me . . . from the wicked who assail me, from my mortal enemies who surround me."

A more intimate evil results from our fallen nature. As the apostle Paul wrote, "Evil is present in me, the one who wishes to do good" (Romans 7:21). That probably wasn't a happy conclusion for Paul, any more than it was for Firebird. Ultimately, only those who are utterly broken before God can really be used by Him.

Kathy Tyers
Montana
September 1999

PRELUDE

Absently smoothing a wrinkle in her snug black pants, genetics technician Terza Shirak pressed her forehead to her scanner and examined a sixteen-cell human morula. She could not allow one microscopic imperfection.

Fortunately, all the visible chromosome divisions proceeded normally. Cytoplasmic proteins were also within tolerance. Terza reached around and carefully returned that culture dish to incubation, then drew the next tiny zygote from its sloshy growing place.

Recently graduated from pre-adult training, Terza worked long hours overseeing these womb banks and embrytubes. Her supervisor, Juddis Adiyn, served the city's new Eldest as a personal advisor. She hoped to be introduced to the Eldest soon, for a vital reason. At her graduation, less than a year ago, they finally told her that Three Zed colony's new administrator, Modabah Shirak, was her own gene-father.

Terza had wondered, during training, if she might be Modabah's offspring. She had his abnormally fair skin, black hair and eyes, and the sharp chin of her half brother, Micahel. She was tall, too, just under 180 centimeters. Still, no subadult conceived in this laboratory knew her parents. The parents never knew her, either, unless she survived training. That objectivity freed the colony to continue its 240-year experiment in genetic engineering. As a named adult, Terza hoped to contribute to Three Zed's strength. To humanity's future.

In such a scheme, there had to be casualties.

Terza stared at the next zygote, then frowned. One chromosome division had stalled, and a delicate chromosomal fibril, which should have divided, dangled through an incomplete cell division instead. The embryo would develop malformed. Absently she inserted a flash probe and vaporized the culture, then removed its entry from her catalog. This no longer bothered her.

Next, she turned to her weekly fertilizations. Fewer than ten percent of zygotes survived to adulthood. The others were culled as malformed embryos or imperfect-response infants, pronounced untrainable at the settlements where they were raised, or killed in training.

As she reached for her touchboard, a barely perceptible temblor shook the ground. Her ancestors had built the Golden City inside an extinct, plugged volcano. The world itself had not quite died.

The tissue-bank list contained her orders for the day, and the first ovum to be fertilized carried the TWS–1 designation. That was her own code—this would be her first fertilization! She sat up straight and flicked black hair out of her face. The odds said this offspring would perish before adulthood, but this was an honor. Her supervisor ordered gene crosses according to hereditary talents and his mysterious ability to predict future events.

Was the cross with Dru Polar? she wondered. The colony's late testing director had been abnormally strong in Ehretan talents. Just last night, her hall-mates on Third South had regaled each other with shivery tales about the trainer who culled so many of their peers. Polar had been found dead twenty days ago, hideously killed, beside Terza's masterful grandfather and another City resident, Cassia Talumah.

Terza grasped her lower lip between her teeth and glanced across the screen, checking her guess. Was it Polar?

No. The ordered fertilization's paternal designation was not Polar's DLP, but the cryptic BDC–5X.

BDC—Brennen Daye Caldwell? Terza clenched a hand. She'd personally cloned that prisoner's skin cells several days before he escaped—but Shirak males made a sport out of thinning his family! According to zealots among his people, a Caldwell would eventually destroy her world.

Terza's people had sacrificed one planet, their home world, to save themselves. Recently, they'd taken a city off the Sentinels' adopted world. They would neutralize the Caldwells if necessary and create more craters, because the timing was urgent. Soon they would be able to offer humanity a gift it wanted at any price: immortality. One world at a time, Terza's people—the unbound starbred—would craft a new human race in a more durable image.

Fortunately, Terza hadn't been involved in selecting the first planetary population to be modified.

She refocused her eyes on her orders. BDC–5X: This would be a female with Caldwell genes, but one who wouldn't carry the allegedly messianic Carabohd name.

This, at least, made sense. Before Dru Polar's interrogations and research ruined him, Caldwell had shown prodigious psionic talent. Maybe her supervisor wanted to create a pool of Shirak-Caldwell embryonic cells.

He could tease apart that breeding stock to create a quick second generation.

Whatever he wanted, she must exceed his expectations. She keyed the stasis unit to deliver appropriate cultures. Within moments, the BDC–5X dropped into the micro-injector on her examining cradle.

Because of its dermal origins, the gamete had no whiptail. She confirmed with a glance that it carried the requisite X chromosome, then injected the gamete into the TWS 1 ovum, creating her own first offspring. Instantly, the smaller cell's nuclear membrane started to dissolve, releasing its genetic contents. Flattening her lips, she transferred the new zygote into a dish of nutrient medium.

Maybe her father hoped to duplicate Caldwell's abilities in his own gametic descendants, the ones who might live forever. Or maybe Terza's lab supervisor meant to test her, to see if she'd obey a distasteful order—this one—or else destroy her own fertilization late in its term. Terza did hate culling late fetuses, whose features looked almost human. Gene technology was dangerous work for a woman secretly more sensitive than most of her fellows.

And this one will carry my genes. Half of all I am.

Appalled by the tug of that new sensation, Terza reminded herself that it would also carry the genes of an enemy. She checked her screen for the next prescribed fertilization.

That day's final order sent her to her supervisor's apartment, several levels beneath Three Zed's basaltic surface. Stocky and small-eyed, Juddis Adiyn looked more like a dark-flour dumpling than a leader of the unbound starbred. He slumped in a brocaded wing chair, clasping stout hands in his lap. Adiyn was old enough—152, by the Federate calendar—to need ayin treatments to preserve his waning abilities. That was one reason her telepathically skilled elders normally spoke aloud. "By now," he said, "you are aware of your primary fertilization. An outcross with the Carabohd-Caldwell line."

Terza rocked from one foot to the other. On the near wall, a glasteel case displayed jeweled offworld trinkets against a frothy lava backdrop. Across the ceiling, red, blue, and green threads of light snaked and writhed. Terza found them mildly hypnotic, and she avoided staring at them.

"You're displeased?" Adiyn asked.

Of course, Terza sent silently. A young underling generally subvocalized, speaking mind to mind on her epsilon carrier wave. *I would have preferred not soiling my father's line with Thyrian genes. But this seems appropriate, considering my profession in genetics.*

"Have you made any guess? Any rationale?"

Something to do with Tallis's announcement, she suggested, taking a shot without a targeting beam. Yesterday, the Federates' regional capital had claimed that the Sentinels had developed a new technology. They threatened to use this RIA weapon against her people, in revenge for Three Zed's pre-emptive strike against Thyrica.

The Federates had good reason to be afraid. Terza was glad to be employed in reproduction, so she would miss the coming horrors.

"You're close," Adiyn said. "It has more to do with your father's scouting trip to Netaia, and with bringing Caldwell back to face justice."

Terza raised her head. Her father gave the fertilization order? She did hope to meet him before the colony moved elsewhere, after a century on this sterile planet. As for Caldwell, he and his Lady stood accused of assassinating her grandfather, the previous Eldest . . . and possibly Dru Polar and Cassia Talumah. No witness to their deaths had survived to testify. A summons had been sent, but no one expected Caldwell to return voluntarily.

Ironically, his people shared her genetic heritage. Because of those psionic abilities, this colony had superb defenses. It had little else, though. Modabah would leave in a few weeks to inspect the chosen planetary system. Netaia had rich assets, estimated at a quarter of the Federacy's. It could be seized relatively easily by altering a few nobly born minds and destroying only one, or maybe two or three, of its cities. Its top-heavy government made it charmingly vulnerable to such a simple approach. There, Terza's people would launch the next phase of their grand experiment. She wanted a pivotal position in that program.

"I assume you've heard that General Caldwell and Lady Firebird will also be traveling to Netaia."

Nudged back to the here and now, Terza nodded and responded, *Some sort of ceremonial.*

"And naturally, your father wants Caldwell back in custody."

She shrugged. Call it justice, or call it vengeance. Eshdeth and Polar had been powerful leaders, poised to destroy the Sentinels' fortress world—

Adiyn raised a hand, cutting off her thought. "Your father prefers to start any operation with several options. If the unexpected occurs, he can be ready."

How true. Down on Third South, her father's love of options had been the subject of some cautious derision.

"Among his options for Netaia," said Adiyn, "is to lure out General Caldwell, preferably in bereavement shock, since he will be there anyway. Modabah requests your assistance."

Terza raised one eyebrow. Bereavement left Sentinels mentally and physically incapacitated, easily seized or dispatched in the following days, because they bonded with their mates at the deepest level of consciousness. But—

Lure him out? she demanded. *A man almost legendary for his ethics?* He wouldn't want illicit power or pleasures.

Adiyn's little eyes focused over Terza's shoulder, toward the ceiling and those eerie light threads. She'd heard that he used them to read the future. "Your primary role will be as messenger, regarding the new Caldwell offspring."

She avoided scoffing, because Adiyn would sense it. *Sir, Caldwell knows we could make him a hundred offspring. A thousand. If we really want to trap him, we should offer him a full case of embrytubes—*

Adiyn raised a gray eyebrow. "Don't display your ignorance," he said tightly.

Terza crossed her ankles. She compressed her lips.

"Sentinels," Adiyn explained, "carry their own young. Apparently, breeding like animals fulfills some kind of psychological need in them." He waved one hand in front of his face. "Caldwell couldn't ignore an embryo that was carried by a woman, particularly a woman highly placed among his enemies. He would try to get her into custody."

Carried by a woman? Custody? "I beg your pardon." Terza spoke aloud this time, dispersing an outer cloud of epsilon static. Normally, she used it to shield her emotions.

"No, we wouldn't let you be kidnapped. We want this offspring for further research and breeding, to say nothing of your own value to your people."

An insubstantial iron band tightened around Terza's chest. He still hadn't explained *carried*. "Sir, you can't mean—"

"If you are unwilling, your father will gladly set you aside and choose another."

The iron band tightened further, and she struggled for her next breath. In colony parlance, "set aside" meant the cold-stasis crypts. There was no escape from that frozen prison, except to a short life as an experimental subject. Modabah wouldn't hesitate to stase one rebellious gene tech, even if she was his own offspring, any more than he would hesitate to order another Federate city destroyed.

Respectfully, sir, she sent, grasping at the first argument that occurred to her, *and I am not saying I am unwilling . . . but if we arrive on Netaia, and circumstances change, the Eldest might not even decide to lure Caldwell out that way. He always has half a dozen options. That would waste . . . my effort....* She could barely imagine the embarrassment, not to mention the discomfort, the blood and pain—

Adiyn clasped his hands again. "Then call it part of your education, Terza. Your contribution to our pending expansion."

CHAPTER 1

TO STRIKE BACK

tema
theme

"And then this is the Codex simulation," said Occupation Governor Danton. "The Electorate sent it down yesterday, demanding that we act."

Firebird pushed long auburn hair back from her face as she leaned forward. Governor Danton's wood-paneled office had two broad, darkened windows and an antique desk, designed to set Netaia's Federate conquerors on equal footing with a snooty nobility. She sat in a comfortable brownbuck chair across from the governor.

Above the media block on his desk appeared an image she would've known from any approach vector: Citangelo, the heart of royal Netaia and its two buffer systems. Between the broad sideways Y formed by the Etlason and Tiggaree Rivers, Sander Hill wore a broad green ring of noble estates, while south of the Y, the central city thrust up ancient towers and shining new constructs. The Hall of Charity stood like a gold-banded cube at the junction of two long green swathes.

Out of midair, a fiery projectile plummeted.

Danton had just shown them an actual recording of the Sunton disaster on Thyrica. Firebird could hardly bear to watch this simulation, but she didn't blink as the projectile—representing a trio of piloted fighters diving from orbit—plunged into the city's southeast quarter near the new Federate military base. It sank through buildings and soil into bedrock. Around it, the city heaved like water into which a stone had been thrown. As the crater blasted two klicks deep, buildings, greenery, and people—everything flammable coalesced in fire. . . .

"Enough," Firebird muttered, turning away. Muirnen Rogonin, Regent until the majority of Her Majesty Queen Iarla, owned the Codex newsnet service. Naturally, he'd sent this to the governor's office as a greeting to Firebird and Brennen.

Governor Danton stroked something on his desk top. The window-filters opened, and Firebird took a short step backward. She glanced out at a heartbreakingly familiar view. An ancient arch framed three distant housing stacks and the central-city towers. Closer at hand, a cluster of tinted glasteel terminals had risen phoenix-like out of Citangelo Spaceport's ashes, evidence of its Federate conquerors' rebuilding program. Webs of gravidic scaffolding surrounded a partly finished ten-meter projection dish that was probably part of the new planetary defense system.

Still intact. Still home.

Governor Danton shook his head. "No one actually knows where they'll strike next?"

Firebird's husband, Field General Brennen Caldwell, sat in one of Danton's luxurious office chairs, lacing his fingers, looking just as sober as Danton. A small, whitening scar marked his left cheek, external evidence of his recent captivity. Brennen had taken terrible injuries at Three Zed. In the weeks since their escape, he'd struggled to convalesce. "I'm afraid not," he answered. "That is the real reason we've returned."

"I don't understand," said the Federate governor.

Firebird pointedly picked up a kass mug she'd left on Governor Danton's desk. She forced down a bitter sip, hating the taste but needing the mild stimulant. With her day cycle shifted eleven hours, this was all that was keeping her awake. Her gesture also cued Brenn that she would rather let him answer.

He set down his own mug. "The Federacy asked us to accept the Assembly's invitation," he said. "When Firebird was asked to return and be confirmed as an heiress of House Angelo, we both wanted to refuse."

Firebird nodded. She wanted that made plain.

"But we found good reasons to accept," Brennen said. "Regional command asked us to make the strongest possible statement that the Federacy supports local governments and their customs."

Danton nodded. "No surprises so far."

Brennen pressed one finger to the scar on his cheekbone, a gesture he'd picked up in recent weeks. "This is the crux, Lee. No one knows where the Shuhr will attack next, and my people have no intention of sending an agent back to Three Zed."

Not after what they did to you, Firebird reflected. Vengeance belonged to the One, but in retrospect, she was glad it'd been necessary to kill Dru Polar to escape. He'd tortured Brennen, then tried to force him to kill her—

"They know Firebird and I will be here in Citangelo for the next six days," Brennen went on. "The Sentinel College has publicized the fact that I was injured and reduced in Ehretan abilities. We hope to draw out a Shuhr agent, take a prisoner, and interrogate." He glanced at his bodyguard, the rather dashing Lieutenant Colonel Uri Harris. "We need to find out their plans before they can strike again," Brennen finished.

"That's why you'll be staying in the palace?" Danton asked. "You'll try to take your prisoner there?"

Firebird nodded and said, "That's plan one. Besides, I'm supposed to show that having accepted Federate transnational citizenship doesn't make me any less a Netaian, or less an Angelo." She managed a smile, despite her queasy reaction to the Codex image. "One Shuhr agent might be foolish enough to think we won't be adequately guarded there."

Brennen, recently reinstated into Regional command's Special Operations force, had just sent twelve of his fellow Sentinels to infiltrate palace staff. Sentinel Uri Harris, his bodyguard, was an access-interrogation specialist, as Brennen had been before Three Zed. Firebird's own bodyguard was a weapons instructor at the Sentinel College.

As the Shuhr continued to step up their raids against military craft, Regional command could draw only one conclusion. The decades-long standoff between Brennen's kindred and their renegade relatives was about to fly apart into open conflict.

Regional command had ordered Brennen's new team to find out where the Shuhr planned their next major attack and to prevent it. He carried sealed orders, to be opened if they could get one Shuhr in custody for interrogation.

Firebird's confirmation gave Brennen's team its opportunity. Confirmation was only a formality, and if she did stay here long enough to go through with it, it would convey no actual power—but Netaia had thrived on spectacle for centuries. In one carefully choreographed alternate scenario, Firebird and Brennen planned to walk up the aisle of Citangelo's great, cubical Hall of Charity . . . as bait for the trap.

"And the new RIA technology?" Danton's voice dropped a little farther, and he drummed his fingers on the desk top. Regional command had announced RIA just over forty days ago. Half the Federacy was now screaming for the Sentinels to use it, to attack Three Zed before the Shuhr could destroy one more city. The other half demanded that all trained Sentinels be surgically disempowered, rather than let them dominate the Federacy.

Danton raised one eyebrow and stared at Brennen. Firebird was willing to bet the RIA announcement disturbed him.

"I promise you," Brennen said firmly, "Remote Individual Amplification poses the Federacy no threat. We will only use it against the Shuhr."

Firebird emerged from Governor Danton's inner office into a narrow lounge. Prince Tel Tellai-Angelo sprang up out of a chair. She hurried forward to greet him.

Tel, widower of Firebird's sister Phoena, was their only ally among Netaia's noble class. Flamboyant in a maroon shirt and knickers, he whisked off a feather-brimmed hat. "Firebird," he murmured. "I just arrived." He turned to Brennen. "Caldwell, welcome back to Citangelo. Are you all right?"

Brennen laid a hand on the smaller man's shoulder. "I'm fine," he said, hastily turning aside.

Firebird sensed his sudden shortness of breath. Ever since Three Zed, narrow spaces like this lounge unnerved him. "Shel," he said, "Uri, this is Prince Tel. He's on the short list."

Uri Harris maintained a cultured air, even when walking behind Brenn at full attention. Keeping closer to Firebird, Sentinel Shelevah Mattason was 170 centimeters of feminine power, with pale blue-gray eyes and a strong cleft chin. She rarely smiled.

Tel raised a black eyebrow. "Short list?"

Firebird threw her arms around Tel and translated, "You're not a potential threat. These are our bodyguards."

Tel pulled away, glanced at Uri and Shel, and said, "Good. I hope there are more where they came from."

Two burly men in Tallan ash gray emerged from Danton's inner office. "Yes," Firebird answered. She couldn't inform Tel about the team infiltrating the palace—not out here, where she might be overheard. "And Governor Danton assured us there'll be extra security, plainclothes. One team will follow us to the palace now."

Brennen led down a passway lined with windowed doors. Firebird hung back with Tel, who leaned down toward her. "How is he, really?"

Firebird pursed her lips. "As well as we can hope." Brennen had done the damage himself, creating amnesia blocks to keep his captors from learning Federate military secrets. Eight weeks had passed since their return from the Shuhr, and he seemed calmer, better able to accept his losses. Besides memory gaps, he no longer had the fine epsilon control that had made him a Master Sentinel. That resulted in a shattering loss of status. The college had asked him to give up wearing his eight-rayed Master's star. His Ehretan Scale rating, once an exceptional ES 97, had restabilized at 83. Normally, only those who scored at least ten points higher were considered for Master's training. "Solid but no longer exceptional" was the new prognosis.

She'd seen him powerless and stammering at Three Zed, where one Shuhr had taunted her, claiming that she never could have had him back, not as she knew him. She was thankful he'd restabilized with this much strength.

She glanced up at Brenn's well-muscled shoulder and the new four-rayed emblem. While this mission lasted, he was masquerading as even more dramatically disabled—an ES 32. If the Shuhr thought he was virtually helpless, they might try and strike.

Almost everyone he met these days looked first at his new shoulder star. He'd told Firebird how plainly he sensed their relief. On the pair bond that joined them, she felt his pained attempts to turn embarrassment into genuine humility. He often succeeded.

Firebird quickened her steps to follow him across the new base. It had a sterile feel, bare of trim and almost surgically clean. As they passed an observation window-wall, she could see little of the aging, dignified spaceport she remembered, nor the vast military installation nearby. *Bombed to slag under the Federates*, she realized.

Would the Shuhr try to do even worse here, or had they set their sights on another world? Lenguad, or Caroli, or even Tallis?

"How are the babies?" Tel asked, pacing alongside her.

Firebird pictured four-month-old Kiel and Kinnor, asleep on their warming cots back at Hesed. "Wonderful," she said. "Active. They're changing so fast, we'll be hard put to catch up when we get back."

Tel touched her arm. "Sixteen more days."

Yes. If this trap caught no one, then at least she might return quickly. It would take six days to finish her electoral business, then ten to travel back across space.

On the other hand, if the trap caught a Shuhr as they hoped, then ten days on a different vector would take them back to Three Zed and battle. Brennen's people were determined not to let the Shuhr blast one more crater or slaughter another innocent twelve-year-old and her family in their home.

Firebird glanced at the small black duffel in Brennen's left hand, sent to Hesed by Regional command. There was a sealed message roll inside. Before he could even open it, they had to catch a Shuhr.

"It's not quite that simple," she told Tel.

They emerged at the command building's main entry. Damp winter air pierced her to the bone. She tightened the belt on her woolen coat, a gift from Sanctuary Mistress Anna. A monstrous indigo groundcar stood nearby, its side trunk open, their luggage automatically stacked inside. Uri walked to the trunk and drew a scanning device from his belt. Shel slid into the car, brandishing a similar scanner.

Beside the front door stood a squat man in indigo-and-black Tellai livery. Tel positioned himself alongside the car, then beckoned Brennen closer. He pulled off his hat and offered it to Firebird. "The height of this year's male couture. What do you think?"

Nestled inside lay two tiny handblazers. "I think it's ridiculous," she said firmly, pocketing one weapon. She would prefer to carry a nonlethal shock pistol, but it felt good to be armed again.

Brennen laughed, a hollow attempt at good humor. "I've seen worse," he said. Firebird didn't see the other blazer leave Tel's hat, but when Tel centered it again on his black hair, it rode lightly.

Brennen stared past Tel's vehicle. Returning to this base felt eerie. Danton's office had looked vaguely familiar, but the long hall was utterly strange, full of foreboding.

He did not regret creating the amnesia blocks. He'd saved vital military secrets and brought down two of the Shuhr's most dangerous leaders, saving Hesed House from destruction. He had to believe that someday he would fully understand why the Eternal One let him be disabled.

He'd returned with irrational fears that were clues to the memories he'd lost. Bladed weapons, anything made of gold—he understood why those things stole his breath. He'd returned with a knife scar on his chest, and in accessing Firebird's memories of Three Zed, he'd seen long golden corridors.

But why did he fear pulsing red lights? He remembered little from that place, with one terrible exception. For three generations, a Shuhr family had pursued his own. A Shirak murdered his great-uncle. That man's son killed his uncles, and the grandson . . .

In a black-walled conference room, surrounded by hostile observers, Micahel Shirak had admitted slaughtering Brennen's brother, sister-in-law, and their children. He forced Brennen's mind open and poured in a memory Brennen wished he could forget.

Brennen clenched a hand. This would be a dangerous double game, to protect Firebird Mari while hunting down a Shuhr. He hoped he might catch Micahel Shirak. That cruel braggart ought to feel the anguish of being probed for secrets that might bring down his own people. Micahel's family still threatened Brennen's children, and their children, and theirs. Micahel might have brothers, or cousins . . .

Brennen frowned. If only he could remember! The Shuhr tri-D summons, demanding he return and face justice, showed only Micahel, sitting at an obsidian desk, promising further destruction if Brennen didn't return.

Regional command hadn't publicly released that summons.

Laying a hand on the car's fender, he stared at the metal-spiked energy fence surrounding this parking zone. He caught an odd epsilon savor at the edge of his new, limited range. Something felt wrong, almost hazy, as if someone were epsilon-shielding their own presence.

Brennen clung to his masquerade, resisting the urge to react. He had to convince the Shuhr he'd lost more ability than he actually had. He'd planted disinformation in the Sentinel College's records, rating himself barely psi-competent. No ES 32 would notice that vague presence. Hardly daring to hope his trap would bring in a Shuhr this quickly, he gripped his duffel strap and forced himself to play the concerned but unaware husband, depending on Shel and Uri for protection. They knew the real extent of his injuries, of course. Special Operations agents had to trust each other.

Firebird leaned close to Tel, speaking softly. The slight young nobleman was half a head taller than Firebird, and her plain gray traveling suit was an elegant contrast to his gaudy outfit.

Shel grabbed her sidearm. Uri hit an alarm on his belt at almost the same moment. They must have finally sensed the intruder.

Brennen curled his hand around Tel's small defense blazer. A brilliant green energy bolt splattered on the door arch behind him, and a foul presence slid into the edge of his mind. He couldn't resist the probe without compromising his masquerade, and so—as planned—he let it take his arm muscles. Controlled from a distance by a lawless stranger's epsilon power, his own arm swung toward Firebird. His thumb slid against his will toward the firing stud.

He seized his right wrist with his left hand and choked, "Get in, Mari." That was his private name for Firebird. If the Sentinel infiltration team was still in the area, this could be their chance—

Where were they?

He forced his rebel fingers open. Tel's little blazer clattered to the pavement.

Uri, Shel, and the plainclothes guards fanned out. As Firebird scrambled into the passenger compartment, Brennen rose onto the balls of his feet and looked around. From some distance away came a pulse of gloating, of shields dropped to reveal epsilon power, a Shuhr agent tossing down a gauntlet. In that instant, Brennen saw himself through other eyes as an easy mark.

He kept anger out of his surface thoughts, where the Shuhr might sense it, but deep in his heart he answered the challenge. *No. This time, we will take you.* Ingrained habits, such as that confidence, proved how deeply he had relied on his own powers, instead of the One he served.

Uri covered a spot near the gate with his own blazer. *No one's close enough to assist*, he subvocalized into Brennen's mind.

"Who was it?" Firebird demanded. On the pair bond, he felt her tension as she peered out of the car's second door.

"Can't tell," he muttered, scooping up the small blazer. "Uri, Shel. Recognize him?"

"No," Uri answered. "We'll see if we can get him to follow."

CHAPTER 2

CITANGELO

fanfare
a short melody for brasses, used as a ceremonial
signal

Firebird tingled with adrenaline as she slid across the seat, making room for Brennen. Tel's chauffeur slammed the car's first door. Tel jumped in front, too, then climbed between seats into the rear lounge. Shel eased around Firebird to take a window seat while Brennen pressed against her side. She hoped she'd acted her role as well as he'd played his. He'd almost convinced her he was helpless.

Uri took another back-facing seat while Danton's men joined Tel's driver up front. "Home," Firebird told the driver, "but not too quickly. We want him to follow." *As if he could lose this monstrosity in traffic!* Danton's plainclothes people would come about half a klick back.

The chauffeur, a lumpish man with shoulders too narrow for his indigo jacket, steered out the base's main gate and turned north on Port Road. Firebird heard a soft trill from the control panel as Central Guidance took over. She almost asked Uri to confirm that the Netaian driver could be trusted, then changed her mind. Tel surely screened his staff. Even if he'd missed a sleeper, Uri knew his job. He'd guarded several high-ranking Federate dignitaries.

She did feel slightly cheated, denied a good view of Citangelo, but she had to get used to moving inside a guarded circle. "Anyone following?" she muttered.

Uri frowned. "No."

One chance lost. Disappointed, Firebird studied Uri's face a little longer. He was Brennen's second cousin, and she saw a resemblance in their fine chins and cheekbones. He had been raised in political circles, which explained his impeccable manners.

Tel fingered a touchpanel on the side console, and the glasteel panel separating them from his driver darkened. "We're privacy shielded now," he said. "What can you tell me?"

Firebird glanced at Uri, then Shel. Shel paused a moment, eyeing her hand-held scanner. "Go ahead," Shel said gruffly. "The car's not transmitting, and the driver didn't react when Prince Tel asked."

Firebird drew a deep breath. "You've probably heard that the Shuhr are raiding again."

"Did Governor Danton show you the Codex simulation?" Tel asked.

Firebird nodded grimly. "Of course. And you do know that the Federacy just announced its new RIA technology."

Tel frowned. "Why?" Tel had gone with her to Three Zed, helping to run an RIA apparatus. Tel already knew most of what the Federacy just revealed—that Remote Individual Amplification would enable a Sentinel to influence other minds from planetary distances, instead of the traditional room's width. It had passed its first combat test when Firebird and Brennen escaped Thyrica, pursued by a Shuhr attack force. Later, it enabled Brennen, then Firebird, to land undetected at Three Zed.

"But RIA was top secret." Tel sounded plaintive. He'd even submitted to voice-command before he left sanctuary, to ensure he wouldn't inadvertently reveal RIA's existence.

Firebird glanced aside at Brennen and caught a glint of keen blue eyes, sober under dark eyebrows. *Do you want to explain,* she thought at him, *or shall I?* Their deep pair bond didn't let them send words, but they were learning to communicate from context and emotional clues.

He opened one hand, gesturing her to go ahead.

She leaned forward on the cushioned seat. "Sentinels have policed the Shuhr for decades," she said. As recently as two years ago, most Netaians hadn't even heard of the Shuhr. There weren't many Shuhr, but it didn't take many to frighten the Federates. "But they've pulled off three raids in the last month."

"Against military ships." Tel glanced up, as if he expected another suicide flight to plunge through the gray cloud cover. Obviously, he'd seen the Codex tri-D.

"Exactly," she said. "They have no military manufacturing. Why bother to build what they can steal?"

Tel nodded again.

"Regional command hopes that announcing RIA might buy us all a few weeks' reprieve. If that slows down their next strike, we might find out where they're headed in time to preempt it."

"Is the Federacy going to attack Three Zed?" Tel asked, looking directly into her face. "Before they can steal RIA, too?"

Again she thought of those sealed orders. She guessed, but she didn't know.

Besides RIA, they would take another dangerous new weapon to Three Zed . . . *if* those were the orders. Ever since Firebird and Brennen escaped from the Golden City, Sentinel College researchers had observed the unique fusion of their epsilon carrier waves. Under certain circumstances, that fusion of mental energy released virtually uncontrollable power. Using fusion, Brennen had sent a swordlike crystace pommel-first from high over Dru Polar's head, down through his body, and into Three Zed's stone floor, blasting out a small crater and filling it with . . . Polar.

Unfortunately, that fusion had sent Firebird into deep psychic shock. The college researchers had also learned that each fusion left scar tissue on the ayin complex deep in her brain, where her epsilon carrier arose. Genetically created by the Sentinels' ancestors, the mental-frequency epsilon wave gave rise to all their unusual abilities.

"I'm sorry," she murmured. "We're not allowed to discuss that possibility."

Tel leaned back in his seat, crossing his arms. Two years ago, Firebird had thought him dull-witted. What sensible person would marry Phoena? In the last four months, she'd seen Tel's courage and intelligence, and his loyalty—one of the highest Netaian virtues.

If the Federacy thought Brennen would lead an attack on Three Zed, why would Tel think otherwise?

She barely smiled at him, then turned aside.

Beneath the shroud of clouds, an elevated maglev rail paralleled Port Road through Citangelo's high-tech manufacturing zone, then bent west toward the fastrans station. Laser-straight avenues and narrow roadways that dated back to colonization crossed Port in the shopping district. An elegant stone bridge vaulted the Etlason River.

"There it is," murmured Shel.

Firebird pressed forward. From this vantage on the Etlason Bridge, she spotted a cubical building at one end of a park: the gold-sheathed Hall of Charity, where her confirmation ceremony was planned.

She might have to leave Netaia before her scheduled confirmation if Brennen made his catch soon enough. Still, if she helped disempower the Shuhr, Netaia might proclaim her a hero even if she left Citangelo prematurely.

. . . Might. There was no predicting the Netaian Electorate.

They passed on into traffic, skimmers and groundcars, mostly controlled by central guidance. Brennen pressed a data chip into the media block on the car's side console. Another half-meter hologram glimmered into existence between the forward- and back-facing seats. Firebird knew every cranny and corridor of the building that appeared. The three-hundred-year-old palace had seven klicks of passways, more than a hundred stairwells and gravity lifts, and two dozen entries. Its governmental and private wings framed formal gardens behind the broad public zone. Behind that columned front, the sovereign—a regent, at present—and other public officials had day and night offices.

Squarely centered between the palace's backswept wings, an elliptical chamber shone off-gold. It was the electoral chamber, heart of power on royal Netaia. Behind it were meeting rooms, galleries, and ballrooms . . .

Firebird glared at the sovereign's night office. In that curtained chamber, her regal mother had given her a last gift—poison, in case she was captured in battle.

Now that Firebird was a mother herself, she could not understand. Back at Hesed, her twin sons were probably fast asleep or enjoying a midnight feeding, Kiel a tiny mirror image of his father, and strong-willed Kinnor with those tight auburn curls, that impish face. How could her own mother, Queen Siwann, order Firebird to poison herself?

Brennen reached into the hologram, creating a double swath of shadow that blacked out several servitors' chambers and the uplevel library. Dozens of small human figures stood inside the two-level image. Nearly all the figures shone the scarlet shade of House Angelo livery, but twelve had been switched to midnight blue. He pointed silently to several.

"You'll have help," Tel observed.

Brennen waved off the media block and retrieved the chip. "That information isn't public knowledge, Tel. I wanted to reassure you."

"Then how do you intend to get a Shuhr in custody?" Tel demanded.

Firebird glanced at Brennen and barely nodded. *Your turn*, she thought at him. Tel had better not hear this from her.

He dipped his chin. "They measure the emotional impact of every action they take," he explained. "As long as they have a chance of catching us in the public eye—"

She sent him a wry half smile. Her confirmation would be public, all right!

He returned a pulse of amusement that only she could feel. "They aren't likely to settle for a quiet assassination," he finished.

Tel dropped his plumed hat. "You're not hoping to lure Shuhr agents into the Hall of Charity."

"To save Netaia or another Whorl world," Brennen said, "we'd prefer to take one quietly, in the palace. But if that fails—yes, Tel. We'll try."

Firebird glanced from one man to the other, hoping Brennen didn't need to put Tel under another voice-command to keep him from inadvertently revealing that information. She hated the idea of violating another person's volition, even for his own protection.

Tel nodded slowly and said, "Now I understand why you came back to Citangelo. The entire Federacy is at risk."

Firebird sensed Brennen's unspoken nudge. "That's part of the reason," she confessed. "There's also the confirmation itself. It is a peacemaking gesture."

Tel smiled wryly. "Well, you've certainly earned it. You've given up more, risked more, for Netaia's sake than any three confirmed heirs."

She agreed, but she couldn't say so. "And I'll be speaking to the Electorate tonight."—Hopefully before the developing Shuhr emergency could call her away!

Tel raised an eyebrow. "I'd thought that tonight's special session was Rogonin's chance to tell you he opposed your return."

"I'm sure he won't miss the chance," she murmured. "But I have more to say than he probably expects."

The car turned north on Capitol Avenue. Fayya trees drooped along the meridian, their leaves winter-dark and rustling in air currents created by traffic. Firebird couldn't see much sky, but she sensed a cold front coming in. It felt good to know she hadn't lost her Citangelo weather sense.

In one way, she hoped the trap didn't spring too soon. If she had to go back to Three Zed, she would love to first rub a few noble noses in her new status as an heir, to face down the young counts and countesses who'd despised a doomed Angelo wastling. She would outrank them now.

It shouldn't matter after all she'd been through, but she couldn't help feeling this way. For all their graceless cruelties, Netaia's noble traditions shaped her life.

On the other hand, she had rejected its strictly external state religion. She'd found mercy in a Singer beyond human comprehension, and she'd seen the evil deep in her own soul, a darkness she could only partially blame on Netaian traditions. That darkness made divine mercy necessary. She hoped she might introduce her beloved common people to something beyond the state-enforced service of Charities, Disciplines, and nine allegedly holy Powers.

"Well." Tel retrieved his hat and replaced it over his dark hair. "I hope you catch your Shuhr and find out what you need to know. But I hope there isn't a pitched battle inside the Hall of Charity."

"It's also possible," Brennen said, "that they might send in an agent who knows nothing important and who could injure anyone who attempted to mind-access him. Or her."

Firebird nodded. They just didn't know enough about the Shuhr's actual capabilities. They needed information on Three Zed's defenses and where the Shuhr hoped to strike. The Federate fleets simply couldn't be deployed to defend twenty-four star systems.

Meanwhile, the new crater on Brennen's home world hadn't finished filling with groundwater. Peaceful, easygoing Sunton, near the single continent's eastern shore, was now a saltwater lake.

Brennen barely swayed with the groundcar's motion, staring as if he were waiting for Tel to speak. He still could sense other people's tension when they prepared to raise uncomfortable subjects. His worst losses were in memory and kinetic skills.

Tel met that stare. "What about Iarla and Kessaree?" he asked.

"Nothing yet," Brennen admitted. Firebird's Angelo nieces—daughters of her eldest sister, Carradee—had been sent away under Federate protection, to be safer from the Shuhr. They never arrived.

Tel frowned and forged ahead. "Some people are concerned that RIA technology could put you people in charge of the Federacy."

Brennen returned Tel's sober frown. Previously, projecting a Sentinel's epsilon carrier wave long-distance could only be done by a planetary fielding team with several rooms full of subtronic gear. Like fielding, RIA's range was planetary. Unlike fielding, an RIA apparatus could be mounted on a single-seat ship.

"People are scared," Tel continued. "After what the Shuhr did to Sunton, every raid is considered a warning. It's that many more suicide ships they could throw at Federate worlds. We need you Sentinels now more than ever."

Firebird wanted to assure him. "The Federacy believes in preserving everyone's freedom. But the Shuhr's freedoms have to end at the point where they threaten other lives. The Sentinels see that as their duty, since they share similar abilities."

Another bridge rose in front of them. To the left and right, hedges marked the boundaries of Angelo property. She sat up straighter as Capitol Avenue crossed the Tiggaree and the chauffeur hit his override. Released from central guidance, their vehicle glided through massive gates tipped with golden spear points.

Firebird bent low to peer ahead as they cruised through a public festival square toward a grand edifice. Six bulky pillars, three left and three right, framed a short flight of wide white marble steps. Two electoral policemen marched down toward the car.

Firebird drew back from the window, almost overwhelmed by her aversion to that uniform. Electoral police, redjackets, enforced the cruel customs that guaranteed the wastlings' martyrdom. Supposedly, she didn't need to dread them anymore.

One tall, crimson-coated man opened the car door on Brennen's side. Freezing air swirled in. Firebird scooted off the seat and stepped onto a white-pebbled pavement.

Half gloved, all in scarlet, black, and gold, the redjacket towered over her. His neckscarved companion shut the car's side compartment. Carrying four large duffels, he strode along the building's front toward an entry in the private east wing.

Brennen followed, carrying that small black duffel.

Firebird's breath glittered as she mounted the steps. At that moment, a tour guide in scarlet-trimmed khaki emerged from the main door, leading a mixed-age troop through the gilt arch. Several reached for pocket-sized camera recorders.

Shuhr? No, tourists. Evidently the palace hadn't tightened security for her visit. She smiled faintly. A few of them smiled back.

Two House Guards in formal red-collared black stood at smaller doors farther on—this branch of service sworn to her family, not the Electorate. Each guard suspended one hand over a golden door bar. Firebird felt Brennen's attentive edge peak, then ebb away. Evidently, the House Guards felt safe to him, but she made it a point to glance around as if she were nervous before she followed Tel into a wide private foyer. Here, especially, they had to make it look as if Brennen had suffered crippling setbacks. Half the palace servitors were probably regency spies. Danton's plainclothes guards entered last.

High overhead, surrounding five ancient chandeliers strung with natural gems, ornate moldings decorated the walls and ceiling with swirls and flower petals. Portraits lined the lower walls. To her right, a staircase curved up to the living quarters. Left, a narrow hall led toward the sovereign's day and night offices.

Shel Mattason strolled forward and took a long look up the office hallway. Her large, wide-set blue-gray eyes did not blink. According to her résumé, Shel held the Sentinel College marksmanship instructors' title, and she was highly qualified in three martial arts. Firebird was glad to have her at right-wing.

Firebird stepped up to the portrait displayed prominently on a screen in midhall. The artfully painted woman wore gold, her dark hair perfectly coifed. Hard lines surrounded her mouth, and her dark eyes had a depth that suggested wisdom. One eyebrow arched slightly.

"Mother," Firebird whispered. There in the eyes, there through the jaw, Firebird picked out her own features in those of the autocratic late queen. *Could I have become another Siwann?* she wondered. If she'd been firstborn, would she have learned to wield power in the Netaian way, disregarding all individuals beneath her station?

Giant white cinnarulias, Siwann's favorite flowers, filled a cat-footed marble table beside the screen. Their scent brought back sharp memories of living here—a proud life, full of pain and desperate striving, and the need to accomplish too much in too little time.

Thank you for taking me away from here, Mighty Singer, she prayed. *But thank you for bringing me back, and for giving me a chance to save my people—from civil war, or Shuhr destruction—*

Quick footsteps echoed along the corridor. A man in Angelo service livery hustled into view. Heavyset with tightly curled hair, he rubbed plump hands together over his white cummerbund. "My lady, let me show you to your apartments."

They followed him up the private stairway, its shortweave carpet muffling their footsteps. Ribbons of gilt edged the banister and floor moldings. A stairwell alcove displayed a bust of the first Angelo monarch, Conura I.

Instead of halting outside the rooms that had been hers as a child, the footman led farther along the balcony, into the crown princess's suite. The high, white-walled entry chamber, with its formal furniture and narrow windows, had been Carradee's sitting room when they were girls. Brennen walked slowly along one wall. She felt how badly he wanted to go to work checking for monitoring devices.

"You will find all the appointments in place," said the footman. "My name is Paskel, of service staff. I live in-house, and you may call for me at any time. My number is six-oh-six." He indicated a tabletop console near the sitting room's door.

The man seemed friendly in a distant, officious way. "Thank you, Paskel," Firebird said. "Should I request dinner a little earlier than His Grace plans to dine?"

"I shall bring dinner up shortly. That will give you time to prepare for the special session."

"Good thinking," said Tel.

The servitor made a full bow. Tel nodded.

Firebird almost laughed. She'd always despised all this nod-and-bow. Definitely, she was home.

"And your . . . personal escort?" the footman asked, glancing at Uri and Shel. "Shall I lodge these in servants' quarters?"

Whether or not Paskel reported to the regent, Firebird wanted it known that she and Brennen were guarded. "No, open the consort's suite that goes with this apartment."

"Very good, Your Highness. Tomorrow, I shall ensure your engagement list is posted to these rooms." Paskel turned toward the door. He closed it silently, without the resounding *boom* so easy to make with heavy doors and ancient, resonant walls.

Firebird stared. He'd *highness*-ed her! She had asked Governor Danton to see that the royal title wasn't used in official releases, but palace staff followed tradition. Was Paskel declaring himself a cautious sympathizer?

Turning his head, Brennen lowered his eyebrows as if he were bitterly frustrated. Firebird knew it wasn't all masquerade. "Uri," he said, "Shel. Please safe the room."

ELECTORATE

promenade
ceremonious opening of a formal ball

Firebird watched the bodyguards walk a slow circuit. Each one paused occasionally, raising a hand toward some innocent-looking object. They passed over the marble firebay and other obvious hiding places for listening and watching devices, reaching instead to touch wall panels, old bits of crystal, a jeweled window-filter. Reaching the far wall, Uri flourished one hand at a priceless, garish South Continent vase, then pivoted on his heel.

Most of those trinkets had been Phoena's, not Carradee's, and now that Firebird considered, that made sense. After Carradee took the queen's apartment, Phoena and Tel had lived in this suite. His Grace the Regent had probably left her Phoena's wardrobe for company.

What did standing in here do to her widower? She turned to eye Tel.

He pulled off his cock-hat and sank onto a pale gold velvette chair. "Here you are, Firebird. The lady of the palace."

Firebird remained standing in the middle of the carpet. She would not sit down until Uri and Shel checked every room. Uri, Shel, or Brennen could also pick up an assailant's focused tension before the attack, so they would have warning of any assassination attempt.

She hoped.

Staying in the palace did make a strong statement on behalf of the Federacy. Even as a transnational citizen, she belonged here.

Or did she? She already felt out of place in her plain gray traveling suit, while Tel's tailored outfit seemed appropriate. "This is more your room than mine, Tel."

"I live in my father's estate. This is a lovely suite, but . . ." He flattened his lips, then spoke again. "You need some time now. I'll be there to support you tonight."

"Thank you for all you've done for us."

Brennen raised his head. "Yes, Tel. You've been a friend where we didn't dare look for one."

Firebird's group assembled in Phoena's second parlor two hours later. The Angelo starred-shield crest decorated both of the study's doorways, and Phoena's furniture seemed oddly placed, with gaps where large pieces had been removed. As Firebird recalled, Phoena had run a resistance movement from this suite before she moved to Hunter Height.

Brennen, Shel, and Uri wore dress-white tunics that made their gold shoulder stars gleam, and the crystaces they normally hid in wrist sheaths rode on their belts. "You look splendid," she assured them.

"You," Brennen said, "look regal." He'd helped select the floor-sweeping skirt and snug velvette blouse, a statement in Angelo scarlet.

She smiled and checked the tiny time lights on her wristband. They should enter the electoral chamber in twelve minutes, at nineteen hundred sharp. Within minutes of that, she planned to interrupt the usual invocation of the nine holy Powers. She must show the electors she was no longer a dutiful wastling. Even the Federacy, which smashed her attack squadron and dismantled Netaia's mighty defenses, had been reduced to waffling against these belligerent aristocrats. Their economic control seemed unbreakable.

Her hand trembled. She stretched it out to show it to Brennen. "I can't look skittish. Touch me with prayer."

He covered her head with one palm. "Holy One, go with Firebird to face these people. Convince them of her wisdom and leadership, and protect her. So let it be." Their eyes met for an instant. "Be wary of pride, Mari."

The name was a private endearment, but she frowned at the warning. He knew what she planned to do. Sentinel College personality analysts had warned her she would always struggle with pride, willfulness, and impatience (Brennen had already known, of course). Still, this was Netaia, and tonight she had to startle the most complacent Netaians of all. "I can't shuffle into that chamber with my eyes on the ground."

"Of course not. Show Rogonin you were born for this. Defy the Powers." Brennen touched her shoulder. "But don't let them tempt you back to the old ways."

She raised her head and strode out.

In the corridor waited another pair of red-jacketed electoral policemen. Beyond them, two uniformed Federate guards waited at parade-rest, Danton's supplemental group. By now, there were probably Sentinels in the kitchens and corridors, looking for Shuhr assassins.

She descended the sweeping staircase, sliding her right hand along a banister and holding her skirt. At the foot of the stair, Paskel stood carrying a servitor's tray. He half bowed as she passed. Despite Brennen's warning, every proud Angelo instinct flamed in her heart and mind. Her adrenaline surged as if she were headed into combat.

Well, she was! Twenty meters along the next corridor, two more redjackets stood at each side of gold-sheathed doors. The doors stood open. Firebird drew a deep breath and walked through.

An elevated, U-shaped table rimmed in gold dominated this elliptical chamber, a room filled with memories. Along one curved crimson wall, beyond a bas-relief false pillar, she spotted a blocked peephole she used years ago to spy on the Electorate. A smooth gold floor medallion carried colder memories. It had felt icy through the knees of her Academy uniform, when she knelt with a redjacket at each shoulder. As a wastling, her birth had helped ensure the Angelo line's survival, but the family's need for her ended when her second niece was born, and so she was ordered to seek a noble death in the name of Netaia's traditions, and for its grandeur. "You are to be praised for your service to Netaia," First Lord Bualin Erwin had intoned the electoral *geis*. "On behalf of the Electorate, I thank you. But your service to this council has ended."

Firebird ground her shoes onto the medallion. She raised her head toward the elevated table.

To be Angelo was to be proud.

Twenty-six elegantly composed faces stared back. The commoners Carradee had appointed were all gone. Ten noble families ruled Netaia as benign despots, treasurers, and demigod-priests for the nine holy Powers of Strength, Valor, and Excellence; Knowledge, Fidelity, and Resolve; Authority, Indomitability, and Pride. Besides House Angelo, there were the barons and baronesses Erwin and Parkai, three ducal houses, and the counts with their countesses. For decades, they had controlled science and shipping, culture and resources, information and enforcement. As Brennen liked to say, their tentacles were everywhere.

At center table, a massive man sat on a gilt chair he'd stolen from her sister Carradee. Firebird half bowed to the regent and Duke of Claighbro, Muirnen Rogonin, but she couldn't keep her eyes from narrowing. "Good evening, Your Grace." *Grace—ha*. His Corpulence was neither gracious nor graceful. All in white with a sash of gold, he glared down through small green eyes.

She nodded left and right. "Noble electors, good evening." Shel remained three paces behind, at the corner of her vision. By protocol, the electors had to allow her one escort. Brennen and Uri remained by the golden door, between Danton's reinforcements and the red-jacketed door guards. The first time she'd seen Brennen, he stood in this chamber as an honor guard. Here they were again!

"Lady Firebird." Rogonin rested both hands on the high table. "You have been summoned by the people of Netaia. Deliver your greeting."

Glancing up, she spotted several miniaturized tri-D transcorders. Black velvette hoods shrouded them. Netaia's three newsnets would not carry this interview.

Actually, that was a relief. She could speak freely.

So could they, of course. . . .

"Your Grace," she called, "Noble electors, I am grateful for the honor of your summons to be confirmed. I am ready to serve Netaia."

Traditionally, that last line ran, *I am ready to serve Netaia and the Powers that Rule.* She expected whispers, and she wasn't disappointed.

Muirnen Rogonin spread his hands. "Then let us invoke the presence of Strength, of Valor and Excellence . . ."

Now! "Before you do," she called, "I have to deliver a warning."

It might not have been the most diplomatic way to get their attention, but it succeeded. Stunned faces glared down at her. Now she spotted Tel, sitting poised and expressionless. "Noble electors," she said, "the Netaian systems are in danger from inside as well as out in the Whorl."

No one answered, and she wondered if these people would ever respect her, under any circumstances. Reminding herself she'd been trained as a soldier, not a diplomat, she plunged on. "On Thyrica," she said, "under a pseudonym, I enrolled at Soldane University. Federate analysts have amassed an enormous database from all twenty-three contemporary systems and several civilizations that fell during the Six-Alpha catastrophe. I have been working toward a degree in governmental analysis."

Count Winton Stele, son of the Duke of Ishma—Dorning Stele had been one of her commanding officers at Veroh—cleared his throat. "What were your motives, Lady Firebird?" Count Winton managed to make her wastling title sound like an insult. "Your Academy education was in military science. We need the military now more than ever."

She frowned up at his sallow face. "I enjoy learning, Count Winton. Federate society embraces many local governments. Each one has a slightly different structure, suited to its own culture."

Bennett Drake, Duke of Kenhing, pressed to his feet. He resembled his brother Daithi, Carradee's husband, though Kenhing wasn't quite as tall. His hairline had the same widow's peak, and his face was almost as round.

Kenhing was also one of the few electors who insisted on being called by his old-style title. When fully dressed, he usually wore a gold dagger on his belt. He wore it today. "Well answered, Lady Firebird," he called. "However, we are most concerned about the danger from this world they call Three Zed. Did Governor Danton show you the Codex simulation?"

Surprised by Kenhing's compliment, Firebird felt her shoulders relax infinitesimally. *See?* she asked herself. *Tel isn't the only elector with some humanity.*

"Yes, he did," she answered him. "Twenty-three other worlds are also desperate to find out where and when the Shuhr will attack again. Several Special Operations teams have been deployed to find out the Shuhr's intentions." *Including this one*—but she couldn't say so. Instead, she returned to her previous topic. "The movement of governments from feudalism to populism has been widely studied," she said. "When I discovered the topic, it intrigued me. The more I learned, the more I worried, because wherever that progression toward representative government has been delayed by force, the downfall of feudalism came by force."

Without pausing, she recited the histories she'd studied: star systems bloodbathed by civil warfare, nations subdued by outside forces . . . *that* gave her a chance to tie the Shuhr threat back in. She used every storytelling skill she'd studied at Hesed House, trying to make those tales compelling, explaining how the Federacy's Regional command could not intervene in cases of internal conflict. She wished she could add music. Mere words didn't convey the terrorized heartbreak of decimated worlds.

"Our people," she said, "appropriated Netaia's ancient mythology and made it a state religion. We adopted a strict caste system and penal laws and called it stability. We set up traditions that perpetuate the transmission of wealth and authority inside a few privileged families. The system has not failed. Our world remains rich in culture, heritage, and resources."

A few heads nodded. Other faces reminded her of blast gates, shut and shielded against her—Wellan Bowman, and young Daken Erwin. The elderly senior baron creaked to his feet. Netaian nobles wore youth-implant capsules under their skin, so First Lord Erwin's hair remained bushy and brown, but even the finest medical technology couldn't forestall aging forever. His formal blue nobleman's sash sagged on a stooped body. He cleared his throat.

That was her cue to stand down, and now she was pushing their tolerance. Instinctively she knew that if she relinquished command of the situation now, she would lose it for good. "For an independent project," she pressed, "I entered cultural and governmental variables regarding Netaia's current situation into a set of equations designed by Federate sociologists, economists, and political analysts. I ran the simulations dozens of ways, altering variables such as subpopulation movements, materials shortages, and shifts in standards of living. Please let me tell you what they predict."

First Lord Erwin made a show of raising both thin eyebrows and spreading his hands. He sat down.

Relieved, Firebird lowered her voice to a confidential tone. "There is a high likelihood of civil war here on the North Continent." Now that Erwin had ceded her the floor, she gave them a moment to picture the crisis. "Disenfranchised classes could take control of the military and our Enforcers, plunging our systems into a period even darker than the Six-alpha catastrophe. Soon. Within months."

"We assume," the regent called, sneering, "that you will now claim that the Federacy can save us."

"No," she said. "You control Netaia's fate, the Electorate here seated." Whispers followed her sweeping gesture around the table. "Without a miracle, there will be war. But you can create the miracle. According to simulations, cultural holidays such as my confirmation tend to preserve cultural unity for a while. But after as little as half a Netaian year, the rising could come. If that rising distracted the Enforcement Corps, Three Zed could seize this world."

"Your husband's kinfolk," said a shrill-voiced countess. "What are you—and he—doing to combat that menace? And where are your nieces? The queen and the crown princess?"

"The Shuhr," Firebird answered, "would threaten Netaia whether or not I had married General Caldwell." She couldn't let them sidetrack her even further, talking about Iarla and Kessaree. "Listen to my proposal. It is incomplete in many ways, but it could give you a framework for your own more thorough designs. You could save Netaia from anarchy, exactly the way our ancestors saved it thirteen generations ago."

The whispers quieted. Really, they couldn't expect her to know where Carradee's daughters had gone. Rogonin, as regent for Iarla, probably hoped they would stay missing.

"For decades," Firebird continued, "the Netaian sovereign has been a legal figurehead, standard-bearer for this Electorate. I propose that all electoral seats gradually become figureheads. Advisors. Do this by stages. Shift control of our navy and the Enforcers to the elected Assembly." Judging from the way several leaned away from the gold-rimmed table, they already disliked her idea—as she'd expected. "The Assembly would remain answerable to the Electorate, but if you . . . shift . . . fifty-percent veto power out of your own hands and to the Assembly, voluntarily, that would show unprecedented faith in your people. You would retain checks on the Assembly. I have also proposed that the noble houses be compensated for this loss of influence." Firebird beckoned, and Shel stepped forward to hand her a recall pad. "I encoded a timetable, along with other aspects of the proposal." She'd spent most of the last two months, while Brennen convalesced and retrained, recording every possible simulation and developing the final document. Over a year ago, she'd made the Federate Regional council a silent promise: spare her life, and she would do all she could to bring Netaia into the Federacy. The time had come.

Rogonin clenched his hands on the table, not into fists but into claws.

"You've been given half a year's reprieve," Firebird said. "Please, for our people's sake, use it wisely." She shifted her weight under the long skirt, hardly believing that she had dared to speak to the electors this way. She almost hated to give up her recall pad and let them commence tearing her ideas apart.

"And who," Rogonin demanded, "would compensate our Houses? Does your considerable influence with the Federacy extend to demanding funds to buy out our seats and our ministries?"

"I have no influence with the Federacy at all." *And you know it, Your Grace*, she wanted to add. "That is one of many details that remain to be worked out. But this is your chance to escape the destruction of a world's way of life. Your estates, your families—the Shuhr would love to take them away from you."

No one plunged into her silence this time. She hoped they were picturing their grand homes plundered, their children carried off to Three Zed or subjected to unimaginable genetic experiments. "You could guide Netaia through a difficult transition," she called. She dropped her voice. "Or you could all die in a terrible bloodbath."

As wretchedly as they'd treated her, she didn't want that to happen. She laid her recall pad on the gold-banded table.

Rogonin eyed it, pursing his lips with obvious contempt. "If civil war threatens," he said, "we will raise additional troops and build more prisons to hold any rebels we choose not to execute. Netaia's strength is Netaia's future, Lady Firebird." He lowered his voice. "You are dismissed."

His arrogance raked her. He didn't care squill for the common people. No surprise there either, really. Still, she'd hoped . . . "Listen to one more request, noble electors—"

"Dismissed, Lady Firebird." The regent raised his voice.

Incensed, she pitched hers to match his. "For the love of your own children," she called, "do not conscript those troops. If you do, they will be the ones who slaughter you—if the Shuhr don't arrive first!" She whirled toward the door, flaring her long skirt. *Dear Singer, don't let them choose destruction!*

She wanted to say so much more. To tell them Netaia's common classes had every reason to revolt. That they deserved privileges that most Federates called rights—the right to earn a decent, stable living, to conduct commerce with other Whorl worlds, to sleep unafraid that city Enforcers might imprison whole families for one member's indiscretions.

But she'd probably said too much already, too forcefully . . . too willfully. Politically, she had probably been utterly ineffective. But maybe a few hearts had listened.

Shel stepped in front of the Netaian door guard. Brennen's eyes flicked back and forth, watching behind Firebird. Uri led out.

Firebird walked with her head upright and her shoulders relaxed, as if she'd chosen to leave, instead of being sent away.

She retired early, exhausted by the time shift, but memories haunted her into the night. Carradee had invited her into these rooms many times. This had been her mother's palace. She lay on her sister Phoena's bed.

It was good to know that Phoena would never torment her again.

She stared at the curtained ceiling, examining the sensation of relief. Finally, she could think about the middle Angelo sister with some objectivity. Despite Phoena's scheming and cruelty, she'd been a sharp stone grinding at Firebird's heart, honing her steel to a sword's point. If Firebird hadn't battled Phoena for so many years, she might not have found the strength to fight Brennen's enemies, or the evil that invaded her own soul.

Her eyes suddenly ached, imagining Phoena trapped at Three Zed. She wondered if at some point, Phoena finally realized that the Shuhr would not help her, that they would take her life and give back nothing at all.

By the Word to Come, she actually pitied her sister.

Shocked, she swallowed. She rolled off the bed and hurried out into the dressing room, where her tears wouldn't disturb Brenn. She caught Shel pacing along the high windows, several meters away.

"It's all right," Firebird managed. "I'm just—finally—grieving my sister."

"Princess Phoena." Shel stared out one window. "I understand. I'm also recovering."

Firebird wiped her eyes and stared at her bodyguard. This was the first information Shel had volunteered since they met, back at Hesed. "You lost a bond mate?" Firebird guessed.

Shel nodded once without turning around.

"How long ago?"

The Sentinel's voice softened. "Six years."

"I'm sorry." Firebird had been told that bereavement shock was devastating. Half of all Sentinels suffered it. Brenn had said it took his mother two years to recover. Still, Shel was young. "Some time," Firebird said hesitantly, stepping closer, "I mean, I would—"

"No," Shel answered. "I'd prefer not to talk about it."

Six years later, she still was tender in a tough line of work. *Shuhr*, Firebird guessed. Many of the Sentinels killed in action were taken down by their distant relatives, by Micahel Shirak and his compatriots.

Then setting this trap was personal for Major Shelevah Mattason, too. Firebird took a few more steps toward her bodyguard, wondering if some gesture of comfort would be appropriate. Shel didn't respond.

Firebird really didn't know whether she hoped they would catch a Shuhr and attack Three Zed, or return to dig in and defend Hesed. Even with RIA, attacking the Shuhr stronghold would be perilous. The last time, she and Brenn had arrived separately, stealing past Three Zed's fielding satellites with single RIA ships. This time they would have to attack in force. They would face the full terrors of Three Zed's fielding technology.

Even at the Sentinels' sanctuary world, fielding defenders could drive off any intruder by directly producing fear in the intruders' minds, and Sentinels followed high moral standards. She didn't like to think about what a Shuhr fielding team might do.

Shel still didn't turn around. Convinced that the Sentinel preferred to keep her grief private, Firebird tiptoed back to bed.

She paused to touch a tri-D cube at her bedside. That touch made it glow with internal light. Her babies might be waking now—Kiel with that squared Brennen-chin and hair that was thickening to Brenn's light rich brown, and Kinnor with his chin pointed like a sprite, his face scrunched in an impish pout. In the tri-D, Brennen's arms wrapped her shoulders, and their hair mingled in a wind that blew out of the rugged mountains around Hesed House. Staring at the cube, she could almost smell kirka trees—

Brennen pushed up on one elbow. "You're all right?"

Firebird slid beneath a silken cover warmed by soft, embedded microfibers. "I am now," she said. "I've buried Phoena. But I can't sleep." If she ever lost Brennen, could she hope to recover? *Please, Singer. One of us must die first, someday. I know this is selfish, but let it be me! Brenn is stronger. He could bear it.*

She couldn't bring herself to relate Shel's story. "I should've asked you to tuck me in," she told him. "Would you help me get to sleep?"

She sensed epsilon energy focusing at one of his fingertips. When he touched it to her forehead, her stressed alpha matrix uncoiled instantly. She sighed, relaxed against his chest, and slipped into dreamless peace.

INTERLUDE 1

"Mistress Anna," said Carradee Angelo, "this is not the innocent request you seem to think. Of course the Shuhr have no sense of honor. I'm not averse to embarrassing them. Who knows, they might even cooperate."

Hesed House's skylights had faded, and silver strands in Sentinel Anna Dabarrah's waist-long hair glimmered by candlelight. Anna frowned deeply and answered, "Even if they offered to help, the Federacy would refuse. No one would work alongside a Shuhr search team, even if they honestly didn't harm your daughters—and I doubt that."

Carradee had let Netaia's Federate governor send Iarla and Kessaree to safety on another world, but they never arrived. Not knowing their fate . . . that was the hardest part. Even now, Federate teams were searching for them.

She pursed her lips. This candlelit dinner table stood near the sanctuary's underground lake, and her husband's mobility chair had been pulled close by. A student-apprentice Sentinel, a *sekiyr*, cut Prince Daithi's umi steak into small bites. Daithi worked manfully to spear them with a fork attached to his hand splint, taking obvious joy in keeping up with his nephews' physical development. Carradee no longer worried whether he would recover from his injuries.

Mouth full, he didn't respond to Anna, so Carradee stared out over the underground lake. Forced to abdicate in favor of her vanished daughter, she'd slid gratefully into the sanctuary's pastoral lifestyle. Sometimes Hesed House seemed far more elegant than the palace where she'd grown up.

When she arrived here, she hadn't understood why even the evil Shuhr would attack her innocent daughters. She'd learned so much since then, about the Shuhr . . . and her sister Phoena.

The events that followed Phoena's departure from Netaia—the explosion that injured Carradee and nearly killed Daithi, their daughters' disappearance—supported only one theory. Phoena had tried to enlist Shuhr help in a grab for the throne. According to what Brennen's captors told him, though he couldn't remember witnessing it, Phoena had paid for her crimes in agony.

The Shuhr must not be believed or trusted. What had she been thinking?

No wonder Rogonin deposed her. "Carradee the Kind," she'd been called, and "Carradee the Good."

"Carradee the Hopeful Romanticist" might be a better title. She arranged a cloth serviette on her lap. One of the Shuhr's announced fields of study was genetic research, and Firebird had proved that one of the Sentinels' distant relatives married into the Angelo line, several generations back. So maybe the Shuhr—

Not even the healing blocks that Master Dabarrah had graciously placed on her grief could strengthen her to finish that thought. She could not envision her precious daughters as research specimens. She would not rest until someone found them. A demand for information had been sent to Three Zed but not answered.

Master Dabarrah leaned over the table. Carradee had grown quickly to respect this psi-medical specialist. He and Mistress Anna supervised Hesed's student-apprentice Sentinels, who in turn helped Carradee care for Daithi and her nephews. This was all the realm she really wanted.

Daithi swallowed his mouthful, then spoke up. "'Dee, Mistress Anna is correct. The Shuhr would be no help. Let the Federates keep their promise. They will find whatever clues can be found." Daithi's diction had almost normalized, thanks to Master Jenner's treatments. He and Carradee often read to each other from the Sentinels' holy book, *Mattah*. That way, they could research their host family's faith while he practiced enunciating.

Back on Netaia, after being injured, Daithi had been under electoral pressure to suicide, leaving Carradee free to marry again. Saving him had been her justification for abdicating. Here, without the pressure to conceive more heirs, they could celebrate each day's millimeter of progress.

Seated on her other side, in side-by-side transport chairs, the Caldwell twins were reaching for bread bits but not quite grasping them—Kiel's fair hair fluffed on one side and Kinnor with a smear of bread crumbs along one flushed cheek. Carradee nudged a bread bit closer to Kiel, who promptly mashed it, then mouthed his hand.

"You're right, of course," said Carradee. "Something about this place makes me too hopeful, I think."

"It was a lovely fantasy," Anna murmured, "but we have no dealings with Three Zed. They are perverse and deceitful. We would attack them in force, except that the Eternal Speaker commands us to hold back until He calls us to destroy them."

Carradee ignored Anna's gloomy analysis and the sideswipe at Brennen's current mission. Anna obviously disapproved of the attempt to trap a Shuhr.

She claimed that the God they served would provide enough knowledge and power to destroy Three Zed when He issued the call. "Very well," Carradee said softly, wiping Kiel's face with her serviette. "I will wait. But it is hard. I want to hold my own children again."

CHAPTER 4

MIRRORS

courante
a quick dance in triple time, with rapidly shifting meters

Fifty-four days had passed since Juddis Adiyn injected the Caldwell-Shirak embryo into Terza Shirak's womb. Waking from a fitful sleep, Terza rolled away from a shipboard bulkhead and pressed one hand to her stomach. *I could almost wish that the Sentinels' god existed,* she moaned silently. *I would order him to smash Juddis Adiyn into sub-biological particles. He owes me. They all owe me.*

She pulled a cover over her head. Darkness held off the inevitable queasiness. It would catch her once she moved, but she didn't want to choke down breakfast while the crew watched and smirked.

If Brennen Caldwell had simply died on Three Zed, this never would have been suggested, even as one of her father's infamous options. The implanted embryo and its supportive membranes couldn't be safely removed, except by childbirth.

She kept to herself on board her father's transport. Beautifully appointed, it might have served the Federacy as a luxury transport before her people took it. From the opulent, enhanced-wavelength shimmer of its corridors to the generously appointed stateroom where she ate and slept, it was a magnificent craft.

On this morning—ship's time—before they were scheduled to arrive on Netaia, she stood for most of an hour inside her vaporbath cubicle, stroking water across sore and swelling breasts. She despised the symptoms that developed as her body adapted to this new role as a container. All her glands seemed to be responding to the half-foreign tissue graft. She'd already learned an important lesson in her chosen field, that the womb-bank was an unspeakably wonderful gift to womankind.

She finished bathing and slipped into formfitting civilian shipboards in a subtle charcoal gray. Superbly ventilated, the shipboards clung to her like a fond dream.

They wouldn't flatter her figure for long.

Abruptly overcome by the completeness with which her life changed with one tissue injection, she dropped onto her bunk and let herself cry silently behind her secret inmost shields. Cursed with the reflective temperament, Terza felt the loss of her freedom, the loss of her few friends at Cahal and in the City. She might have—no, she *would have* been culled in training for her temperament, if not for those inner shields. Even Director Polar hadn't detected them. Discovering them had been an accident, when as a seven-year-old she'd been in danger of severe discipline.

She ought to report them to Juddis Adiyn, who was always looking for new epsilon abilities. He bred them carefully into the next generation. Still, self-preservation was mightier than scientific curiosity.

Her door buzzer sounded. "Go away," she whispered, but it buzzed again.

She rocked to her feet. She checked her dark hair, pulled conservatively into a holdfast, in a freshing cabinet mirror. Then she touched a tile that opened the door.

Her half brother Micahel, cleft-chinned with strong cheekbones, shoved something that looked vaguely edible into her hand. *Come,* he ordered subvocally. *Father wants to meet you.*

That thought no longer delighted her. Terza shoved the doughy lump into her mouth. *Why now?* she asked in the same way. *I'm barely awake.*

His eyes, like her own, were so dark they nearly looked black. She and Micahel also had the same extremely fair skin, but his hair made a thick cap of curls on his head, while hers hung limp over her shoulders.

He smirked. *You have an order. Better come.*

She followed him up the ship's shining passways to a guarded door and stepped into an enormous stateroom. All its walls—she couldn't think of these as bulkheads—were mirrored, reflecting endless rooms in all directions. The ceiling reflected images, too. So did the floor, though it yielded like soft carpet as she walked forward.

The tall man she knew from tri-D images as her father, Modabah— barely gray at his temples and oddly stooped—stood at the crux of a row and a column of reflections. Terza inclined her head and dissipated her habitual epsilon-energy shields, proper signs of submission. *I am honored to meet you, sir.*

He returned the gesture, dropping his own shields. She expected him to speak aloud. Instead, a blast of epsilon power gusted through her. Something in the smell of that wind was familiar and self-like. Something else came across as unbalanced, insane, inhuman. As she cowered against the

assault, discontinuous images flashed through her mind—scenes from unfamiliar military bases—satellite images of a world she knew as Tallis, the Federates' regional capital—

Voices surrounded her, too. Her father's: "No feints, this time. Cripple
them before they can use RIA anywhere except Thyrica or Hesed." Her
brother, answering: "I've said it all along. Kill him. Kill the whole family."
Her father again: "After we find out how they escaped." His voice drew
closer. "Lure him to us, little Terza. Bring him in."

Threads of her mind tore loose. The presences scrutinized and rewove
her thoughts and memories. Their otherness thrust deep into her mind. She
screamed, and screamed . . .

Terza looked up, disoriented, not sure whether she'd fallen on the mirrored floor or still stood upright. Her father and brother hovered over her.
She felt their probes thrust through her again, examining their work. . . .

Then another probe, like a garrote, choked her memory. It squeezed off
the moments she'd just experienced. She struggled, but she didn't dare
think about using her inner defenses. The memory danced away, faded, and
was lost.

Her father helped her onto her feet, gently holding her shoulders until
she felt steady. "You must have fainted," he murmured. "Have you eaten
breakfast? This room has an odd effect on many people the first time."

Sorry, sir. She nodded respectfully. Her father's epsilon shields seemed
to sparkle in the mirrored cabin.

You have accepted all my requests, he subvocalized, spending epsilon
energy in a formal greeting.

As . . . willingly as can be, she answered in the same way. She felt oddly
weak, dizzy, as if something more than the strange mirrored room had
struck her. Something had just happened. Something strange—something
she ought to remember . . .

The tall, handsome man raised a dark eyebrow.

I serve our people, she said, *as you do*.

"Show me your thoughts," ordered her father.

For some unremembered reason, Terza felt that his probe ought to feel
like a wind. Instead, it pierced like a knife, stabbing through her alpha
matrix, cutting multiple breaches.

She struggled to keep looking his way, focusing on his real face instead
of his many reflections. She slowed her breathing and straightened her back.

She scarcely remembered returning to her cabin and falling onto her
bunk. Hours later, she awoke sick and dizzy again.

She lay on the broad bunk and stared, shrouding her despair and humiliation under a layer of hatred, but hatred only amplified the gnawing pain in her gut. She must have missed a meal. She couldn't do that anymore.

She swung her legs over the side of her bunk and waited for lightheadedness to pass. Like it or not, she carried her enemy's genetic offspring between her hipbones.

Her enemy . . . her prey. She almost pitied him. Like Caldwell, her destiny had been determined before she was born. Her life had been choreographed by others, and now even her body wasn't her own—or her mind! What had her father just done to her, there in his stateroom? She knew enough about memory blocks to know one had been placed. She dug as deeply as she could manage, wishing she could escape this predicament.

A new thought brought her head up. What if the disquieting new theory was true? RIA technology was disturbing enough, but another rumor had surfaced just before they left Three Zed. It was suggested that Caldwell had developed some terrifying new epsilon skill, something that killed Testing Director Dru Polar. Now it wasn't just justice that required them to take him down. There was also fear—

But that rumor couldn't be true, to her way of thinking. Caldwell had already been epsilon-crippled by the time Director Polar died . . . and besides, it was dangerous to harbor seditious thoughts and fears. Her father might send quest-pulses up and down the corridors, checking the thought life of others on board.

But would Caldwell help her escape? The idea would not go away. What if somehow she could shield her fetus from her supervisor's inevitable experimentation, even deliver it offworld? Give it—give her—a life in some other place, where she might grow up happy and unafraid . . .

Her? That disgusting fifty-day tissue *blob* had become female in her mind?

Stop! she commanded herself, panicking. *Don't even think such things!*

The Shiraks' landing shuttle set down in a rural area not far from Netaia's capital, three hours after local midnight. Within two more hours, Micahel Shirak stalked into Ard Talumah's topside apartment and took a good look around.

Netaians did not live underground. Outside Talumah's windows, stars glimmered, distorted by a blanket of air. It wasn't as thick or as moist as Thyrica's, but it still looked eerie to Micahel's senses. Inside, poorly cured duracrete was daubed with orange paint. The apartment smelled musty and was furnished with cheap sling chairs.

At least it was half a klick away from the elegant midtown flat where a dozen of his father's lackeys were unpacking. As soon as they arrived, one of Modabah's crewmen called Talumah to get a preliminary report, since he'd been living on-site. Couched in his answer was the offer of a spare room, and after eleven days in close quarters with his father, who was constantly dithering about his half-made plans—and too close to that pitiful, pregnant half sister—Micahel jumped at the offer, even though he barely knew Ard Talumah.

Micahel's late trainer had called Micahel a renegade, with unpredictable tactics that made him almost a liability. Maybe he shouldn't cultivate Ard Talumah, but he didn't care shef'th about the long-standing ill will between his and Talumah's families. Talumah's deep mind-work specialty put him outside the Shiraks' chain of command. That made them more or less equals.

As for this survey mission, those ludicrous options, and the shifts in policy from his grandfather's regime to his father's, Micahel only cared that he would see Brennen Caldwell stripped of any RIA intelligence he still remembered, or had relearned, and then killed in a creative manner. He prided himself on artistry.

He glared at an electronic ceiling grid. "What's that?"

Ard Talumah waved a hand, dismissing his concern. "It's taken care of." He pointed at a subtronic device that sat on a scarred table. "Local enforcement looks in now and then. This shows what they want to see." To Micahel's surprise, he used the Federate trade speech, Old Colonial.

"They spy on their citizens?" Talumah was probably right to use Colonial, in case someone might be listening. The rich, ancient tongue of Ehret could give them away.

Talumah nodded. "Here in Citangelo, they do. They can only check one in ten thousand, but the risk is enough to keep some people in line. This way is the kitchen."

Micahel followed Talumah into the last room, with a servo area along one wall and a table on the other.

"I've taken in lodgers before." Talumah backed away from his servo, holding a slender blue bottle. He had the long face of many Ehretans, with a pouting lower lip and long, nondescript brown hair. He sat down on a high stool, opened the bottle, and sipped. "Help yourself, if you want. The local wines aren't bad. I recommend the joy-blossom."

Micahel shook his head. According to Modabah, Ard Talumah had lured the local princess Phoena to Three Zed. Traveling as a trader in rare commodities, he had also fired the blast that ripped open a certain missing shuttle as it emerged from slip-state. Queen Iarla Second and her infant sister, Kessaree, were as dead as deep space. For now, Modabah forbade releasing that information. Keeping information from his enemies gave him more options.

Modabah's dithering kept him paralyzed, to Micahel's way of thinking. It was time to take the next bold step. The Carabohd family was his rightful prey, and this pair humiliated him at Thyrica. His most vivid memory of the late director Dru Polar was a scornful subvocalization: *Undone by a pregnant woman. Shame, Micahel.*

They had disgraced him again at Three Zed, escaping before he could return from Cahal to the Golden City. There would be no third escape.

"So." Micahel took a sling chair. "You've lived here a year—"

"Two years," interrupted Talumah.

"What do you think of Netaia?"

Talumah pulled on his bottle. "Open air. Resources to waste. We've survived for a century taking goods from the Federacy. Why not take a planet?"

"Well put." He liked Talumah's practicality. Adiyn and his aging cronies could babble about serving humankind by giving them immortality, but their starbred ancestors created the superior genes. Their own kind would rule the new civilization.

Talumah gestured toward the cold cabinet, and Micahel shook his head again. The unbound starbred did not trust their most gifted young people. Only a few potential leaders were ever conceived, and they learned not to turn their backs. Until he felt sure he could either trust Talumah or dominate him, he would avoid recreational depressants. He dug into his duffel and pulled out a scan cartridge. "I assume you saw this?"

Talumah loaded the cube into a tabletop viewer, read a few lines, and laughed. "Oh, dear," he exclaimed. "Tallis promises military retaliation . . . unprovoked attack on the Federate world of Thyrica . . . Sunton destroyed . . . new technology . . . Micahel, you're famous."

Another scoffer. "Evidently you didn't read the part under 'new technology' carefully enough."

Talumah waved a hand. "Believe me," he growled, "I've read every release on RIA technology. I could quote them all."

"We need to get it. And stop Tallis from using it."

Talumah shrugged. "I think we can take Netaia peacefully, from inside, without leaving a single crater. We'll have to discipline Tallis, though." He sent Micahel a subliminal nudge, replete with respectful undertones.

Micahel smiled slightly. Talumah respected his methods? Maybe that was why he offered the room.

"After that," Talumah continued, "we can give each Whorl world a choice when its time comes. I don't think you'll have to waste too many suicide ships."

"It's a good time to be coming into our own." The Whorl only had two real powers, and Micahel believed he and Talumah would live to see that reduced by one.

"Well," said Talumah, "now that Caldwell scores thirty-two instead of ninety-seven—"

"I won't believe that without better evidence."

Talumah shot him a tolerant half smile. "Berit, on their campus, cracked the data base, and I got a shallow probe into him yesterday as they left the governor's camp. I can tell you Brennen Caldwell is no longer that kind of threat."

"Really." Micahel grimaced, glad for the information but resenting Talumah's success. If Dru Polar could've kept his prisoner semiconscious in the interrogation lab, too drowsy to focus on complex tasks like amnesia blocking, they would've had RIA from him—and now he would be dead.

"And the lady," said Talumah, laying down his viewer, "is a seventy-one, according to Berit. Nothing remarkable. So Polar must have been blasted by something else, something new. Did your people turn up any more clues as to how they escaped him?"

"No." Micahel frowned. "But I never liked the theory of Polar destroying himself. Polar was too smart."

"I agree," said Talumah.

Micahel rubbed his chin. The Sentinels refused to breed for talent and even married outsiders. Over recent decades, his own people had grown measurably stronger while the Sentinels declined. Polar had reported that their strongest Master was easily dominated. Debilitated by his own amnesia blocks and drugged to the gills with the epsilon-blocking drug DME-6, he shouldn't have been able to escape.

Talumah widened his eyes and let his face slacken in an idiotic expression. "I know!" he exclaimed. "Their all-mighty god has finally gotten mad enough to slap us down!"

Micahel ignored the mockery. "I'm less interested in Ehret's god than Netaia's regent. You have contacts on his staff, don't you?"

"Yes. I could call—"

"Not yet." Micahel paced to the window and stared out at the unsteady stars. "First, I want to test Caldwell's other defenses, his reinforcements. To see what I can scare up, with a feint."

CHAPTER 5

CONSPIRATORS

allemande
a stylized dance in moderate duple time

That same morning Firebird steered a small, unmarked skimmer up a ramp into a residential block's parking stack. Tel's town apartment was half of an impressive granite-block complex, and they'd agreed to meet him early. Followed by Brennen at one hand and Shel at the other, she sprinted up the steps and touched the door. Uri came last. Danton's uniformed team followed in another vehicle.

The first meeting on today's agenda had nothing to do with the Shuhr. Firebird had already delivered a vital message to the noble class. She hoped to send one more to the rest of Netaia, to people she'd known in downside Citangelo, huddled in back rooms together—her fellow musicians and the people who passed on their songs.

A tri-D image appeared on the door's central panel. "Come in," said a woman wearing a stiff blue apron. The door swung open.

Firebird spotted movement behind Tel's servitor. Shel swept around her, one hand grasping the butt of her blazer, and stared up the paneled hall.

Tel strode into view, dressed in casual slacks and a natrusilk sweater. "Come in, come in." He led through a wood-and-stone door arch. This long room had a massive stone firebay at its center, surrounded by deep chairs and loungers. Firebird's feet sank into longweave carpet.

A woman stood up quickly. "Lady Firebird," Tel said, "this is Clareen Chesterson, a versatile bassist and arranger who sings like a brook sprite."

Firebird clasped the woman's hand. Gold-blond hair waved around Clareen's shoulders and fell to curls near her waist. She wore a floral tattoo under one eye. Her grip was strong, with rough fingertips.

"Clareen," Firebird said, "I'm honored to meet you."

"And you," said Clareen. "And General Caldwell." She turned to Brennen, offering her hand again. "I was raised on Tallis," she said. "I'm a consecrant and deeply honored to meet you, sir."

Brennen bowed slightly over their clasped hands. Firebird back-stepped.

She'd asked Tel to find a competent performer and arranger, but she hadn't specified "Netaian." She'd assumed . . .

"I've lived on Netaia almost a year," Clareen told Brennen. "I've been trying to get a Chapter room established or a house built. I hope you might help me negotiate the legal tangle."

"I wish we could," said Brennen. "I can at least contact Shamarr Dickin with your request."

"That would be a help. These people are desperate for mercy."

"I know," Brennen said, and Firebird felt the gentle warmth of his pity on the pair bond.

Clareen released his hand. When she became a consecrant, Clareen would have been told about the prophecies regarding Brennen's family. Besides destroying a "nest of evil" that sounded strikingly similar to Three Zed, some Carabohd descendant would wield the creative power of the One who sang all worlds into existence. In that person, the Mighty Singer would complete a reconciliation that none of His other servants could attempt.

Firebird still didn't understand all those prophecies. She suspected they weren't meant to be fully comprehended until after the fact. Still, she liked Clareen's sense of priority.

Brennen sat down on one arm of a long lounger and motioned the musician to a nearby chair. Firebird took a seat next to Brennen. "Clareen," Brennen said, "you must understand that we need to check your intentions."

Here we go again, Firebird thought glumly. "This isn't deep mind-access," she explained. "It isn't interrogation. Sentinel Harris—Uri—can simply make sure you don't mean to betray us. He can make sure you won't, too," she added, trying to sound lighthearted. Voice-command, the violation of another person's will, was no laughing matter. "But as for prying into your secrets, that's just not done. It's only . . . uncomfortable," she admitted. "The first time someone did it to me, it turned my stomach."

Clareen frowned and sat down. "Since I'm one of your fellow believers, you might simply take my word. I am on your side."

"Certain parties on Netaia," Firebird said carefully, "would consider this kind of music seditious. If you're suspected of involvement with us and questioned, voice-command will protect you. You won't be able to incriminate yourself." She flicked back her hair. "Believe me, I understand how most people feel about mind-access." She barely resisted shooting Brennen a glance.

His amusement came through, though, followed by a rueful sense of apology.

Long forgiven, she thought at him. *Don't worry about me. Clareen's our concern at the moment.*

Clareen folded her long, slim hands in her lap and exhaled heavily. "I should have known. Your lives are at stake, aren't they?"

"I'm afraid so," Brennen said softly. "I do apologize. My people have been made stewards of abilities that many of us dislike. We try to use them responsibly."

"Then you have my permission, General."

"I can't," Brennen insisted, but Firebird felt a ghost of his former self-confidence. He'd lost abilities, but nothing could change his standing as the Mighty Singer's eldest heir. "Will you permit my bodyguard, Lieutenant Colonel Harris?"

Clareen's lips tightened, but she said, "Of course."

Uri moved a second chair close to hers. Firebird hardly knew where to look as Uri gave Clareen basic instructions—to get comfortable, try to relax, look into his eyes. While the silent mind-access lasted, an ancient clock ticked over the mantel between a pair of beautifully executed portraits. She suspected Tel had painted them, though she didn't recognize the subjects. On the pair bond, she felt Brenn focus tightly. Again, he had to rely on someone else's abilities. Firebird faintly sensed his frustration.

Uri broke the silence. "Thank you, Clareen. I don't need to go any deeper." His voice sounded slightly fatigued. "Welcome to the conspiracy to give Netaia back to its people."

It was exactly the right touch. Clareen smiled weakly, wrinkling the floral tattoo. "A lofty goal. Very Federate." She turned back to Brennen. "All right, General, Lady Firebird. How may I help?"

Firebird reached into a pocket of her loose, blue Thyrian skyff and pulled out an audio rod wrapped in bio-safe cloth, which she passed to Brennen. Without touching the rod, he pushed it onto the arm of Clareen's chair, then pocketed the cloth.

"I've put together several songs," Firebird said. "Some are better than others, but I think the melodies are catchy—"

"Wait." Tel remained standing, close to his massive firebay. "You put them together? You wrote them?"

"Yes, but I don't want that known. They're about Netaia, Clareen." She pulled one leg up on the lounger, trying to recapture the casual, cordial air they'd lost by insisting on an access check. She explained to Clareen that she'd written them carefully, including lines about seeking freedom in the right way and giving it to others. Most freedom ballads were spark in tinder. She wanted to prevent a war, not start one.

"Prince Tel told me about your presentation to the Electorate," Clareen said somberly. "I came here hoping to research popular ballads like you're describing. I'm particularly interested in the Coper Rebellion period."

It was Firebird's turn to smile weakly. Two centuries ago, Tarrega Erwin—regent for the infant Queen Bobri—had killed eighty thousand people, putting down that coup attempt. Two young noble offspring had led it, and Netaia's wastling traditions began shortly afterward. "I know those songs," she admitted. They'd been some of her favorites, years ago. " 'Northpoint,' " she suggested. " 'The Bridge of Glin,' and 'Bloody Erwin.' "

"Yes!" Crossing her ankles casually, Clareen raised the audio rod. "What would you like me to do with these?"

"That," said Firebird, "is a recording of chords with a synthesized voice. The songs can't be traced this way, but no one would change her political views from listening to them. They have no soul. Still, I think—I hope—that the melodies have broadcast quality. I have to trust your judgment. If you don't think they're up to par, destroy the rod. But if you think they might influence people, can you record . . . can you release?"

"If they move me," Clareen said soberly.

"Perfect." Firebird touched her hand, relieved, suspecting Clareen would deliver a quality performance or none at all. They discussed instrumentation, Firebird suggesting a double conchord, a wide-necked instrument with four pairs of strings, two pairs tuned an octave apart. It put a soul-digging "chunk" in every note.

Clareen pulled back her hair with one hand. "Is there a chance you could make an appearance this week? You'll change more minds and win more friends with one live concert than a dozen recordings. People who have sat in the same room bond to you."

"They do." She knew it well. Her secret performances, years ago, showed her how much a wealthy but doomed wastling had in common with poor laborers. But security had to take precedence.

"And you don't want to encourage an uprising?" asked Clareen. "I think you should. Songs can only do so much. If there's no other way of getting Rogonin out of office, there has to be violence—"

"No!" Firebird's stomach churned at the thought. "No more Coper Rebellions, Clareen. You've seen the Codex simulation of what a Shuhr strike could do to Citangelo? A civil war would do worse. The Coper ballads make warfare sound noble and exciting. It's brutal. Good people die in horrible ways." *Eighty thousand of them . . .*

Clareen stared at her. "I respect your point of view," she said. "You have been in combat. You . . . don't want the regency ended, either?"

Firebird laughed. "I'd love to see Rogonin tossed out. But someone else should take the regent's rod. Someone who could cooperate with Governor Danton and gradually shift power away from the Electorate. Slow changes tend to be permanent."

"But if you became queen—"

"That won't happen." Firebird spread her hands for emphasis. "I'm being confirmed as an heir, but that's just for show. The Electorate controls the crown. They wouldn't give it to me, and I wouldn't take it. Anyway, Brennen and I expect a transfer back to Regional command on Tallis as soon as we finish here." He *had* been reinstated to Special Ops. "I hope to set up a cultural exchange program and work toward covenant there."

The woman toyed with the curling end of one long blond lock of hair. "Don't worry, Lady Firebird. General. I won't let you down. And I would never betray the Carabohd line and the Word to Come. General," she said, "maybe you're the one who'll end the Shuhr threat. I hope it happens soon. People are frightened."

Brennen opened his hands. "I wish it could've been ended before they killed my brother and his family and Firebird's sister. Don't look to me, Clareen, but remember us in your prayers."

"From this day on," Clareen declared.

As his servitors escorted Clareen to the door, Tel swept an arm up the other hall. "Would you join me for an early lunch? My staff prepared a meal. Nothing fancy."

"That would be wonderful." Uri and Shel had tested the palace-delivered breakfast, and Firebird's biological clock had been ringing "dinnertime" ever since she rolled off Phoena's bed, but she'd barely touched the palace meal.

Following Tel's gesture, she strode into a timber-beamed dining area. At its far end, double doors hung open into a kitchen. High curtained windows let her see Citangelo's streets. The inlaid wooden floor would have cost a high commoner two years' wages, and this was only one of the Tellai family's Citangelo holdings.

Uri and Shel walked slowly around the room, and then Shel took a parade-rest stance near the hall door while Uri moved behind Brennen. A servitor laid out steaming dishes. Though Tel insisted the meal would be modest, Firebird found familiar foods well prepared, their flavors a cauldron of memory: pied henny baked in a tender crust, crisp multicolored slivers of marinated vegetables, and the traditional steaming mug of sweet, spicy cruinn.

She attacked this target with enthusiasm.

"Firebird," Tel said gently, "if you would ever want lessons in, ah, diplomacy, I would be delighted to assist. Waiting for the right moment to speak last night might have won you more allies than shouting down Erwin and Rogonin."

Amused, she washed down a bit of pied henny with a sip of cruinn. "Tel, they remember seeing me kneel on that floor and agree to go out and die nobly. I had to prove that I wasn't their wastling anymore. I'll be more respectful in the future."

"They already know you're no wastling." His dark eyes gleamed—fondly, she thought. "But to get people to really listen, sometimes you have to speak in the right way, at the right time."

Pride, willfulness, impatience. There they were again—

"Thank you, Tel," she said, trying to sound gracious. "Maybe we will have time to get together again."

Brennen sipped his cruinn and made a face. He'd never liked the sweet, spicy Netaian beverage, which was fine with Firebird. She barely tolerated the ubiquitous Federate kass.

The servitor brought a soup course, then disappeared into the kitchen. Tel leaned close to Firebird and murmured, "Firebird, Brennen, it's my turn to bring you into sedition. Don't tell people you would not take the crown. There is a growing alliance to restore the monarchy, mostly among high-commoners. Something must be done to get rid of Rogonin. I feel strongly about this. Better you were on the throne . . . than him."

She'd been half afraid Tel felt this way. Something at the back of her mind adored the idea. She sat on it. Hard. "Tel, if I took the crown, I would try to change one thing immediately. No one would worship the Powers, even though people could still respect them as attributes. Do you want that?"

"Service to the Powers has never been a matter of faith," he said. "Only action."

"Be careful, Tel. You almost sound like a heretic."

He smiled broadly. "I am. I want an Angelo in the palace again. Danton's reforms make sense, but a low-common rabble cannot run our government. As queen, you would have the support of many of the noble class—"

"Tel, they despise me. And not all low-commoners are rabble—"

Tel's blue-aproned servitor hurried back in, and they fell silent. On the woman's tray, three mounds of granular white powder burned orange on individual dishes. "Flamed snow!" Firebird exclaimed. "Tel, it isn't Conura Day." On that holiday, Netaia's nobility celebrated the accession of the first

Angelo monarch, who freed Netaia from out-Whorl invaders.

Tel arched one eyebrow. "You've missed Conura Day for two years."

The serving woman slid a plate, still flaming, onto the tapestry table-cloth. "The trick to eating this," the woman told Brennen, "is to keep it alight. Blow out each bite just before you take it into your mouth."

"I see," he said dubiously, trying to spoon into it. He lifted the bite, and it extinguished.

A faint bell chimed behind Shel's back. She stepped aside as Tel's servitor hurried up the hall.

"Do this." Firebird slid a spoon into the center of her portion, let granules spill in, then carefully raised the bite, still flaming.

The blue-aproned woman reappeared beside Shel. "Your Highness? Crosstown link."

Tel pursed his lips. "Right in the middle of dessert. Wouldn't you know?"

"I'll make you another, sir," the servitor said as Tel brushed past her. She remained in the room, eyes averted from Tel's guests, so Firebird didn't speak. The sweet, rich dessert had a perfumy taste.

Less than a minute later, Tel returned, frowning. "Evidently," he said, "they really want to speak with you, Firebird."

"Who?" she asked, glancing at Shel.

Tel folded his hands. "He didn't give a name."

Frowning, Firebird followed him to his crosstown station. A feather-weight headset dangled from a wall panel that could display a caller's face, amplify a voice, or show informational displays.

Shel's footsteps came close behind.

Tel lifted the CT headpiece. Firebird hooked it over one ear as he hurried back to the dining area, and then she made sure his link wasn't set to transmit visuals. "Hello," she said toward the blank wall panel.

"Lady Firebird." It was, as Tel said, a male voice . . . and no face appeared. The caller hadn't set to transmit either.

"Speaking," she answered.

"Greetings from Three Zed. We've missed you."

Firebird's blood turned icy. She whirled to lean against the wall and stare into Shelevah Mattason's blue-gray eyes. As Shel pulled a subtronic tracing device out of her tunic pocket, an epsilon probe slid into the back of Firebird's awareness. The sensation made Firebird wish she'd eaten less—and made her sympathize with Clareen Chesterson. "Go on," Firebird said, not bothering to turn her head. The pickup was omnidirectional.

"So you dislike idle talk, too. Good. Are you familiar with a phenome-non called the *shebiyl*?"

Firebird thought back to something Brennen had once mentioned, a practice forbidden in the older holy book, *Dabar*. "Alternate paths of the future," she said crisply. *Keep talking*, she urged him as Shel held her device close to the CT unit. Danton's plainclothes agents had been assigned to cruise this neighborhood in a second car. Shel would alert them.

"Very good. We have seen on the shebiyl that your presence could lead to Netaia's destruction. We've seen this world as a cold cinder spinning in orbit. If you really care for your people, you should leave quickly."

She silently cried, *Liar!* but the mental image made her tremble, espe-cially after watching that Codex simulation and hearing Tel make plans on her behalf. Could she live with herself if she caused—

Could *she* spark the uprising?

"Nothing to say, Lady Firebird?"

"Who are you?" Was this Micahel? Whoever had emerged from the shadows, Brenn needed his location. They also needed to know how the Shuhr tracked them here.

"You wouldn't know my name, Lady Firebird."

Disappointed, she said, "Go back to your own world. This is mine."

The voice laughed. "Yours? I believe it belongs to your countryman, Muirnen Rogonin."

Firebird rolled her eyes. Shel adjusted her device.

"Do enjoy your visit home. And your bond mate, while you have him." The connection clicked off.

Chilled, Firebird dropped the headpiece onto its hook. *While you have him?* "What did you get?"

Shel cradled her tracer on one palm. "Frequency, range, heading, and a voice profile. He's close, maybe half a kilometer." She reached for the CT link. "I'll relay this to base and our auxiliaries. Maybe we can take this one."

Firebird marched back toward the dining area. Brennen stood in the hallway, Uri at his shoulder. Firebird wondered how much they'd heard. "Shuhr," she murmured, "and Shel says he's close. Half a klick. She has the base trying to trace the call." She slipped back into the dining room and sat back down. With one puff, she blew out her dessert. "Tel," she said, "we just had a call from one of the Shuhr."

Brennen followed her in. "Governor Danton will get you a guard in minutes," he told Tel. "Meanwhile—"

Tel's expression darkened, and he lowered his eyebrows. "Not necessary, Cald—"

Shel emerged last from the hallway. "I've got a trace on the call. The auxiliaries are on their way."

Tel glanced up. "I have a bodyguard of my own, uplevel. I gave him some time off while your shadows take care of me." He touched a control on the table's edge.

Brennen blew out his own dessert, a smoldering cinder. An image sprang into Firebird's mind—Netaia, blackened like that burned-out dish of flamed snow.

Liars! They couldn't be trusted, but the image wouldn't leave her mind.

A liveried man appeared in the hall doorway, imposingly square-shouldered, impressively quiet. Tel turned to him. "Paudan, the threat is outside. Watch the front door."

The big man half bowed and slipped out.

With a sweep of double doors, Tel's servitor pushed through again, three more dessert portions gleaming on her tray. "Let's try this again," Tel said cheerfully.

Shel moved to the window and stared out, resting one hand on her holster. Before the servitor finished setting down the desserts, Shel murmured, "There he is. That's no pedestrian."

CHAPTER 6

THE BEST ANSWER

galliard
a vigorous dance with repeated leaps

Firebird sprang up and followed Brennen to the window.

He'd already pulled an interlink off his belt. "Tel," he said, holding the link aside, "how many entries do you have?"

"Three." Tel pointed toward the kitchen. "He seems to be headed for the service entry. Side door's in the firebay room, and there's the front way, where you came in."

As Brennen relayed Tel's information to his other forces, Firebird pulled Tel's small blazer from her deepest pocket. Brennen drew an oddly shaped weapon, designed to be concealed in his palm. It contained ten tiny injector darts, each loaded with two drugs. One was a rapid sedative. The other, a chemical called DME-6, temporarily blocked all epsilon abilities. Brennen had refused to touch the darts but let Danton's nongifted aides load his pistol. Firebird, who'd struggled with a needle phobia all her life, literally could not carry the weapon. "Don't get separated from Shel." Brennen touched Firebird's elbow. "You two, firebay room. Tel, can you and your man handle the front door?"

"Yes."

"All we need to do is keep them busy until Danton's reinforcements arrive." Brennen turned to Uri. "We'll take the service entry." He loosened his crystace in its wrist sheath, then glanced toward the back door.

"What makes you sure there'll be more than one of them?" Tel asked.

True, she thought at Brennen. *He came alone that night at Trinn Hill.*

Brennen shook his head slightly.

All right, then. Brennen, at ES 83, was still better equipped than Tel and all his servitors to deal with Shuhr until reinforcements arrived. *And what about windows?* Firebird wondered.

Following her bodyguard, Firebird hurried back up Tel's hall, past the link station and into the room where they interviewed Clareen. Now she saw it with an eye for defense. Its windows faced downhill. Across from the windows loomed the massive stone hearth, and then one more heavy wooden door beyond the hearth, at the room's end.

"Watch the window," Shel said. After propping the inside door and examining the outside door's palm-lock, Shel took up a position against the firewall.

Firebird eased toward the outer wall between window and door and peered through the edge of the glass pane. Or was it glasteel? Would it hold until a Sentinel force arrived? There were more ways into this apartment than through doors. Her stomach tightened on Tel's "modest" food.

She saw movement outside. A bony, dark-haired man—she didn't think it was the assassin she'd glimpsed at Trinn Hill—mounted Tel's steps.

He hadn't gone to the service entry after all, but straight to the door that no Sentinel guarded.

"Shel," she whispered, drawing back. If she could see him, he could sense her by her individual tang of alpha-matrix energy. More than ever, she wished she could shield her mind against the gifted. She'd only learned to turn inward and touch her epsilon carrier, and unless she coupled it with Brennen's, she'd only managed to kill two assailants who attacked her psyche. She prayed she would never again get that close to a Shuhr.

The door chime rang.

The ancient mantel clock's pendulum swung in slow arcs. On one side of the firebay, a covered canvas lay on an easel, probably one of Tel's projects. Traffic hummed in the distance.

The caller knocked lightly at first, then harder. Just inside, beyond the propped parlor door, Tel squared his shoulders beside his broad-shouldered shadow. Firebird wiped moisture off her palms, cringing. Brenn hadn't wanted to involve other non-Sentinels in their trap.

An eerie wail started overhead. Shel's head jerked up, her blazer wavering between door and ceiling. As the wail grew in volume, Firebird jammed a finger in her left ear. Sonic weaponry? Or

Down the chimney came a rattling shriek. *More ways in than the doors!* Simultaneously, something slammed against Shel's side door. *A second assailant, attacking while we're distracted.* Shel crouched, shutting her eyes and flattening her palm against shuddering dark wood.

Out of the hearth burst a shrieking flock of black saucer shapes. Spinning and sputtering, they scattered. Firebird dropped to a crouch, steadied her little blazer two-handed, and tracked one saucer. She fired. The saucer exploded, scattering metal fragments over a narrow radius, showering Tel's longweave carpet and some of the furniture, and piercing the covered canvas with a *pop*. She tracked another saucer and fired. They had to be close-quarter drones, the kind that adhered to a victim and then exploded. If caught midair, they wouldn't throw much shrapnel—

Three of them whirled toward Shel. Two more whizzed at Firebird. Her blazer quivered in her hand. She got one, missed one . . . ducked . . . caught it as it spun back toward her, then picked off the others.

Tel shouted a challenge from the entry. Had she missed another saucer? A hasty glance back showed Shel still crouched at the side door, left hand raised in voice-command. Someone had to be outside that door, pitting his epsilon strength against hers. *Mighty Singer, where are those reinforcements?* So much for their assumption that the Shuhr would wait to attack publicly!

There *was* another saucer in the entry, diving at Tel. Tel's servitor fired, missing Tel by centimeters, too close to hit the swooping drone. Firebird tracked the drone and fired again. Metal exploded with a flash that seared afterimages on her retinas. Tel fell back, one arm flung up to cover his eyes. His other servitor huddled in a corner, holding her sweeper aloft like a weapon.

Outside, an engine roared up and stopped. Shel shouted through the parlor, "They're here!"

The clock's ticking seemed to grow loud again. Firebird listened hard. Running feet and shouting voices passed by . . . outdoors. She blinked, trying to clear smokelike puffs from her vision. A weird chemical smell filled the hallway. Shel pulled an instrument off her belt. "Nothing toxic," she assured Firebird. "Just explosives."

More light footsteps ran through the dining room. Brennen and Uri appeared in the hall. Firebird felt Brenn relax when he saw her unharmed.

Tel lowered his arm. Two short scrapes oozed blood on his forehead.

"Are you hurt?" Brennen asked.

"Scratched." Tel frowned as the door chime rang. "Do we let these men in?"

"Yes." Uri reached for the interior lock panel. The front door swung open. "Did you—?"

A uniformed Sentinel shook his head. "We were too late. Couldn't pick up a trail. How many—?"

"Two of them," Shel broke in.

Leaving Shel with Firebird and Tel, Brennen and his cousin walked four new arrivals around the apartment's perimeter. Tel's manservant biotaped his scrapes.

"I'd heard you were a good shot," Shel murmured, smiling. "Well done."

Firebird shrugged, wishing Brenn's reinforcements would have arrived three minutes earlier. He and Uri would be restraining an epsilon-blocked Shuhr for interrogation in Tel's parlor and sending Shel back to the palace for those sealed orders.

Tel inhaled deeply. "Ventry," he said, relieving the serving woman of her sweeper, "could we possibly try, one more time, to eat a quiet dessert?"

Firebird thought she heard the woman groan.

A carload of Sentinels escorted them back to the palace, then remained on watch, parked in the public square.

Firebird's afternoon commitment to the elected Assembly wasn't for two more hours, and she knew she'd better consider every trip outside these walls as a perilous opportunity. Brennen put Shel to work on the voiceprint, tracing calls through the crosstown network's memory banks.

Brennen was also making plans to fly a search grid, hoping to spot those Shuhr agents by their stray flickers of epsilon energy. Firebird doubted he would try such an overflight more than once, if at all. Flying surveillance would be risky and difficult.

She decided to make one pilgrimage inside these walls before her Assembly appointment. Shadowed by Shel, she padded up the private hall and around a corner. She palmed the locking panel on her old rooms. The door didn't budge.

Unsurprised, she stepped back to look around. Down the stair, a servitor hurried across the wide hall—and she recognized him. She'd heard Brennen assign this blond-bearded Sentinel to kitchen staff, back at Danton's office. He was one of their undercover agents. "Hello," Firebird called down. "Good afternoon."

The young man paused. "Good afternoon, Lady Firebird," he answered stiffly, mimicking palace-staff decorum.

Not bad, she observed. Following protocol was his best chance of going unnoticed. Higher-ups on the staff, having served together for years, couldn't be impersonated—but lower echelon servitors came and went regularly. If this Sentinel diffused his epsilon shields, he would sense her approval. "I'm sorry to bother you," she called, "but I would like to look in on my old suite."

He turned away. "I'll find someone to deactivate the lock."

Five minutes later, Firebird stepped into a sitting room she could've crossed in the dark without stubbing her toe. Shel followed, silently shutting the door.

The furniture remained, but otherwise the sitting room had been scoured of all evidence that Firebird ever lived here. Her parlor and bed-room were just as tidy and soulless.

Still, her mind saw a row of Academy trophies, a stack of tri-D souvenirs, and her brownbuck flight jacket flung over the ornate desk chair. This suite reappeared regularly in her dreams. She stroked a tiny pit in the stone wall, then traced a mineral vein with one fingertip, letting the sad sweetness of actually standing here roll over her.

She'd lived simply at Hesed and liked it. She wondered if five days in-house would leave her a spoiled aristocrat. It occurred to her that she'd been raised wealthy, never lacking anything she really craved. *Except faith, except security, except love,* she realized. Even her first clairsa was the work of a master instrument maker. The family had paid for her Academy training, knowing Netaia would never recoup that investment.

Maybe it would. Maybe she would serve her people better than her mother ever dreamed, steering Netaia toward Federate covenance and the Ehretans' faith.

She pushed open the last door. Her music room, a narrow chamber with only one window, had been utterly stripped. Not even the high stool and transcriber table remained.

Shutting her eyes, she leaned against the marble wall and wrapped her arms around an imaginary clairsa. She'd written her first songs on this spot, sitting here with her transcriber running. She'd collected other instruments, enjoying the challenge of learning to chord or pick out melodies.

Sighing, she opened her eyes and turned to leave—

And looked into her own image beside the door. For one instant, her brain registered it as a mirror. Then she recognized the portrait. Painted when she was sixteen, seated in a royal wastling's pose, the portrait showed her wearing a smaller diadem than the one she would accept in five days. The artist had somehow created an odd, haunted sadness in the eyes, con-trasting with the proud uptilt of her chin.

Who hung it here? Firebird wondered. Carradee must have done this, consciously leaving a ghost of her presence in the one room where she'd dared to hope she might survive a wastling's fate in the songs she left behind. Even Rogonin's staff must've felt it appropriate to leave the portrait here, or else they simply hadn't bothered to take it down.

"Nothing has changed," Firebird whispered. She still hoped to touch her people's hearts—not the detached, unflinching electors, but the people who truly were Netaia.

Would anyone listen? She was a convicted criminal. She wished she could ask for a fair retrial, besides her gubernatorial pardon. After covenance, maybe. Before the Assembly instead of the Electorate.

She stared at the picture, grateful for one more of Carradee's kindnesses. Mentally, she retraced her route through the portrait hall. She couldn't recall seeing Carradee's image. When Carrie abdicated, they must have removed her portrait from the entry, replacing it with Siwann's.

If anyone ought to have pride-of-place down there, it should be Carradee's daughter, Iarla Second. Surely the four-year-old's portrait had been painted before she vanished.

Firebird hung her head. Almost without question, the Shuhr had found Iarla and her sister. If they were alive, anywhere, surely they would have surfaced by now.

But if the Shuhr had destroyed them . . . then with Carradee abdicated and Phoena dead . . .

Firebird pushed away the thought. The electors would continue their mockery of a regency for decades, if necessary, to keep her from ever coming back.

She pushed away from the wall. Shel, standing against the door, raised an eyebrow.

"Nothing, Shel. I've seen enough. We have work to do." Firebird felt half-complete when Brennen wasn't close, bad enough without adding a burden of memories. She turned away from this place that once vibrated with music. Leading her bodyguard, she hurried back to the crown princess's suite.

When they left the grounds headed for the Assembly, two small, dark cars pulled up alongside their limousine, and she saw midnight blue uniforms inside. A phalanx of Citangelo Enforcers surrounded that unit and delivered her to a hall in the central city. For most of a glorious hour, she sat in a balcony listening to a re-creation of the vote that brought her here. To override the inevitable electoral veto, she'd needed ninety percent of the popularly elected representatives.

She took ninety-four. This time, the Assembly representatives also made short speeches, praising Firebird for entering the single "nay" when the Electorate voted to attack Veroh, and demanding pledges that the Federates would protect their cities from Shuhr suicide attackers. Firebird answered with assurances, then delivered her cultural-exchange proposal. That drew polite applause.

Afterward, an ice-mine director, a metals stamping robot operator, and a woman who operated heavy machinery by virtual remote—all of them elected to represent working constituencies—joined her in a small private room.

Firebird tried to explain Federate covenance and the process by which free elections would lead to an application for Netaia's membership in the Federacy. By careful questioning, she learned a little about postwar living conditions on the North Continent. Metal and technology items had become scarce with so much manufacturing destroyed. The rich weren't suffering, but low-common and servitor classes pieced together a harder existence.

The pale, dour ice miner asked about Federate wages and rights.

Firebird admitted, "I've seen the Federacy make mistakes. I can't say covenance would end everyone's troubles, but living conditions would improve."

The ice miner lowered her voice. "Under Rogonin?"

Firebird longed to say she'd love to boot Rogonin out of her mother's office and over one of the moons. *Diplomacy!* she reminded herself, but lyrics danced into her mind, set to an old bugle call. *He's back, Bloody Erwin is back. . . .* She hadn't recorded *that* composition for Clareen Chesterson.

The other woman kept her arms crossed. "Governor Danton," she said, "sends inspectors. He makes promises. But so far we haven't seen anything change. We're almost as fed up with him as we are with the Electorate."

"He has only peeled away the surface layer," said Firebird. "This system has lasted for two hundred years. There will be more changes."

The ice miner spoke softly again. "If there's rebellion, the Enforcers will be key players. They're electoral employees, but they're mostly low-common. What would it take—"

"War is never the best answer," Firebird insisted, shaken by this proof that already Netaians were bracing themselves to rebel. The Enforcers, whom Federates would call a hybrid between police force and standing army, maintained order in the cities. What would it take to get their loyalty? Rogonin's wages fed their families. Idealistic songs wouldn't soften them. *Could* she enlist them, if—

What was she thinking? She could not, would not lead an uprising!

The door opened slightly. Shaken by her own thoughts and how easily they turned to war, Firebird reached for the ice miner's hand. "I think we're being told that this meeting is over. Contact me through Danton's office if you have other questions about Federate covenance."

That evening, the Assembly's Pageantry Committee filled the wood-floored west dining hall, applauding and drinking the regent's wine . . . or was it hers? She suspected Rogonin would bill every possible expense to her modest new heiress's allowance. She managed to greet all eighty-five guests, mostly high-commoners. She followed their conversations, depressed by the class prejudices that colored their attitudes.

Interstellar diplomacy, she'd found, also revolved around money, pride, and influence. Class differences just weren't as obvious out there—or as permanent.

CHAPTER 7

ESMERIELD

gavotte
a dance in moderately quick quadruple time

"The Countess Esmerield Rogonin of Claighbro has passed the main gate," intoned Tel Tellai's footman, "with an escort of her House."

Tel paused at an indoor trellis, halfway across his estate's dining balcony, and stretched out a hand. "Cutter, Gammidge."

A gardener in black-and-indigo livery handed Tel a small laser cutter.

Tel whisked six buds from a jantia vine's tip. "You've let this runner try to support too many blooms."

His bodyguard, Paudan, remained at the town house, supervising cleanup and interviewing two dozen muscular commoners. Tel could afford to increase a security force for his properties. With Phoena gone, overseeing his homes and their landscaping gave him something to care about.

It no longer mattered whether the other electors approved of him. As he told Firebird this morning, Netaia needed an Angelo ruler. The figure-head role, on behalf of the mighty Power of Authority, had been passed down for thirteen generations. It was a psychological need of this culture. Really, though, he'd never cared whether the Powers, Electorate, or Assembly kept Netaia prosperous. His worship had gone to Authority and Excellence, in the person of Phoena Angelo. . . .

Since returning from Three Zed and Procyel, Tel had required his servitors to keep the Charities and Disciplines whenever possible, but he no longer felt like a representative of the Powers.

He handed off his shears. "Dismissed, Gammidge."

Straightening a gold-trimmed blue sash over his pale blue sateen tunic, he walked to the dining balcony's edge. He'd dressed for Esme Rogonin's protocol visit. They both had postponed this to the last possible evening before her presentation ball. By tradition, the head of each noble House must be invited to a debut ball during an informal dinner.

A man in Angelo scarlet plodded out of the gravity lift at one end of the dining balcony. He had Rogonin's size, but not his figure, and a black cap tucked into his belt over a crimson tunic. Rogonin's eighteen-year-old heiress followed. *Using a palace redjacket as Escort of the House!* He might be entitled, but this was another deliberate affront to the Angelos. Regardless, Tel had to stand and bow. "Countess Esmerield," he intoned.

"Prince Tel," said the young woman. She pushed past him to his table.

Tel's butler pointed out a place to the redjacket, who seated Esmerield and then stood behind her. Tel took his own chair, glanced out through stately gold-framed windows toward the gardens, then back to the countess.

A final growth spurt had stretched green-eyed Esme, giving her attractive proportions and making her almost as tall as he. As soon as the butler poured tiny glasses of gold-white Southport wine, Tel toasted her.

The green visiting gown made her eyes shine like emeralds—or poison, which was a better comparison, considering her father—and like the regent, she eyed everything as if she either despised it or wanted it. Without waiting for Tel's staff to lay out their first course, Esmerield flicked a rolled and beribboned paper up the table. "My father bids you come to my debut ball tomorrow night, as head of your House."

Efficiently done! She could leave now, if she wished. He didn't often think of himself as the head of House Tellai, but when Phoena had been absent for two years, he would be ordered by the Electorate to remarry and start producing Tellai heirs—wastlings, too—so the line would not die out.

For now, Tel missed Phoena too badly to feel any interest in remarriage. He would honor her memory by fighting for her sister's rights, though Phoena would not have found that appropriate. Counseled and healed by Sanctuary Master Dabarrah, he'd come to realize his late wife was selfish, ambitious, and cruel. . . .

But regal and proud, and breathtakingly beautiful. She would have made a better goddess than queen.

He would've begged her not to go to the Shuhr if she'd stopped to say good-bye. His last memory of Phoena framed her sitting on their octagonal bed, knees to her chest, fuming over Firebird's dishonorable pregnancy—wastlings were not allowed to marry or bear children—while he drifted, frustrated as usual, toward sleep.

Mustn't let my mind wander this way! "My thanks to your father," he answered Esme, "and the House of Tellai will most certainly be represented."

Having concluded that business, Tel reached for his fork. The first course, a rich and beautifully constructed soufflé, had arrived while his thoughts skipped back.

"As I hear it," Esme said, "our current discomfort began at the United

Session, when the Assembly voted for Firebird's return."

So she meant to stay a little longer? Tel glanced up at the redjacket before he answered. The big man stared back. Tel didn't feel threatened. One of his own bodyguards sat in a hidden observation room, controlling several remote security devices.

He had nothing to lose now. He would not be Rogonin's flunky anymore. "Originally, Countess, I only presented Carradee's request to restore Lady Firebird's Netaian citizenship. The Assembly took that issue a step further. Carradee might have made a capable monarch," he added, "in time, if things had gone differently." Tel would still serve an Angelo queen, gladly. But not Muirnen Rogonin, never again.

"Time." Esme tapped her plate's edge with her fork. "Netaia has little time, Prince Tel. In a year and a half, we could be absorbed by the Federacy. Meanwhile, their occupation taxes are ruining us."

He knew that Esme only echoed her father, having no opinions of her own yet. Tel wanted to remind her that the nobles' taxes were rebuilding defenses that the Federates shattered in response to an unprovoked attack on Federate space, and that the Federates were paying fifty percent of that expense. By the time Danton's engineers finished rebuilding, this world would be better defended than ever. He hoped they hurried.

"We must walk a careful path," he said, deliberately oblique. Rogonin had to be deeply displeased about the timing of Firebird's return. Her confirmation was overshadowing Esme's festive debut. Protocol demanded that she and Caldwell attend the ball.

"Why," Esme demanded, "don't Caldwell and his mind-crawlers just fly to Three Zed and eliminate those people? Why are they wasting time here?"

So that's what she wanted. He could answer part of her question. "Three Zed has defenses that even the Sentinels can't pass easily. Unless they do it right, it would be suicide."

"Obviously, the Shuhr don't hesitate to fly suicide missions. Losing most of the Sentinels wouldn't bother me at all."

He considered telling her about voice-command, and how a Shuhr pilot could be forced to act against his or her will. That, he decided, would only encourage her hatred and fear of Sentinels. He held his peace, finished the last bit of his soufflé, and sat back. Servitors removed his plate and brought sherbet glasses of tart eden fruit, round and pink, seeded and syruped, to cleanse their palates for the next course.

"Thank you, but I'm quite full." Esme raised one finger at her escort. The redjacket drew back her chair.

Fine. Leave. Tel dismissed her mentally but not without a twinge. He did sometimes miss the placid assumptions of his youth—the lifestyle he'd been raised to expect and the absolute certainty that a nobleman was a superior being. Rising, he bowed again. "Please convey my thanks to your father," he said, "for the pleasure of your company."

Esme's cheek twitched. She dropped a half curtsey and bounced down the balcony stairs without bothering to ride his lift.

Esme's father, His Grace the Regent, sat in his night office and watched two strangers stride past his uniformed door guards. Bypassing the enormous, internally lit crystalline globe of the home world, the wiry young black-haired man stared malevolently. His long-haired partner, slightly shorter, looked vaguely familiar.

Rogonin frowned down at them.

"Thank you for receiving us, Your Grace." The second man made a full, courtly bow. He spoke with a throaty accent so deep that his *R*s almost gargled. "I am Ard Talumah. I have worked on Netaia for some months as an independent trader, representing a non-Federate concern. My colleague, Micahel Shirak, arrived on Netaia early today." His glance darted toward the taller man. An instant later, Shirak bowed, too.

Muirnen Rogonin's stomach gurgled, and he covered it with one hand, pressing through folds of flesh. These people had demanded an audience on one hour's notice. He wouldn't mind if the Shuhr ejected Occupation Governor Danton and all his ilk from Citangelo, but not by destroying the base, as in the Codex simulation. He had no intention of dealing with a mind-crawling, gene-fixed, offworld trader. Not long ago, offworld trade had been strictly illegal. "Whatever you have to say, you will listen to me first. Any threat against Netaia, or any of my subjects, will not be tolerated. Am I understood?"

Talumah spread his hands. "I give you my word, Your Grace. We have designs on only one of your subjects—Mistress Firebird. Why in all the worlds is she being honored in Citangelo?"

"Not honored. Only confirmed." Rogonin balled a fist. In principle, he approved of the confirmation of wastlings if tragedy struck a noble family. That was why they were born. Each privileged family had to raise wastlings along with its heirs and instill a willingness—even eagerness—to die for Netaia's glory as soon as elder siblings secured the succession. That system, coupled with strict isolation, had kept Netaia stable for decades.

But the notion of restoring Firebird Angelo Caldwell to the royal succession soured his digestion. She'd proved herself poisoned by Federate ideals. Last night she'd shown how eager she was to poison others.

Talumah took one step forward. Rogonin watched him closely. One more step and the offworlder would feel a House Guard stun pistol.

"Despite our political differences," Talumah said, "we are also a people who do not bow to the Federacy, and we are deeply concerned with justice. Firebird was found guilty of treason, was she not?"

"Treason," Rogonin pronounced, "sedition, and heresy—but what do you know of the nine holy Powers?"

"Strength, Valor, and Excellence," recited Micahel Shirak. "Knowledge, Fidelity, and Resolve; Authority, Indomitability, and Pride. Laudable attributes, Your Grace. They should be served by those born to represent them. Such as—her."

Rogonin raised an eyebrow. Maybe he'd misjudged the young man. "That is correct. But I can deal with Lady Firebird without outside help." His greatest fear, after losing his family's position, was the danger of Federatization. Netaia's high culture, directed for centuries by a knowledgeable elite, could drown in a sea of low-popular influence. He would hate to see his people reduced to the homogenous culture of other worlds while others carried off Netaia's wealth. Obviously, Firebird was cooperating with those forces.

"Reconsider." Micahel Shirak's voice sounded brittle, even icy. "The Netaian systems are preparing for pageantry. Would you find it satisfying to substitute a state funeral?"

Rogonin's eyes narrowed. He wanted to ask if Princess Phoena really had died on their world, or if that was Federate fabrication. He'd admired Phoena. Still, she was one more Angelo, and she would have stood between him and his new personal hopes. "I don't need your help," he repeated. "My legal agents—"

"You must understand," Talumah interrupted, "that when it is necessary to take a life of public significance, the event should be arranged to bring the maximum benefit. Firebird Caldwell's death could guarantee permanent Netaian independence from the Federacy."

Rogonin frowned down at the long-faced man and his icy compatriot. Independence . . . permanent . . . As the words circled each other in his mind, he linked his fingers again. Could these people break Netaia's Federate chains and dispose of the dangerous wastling without implicating him? After all, those reports of the Shuhr threat to Citangelo came from Federate sources.

Maybe he'd misjudged that, too.

He waited to see if they would react to his shift in attitude, even before he spoke. Caldwell had shown they could read his emotions.

They gave no sign of having probed him. After several seconds, he accepted their apparently respectful silence (and mentally cursed Caldwell, who had forced mind-access on him twice). "You interest me," he admitted. "But you, too, have your own resources. You may threaten, even dispose of that Netaian subject, but do not implicate me, and do not come back to this palace again." He started to raise a hand, gesturing to his guards. He glanced at Talumah's eyes.

Something warm, like good brandy, threaded through his brain. It lulled and comforted away his desire to see them gone. *What harm in hearing if they have anything else to offer?*

He laid down his hand.

Shirak seated himself on the grand desk top, dangling a leg. "Your Grace, what is your present military strength? We assume the Federates have done pitifully little to help you rebuild."

What harm in letting them sit? Rogonin reached for his touchboard and called up data. As he read it off, Shirak shook his head.

"That," said Talumah, "is disgraceful. They have left you virtually helpless."

"But we will never bow to them."

"Neither will we, Your Grace." Talumah jerked his head to one side, and Shirak slid down off the desk. "Our people's goal is to save humanity. Civilization barely survived the first Six-alpha catastrophe. If that binary emits another radiation storm, we will all be better prepared."

Rogonin raised one eyebrow.

"But the Sentinels oppose us. The last thing they want is for humankind to become immortal. They want us all to settle for life after death, if such a thing exists."

Immortal? They had his attention now!

Shirak gave the crystalline globe a spin. "We started testing Caldwell's defenses this morning, at Prince Tellai's town home. Since we are sharing information, you may want to know he and Lady Firebird are defended by at least three plainclothes remote teams."

Rogonin laughed shortly. "I saw two this morning myself."

"Now you know of another," said Talumah. "And there are more. Here, inside the palace."

Rogonin jerked up his head. He eyed the House Guards at his doorposts. "They wouldn't dare."

"They wouldn't dare come here without bringing assistance, Your Grace. I would suggest rescreening all palace employees. We could help," Talumah said softly. "We know *them* when we see them."

With his daughter's ball impending—should he?

"No," he said. That would be collaboration. "Thank you for the information, but my security staff will investigate."

"As you wish, Your Grace." Shirak chuckled.

His laughter shattered Rogonin's temporary languor. He sat upright. "I can spare no more time." He flicked his fingers in dismissal.

Talumah bowed and turned away, but Shirak stood his ground. "Do you remember," he said, "that General Caldwell's brother and his family were murdered?"

Drawn oddly to the man, Rogonin answered, "Of course. That came over Federate newsnets. Though we distrust the sources, we did use Caldwell's bereavement as an occasion to open a case of old southern wine. Is it true?"

Shirak crossed his arms. "I killed them. I will kill again, this time for you. Set aside a case of old southern wine to drink with me. When *she* is dead."

Rogonin raised an eyebrow.

Shirak pivoted and strutted to the door.

Rogonin watched until the massive gold panels shut them out. Yes, he decided, Shirak looked like a murderer and a braggart. Deciding to have him tailed, Rogonin reached for his desk pad.

Oddly, the screen glowed with military information. He didn't remember calling that up.

He frowned, blanked it, and tapped out an order to Enforcement.

CHAPTER 8

QUEST

sarabande
a dignified dance in triple meter

Early the next morning Brennen's interlink gave off a soft tone. Firebird rolled aside as he retrieved it from the nightstand. "Caldwell," he said.

"Good morning, Caldwell," she heard. "Danton. Nothing new on yesterday's callers to Tellai's house, but one of your quiet help reported suspicious presences last night. There's a chance the Shuhr have tried to contact the senior authority."

Firebird blinked. The interlink channel was supposedly secure, but neither Brennen nor Danton would refer to Sentinel infiltrators in the palace.

"No changes to our staff? We'll have a quiet morning and an afternoon fitting. The Rogonin ball is tonight."

Firebird sat up, and Brennen's amusement followed her delight like an echo. He had no intrinsic interest in meeting that protocol requirement. She, on the other hand, might have been tempted to interpret protocol a little too strenuously for the chance to dance a triplette in his arms—

But as their second most public appearance, it was one more chance to draw out a Shuhr agent without endangering too many civilians. There would be thousands in the Hall of Charity. Already, their palace-staff infiltrators would be jockeying to serve on tonight's shift. Her own assignment was simply to be as visible as possible, and the dance floor would serve nicely.

"We'll be ready," Danton said. Brennen thumbed off the interlink.

The "quiet" morning would give Firebird one more chance to prepare herself, mentally and spiritually, for the days ahead.

First, she spent half an hour at her studies in *Mattah*, the Sentinels' holy book. She'd been battling with the issue of atonement. Self-sacrifice was something she'd always understood—but for her full and final justification, according to *Mattah*, she must trust in an atonement the Eternal Speaker would make . . . someday, in the Word to Come's time. That was less clear.

After reading several chapters of the historical Second Confessions and one in the meatier Wisdom of Mattah, she set the book aside. Again, she'd found more questions than answers—but Brennen had gone out. Intellectually, she could understand the idea of substitutionary death, of escaping the consequences of her own actions thanks to someone else's sacrifice. She knew that the Singer had laid a covering over her so she could stand in His presence. Still, in her heart of hearts, she felt that if a sacrifice needed to be made for her full and final cleansing, she must make it. Herself.

This was progress. Back when she honored the Powers, she'd had to be the sacrificial victim.

She took a fast turn in the vaporbath, then settled in Phoena's parlor with Shel. After months of effort, she'd learned to touch her epsilon carrier. It was the first skill all Sentinels learned.

This was pathetic progress, but because of her oddly polarized epsilon carrier, it allowed the unprecedented explosion of power they now called epsilon fusion. RIA alone wouldn't guarantee their safe passage through the renegades' fielding net. They would need her—and fusion. College researchers had all but proved that she'd killed the Shuhr who attacked her by fusing carriers and amplifying their deadly intent.

The researchers had also measured considerable scarring to the ayin complex in her midbrain. The more she practiced fusing carriers, the sooner she would destroy it altogether. That made her more determined than ever to learn how to shield her mind from attack.

Shel sat in a straight-backed waiting chair. "Try this," she suggested. "Think of the air around you as neutral, uncharged. With your carrier, you want to charge it positively, so it will repel other positive energy. Can you think at the electrical level?"

"Perfectly," Firebird answered, "if it's pertaining to a shipboard console."

"Go ahead, then."

She quieted her thoughts and forced herself to relax. Turning inward, she first faced the flaming darkness, the taint in her soul that surrounded her epsilon carrier. She no longer felt compelled to find an intellectual explanation for its existence. She was learning to focus on the Mighty Singer instead, and to be grateful He could use her flawed gifts. Cautiously, she touched the carrier itself.

Colors suddenly brightened, while common sounds developed a deep, eerie music. Holding that mental posture, she tried Shel's suggestion, envisioning air molecules charged with energy. She tried imagining them turning different colors. She tried shifting them into sound waves.

Nothing happened.

She let go of her epsilon turn and drooped against the back of Phoena's deep chair.

Shel shook her head. "I can't tell if you have the idea," she complained, "not when I have to stay shielded this way."

Firebird understood the danger. If she and Shel accidentally created fusion, Shel might be killed. Cassia Talumah and Harcourt Terrell had died this way, according to the Sentinel College's current theory.

"I understand," Firebird said. "I'll try again."

Several attempts later, while holding the depth of her turn, she remembered the visualization she'd first used to find her carrier: the stone wall surrounding the Angelo estate at Hunter Height, where Phoena nearly executed her. In her vision, that barrier walled a perpetual inner darkness away from conscious perception—and with it, the carrier.

What would happen if she tried to take part of the wall down?

She imagined herself drifting alongside, considering its lichen-crusted strength.

What if she imagined a crack?

Wanting to find it, longing to find it, she wasn't surprised when a crack appeared some ways ahead, between stone blocks. She forged a firm link between her point of consciousness and the convoluted cord of energy behind her. Grounding herself in that power, she thrust at the crack. Thrust, again—

And fell back in her chair. "I almost had it." She shoved hair back from her forehead. "Did you feel anything that time?"

"No," Shel admitted, "but if you felt that was progress, try again."

This time, when Firebird shut her eyes and rested back in her chair, Shel Mattason dispersed her shields. Like most Sentinels, she'd picked up her basic skills without weird visualizations—but Firebird was notoriously unique. Shel had been warned to avoid creating any situation that might produce the potentially deadly fusion, even though the masters' research reassured everyone that Firebird could now control whether or not fusion occurred.

The faintest tendril of epsilon presence touched her. Instantly, Shel shielded herself.

Firebird had gone stiff again, her hot brown eyes open wide. "What was that?" she exclaimed. "Something happened."

"I don't know." Startled, Shel sat back down. She didn't remember standing up. "It was no shield, but I think it was almost a quest-pulse. Could you do it again?" This time, she shielded heavily.

Firebird shut her eyes. This time, the only outward sign of her effort that Shel could see was a bead of perspiration that trickled down her forehead, along her left eye, and then down the edge of her cheek.

She was trying. Desperately. She couldn't make it happen again. Eventually, she gave up.

"I think," Shel murmured, "you're too tired to go on. Do this, though—remember what you did the first time. Let me watch you remember. Just don't pull me into your turn."

"I won't." Firebird felt the weird otherness of Shel's epsilon probe slide into place. As soon as she knew the Sentinel could observe, she touched her epsilon carrier. She recalled the effort of thrusting at the chink in that everlasting wall, battling until a tiny granite chip split off its surface. She was through! On the outside, she felt the slightest echo of another epsilon presence.

She opened her eyes.

"That," Shel pronounced, "was a quest-pulse. Not very strong, but it was real. Well done!"

Firebird cocked one eyebrow and barely smiled.

"Take a minute to let your carrier rebuild, then try again while your memory is fresh. Do it over and over, until you can do it under consistent control."

"What good is it? That slowly—that weakly—I need to be able to shield, Shel! To put out fifty times that much energy." And to hold on to consciousness after fusion. She hated the thought of sparking fusion for Brennen, deep in enemy territory, and then falling unconscious.

Shel frowned. "Sometimes, the Holy One gives us only one skill for a number of months. It's like His call on our lives. We don't necessarily understand, but He'll give us whatever we genuinely need, and always in time."

Firebird gripped her armrest. Coming from the bereaved Shel, that encouragement carried considerable weight. Surely these infinitesimal achievements wouldn't feed pride, not the pride she would feel if she saved Netaia, even if achieving that glory cost her life—

Whoops! Again, she caught herself in Powers-based thinking. She could not shake the idea that if any sacrifice had to be made for her sake, then she must be directly involved or it would count for nothing. It was a virulent Netaian sort of pride, the exact opposite of the future atonement taught by her Path instructor, in Second Confessions, and in the Wisdom of Mattah.

Intellectually, she had almost grasped it. Obviously, she still believed otherwise.

"So practice," Shel said. "You'll build speed that way."

Firebird pushed away her theological reflections. "What good is a quest-pulse, Shel?"

"Controlled, it can be used to find a person whose mental savor you know, or to send energy in small packets, or communicate your presence. Brennen will be delighted," she added. "And sorry he wasn't here to see."

Brennen was engaged in his own struggle. In Uri Harris's elegant parlor in the adjoining consort's suite, they both sat in straight-back chairs. Brennen was relearning to remotely lift simple objects—starting with a shoe, then his crystace. They'd progressed to nudging pieces of furniture away from the walls and then back. Even the precursor skill, focusing epsilon energy in his hand's long nerve bundles, no longer came consistently. Once, all this had been so easy that he could control his own rate of fall.

Now it felt like trying to fly through syrup. His spiritual father had recently said, "Rarely do we experience a true spiritual victory without afterward being tempted to believe we have lost something precious. Other temptations will come, too, because the Adversary tries to avenge his losses. You won a great victory at Three Zed. Do not forget that."

Brennen exhaled heavily. In one way, it was a relief to lay down some of his ancestors' burdens, the psi powers that resulted from unconscionable gene tampering. His losses, and his new fears, must strengthen his faith. He must focus his reliance on the Holy One.

That wasn't easy for a gifted man. He had to sympathize with Mari's struggle against the pride that kept her from dying to willfulness and being fully used by the Eternal Speaker. As the Caldwell-Carabohd family's eldest surviving heir, he had to live by that highest standard of humility. He'd been tempted by a conqueror's pride, back before he lost so much epsilon ability.

Guide me, Holy One. Help me walk this new Path.

Uri rested his chin on one hand. "Before we try springing this trap at the ball," he said, "you and Lady Firebird ought to try fusion again. Shamarr Dickin was firm about being prepared. All this, everything else we've tried, strikes me as avoiding the real issue."

"And no one has heard the call," Brennen pointed out. It had been decades since Sentinel forces found the enemy's stronghold, and still they waited. Previous shamarrs, speaking on behalf of the Holy One, had warned them to hold back until the chosen moment.

Uri nodded. As commissioned officers, they should obey Federate orders, even to a premature strike, if there was no overwhelming moral reason to disobey . . . but Special Ops had already warned Regional command that sending a Sentinel force too early might result in losing it.

Brennen hoped his orders might include a discretionary provision. That could be granted under extraordinary circumstances. Assuming they gave him command, he might have several hundred lives resting on that judgment call. Uri, for example—the son of parents with ES scores too low to qualify for training—really hadn't wanted to become a Sentinel at all, but acquiesced to his parents' wishes. Brennen might have to decide whether to risk Uri's life.

"Hiding our gifts," Uri said, "is one way of misusing them."

Brennen rested his head against the wall behind his chair. "So we have the Codes." He had only to look at the Shuhr to see what his people would be without those restrictions on using their skills. "I wonder," Brennen said, "if they are already cloning offspring from Phoena's cells. If she inherited a reversed carrier, too, that might give them fusion-capable warriors in just a few years."

And my own cells? Would there be Caldwell offspring among Three Zed's next generation?

He must not think about that.

"And passive fusion-partners even sooner, if they manipulate development." Uri stroked the side of his chin with two fingers.

If the Shuhr attacked Federate worlds using RIA and fusion, they could take anything. Everything.

They *must* catch one Shuhr. Maybe then they would be called. This, not Mari's inexplicable passion to try dancing with him, was the real excuse for attending Esmerield Rogonin's ball.

"If I could wish," Brennen said, stretching the kinks from his back, "I would wish there were some way to show mercy. To win them to truth. To show we could destroy them but would rather hold back." He'd toyed with one perilous idea. If Three Zed's fielding could be taken down, he might go in under a flag of truce and try to negotiate, even knowing he might be killed by his own forces if the Shuhr refused to cooperate and the Federates had to attack. He hadn't forgotten disobeying Federate orders to go to Hunter Height. That incident had put a count of insubordination in his master file.

But if the true call came, he would not disobey, even to save his life. He couldn't save it, anyway . . . only lengthen it. *Let a door open to mercy,* he prayed, *or else show us your will. Plainly.*

The bedroom door opened, and Brennen peered through. "Are you ready?"

Firebird frowned. "Not really." Brennen and Uri had interrupted her session with Shel, reiterating the urgency of practicing fusion before tonight's potential encounter. She'd demanded ten minutes to rest and pray.

"Uri and Shel will wait in the next room, shielding." Brennen sat down on the bedside, casual in a skinshirt and trousers.

Firebird dropped her copy of *Mattah* on the bed. She was learning to tell when Brennen would not back off, and he was right about this. "Let's get it over with," she grumbled. "Do what you can with the excess energy. See if you can restore any of those lost memories."

"I'm going to try," he said, "simply to keep you conscious."

"I need to do that myself. After all—"

"The longer we procrastinate, the more frightened—"

"Yes." She shut her eyes. She envisioned the granite wall and pushed her point of consciousness inside, irked as always by her slow motion turn. At the heart of the flaming blackness, she spotted the glimmering epsilon nebula. She felt a smoky-sweet presence follow. That had to be Brennen, already holding a turn.

Help, Mighty Singer!

She touched the nebula and then latched onto Brennen's epsilon presence. For one moment, she felt herself as an explosion, expanding at horrific speed, blasting through everything around her. She was a compression wave, or the gas shell of a star going nova. She was Sabba Six-alpha, flinging energy storms into space, atomizing every molecule for light-years. She . . . was . . .

She was a small woman, struggling to open her eyes. Finally, she focused on a blur that became Shel Mattason's face. Uri and Brennen stood close.

She drew a deep breath. "Brenn, are you all right?"

"He's fine," Shel said curtly. "How do you feel?"

"Dizzy. How long was I out?"

"Twenty-six minutes."

The best yet, but still pitiful. "Did you need to bring me back? Out of psychic shock?"

Shel nodded.

Firebird bit her lip. She hadn't yet revived without help. "I'm not going to be much help in a crisis."

"Yes, you are. You're the key we've been given for this time. Everything is falling into place," said Brennen.

Glittering gold tracery hung from the ceiling high overhead. The tour guide's ludicrous white gown had tripped him twice, and Micahel thought it might tangle the simpering fool's legs again momentarily.

Rogonin's Enforcement tail had been pitifully easy to lose.

"The nave, of course," whined the guide, "dates from the late second century of settlement. Notice the exquisite parabolic arches, and how they meet delicate ceiling tracery at precisely calculated angles to create the impression of an infinite golden distance."

Micahel stared upward, paying attention to detail that surely gratified the tour guide. Following those arches, Micahel imprinted every angle on his trained memory. Among those gaudy traceries, he should easily find a sniping loft.

The Hall of Charity was really three halls. He stood in the central nave. The North Hall, with its separate entrance, tight seating, and low ceiling, was normally used by the low-common class. Similarly, the South Hall accommodated servitors who cared to worship their oppressors, the noble electors, in their capacity as priestly demigods. The high-common class was entitled to enter the nave, in sight of the "holy" electors.

The mincing guide led his troop up the nave's long aisle. At the front, five steps led up onto a stage ringed by curved seating. "Here in the sanctum," he intoned, "the noble electors take their places. On the left, the Houses of Tellai, Drake, Gellison . . ." As he spoke, he touched a tri-D projector. A host of ghostly images appeared, holographic portraits of long-dead electors who stood wreathed in heavy floral incense.

Still staring at the ceiling, Micahel jostled a frowzy-haired woman. High rafters crossed the main arch. According to his diagrams, he thought he'd seen . . .

Yes. Near the left pillar, at the sanctum's edge, a gilded beam protruded, concealed from all other angles.

Back at Talumah's apartment, Micahel studied detail maps of the nave, palace, and Federate occupation base. "Borrowed" from Rogonin's files, the first two maps had the look of antiques, printed in two dimensions on thin, brittle wood-pulp paper.

Long-faced Ard Talumah hovered near Micahel's shoulder. He hitched one hip up to half sit on the table. *Did you ever meet our would-be monarch, lovely Phoena?* he asked.

Struck by the way one portion of the map nudged his memory, Micahel matched a balcony-level overlay of the nave to its lower story, running one finger along ceiling beams, studying scanner angles. From beneath, it seemed to vanish. *Yes, Ard. I saw her so-called execution.*

What does Adiyn mean to do with her? Talumah demanded. Dark brown hair drooped onto his forehead, almost into his eyes.

"Keep her in stasis," Micahel muttered aloud. He'd spoken Old Colonial so much lately that he was starting to think in the trade language. "She's just a gene specimen."

Talumah followed his shift to vocal speech. "How seriously damaged was she? Really?"

He shrugged. "If Adiyn ever revives her, it won't be out of kindness. There's not much left of the mind when the body's gone through that." Sipping his kass, he eyed the map again.

"I met Phoena," Talumah rambled, "at the queen's birthday celebration, here in Citangelo. Caught her alone for one moment, proud and angry, superbly open to suggestion . . ."

The thought nudged Micahel out of his concentration. Tonight there would be another ball.

Talumah paused. "What?" he demanded. He must have sensed Micahel's turn of emotion, but he knew better than to probe uninvited.

"The debut tonight. Caldwells are required to attend, aren't they?"

"By protocol, yes. Anything less would be an unforgivable insult to the Rogonin family."

"Then tonight, we'll find out which so-called palace servitors are actually Sentinels. They'll all be there, protecting that pair." Ten or twelve Sentinels, two of them. Acceptable odds. Caldwell's high-ES bodyguard would recognize him, of course. There should be a microsecond's delay between the guard's warning and Caldwell's reaction, if Caldwell really were disabled.

The Sentinels might even try to grab him.

He smiled at Talumah, envisioning Caldwell sprawled on a restraint table, stunned by bereavement shock. That had been the plan back at Three Zed.

If Caldwell's imitation palace servitors attacked him, he might take one down. Violence at the regent's daughter's ball would guarantee an interstellar incident. It might even spark a war. His people could step in, becoming Netaia's saviors. He was willing to bet Modabah hadn't thought of *that* option.

Yes. Tonight, he would dare Caldwell to go through with his mate's mock coronation. He would scare them and slip away. He'd enjoyed the outcry over Sunton. Publicity went to his head like a drug.

He wanted more.

Modabah Shirak's rich apartment, on the other side of midtown, had too many windows for his gene-daughter's taste. Seated on a lounger near an inside wall, Terza listened to voices speaking Colonial in her father's room. He often closed her out. For a while she'd hoped that by impressing him she might advance her career. He scarcely talked to her, closeted with on-site agents or poring over travel documentaries with other members of the crew that had brought them here. Apparently, Netaia was all he had hoped.

A youth of fifteen or sixteen scurried past her, carrying a carafe of fresh kass. Terza kept her shields steady. She didn't want to feel the youngster's fear. She'd been a subadult too recently, and the sensation might bring back her nightmares. Her father, or any adult of leadership status, could order a trainee sent back to the settlements—or culled, if she were judged inept or dangerous.

Then was Terza, even as a named adult, only a specimen to be sacrificed for others?

Never!

She tightened her inner shields to stifle that cry, then picked up a primitive data desk. With no work to occupy her, she had accessed the Federate register and researched the Carabohd family. She understood Micahel better for it. Terza couldn't fantasize with her father around, but whoever destroyed Caldwell would enjoy unusual pleasures. He would obviously try to die faithful to his god. That kind's despair, as death and defeat sucked him down, should be sublimely sweet.

So she'd been taught. Now even that notion was losing its appeal.

Other details in Caldwell's biography intrigued her. Unmarried until he was thirty by the Federate calendar, he must've been unable to find a connatural Sentinel mate.

Terza wondered what set him apart. Speculating kept her from utter boredom.

And nausea. Always, the nausea.

CHAPTER 9

REGALIA

pavane
a court dance in slow duple meter

A different kind of duty took Firebird downstairs that afternoon to a windowless first-floor room in the west wing. She vaguely remembered a diplomatic reception here years ago. Four meters by five, it was adequate for this purpose.

Brennen sat quietly, almost invisibly, in a chair against the wall. In the end, he'd decided against flying that surveillance grid. There was simply too small a chance for success compared with the risk of being shot down.

Three women bustled around boxes piled on chairs and tables at the room's opposite end. These women were genuine palace staff, too highly placed for Sentinels to impersonate. Shel stood at one heavy wooden door, Uri at the other, twin midnight blue shadows in a chamber frosted with gilt. Brennen wore his uniform, as he'd done during every public appearance, as if he too were on guard duty. He also needed to show off that four-rayed star.

He shifted on his chair as someone hurried past Uri's door. They'd insisted on a room with two entries for this fitting. Though it might be less private, it would be easier to escape . . . in case. She sensed that Brennen didn't like its closeness, nor the number of strangers. His dislike fell short of phobic panic, though. She wondered which one of the Adorations he was silently reciting.

"Over here, please, my lady."

Startled by the chief dresser's contralto voice, Firebird walked her direction. One helper dragged a spiral-legged table underneath the room's central chandelier. The stout dresser gently laid down a box, lifted its lid, and drew out a garment of shimmering pale gold.

Firebird felt Brennen's tension focus. He was already bracing himself to face the gold accouterments in the great Hall of Charity.

"Undertunic, my lady," said the deep-voiced dresser. "If you won't mind slipping out of that skyff, we'll check its fit. If this hangs well, we won't worry about the gown for tonight. It's not quite finished."

Shel and Uri stepped out through their doors and shut them, leaving Firebird alone with Brennen, the dresser, and her assistants. She appreciated their concern for her modesty.

In the middle of undressing, Firebird glanced back at Brennen. He leaned forward on his chair, hands clasped over his knees, watching intently. She knew his attention had nothing to do with watching her disrobe. He would be entirely open to sense her mood. She wondered if the ceremonial significance of these garments had started to mean anything to Brennen. His upbringing was so different.

His bird-of-prey medallion dangled down her chest as the tunic slithered over her shoulders. At her sides, the assistants pressed seams together to fit it.

Firebird smoothed the undertunic's front and lifted one heel to eye its length. The long-sleeved garment rippled to her ankles.

The stout woman brought up a second parcel. "When your sister Phoena was confirmed," the woman huffed, "we had to try these six times. I do hope you're easier to fit, my lady."

"I doubt the problem was your workmanship," Firebird muttered. Phoena had terrorized palace staff.

The dresser twisted one corner of her mouth upward. "If you wouldn't mind stretching out your arms, my lady."

Three women draped a sleeveless crimson gown with open side seams over her shoulders, then girdled it with a belt crafted of interlacing emblems, finely worked in gold, a relic of the House. Each emblem symbolized an heiress confirmed more than a century ago. "We've kept this regalia under all-day watch," said one woman. "Several small but valuable pieces are missing from the state treasury."

Another said, "Some people say the Federates are stealing things."

Firebird frowned. "I doubt that. But I wouldn't put it past the Shuhr." She fingered the belt while a length of crimson fabric, fastened with a gold brooch to each shoulder of the gown's open neckline, was dropped behind her and draped. The emblems stood for her heritage, her responsibilities, her rights as an Angelo heir.

She looked around for a mirror and found none. She was surprised by how much that peeved her.

The woman pursed her lips. "The overgown seems to fit," she said. "I'd have thought we might have to let it out again. You should be proud, my lady. You've had twins."

Firebird straightened her shoulders. She hadn't worked to get her figure back. She'd lost all that weight worrying while Brennen was a prisoner.

The dresser's attendant brought up a final box, smaller than the rest, made of dull metal. The stout dresser touched its latch and lifted out a tiara sparkling with large, square-cut rubies—at least a hundred of them—and a single diamond drop, dangling at center, to touch the wearer's forehead.

Archivists called it the Crown of Fire, more delicate than the heavy, jeweled Crown of State, the dressy goldstone Iarla Crown, or any of the others. Phoena had worn this tiara, an elegant nine-year-old with her chestnut-colored hair elaborately coifed, her small chin high and forward, when seven-year-old Firebird witnessed her confirmation.

The woman set it on Firebird's hair, far forward, then eased it back toward the crown of her head. It squeezed uncomfortably. The diamond drop tickled her brow.

The woman backed away.

Firebird took a tiny step to her right, facing Brennen. *I used to want this desperately*, she thought at him. *How silly do I look?*

He stood up. On the resonance of the pair bond, she felt an uneasy concern. He paced around her, clasping his hands. "She'll wear low shoes, like these?" he asked the dresser.

"It's been fitted for low shoes," she answered. "The costume's normally worn by a preadolescent. She's small for an adult, so it suits her."

He paused in front of her, looked her up and down, then extended a hand. She took it, not quite sure what he intended, or what bothered him.

He raised her hand and kissed it formally. Then he touched one fingertip to her forehead.

An image flooded her mind. With Brennen, she stared up and down at herself as she stood in the costume, taking in its rippling scarlet train, the disquieting shimmer of golden undertunic snaking down the gown's open sides, and the high-waisted fit of the belt. He stared longest, for her sake, at the ruby confirmation tiara, its diamond drop glittering over her forehead.

She was still lost in that image when she and Brennen took an early dinner at the Tellai estate. Tel had invited several local dignitaries, but after Firebird managed a few words of thanks and greeting, those people engaged each other in conversation, excluding her . . . to her relief.

She'd fulfilled every wastling's dream. She'd survived to be confirmed, and tonight—just for tonight, she promised herself—she would bask in this pleasure, here at Tel's reception and later at Esme's ball.

Shel remained at one door of the indoor dining balcony, Uri near the other. Tel's staff paraded past, serving a light soup garnished with fresh herbs sprinkled on floating dollops of set cream.

Firebird spotted one uniformed Federate turning aside to speak into an interlink. Two minutes later, the woman beckoned.

Brennen still seemed oddly distant. He pushed back his chair. "Excuse us for a moment, Tel."

Tel made some polite reply that Firebird scarcely heard as she sprang up and followed.

This aide wore the khaki uniform of Carolinian forces. "Another raid," she said somberly. "Two picket ships got too far behind a trade convoy from Beda to Inisi. Inisi is investigating."

Two more ships! Firebird glanced back toward the table. Several of Tel's other guests had fallen silent, staring in this direction. "This isn't classified, is it?" she asked.

The Carolinian shook her head. "It's going out over the newsnets."

They returned to the table, and Brennen relayed the news to Tel and his guests. Firebird went back to eating, watching faces turn sour lipped and narrow eyed as Brennen spoke. As soon as he finished, Tel's clairsinger ran his fingers lightly up and down his instrument's strings and took up a prim art song about picking herbs in springtime.

Netaia! Firebird fumed silently. Sabba Six-alpha could blast out another radiation storm, and most of these people wouldn't even notice. They clung to their ways like limpet mines to a destroyer.

Yet all these things—the balcony, the art song, the servitors—were part of her heritage, like the small Crown of Fire. "I could help Netaia. I could," she murmured over her soup. She could accomplish things here that she never could do out in the Federacy, and be honored for them. She had every right to wear the Crown of Fire.

"You could." Tel folded his hands on the tabletop across from her, then glanced aside. The dignitaries remained busy with their own conversation. "You must consider your people, Firebird."

"I could at least help them wake up."

Tel plucked a fragrant purple jantia blossom from the nearest table bouquet. "Don't ever give up on us." He leaned toward Firebird with it. Then, appearing to change his mind, he handed it to Brennen. She felt a flicker of surprise before Brennen passed it along to her.

She glanced from one man to the other, unsure of what had transpired. Neither of them explained.

Back at the palace, Brennen took her coat as Shel and Uri disabled a new set of listening devices. "What was that with Tel and the flower, Brenn?"

He laid her coat over a chair. "He wanted to give it to you. He decided that might not be appropriate."

"I can take a flower from a friend. He's just trying to court me for the . . . no, don't tell me he's . . . no," she said, disheartened. "No, Brenn. I know I look like Phoena, but Tel's too intelligent to mix me up with her."

"He admires you for what you are." Brennen slid an arm around her waist. "Mari, be careful. Pride has no place in our hearts. You are lovely, and regal, but—"

She laughed sharply, realizing what had been bothering him. "It's only a costume, a role. I'll take it off when that day's over and never wear it again."

He raised one eyebrow. Then, to her surprise, he leaned down and kissed her forehead.

She shut her eyes and pressed toward him. Brennen's lips almost pulled away, then pressed again, as a smoky-sweet presence hovered at the edge of her mind, enjoying her sensations, amplifying them. "I really am looking forward to the ball," she whispered, kneading the small of his back. He particularly liked that. Now his pleasure, too, echoed in the bonding resonance. "Dance one triplette with me, just one, as soon as we get there. If we're supposed to be visible, let me enjoy it before anything else can happen."

"I don't know the triplette," he murmured against her ear. He'd pulled off his coat, and a faint scent of leather clung to him. In an hour they would bathe and dress to go downlevel. In the ballroom, their kitchen infiltrators would coordinate every supply run with rotating door guards and footmen, to ensure security coverage at all times. Shel and Uri would run the actual intercept if possible, allowing those Sentinel backups to remain inconspicuous in case they were needed again.

"We can easily create the illusion," she answered. "A little mind-access on your part, a little reminiscing on mine, and you can anticipate anything. The court will be so impressed."

"Using mind-access," he said softly, tangling his fingers into her hair, "to create the appearance that I know how to dance, falls very close to 'capricious or selfish' use of epsilon abilities."

"Not selfish," she insisted. "It's not for you, or even me. It's for the mission." He couldn't argue with that. She tilted her chin, wordlessly asking to be kissed on the lips.

Instead, he reached in through her hair, stroking her throat with both palms. "And for us, my lady."

"Don't tease," she murmured.

His voice turned solemn. "This intercept," he said, "could be the riskiest moment of our trip."

"Second riskiest," she whispered. "There's also Three Zed—"

The crosstown link chimed before their lips could touch. Scowling, Firebird reached for the receiver.

Brennen raised a hand. "Shel?" he called through the marble wall.

Firebird waited silently, wondering if Shel heard the sensuous huskiness Firebird felt in Brennen's voice. Guarding a pair-bonded couple must be torture for a bereaved Sentinel.

Brennen walked to the room's end and opened the door.

"Good evening." Firebird heard Shel's voice, then silence.

Standing just inside the archway, Brennen raised one eyebrow, and then he frowned. "No one there," he relayed to Firebird, his sweet physical tension fading.

The CT chimed again. Irked, Firebird joined Brennen in the door arch.

Shel held the earpiece on one side, her wide-set eyes cold. "Good evening," she repeated. Firebird waited a slow ten-count, then Shel jabbed a key to break the connection. "Would you suggest calling palace security?" she asked Firebird.

"It could be palace security, harassing us. Redjackets, or House Guard. Or other friends of His Grace."

"Or Shuhr," Brennen said.

"By now, they could be working with him," said Firebird. "Nothing Muirnen Rogonin did would surprise me."

"It occurred to me," he admitted. "Rogonin has tried nothing against us. He could be waiting, collaborating—"

"If he's caught collaborating, the Electorate will throw him out. That's treason—"

Chime, again.

"Shall I?" Firebird moved toward it.

"Let me." Brennen extended a hand. "Yes?" he asked the wall-mounted pickup.

. . . nine, ten. Brennen switched off.

Chime—

Brennen lifted the earpiece, keeping it away from his head. "If you have a message for Lady Firebird, I'll relay it." He stared at the floor, glacial-ice blue eyes gleaming. "Nothing." He hung up.

"I'm going to bathe," Firebird said firmly, glancing over her shoulder toward the master room.

Brennen held the earpiece, looking ready to originate a call himself. "I'll come soon."

She undressed, then lay down on Phoena's bed. The Shuhr were flaunting their invulnerability, she guessed. Much more of this, and protocol or no protocol, appearances or no appearances, she would move out of the palace and down to the base, with its better security.

Not that she wanted to! She'd been homesick out in the Federacy. Netaia wouldn't like her moving out, either, unless some incident proved she was in danger.

Maybe that was why Rogonin held back. Maybe he knew he'd get only one shot at her, so he'd better take a good one. If only he knew how easily she and Brennen could destroy him!

She closed her eyes and turned inward. Holding her epsilon carrier, she probed the visualized wall, looking for that flaw. She grasped the carrier, looped it around her point of consciousness, and thrust at—not through— the tiny crevice's edge. A new crack appeared. She beat against it, widening it by a millimeter. If she hoped to really use the quest-pulse, she had to learn to create it without using this visualization. She had to—

Gasping, she relinquished the turn. Brennen's voice filtered through the wall. He paused, then spoke again.

She centered her next thrust at the enlarged breach. The carrier's eerie gleam dimmed momentarily, and she thought she sensed a warm, smoky presence. When she opened her eyes, Brennen stood inside the doorway, clutching the hem of his shirt. With a smooth motion he pulled it off. "You called?" She heard delight in his voice. She felt it in her soul.

Progress at last! "What did you find out?" she asked. "Who did you contact?"

"House Guard. The calls originated outside, but they didn't appear on their switching monitor."

"So the House Guard claims."

Brennen sat down on the edge of the bed, then stretched out beside her. "Yes. So they claim."

Micahel Shirak smiled as he reentered his apartment. For now, it was enough to know that this afternoon, without any manipulation, Rogonin had provided the correct CT number for Firebird's rooms. The information itself was unimportant. More vitally, Rogonin was starting to cooperate. If he seemed to support them before they took his volition, the change in him would be less noticeable.

Micahel did hope he hadn't frightened the Caldwells out of attending tonight's ball. He'd found a wonderfully garish outfit.

Nineteen hundred arrived. Firebird tugged the shoulder seam of an electric blue gown, almost wishing she'd taken the couturier's suggestion and hired a personal girl to help her get it on, but she'd dressed herself for almost twenty years. Even when the Angelo fortune supported her, she hadn't rated a dresser. No ball gown was going to defeat her.

Finally, tonight, she would dance with Brennen. She matched her shoulder hems before setting the bodice stays. This really would be the perfect time to get a Shuhr in custody. Then she could enjoy her confirmation uninterrupted.

But one slip of attention tonight could leave her lying dead on a black marble dance floor. Danton would send half a dozen auxiliary plainclothes guards. She wondered how obvious they would look in a ballroom full of aristocrats in full finery.

She adjusted the chain of Brennen's bird-of-prey medallion around her neck. Shortened just . . . so . . . it dangled dramatically, several centimeters over the gown's neckline.

A muffled step caught her attention, and Brennen's image appeared in her mirror. He looked princely in dress whites with the red-and-blue Federate slash on his chest, even with his plainer shoulder star. Before their marriage, she'd observed that he moved with a dancer's grace. With him, she'd done a hundred things beyond her childhood hopes . . . but this would be their first chance to dance together.

His more moderate sense of expectancy dimmed hers. Like Uri and Shel, he'd concealed his crystace and a dart pistol under his uniform. "Stay close to at least two of us," he reminded her, "until they make a move."

She slipped Tel's little blazer into a deep side pocket. If she managed to carry it in past door guards, who ought to be wearing weapon sensors, she could encounter others there who might be armed as well. "We'll do this," she said. "I intend to live to see Kiel and Kinnor again."

Behind her, Shel peered through the near arch. Shel had consented to wear one of Phoena's gowns, sorting with Firebird through still-full closets until they found a pale blue creation less formfitting than most.

"I'll be just a minute." Brennen headed into Uri's rooms, probably to finalize plans by interlink.

Firebird walked out to the study. Pausing in front of a mirror, she pulled her shoulders back to carry off the ball gown's draping. When she'd been younger, she had always felt more comfortable in her Naval Academy uniform than in fancy dress, and she often tweaked tradition at gala occasions.

But tonight she represented the Federacy, Brennen's people, and even the Mighty Singer. She'd tried to gown up properly, had even called the palace tresser and submitted to a hurried coifing.

She stood a moment longer, studying the effect. *Just for tonight*, she'd told Brennen . . . but playing this role felt fabulous. With the red-brown waves of her hair chemically controlled, whisked up at the crown and swept low across her right eyebrow, she might have been mistaken for Phoena. It had happened more than once when Phoena was alive.

Guilt made her slump. What would seeing her like this do to Tel?

"Ready, Mari?" Brennen's image appeared beside hers, his shoulders broadened by his dress whites.

She smiled and whirled, trailing her stiff blue skirt on marble flooring.

Uri entered with Brenn, matching him in dress whites. Poised in his posture, urbane in his slight smile, Uri looked a noble escort to Shel, who wore Phoena's heavily embroidered gown with surprising grace. Shel's usual gait had no female sway. Firebird guessed that normally, if unconsciously, she tried to repel male attention.

Brennen looked hard at Uri, then Shel. "Stay with us until you spot a target. We'll draw him on. Don't be afraid to signal the backups for help. That's why we have them."

Uri nodded gravely.

Firebird took a last glance at her party. A thousand snares of etiquette awaited, but she couldn't drill them in inconsequential nonsense. Tonight was their first serious chance to catch a Shuhr. "Don't worry about fitting in," she said, drawing on her pale blue gloves. "You're expected to behave like offworlders. As long as you make it obvious that you're trying to observe the niceties, you'll please anyone who's willing to be pleased. There's nothing we can do about the rest of them."

A whiff of festive spices blew through the hall door. Paskel stepped through. "My lady, here is Prince Tel." As Tel strode past him, Paskel crossed the formal sitting room in his inimitable palace-staff strut. Tel swept off his indigo-plumed hat and bowed, holding the pose long enough to confirm Firebird's apprehension. "I'm sorry," she said, adjusting her gloves. "I can't help looking like her."

Laughing weakly, Tel drew a hand cloth from one pocket and dabbed at his face. "No, you can't," he said. Pocketing the cloth again, he straightened the ends of his gold-edged sash with a gesture so automatic she envied him. He replaced the cock-hat, then offered Shel his arm. "Are you ready?"

Firebird linked her hand around Brennen's arm. "Tel," she murmured, "there could be some excitement tonight."

"Again?" he asked, raising his head.

"Possibly," Brennen said. "Just be ready to dive out of harm's way, in case our visitors come back."

"Paudan will be there," Tel assured them. "I'm covered."

Paskel held the door open.

Arm in arm with Brennen, Firebird strode out the door, along the balcony, and down the long curving stair toward the main ballroom. Soft footfalls behind her assured her that Shel, Tel, and Uri followed.

CHAPTER 10

ONE TRIPLETTE

valse noble à cinq
waltz in the aristocratic style—for five dancers

Firebird paused as Tel left his hat with a scurrying servitor in the portrait hall. After that, rank and decorum decreed she must lead into the ballroom. A footman announced them, crying first, "Lady Firebird Angelo Caldwell and General Brennen Caldwell."

A hundred stares turned toward the door like targeting lasers. Firebird walked one step ahead, directly down the right side of widening stairs carved from gold-shot black marble, as the footman announced Prince Tel Tellai-Angelo, Major Shelevah Mattason, and Lieutenant Colonel Uri Harris.

His Grace the Regent stood at the foot of the steps, resplendent in a fully formal white brocade jacket, with his House insignia of three stacked platinum triangles pinned at his throat. His thin eyebrows arched regally.

Mindful of the press cadre, Firebird composed her face to respectful solemnity. *Here we are*, she thought at Rogonin . . . and the door guards. *Get a good look.*

No one moved to take away her blazer.

Muirnen Rogonin looked broader than life in brocade. Dark blond Esme stood at his side, a rich spring green gown artfully revealing her flawless shoulders. Until this trip, Firebird had only seen the girl from a distance. Her father's round face was softened through Esme's cheekbones by her mother's Parkai blood. Duchess Liona stood third in the receiving line—

Parkai . . . Chilled, Firebird realized she had killed the girl's grand-uncle at Hunter Height. It had been accidental, in self-defense, but no one here believed that.

It galled Firebird to curtsey to Muirnen Rogonin. Still, she dropped a full one, forehead to her knee, before bowing to Esme. Out of the corner of her eye, she saw Brennen give a full bow behind her. As she rose out of her obeisance, Rogonin smiled down with an expression she'd last seen on Dru Polar, testing director of the Three Zed colony—a greedy, deadly hunger.

"My lady," he said, clasping her gloved hand. "Let me ask privately, what are your plans for Netaia? Will you stay with us beyond your confirmation?" Through his white gloves and her blue ones, his hands felt unclean.

"I've come back only because the Assembly called, Your Grace. My future is with the Federacy."

"If Netaia covenants to the Federacy, all your troubles will end. Am I correct?" His breath already reeked of liquor and spiced hors d'oeuvres.

"I will never put my own convenience before my people's welfare. The risk of civil war is substantial. I would have sent my proposal, even if I couldn't have come in person."

Rogonin glanced past her right shoulder, and his eyes narrowed. She felt Brennen's disgust for the man who had twice tried to kill her.

The regent seemed to be enjoying himself, though. Still gripping Firebird's hand, he lowered his voice. "My Lady Firebird, if you will sign something for me, I will personally see you protected during the length of your stay, and I will ensure that you leave Netaia safely."

Was that a veiled threat? "What do you want?"

"A pledge. A promise that on your honor, and despite any public statement you may make, you will use your influence to free the Netaian systems from all Federate influence."

Her diplomatic resolve had almost run out. "Your Grace, that would be a disaster. The Shuhr would devour Netaia like a choice morsel if the Federates withdrew—"

"And who destroyed our defenses, Lady Firebird?"

"My mother did," she snapped, "by attacking Veroh. My pledge to you is that I will not interfere with the peace of your lawful rule." She turned her head and looked pointedly at Brennen, who stood waiting to pay his formal respects. She curtsied again, feeling too angry to offer any more pleasantries. The prim opening strains of a gavotte fell into her silence.

She shuffled to her left, gave Countess Esme the ritual kiss, and whispered, "Congratulations, Countess. You are beautiful tonight." She curtsied again and stepped to her left. "Duchess Liona."

Esme's mother glared.

Shel murmured in her ear, "Go ahead and move out. I'm at your back." She plainly felt Brennen at full-defense readiness. Glad to show the Rogonin family the gathered back of her skirt, she took Brennen's arm and led into the room. She sensed Uri and Shel falling in behind, each slightly to one side. *Just like flying in formation.* Were the Shuhr here yet? Were they watching?

As she walked she stared around the ballroom. Beyond the mural of Conura First's coronation, ranks of crimson curtains stood open. Brilliantly lit formal gardens showed beyond the porticoes, between lawns where she once played touch tag with other wastlings. The palace orchestra filled the dais, its conductor wearing the gold-trimmed black of a servitor assigned to public performance. His graying curly brown hair was caught back in a tail. The tip of his baton flicked toward Firebird in midsweep. He nodded a greeting.

She let her stare travel clockwise, picking out one of Danton's plain-clothes people, discernible by his conservative clothing and less arrogant face—and then recognized two Sentinels in Angelo livery, balancing trays full of wine goblets. They played the servitor's role surprisingly well.

Quadruple doors at the far end stood open. They admitted more tray-pushing, liveried servitors and a heavenly aroma. Glancing over the shoulder of one "servitor," actually a Sentinel she'd met shipboard, Firebird saw a refreshment table laden with crystal plates and bowls, and she spotted several of her favorite delicacies. Red gem tartlets, nut wafers, pastry wings with various spiced fillings . . . her mouth watered.

Not yet. She stepped away regretfully. *Maybe not even later.*

Slowly she crossed the ballroom, pausing to curtsey and exchange a few words with the nobles and high-commoners who were willing to tolerate her. Only one group tried to extend greetings into something like conversation. "Lady Firebird, is there any news at all about Carradee's daughters?"

"No news," she admitted, "but there are eight teams searching the Inisi system and surrounding space. The Federacy is committed to finding them."

The high-common woman flicked a strand of hair out of her face. "How long do they think that will take?"

"Frankly," Firebird said, "in an area that large, even if they can be found, it could take months or even years."

At an uncrowded spot near the tall windows, she was hailed by a man and woman, both tall and extremely thin, who carried themselves with aristocratic poise. Curtseying, she wracked her brain. She could have sworn she knew every member of all ten noble families. . . .

"Cometesse Verzy Remelard," the woman introduced herself, "and my husband, Comete Noche. Our home is on Luxia. We are ambassadors to Tallis."

Firebird had heard of the Luxian nobility, but these were the first she'd met. "Welcome to Citangelo," she said solemnly.

"Thank you. We have come to see you confirmed and to acquaint ourselves with our peers in the Netaian systems."

"You've had an opportunity to meet the regent, then," Firebird guessed. "As you entered."

They turned to each other. "Yes." The comete's mustache waggled as he spoke. "We weren't quite snubbed."

The cometesse turned to Brennen. "Has anything been heard about Her Majesty Iarla or Princess Kessaree?"

Distracted by a change of music, Firebird let Brennen answer. She seized a goblet of water from a passing servitor's tray. From this spot near the windows, she had a good view of the celebrants. Besides the occasional Sentinel infiltrator, she recognized many young nobles who had posed hazing threats to a wastling child. She had never felt truly safe from them until she enrolled at the Naval Academy. Heirs left military wastlings strictly alone.

The conductor's reedy voice caught her attention. "Noble electors, honored guests. We play tonight for His Grace, Regent for the Crown, and for Countess Esmerield . . . a lovely young girl, and this night—a woman."

As a triplette began, and Firebird reached toward Brennen's arm, a huge man passed between Firebird and the conductor. Firebird set down her goblet and stared. She had never thought to see long-faced Devair Burkenhamn again. Once the First Marshal of the Netaian Planetary Navy, he'd stood as a witness when she vowed away her allegiance to Netaia.

He had also signed Netaia's surrender.

He headed straight for her. "Marshal," she said softly, half curtseying. She felt Brennen and Uri ease closer. Taller than anyone else in the room and heavy with muscle, Burkenhamn projected disciplined power.

He grasped her hand and spoke softly, though his posture never loosened. "My lady, welcome back. His Grace will not be pleased if he sees us speaking. Call on me in person tomorrow, on base, for a few minutes. My secretary will admit you at any time." He strode on toward the refreshment tables.

Dumbfounded, Firebird tracked him. She had admired Marshal Burkenhamn, and he always treated her with respect. "We need to talk to him," she told Brennen. Even if Burkenhamn gave her a dressing-down for her failures at Veroh, he might help their present cause.

She felt Brennen's amusement rise.

"What?" she asked.

He inclined his head toward the dance floor.

Out on the glimmering marble surface, Esme Rogonin minced through the triplette's sweeping steps, engulfed in her father's arms. He moved ponderously, without regard for the beat. "Rogonin couldn't dance a triplette if he had three legs," Firebird muttered.

To her surprise, the couple finished their triplette near Tel, who lingered with his sister Triona and her husband, Count Winton Stele. Esme and her father bowed and curtseyed to each other, then turned simultaneously toward Tel.

"Do you think Tel needs help?" Firebird pivoted half aside, not wanting to stare, not wanting to lose sight of them. Rogonin laid Esme's hand on Tel's arm and backed away. The orchestra started a bourrée. "What is he up to?"

"Fishing," Shel suggested.

Brennen's eyes darkened. "Tel is under full voice-command," he reminded them. "He's safe from any 'fishing' attempts."

Firebird stared around the ballroom. Fifteen-year-old Grand Duke Stroud Parkai took the dance floor with Winton Stele's sister, Countess Alia. Lace cuffs drooped over the young dandy's hands, and a matching jabot cascaded down his shirt front. Near those two, the elegant Duke of Kenhing swept his duchess into his arms. Firebird glimpsed Kenhing's dagger, this time with the slightest shudder. Muirnen Rogonin had tried to bring her just such a dagger when she'd been in protective custody on Tallis and the electors expected her to suicide.

She glanced over her shoulder at Shel. "Ready?" she asked.

Shel barely nodded.

She touched Brennen's arm. "The next triplette?"

He pursed his lips, then said, "You really want to do it this way."

She laid her gloved hand on his shoulder. "More than even you can imagine."

"All right," he said gently. "The next triplette. Until then, we need our backs to a wall, not a window."

Firebird nodded. She led the group to a section of floor between windows, again with a good view of the dance floor and Esme Rogonin.

Poor Tel.

Brennen winked, dimpling the scar on his cheek.

Tel couldn't escape the evening's honoree. This was too high an official obligation.

But perhaps it was a chance to chip at Esme Rogonin's shell, or at least to see how thick it was. He held her small hand with detached firmness.

She took his lead well, following through the bourrée's quick, light steps. After half a minute, she blurted, "Your Highness, may I ask an impertinent question?"

Now he was glad for the secret moments with Caldwell. "I will answer if I can," he said, smiling to himself at the double meaning.

Her lips crinkled. "You probably think Father ordered me to ask half a dozen questions."

"It occurred to me."

"Oh, he did. But I know you won't answer any of those. When we spoke last night, I should have asked if those mind-crawlers ever did anything to your brain."

Tel raised one eyebrow. A sort of fatal curiosity gripped Citangelo's nobility, but no one else had dared to ask. He liked Esme's courage. "I assume you mean General Caldwell."

She nodded. Her steady gaze assured him she really wanted to know . . . had Tel's mind been violated?

Thinking back almost five months, he steered her out of the path of Kenhing and his full-figured wife. "When I first arrived on Thyrica," he said, "General Caldwell was naturally afraid that I might have come intending to harm Lady Firebird. He did examine my intentions. He is . . . was . . . highly skilled."

"Mind-access," she said, frowning.

Tel nodded.

"I'm told it's uncomfortable."

"Certainly that." But unavoidable.

Esme glanced toward the Caldwell party, virtually ostracized between the tall windows. "Is he really as badly crippled as we've been led to believe?"

"Yes." Tel couldn't expect her to understand how tragic that was. "The Sentinels aren't evil, Esme. They are committed to serving other people, just in an unusual way. Just as you and I both are committed to serve Netaia, though we have different opinions about how best to do it."

Esme's hair, loosely coifed, rustled as she tossed her head. "Lady Firebird seems civil enough. Father says she killed Grand-Uncle in cold blood."

"Accidentally."

"Of course she says that."

"I'm convinced," Tel said.

"You've seen her in battle, I'm told. Does she enjoy killing people?"

"Not in the least."

"Hmm," Esme said. Her skirt swirled on the polished floor. "But wastlings are all a little unbalanced, aren't they?"

"If they are, Countess, we made them that way."

Her nose wrinkled in perfect court coquettishness. "Perhaps you've hurt wastlings. I've done nothing."

"If your conscience is clean, Esme, count yourself fortunate. Mine gives me no such peace. By refusing to insist on their safety, I am as guilty as . . . others," he said, squelching distasteful memories. "What are our true motives in demanding their deaths? Have you spent time with your little sister and brother? Do you want to see them die?"

"I have been taught to look the other way," she said tartly, "and so have you. That is only common decency."

The bourrée had nearly ended. He steered her toward the refreshment table and her father, glad to escape, wondering if he'd accomplished anything.

Scarcely pausing after the bourrée, the conductor swept up his baton and directed the opening chords of Firebird's favorite triplette. Those chords sang irresistibly. *You belong here. You are one of us. You were born to this.*

She seized Brennen's hand and tugged him toward the dance floor. "I assume," she murmured, "you watched the first triplette?"

His arm slipped around her waist, warm and steady, and he gripped her hand. "And I assume you haven't forgotten how."

"Not at all."

"Then close your eyes. Visualize dancing with someone very smooth."

The smoky-sweet tendril threaded into her mind. She back stepped onto the floor as if Brennen were leading. She felt him follow, felt his warmth press close. In her mind, he led her left in an arc (*Watch out for other couples, Brenn!*). His legs moved close to hers, perfectly synchronized.

Was this a dream, or was it really happening? Her eyes flew open, and she felt her cheeks cramp with the effort of smiling so broadly. Other couples had taken the floor, but several backed to the edge, standing, watching them.

"Concentrate, Mari," he whispered.

She grinned.

Shel didn't have to use Sentinel skills to see the rapture on Firebird's face. Her own memories wrenched her. She was no dancer, but years ago she and Wald had joined an open-hand drill club. Already pair-bonded, they relished the grips and the throws, the strikes and blocked punches. It had been very much a dance—

A newcomer distracted her. This young man, wearing velvette knickers and cascades of ruffles on his pale green shirt, seemed ostentatious even for a Netaian aristocrat.

Then Shel caught a momentary blurring of his aquiline features.

Without hesitating, she sent Brennen a cautionary quest-pulse.

He paused in his dance step and followed her pointing finger toward the stranger, now standing at the dance floor's edge.

For one second, Shel clearly saw the intruder's curly black hair and a sharp, cleft chin—and the startled look in Brennen's eyes. Clutching Firebird's hand, he backed off the dance floor.

Shel picked a path that positioned her between Firebird and the newcomer. She reached into her ball gown's wide belt, seized and palmed her dart pistol, and slipped closer. Deadly risks didn't bother her. When the inevitable happened, she would simply join Waldron.

Brennen's pulse thundered. Cringing like a helpless ES 32 facing his executioner, he shielded his mind, and Mari's, with minimal energy.

It wasn't hard to fake panic for Micahel's sake.

Firebird clung to Brennen's hand. Uri sprinted toward them, and several women craned their necks to watch Uri. Two false servitors set down their trays and headed for exits, cutting off someone's escape. Brennen's handclasp shifted to a vise grip. He backed toward one of the windowed doors.

As the orchestra played on, her pulse did a full symphonic accelerando. *Where?* she thought at Brenn. *Where is he?*

Uri whipped an interlink from a pocket. Firebird followed Brennen's stare. At the back of her mind, his emotions had gone to knife-edge. With Muirnen Rogonin stood a thin young man in elegant knickers, staring back at her. He smiled, showing teeth. He didn't seem to see Shel, edging toward him around knots of socialites, or notice the servitors who had moved to the glass doors along the colonnade.

"Micahel Shirak. Side door. Now." Uri's hand went to Firebird's waist.

Aghast, she hustled to the nearest open door. This was the man who had murdered her niece—her nephews—their parents. She let Brenn tug her out into a chilly evening, but her hands clenched into fists. He led down three marble steps off the porch, then aside, out of the brilliant lumibeams on a glistening lawn. Uri took up a post near the door.

Over here, she urged silently. *This way, Shirak. One good shot with a dart pistol, and we have you.*

"You're not going back in there," she muttered to Brennen. "Not until somebody gets blocking drugs into him."

He drew his short-barreled pistol.

"Stay out here, Brennen," said Uri.

She seized Brenn's hand. "He'll shoot to kill, Brenn. It's your family he attacked."

A gust of wind tossed the fayya trees as Brennen pulled his hand out of her grip.

"If you go back, I'm going with you," she declared. "If he attacks, we might have to use fusion."

Finally, Brennen focused on her. "We can't do that in public."

She shook her head. "If your life's at stake, your orders mean nothing to me."

Firebird felt an unspecific rumble she'd learned to interpret as Brennen thinking quickly. Then he said, "Come on, then. Both of you."

Firebird eased along the exterior wall, back toward an open glass door. Capture if possible, kill if necessary. . . . *Come on, Shirak*, she thought at him. *Here we are. It all comes down to this.* She shivered.

Uri's shoulders went stiff. He shook his head and looked to Brennen.

Shel hurried out the door. Instantly, she turned toward them. Brennen backed against Firebird as if hiding her behind his body.

Shel reached them a moment later. "He got away," she said. "He ran out through the main entry, and we lost him."

Firebird drew a quick breath. "Did our people miss a door?"

Shel shook her head. "One's down. Shock pistol."

Was Micahel doubling back, then? Behind the curtained windows, richly dressed silhouettes stalked back and forth. "Hiding?" Firebird whispered. "Or gone?"

Straining to listen, she heard the soft buzz of small hovercraft approaching out of the south, probably more reinforcements from Governor Danton.

Uri stepped into the lights and held perfectly still.

"I can't tell," Shel said flatly. She turned her back and stared out into the night, on guard.

Firebird flattened her lips in frustration, then seized her skirt. The hem had turned dark with moisture from the lawn. Her feet felt clammy. "Good try, Shel," she said.

Brennen caught her hand. "Now we know they have camouflaging skills. We only suspected it before. We'll be able to seal the Hall of Charity better than this."

"He didn't even try to attack," said Firebird. "So what was he doing here?"

The hovercraft descended toward the festival square on the palace's south side. "I suspect," Brennen answered, "he came to check on me. On my disablement. The last time I saw him—"

"And you were dancing," she interrupted. "Linked with me. A thirty-two could do that."

"Ye-es. I didn't notice him until Shel alerted me," he admitted. To her surprise, she felt embarrassment behind his irritation. "If he was testing me, I probably passed—thanks to you."

She wriggled her damp toes, which were growing painfully cold. "We should report this to Danton's people. For us, the ball is over."

"We should do more than report." Brennen glanced up at the white marble facade. "This is no good anymore. Too many entrances, too many spies. We've made our statement. You do belong here, but I think they've found out we're too well guarded. Staying here any longer would only put you in unnecessary danger from Rogonin."

"You're right," she admitted, though it made her feel wistful. "We'll go back to the base and stay there—until tomorrow afternoon's rehearsal." She glanced up at the private wing's windows. She couldn't bear to walk past her old doors once more, knowing it could be the last time. "I'll have Paskel send over our things."

INTERLUDE 2

Light-years from Netaia on the Sentinels' sanctuary world, Carradee Angelo grasped her nephew's round little hand and counted off fingers. "One, two, three." Three days ago, Master Dabarrah had sent her request to Three Zed, diplomatically couched as an offer to open talks at a neutral site. Assuming it reached that system, and assuming someone might deal with her request, how many days would it take for a response to come back? Transport time, minimum, from here to Three Zed, was reportedly nine days. "Well, Master Nearly-a-Prince Kinnor Caldwell, it looks as if we shall need your toes." She reached for one foot. He shrieked with laughter, kicking and kicking.

Anna was probably right, though. Any response to her request would probably be deceitful.

Oh, my Kessie. Little Iarlet. Is someone holding you tonight? Do you sleep in medical stasis somewhere . . . or are you holding an angel's hand, exploring the hills of paradise? Every day the searchers found no trace, it was easier to believe there'd been a tragedy.

Little Kiel sat in the crook of Daithi's arm, nestled in the adjustable bed.

Today, the scanbook gleaming on Daithi's lap was *Mattah*, the Sentinels' holy text. "'Dee," Daithi exclaimed, "listen to this. I've found another triple name for the deity. 'The Wisdom, the Love, the Power,'" he read. "How does that match the Shaliyah?"

Mistress Anna had spoken of the three ways God showed himself. "The Speaker . . . I suppose that would be Wisdom."

"I got that far," said Daithi. "But the other two don't fit quite as well."

"Power," Carradee mused. "That would have to be the Voice, wouldn't it? But that would leave Love as the Word, and . . . no, I think I have those backward. The Word they expect—the personal incarnation—is supposed to come in power. Some of their teachers say He will destroy evil wherever it exists. Some of them think the prophecies refer to more than one person, but one in particular." What a tremendously complex, majestic entity this god of theirs seemed to be. There would be no end of learning about Him, even if she lived forever.

Kiel gurgled loudly and reached for Daithi's chin.

"What would you know about that, little man?" Daithi asked his nephew.

Kiel babbled again. Carradee laughed, heart-happy. Like her girls, these babies spoke in full, unintelligible sentences long before their lips and tongues could form words. "Daithi," she said, "everything we've read, everything they've said about this deity rings true, even when I don't understand. There is a magnificence here, a grandeur beyond anything mere humans could have imagined." She laid Kinnor on the bed. Instantly he took off, scooting toward his brother and uncle. "They say there's a leap to make, trusting and blind," Carradee reflected. "I feel like leaping today."

Daithi dropped the scanbook on his bed sheets in time to save Kinnor from a tumble. "So do I," he said. "So does Kin, obviously."

Carradee pulled Kinnor back to her shoulder and rocked to her feet. Kin gurgled and kicked, demanding to be set back down. "I'll speak with Master Dabarrah," she said.

"Aaaaah!" That was Kiel's voice behind her.

She turned around quickly. "What did you do to that child?"

"Nothing," insisted Daithi. "He just bellowed. I don't think he's in pain."

Carradee eyed her nephew. The little boy did look blissfully happy. She smiled at her beloved husband and daredevil nephew. These twins were exceptional . . . something about them, perhaps their latent psionic abilities. *But no one will ever take my girls' place—except, maybe, you.* She found it amazingly natural to talk to someone she couldn't see, couldn't even comprehend. "We'll be back in a few minutes with Master Dabarrah," she told Daithi and Kiel. "Won't we, Lord Kinnor?"

INTERLUDE 3

The Inisi system, near the counterspinward edge of the Federate Whorl, had collected the usual amount of debris—long-dead prospecting probes, defunct satellites, and trash jettisoned by uncaring freighters or passenger haulers. Second Lieutenant Aril Maggard slipped into her seat on *Babb*'s crowded bridge and entered a tick mark at one corner of her com console. Major Charin Dunn had just relieved another search ship. Her crew of eight was buoyant, expectant. The diplomatic shuttle that Governor Danton had sent to Inisi, with the little Angelo girls and their servants on board, had carried emergency supplies for several weeks. Even after this long, it was quite possible that the transport crew and its passengers were alive, stranded by a malfunction, unable to answer hails.

Babb lurched as her pilot fired braking thrusters. "Almost on sector," he announced.

Aril activated her scanners and leaned over her tracking board. "Hang on, little ones," she whispered. "We'll find you."

cotillion impromptu
a complex ballroom dance, with improvisation

Esme Rogonin lingered, watching musicians pack oddly shaped gear. Her father strolled back down the short flight of entry stairs, having seen their final guests through the doors. When she last checked the time, it had been just after three hundred. She hated to see the evening end. This had been almost pure pleasure. Even the Caldwells' indecorous exit kept her blissfully entertained.

Her father took her hand. "You were lovely tonight, Esme, and so gracious. Your mother and I are extremely proud."

She patted his arm. "I hope you got what you wanted from Lady Firebird. Dancing with Prince Tel was not what I came for."

Smiling, her father kissed her fingertips. He looked so grand in white. "We shall see," he said. "She disrupted a triplette for no reason I ever saw, and she has not returned to her rooms. Furthermore, we seem to have picked up a number of false servitors. The House Guard will be busy tonight, checking records."

Esme couldn't be bothered by servitor problems. She yawned. What a grand night—even her formal introduction to Netaia's most notorious wastling, a woman still technically sentenced to die if she lingered in Citangelo. Esme couldn't wish death by lustration on anyone. "I thought she was actually quite civil."

As rain spattered the tall windows, her father leaned back in a tired stretch. "She's biding time. She'll live up to her reputation, child. You'll see."

"She's pretty." Esme sniffed. "And spirited. I almost like her."

"She stands between us and the life we cherish, Esmerield. Between you and a fortune."

Firebird blinked hard. Why was the bedroom window over *there*?
Then she finished waking up. She lay beside Brennen on a bed half the

size of Phoena's, in a bare off-white room. Late last night, base staff had escorted them to a small apartment with a view of the new Memorial Arch. This really was necessary, she guessed. Their first attempt to catch a Shuhr had failed. Their enemies were moving, and it wasn't difficult for starbred individuals to infiltrate palace staff.

She stretched, then looked across the pillow into Brennen's blue eyes. "Good morning," he said. "Could you manage an early start?"

"Something urgent?" she asked, feeling bleary. She could use one more hour of sleep, even though she had promised to drop in on Marshal Burkenhamn. "About last night, I suppose."

"Governor Danton wants to speak with me." She felt his regret like a warm cloth wrapped around her shoulders. "I suspect his call woke you up."

Firebird yawned. The electoral schedule makers had decreed that she should rest this morning, and for once she liked their choice. This afternoon there would be a rehearsal for her confirmation. "Ask for extra guards today." She heard Shel and Uri talking in the front room.

"I'll do that."

She threw off the gray bedcover and dropped her legs toward the floor.

Brennen busied himself in the freshing room. Firebird gazed out toward the spaceport and a rain-washed winter morning. An early passenger craft roared in, one of the flattened-oval Federate landers—dropping toward the field, bringing more people into Citangelo.

And more Shuhr?

Frowning, she fingered the coarse curtain. Defeating the Shuhr at Three Zed would require fusion, RIA, and everything else the Federacy could throw at them. Fusion still was the weak link in that chain, and she hated being the weak part of anything. While Brennen spoke with Lee Danton, she intended to sit in a lounge and do some more experimenting. Then they could speak to Burkenhamn together.

A guard waved their shuttle to a parking area near the new three-level command building's entry. As Shel steered into a slot, Brennen spotted the massive projection dish he'd seen on their first day on Netaia. The scaffolding had been peeled away, revealing a honeycombed parabola, part of a new civic particle shield. *One more response to the Sunton catastrophe*, he observed. Downtown and in the suburbs, Danton's people were building more projectors.

Was Three Zed also bracing for war? he wondered. He left Firebird in a lounge, and an aide took him into the occupation governor's office.

Lee Danton stood at the side of his desk, in front of one of the broad windows. He rolled a cross-space message cylinder between his hands. An auxiliary bluescreen gleamed alongside his memfiles, and its glow cast a bluish light on the right side of his angular face. "Come in," he said.

Catching an uneasiness, Brennen dropped his epsilon shields. He and Danton had worked together during early occupation. He'd foiled four attempts on Danton's life before the angry Netaian separatists realized it was no use trying. He and Danton respected each other. Now either the governor believed in Brennen's disablement or he wasn't trying to hide his tension.

Pretending ignorance, Brennen took a wide stance at midfloor. "Good morning, Governor. Tell me how I can serve you."

Danton dropped the message roll onto his desk. "Sit down, Brennen. You can see I'm somewhat nervous."

Brennen took a side chair near the memfiles. "I hope I can reassure you."

"Mm." Still standing, Governor Danton touched the message roll. "Four hours ago, my aide received a scan cartridge by special courier. According to cover information, the original was sent to Regional command from Thyrica."

Now he was thoroughly puzzled. "Yes?"

"The cartridge contained an eyes-only memo concerning research that has been conducted at Hesed House and at Sentinel College, regarding a phenomenon they're calling 'epsilon fusion.' "

Caught off guard, Brennen reached toward Danton's auxiliary bluescreen. Then he saw the pulsing red light on its control surface. He jerked back his hand.

"What is it?" Danton stepped closer.

Embarrassed, Brennen inhaled slowly. "Forgive me. I came back from Three Zed with some illogical fears. Red light is one of them." At the back of his mind, he was already thrusting down wounded pride, examining his mental state for too much self-confidence. *Power and might are in your hand, Holy One. No one can stand against you.*

"I could cover the panel."

Unshielded, Brennen felt Danton's embarrassment like a fainter echo of his own. "No, I'm all right. It just startled me." *My peace is in you, Eternal One, and you are my power.* Sentinels were trained in emotional control.

He placed his thumb over the indicator light.

The memo was indeed eyes-only, thank the One. "It's our best chance to strike back against Three Zed," Brennen said after skimming the address and heading codes.

"You and Lady Firebird."

"Yes."

Danton took a step closer. "Now I see why you both might have to leave on a moment's notice. Go ahead, read. Then you'll know what we're free to discuss."

Brennen scanned quickly. The memo explained that the fusion phenomenon seemed to rise out of Firebird's oddly polarized epsilon carrier wave. It did not say she'd killed two assailants, but it mentioned concern that the Shuhr could have taken genetic specimens from Princess Phoena, and that they might breed individuals capable of this kind of fusion.

That research was one more reason Brennen dreaded those sealed orders. In light of those programs, he might be ordered to sterilize Three Zed down to bare rock. His ancestors had already destroyed one world.

He turned back to Danton. "You didn't call Firebird in."

Danton stroked his chin. "I'm half afraid to."

"It doesn't happen accidentally." Brennen pointed out the paragraph that explained its near-fatal effects on Firebird Mari. Missing was any mention of the scar tissue accumulating cell by cell inside the ayin complex at the middle of her brain. Naturally, the Federacy worried less than he did . . . about that and about the self-focus that had seemed to infect her when she put on that confirmation costume. He'd paid dearly for his own self-reliance. He wanted to spare her from that kind of disciplining.

"I would hope," said Danton, "that by using RIA, coupled with this other development, the Federacy can move quickly against Three Zed."

"As soon as we know how to take down their fielding team, we can get close enough to slip effective payloads past their particle defenses."

"Finding that out is half of your mission here, as I recall."

"Besides getting a handle on their long-range plans."

"And appeasing Councilor Kernoweg's crusade to see Netaia covenant to the Federacy. I don't suppose your Shuhr hosts exactly took you on a tour of their fielding unit," Danton observed.

Brennen heard and felt the good humor creeping back into Danton's mental stance. "If they did," he confessed, "I've forgotten."

Danton winced. "Understood. I was hoping that your disablement is . . . somewhat less than is being publicly reported."

It wasn't really a request for information, and Brennen didn't volunteer any. Until they had a Shuhr captive, he would not tell one more soul his actual ES rating. "Thank you, Lee. I wish I could tell you I'm fine, but I'm not . . . as you just saw." He slid his thumb off the pulsing red light.

Danton stroked his chin. "With the kind of power this fusion report implies, no other authority in Federate service will be able to control you and Lady Firebird. Some will want to separate you."

"Lee, the same vows that protect you from capricious use of an RIA apparatus—"

Danton cut him off. "Sometimes those vows are no control over your people. You do swear loyalty to your kindred above loyalty to the Federacy."

Brennen studied the governor's face, feeling no hint of sympathy. "That is the vow," he agreed.

Silence dampened the air. The Federacy barely trusted his people. That had been one major argument against revealing RIA to the Federacy, and this new development made him and Firebird, personally, into potential threats.

"We could demonstrate fusion at your convenience."

The governor exhaled. "Thank you, that won't be necessary. How can I facilitate your strike at Three Zed?"

Brennen relaxed into his chair. "My orders are sealed. I'm assuming they are to strike, but I will open them only when we have that prisoner."

Danton stared off into space for several seconds. "Is Lady Firebird fighter-rated for Federate ships?"

"No. She and I would fly together. Thyrian fighter-trainers are notoriously underpowered, but—"

Danton leaned toward his com panel. "Maybe," he said, "I could give you one more option." He touched the panel. "Major Harthis, give me Marshal Burkenhamn's office."

Firebird sat in the third-floor observation lounge, ignoring the view. She was distracted by wondering what Governor Danton wanted with Brennen.

Hearing footsteps, she looked up. Beyond a cluster of angular, upholstered chairs, a man came striding up the corridor. He wore Netaian cobalt blue trimmed in red. In the next instant, she caught a red glitter on his collar, the ruby stars of a first major—her own former rank in what seemed like another life. She'd been so proud to wear that uniform.

He marched into her lounge. Shel sprang up.

Firebird rocked onto her feet. Even if she'd been in uniform, she couldn't have saluted. She'd been dishonorably discharged as soon as the Netaian Planetary Navy learned she was captured instead of killed at Veroh. She was lucky they hadn't court-martialed her, too. Evidently her electoral trial sufficed for all offenses.

"Lady Firebird," said the major, "Marshal Burkenhamn wants to speak with you. I'll take you downlevel to his office."

Shel stepped forward. "Is that office secure, Major?"

"Yes. You're also welcome to escort her, naturally."

Firebird glanced from one to the other. Of all places on Netaia, this base was probably the safest for her. Still, it was good to see that Shel took nothing for granted.

They rode the lift back downlevel. As she walked up the corridor with the major on one side and Shel on the other, she composed a formal apology. If ever she felt guilty about betraying Netaia during the Veroh war, Burkenhamn's was the face she'd seen. At Tallis, he had helped save her life by refusing to endorse a proposed execution—and she'd promptly snubbed him by taking Federate transnationality.

He'd accepted a position under the occupation government, so maybe he wasn't entirely anti-Federate.

A windowed door, lettered NETAIAN FORCES—MARSHAL BURKENHAMN, slid open. "He'll see you immediately." The major stroked a panel on the clearing room's desk, and a second door opened.

Firebird glanced at Shel, squared her shoulders, and walked in.

Behind a red-grained leta-wood desk, Devair Burkenhamn was rising to his feet. Something whirred on his desk top, spewing hard copy. The silver fringe of hair behind his ears seemed thinner than before, and she saw deeper lines between and over his eyes. He extended a huge hand, and she clasped it over piles of scan cartridges, chip stacks, and more hard copy, the typical flood of administrative busywork.

"Good morning, sir. You asked to speak with me."

He sat down, and as she took the opposite chair, she flattened her hands in her lap. Marshal Burkenhamn must make the first move in this new, awkward game. She'd always been his student and very junior officer.

Though he was one of the few Netaians whose body couldn't tolerate anti-aging implants, he remained superbly trim, his broad shoulders looking as solid as ever. "Lady Firebird," he began, then he paused. If he'd addressed her as "Major," she might've expected a reprimand. But calling her by her title seemed conciliatory. "I said this last night, but I mean it sincerely. Welcome back."

She hated to humble herself like this, but she had to. "Marshal, the last time we faced each other, I—"

Burkenhamn waved a broad hand. "I wish to discuss the future, not the past. Would you be so kind as to say nothing about previous events?"

Relieved, Firebird sat straighter. "As you wish, sir. I would like to be numbered among those who support you wholeheartedly."

Burkenhamn smiled sidelong. "That is refreshing to hear. I tried to help with the . . . disturbance last night. I'm afraid I accomplished nothing."

She hadn't read a follow-up report yet. "Thank you for trying, Marshal." Oh, the memories this man's long face and rich baritone brought back! "I'm sure you made an impression."

He spread his broad hands. "Please, let me explain why I called you here."

She nodded formally.

"Governor Danton has just asked me to offer back your fighter rated status in the restored Planetary Navy."

He couldn't have immobilized her more effectively with a shock pistol. After four or five seconds too long, she found her voice. "Marshal, I'm . . . I have commitments. I couldn't accept a military position here."

"I'm not sure I understand Danton's request." Burkenhamn half smiled. "He asked in confidence, and I must assume your bodyguard is also sworn to silence."

"Yes, but—"

"Your husband's name was also on the request," said Burkenhamn. "Governor Danton implied that this has something to do with our general assumption that Sentinel forces are being assembled for a possible strike."

"Oh," she said softly, and her mind whirled forward. If she were fighter-rated, she and Brenn could each fly into fielding range. That would give them the combined power of two RIA units. "Maybe the Federates would like to have all Federate worlds represented, even an occupied one, in any case," she suggested. She couldn't confirm his guess. He wasn't directly involved, and officially, no such order existed yet. "What fighter, sir?"

"The governor sent down simulator training materials for something called a Thyrian Light-Five. Are you familiar with it?"

"I've seen them. Federate cockpits are engineered to standard specs." But every fighter would respond differently. She would need sim time.

"Very well." He rested his elbows on the desk. Old habits made her answer his gesture by coming to seated attention. "I would also like to take Danton's request one step further. I want to offer you a field promotion . . . an honorary title, more or less. If you accept, it will become public knowledge."

One of her hands did an involuntary flutter in her lap. "Go on," she murmured.

"Your discharge has already been canceled, by my order. I want to offer you the rank of second commander, subject to eventual approval by the First Naval Council."

She felt her eyes widen. That was a full rank, probably three years of service, above the first majority.

"I will present it to the electors as a symbolic gesture." His stiff back relaxed. "If Netaia can only send one soldier against Three Zed, we should be proud to send our best. Firebird, you acquitted yourself honorably at Veroh."

"Sir," she managed, "thank you, but from the standpoint of Netaian honor, I failed miserably at Veroh."

"I disagree." He leaned away from her. Trying to look casual, she guessed. "Governor Danton only asked that I get you rated for that particular fighter, which would automatically make you Federate personnel. If you prefer, you may accept the rating at a lower rank."

Firebird took a closer look at his cobalt-blue uniform. Sure enough, the Federate slash had been added over his breast. "You know me too well for that, Marshal."

"Yes, I do. You were one of the few high achievers who consistently gave more than necessary. If you accept my offer, that will only improve Netaia's standing with Regional command. As a transnational citizen, you will represent both Citangelo and the Federacy."

How thrilling! But . . . *This promotion feels like a temptation, Mighty Singer. Is it?* "Appointing me commander of whom?" she asked carefully. "Sir, I have family commitments. I will not choose to leave my children to serve a tour of duty." Leaving them for a little while was hard enough.

Burkenhamn leaned against one armrest of his chair. "You've seen heirs take honorary positions."

"Well, yes." Here on base, she had trouble thinking of herself as an heir. Heirs who wanted to wear a uniform were given an empty rank and a few speeches to make. Wastlings trained at the Naval Academy. They saw frontline combat and died.

"Your real experience would be valuable in a training and liaison capacity . . . and, yes, in our reserve defenses. Tallis is letting us reestablish an active force, but I'm only a figurehead. You'd be more effective in that role, especially after your confirmation. I've made arrangements for heirs' occasional reserve schedules. I would find it a pleasure to do that for you."

Firebird's mind sprinted ahead. What if civil war erupted? With a military rank, she might actively shorten the conflict. She could only imagine the ballads that might be sung about the wastling who saved Netaia.

"Marshal Burkenhamn," she said solemnly, "for two years, I've suffered whenever I thought of you. I owe you a debt of honor."

Burkenhamn extended his hand. "Then you accept?"

His fingers surrounded her palm. She gripped the edge of his hand with her fingertips. "Yes, Marshal. Thank you." *Second Commander.* Picturing three gold moons on her cobalt blue uniform collar, she couldn't help smiling. *Commander Caldwell!* Or would they call her *Angelo?*

Terza Shirak sat at a servo table, staring out the window, feeling like a neglected pet—or a breeding animal. Her father's apartment had several sleeping rooms off a short hall, but she spent much of her time in this south-facing dining area. Her appetite had returned with a voracious vengeance. Ever since leaving the Golden City, she'd done nothing but swell. Others might not notice the signs of her pregnancy, but to her they were becoming obvious. She felt like one of the ceremonial kiprets that her overzealous ancestors used to fatten and then butcher for sacrifice. She missed her station in Adiyn's laboratory, her womb banks to tend, her cultures to fertilize and check. She had loved achievement, exercising her own small control over the next generation. She missed the Golden City.

She glanced down. The only visible mark of her . . . pregnancy (she still hated the word) . . . was the tight fit of her clothing, especially her shirts. But its chemical effect on her brain astonished her. Though her father still frightened her, she felt a growing sense of familial identity, of pride to be called by his father-name. If he'd shown any sign of returning that pride, she would be sleeping easier. Also, the mundane touch of human skin had become almost a fetish, the softest, most appealing texture imaginable. She kept close control on that notion. Preoccupation with the physical was vulgar.

She pressed both hands to her middle. For all the discomfort she would have to endure, she wanted some return . . . some assurance that her embryo would thrive.

Her embryo? Half the chromosomes, maybe. But the zygote, like all subadults, belonged to Three Zed colony.

She felt less certain of that every day. Making a gestational mother of her had been Modabah Shirak's mistake, if he hoped to maintain her objectivity.

Maybe he didn't. Maybe he meant to sacrifice her. Again she thought of the half-witted creatures her ancestors took to Ehret's great temple.

Cautiously, she looked around the dining area and lounge. One of her father's dozen lackeys bent over the servo, ordering a preprogrammed Netaian specialty. Another stood close to the view window, reading something on a recall pad. Across the living area, on a long animal-hide lounger, her father sat with another stranger, who was describing Netaia's cultural museums.

If the man could have guessed Modabah's intentions for the contents of those museums, he might not have come to this apartment. But once inside, under voice-command to speak freely, he might as well deliver the artworks.

She frowned, pitying all Netaians. Juddis Adiyn had remained on Three Zed, but he would travel here sooner or later. Once her people had the Sentinels' RIA technology in hand, they could take control of Netaia's resource base.

Then Adiyn could expand his staff and set about modifying the planet. Three Zed retained centuries-old genetic weapons that had already sterilized one world of human life, but her grandfather's long plan had been superseded by Adiyn's. Here, Terza might be ordered to assist in the release of other agents, viral organisms that would infect all Netaians, turning them into carriers for whatever genes Adiyn selected.

Early die-off would come first, naturally. Their altered descendants wouldn't need to fight another war, like the one that devastated Ehret. That had been a hard lesson.

Brennen Caldwell, who would give them the key RIA technology, had been carried in some starbred mother's womb. Lady Firebird had been a noblewoman's child, though not a cherished offspring. How could these "nobles" sentence their own named youths to die, simply to preserve their wealth? It was bad enough in the Golden City, where inferior or dangerous youngsters *must* be eliminated.

Mustn't they? Now she wondered if she could still approve even that. Infecting an entire world's population, even with an eye to their descendants' immortality, no longer sounded generous.

She had to hope Micahel succeeded in the Great Hall and took Caldwell down. If that option failed, her father might use her next—to dangle as bait.

Micahel reported to his father's apartment after stopping midtown for a noon meal. Netaian food, fresh and varied, did impress him.

Modabah sat slumped over the servo table, eyeing its inset bluescreen. He must have sent Terza and his crewers away. Only Talumah sprawled on the lounger.

"So," said the Eldest, "no fatalities reported at the Rogonin ball. Did you have an off night?"

"I accomplished what I set out to do." Micahel straddled a stool, putting the sun at his back. "I tested his defenses. They had more support than I expected."

"What about Caldwell's powers?"

"He actually reacted as a thirty-two would," Micahel admitted. "I could have killed him. He didn't even see me arrive. He was *dancing*," he sneered. "Making love in public. If Talumah had gotten closer, he'd be ours."

"So it's Talumah's fault?" Modabah swept one hand over inset controls, darkening the bluescreen. "I'm still surprised you didn't leave a few bodies."

"Too much support," Micahel repeated. He'd been grabbed by a huge Netaian man—a long-faced, balding military type—and flung bodily toward a wall. He'd barely stopped his flight in time to keep from being knocked senseless. He had fled, irked to find Talumah outside and unhurt.

"How did they stop you?"

He would *not* mention the big Netaian. But he would have revenge. *All right, I had an off night.* Micahel switched to subvocal speech, with its implied subservience and layers of emotional overlay. *They were waiting for us. They were prepared.*

"They'll be prepared at the Hall of Charity," his father pointed out.

There, we expect them to be prepared. A kill is easier than a capture.

You could wire the headpiece, Ard Talumah insisted from across the room. Micahel glanced toward the lounger. Talumah hadn't even opened his eyes. All along, he'd wanted to redesign the confirmation tiara with miniature explosives, sensitive to body heat. Blowing the woman's head off by remote would terrorize Netaia. With Sentinels so nearly involved in its government, that could throw all sorts of suspicions. Possibly set a large Federate element against Thyrica.

"No," Modabah called over his shoulder. "Not the tiara. Standing close, Caldwell could sustain injuries."

"She's mine, Talumah." Micahel shifted. Sun on his back, even weak winter sun, felt strange. "With the lady dead and Caldwell in shock, with the side entrance covered . . . we'll take him." The public press could be counted upon to sear images on the public mind, images that would prepare Netaia for its regent's capitulation to Modabah. Micahel grabbed a bottle off the servo counter, poured a glass of joy-blossom wine, and raised it. "And this time, we'll keep him."

Talumah sat up on the lounger. "Then I have another contribution. One of my suppliers just dropped off a multifrequency disruption grid. I think you could use it."

CHAPTER 12

PERFORMER

ballade
a composition suggesting the epic ballad

Firebird's simulator screen faded to gray, and she exhaled hard, relieved to know she hadn't lost all her reflexes.

Someone stood beside her booth, and she felt a welcome presence. She refocused her eyes on the real world.

"Second Commander," Brennen said gently. "Congratulations. Marshal Burkenhamn reported back to Governor Danton while I was still there." He extended a hand, and she grasped it, leaning on him to unfold herself out of the booth. "What are your orders?" he asked.

"For the moment, I'm only rated to start training again." She hadn't wasted a minute, either. She pulled her hair out of the catch at the nape of her neck. "But step by step," she murmured, "we're getting closer to Three Zed."

—And its planetary fielding team. No matter how thoroughly she trained, fielding operators could attack the areas of an interloper's mental matrix that responded with the deepest torments of fear.

Still, she had some confidence in her ability to endure terror. She'd already faced the darkest side of herself. What was left to fear?

Firing on friendly forces, for one thing. Or if they couldn't terrorize her, they could try to drive her insane. If she had to lay down her life there, so be it. But if they stole her sanity . . .

Better not to think about that. She peeled out of the heavy life suit Danton's people had issued for sim use. "And you?" she asked.

Brennen reported on Danton's fusion memo.

"Sounds to me," she said as she returned the life suit to an adjoining locker, "that he took it rather calmly."

"He's nervous." Brennen glanced out the nearest door. Beyond several other sim booths that were closed down for use, Firebird spotted one of their plainclothes guards.

"The Shuhr haven't missed a chance," Firebird said. "It could be an exciting rehearsal."

"They haven't seriously tried yet," Brennen answered. "When they do, we'll know."

She frowned. "I want a bath before the rehearsal."

He slid one finger under his collar. "Actually, so do I."

They hurried back to the apartment.

Shortly, a large car with base markings pulled up outside the housing unit, and Shel and Uri escorted them to the vehicle. Four Tallans in ash gray uniforms, sidearms prominent on their belts, rode along this time. Two additional cars served as outriders on each side. Brennen sat silently, watching the roadside pass.

He'd sent a decoy car ten minutes ahead. Along Port Road traffic flowed smoothly, with no sign of any disturbance.

He frowned. His agents still had no luck finding the Shuhr's nest. Shirak and his compatriots could hide and shield themselves too well to be found that way. They must be lured in.

He glanced up at the clear sky. There was probably enough Federate force deployed here to prevent a suicide strike, even if more Shuhr arrived with an attack group.

No, the confrontation would be personal, and he guessed he knew when it would come.

At the Hall's security blockhouse stood a line of groundcars, their doors marked with House insignia. From several vehicles marked with the crimson Angelo-starred shield, staffers unloaded long, stiff bundles, covered trays, and crates and boxes of all sizes. Uniformed security guards examined the bundles.

Firebird stepped out of the base car between Shel and Uri. A line of servitors steered laden carts toward the tunnel entry while Enforcers in city black stood sentry. The servitors stepped aside and let her group board the lift.

As an inquisitive child, Firebird had explored the downlevel tunnel while others thought she was obediently discussing Charities with her Discipline group. She hurried along, sensing Brennen's disquiet as they passed storerooms, sacristies, and vestries. He too must be badly distracted if the narrow tunnel was bothering him.

Up a stair, through the broad narthex, then down a long straight aisle. Nearly thirty people already stood at the foot of the sanctum. She didn't see Muirnen Rogonin, but she did spot midnight blue figures at several stations.

"Good." First Lord Erwin straightened slightly, and his voice rang out in the nave. "Here you are at last. Gather close, please."

Shel led to the front. Firebird mounted five steps to the stage-like sanctum, then glanced back again. Servitors worked in teams, using telescoping
booms to hang wide streamers of scarlet velvette from the sloping side balconies and spiraling them around gilded columns. Twenty-two of those pillars lined the side aisles, then pierced the balconies, to split treelike and form
limbs of gold tracery.

Other men and women, at least twenty of them, sat and watched the
servitors. More Federates, she realized. *Thank you, Governor.* Shel and Uri
had unquestionably dropped their shields to listen for any hostility, too. But
in Brennen she still sensed the faint underlying panic.

Gold, she understood. The nave was full of it.

Memories leaped out as if they'd hidden between pews, images that had
remained lost to him until this moment.

. . . Golden corridors, with ceilings that arched close overhead. A lanky,
black-haired man with lashless eyes walked at his elbow. . . .

. . . A tiny black room with pitted walls, its door a glossier black shadow.
A single white lamp hung over his head, and he lay on a narrow black
shelf. . . .

. . . Another face, younger, eyes brimful of hate. A firm mouth, a cleft
chin . . .

Micahel.

His throat constricted, and breath came hard. He'd studied chapters and
chapters of scripture that he once could've called instantly to mind. He'd
come across one that must have been a favorite, from the number of marginal notes he'd made:

> *I will be with that remnant.*
> *I will refine and test them as meteor steel*
> *And make them a sword in my hand.*

Loose sword, he found in his own penmanship, *useless. Effective only in
His hand.*

He had to fall into the Holy One's power when terror unbalanced him.
He could not fight these irrational fears alone. Deliberately, he relinquished
himself—and the situation—to One whose strength was broad and deep.

Then he could breathe more easily. He eyed the high golden ceiling with
a practiced eye. During this rehearsal, his own forces would run a final surveillance from assigned positions—at exits, or seated where they could wield
scanning imagers, behind tapestries.

He would have that ceiling, those tapestries, and every individual who entered the Hall thoroughly checked. Intercepting an assassin "incoming" would be the ideal scenario.

Catching one during the ceremony—an agent with enough tricks and abilities to penetrate his perimeter—might be dramatic, but at this point the idea had considerably less appeal.

Firebird faced forward again. Ornately carved seating boxes surrounded the sanctum's main stage. Behind them, in corners along the front wall, two musicians sat at banks of keys, panels, foot pedals, levers, and sliders. The Hall's organum wall could drown out a full choral orchestra or fill the nave with soft, meditative strains. She wished she'd been consulted on the choice of music. . . .

Then she changed her mind. Distracted by a favorite march or air, she might stop paying attention. It would take only a moment to unbalance their fragile trap and let Micahel Shirak take his bait.

She sidestepped closer to Brennen and frowned up at the statuary. She couldn't remember, because she had never noticed, how much of a part the graceless Netaian faith had played in Phoena's confirmation. It hadn't mattered back then. Centuries ago, the Netaian government deliberately corrupted its people's faith. Now it mattered very much.

The stooped first lord read a few lines, then set down his recall pad. Firebird listened, reluctantly impressed, as he recited her lineage from Conura I to her mother without glancing at the pad. ". . . who bore to Netaia four daughters: Carradee Leteia Authra, Lintess Chesara Solvé, Phoena Irina Eschelle, and Firebird Elsbeth, Lintess and Phoena now deceased."

Firebird barely remembered Lintess. The family had lost her in a childhood accident, but even then, Firebird suspected Phoena. If only she'd been stopped as a youngster and disciplined. How might their lives have been different?

Firebird would never know. *Only one Path*, her instructor had said, *can be walked or understood*.

First Lord Erwin turned to her, and she shook off memories. "You who stand in the sanctum to be confirmed, tell your name and your lineage, and your right to stand here."

She cleared her throat and raised her head. "I am Firebird Elsbeth," she said, "and you have told my lineage."

"Yes, good." The ceremonials director stepped forward. "But keep your body straight ahead. Try that again."

Firebird compressed her lips, came to military attention, and repeated her line.

"Better." The director stepped back. "All right. Continue, Baron Erwin."

"At this point," he said, "I make a rather long speech that my writers haven't finished. I end with the big question, Lady Firebird. Here it is. Will you stand ready to serve, should the high calling to which you are now declared an heiress ever fall to you?"

"And I answer," Firebird said firmly, "I live to serve Netaia." A five-year-old could master that declaration. During the ceremony, though, she meant to change a few words. From *live* to *hope*, and from *Netaia* to *Netaia's people*. She *hoped* to serve *Netaia's people*. Small words were important.

"Then I reach around," said the director, "to the table, for the tiara. You will kneel."

Firebird back stepped into a deep curtsey. She took it deeper yet, then dropped one knee onto the carpet. Once steady, she dropped the other knee. This would be awkward in costume.

Baron Erwin pantomimed laying his hands on her head, sliding the tiara into place over her hair.

"In the holy names of Strength, Valor, and Excellence," intoned the baron—

Firebird jerked her head up. Baron Erwin droned on, asking a complex blessing in the names of all nine holy Powers. To Firebird, it sounded like a curse. She'd spent much of her life flaunting insignificant Netaian traditions. This no longer seemed insignificant.

She must speak with Baron Lord Erwin. Surely he could be reasonable about shifting a word here and there.

He finished.

"Questions?" asked the director.

Now, urged a voice at the back of Firebird's mind. *Object!*

She hesitated. She'd already disrupted Esme's ball. If she spoke up now, there could be a loud, unnecessary fight.

No. Now.

"May we talk about that blessing?" Firebird stared hard at the baron. "Later tonight?"

He nodded slightly, pursing his lips. "And I have a question for you, Lady Firebird. Do you intend to disrupt this ceremony and disgrace us, or have you finally accepted your role in Netaian society?"

"If there are disruptions," she said carefully, "they will not come from me or the Federates."

He glared at Brennen. "General, I demand your word of honor that your people will not use this solemn occasion to further their own agenda."

"The Federacy," Firebird interrupted, "asked that I accept this invitation. They will not—"

"General," snapped Erwin. "Your word."

Brennen's hand clenched down at his side. "I will protect Lady Firebird with my life if necessary. Otherwise, I will be silent and decorous. You have my word."

"See to it."

And maybe, just maybe, the Shuhr wouldn't show up. Brenn had mentioned putting a decoy team in the motorcade to the Hall.

The director stepped forward, clasping her hands over the front of her white gown. "After the recessional, we will motorcade back to House Angelo. There will be a formal luncheon. Lady Firebird, you will be given your heir name and make gifts to your chosen charities."

She nodded. Heirs had two middle names, and the second usually honored one of the Powers. She hoped the pageantry committee had been kind. She'd requested *Mari* instead.

"There will be time for all celebrants to rest after the luncheon," the director continued. "Dinner in the main hall for electoral families—"

Firebird was not looking forward to that.

"—and the day will end with the confirmation ball."

Finally, finally! Compared with other concerns, this was insignificant, but she still hoped to finish that dance with Brennen before heading to Three Zed. Let this trap spring successfully, and Rogonin wouldn't dare accuse her of sedition. She'd be a hero.

Don't forget, she reminded herself. *Only the Electorate can save Netaia.*

Riding back to base, she spotted five Enforcers on street corners. She'd never seen so much patrol activity.

Maybe His Grace was nervous.

She leaned against Brennen's shoulder. "I suppose they expect me to retire early that night, exhausted."

"You will be," said Brennen. "Or else you'll be shipboard."

"I wonder," she murmured, still later as she eyed a stack of luggage, delivered to their four-room apartment on base, "if our exalted ceremonials director or Lord Erwin have any idea who really might disrupt the ceremony."

"They'll be warned tomorrow night and informed of our precautions.

No point frightening them any sooner than necessary."

Twice during Firebird's evening session with law advisors, who read her every regulation that concerned her conduct as a potential elector, she halted the proceedings. She hurried to the base lounge's CT link, called House Erwin, and asked to speak with the baron. The first time, he'd gone out to dine. The second time, he'd gone to bed.

At nineteen hundred? *His youth implant must've expired*, she fumed as she returned to the briefing room. Brennen raised an eyebrow. She shook her head, then turned to her second counsel. "Go ahead," she said. She still had all day tomorrow to reach Erwin.

When the counselors finally finished, she flicked the CT board again and found a call from Clareen Chesterson, the bassist. "Firebird," the singer said, "there's a sing at Nello's tonight. Can you get away?"

The message ended.

"Nello's?" Brennen raised a dark eyebrow.

Dozens of memories rushed back. "Most nights, it's a factory ware-house. But a group uses it for impromptu concerts, very much frowned on by the noble class. Wonderful music, with the heart of a world in it. Exactly the kind of place where . . ." She halted. Really, there was no use hoping to do this. The Shuhr had proved they weren't waiting for the ceremony. "I used to go to Nello's every chance I got," she said wistfully.

"You'd like to go tonight."

"Of course. But it would be foolish." She could've been among real people, common folks. "There's no point trying to make it a trap, though. Too many bystanders, too little advance warning."

She felt his amusement.

"But there might be one thing we could accomplish," she realized, and suddenly the risk seemed worthwhile.

"What?"

Firebird leaned against the windowbar. "I've discovered something more profound and real than the nine holy Powers—"

"Mari." Brennen frowned. "I know you haven't been vested, but it's still not allowed to proselytize, unless someone inquires—"

"I'm not even Thyrian—"

"You have Ehretan ancestry. You've been consecrated in the faith, and you have epsilon powers—"

"What powers? I can barely quest-pulse."

His eyebrows lowered. He covered his mouth with one hand, and she felt his intense disapproval. "You and I, together, have an ability that—"

"I want to help my people, Brennen—"

"Of course you do. How do you think we feel about other Thyrians? Even some of the Shuhr probably aren't beyond redemption. But we are commanded. If others inquire, then we can tell them what we believe. Otherwise," he said, gently prodding her chest, "you would have heard plenty before you ever set foot on Veroh."

Irked, she stood staring at him, working one finger against the side of her thumb. Even when she experienced his emotions, she didn't always agree with them.

His voice softened. "If you cannot obey our codes, we cannot train you. Obedience is all that sets us apart from the Shuhr. This command will change, one day when we've learned patience."

"I could sing to them," she insisted. "There's no commandment against performing an old ethnic hymn. Is there?"

He shook his head, still unsmiling. She could almost feel him thinking, *Pride, willfulness, impatience.*

She did recall how patiently he had waited for her to ask about the faith. He hadn't broken his codes, not even for her sake, not even when he desperately wanted her to ask.

She ought to feel honored, by an honorable man. Still, she would like to have known more—sooner.

Maybe she could arrange for Clareen's Chapter house to be built in Citangelo. She would soon have an heir's allowance.

Abruptly, she realized that Clareen would be there tonight, and Clareen was under no prohibitions.

Getting off base proved simpler than leaving the palace. Brennen enlisted a Federate aide, who drove a midsized groundcar to a quiet street, then parked and walked back to the base. Five minutes later, Firebird pulled off the blanket that covered her and looked around from the backseat. "We're clear, Shel. I'll direct you from here."

In an urban area that smelled of industry, at the back of a brown-brick commercial plant, Uri softly voice-commanded a watchman to turn aside. Firebird led the way in.

Two hundred people, most of them dressed in drab, working-class coveralls, sat in chairs or on the floor, surrounding two singers and a lutenist. They were performing a love song Firebird hadn't heard in two years. Months and light-years retraced themselves. Now she marveled at how well the lyrics described Brennen. Some of her irritation with him flowed away.

She edged toward a short stretch of standing room along a wall. The cavernous room smelled of sweetsmoke and sweat. Shel's eyes didn't stop moving, and Brennen's emotions were at fever alert. They couldn't stay long.

The song ended. As the last chord faded, a man jumped to his feet. "Firebird!"

Again, the stares were like targeting lasers . . . this time, friendly ones. Shouts of "Welcome back," and "Sit here," and "Introduce your friends," echoed through Nello's back room. Someone tugged Firebird to the trio's chairs. Shel squeezed forward with her and sat down. Uri and Brennen—dressed in black civilian clothing—stood thirty degrees apart, along the wall. A high-headed small harp was passed hand over hand to the front.

"Introduce your friends," somebody called again.

The place stilled. Its high, smooth ceiling gave it a lively, bright acoustic presence she remembered well.

Most of these people had seen few offworlders, and never a telepath. "This is Shel Mattason," Firebird said. "She's . . . well, I don't go anywhere without her this week."

Laughter bounced out of one corner. Someone asked, "Can she sing?"

Shel glanced left and right, looking no less intense in her casual white pullover than in uniform. "I have no sense of pitch."

Uri extended an arm, calling, "I don't sing, either. But I enjoy listening—and it's my job to watch."

"And this is my husband," Firebird said steadily. Brennen took a short step away from the dark gray permastone wall. He *could* sing. She loved his light, pleasant tenor. Her musical training intimidated him, though, and he rarely sang in her presence . . . except at Chapter. "Brennen Caldwell saved me from a wastling's death. He has given me hope, and love, and shown me how very much more there is to the universe than I found inside palace walls. We have two beautiful sons." What else, what more could she tell them? Brennen had been Danton's strong man, lieutenant governor for the occupation. They'd already formed opinions about him. "I owe him more than I could ever repay," she added, and the truth of that statement washed away the last of her irritation. "And no," she said, "none of them can read your minds without your being aware of it."

Old Tomm Shawness pushed away from a nearer wall. Tomm had taught Firebird some of Netaia's best historic ballads, and though his singing voice creaked, his interpretations always drew cheers. "Sentinel Caldwell," he said, "if all she says is true, then we owe you a debt, too. On behalf of us all, thanks."

To Firebird's delight, most of the others applauded.

"Iarla!" Clareen's voice came from the floor, near her feet. "Firebird, give us the Iarla song!"

Wondering where the Tallan researcher turned up that two-year-old ballad, Firebird placed her hands on the clairsa's strings and played a few experimental chords. This instrument was painted with stylized vines twining up its bow and upper arch, leaving the sound box plain. She tweaked a sagging bass string, then sang her ballad with only one pause to clear her throat, and after the applause settled, she led a boisterous chorus about working conditions in places like Nello's front rooms, adding a few nontraditional chords to keep things interesting. Ballads that had survived the passage of time were anything but ordinary. The real workers sang along. Behind them, Brennen leaned back, appearing to relax.

It was too bad she didn't actually want to incite a rebellion. It could be so easy. A song from the Coper Rebellion, a short speech—

Was there a chance, after all, that her destiny lay along musical lines? She could almost feel energy coursing into her, drawn from her audience. If it hadn't been for her wastling fate, she might have pursued this kind of career. Now that she knew a mightier Singer, this almost felt like a call on her life.

She glanced down at Clareen, then over at Brennen, determined not to waste this chance at center stage. She fingered a soft arpeggio and said, "I want to tell you something wonderful, from beyond the Federacy."

Brennen raised a dark eyebrow.

"But I can't," she said. "Here's a woman who could. Clareen?"

As if she'd been waiting for just such a chance, the bassist sprang up. "There is something much better than the Powers," she said. "They're only personality traits." Someone hooted from a dark corner.

"Your electors are only people like yourselves." She touched Firebird's shoulder.

"Most of them are a lot worse than she is." That from another corner, near a gridded ventilation chute. Catcalls answered it.

"But all this"—Clareen's long hair rippled as she gestured toward both sides and up toward the sky—"came from somewhere. An infinite being is Sovereign over everything that exists. There wouldn't be time tonight to tell you about Him . . ." She looked toward Firebird.

Firebird pulled the clairsa against her shoulder. "Here's a song from the Thyrian tradition."

She tried to focus her heart on the original Singer, praying even while her lips formed lyrics. *Let these images catch in their memories. Let* me *bring mercy and light to my people.*

Before the long dreams of eternity flowed
He stood matchless, alone and sufficient
And out of the Word of His speaking
Made light, life, and time, made all things
So that over all living
He might justly command our obedience.
He is beyond time, more brilliant than light
In Him is no darkness at all.

Shackled by our selfish lust to be gods
We stand powerless, alone and despondent
And only beginning to fathom
The majesty and flawless power
Of this highest of judges
And His right to condemn us to sorrow
For we disobey, and we smother the light
And the darkness falls over all.

Holy One who made time and the light and all things—
Brilliant paradox, transcendent judge
Who promises undeserved mercy
To your servants, flawed as we are!
Holy Speaker, Shaliyah,
With your own hands lift us past sorrow
To your land beyond time, where you are the light
And there is no darkness at all.

The hymn translated jerkily into Old Colonial, but Firebird was glad that the translators had aimed for textual accuracy instead of forcing the lyrics to rhyme. For several seconds, the room remained silent. Firebird carefully avoided looking at anyone, but gave them time to reflect on what they'd heard.

Then out of a corner, someone asked, "Would you sing it again?"

Firebird did, gladly. Then, nudged by Brennen's growing unease, she handed off the clairsa and touched Shel's shoulder. "Let's go."

"Escort," ordered a small, middle-aged woman near the door.

Instantly, the people nearest the woman surged out into the night. Others surrounded Firebird as her group emerged. She felt Brennen's confusion, then his amusement, as servitors and low-commoners preceded, guarded, and followed them, ten deep in places. It was an honor they'd accorded her before, when they were concerned for her safety. This way, she couldn't see a potential assailant, but he couldn't see her either.

As they approached the door, one woman slipped into the open space around them, glanced at Shel, and kept a cautious distance. "I would like to know more about the Thyrian hymn tradition," she said. She blinked small brown eyes, then added, "And that transcendent judge."

I told you, Brenn! I told you! Firebird turned around, rose onto her toes, and pointed back into the room. "Do you know Clareen Chesterson, the bassist? That woman with the long blond hair? She can tell you more."

"I will ask. Thank you." The mob moved forward, hiding the woman once more.

Shel stayed close as Uri steered the mob to the unremarkable base groundcar. Netaians lingered while he activated the engine, and a sea of Netaian faces parted only a few at a time as he steered through the workers' parking zone. Others surrounded the gates. Uri emerged from the crowd to join traffic.

Firebird craned her neck, staring back at the crowd. "Now you see, Brenn. Now you understand why I love these people. These are the ones Rogonin sees as subhuman. These are the ones Carradee and Danton have tried to help. The people," she added as Uri turned the car out onto Port Road, "who would die in a civil war."

"And you see how little interest most of them showed in the truth."

"They listened," she said. "They were silent. That is a wonderful hymn from an artistic standpoint, too." Still, he was right. The Sentinels' Ehretan ancestors had disqualified themselves to proselytize when they gene-altered their children. She did share that heritage.

She shook her head as a maglev train sped past, one long white streak in the darkness. She couldn't help basking in the sense that she'd done something splendid. "I'm sure Clareen will talk with that woman," she said. "And they may attract others."

Brennen rested one hand on her leg. "The time will come," he said, quoting, "when truth will come in like the tide. No one will be able to deny it in that day."

In Kiel or Kinnor's time, maybe. His family would ride the crest of that tidal wave. Dozens of prophecies said so, and now she was part of that magnificent heritage. "Maybe that time is now." She stroked his hand. "Maybe the place is here."

INTERLUDE 4

Carradee opened her eyes and peered up at a skylight. At last, she and Daithi would begin Path instruction today. She rolled onto her side and eyed his therapy bed. He snored softly under a long regeneration field projector, one of Hesed's few concessions to modern technology. The twins slept in an adjoining room, which she'd vacated to move back in with Daithi.

Today.

She hadn't waited for Path instruction to start praying, though. *Eternal Speaker, Firebird's day is almost here, too. Bring her and Brennen safely through danger. Save her from the unholy Powers.* It felt wonderful to say that, even silently! *Save her from her enemies.*

Then a more personal plea. *Guide the searchers to find my daughters' real fate. Protect Hesed and everyone who lives here. Lead Netaia out of darkness. By the power of the Holy Word to Come, let it be.* Then, *Go on healing Daithi . . .* His body was starting to respond in surprising ways.

She slipped into a nightrobe, laid one hand on the regenerative projector over his bed, and kissed him awake.

He opened his eyes and said, "'Dee. I've had an idea."

She raised the projector and stroked curly brown hair off his forehead. "You wake up so quickly. I envy you."

"I read something yesterday that stuck in my mind, about the power of prayer, illogical as it seems. If the Speaker truly wants us involved in the workings of the universe, we should ask everyone here to fast tomorrow. To fast and to pray that Firebird's confirmation will proceed safely. It could be urgent."

"Tell Mistress Anna at breakfast," she said softly. "That is an excellent idea."

The strangest sensation came over her, a sense of approval and rightness. *Is that you, Speaker?* she asked, delighted. *Are you truly here in this room?*

Dust motes sparkled under the skylight, as if the sun were directly overhead.

INTERLUDE 5

Juddis Adiyn strode through Three Zed's central meeting chamber, hardly sparing a glance toward the vaulted ceiling, barely looking into the volcanic depths beneath the chamber's transparent gray floor. Onar Ketaz, commander-in-chief in Modabah Shirak's absence, had called him to the fielding station across the colony from his apartments.

The city ran smoothly in Shirak's absence. Adiyn had seen a marked decline of wisdom and focus in the Shirak family, despite his lab's best efforts. His young tech, Terza Shirak, had seemed stable enough, but Modabah had informed him Terza would not be returning, and the shebiyl confirmed it.

He did not like or trust Micahel. No longer sure the Shiraks could lead an assault on the Federacy, he might have to repair the strain or remove it. He would not order his techs to breed Micahel a son. The next namable Shirak would come from Micahel's grandfather's banked gametes.

As he passed his laboratory, he glanced in. A security lamp gleamed, lighting rows of womb-banks and embrytubes. Behind its locked inner door, in a vast cold room, lay dozens of stasis crypts—Golden City residents awaiting medical treatment, subadults culled for experimentation—and a few genc specimens, including the faithless princess who had briefly graced Three Zed with her presence. Smaller cold cases held specimens taken from Phoena's nieces. Unfortunately, no one had taken samples from the sister Firebird. No one thought she would leave here so suddenly.

So rarely was a new Ehretan family line found that Adiyn's senior staff had focused on decoding the Casvah-Angelo genes. He did have the feeling that something vital could come from the reunion of Caldwell-Carabohd with the Angelo-Casvahs . . . here, in his laboratory. He always attended to those feelings.

At 152 years old, Juddis Adiyn had reached his productive middle age. Three Zed's bioscientists had almost given this people immortality. Unfortunately, epsilon powers still deteriorated, and this laboratory's day-to-day concern was to provide injectable tissue suspension for revitalizing the ayin . . . hence the embrytubes. He'd had a few flickers himself recently. He was due for a fresh treatment.

Beyond and beneath the cold room, a deeper lava chamber housed his ancestors' biological weapons. Though his ancestors destroyed the non Altered residents of Ehret along with most of their own kindred, his people were now humankind's best hope of survival. The trade worlds had barely survived the first Sabba Six-alpha catastrophe, when that binary star spewed radiation storms out into the Whorl, disrupting travel and trade, destroying technology. Adiyn's people couldn't prevent further storms, but their potentially immortal descendants would be compelled to solve that problem. In time, they would become gods. Their servants-elect on other worlds would be altered over generations. On each world, the first new generation's genes would be manipulated to ensure die-off as soon as the second generation came to maturity. A second generation could carry any gene he chose to introduce. In the truest sense, they would be his own people's descendants.

He did hope he would live to control that phase of the experiment. After death, he expected nothing. Bliss, the Speaker's Country, and all other "spiritual" hopes for eternity were the hopes of a short-lived people, sops to their outraged sense that there ought to be more than a hundred or so years of existence.

He could do nothing for them. For Onar Ketaz, he needed to check what seemed to be a manifestation of the shebiyl.

He backed out of his lab and strode on.

The City was silent tonight, except for low voices here and there. His people wasted little time with sonic entertainments, and infants conceived in his lab lived in distant settlements until subadulthood. The Golden City was no place for youngsters, whose budding epsilon potential made them more nuisance than use.

He found Ketaz in the fielding station, not far from the main north airlock. Inside a ten-sided chamber, teams of three sat in five rounded wells, wearing gray-green shipboards and headsets, watching vast fields of space projected on ten continuous overhead panels.

Ketaz strolled toward him. Square-faced and stocky, the man was about to celebrate his ninetieth birthday. He looked forty by most worlds' standards, another triumph of Golden City genetics.

"Adiyn," he said. "I was simply standing here, watching the screens. I saw two large ships and half a dozen small fighters coming in. When I looked again, they'd vanished. The mass detectors picked up nothing."

Only a few were born with Juddis Adiyn's exceptional ability to foresee the future, along branching paths or streams of alternate reality. He could also tell, with ninety-nine percent accuracy, whether another individual's seeming shebiyl experience was genuine.

He had not bred himself any descendants. He didn't want any potential rivals yet.

He took the seat Ketaz offered.

Ketaz scattered his epsilon-energy static, and Adiyn focused a probe. Ketaz brought up the memory. Adiyn watched, second-hand, as the ships appeared to approach. They had Federate markings . . . Thyrian, in fact.

The vision flickered, looking lifeless and two-dimensional. His own glimpses had the texture of reality. This must be an illusion, created by fear and excitement.

"No," he said. "You were right to call and have it checked, but this is false. You are under stress, and the colony needs you at peak objectivity. I relieve you."

Ketaz narrowed his eyes.

"Report to second-level south," said Adiyn. "I'll call ahead."

Adiyn sensed that Ketaz wanted to object. At Second South, the colony's medics could readjust brain chemicals to ensure peak performance. He'd had it done once. Unsettling, not at all like the multisensory blast of ayin-extract injections.

Tomorrow, he promised himself.

CHAPTER 13

CRUX

subito fermata
sudden stop

For Firebird, after the excitement at Nello's, sleep came slowly. Midnight passed, and then one hundred . . . two hundred . . .

She lay awake in the dark, not wanting to nudge Brennen and ask for a calming touch. Behind her eyelids, black-haired Micahel Shirak stalked up their hallway at Trinn Hill . . . and this time, she imagined waiting for him with a dart gun.

This would be her fifth day on Netaia. Not today but tomorrow, the ceremony—then she'd have one day to conclude her charitable obligations. After that, she might fly back to Hesed and her sons, or on to Three Zed.

Actually, she'd half expected to have that fielding information by now.

She reached over the edge of the bed and touched her tri-D, wondering if Carradee thought about her as often as she missed her sons. She hoped she would return to them with the best possible gift, an end to the Shuhr menace.

She slept a little.

Her schedule had been left empty, this last day before confirmation. Tel called early and invited her and Brennen back to his estate, mentioning his newly expanded security force. She leaped at the chance to get off the sterile, unfamiliar new base—but at Tel's, she had trouble settling into any one room, and soon she regretted her choice. At the base, she could have been logging sim time.

Brennen had notified Danton of their whereabouts, and the steady hum of low-flying surveillance craft did nothing to settle her nerves. Guards in Tellai indigo and black stood at every door and sat on Tel's rooftop. She only had to stay calm and let time pass.

Impossible.

Her old palace physician, Dr. Zoagrem, arrived at ten hundred. He diagnosed stress and imminent exhaustion and insisted that this laid her open to several mutant respiratory viruses making the rounds.

If she got sick on the way to Three Zed, she could have trouble using her epsilon carrier. She had to let him give her a series of three lung-strengthening injections, an hour apart. Only Brennen's epsilon touch helped her sit still for a needle. Even Brenn had been unable to help her overcome that old phobia. They'd never dug deep enough to find its cause.

She spent the last morning hour closeted with him, locked away from Tel's hovering servitors, trying to develop a shielding visualization. Again, the quest-pulse was all she could muster . . . and it was weaker than before.

"Distracted," he observed.

"Well, yes." She rubbed her sore arm.

She tried calling Baron Erwin from a CT station surrounded by bubbling fountains. *Still in bed*, she was told, but she no longer believed it. He knew what she wanted. He refused to cooperate. Like it or not, she would have the Powers' blessing.

Brennen sent out another decoy team, and between taking their reports of a disappointingly uneventful day, he heard her recite the first quarter of her second codebook. He corrected her stumbles with uncanny patience. They nibbled exotic sweets that Tel's servitors brought on trays. She even locked herself away with a clairsa lent by Tel's staff clairsinger, but after she loosened her fingers with long-memorized scale and arpeggio exercises, nothing she played expressed anything but discordant tension.

So she ate and paced and explored the grounds with half a dozen of Tel's stiff-backed new guards. Behind her, one of them quizzed Shel about Federate training techniques. Tel walked beside Firebird like a gallant out of some old story, paying court to her ego, trying to revive old dreams of the Netaian throne.

He was almost succeeding. She could accomplish so much if she stayed here. Halting beside an artificial waterfall planted with exotic silverthroats and trailing oncidia, she turned to him. "Tel, remember what I told you. If some combination of circumstances put me on the throne, I would do everything in my grasp to introduce an alternative to Powers worship. Could you support that?"

He glanced back and aside at his guards, then crossed his arms. "I ask my servitors to keep the Charities and Disciplines. I've never punished one for neglecting them, though. Their spiritual status is their business, not mine. I simply want an Angelo in the palace again." He half bowed and then stalked back up the lawn toward the estate house. Two of his guards followed. The rest stayed with her.

She trailed one hand in the chilly cascade. She hated to think of Netaia's future resting on her shoulders. It was a weight she didn't want to carry.

Still . . . maybe the Mighty Singer had brought her back to show Netaia the difference between faith and legalism, and to save her people from civil war. Maybe she was meant for the throne.

One of Tel's guards struck a pose at the top of the two-meter falls on a newly landscaped artificial hillside. Two more stood down on the lawn, while one remained close, with Shel.

Suppose she did stay on. She would need a personal security force. The Electors had their redjackets, and every noble House had its House Guards. She should've asked for more Sentinel escorts.

A vague suspicion nettled her. Brenn wouldn't like to catch her entertaining these thoughts. He'd accuse her of the usual offenses.

But she could do so much here. She was capable. She was trained. She had the common people's support.

Hearing a step at the library door, Brennen turned around. He didn't shut the leather-bound volume he'd been scanning. Tel stood framed in the doorway, hands behind his back.

"Thank you again for the invitation," Brennen said. He reached for a velvette page marker, then closed the book, using that time to dissipate his shielding cloud of epsilon static.

Tel raised one eyebrow, curious. Brennen showed him the biography's cover. It was *Iarla of Citangelo*.

He'd enjoyed Firebird's singing last night, and he'd felt surprisingly comfortable in that warehouse after cozying up to too many swaggering nobles. Her sweet voice had carried him up and out of the demands of his mission, into a Hesed-like realm of contentment with the eternal.

Still, she must obey the codes. She must not put herself above those laws, or according to all he'd been taught, the One himself would bring her down. He needed to speak with her about pride, too. That subtle glow after the fitting had grown stronger.

"I had that out for research." Tel moved toward a long ebony table. "I've been painting Iarla First. A confirmation gift, though I suppose Firebird might not have room to pack it back to Hesed House." He lifted a cover from a large canvas square.

Brennen eyed the image underneath. The dark-haired, fiftyish woman wore Angelo scarlet, and her eyes glimmered, with amber sparkling through brown. Brennen knew little about painting, but the image impressed him as lifelike and lively. "She'll love it."

"Can anything more be done to ensure her safety tomorrow—and yours?" Tel moved closer and glanced at a long indigo lounger, but he remained standing.

"We'll have guards at every imaginable station, and new equipment, but security is stretched. The best we can do is to ensure tight protection right around us. Like this." Brennen gestured toward two corners of the estate. "Thank you again. We appreciate this deeply. It is much more pleasant than base housing."

Unclenching his hands, Tel leaned forward onto the table where Brennen had laid his book. "I'm beginning to feel responsible, to wonder if you two should have come back to Netaia at all." Tellai's sincere concern gave him a twinge of sympathetic worry. "What about the new technology, the RIA? Can you use that to defend us?"

It still felt strange to discuss RIA publicly. "Yes, but you—and everyone you can convince, on the Electorate and in the Assembly—can do more than we can to bring stability," said Brennen. "Only a unified Netaia can defend itself. Remember Firebird's simulations. Even without Shuhr interference, there's a strong possibility of civil war. Firebird's confirmation came through on the equations as a stabilizing event."

Tel shook his head, frowning. "I hadn't forgotten. I'm glad she came. I'm amazed by how little I care if the Electorate approves of me now."

"You were a follower," Brennen said. "You're emerging as a leader."

Tel chuckled. "I doubt that."

Brennen backed away. Several other portraits lined a shelfless stretch of Tel's wall. Aristocrats all, from their haughty faces and blue sashes. Brennen wondered how many Tel had collected and how many he'd painted.

That couldn't distract him for long, either. They had failed to capture a Shuhr at the palace, and the decoy groups had been ignored. Tomorrow he must be ready to step into Micahel Shirak's targeting scope. *Holy One, protect us. Take us home to our sons.* He'd half expected Firebird's physician to diagnose him, too, as stressed.

"I love her," Tel murmured, his head bowed. When he raised his chin to meet Brennen's sudden glance, he exhaled. "I assume you know that, Caldwell. I have, since—"

"Don't." Brennen tried to say it kindly.

The nobleman snapped his mouth shut.

"I knew. It will go no further."

"Not to her."

"Never to her," Brennen said, knowing Firebird had already guessed. "I've been burdened professionally by many secrets. I have reason to sympathize with yours."

Dinner started as a quiet affair, spent watching news at lap tables in defiance of court etiquette. Rogonin's network, Codex, used the occasion to chronicle the few production quotas that had declined under occupation. There'd also been high-common class protest against Firebird's return, mostly in southern cities and out on Kierelay Island. Codex reporters accused the Federates of complicity in Iarlet and Kessie's disappearance. One netter smilingly detailed an accusation that Firebird murdered Phoena herself, that her half-alien husband was using her for mysterious purposes, and the story that she'd birthed sons was fabrication. Where were these mythical princes?

Firebird glanced aside as one of Tel's servitors brought in a carafe of cruinn. "Still no luck, my lady," she murmured as she poured for Firebird. "His Grace must have gone to the country for a day."

Firebird frowned, and then the tri-D caught her eye again. A woman in drab worker's dress was speaking out against the aristocratic tradition that would spend so much money, waste so many worker hours, on one day's pageantry. "I can't believe Codex carried that," Tel said from the depths of a brownbuck chair.

Firebird agreed, but next, the announcer skipped to four men and women who wondered aloud how much of the Angelo fortune would fall Firebird's way, and how much would be hers to take offworld, after her confirmation.

She tossed a lounger pillow idly. They *would* worry about that. Frankly, she wasn't counting on a torn credit-chit after the bills came in—but it would be gratifying to build that Chapter house.

If only she'd demanded that First Lord Erwin change his blessing right then, at the rehearsal when that small Voice prompted. Now she was trapped, with no escape except to try counteracting Erwin's wretched invocation with her short speech afterward.

The other newsnets—Affiliated, a public corporation, and Drong, which had been family owned for centuries—were making a gala out of anticipation, interviewing souvenir hawkers and running old clips from Firebird's adolescence. On screen, she relived her triumph at the Naval Academy's war games, where she'd been nominated for top graduate. She felt Brennen's pleasure as it ran—and his amusement to learn that her all-Academy flight simulator record still hadn't been broken.

Then Marshal Burkenhamn, interviewed live, announced her recommissioning in the NPN. Newsnet analysts took off from that in all directions. One called it "another step toward the Federatization of Netaia."

Tel laughed. "Congratulations, Commander," he exclaimed, attempting a salute.

She grinned.

Another spin-off showed the Hall of Charity's interior, with guards at every entrance. That image metamorphosed unexpectedly into another newsnetter. "There have," he said, "been warnings that Second Commander Angelo's confirmation ceremony might be disrupted by offworld elements, despite all assurances from the Federacy. As a result, the Electorate was polled by CT. Our holy electors will not observe from the sanctum, as scheduled, but from the adjoining North Hall. His Grace the Regent wishes to inform ticket holders that tomorrow's ceremony will be segregated not by class but by preference. To accommodate all comers, the Hall will open at seven hundred tomorrow morning."

"Oof," Tel exclaimed. "No electors in the sanctum? They're scared, Firebird."

"Didn't they call you?" she asked.

"No," he said grimly. "Obviously, they know I'll be there. Did you notice how quickly they picked up on Marshal Burkenhamn's announcement?"

"Yes." Firebird glanced at Brennen. "And if we can pull it off, do you realize what this means? We could have a nave full of people who actually care what I'm doing." A nave full of sympathetic witnesses, if they managed to capture one Shuhr. Those witnesses would tell their children, and grandchildren, about watching Firebird and her security force catch a terrifying enemy. *Second Commander Angelo*. It sang at the back of her mind. *Commander, Commander, Commander . . .*

As Brennen discussed the early Hall opening with security people, Firebird called the palace and asked for six-oh-six. Paskel spoke softly. There'd been talk of delaying the ceremony one day, he admitted, but all parties—even Rogonin, consulted via interlink—decided to go ahead as planned. Paskel believed that Rogonin was anxious to see the ceremony concluded and Firebird sent back offworld.

She spent the silent ride back to base rehearsing her lines for tomorrow. *Commander*. Now that it had been announced, it felt real. She hoped Burkenhamn kept his promise about making it temporary.

As she climbed under the bedcovers, she felt a disquieting tension in Brennen. "Mari," he said softly, laying his arm over her. "Don't let all this distract you from the real call on your life, and your responsibilities. Not even catching a Shuhr is as important as one immortal spirit. Our humility is crucial, before the One."

She yawned. "Can we talk about this in the morning?" she mumbled. She rolled aside before he could answer.

She felt as if she'd barely fallen asleep when her dreaming mind was snatched into a reality more vivid than life. She sat on a gilt chair, suspended from space over Citangelo—except that it wasn't Citangelo, but an eerie transmutation of the metropolis, built over a basalt mountain that reminded her of the Shuhr's Golden City.

A Voice sang from everywhere, a Voice she'd heard like this once before, flinging the worlds into existence. This time, it addressed her, singing deep and sonorous, *Strength, Firebird. Whence your strength?*

She trembled at the solemn sound. "My strength is from you, Mighty Singer." Her feet dangled over thousands of meters of empty space. It would be easy to fall to her death.

The Voice rose one note of the scale. *Valor, Firebird. Whence your valor?*

"From . . . you." Her own voice sounded pitiful, breathy.

One by one, the Voice thundered the Netaian Powers. Each time it spoke, it ascended one note of a modal scale like the Sentinels used in worship.

Silence rang in the heavens with one Power left. Firebird clenched both arms of the gilt chair . . . her mother's chair. Her sister's chair. The chair Muirnen Rogonin had stolen from them.

Now the Voice sang in a whisper, all notes of the scale and the half steps too, a dissonant tone cluster. *Pride, Firebird. Whence your pride?*

Other voices sang a chorus out of her memory, her own thoughts and words.

Pride, impatience, willfulness.
To be Angelo was to be proud.
The pride she would feel if she saved Netaia . . .
If only Rogonin knew how easily she and Brennen could destroy him!
She could only imagine the ballads that might be sung about the wastling who saved Netaia.
Let me bring mercy and light to my people.
She could accomplish so much if she stayed here.
Maybe she was meant for the throne.
Commander, Commander, Commander . . .

And she'd turned away from Brennen tonight when he gently tried to warn her.

Of all the nine Powers, Pride was the only one *Dabar* and *Mattah* rebuked. It was her birthright and her burden. It was the Adversary's claw, caught in her soul.

—By her own permission. She'd forsworn too much of her upbringing to cling to that as an excuse, when it came down to pride.

"From myself," she admitted. The relief of honest confession balanced her pain. Maybe pride fueled that flaming, dark taint on her soul.

Pride brought you here, my child.

He did not disown her. He still called her His child.

Silence rang, a grand pause deeper and longer than Firebird could bear. She whispered to break it. "Forgive me, Singer. I wanted to save Netaia myself. I wanted—I still want to catch the Shuhr who murdered my niece, Destia." And there was more. "I want to be seen and admired, and respected . . . saluted." She'd explained to everyone that she came to serve Netaia's people, but deep in this dream, her buried reasons clamored for recognition.

Without truth, said the Voice, *you are vulnerable.*

"And . . ." Would this dream never end? She couldn't bear this. "You may have called Brennen here to get the intelligence he needs, but you didn't call me. I . . . wanted . . . I still want," she managed, "revenge. For Destia and her family."

Revenge is mine, sang the Voice.

"But I do want to help my people," she insisted. "I want to save them." She knew what she must add. She resisted. Disappointment hung in the heavens, so keen and loving that she couldn't hold back. ". . . Myself." She let it out, almost choking on that admission. "I want to save them myself, without giving anyone else the chance to do it."

The sky rejoiced again, billions of molecules dancing to music she could not hear.

"But, Singer, you brought me into this royal family. You gave me this longing to achieve and the abilities I would need. I could help the common people. Truly, I could." As she argued, her chair rose higher, and loftier, until the sky around her darkened toward black. The fall, deadly before, now looked twice as terrifying.

Pride, sang the voice, *brings a long, long fall. But never so far I cannot catch you. You are mine. Forever, I have called you. The final price is mine to pay.*

But the consequences are yours. I shatter the proud heart, so that you may wear my image.

Slowly, the gilt chair tipped forward.

But I give grace, and true peace, to the humble and contrite. To the obedient.

The chair kept tipping. Firebird scrambled around to seize its ornate back. The farther it tilted, the harder her cheek pressed against the starred-shield Angelo crest. Her body slid, first a few centimeters, then farther. "Singer!" she pleaded. "Help me!"

Know this, sang the Voice. *Even in tragedy, I am God. I am not surprised.*

She woke in a puddle of sweat.

Brennen lunged for the nightstand, where he'd concealed a blazer.

"No," she groaned. She touched his arm. "It was a dream."

"Mm," he mumbled into the pillow. Then he rolled over. "You don't feel," he said slowly, "like you had an ordinary dream."

"No." The word came out in another groan. "Brenn, I . . . I may have made a terrible mistake."

CHAPTER 14

GREAT HALL

pavillon en air
brass instruments' bells are to be directed upward

"Show me," Brennen said gently.

She buried her head against his chest, clinging to him as his presence filled her, comforting, seeking, observing. Safe in his arms, she watched the dream unwind again. Meanwhile, more accusations rattled through her mind. Her self-absorbed whining at Hesed while Brennen faced the Shuhr at Three Zed. Her eagerness to accept the Assembly's invitation, and rub noble noses in her new status, even before Brennen's people conceived the entrapment mission. Even her hope to wear Netaia's colors at Three Zed, supposedly for Netaia's honor.

Our humility before the One, Brennen had said. He'd been trying to tell her this. Pride still dominated her mental habits. If only it weren't such a long Path from the first sheltered steps to actually arriving!

When the dream ended again, she gripped Brennen tightly, still terrified by her self-imposed height.

"What can I do?" she asked, knowing there was no easy answer.

"What do you believe you should do?" His arms pulled her closer, chest to chest, until her chin rested on his shoulder.

"I don't know. Yes, I do," she realized. "I have to pray."

"I will, too."

Clinging to Brennen, she begged the Infinite for wisdom, for direction. Should she retreat, after all? Fly back to Hesed, resign her new rank ignominiously, and cancel the ceremony? That would be the ultimate death of her pride. She could never show her face on Netaia again.

No. She must not back down. Brennen needed that information. They must take a Shuhr. . . .

And couldn't that be done some other way? Danton's people, accompanied by plainclothes Sentinels, had fanned out across Citangelo—but they had turned up nothing.

Quieting her mind, she waited for an answer.

It came softly.

She could not save Netaia. Only the Electorate could do that . . . but she had offered to serve the Federacy. She had also sworn to Burkenhamn that she would serve Netaia, and she must keep those promises. At least, she had to try. The Singer would bring success or failure and show her the consequences of stepping out in pride. *I shatter the proud heart. . . .*

Do what you wish, she prayed, clenching her hands behind Brennen's back. She felt the pulse in the side of his warm neck. *But don't, I beg you, don't let Brennen suffer. Or Kiel, or Kinnor. Spare my loved ones. Everything I have . . . it's yours. Take my life, or my self-absorbed happiness. I will try to serve you.*

She pulled away from Brennen.

He kept one hand on her shoulder. "We're going ahead, aren't we?"

She nodded miserably. "Maybe He'll be merciful. Maybe I've repented in the nick of time."

" 'We are called to a higher standard,' " he quoted solemnly. "And, Mari, we'll have the biggest guard force Citangelo ever saw. He didn't tell you the Shuhr would actually take either of us."

"No." She stared into darkness. "If I backed out now, that would be the ultimate insult to the Assembly, the Electorate . . . to Netaia itself. Not to mention Governor Danton, and the Three Zed situation—"

"I didn't say you should back out. I think you're right. We have to go ahead, and we've been warned that if anything happens, it will be a natural consequence of what we've already done. Both of us. You aren't here alone. The real price, Mari—the final debt—is paid for us."

"I understand." . . . *I think*. For all her intellectual assent, she still flinched away from accepting someone else's atonement.

Brennen rolled away from her, sliding off the bed.

"Where are you going?"

His answer came out of the darkness. "I'm going to spend the rest of the night praying. Get your rest."

A vigil? Good idea. Excellent idea. She wished she'd thought of it first.

She rolled off the bed and onto her knees beside him. She could think of only one thing the Shuhr might do that would utterly break her proud heart.

Please, she begged. *Don't let them take Brennen!*

Some hours later, she stumbled out of the bedroom bleary-eyed. After a minute of shuffling through duffels, she picked out a simple dark blue outfit to carry into the freshing room. Halfway through her vigil, she'd found her recall pad, loaded the Soldane University simulation program, and run two more projections through the complex equations. Sure enough, Governor Danton could count on another half year of peace if she went through with the ceremony, whether it ended in celebration or disaster. Then, struck by a horrible thought, she ran a different chain of events. Sure enough, a Shuhr attack would also stave off civil war—but probably destroy Netaia.

Surely that wasn't your plan, she reflected. *Surely we were right to come back.*

From the adjoining cubicle, she heard percolating sounds. Brennen was already in the other vaporbath.

According to her Path instructor, acting out of pride was the spiritual equivalent of proclaiming that she was her own little goddess, her own holy Power.

I thought I'd shaken loose from them!

Fear came straight from the Adversary, though. She counterattacked with an Adoration she'd memorized before leaving Hesed.

Do battle with those who attack me.
Rise up for my help, and let them be ashamed,
Drive them off with your mighty weapons.
My soul shall rejoice in your salvation.
Who is mighty like you, rich with mercy?
Who delivers the weary, and binds up their wounds?
Clothe my enemies with shame and dishonor,
But let those who love me shout joyfully,
"Exalt the One, who defends His beloved!"

That calmed her. Live or die, they remained in the Singer's hands. Nothing could touch her, or Brennen, without His permission. *His sovereignty*, Master Dabarrah had said, *cannot operate independently of His love.*

I'm only your servant now, she prayed, and this time, she felt a difference. There was no thrill in the thought of confirmation now. She must trust the Singer . . . today like every day . . . but today, it would be much harder than usual.

Two minutes with a hot brush dried her hair. Tressers at the Hall would worry it into a style of their choice. Her physical person was only raw material to be costumed.

During their swift ride across town in an armored base car, she fought an unseen battle. Her imagination roiled, suggesting possible consequences. Death, injury. Catastrophe. A sprung trap, with no one caught inside.

She fought back: *Exalt the One, who defends His beloved!*

Streamers hung from buildings, draping them in gold and Angelo scarlet. Netaians loved pageantry.

She sent off one last frightened prayer. *Take me, if there has to be a sacrifice, like long ago in your temple. He could survive without me, but . . .*

She glanced sidelong at Shel, imagining herself six years from today, still recovering.

Brenn murmured, "You're all right, Mari?"

Staring ahead, Firebird could see his reflection in a panel that separated them from Uri and a base driver—the fine chin, the dark eyebrows framing his blue eyes. He pressed a finger against the scar on his cheekbone. Outside, the air was cold and still, a typical winter morning. Knots of people stood on street corners.

"Yes," she answered. She would not give in to fear. "Are you?"

He said, "Yes." She couldn't tell if he too was struggling.

After confirmation, and before tonight's ball, she was expected to bestow charitable gifts from her new allowance. Giving away as much Angelo money as possible seemed a worthwhile goal . . . and finding an architect. She'd meant to do that, anyway. Rogonin would be into the Angelo accounts soon, if he wasn't already.

As Port Road dead-ended on Capitol, she spotted a long line of huddled forms along the roadside, people who'd slept beside the street anticipating the traditional motorcade back to the palace.

Sadly, she wouldn't see them again. There would be a decoy car in that motorcade. She and Brennen would be flown over by Federate shuttle.

The golden cube with its ice white columns loomed ahead. She felt Brennen's dread at the sight of it, and this time, she couldn't steady him.

The Shuhr wanted him dead, not her. He was the Carabohd heir. To them, she was just a distraction.

She caught a flicker reflecting off his eyes as he glanced at her. He must've caught her worry, because instantly his dread changed to a slow, relaxed drone she recognized from Chapter worship. He'd gone beyond reciting Adorations to focusing on the Singer himself and praising Him.

She should do the same. In the Adorations, praise led to deliverance and victory.

And victory—eternal victory—had been guaranteed.

The car whisked them to the blockhouse. Black-uniformed city Enforcers escorted them through the tunnel. At a turning near the main gravity lifts, Brennen's escort urged him forward while Firebird's Enforcer waved her to the right. "I'll be a little while," Brennen said, and he walked on with Uri.

Ten meters along that corridor, the man in black opened a door. Firebird pushed through, followed step for step by Shel. Two women who'd been sitting on a bench scrambled to rise and half bow.

Now Firebird was only a player on a magnificent set, and she might as well try to enjoy what she'd come here to do. Everything lay in the Singer's hands. She must trust Him, put on confidence—that was allowed, when pride wasn't!—and walk open-eyed onto the trap's trip plate. Governor Danton's people, Thyrica's people, and even Citangelo's Enforcers couldn't catch Micahel if she and Brennen didn't lure him out.

But maybe she still could try one thing.

She turned to the nearest servitor. "I need to get a message to First Lord Erwin." She dictated her request one more time, this time as a flat refusal. She would not accept the Powers' blessing.

Then she moved toward a table piled with pressboard boxes. "All right. Where do we start?"

"With this, evidently." One woman held up a shimmering silver-white garment. "Compliments of His Excellency, the Governor."

The body armor she'd requested! She reached for it. "Decorative, don't you think?"

"He asked if you would return it undamaged."

"He sent one of these over for Brennen, didn't he?"

"I don't know, my lady."

"Have someone check. Please."

Another servitor was dispatched while Firebird submitted to undressing. The first woman went for her hair while the second slipped soft, cold, shimmering armor up her legs and arms and down her chest. It covered her body from ankles and wrists to a wide V neckline that she guessed matched her regalia, barely exposing her collarbone. "I've never seen anything like it, my lady. The Federates have wonderful technology."

"Yes, they do." Firebird had never seen anything like it, either.

An hour passed. She relaxed in the cloth-of-gold undertunic, washed down a roll with hot cruinn, and let the women arrange her hair, apply makeup, and finally dress her. She wore Brennen's chain long today, hiding the medallion low but determined not to take it off. Considering how little she'd slept, she felt thoroughly awake. Two more times, she sent servitors with messages for First Lord Erwin. Nothing came back.

The older woman held the crimson train in place for the younger to pin with shoulder brooches. This was truly Firebird's last chance to gracefully back down. She reviewed her choices, weighing the risk they were taking against the hope of capturing Micahel Shirak or his comrades—if even a

Shuhr who could blur his face to a mob was overconfident enough to walk into a building full of Federate guards! Brennen might as well still be a Master Sentinel, for all the Shuhr's chance of striking undetected.

But Brennen had said that an ES 97 Master could detect epsilon-energy uses that a room full of 32s or 50s might miss, so maybe a Hall full of guards wouldn't keep Micahel home today. Plainly, the Shuhr had waited for this moment.

Her hands shook as a servitor slipped a house signet ring onto her right hand. The women had the good grace not to ask if she was feeling all right. They knew now that there was a threat of disruption. Shel remained by the door in an attentive stance, her Sentinel midnight blue a shock in these surroundings.

More shocks like that one would be reassuring.

I trust you. You only. Yes, Brennen's obedience at Three Zed cost him terribly—but the Singer preserved his life. He'd accomplished his real purposes.

Let us serve you today, too.

Rogonin would probably watch on tri-D from the North Hall. She doubted he'd miss a chance to wear his robes of office. He valued pageantry as much as any other elector. The high-commoners who chose to attend in the North Hall's safety would still get their eyes full of electoral finery.

"Perhaps my lady would like a final chance at the freshing room?" asked the older woman.

Firebird pushed up a golden sleeve and checked tiny lights on her wristband. Two hours had passed since their arrival. Brennen had said he'd be only a little while. She hoped nothing had gone wrong with security details.

She took her smallest duffel with her, and after taking care of her most pressing business, she pulled out Brennen's old leather wrist sheath. The undertunic's sleeve was tight, but she buckled on the sheath and slipped in her night-black dagger. Also from the duffel, she pulled out Tel's tiny blazer. She checked its charge and slid it into a deep undertunic pocket. This would take a little maneuvering to draw, but she practiced, avoiding the gown's side ties and hitting that inner pocket, where she was expected to keep only a cloth for dabbing at tears of sincere emotion.

She paused in front of the mirror. What a costume, all scarlet and gold. As she slipped back out through the freshing room door, the heavy regalia steadied her stride.

To her relief, she sensed Brennen nearby. It was a splendid stranger she saw, though, standing with Uri just inside the dressing room. Could this be

Brennen Caldwell, who never wore more decoration on his uniform than a Sentinel star and the Federate slash?

Over a magnificent sapphire blue dress tunic brocaded in pearl white thread, two wide black belts crossed each other at his waist. On one belt he openly wore a holstered blazer, handgrip exposed. A dress rapier, basket handled with its blade hidden in a long silver-trimmed sheath, hung at his left hip. Midnight blue trousers vanished into supple, high black boots. At his collar, to her relief, she saw a thin rim of silver-white fabric like the body armor Governor Danton had sent her.

"My lord consort," she murmured, dropping a half curtsey. "Pray, would you grant me the first dance tonight?"

He glanced down and touched the sword hilt. "I think this part of the costume was created for sound effects." He jingled its harness. "The blade is sharp, though." He smiled faintly. She knew how he felt about bladed weapons since Three Zed.

She eyed his high boots. "You'll be able to run, at least," she said. Ruefully, she tugged her scarlet gown. "If I leave Netaia without a tri-D of you looking like that, it won't be for want of trying."

His tense smile relaxed into something more sincere. He strode closer and took her in his arms. She felt his crystace, solid and hard through his left sleeve. "The grounds have been sealed and searched, and everyone who arrives is searched, too. There's a good chance they'll have him before we walk out into the aisle."

She kissed the side of his neck. "Brenn, we could still back out. If you want to, I will."

"No," he said firmly. "For Kiel and Kinnor's sake, we will take down these murderers." Ignoring the dressers and both their bodyguards, he kissed her deeply. He had told her that before Three Zed, before Veroh, he enjoyed the challenge of hazardous missions. She'd complicated his life . . . for the better, she hoped.

To Firebird's satisfaction, the door guards admitted a tri-D man half a minute later. For fifteen minutes she struck poses, several of them with Brennen. If Rogonin had ordered portraits done now, instead of later, he probably planned his own interruption for the ceremony.

The Federates were ready.

An electoral policeman slipped in, holding the door with one half-gloved hand. "Any need to delay, my lady?"

"No," she said in a firm voice. "I'm ready. . . . Almost," she added after the redjacket left her dressing room. "Kiss me once more. Please?"

He took her in his arms and held gently, kissing her eyes with his stare before touching her lips. She felt a gentle quest-pulse assure him of her decision. Then a wash of smoky-sweet calm started beneath her consciousness and welled upward until all doubt dropped away.

"Thank you," she whispered.

"I want you standing tall."

"Me? Tall?"

He leaned down and pressed his smooth cheek to hers. "You, Firebird Mari. Show them you were born for this, whether or not they let you claim it. You can demonstrate that without pride. Anything less would be false humility." He looked left, then right. "Uri? Shel? Ready?"

"Yes," said Shel. Firebird saw Uri nod at the corner of her vision.

Brennen held the door open, and they rode the lift together. In the long narthex, the procession was forming. A redjacket led her to her place in line, behind six skirted heralds. His red coat looked drab against the rich scarlet train Firebird's dresser carried, draped over one arm.

Shel and Uri stepped back to stand flanking Brennen. Slowly, the line moved forward. Heads approached an archway ahead, then disappeared. This morning, she couldn't hear the organum from back here. A nave full of bodies deadened its acoustics.

She stepped along the narthex. On both sides of the entry, waiting for the procession to pass, stood men and women in midnight blue, her honor guard. Now she could see that Brennen's task force had raised a glasteel arch, turning the aisle into a long, clear security tunnel. She still felt uncannily calm, steadied by Brennen's epsilon blessing.

She edged forward again. Now she could hear ceremonial music swell out of the nave. She'd despised many of Netaia's formalities as a child, but never its music. A commissioned composer could push for drama at the confirmation of an heir or heiress. The swell of the Hall's massive organum wall, brass and string banks pealing together, reminded her of a Song she'd heard once, in a vision . . . though not nearly as grand as that had been. Firebird had attended services in the Great Hall whenever her duties required it, and watched tri-Ds of her mother's coronation, and—of course—attended Phoena's confirmation.

Odd that she'd seen no tri-Ds of Carradee's coronation. She must ask a palace staffer to send over a copy.

And where was Carradee's portrait?

Still no one hurried up with word that they'd found an intruder.

The glasteel arch opened to her. She moved into position and stepped onto the main aisle. She paused, looking down its scarlet shortweave carpet toward the sanctum steps. *Here I am, Shirak. Show yourself.*

The Assembly stood.

CHAPTER 15

SANCTUM

lira tutti
use the full organ; pull out all stops

Guard my heart, Singer. Protect me from pride. Feeling like a character in a myth, Firebird followed her golden-skirted heralds into the aisle. They raised their horns and answered the organum's peal of chords with a harmonized blast.

Then she walked the aisle.

She wouldn't stumble. She'd rehearsed her lines. There would be cues, too. The aisle seemed a kilometer long. Maybe it was. She let her feet follow the music and glanced side to side, through the glasteel, past security posts, into a blur of faces. High-commoners in their finery stood next to the low—and even servitors—in their cheapside best, for the first time in the Hall's history. What a gesture to offer the Federacy, a truly unifying event.

Step on, measured and slow. Had the Shuhr gotten an agent inside after all? She felt Brennen behind her and guessed he, Uri, and Shel walked in cadence, scanning the hall with their epsilon senses. Nearer the sanctum, but short of the now-perilous electors' boxes, several sashed nobles held cockhats like Tel's against their chests. She spotted Tel between a black-coated Enforcer and his bodyguard, Paudan.

She didn't see one empty seat.

First Lord Erwin stood at the broad steps' right, dressed in his white ceremonial robes. To her surprise, he clutched the rod of regency across his chest. *Rogonin's presence by proxy,* she realized.

He wouldn't be any friendlier.

Maybe Micahel, seeing their security arrangements, was waiting for the motorcade, larger crowds, and easier escape routes.

She wouldn't be in that palace car, though. She let herself relax slightly as she mounted the steps. Smoke drifted down from a censer, acrid and invigorating. A half circle of motley faces grinned down from the electors' seats. She couldn't help grinning back. Then she hastily composed her face. Who, she wondered, had selected the people to sit up here? Maybe the first arrivals were given that option, or Hall staff chose them at random. She hoped the Netaians hadn't minded *too* much when Federate guards searched them.

With a final crescendo, the march theme ended on three crashing chords. She stood on the trap's trip plate. She could almost feel the winding of springs.

She spoke her lines in a satisfyingly firm voice, substitutions and all. Near the end of First Lord Erwin's speech, his words nudged her out of the overwhelming spell of organum music. "And you shall consider yourself at the mercy of your people," he called in a theatrical, subtronically altered bass-baritone, "should they call upon you to assume the throne. Will you stand ready to serve, should the high calling to which you are now declared an heiress ever fall to you?"

Firebird glanced at the redjacket who stood behind the gowned ceremonials director, guarding the tiara that gleamed with square-cut rubies. Never the throne. Not unless all twenty-six electors changed their minds about her.

But she gave the ritual reply, knowing that even modified, it legally bound her. "I hope to serve Netaia's people," she called in a clear voice.

Frowning severely, he nodded. The director reached around for the tiara. A servitor at each side of Firebird offered an arm, and they steadied her against the costume's weight as she knelt. First Lord Erwin slid the tiara above her ears. "Let us then invoke the Powers that you shall represent," he said.

He'd made a small change in his own lines, adding *that you shall represent.* Firebird jerked her head up. "No," she said loudly. "Lord Erwin, I will not—"

As if he hadn't heard, he droned on. "Fill this your servant, O Strength . . ."

The servitors had backed away, so Firebird couldn't even stand up to make her objections heard. She could only glare and refuse to listen. Instead, she thought ahead to her Naming. *Not something horrible, like Indomitability. Please make it Mari.* Brennen's boots shone on her right, Shel's low shoes on her left.

Maybe by now, Danton's people had caught Micahel or another infiltrator—outside. That would be better than her happiest dream.

The tiara's weight forced her balance forward.

She tuned back in to Baron Erwin for a moment. He'd gotten past Resolve to Authority. Two Powers to go. Firebird strained to look up, but she couldn't see the tiara's diamond drop.

Erwin's voice droned on. "Let this woman show your face to all the worlds, Mighty Indomitability . . . and Pride, let yours be the Power that fills her spirit and mind." He raised his head, then gave a quick, self-satisfied nod.

Like a meteor burning down from the sky, something drove into Firebird's shoulder.

Brennen flung her toward the nearest wall before pain even registered. Fiery pressure tore through the muscles near her neck and deep into her chest. As from a distance, she heard shouts.

Brennen fell to his knees and seized hold of her shoulder. Mixed with the gentler heat of his access, she felt his horror.

Past Brennen, she thought she saw First Lord Erwin—someone, anyway, a white blur trying to shout orders. Tel dashed up the steps to stand behind Brennen, his own small blazer already drawn. Then a midnight blue cordon blocked her view.

So this was how it felt to be shot. *Catch him*, she begged, more of a plea than a prayer. *Catch him! He's here!* "It . . . burns," she told Brennen, reaching into her side pocket for that square of cloth tissue, "but—"

"Don't talk unless you have to." He still knelt, closing his eyes. Uri crouched beside him, covering his efforts. Firebird hoped he was remembering to look helpless. *The media's here, Brenn!* She felt a deep drain on his nervous system. When he opened his eyes, his cheeks looked pale, his scar dark. "It's an explosive projectile."

Uri nodded grimly.

She objected, "But it didn't exp—"

He seized the cloth and pressed it firmly against the top of her shoulder, close to her neck. The pressure made her gasp. "Shuhr work. It has both a shield and a timer."

Tel dropped down beside him. "Timer?"

Brennen glanced sharply at Tel and told him, "It's lodged in her upper lungs. They—" She felt the resonance vanish as he blocked fear from her perception. "It's designed to explode well after impact, and the mechanism is epsilon shielded. But they made sure I'd be able to count it down if I weren't really disabled."

Inhaling was agony. Exhaling was worse. "How long?" she asked.

"Just under five minutes," said Uri. He stood over Brennen, shielding them both with his broad back.

Tel sprang to his feet. "That's barely long enough to get her out the south door. What can we do?"

She felt queerly clearheaded, possibly from the acrid incense, maybe from adrenaline—or whatever Brennen had done to her alpha matrix before the processional—or maybe from the realization that pride had put her here.

She lay still, staring up at the men, not daring to move for fear she'd set off the . . . the tiny . . .

There was a bomb in her chest?

The gown's broad neckline and her bowed head had given the sniper a clear shot from above, despite Danton's body armor. And cruelly, he'd waited for the end of the Powers' blessing.

"Dig it out with a crystace." She looked down, coughing. Shiny blood pooled below her shoulder on the red Hall carpet. As she watched, another stream trickled down to spill over the step.

"That would kill you," Brennen said.

She had to ask, "Five minutes?"

Brennen's chin firmed. "Four. Uri, can you move it?" He shut his eyes again. She watched Uri raise a hand, felt something tug deep inside her. She gritted her teeth to keep from crying out.

Uri's hand shook. "It won't come cleanly. It's expanded in the tissue. No one can command it out without bringing most of your lung with it."

From between two other Sentinels guarding the foot of the steps, Dr. Zoagrem rushed forward. "Caldwell. How bad is it?"

"She's conscious." Brennen clenched her shoulder. Anguish started to fray the edges of his control, even his shielding. Several Sentinels stood aiming their weapons upward.

Another shot fell from the ceiling. Brennen twisted aside, flinging his arms wide. A tiny dart drove into the carpet between them, pinning Firebird's train to the floor.

They'd set a trap, too! They wanted Brennen—not dead but alive, and crippled by bereavement shock.

Her quest-pulse would accomplish nothing. "Fusion," she gasped to Brennen. "Can I help you? Is there something we can do—unless—" They'd been ordered not to use fusion energy in public, but . . . but the Mighty Singer knew she wanted to live! She felt almost giddy with relief that they didn't want Brenn dead after all. His guards would keep the Shuhr from seizing him. These consequences of her pride were hers to bear . . . except . . . *Oh, Singer, he'll suffer if I die.* She glanced at Shel, then back to Brennen.

Zoagrem pushed something against her shoulder. The sting made her gasp.

Brennen's stare refocused onto some unknown distance. Fusing energies could kill her this time, since she was already wounded—but if they did nothing, she would die. Absolutely.

"No time to experiment," he said. "We'll have just one chance." He touched her temple. "*Can* you turn?"

Doubt sickened her. She'd almost failed to turn under pressure at Three Zed. And could Brennen think clearly? She couldn't. He must choose between her life and his orders, but unless she survived, he couldn't use fusion to strike at Three Zed.

She clenched her teeth. "Don't . . . if there's a funeral, Brenn, don't let them invoke the Powers. Please."

"Never," he declared.

Shel, who'd been speaking over an interlink, hurried up. "Forgive me, Brennen, this is asinine, but His Grace insists the crown be removed."

The ruby half circlet mustn't be damaged. Firebird reached up, but she couldn't raise her right arm far enough. Shel carefully slid off the tiara as Firebird released the belt of emblems.

Zoagrem held the stinging substance against her shoulder. A Sentinel shouted orders.

Catch him, she pleaded silently, *trap him up there—just don't let him get away!* She heard more shouting out in the nave.

It took less than one of the minutes she had left to beg the Singer to care for Kinnor and Kiel. Her head swirled with disconnected thought, as if she already lay halfway Across into the Singer's world. "What are you going to try?" she whispered.

Brennen's inner shields were fully in place, and that frightened her worse than anything else. "Commanding it out, unless . . . no, there isn't any alternative. It'll wound you, but Zoagrem's here, and Uri or Shel can put you in t-sleep until we get back to base. If I get it out, though, the projectile will explode here on the dais." He wiped his mouth with one arm. "Uri, have Tel and Dr. Zed move away."

Neither budged. Tel stood between Brennen and Paudan while Zoagrem fumbled in his case. She wondered if Codex newsmen were moving into balcony position for spectacular, grisly imagery.

Brennen had trouble remote-moving objects. Even using fusion, *could* he—

"Brenn. Brenn," she said, and this time, inhaling deeply made her grunt.

"What, Mari?" He bent close to her lips. Glints in his eyes made a blurred, fiery dance in her vision.

"Could you . . . instead of trying to move it, could you make a field, a shield . . . around it? To try and absorb the . . . explosion?"

He looked at the time lights on his wrist, then back into her eyes, projecting controlled assurance that wobbled with each of his heartbeats. "Is that what you want me to try?"

"I don't know," she moaned, and then she regained control. If this was death, she didn't want Brennen remembering her weak and frightened. "Yes," she said. "Try it. Thank you, Brenn."

"By the Word, I love you." He turned his head. "Zoagrem. Give her something for pain."

She scarcely felt the jab. Hypnotized, she watched time lights change on Brennen's wrist. Twenty seconds. Fifteen. She gathered herself for the effort and felt him do the same.

He clutched her hand.

As she groped for her carrier, she felt Brennen breaching to access. Energies fused. With all the strength left to her, she clung to his point of presence, hiding from death with Brennen's strength. He would not let her see it.

Tel couldn't believe this was happening. Shel ran along the sanctum steps, shouting and shoving people away. Another pair of Sentinels tried to fire toward the traceries, but their weapons kept malfunctioning.

Did it only take one Shuhr to render them all helpless?

Paudan seized Tel's arm and pulled him down the steps to crouch behind a golden anointing font. *Ten*, Tel counted to himself. *Oh, please. Seven . . .*

Then a second tiny dart dropped from the ceiling, striking Brennen's neck, near his hairline.

"No!" Tel cried, leaping forward. As he batted off the dart, a golden figure plunged out of the tracery into the pews. Midnight blue figures converged on him from three directions as several small explosions started people screaming again.

Tel only had eyes for Firebird.

Her legs convulsed. Brennen drew up straighter, then crumpled across her. Zoagrem plunged forward and attended to Firebird. Tel pulled Brennen's shoulder up. The Sentinel's sapphire blue sleeve was soaked in blood. Tel couldn't look down any farther. Another center of shouting and scuffling erupted near the south door.

Brennen's eyes barely opened as he pushed up to crouch. Shel Mattason hurried to his side.

"No pulse." Zoagrem reached into his case for another injection ampule. "Did you . . . could you contain the—?"

Caldwell exhaled, shaking. "Not completely."

Tel looked now. Where he'd feared to see her torn open, she lay unconscious . . . no, Zoagrem said her heart had stopped. Dead? Her eyes rolled upward. Her lips had drawn back, showing her teeth.

Zoagrem pressed the ampule to her shoulder, watching his scanner. "It's trying to beat and can't. The sinoatrial node must have been destroyed, and Powers only know how much heart and lung."

Caldwell rubbed his mouth with one sleeve again. This time the sleeve left a bloody stripe across his chin. "Shel," he managed, "I've lost my turn. Put her in t-sleep. Hurry." Then he collapsed.

Tel turned around. To his horror, the golden figure came on, seemingly striding a meter in the air—leaping along pew backs, mowing down guards and spectators with a projectile gun. No one else's weapon seemed to be firing. The intruder wore a cloth-of-gold hooded skinsuit, his face and hands glimmered, and even his eyes gleamed the unnatural shade. Netaians scattered, trampling those who had already fallen.

Midnight blue figures fought the fleeing crowd, trying to reach the gold man with their crystaces. On the sanctum, the Caldwells' bodyguards crouched close to their fallen charges. Zoagrem shouted orders to arriving medical aides.

The golden figure leaped down into the open space in front of the sanctum.

Well, if he's got some way to freeze our blazers—

Tel drew his dress sword and stepped into his path, determined to buy Firebird two more seconds of life if he could do nothing more. For the second time, he looked down the sights of someone else's weapon—

Then popping noises erupted from several directions. As Paudan charged, the gold man changed course, headed for the south door. Tel lost him in the crowd.

Distant sirens wailed.

Terza watched live tri D coverage over her father's servo table in the apartment across town. An aerial shot followed an evac van speeding up Port Road toward the Federate base.

She doubted Caldwell was in it. An atmospheric shuttle idled on the roof, ready to transfer Micahel's prisoner to their transport ship.

A tone sounded, indicating the security garage had been breached. Two crewers were downlevel, guarding that entry. Another sat between Terza and her father, while two others readied the shuttle.

She stepped away from the servo table. At any moment, she would see her child's gene-father.

To her horror, she did think of her hypothetical daughter as a child—no morula, no embryo, none of those comfortable, distant terminologies. The cells growing, dividing, and (by now) differentiating inside her were the building blocks of a life.

She wanted to shriek, to deny the change in her soul. Instead, she buried it behind her deepest shields. Few of the unbound ever bonded to any other. Under Testing Director Polar, she'd been taught how to evade pair bonding; otherwise, it was an inevitable consequence of sexual liaison. But Terza had formed a bond of exactly that sort, the kind breakable only by death.

Her father also stood, and he stepped toward the lounge area.

Micahel swaggered through the rear entry alone.

Modabah blocked his son's path. *What happened?* His question, freely broadcast, echoed through Terza's mind.

She's dead, came the answer, *but I couldn't get to him*. Micahel stalked to the table, took Terza's vacated chair, and sat down.

Dead, Terza reflected. The woman was gone, and Brennen Caldwell would be half dead with bereavement shock. Evidently he *was* in that evac van, riding beside whatever remained of his mate.

Then would Modabah send Terza onto the base to draw Caldwell out? She dreaded what Talumah might do to her mind, preparing her and protecting her compatriots.

Affiliated News still blared over the tri-D set, playing and replaying key moments from the interrupted ceremony. Micahel fell silent, watching. Terza looked over his shoulder. Modabah rubbed his chin.

The Angelo woman knelt. Close-up, headshot—she blinked once as the tiara was set on her head, then stared forward.

At least she died a princess. Or did she? She'd worn the tiara, but they never made the official proclamation.

As if it mattered now. In slow motion, the projectile tore into her flesh. It seemed to take her several seconds to gasp and tumble out of closeup range. The field widened to show her lying prone, her supporters dropping to their knees.

"See that?" Micahel demanded aloud. "That was a marksman's shot. The explosion killed her. I darted Caldwell, but I couldn't get to him. He won't show himself, won't move, for days or weeks. In that much time, we can easily infiltrate the base and take him. Easily. We'll own the RIA technology and then the Federacy. All that with one shot."

Hearing the defensiveness in his voice, Terza avoided looking at him or their father.

The image played once more. Terza leaned closer, still surprised to see so little blood. The image shifted, showing a scuffle near one of the hall's side doors. She recognized Ard Talumah, costumed as a nobleman, clearing a path for her brother's escape.

"They haven't announced her death," Modabah said gruffly.

Micahel raised his chin. *What's keeping them?* he wondered without shielding.

Their father sat back down, settling onto the last vacant servo chair. "Official announcements require protocol here. Or she might not be dead."

Micahel laughed. *Not this time.*

The security tone sounded again. This time, Ard Talumah slipped through the inner door, clothed in celebratory scarlet. A nobleman's blue sash completed his costume. He touched his forehead in salute and sent, *Congratulations, Micahel.*

Your disruptor grid worked, Micahel sent with a magnanimous sweep of both arms. *I got into position before they closed the hall for security, set up the grid, and stayed behind my own personal shields.*

Polar had excellent shields. Obviously, you studied with him. And skinsuit armor looks good on you. Ard Talumah poured himself a drink. "Look, there you go." He pointed back to the tri-D image.

Terza watched Micahel flee in miniature, saw Federate guards close in at the south door. This time, she spotted Talumah sooner. "Why didn't you just stay up there?" she asked Micahel.

He shrugged. "And miss this?" He stepped closer to the tri-D. "I changed clothing down in the tunnel, and then we separated—blended into the crowd. I looked a Sentinel straight in the eye and ducked a sorry excuse for an epsilon probe. It was almost too easy."

Terza managed to smile.

The replay shifted to real-time. As the evac van vanished into a tunnel on base, an announcer tolled the names of dead Netaians.

She only half listened. On the sanctum steps, there simply had not been enough blood, if that projectile had exploded.

A new face appeared center-screen, the sandy-haired Federate governor. "Not Rogonin." Micahel turned to Talumah. "He must be opening old wine."

"I have an update on Second Commander Firebird Angelo Caldwell's condition," Danton began.

Terza felt Micahel's alarm. *No! An announcement! You want to make an announcement!*

Modabah glanced his direction and said, "Hush."

Danton hadn't stopped speaking. ". . . lodged in lung tissue, four centimeters from the heart." Another picture replaced Danton's face. Diagnostic imagery of a ruined lung roused Micahel's pride, and he let everyone in the room feel it. He had placed the cartridge perfectly. But—

"Her chest should've exploded," he protested. "You gave me a defective cartridge—"

"Shh," said Modabah and Talumah.

". . . Caldwell evidently was able to partially contain the explosion. Again, Lady Firebird Angelo Caldwell has been rushed to Citangelo's Federate military base, where she remains in critical condition. . . ."

"*Contain* the explosion?" Talumah demanded.

Terza stared.

Modabah straightened his stooped back, sitting as tall as he could. "Then Caldwell is no ES 32. They falsified college records. Harris must be a Master, too. Or Mattason. They must have linked. And obviously, you missed him with that drug dart."

"It hit his neck. Left side, back." Micahel picked up a writing stylus, broke it in half, then broke each half again. "He couldn't have contained that much physical force. Not even a Master could do that."

"There was something else," said Talumah. "I was less than twenty meters away. Someone did expend energy."

Modabah craned his neck. "Why didn't you say something?"

Talumah raised his glass. "I only now realized it was epsilon power. I thought it was a blast wave from the explosion. I felt it as a physical force. It was huge, enormous."

"The RIA technology?" Modabah suggested. "Shef'th," he swore, "have they already learned to miniaturize it?"

"I don't know." Ard Talumah drained his drink, then yanked off his blue sash.

Modabah steepled his fingers. *We need to get onto that base*, he subvocalized slowly, *before Caldwell can get off it.* He turned to the wide-eyed lackey next to Terza. *Get every operative on world here, in this room*, he ordered. *Tomorrow morning, before six hundred.*

Then his glance rested on Terza, and she lowered her eyes.

Five hours had passed since the shooting. Brennen stared down at his bond mate's pale face. She lay propped against a large pillow, and a slender tube drained fluid from her chest. Beneath the microfiber blanket he'd raised to cover her, her torso was bruised from neckline to hip. Meds had clamped a regenerative field source over the cauterized new suture that crossed her ribs. Arching from one side of the bed to the other, its green-and-white surface was interrupted only by a control panel and a series of monitor lights. Besides hastening the cardiac muscle's self-repair, it would speed thoracic healing: the torn muscles, the microbreaks in her ribs. She was already well beyond physical danger, but if they hadn't achieved fusion before that dart hit him, she would be dead.

The small bruise on the back of his neck was his only injury. Ultradialysis had cleared the dart's dose of blocking drugs from his system even before Mari emerged from reconstructive surgery.

A twisted mass of scorched metal fragments and several grams of spent explosive had been extricated from her chest cavity before the base surgeons repaired her inner wounds. She was expected to recover quickly, but Micahel's slug-thrower and the resultant pandemonium had killed sixteen Netaians. Twenty-eight more lay seriously wounded. According to Uri, a second Shuhr had hidden in the crowd near the south door, dropping his camouflage only when it looked as if his partner might be taken. No one saw them leave the Hall, though Federate and Netaian security—working together, one small miracle in the midst of these failures—had kept the grounds sealed and released spectators in small groups after weapons inspectors cleared them. Grim-faced Sentinels, sensitive to any flicker of epsilon-energy use, backed up the inspectors.

A miniaturized field projector, found smashed in the overhead tracery, was suspected of disrupting all the energy blazers.

How had he gotten in past security?

Brennen exhaled heavily. *Was this the cost of our pride, Holy One?* Sixteen Netaian lives, two Sentinels among the seriously wounded . . .

And empty hands.

He stared down again, assuring himself that Mari was only sleeping off a surgical anesthetic. Her chest rose and fell against the bridgelike field generator. She would have been ripped in two if that dart had hit him one second sooner, preventing their fusion.

In hindsight, maybe he could have penetrated the device and defused it. Maybe he could have spared her some of this. Could have . . . but how?

Standing beside him, Zoagrem shook his head. "That injection series she took yesterday gives us another advantage. Her lungs started regenerating almost instantly after penetration. Pulmonary damage will be minimal."

"But her heart . . ." Brennen trailed off.

He didn't have to drop shields to see Zoagrem's satisfaction. "The cardiac nerves have been replaced. Parts of the right atrium and ventricle temporarily lost contractile ability, but the surgical team had them beating again within the hour." He frowned. "There's been considerable thoracic trauma, though."

Psychic trauma, too, though the Netaian couldn't see that. Brennen had sensed the breaks that smashed across her alpha matrix as fusion energy coursed through her at the moment that should've been her death. Maybe the alpha-matrix trauma was what kept scarring her ayin.

And the assassins had escaped. *Bedim them!* Had Micahel Shirak chosen to dress in gold because of Brennen's fears, or was that just a coincidence?

"She's a fighter," said Zoagrem. "Always has been." The palace med glanced nervously over his shoulder as someone walked down the base infirmary hall. "In a day, we'll have a more specific prognosis. But I wouldn't worry about her long-term chance of recovery."

Not unless the Shuhr penetrated this base! The Federates were absolutely right to fear those people. His own kindred lived under so many restrictions that no one could have guessed—until the Shuhr showed them—what they might have become.

Brennen sensed someone else at the door behind him. He looked around to see the infirmary administrator, a broad-chested man whose cleanly shaved head gleamed under hallway lights. "An announcement must be made," he told Brennen. "Governor Danton insists you approve the wording."

Reading the recall pad, a common media release detailing his Mari's near-death, he shuddered. "Strike this," he said, pointing to a suggestion that he had helped her survive. That must not be publicized. "If I could have helped her, she wouldn't be here. She would be . . . with me," he realized. "On a dance floor."

CHAPTER 16

SURVIVAL

molto rubato
taking great liberties with tempo, as expression
demands

Firebird blinked up at an institutional white ceiling. The upper half of her bed was tilted to make breathing easier, but the humming metal-and-composite arch of medical machinery wedged her down. She could move her arms, but not far. She'd been medically dead for a quarter of an hour.

The Shuhr had almost taken her—and Brennen had recognized the golden face in newsnet broadcasts. Micahel was there, himself. But he'd gotten away!

Though the "news" was now eight hours old, all three nets were still playing and replaying the shooting from every angle imaginable. Brennen had looked princely, poised. Elegant.

Why hadn't the guards looked up? Or had they, and had Micahel Shirak shielded himself from sight? They now knew Shuhr could blur their faces in an observer's vision. Was that how he got past the exit screening?

The small woman above the tri-D projector fell. A scarlet train wrapped her like a shroud. Blood pooled beneath her. Close-up, freeze frame: It had been a master sniper's shot, missing both collarbone and shoulder blade to penetrate her chest.

Nauseated, she waved off the set. The ragged entry wound in her shoulder burned under a layer of biotape.

She couldn't as easily wave the sniper's image out of her mind. At Trinn Hill, his face had been blackened. This time, it glimmered with gilt.

Firebird groaned, shifting on the pillow. Pain blocks made her restless. So did the notion of lying here while the regen field accelerated her recovery.

But if she checked out of regen therapy, she'd have no chance of being cleared to fly combat at Three Zed—if ever they could get a Shuhr in custody.

Dear Singer, she sighed, *thank you for taking us out of there alive. Deliver my people from the threat of war.*

But, my Lord, will you stop at nothing to keep me from dancing with Brennen? She sighed, hoping the Singer wouldn't think that irreverent. She'd been taught to be honest in prayer.

She felt dead from hip to neck, due to the pain blocks. She wished she'd struggled up off her knees and challenged First Lord Erwin about that blessing, right there in the sanctum. She nearly had died, with those words almost the last ones she heard. From now on, she would be more outspoken about her faith.

And on the subject of speaking . . . though Firebird had sworn no one would ever use the title, netters were calling her "Princess."

Not for long! They could call her "Commander," if they had to call her anything. Her shallow, half-pretended nonchalance toward that high gilt chair had turned to real aversion. She reached toward a call button, then fell back on her pillow. It hurt to raise her arm.

He'd gotten away. Anna Dabarrah was right—she should've stayed at Hesed with her babies.

Sixteen Netaians were dead. She wanted justice for them, not revenge on the one who had done it. Something inside her had changed . . . no, the shift went even deeper. Something had died. Pride, maybe.

Half a dozen more Netaians might die before morning. She could never compensate their families for that loss, not even if she'd inherited the entire Angelo fortune instead of a token allowance.

Near midnight, Brennen squeezed her hand, relieved to find it warmer than before. She scowled and struggled to shift under the humming regen projector.

From a pocket in his wide belt, Brennen pulled the bird-of-prey medallion on its chain, its wings swept back almost to touch each other. One of the surgeons had brought it out to him. He no longer cared if it was gold, silver, or lead.

"How do you feel?" he asked.

"You of all people don't need to ask," she muttered.

He did feel her frustration and remorse, and even some of her numbness came through as a vague dampening of sensation. He dropped the medallion on her bedside table, carefully coiling the chain in a spiral.

She added, "I'm sorry. I make a rotten invalid. How soon can I get back in the flight simulator?"

"Not today, Mari." She *must* be fit to fly before they could get to Three

Zed—but were all their hopes built on a false assumption? Maybe the Shuhr were genuinely untouchable.

"It could be close, couldn't it?" There was a plaintive note in her voice.

"Your medics have planned a regimen. You've got to stick to it." Regen time, a gradual increase in physical activity, and a return to sim training had all been mapped out, hour by hour. "You need twelve days, minimum." Or she'd be a liability, not an asset, at Three Zed. Assuming those were his orders.

"Like a limpet mine," she declared. "And thank the One for onboard gravidics. Without those, I'd be grounded for good."

"There's one man I want to ground for good." He touched the pocket recorder he'd added to his belt. "Danton sent out some of our currently unemployed infiltrators on surveillance teams. They'll find him. One of the Sentinels at the Hall did let him leave."

"I don't understand. Did the guard remember him later?"

Brennen nodded. "That implies that the Shuhr can cause temporary amnesia, besides their permanent memory blocks." *One more ability we never suspected.* "But we finally have Micahel's alpha-matrix profile. He's detectable now, if he turns up in public."

"And how did he get in?"

"It looks," Brennen said, "as if he'd been in position for some time, possibly in t-sleep. No one sensed him there."

She sighed. "What about your cover? Your epsilon rating, the fusion . . ."

"I think it held. I want to go check, though, if—"

"Please stay." She reached toward his hand, and he saw how the effort made her wince. "I was afraid you would die in there. I can't imagine why he aimed for me instead of you."

But Brennen had been trained to notice deception. He saw it plainly now.

"I can," he said grimly, "and so can you. RIA. They want me alive, just like we want one of them." He reached for her hand. Her proud heart really had been broken—literally—but someone, somewhere, had covered her with prayer. "Promise me you'll rest and not fight the regen arch or demand to watch Rogonin's version of the news."

The sensations radiating from her reminded him of a trapped animal, panicked and unable to stop struggling. She stared straight ahead when she said, "I promise."

He laid a hand on her forehead and stroked her alpha matrix, in the tender way only he could calm her. Eyeing the humming arch, he wished such technology could've repaired his own injuries. Certain tissues, such as cardiac muscle, responded with amazing speed to regen therapy.

But the mind was more than nerve cells and electrical impulses. No physical device could repair what he'd done at Three Zed.

He glared at the bird-of-prey medallion, willing it to rise on the bedside table. The chain barely rustled. Even that effort made his temples ache.

Too tired, he reminded himself. He, too, needed sleep.

"Please read me an Adoration," she mumbled. "I left my *Mattah* back at our quarters."

He didn't want to wave on a light, and anyway, he'd been meditating on one Adoration for most of the last ten hours, praying that if this truly was the time to strike Three Zed, that divine call would come. " 'The Holy One,' " he quoted, " 'long-suffering and just, will one day release His vengeance. If the wicked will not repent, He will sharpen His sword. He has prepared for himself deadly weapons. . . . ' "

Firebird smiled faintly.

Another woman sat up late, watching a rebroadcast. From a bedroom in her father's apartment, Terza Shirak stared into the space over a media block. Her eyes fixed on the small, handsome figure in sapphire blue. He knelt with his eyes closed in concentration, then fell prostrate across the woman who ought to be dead.

She'd give a hundred Federate gilds, a thousand, to know what he'd done. Once, he'd been rated ES 97. *Would his gene-daughter inherit that carrier strength?* Terza wondered. But no Master Sentinel, regardless of potential or training, could have defeated that exploding shell, so well lodged.

This must have been a demonstration of the Sentinels' RIA technology. She wondered when Tallis would announce that.

Sighing, she turned away from the screen.

With that kind of power . . .

Alarmed by the thought that whizzed through her mind, she raised her inner shields and trapped it for future consideration. She glanced at her door, then extended a quest-pulse through it.

The others had gone out, undoubtedly assembling their forces. Now they must penetrate a military base. Impossible by nongifted standards, but Terza didn't doubt they would succeed.

She let the thought rise again.

A man with abilities like Caldwell's, assisted by RIA technology, might— might—be able to stand even against her father and brother. Might be able to shelter one woman's attempt to escape from the Shuhr.

There. She'd thought it at last. Escape . . . and she'd called her own people *enemy*, by using the Sentinels' word. In their ancient common tongue, *Shuhr* meant foe, adversary.

Squeezing her eyes shut, Terza gripped the edge of her bunk. Unknown by her consciousness, the urge to escape had grown stronger while she held it down under her inner shields. Stronger, and more complex. To live free on Thyrica, where her daughter might have the casual happiness Terza never knew . . . where she might grow strong in the wind and sun, instead of banks of lights . . . on a world where the most severe penalty for weakness was the denial of training, not immediate death. . . .

She'd had one friend as a little child. One of the few light-haired youngsters at Cahal, Caira always let Terza choose games and usually let her win. When the first competence evaluations were given, Caira vanished.

Terza's stomach fluttered. She hadn't eaten in hours. She reached for a tin of fruit biscuits she'd stashed beside her bed.

When they sent her to the base, they would watch-link her mind in such a way that she could bring others inside the link, so Modabah or Talumah could observe and control her. She didn't dare wonder if her inner shields might give her some defense against that strategy.

Adiyn had said that they wanted the child she carried—for breeding stock. He'd talked mockingly about creating antimessiahs, using Caldwell's genes.

Terza couldn't move openly, but for his own child's sake, Brennen Caldwell might help her escape. That had been compassion she'd seen in him . . . plain, raw grief . . . as he knelt above his fallen bond mate.

A bond mate Terza never would be, but her child carried his essence in every cell.

She shut her eyes and cursed pregnancy hormones.

Well past midnight, Brennen lay awake on a cot that base staff had wedged into Firebird's room. Shel had only left this door when Brennen lay down and Uri took over.

She *would* recover, he reminded himself. He'd sent reassuring coded messages to Dabarrah and Carradee via the first messenger ship leaving Netaia. For the first time, though, he doubted the wisdom of bringing her to Three Zed. They hadn't taken a prisoner yet. The strike might be delayed indefinitely. He had to hope so, for her sake.

On the other hand, every day they delayed gave the Shuhr more time to attack other worlds—and get RIA technology.

At least Danton's watchers in low-common neighborhoods were sending good news. For the moment, Citangelo's people had united in concern and in anger that the same Shuhr who cratered Sunton had struck in Citangelo. They were in no mood to throw off the electors. For the moment, they were blaming neither Firebird nor the Sentinels for drawing an attack. Some were even demanding a stronger Federate presence.

One newsnet report, though, quoted rumors that Firebird had died, and the Federacy was covering up. Brennen guessed that was an attempt to draw her out into a vulnerable position, so Micahel Shirak might try again.

Not here, Brennen vowed. *Holy One, salvage this situation. You can use even our mistakes for a greater good.*

This base could withstand a siege by conventional weaponry, but not for long. How long could it hold back the Shuhr?

At least none of the most disquieting reports would reach her. Danton's people had scrambled Codex on her set.

He shifted on his cot, unwilling to look away. When he closed his eyes, he saw her crimson blood. She slept restlessly, but at least she slept.

So this was His Grace the Regent, Muirnen Rogonin.

A dim winter's sunrise filtered into the sovereign's day office through its east window. As Terza followed Talumah and Micahel down three carpeted steps onto an inlaid wooden floor, she wondered if he depended on props, such as the five translucent world globes suspended over this sunken floor, or the elevated platform on which his desk stood, to command respect. He was neither attractive nor wise-eyed, and though his vanity implant created a youthful illusion, overconsumption was his obvious weakness.

With Firebird gone from the palace, the ten-plus epsilon presences had also vanished. Muirnen Rogonin would never know that his rival's presence had protected him—briefly—from his real enemies. Today marked the end of his volitional independence.

Micahel walked across an inlaid sun, complete with solar prominences, that had been created in some gold-grained wood. He stepped up to desk level and reintroduced himself and Talumah, then presented Terza.

On cue, she stepped forward. "I bring my father's greeting," she said, as ordered. "He is Modabah Shirak, hereditary head of all the unbound starbred."

In Rogonin's terms, that made her royalty. He raised his head. "What is your title, then, as his daughter?"

"No title is necessary."

"Then I am to call you. . . ?"

"Terza. Terza Shirak."

He glanced at Micahel. "Are you . . ." He flicked a finger back and forth. "Related?"

"Distantly," Micahel answered, and Terza spotted disdain in the narrowing of his eyes.

Disquieted, she looked away.

"Very well, Terza," said the regent. "Sit down. Tell me more."

One of his attendants pushed a chair away from the wall at one end of the platform, and she sat down across from him. A minute ago, he'd been openly suspicious. Now he meant to flatter her.

Talumah remained standing beside her, under one of the five globes. She'd been told that they stood for Netaia, two other settled worlds in this system, and its two buffer systems. "Our people," he said, "wish to establish an observation post in this residence." Terza felt a flicker of protest, then the counterflicker as Talumah smoothed away Rogonin's objection and went on speaking. "We are disappointed, of course, that Lady Firebird survived our attack yesterday."

"Disappointed?" Rogonin's cheeks flushed. "You killed sixteen of my subjects. That is inexcusable, unforgivable—"

In that moment, Talumah thrust a breaching probe deep into the regent's alpha matrix. Terza felt the backflash. Rogonin sat motionless, wide-eyed, clutching both arms of his throne-chair. Talumah worked swiftly, manipulating Rogonin's will exactly as he'd mind-altered Princess Phoena.

Exactly as he would manipulate her if they discovered her secret hope.

The silence lasted ten minutes, and Micahel kept his stare on Ragonion's attendants. Then Terza felt echoes of epsilon activity fade away. Rogonin's contorted face relaxed. He drew a deep breath.

Memory block firmly in place, she understood.

"We now wish," said Talumah, "to penetrate the Federate military base. Help us only a little, and we will eliminate your Federate overseers."

Rogonin spread his hands. "Gladly. Tell me how."

Micahel stepped toward the long desk's other end. "We want to take the base in two stages, probably an hour apart. First, it is still crucial to kill Lady Firebird and take General Caldwell prisoner. We still assume you would not regret losing *that* subject."

The regent straightened in his gilt-crusted chair, clasping fleshy hands. "No. I would also be pleased to see the lord consort gone, permanently. Terza," he continued, looking back at her, "tell me, and the secret will go no further. What really happened to the young queen whom I serve as regent? Carradee's daughter, Iarla Second?"

She glanced up at Micahel, who was deeper inside their father's confidences.

Go ahead and answer, he sent. *This is one secret he'll keep.*

She turned back to the regent. "Iarla and her sister are dead, Your Grace."

He inhaled slowly, smiling. "Tell me more."

Disgusted by his delight in child murder, Terza used her inmost shields. "Step forward, Talumah." The taller man made a mocking half bow to the regent. "My co-worker," Terza said, "intercepted a Federate shuttle carrying them to the Inisi system. He destroyed it as it reentered normal space." She didn't tell him about the tissue specimens preserved in her laboratory, nor her supervisor's interest in the Casvah genetic line.

Casvah. A thought struck hard. What if . . . what if it were *Firebird* whose epsilon potential saved them yesterday? Or maybe, some psychic union of the Casvah line with the Carabohds? If so, then those Casvah specimens in Terza's laboratory could have the same potential. They might give her people the powers that had just saved Firebird from certain death.

Talumah stared down over her shoulder. She felt his epsilon probe lick up that thought. He raised one eyebrow, radiating pleasure. *Yes*, he sent, *that is possible!*

"And then?" Rogonin asked Micahel. "What about your second stage?"

Enraptured by his own destructive fantasies, Micahel seemed to have missed Terza's exchange with Talumah. "We will destroy Citangelo Occupation Base," he said, "just as we hit Sunton on Thyrica."

Rogonin's fleshy face turned pale. "Yes, we heard about Sunton . . . but . . . Citangelo . . ."

"This time," Talumah said slowly, and Terza felt the calming overlay, "we will not take out the entire city. There is enough distance between the base and this district that the finer homes will be spared."

"How soon will you strike?" Rogonin asked, clenching the arms of his chair. "I want my family sent out of danger."

"There is no danger." Micahel spread his hands.

"How . . . soon?" Terza felt the effort that question cost Rogonin. His will was strong to be able to question them at all.

"As soon as you can give us ships capable of this kind of attack. Sooner, I think, than Lady . . . *Princess* Firebird," Micahel taunted, "and her lord consort can leave the base. She may not be dead, but she shouldn't be moved."

"Excellent." Rogonin finally succumbed, touching a desk control that lowered the large, central globe to just over head-high. Now Terza recognized the coastlines of Netaia's North and South continents. Another flick of his finger created a glowing zone on the globe. An enlargement of the glowing area focused over his right shoulder, on a projection panel she'd mistaken for a wall. "The spaceport district," explained the regent, "is badly in need of urban renewal."

Micahel smiled slowly. Terza choked on the urge to tell Rogonin that his spaceport district, if Micahel got several warhead-loaded ships through, would be the rubble-strewn deep spot of an uninhabitable crater.

"Regarding your first stage," he said, "I have a suggestion. First Marshal Devair Burkenhamn of the Netaian Planetary Navy has gone over into Lady Firebird's camp. I saw them speaking at my daughter's presentation ball, and he just reinstated her into the Planetary Navy. With a promotion," he added, frowning.

"So we heard," said Talumah.

Rogonin nodded. "Since she has reason to trust him . . ."

Terza plainly felt his last struggle for independence. Then he blurted the words, "Could your people use him as an assassin? He lives out in the city, but he works on base."

Terza raised one eyebrow. Ard Talumah wouldn't have planted that suggestion but commanded Rogonin to serve them with full loyalty and his favorite "impossible" ideas.

For all Micahel's murderous skills, Modabah seemed reluctant to let him penetrate the base at ground level. So he would send in Burkenhamn—and Terza.

"That bears consideration," Talumah said slowly.

Rogonin stared down at Terza. "Are you all right, my dear? You look pallid."

"Your Grace is a fine strategist," she said stiffly.

"Obviously, I have employed fine agents." Rogonin spoke firmly now, his alpha matrix reorienting to its newly imposed loyalty. He called up another map projection. "For your second stage, I suggest using Sitree Air Base. I can give you access codes. You can get other information when you . . . when we interview Marshal Burkenhamn."

"Excellent," said Micahel.

Terza looked aside, at Talumah. He paid Rogonin's props no attention at all. She could almost feel his mind racing.

Casvah-Angelo and Carabohd-Caldwell, Terza reflected again. Casvah and any Ehretan line, maybe. The Angelo woman might be key to their victory, after all. Firebird . . . and Terza's child, to get them to Caldwell.

INTERLUDE 6

Second Lieutenant Aril Maggard dropped into her seat on *Babb*'s crowded bridge and entered another tick mark at one corner of her com console. They had been eighteen days in Inisi space and found no trace of the little girls' shuttle. Curious by nature, Aril had studied the Federate register between watches. She guessed she'd learned more about Netaia's customs and its noble families than most other Federates knew about their home worlds.

With this much time gone, though, hope had faded. The diplomatic runner's supplies would have run out some time ago. Aril's best remaining hopes were to see a footnote entered in Netaia's history . . . or better still, to go back to Lenguad and get on with her life.

She really would prefer someone else found them now, if they were in Inisi space.

The salvage ship lurched as *Babb*'s pilot fired braking thrusters. "Almost on sector," he announced.

Aril activated her scanners and leaned back, stretching.

An hour later, the shift's first *ping* brought her upright. The second curled her forward over the scanning screen. "Debris," she called. "Metallic, irregular. Considerable mass."

Major Dunn leaned over her shoulder and ordered, "Block the quadrant and rescan. Transponder check and mass estimate."

"Transponder check and mass estimate, aye." Aril stroked her controls, first defining a scan volume, then collecting data. She read off a mass figure, then craned her neck to look up at Major Dunn. "Transponder confirm, ma'am." This was the missing shuttle.

Could they still be alive?

The officer frowned. "Check life signs."

Aril had already flicked another scanner. A red light glimmered on her board. "Negative, Major." She said it calmly, but her chest went tight. She had several young nieces and nephews.

Maybe they'd gotten away in a rescue pod.

Major Dunn took the command seat. "Helm, take us closer. Scanners, spotlight whatever there is to see. Com, call Inisi base. I'm afraid we may have found them."

Minutes later, Aril's neck and shoulders ached from sitting in one position, staring, waiting to activate the big lights. At last, she switched them on.

The underside of a Tallan courier appeared, rotating slowly. Even from this angle, Aril could see that several steering units had been blown off. "Confirm battle damage," she said. She'd seen this before. It had never affected her quite so deeply.

"Match speed and rotation," the major ordered.

On the main screen, a long, gaping tear with metal and composite hull curled back from its edges drifted into view. The cockpit had taken a direct hit. Aril stayed at her post while two salvage workers donned extravehicular suits and exited the main lock, carrying rescue bags and remote imaging equipment. She touched a control that split the main screen. It continued to display the damaged courier's exterior but added a view from the salvage team's imager.

Avoiding the tear, they approached the main lock.

It hung open.

"This ship has been boarded since impact," said a young male voice on the cabin speakers. The image on Aril's screen bumped and shifted as the imager jiggled, then floated steadily inward. The powerless shuttle had naturally lost all gravidics. "Crew of six on station, no life signs," the voice said dispassionately. He didn't swing his imager around to show bodies. His partner would be taking those recordings, using a different instrument. "Significant toxic residues on the bulkheads."

Aril tried to comfort herself with the fact that there'd been no accident. No mishap would be blamed on Federate ground crews. "Shuhr," she whispered. The fiends! She brushed moisture off one cheek.

"Look for a private compartment," Major Dunn directed.

The image floated up a short corridor. The first starboard hatch hung open, damaged. Aril's chest tightened again as she spotted a soft, brown stuffed animal—some domestic Netaian creature—floating in a corner between bulkheads. This had been a child's private cabin.

"They're not here," the male voice concluded several minutes later.

"Rescue pods fired?" Major Dunn asked.

"Negative."

What could the Shuhr have done with two small children? Aril wondered. The ship had been boarded. Were they kidnapped? Acting on a hunch, she activated one of her other scanners.

Something cold seemed to settle on her chest and shoulders. "Biological debris," she announced. "Eighty meters aft, drifting."

Major Dunn relayed that report. The salvage crew exited the shuttle, and on the main screen, Aril saw the faint red glow of EV suits' steering units.

The remote image remained trained on the starfield.

"Yes," the voice said softly, angrily. "We've found them."

"Com, inform Inisi base." Major Dunn sounded weary. "Tell them to notify Hesed and the Netaian Electorate."

Aril did a quick mental calculation. Because of the relative distances to Hesed and Netaia, Carradee would receive the news first.

CHAPTER 17

BEQUEST

intermezzo, piu agitato
interlude, slightly agitated

Tel pressed the CT earpiece in tightly, then cupped a hand over it. "Yes, Solicitor Merriam, I remember you." The elderly man was the sovereign's legal counsel. "Could you speak louder?"

"I'm sorry, no," said the husky voice. "The regency has been monitoring my office for days. I'm not certain my home is clean. It's urgent I speak with Firebird, but the base is allowing no one through. Can you have her contact me immediately?"

Barely awake and less than half dressed, Tel leaned against one wall of his spacious wood-paneled bedroom and peered at a clock. What time was it—six, maybe seven hundred? "I will try, but I was unable to get through myself. The base is taking no chances." The implications—that Shuhr agents might find and influence him so that he might harm Firebird—were chilling. Still, he had plenty of loyal bodyguards now. He felt safe enough.

"It regards Carradee's will." Merriam's voice—or was it even Merriam?—dropped until Tel strained to catch words. "I am leaving the city for my own safety. I will drop certain documents by Your Highness's estate in half an hour. You must see them delivered."

The connection went dead. Through a force-screened window drifted the song of an awakened bird. Tel replaced the earpiece in its uteh-wood box, then slipped on a pair of warm house shoes. If these documents were genuine, then by the urgency in Merriam's voice, Tel guessed they would cause a sensation—and bring Rogonin's redjackets to his door.

Alarmed on all counts, he picked up the earpiece again and put through a call to base. He still couldn't persuade the staff to let him speak with Firebird—no one wanted to wake her—but Caldwell's bodyguard, Uri Harris, intercepted his attempt.

Tel liked Lieutenant Colonel Harris, who moved and spoke with upper-class grace and self-confidence. "If you could reach my estate in twenty minutes," Tel said, "there will either be extremely important documents delivered that are meant for Firebird, or else an attempt on my life." As he spoke, he stared up at the portrait over his bed. His late wife wore orange, which represented Excellence in Netaia's symbology. Heir-named *Eschelle* for *Excellence*, she had always called that "her own" Power.

The imperious tilt of her head balanced the grace with which she clasped her long fingers. She'd sat willingly, letting him adore her on canvas.

To his chagrin, this morning he could look at that portrait without longing for her. She'd brought Netaia to the Shuhr's attention. Because of that, they threatened to take the world—and they nearly killed Firebird yesterday.

"If this is real," he told Harris, "and if His Grace at the palace is watching the solicitor's home, I will not be secure with those documents in my hands. Please come and take them."

"I can't leave my post," said the Sentinel, "but I can send another courier. She'll be in uniform, with my personal clearance code."

"Again," ordered Modabah.

One of the ship's crew who'd brought them to Netaia toggled a control. Over the media block, the familiar tableau appeared: Firebird Caldwell knelt at center stage with her Sentinel beside her.

The projectile drove her to the floor. Caldwell all but collapsed.

"Not yet," said Talumah. "Keep going. . . ."

Terza watched Talumah watch the tri-D. His eyes fell half shut. The miniature figures huddled—

"Now," Talumah exclaimed. The crewman froze the image.

But they're just lying there, Terza said.

Modabah occupied the largest chair. He brandished a recall pad. "Listen to this." He read off several paragraphs couched in self-assured prose that reminded her of Dru Polar. "Polar's research," Modabah explained, confirming her guess. "Just before his death, he was working with the idea of fusing two epsilon carriers, one artificially repolarized to an unusual conformation. His theory was that joining two such carriers would release a flood of energy. He called his theory 'antipodal fusion.' "

Micahel spoke first. "Do you suppose Caldwell stole Polar's idea and perfected it? This looks like—"

"How did you say it felt, Talumah?" Modabah demanded.

"Like an explosion of pure energy."

Modabah flung the recall pad against the wall. "That's what they're doing. Caldwell and Firebird, somehow. The Angelos have been isolated here for over a century. There must have been a mutation. Something altered their epsilon potential."

"Kill them," declared Micahel. "Separate them first. Then we can kill them both."

Modabah slicked back his hair with both hands. "We still could take him and use him. But yes, finish her. If she has that kind of epsilon carrier, and she inherited it, then he couldn't do this with anyone else—except Carradee, the one who abdicated."

She would've taken a vanity implant, Terza pointed out. *Her ayin is probably destroyed.*

"Good, Terza," said her father.

It was the first time he'd ever praised her.

Ard Talumah turned his back on the tri-D image, crossing his arms over his chest. "So nothing has changed. Kill her, dart him, and grab."

Modabah scowled. "Something has changed," he insisted. "If our assumption about the Angelo line is wrong, then other Sentinels might be learning this technique. They've undoubtedly studied whatever it is these two have been doing. We can't give them one more day."

"Yes," Micahel hissed. "Hit Thyrica. Take down the college. And I tell you, Hesed can be attacked. All we need is one Thyrian ship with RIA technology—"

"We've tried. They're guarding those ships too closely. Take an order," Modabah called to the crewman, who pulled his own recall pad off his belt. Modabah rocked forward on his chair, clasping both hands. "This is for Adiyn, by fastest courier."

The crewman nodded.

"Adiyn," said Modabah. "Mobilize. Deploy to Tallis," he stressed, glaring at his son. "To the capital city, Castille. I want a crater twice as deep as Micahel left at Sunton."

One side of Micahel's mouth quirked upward.

Modabah gripped air with one hand. "Make it look like a Sentinel attack—use the Procyel-Tallis approach vector, and transmit from Thyrica that Tallis's inaction after Sunton could not be tolerated. Turn them on the Sentinels at all cost."

Terza quivered behind her deep shields, staggered by the loss of life he was ordering.

"Second order," said Modabah. "Those Casvah gene specimens could be priceless. Get them into the deep vault under the main chamber. I will follow close behind this message, as soon as Caldwell can be taken. End message." He glared at the crewman. "Get moving."

Then he turned to his son. "The third order is for you. Get on your way to Sitree. I'll transmit specific orders as soon as we have Burkenhamn. Get three fighters. Heavy ones, long-range. Load up, stand out, and await orders. As soon as we take the Angelo woman down and Caldwell out, demolish that base. Pick two pilots from the settlements. You know the drill."

To Terza's surprise, Micahel didn't seem delighted by his assignment. He stood cracking his knuckles. "For once," he muttered, "just once, I would like to be present when Caldwell is brought in. He is mine. So is Burkenhamn, after he roughed me up at that ball."

Terza watched her father hesitate. After all, one day Micahel would lead the unbound. He had the right to take this generation of Carabohds. . . .

"I can't promise you Burkenhamn," Modabah said. "But I will say this. No one will kill Caldwell until you arrive."

Firebird woke herself midmorning, thrashing, trying in her sleep to find some position that eased the main weight of that field generator off her chest. It was only twenty centimeters wide and ten thick, with rounded edges, but after just one day, she'd started to think of it as an instrument of torture. It hummed incessantly, not quite a true pitch. She also had a new, nagging itch at her left wrist. The base's chief med, a Tallan named Adamm Hancock, had secured a life-signs cuff. She would be wearing that little bracelet, too snug to be removed, until the surgeons pronounced her fit to fly.

She felt stronger already. Something else had changed, too, back at the sanctum. Along with her pride, that asphyxiating fear . . . for Brenn, for herself . . . had vanished. There remained terrors to be faced, but she couldn't bring herself to care. Mightier hands than hers, moved by a wiser will and a richer love, controlled her destiny. It was obvious now.

She just wished she felt stronger yet—and more comfortable.

The door slid open, and Shel slipped into her room.

"Where's Brenn?" Firebird asked.

"Uri says he's been up since two hundred. I don't think either of them slept. May I ease you?"

"Yes, thank you."

Shel walked over and locked stares with her. Nauseating otherness swept across Firebird's alpha matrix, but it leveled peaks of discomfort. "Thank you," she repeated.

Though the deep, infuriating itch faded, the generator's weight still tormented her. According to her regimen, in a few hours she could get up for a while. That couldn't happen soon enough. "Did they find any more traces of Shirak overnight?"

Shel took the bedside chair, leaning away from her hip-holstered blazer. "He left a few skin and hair cells on the overhead beam. They took a full DNA tracing and cross-checked the Netaian medical database. That only proved he was offworld. *His* people don't publish referents. Nothing else on the search. Rogonin insists the palace is cooperating, but we have doubts."

Firebird nodded. She did, too.

Shel slipped out.

Only a few minutes later, there was a quick rapping on the door. Firebird straightened her hair over her shoulders and called, "Come."

Uri and Shel pressed through together, along with a third Sentinel Firebird had met yesterday on guard shift, Lieutenant Rachil Mercell. Slender with short brown hair, she'd sat and talked music, describing herself as a lapsed brass player.

Uri held a sealed message cylinder under his elbow. "We've safed this," he said, sounding slightly less composed than usual, a little more tenor than baritone. "Lieutenant Mercell picked it up at the Tellai estate, with instructions from an older gentleman to greet you in the name of Solicitor Merriam."

"Merriam's afraid." Lieutenant Mercell stood against the door. "I've applied to Governor Danton for his protection."

Startled, Firebird forgot where she lay and tried to sit up straighter. The field generator held her down. "Did Solicitor Merriam say what this is?"

"Not to me," the lieutenant said.

Firebird thumbed the seal, and the cylinder's halves fell apart. She fumbled out several sheets of rolled parchment. The smallest, in Tel's hand, dropped free. "I believe you need to know," she read aloud, "that the Ceremonials Committee turned down your request. Your heir name is Domita." *Not Mari*, she reflected, *but at least they shortened Indomitability.* Two years ago, she had hoped to be remembered for indomitably facing her wastling fate.

She eyed the other sheets. "These look like original documents," she began, then she realized, "They are. Heatsealed." She turned over the loose roll. It was illegal to break a heatseal unless authorized, but above the seal was printed, "Firebird Elsbeth Angelo, upon her Confirmation as an heiress of the House."

That looked like Carradee's scribing.

She punctured the seal with one thumbnail. "Testament Upon Renunciation of the Throne," she read aloud. Then, sobered by the realization that these documents were vital family property, she scanned the top page.

By the time she started reading the second, her heart thumped under the field generator and the life-signs cuff gave off a pale green light. The Angelo fortune—the entire wealth of Netaia's most powerful family—was to be placed under her administration, if she were ever confirmed as the heiress.

No wonder Solicitor Merriam feared for his life. She couldn't waste a minute. She could accomplish something for Netaia right here in the infirmary, and pride had nothing to do with it. Carrie had arranged this even before leaving for Hesed. She'd kept it secret, too, and explained why . . . right there in the fifteenth clause. "So that no one might accuse Firebird, now or ever, of monetary motivation in accepting confirmation."

That explained Carrie's delight over her decision to come back here, though. She'd practically shoved Firebird up the shuttle's boarding ramp.

"Uri," said Firebird, "is there a legal consul on base authorized to access civilian programming?"

"I don't know."

"I need to speak with one right away. And can you access him, to make sure he's not under Rogonin's influence?"

"That depends. We're only allowed use of our abilities—"

Under strictly controlled circumstances, she chorused mentally as he spoke. "All right," she said. "This solicitor is about to be asked to do several things. He must have Tel Tellai-Angelo authorized on these documents as my Netaian representative—and executor, if necessary," she added, determined that whether she lived or died, Muirnen Rogonin would no longer leverage the Angelo fortune.

Her voice rose with excitement. "I also need documents of incorporation, so that moneys I now control can be distributed without certain parties' knowledge or interference. I mean to use Angelo resources to end the electors' stranglehold on Netaia's economy, Uri. Is that circumstance enough?"

She saw a hint of Brennen in Uri's half smile. Second cousins, weren't they? "I believe it is," he said. Then he added in a teasing tone, "Commander Caldwell. I'll send down breakfast, too." He left with Lieutenant Mercell. Shel stayed at the door.

Firebird stared at the far wall. Tel must examine the family portfolio— no, first he would have to *find* it—it was probably at Merriam's office and might have been stolen.

She could withdraw enough funds to build a Chapter house, too, and bring non-Sentinel Path instructors to Citangelo.

Smiling, she shut her eyes and relaxed against the field generator. What *was* the pitch it had hummed all night? Not quite a C-sharp, but a sharp C-natural . . .

Another idea rose to tantalize her. All her life, she'd wished she could be remembered as a patron of musical arts. It would have been lovely to establish a conservatory scholarship in perpetuity. Or an orchestra . . . she'd always wanted to found a new orchestra. This one could be dedicated to diverse programming.

Could be. She couldn't afford to think in those terms yet. Resting her recall pad against the regen arc, she keyed up her list of official charities, side by side with a compilation of Netaian industries that had cooperated with Governor Danton.

Muirnen Rogonin made a chopping motion with one hand, and his servitor hastily waved off the media link, choking out the irritating new song. He wished it hadn't taken his people three days to recognize its deadliness and how far such songs might travel before they were stopped.

But now he had a prisoner.

She stood on the inlaid petitioners' floor below his desk, wearing a baggy, unflattering low-common dress and wrist restraints. Her left eye twitched above a floral tattoo.

"Clareen Chesterson," he said slowly. "If you will cooperate, this interview will be far less uncomfortable."

She adjusted her stance, straddling an inlaid inner-world orbit. "I have nothing to say, Your Grace. I have done nothing wrong."

Rogonin raised one eyebrow. "Is that so? I have here," he said, raising one sheet of hard copy, "testimony of a subtronic trace. A transmission was sent from Prince Tel's residence to yours on the twenty-third of this month. Again," he said, sliding another sheet to lie on top of the first, "a high-commoner willing to swear he saw you the next day, going into Tellai's town apartment less than an hour before Lady Firebird entered."

"That has nothing to do with Your Grace's accusation."

"I think it has." He popped a mint under his tongue to cool and burn and soothe him. "Here is another testimony, stating that you were seen entering the Tellai estate on two other occasions. Prince Tel is known for unconventional monarchist views."

"That has nothing to do with me, Your Grace."

"Is that so?" His new friends had warned him that if she'd collaborated, the Sentinels would have voice-commanded her, making her truly unable to reveal information, even under pharmaceutical or physical persuasion.

Here she stood, though, an instigator of the Federatization he feared.

He regretted that harsh steps were necessary. He dreaded the purge that must come. It soiled his regency, it soiled his House, but for Netaia's sake, he would not back down. He would build new prisons with the Angelo moneys he still leveraged, as regent. . . .

From behind her, near the Coper Rebellion mural, Talumah purred, "She is afraid, when you question her."

Her head whirled toward the voice, and she stared—either at Talumah or the mural, worked in jewel dust over a translucent screen.

"Give us what we want." Rogonin rose out of the day office's chair. "Identify Lady Firebird as the writer of that vile, juvenile ditty. If you do, we will free you. If not—" He laced his fingers across his midsection. "You will vanish from Citangelo."

Clareen Chesterson clenched her crossed hands. She gritted her teeth, looking as if she wished she could rip off her wrist restraints and jump him.

Hinnana Prison was full of the likes of her. He also had detention facilities at Sander Hill Station and under the palace. As of yesterday, he also had new allies who surely could convince her to confess.

"Talumah, escort our musical guest downlevel. Send Burkenhamn in on your way out."

Terza sat in the dank new downlevel observation post, a long, thin chamber between storerooms, stuffed with eavesdropping gear the crew members had brought from Three Zed. She tugged a sleeve of her awkward House Guard uniform. It rode up her arm with a will of its own, instead of following her motions like sensible clothing.

Micahel was headed southwest by superspeed commercial transport, and Talumah was uplevel with the regent. Momentarily alone, she wondered if Talumah had already altered her alpha matrix, either shipboard or since she arrived here. Her father had a reputation for making plans within plans. Maybe her upbringing included subtle pushes toward rebellion.

Or was this growing urge to escape simply the unstable Shirak personality, as her old supervisor Juddis Adiyn called it? Tallis was doomed, the Federacy about to fall.

Think in one straight line! she commanded herself—*escape!* Modabah Shirak might guess that his daughter could try to defect. Or, more sinister, he might be pushing her toward defection. If her alpha matrix had been twisted, she wouldn't remember. That also was standard procedure.

Maybe she, too, was being maneuvered into position to destroy Brennen Caldwell's bond mate, without her knowledge or consent.

She covered her abdomen with both hands. If she killed Lady Firebird,

Caldwell would never—never—help her escape.

But she had to get to him, even if that was exactly her father's intention.

Out in the north corridor, footsteps passed. Terza peered through the storage room in time to see Talumah pass, escorting a manacled woman.

Netaia's seizure was beginning.

Outside, it was cold midmorning. Muirnen Rogonin stood behind his day desk and listened to Devair Burkenhamn abase himself. The marshal stood at the flaming, inlaid sun's center, at rigid attention. "Your Grace," he concluded, "I am oath-bound to come to you in time of conflict. You called, so I must offer my services."

Here was one more traitor to Netaia's lasting grandeur . . . but this traitor would be of use. No Sentinel would have dared to put voice-command on First Marshal Burkenhamn, the way they got to Clareen Chesterson. Behind Burkenhamn, almost invisible against the older mural—of Conura First's victory over the outsystem invaders—stood another one of Rogonin's new House Guards. Rogonin returned the man's slight smile. Burkenhamn—with his size and strength, and Firebird's trust—would make an ideal assassin.

He returned his attention to the beefy marshal, who looked rather like a target standing at the center of all those inlaid orbits. "Thank you for your timely arrival. I assume this is a difficult gesture for you to make." *You still want her back in the palace, don't you, Burkenhamn? She'll be there, all right. Lying in state, thanks to you.* "I want you to deliver messages to the occupation governor and Commander Angelo."

Burkenhamn barely inclined his massive upper body.

"First, you will need a strategic briefing." He beckoned another one of his new employees away from his post by the east window. They had promised him Burkenhamn would remember nothing from what they were about to do, except having been brought to their new observation post. Rogonin did not want Netaians carrying memories of their foul treatment. Burkenhamn's suicide would be honorable, too. Rogonin would slip him a dagger in custody after they arrested him for murdering Firebird.

CHAPTER 18

BURKENHAMN

tutti
for the whole ensemble

Ard Talumah called Terza into the south storage room. "Look over what I've done," he ordered. "I need to send Micahel some intelligence." Then he stepped out.

Lying unconscious on a dusty, marble-topped table, Devair Burkenhamn looked like a monument carved from stone. Terza focused for access, probed for the breach Talumah had left, and slipped through.

Twisted threads of Burkenhamn's alpha matrix, linked with recently inserted suggestions, showed how subtly Talumah had blocked the memory of interrogation, preparing the marshal to return to full consciousness only when taken inside their observation post. Deep beneath Burkenhamn's consciousness, bird's-nest knots of thought and emotion would be Talumah's preparation for betrayal, murder, and finally suicide.

Talumah was a master.

Again, she wondered—had he already done this to her? Shipboard, or just moments ago, between her arrival in the storeroom and her first glimpse of Burkenhamn? Talumah could have rethreaded her entire alpha matrix after calling her in, and she would remember only the sensation. She turned inside herself, trying to see if anything felt different.

She found it only when she slipped behind her secret shield. Talumah had prepared her, too, for the attack. Trembling, she made sure Talumah really had left her and Burkenhamn alone. To be absolutely safe, she raised her inmost shields once more. Then she examined the preparatory locus in Burkenhamn's alpha matrix, where Talumah had subverted volition at the deepest possible points. As terrified as she was, not knowing exactly what Talumah had just done to her, she knew she must try to thwart Firebird's murder. That was the only way she could get Caldwell's sympathy and help.

With utmost care, because this kind of work wasn't her specialty, Terza loosened the critical locus like a knot. She didn't dare do more. If Talumah caught her meddling, her father would take her alpha matrix apart thread by thread, then blast her out the nearest airlock. This effort would be her signature, her proof to Caldwell that she'd tried, at least, to circumvent their murderous plans.

She could do nothing for herself. She only hoped Caldwell still was capable of detecting what she'd just done to Burkenhamn.

But did she really want to defect? What would it accomplish, what would it prove?

In that one reluctant thought, Terza found her own proof. Her father must've once wanted to plant her among the Federates, maybe to assassinate Caldwell. Now he had other plans for her. He'd ordered Talumah to create new doubts as to whether she wanted to defect.

Then Talumah would have watch-linked her already. The transport that brought them here surely carried the requisite gear. Talumah and Modabah would be able to monitor all her uppermost, unshielded thoughts.

All right, Father. She formed the words clearly, desperately glad she'd shielded herself before tampering with Burkenhamn's alpha matrix. *I am not deceived, but I will serve you.*

Carefully controlling all further thought, she shook back her hair, straightened the uncomfortable sleeves once more, and shut off the restraint table's immobilizing field. She angled a hand to use voice-command. "Open your eyes and sit up."

The monument shook itself. Burkenhamn rose, staring, his eyes processing only enough information for physical function. She dusted the back of his cobalt blue uniform with her crimson sleeve, then nudged him toward the observation post. Talumah sat finishing a late, elegant-looking cold lunch. *Yours, Talumah*, she subvocalized.

Talumah grasped the unseeing marshal's elbow. "Inside, large one," he ordered. Then he subvocalized to Terza, *Satisfied?*

She nodded.

Today, Talumah sent, *we show Caldwell that his God has a short reach.*

Burkenhamn revived all in a moment, bending forward to stare at the nearest bluescreen. The post had three visual monitors, one currently showing the palace's north grounds, another displaying airspace over Citangelo. The third was blank.

Crooking one finger for Terza to follow, Talumah glided toward the opposite door. The storeroom that accessed this post from the north corridor was piled haphazardly with clear-wrapped uniforms in black, gold, and scarlet, moved out of the inmost room to make room for surveillance gear.

He handed her a recall pad. *The rest of your orders.* Then he slipped back out.

She sent the door shut, then touched the ON button and read.

> Burkenhamn will be quick—a simple strangulation, a blow to the head, break her neck, anything—but it must be his doing, not yours. Do not interfere.
> Once that is accomplished, you and Talumah will still have Burkenhamn as hostage for a safe exit. Deliver our ultimatum to Danton. Caldwell will be experiencing bereavement shock. He may be entirely without control. Again, be quick. Dart him. Drag or carry him toward the main gate. We'll pick you up.

Yes, Father. Again Terza formed words with deliberate care. Behind her innermost shields, she wished Talumah weren't coming. Sending her alone onto the Federate military base would be foolish, though, even with new subliminal orders to leave the base. Her father was no fool.

The vision of Ard Talumah as a malformed embryo flitted across her mind. She dismissed it hastily and read on.

> I'm ordering Danton to withdraw all forces from these systems. Instantly. He is granted his personnel's lives, but he must leave all maté-riel. Micahel is prepping two crewmen for the clean-up mission. Don't worry—we'll be far out on the plains in less than three hours, before Micahel can get back.
> Bring Burkenhamn out with Caldwell if you can, but don't delay for Burkenhamn's sake. Only Rogonin cares if the marshal is killed on the base or if he suicides. Rogonin is cooperating fully.

Terza stared at the device. *Well planned, Father,* she thought hard.

> If Caldwell cannot be drugged, the second threat to be leveled against him will of course involve the fetus. If you leave the base without him, it will be flayed and dismembered at a viable stage, and the remains delivered personally into his hands. The procedure will be transcorded for general Federate consumption. If he has already lost a bond mate, I don't think he'll resist this threat.
> Once more, do not delay. You must not be on base in three hours.

The message ended.

Nauseated, Terza squeezed the OFF panel. She frowned, covering another shielded reflection with surface gratitude. She should be thankful that Modabah meant to get her out of Citangelo before Micahel sent in his suicide pilots. Did he know—did he guess that her heart, betrayed by the workings of her own body, really had chosen against him?

He couldn't think otherwise. He'd just threatened to abort, torture, and callously dispose of her child. Short weeks ago, she had destroyed human embryos with no more remorse than he showed now.

Excellent, Father. I am ready. We will defeat the Federates from our new base on Netaia. I would like a rural estate, south of here, near a river.

She dropped the recall pad onto a clothing stack, then strode back to the inner door.

"Ah," Ard Talumah said when she emerged into the observation post. "Here is our other escort, Marshal Burkenhamn. Terza," he added in a clipped, authoritarian voice. "The marshal is to deliver messages to Governor Danton and Commander Angelo Caldwell. We will see that he passes safely onto the base *and safely returns.* We are his Netaian escort, from families he knows well."

"Sir." Terza dipped her head to Burkenhamn. "I am at your disposal."

This is for you. Talumah dangled a lens-shaped tri-D pickup, swinging like a lavaliere on a short golden chain. *A gift from His Grace. He wants a recording of Firebird's demise.*

Then he slipped her a silvery injector. She made sure it was sheathed before pocketing it. She spotted a standard dart pistol tucked into Talumah's belt.

Well planned, Father. Well planned.

Talumah led out, his long face pointed confidently forward. *Here we come, speaker-god. Stop us if you can.*

Terza followed Burkenhamn up the north corridor, then out an echoing white tunnel to palace garages. The heavy lavaliere lens pressed against her breastbone. The Netaian marshal slid behind the driver's seat of a palace groundcar as easily as a smaller man might move. His strength had to be tremendous.

Talumah joined him in front. Terza took the place behind Talumah, determined not to watch him too closely. They emerged near the spear-tipped gates and accelerated down into Citangelo. The city streaked past under a winter blue, late-afternoon sky.

Deep behind her shields, she let the thought rise: At the surface, she no longer wanted her freedom. But how deeply could her father affect her will? Somewhere in Modabah's web of counterplans, did he want Ard Talumah disposed of? And if so, why?

Did the law-bound Sentinels live like this? she wondered, still hiding her thoughts—each one suspecting all others? Or was their propaganda based on truth, and did their allegiance to a higher cause make them a truly different people?

Her daughter had little chance of reaching maturity if she returned to Three Zed. She would probably be aborted anyway, or euthanized, and her cells cloned as breeding stock. Yet the hereditary abilities of Modabah Shirak and Brennen Caldwell could've made that child great for either side. A treasure had been thrust into Terza's hands.

She would guard that treasure if it cost her life. If the Federacy's new weapons might be used to turn the Golden City, like Sunton, into dust and rubble, then her child must not be there.

She thought of her lifetime's work—all those genetic samples—and Three Zed's armory, its records, its Ehretan artifacts—the treasures stolen from Federate worlds—must they be destroyed? Could she carry that burden?

She clenched one hand. *Of course not, Father.*

Automatically braked by central guidance at the end of city-controlled roadway, the car slowed. Ahead, Terza saw massive energy-fence walls. She loosened her blazer in its holster.

Two Federate watchmen guarded each side of the base's tall main gate. Behind them, a fifth man sat half shielded on the gunner's seat of a huge new energy projector. A man in midnight blue stepped to Burkenhamn's side of the car, followed by one in Verohan pale blue.

Burkenhamn opened his windscreen to answer. "I need to speak with Governor Danton." He handed out an ID disk. "You may tell him I'm here."

A gust of breeze lifted the Sentinel's dark blond hair. He stared at the Netaian officer, then glanced in Terza's direction.

"My aides," Burkenhamn declared.

Terza slipped complacency into the suspicious Verohan's midbrain, letting Talumah deal with the Thyrian. He'd proved he could deceive Sentinels when he escaped the Hall of Charity.

The Sentinel rested his left hand on Burkenhamn's door. "One moment." He lifted a tiny subtronic device, backed away, and spoke rapidly. Terza caught the word *Burkenhamn.*

Then they waited. Terza might have dashed past the guards to a cluster of gray buildings beyond the perimeter, but that energy projector looked capable of ground-to-air defense. It wasn't something she wanted to tackle.

The Sentinel removed his headset. "I'm to accompany you. Unlock a rear door, please."

Danton probably realized Burkenhamn was in danger, even on base. Terza rested her hand near her blazer as the Thyrian slid in.

Half a meter separated her legs from those of someone who had been raised to kill her kind on sight. She mustn't provoke the Sentinel, not this time. She must not make enemies.

Burkenhamn steered the vehicle toward the L-shaped main building.

Brennen reentered the base's command center after a quick break. Several Sentinels that had been withdrawn from palace infiltration stood at guard posts. He was pleased to see Firebird reclining in a mobility chair, studying the tri-D well with Governor Danton.

She glanced up at Brennen. "I'm barely moving. *Largo*," she joked feebly. "We're drawing up an evacuation plan for Citangelo's civilian population."

This was her transitional day, slowly working up to walking again. Brennen turned to Danton. "Any word from Marshal Burkenhamn?"

"On his way. Just passed the gate."

Burkenhamn saluted a quartet of door guards, two of whom stepped forward as he approached. "I must speak with Governor Danton," he said calmly. "Direct me, please."

One in Tallan gray saluted again. "Follow me, Marshal."

Terza came behind Talumah and Burkenhamn, and though Terza was taller, the Sentinel guard paced her step for step. The other Federate guard followed.

How many minutes might I have to live? she wondered, down deep. Then she thrust the thought aside and pointedly recited, *Get the drugs into Caldwell. Cover Burkenhamn while he kills Firebird. Get Caldwell off base.*

Well planned, Father.

Their Tallan guide led down a soft-tiled hall, past doors on the left and right, all closed. The guide's home world, Tallis, would be struck—probably within fifteen days. Terza wondered if he had family.

Ahead, double doors stood open, guarded on both sides. Terza touched the tri-D pickup around her neck. Now it would record, though it wouldn't transmit, so far as she knew. Netaian transcorders were larger and heavier than this.

Striding in, staying on Burkenhamn's left, she took in the instrument panels, display monitors, and other accouterments of military power. Half a dozen Federate staff stood or sat at various stations, flanked by several uniformed Sentinels, undoubtedly the ones withdrawn from the palace—

Her sweeping glance snagged at the sight of a man she recognized from Three Zed. Caldwell had a slightly squared face, with one cheek faintly scarred and alert-looking blue eyes. He stood beside the Federate governor, near a tri-D well. His epsilon savor was plainly muted, weaker than she'd imagined. He wasn't as tall as she'd pictured him, either . . . nowhere near as tall as her brother. Slim shouldered, he retained the presence that had carried authority—but without the hard, arrogant edge that marked Three Zed's leaders.

Burkenhamn saluted the Federate governor, then looked aside.

And there *she* sat: Firebird Angelo Caldwell, white medical coveralls bringing out the flame in her hair. Her face looked flushed.

There they were together, her daughter's gene-father and the mother of the only children he ever would acknowledge—his prophesied heirs, miraculously safe at sanctuary.

Burkenhamn saw Firebird, too. Smiling, he strode toward her mobility chair as Talumah palmed his dart pistol. Terza felt Talumah gloating, taking mental aim at Caldwell, measuring his range. Burkenhamn picked up speed as he crossed the room.

"Marshal." The Angelo woman smiled warmly. "We needed to talk with you about—" Welcome faded from her face. It would have been easy to let Burkenhamn reach her. Easy, and right—

From behind her inmost shields, Terza brought up the cry, "Stop him!" Against common sense, against all sense of loyalty, she leveled her blazer at Talumah's back and kept one eye on Burkenhamn. "Caldwell!" she forced out the words. "He's under command to kill her!"

Burkenhamn lunged. Firebird flung herself off the mobility chair. A cleft-chinned woman Sentinel sprang toward Burkenhamn. In the same instant, Talumah pivoted.

Terza shot him in the chest.

Firebird landed hard and rolled over with impressive speed for someone so recently and severely wounded. *Pain blocks*, Terza guessed, *and regen therapy*—

The Sentinel woman landed a flying kick on Burkenhamn's left hip, knocking him aside. She hit the floor in a tuck, somersaulted, then lashed out again from a crouch. Caldwell and another Sentinel closed in on the big Netaian, raising their hands to use voice-command. Two guards in mismatched Federate uniforms caught Burkenhamn's arms.

Other men and women scattered. Terza opened both palms and extended her arms. Her hands trembled with self-reproach. Her blazer hit the soft tile, bounced once, then lay still. She fixed her stare on Brennen Caldwell's eerily blue eyes, holding it there even when someone seized her right shoulder from behind and pressed something hard against the base of her skull. "Don't move," said a woman's voice. Other hands fumbled at her belt, then patted her down. Someone pulled the lavaliere pickup over her head.

She drew a deep breath, smelling charred fabric and flesh. Talumah's flesh.

I'm sorry, Father. There are things even I have to do. Good-bye.

A Sentinel knelt beside Firebird, supporting the small woman in a sitting position. The female guard who'd intercepted Burkenhamn stood over them, brandishing a blazer. The room quieted. Controllers and com techs returned to their stools and sat motionless. Burkenhamn blinked as his mismatched guards helped him stand up.

Caldwell stepped in front of his bond mate, defensive fury in his eyes. Did he realize how narrowly she'd just escaped assassination . . . again? Finely muscled, he moved well, and the savor of his presence had an uncanny peace. When he stopped two meters away, she dropped her shields in submissive greeting.

His dark eyebrows arched. She felt him focus the remnants of his epsilon shield. She waited, passive but tingling in every nerve, for a thrust of mind-access.

"Who are you?" he demanded.

The voice, too, surprised her. It wasn't as deep as she remembered from Polar's interrogation files. Did Caldwell sense nothing? Her desire, her intentions, her . . . the state of her body?

Three med assistants in yellow tunics dashed through the door, pulling a medical litter. One knelt beside Ard Talumah, touched a hand to his chest wound, then shook his head at Occupation Governor Danton, who hung back between two big-muscled Carolinians.

Other meds helped Firebird back into her reclined mobility chair, where she kept her eyes trained on her bond mate.

"Who are you?" Caldwell repeated. "Who is he? Why did you kill him?"

She wondered what Juddis Adiyn saw at this moment on the shebiyl, back on Three Zed. Surely a dozen possible futures snaked off from this nexus. Her voice shook when she answered, "My name is Terza Shirak."

His eyes widened.

"I am asking . . . requesting asylum. I believe your people hoped to take a prisoner, just as mine did. Guarantee my safety, and my memories are at your disposal." Was she really saying this?

He stared, and still she felt no probe. Maybe he thought she was insane, or illogical, or hurried over the brink of competence.

"Asylum?" came a feminine voice from behind him.

Caldwell stepped aside, glancing down.

That had been Firebird's voice. Her bodyguard remained close, holding that blazer.

The weapon Terza couldn't see pressed hard at the base of her neck. Still shieldless, she felt Firebird's curiosity and gratitude mingled with suspicion. Neither she nor Caldwell accepted Terza's plea . . . yet. Terza would have scorned them if they had so quickly.

Terza indicated Talumah with a flick of her eyes. One of the meds unfurled a body bag over him. "His name is Ard Talumah," she said. "I killed him because he would've killed me, once he understood that I mean to defect. Believe that or not, as you will. But I am not acting under orders now. I am breaking them."

Firebird pursed her lips and raised her chin.

"He deserved to die," Terza said softly, pitching her voice so that only Firebird and Caldwell would hear clearly. "He mind-altered Burkenhamn to kill you. He also murdered your nieces. The Angelo girls."

Firebird's eyes narrowed as if she remembered something. "Talumah," she muttered. "Cassia Talumah's brother?"

"The same." Cassia, who died when this pair escaped Three Zed, must have bragged about Ard's attack. "I have something else to tell you." She focused on Caldwell again. "It will be better if you hear it alone."

He barely shook his head, perhaps distracted by a second burst of unshielded realization from his bond mate. Carradee gone, then Phoena, and now Carradee's heiresses—

"You have every reason to suspect treachery," Terza said softly. "I am almost certainly watch-linked. I'm also sure my alpha matrix was manipulated. And one other thing has been done to me. To my body. I am—I was—a genetics technician. The plan was to lure you in."

To Terza's satisfaction, Firebird glanced directly at Terza's belly. Again, comprehension burst out of her. Naturally, the woman would understand first. She was a mother and a bond mate. She stretched out one hand toward Caldwell.

He leaned down, letting her whisper into his ear. His stare whipped toward Firebird, then back to Terza in horror and . . . was that hope?

I want the child to live, she projected, using minimal carrier strength. There were other Sentinels present. *That's why I'm defecting. I'll tell you everything I know or have been led to believe. But then you must find a way to see that I can't harm you, or else the tragedy will have only begun. They want you.*

The governor stepped forward, sandy hair dangling across his eyebrows. "Do you know this woman, General Caldwell?"

"No." He tilted his head back, exhaling slowly, his every movement caution. "But I know her family."

"Not—" the governor began.

Caldwell nodded curtly.

Again, Terza felt faintly nauseous.

One of Burkenhamn's guards held the lavaliere pickup. He pointed it back at her, and she spotted her own injector in his other hand. "Would you submit to blocking drugs, Terza Shirak?"

She bit her lip. Blocking drugs might break the watch-link, but they could also damage her child's neural system. She held her breath, wondering if Caldwell would let that fetus be mentally crippled, to render Terza harmless. If so, he was more like his *shuhr* than she'd thought. "I will submit," she said, letting Caldwell feel her anxiety, "if General Caldwell orders drugs."

The hostility in him dimmed. Maybe he hoped she might be genuine. He flicked one hand, and the pressure against her skull eased off. "Go with Sentinel Mercell, Terza. She will make you comfortable. I'll follow as soon as I can."

The guard behind Terza grasped her elbow.

"Lieutenant Mercell," Caldwell added.

The Sentinel woman turned around.

"No drugs," he said. "That is an order."

Esme Rogonin sat at table, clutching a cloth serviette in her lap as she silently finished her soup. Her father had actually invited one of his mercenaries to dine with them. Esme was trying—vainly, she feared—to hide her disgust. This was the father of that sniper who nearly killed Lady Firebird, eating Netaian food in the palace's most elegant private dining room! Until this hour, Esme had been able to pretend that her father hadn't collaborated to commit murder.

And something was terribly wrong with her father. In place of his usually regal manner, he was cordial—even effervescent—with the intruder and his aides. Esme had warned her mother, who was visiting the Parkai estate, by CT link. Duchess Liona had dispatched a driver to pick up Esme and her other children, but he had not arrived. Maybe the mercenaries wanted hostages.

It *was* odd for all four Rogonin children, heirs and wastlings, to eat together. Beyond Esme at table, her young brother Kelsen catapulted bits of food at Lady Diamond, the youngest. Thank the Powers, Esme could still pass for fourteen. She made a point of slouching, looking intimidated. If they thought of her as a child, they might not consider her a threat.

"Until this incident," said the oddly stooped chief mercenary, "we had no idea how dangerous Firebird is. I guarantee that she will commit no further treachery."

Esme kept her fork moving. Her father laughed merrily, and his guest watched him . . . instead of his eldest daughter. A good thing, because if they really could read people's emotions, her horror might attract attention.

What would her life be like as heiress to a seized throne, controlled by offworld interests? It was clear to her, if not to her father, that these people were about to grab all Netaia. Did she have to choose between collaborating with these murderous "unbound" or with Prince Tel's Federate friends?

She never, never could take a warning to the Federates. That would betray all she believed. But Prince Tel had pricked her conscience at the ball, talking about wastlings, and motives, and . . . and her little brother and sister. Her father's actions today were *wrong*.

She shivered over her hot soup.

INTERLUDE 7

Carradee woke up wreathed in a strange feeling of peace. She checked the time—three hundred forty. For a while, she listened gratefully to the soft hum of Daithi's spinal regen apparatus and his slow, steady breathing. Then she rolled out of her bed toward the twins' chamber. A small luma glimmered there, and a watch-keeping sekiyr lay on the bed between warming cots. Her nephews slept peacefully. Tonight she plainly saw Brennen in Kinnor's relaxed expression. That was unusual, but she knew an Angelo from a Caldwell.

Silently she dressed. She couldn't have said why. She slipped out of the medical suite and walked onto the waterside pavement. A pale turquoise band rimmed the vast pool, shadowed by islands and square stepping-stones but casting enough light to walk by.

She followed a stepping-stone path to an island and sank onto a stone bench. There, she gazed into the water until memories came: Iarlet tottering onto her feet and then, seemingly only a day or two later, dashing naked out onto the palace balcony. Kessaree shrieking with laughter at her sister's face-making. Iarlet explaining soberly why she would not, could not, wear the same-colored skinshirt two days in a row.

It felt good to weep.

Half an hour later, Master Jenner strode out onto the stepping-stones, and Carradee knew what he must tell her. She was as ready to hear it as a mother ever could be. She'd cried herself dry.

"They have found your girls' bodies," he said as they sank back onto the bench, "and the wreckage of their shuttle. It was attacked, Carradee. I am sorry. They were . . . murdered. We should receive more details soon."

She shook her head. "They are with Him," she murmured. "They are safe. No one can hurt them now. But pray for me, Master. And for Daithi."

"Shall we move the twins from your suite, to give you time to grieve your daughters?"

"No!" Carradee cried.

CHAPTER 19

ORDERS

prestissimo
as quickly as possible

Firebird's pulse pounded as she sat and watched the tall, pale woman walk out. Signs of early pregnancy—the full, high breasts, the barely darkened mask across her cheeks—were there for any observant woman to read. Terza Shirak's statement, "The plan was to lure you in," told her the rest of the story.

Could anyone call this Brennen's child, since he had no role in its conception?

At least Terza was trying to see that no one found out except Brennen and herself. Firebird tried to imagine Brennen's eyes, Brennen's personality . . . Brennen's abilities . . . imprinted on a baby that wasn't hers, too. They knew that the Shuhr carried on the Ehretan tradition of genetic research. They'd discussed the possibility that his cells might have been cloned. Now ramifications were occurring to her that she hadn't considered. Especially . . .

Was the child genetically Terza's, too? A Caldwell-Shirak? *Mighty Singer, what is this?* Her arms and shoulders still trembled with her body's reaction to danger. She hadn't lost her maternal instincts, either—she wanted to rush home and grab Kiel and Kinnor, to never let them out of her sight again.

Terza's other revelation, alone, would have stunned her. Cassia Talumah had told the truth when she claimed her brother "brought in tissue samples" from Iarlet and Kessaree. If that man, Terza's victim, really killed them, then . . .

Poor Carrie!

Then Firebird's promise in the Hall of Charity could shackle her to a gilt chair and the weight of a world. She no longer wanted that, not even as a reformer.

Mighty Singer, send me back to Hesed, to my children, my new life. I was wrong to try to return to this.

Then she thought of the ice miner and thousands of other commoners struggling for a share of Netaia's prosperity. She thought of monstrous Hinnana Prison and wondered how many children's parents languished inside.

Singer, what do I do?

She knew one answer from Path instruction: Commit this day to His will and live it. She would be grateful for specific guidance, though.

Brennen looked in her direction, and his lips tightened again. She could almost read his thoughts: *You shouldn't have been here.* His next glance was at Burkenhamn. The big marshal stood motionless, covering his face with both hands. Governor Danton leaned against the tri-D well, staying close to his guards.

Surely he hadn't heard Terza's revelations.

"You have your prisoner," said Danton. "Finally. Who's your strongest Sentinel here?"

"Firebird's bodyguard, Major Mattason, has the highest ES rating." Brennen said it without hesitating. "But Lieutenant Colonel Harris is better qualified for access interrogation, and even before he begins, I have orders to open." He raised an eyebrow to Uri. "Marshal Burkenhamn," Brennen added, extending a hand, "my sincere apologies. You must not doubt what the Shuhr woman said about her compatriots planting that suggestion."

"Not at all." Burkenhamn cleared gravel from his voice. "I felt it as she shouted. I deeply wanted to kill Commander Angelo, whom I respect."

"Commander *Caldwell*," she murmured.

Burkenhamn didn't seem to hear. "And it . . . still . . ."

Burkenhamn's guards seized his arms, but he threw them off. Shel stepped toward him, blocking Firebird's view. Uri hissed a word of command.

The marshal came no closer. Firebird saw only his legs, working as if he were trying to walk in mud. "Not my doing," he muttered. "Help me, Sentinel."

"Gladly," said Brennen. "And I need one thing from you, sir. I need a set of orders, for Second Commander . . . Caldwell," he said after a moment's hesitation. "I need her to report to me, for the duration of an upcoming operation."

"Yours," said Burkenhamn.

Shel stepped aside, but not far, and she kept her blazer ready. Now Firebird had a clear view of her marshal and the anguish on his lined face. "Commander," he said, "report to Field General Caldwell for the duration of operation . . ." He broke off, glancing at Brennen. Getting no response, he turned back to Firebird. "You will remain under General Caldwell's orders until he dismisses you back to me."

Chain of command wasn't so different from palace nod-and-bow, really. Firebird raised her right arm stiffly, touched one eyebrow, and murmured, "Y'sir."

Brennen glanced to one side. The Sentinel at Burkenhamn's right shoulder nudged the big man's arm. "Come with me, Marshal." Two more Sentinels followed him out, through a different door from the one the Shuhr woman's guards used.

Brennen's glare softened, and Firebird felt his concern. "Commander," he said, "your first order is back to sick bay. Your exercise interval ended five minutes ago. I'll join you there," he added.

Her medical aide drew out a hand controller for her mobility chair. Firebird still heard her pulse thudding in her ears. She raised her wrist and saw that the cardiac monitor's display had gone red, into the danger zone . . . as if that would surprise anyone. She felt aged, decrepit—

And bitterly resentful, that the Shuhr used Marshal Burkenhamn against her. Once again, her new rank and honor nearly led to tragedy. *I see your point, Mighty Singer. I get the message. Enough!*

As the aide steered her back up the corridors, her thoughts fled to Hesed House. *Poor Carradee! Who will tell her she has no daughters?*

Brennen waited until she'd passed out of the range where they could share each other's feelings, then clenched a fist. This situation wasn't developing remotely as he'd anticipated.

Glancing around, he beckoned the nearest remaining Sentinel . . . not Uri, who couldn't leave him, but the next closest. "Lieutenant Cowan?"

The young man with the blond beard hustled forward.

"In my quarters, on my work desk. Sealed message roll. Meet me outside sick bay with it."

One more Sentinel left the command center. It was becoming almost private in here. . . .

Then he sensed a tracking tech's alarm from over near the tri-D well. "Sir." The woman stared at him, not the governor. "Messenger ship outbound, heading six-one-two point one-two. Refuses to ID."

Brennen hurried to the three-dimensional cylinder that represented space within the primary Netaian system. Green spheres were planets, silver dots meant satellites, and gold pinpoints represented friendly ships.

The tracking tech pointed toward a gold pinpoint streaking outsystem. According to characters displayed alongside, the ship was a DS-212 Brumbee messenger, launched from the NPN's Arctica Base, accelerating too quickly for any hope of intercept.

"On that vector," Brennen said softly, "it could be headed for Tallis, or Caroli—or Three Zed." That system lay north-spinward of Caroli. Shuhr agents here could be reporting on events in the Hall of Charity.

What had they concluded?

"Keep trying to reach him by DeepScan," said Governor Danton. "If there's any other unscheduled activity, either on or offworld, notify General Caldwell and myself."

Medical supervisor Adamm Hancock's dark eyes and sharp chin framed a frown as he tucked a microfiber blanket around Firebird's legs and chest, bathing her in warmth. She started to relax. "You're supposed to be working back up to walking," he said, "not trying to get killed."

Her cubicle's door slid open. Brennen stepped in, clutching the silvery message roll down at his side.

"Thank you," Firebird told Med Hancock. "I really didn't plan—"

"Of course not."

"May we have a few minutes alone?" she asked. Over her chest, the regen arc felt oddly warm, almost comforting.

"Ten minutes, General," said the medic. "Then I'm going to sedate her. That'll put her back on schedule."

"Excellent," Brennen answered.

Hancock scurried out. After the door slid shut again, Firebird raised a hand. Brennen seized and stroked it. "You're cold," he said.

"You're warm. Open your orders."

"I will, as soon as I've cleared you to hear them." He set down the message roll to pull the new pocket recorder off his belt, thumb it on, and recite date and time. Then, "Second Commander Firebird Angelo Caldwell, Netaian Planetary Navy, now under my orders, hereby designated my forward attack subcommander." He returned the tiny recorder to its place, then thumbed the cylinder's security seal and twisted the halves apart. "Breathe, Mari," he murmured.

She hadn't realized she was holding her breath. She took a deep, slow breath. Then another.

He unrolled the sheaf carefully. His eyes flicked left and right several times. "Operation Yidah," he read softly. "We're . . . hmm." He frowned.

"What, Brenn?" she demanded.

His displeasure came through strongly. "We're to take off, with prisoner, and interrogate en route to a rendezvous point north-spinward of Caroli."

Hastily, she calculated travel time against her retraining schedule. She could do it—barely—if they really were headed to Three Zed. " 'Yidah' sounds Ehretan," she said.

"It is," he murmured, still scanning. "It's one of those prime words with half a dozen meanings. Various uses of the hand—to throw a stone, cast out, offer praise . . ." He lowered the roll, widening his eyes. "Or thanksgiving. Or to bemoan."

"The hand," she said softly. "A sword in His hand."

He shook his head as if to clear it. "We'll leave today. You'll have ten days en route, and that doesn't give you any leeway at all. I'm ordering you to stick with that schedule."

"I will." Firebird knew which system "ten days en route" indicated. "Then we are ordered to Three Zed."

"Of course." He curled the sheets between his hands and slipped them back into the message roll. "As directly as possible. No devious attack vector, no warning. The Federacy wants us to burn it to bare rock."

Her breath caught. This went further than she had expected. Clearly, the Federates were so terrorized by the Shuhr's destruction of an entire city, and by their uncontrolled use of epsilon talents, that they felt this was justified. Even Brennen's people had been warned that they would be called to this task one day.

"But is there a discretionary provision?" she asked. That holy call still had not come.

He shook his head, washing her with a dizzying mixture of reluctance, eagerness, anger, and pity. "Even if our force is wiped out, the Holy One always keeps a remnant alive. Only sixty-two of the faithful survived Ehret— Mattah and his family, their friends, and the orphans."

"Then at worst, Kiel and Kinnor will be part of the next remnant," she murmured. He'd obviously thought this through.

"They sent a roster of ships and personnel waiting to rendezvous with us." He ran a hand over his hair. "My first job is to get a transport with a full med suite, and a secure room to hold . . . Terza."

"Quickly," she said. "Once they know she defected, they're likely to throw everything at this base."

She still felt his uneasiness. He leaned down and brushed her lips with his. He smelled of kass. "By the time you come out of sedation, we're likely to be en route. Is there anything you need to accomplish first?"

"Yes. I've still got some business for Tel." There had to be some way she could disinherit herself. But when Terza's news about Iarlet and Kessaree reached Netaia from other sources, the electors would have to either acclaim a new monarch or else give the crown to Rogonin.

"Finish it," he said, and his eyes softened. He'd probably guessed half of the thoughts that just blasted through her mind. "You're prone, you're under regen. I'll hold off the med for a few minutes."

He sent a sick-bay aide for her recall pad as he left. When the aide returned, Firebird dictated a new will, with orders for copies to be sent to Hesed, the Netaian Electorate, and Prince Tel. If she died at Three Zed, Tel was to distribute whatever remained of her allowance to Kinnor and Kiel, pending their confirmation as heirs. If by some miracle Carradee conceived again, he was to petition the Electorate to restore the throne to Carradee's line. Three days ago, she wouldn't have requested that. *Dying does change a person. . . .*

Finally, she outlined her plan to reconfigure the Angelo portfolio to support eventual covenance with the Federacy. Effective immediately, Tel was to divest her of hidebound, nobility-based trade and industry, using the family wealth to support offworld trade and programs that would strengthen the common classes.

If he hurried, they might prevent civil war after all.

In the two hours estimated to convert the Luxian diplomatic transport *Sapphira* for his needs, Brennen had to do two days' work. The heavily armored, adequately armed transport had been assigned to the Luxian ambassadors, Comete and Cometesse Remelard. Brennen's message roll did include a *commandeer* order from Regional command, and on seeing it, the mustachioed comete instantly relinquished claim to his ship. Danton's top engineer went to work, removing most of its comforts to make room for additional quarters and converting an inner cargo hold to a reasonably comfortable brig.

With work teams dispatched, Brennen paused in a secure room off the corridor and reread his orders, trying to commit all salient points to memory. Even after all the Shuhr had done to his family, and to the rest of the Whorl, he did not want to command such a brutal operation without divine confirmation. This could also be the end of Special Operations as a significant group if his force was defeated. Most of the rest of Special Ops, and Thyrica's Alert Forces, waited at the rendezvous.

Please confirm this, he begged. *Send us with your blessing, or else show me I must disobey Federate orders again. You know I will obey either call. The Federacy is afraid, but you are above fear. We all live by your unconscionable grace and mercy.*

He'd given up his chance at the Federate High command by disobeying an order he couldn't follow in clear conscience. He would do that again, if necessary, to save Sentinel lives. That would mean a permanent dismissal from Federate service. At least.

Firebird was the last Angelo, though. The Electorate would undoubtedly call her back to Netaia. He was willing to serve wherever the Holy One sent them. If only he knew . . . clearly . . .

He waited more than a minute, resting his forehead on clenched hands. Nothing came.

Then he would have to wrestle with his conscience en route. Meanwhile, he did have orders.

Most of an hour later, he and two other Sentinels were testing epsilon-fielded locks on the new brig's windowed door and every other escape route, logical and illogical. He'd also arranged for Terza to be watched clock-around from a guard station just outside the brig and by in-cabin monitors. Only the One knew what other compulsions her people had put on her, besides the watch-link.

As he stepped through the crew lounge, past a triple bunk that workers were bolting to a bulkhead, the door to his own forward quarters slid open. Shel stepped away from the hatch and stood aside. Two med attendants came steering a medical litter up the port passway. Firebird lay on the litter, unconscious under the regen arch. He lingered at the hatchway, watching the meds squeeze alongside a newly installed forward berth in his cabin. Marks on the deck and bulkhead showed where other furnishings had been removed.

"I want medical monitors at my bridge station," he said, eyeing her face. A faint flush warmed her cheeks, and those delicate features never quite relaxed, but carried a hint of her determined spirit. He wanted to protect her, not take her to—

"Installing them next, sir." The meds raised the green-and-white arch, rolled his bond mate onto the new berth, then set about installing the arch in its new position. "Barely room to swing this aside, sir."

"We'll manage," he told them. *For five days, until we get to the rendezvous point and aboard a bigger ship.*

Back out in the passway, Sentinel pilots hauled duffels into assigned cabins, singles reconfigured as doubles. *Sapphira's* redundant life-support suites would support them, and he wanted every combat-trained Sentinel on board to crew RIA ships. According to his orders, he would command the attack cruiser *North Ice*, the fighter-carrier *Weatherway*, and their complement of RIA-equipped scouts, bombers, and fighters.

He flexed his hands and stepped onto the bridge. Pilot, nav, shields, and sensor/com officers were already there, running preflight checks, cross-programming the escorts' navigating computers.

A tone sounded on *Sapphira*'s com board. The Sentinel running checks touched a tile. "*Sapphira*, Lieutenant Mercell at Sensors."

Danton's voice came through clearly. "If General Caldwell's on board, send him back to the command center. All haste."

"On my way," Brennen called, already jogging.

Lee Danton gestured toward a wall screen. "We're getting a picture from . . ." He stared a question at the nearest controller, whose headset dangled from one ear.

"Satellite outsystem, sir."

The governor frowned, drawing his eyebrows down almost to touch at center. "We've got an unauthorized rollout at Sitree Air Base."

Brennen eyed the screen. Sitree was twelve hundred klicks west-southwest of Citangelo. Well within striking range, three long-range fighters had been rolled out of their hangars and were being serviced.

"According to Sitree Command, they're being fueled and fitted by Marshal Burkenhamn's order," said the controller, "but Burkenhamn insists the order didn't originate in his office. Not that he can remember."

"The Shuhr could've had him authorize any number of things." Brennen cast a glance around the command center. "Sir, you'd better go to full alert."

"Gambrel Base is scrambling regular crews to fighters," Governor Danton assured him. "But how many ships did the Shuhr throw at Sunton?"

Brennen silently raised three fingers.

Danton touched his collar mike. As he called for a second-stage alert, Brennen sprinted back into the corridor.

Tel Tellai glared at a tri-D image. He couldn't believe this Codex propaganda! Firebird, dead by Burkenhamn's hand? And Caldwell, sheltering a woman who carried his child?

Ridiculous.

". . . as proof Caldwell's treachery started months ago," the Codex commentator intoned, "proving again that Netaia's former lieutenant governor has been a covert leader of the Federacy's attempt to enslave the Netaian systems. His Grace the Regent is in emergency session with the Electorate, considering a declaration of war. A further announcement is anticipated at any moment."

Another electoral meeting, called without him—illegal!

Tel strode across his study and poured a glass of mitana, an eden-fruit liqueur. Rogonin's loyal commentator had to be lying. Surely Devair Burkenhamn hadn't killed Firebird, not after all she had survived at the Hall of Charity.

He sent a servitor to bring his remote CT link, then tried to ring the base. Again he was told Firebird could not be reached.

So he paced his portrait-lined library. Caldwell never would have been unfaithful, any more than Firebird could have been. Yet the unknowing Netaian would react with savage insistence that the Angelo dynasty had been cuckolded.

Another face appeared over the projector, again no spokesman, but Lee Danton himself. Sipping the perfumy liqueur, Tel stalked back to his media block. According to Danton, Rogonin's announcement was proof of the regent's treachery, not Caldwell's. Firebird was not dead, he insisted. Burkenhamn had been sent to the Federate base, ordered by Rogonin's mercenaries—there was some confusion on that point—to murder Firebird. The offworld woman had been impregnated against her will with cells cultured from an unidentified donor's skin, using a well-known *in vitro* technique. She had been granted asylum.

Had Shuhr agents told Rogonin's office that the unwilling "donor" was Caldwell? It was possible. He'd been their prisoner.

My fault. Tel passed a hand over his eyes. *And Phoena's*.

Additional imagery followed. It appeared to have been recorded inside a military base, and the image bounced as if it had been made with some kind of hidden equipment. Even now, certain panels were obviously blurred for transmission. There was Burkenhamn, pressing toward Firebird. She looked considerably less pale than Tel might have expected. A garbled shout from behind the pickup brought in guards. Sentinel Mattason made a spectacular flying intercept. Two Federates seized the huge marshal. Imagery shifted to show a tall, black-haired woman with a strikingly sharp chin leaving the room under guard. "Bravo!" shouted Tel.

"Lady Firebird took no further injury and is resting comfortably. We return you to scheduled programming," said an unprofessional voice, some tech maybe, at the Codex studio.

Tel shoved his liqueur aside, rang for cruinn and sank onto his most comfortable lounger, pondering his next move in an increasingly dangerous field game.

His footman broke into his thoughts. "Prince Tel, the Countess Esmerield and Duke of Kenhing are here."

Tel sprang to his feet.

The slender dark blond woman swept past his servitor, wearing thrown-on clothing. Her hair and face were lovely for not having been coifed or shaded. "Dismiss your servitor," she ordered, panting. Kenhing followed several paces behind her. Immaculately dressed in dark green, he looked startlingly like his brother Daithi. It had to be his hair, waving slightly out of control, that emphasized the resemblance.

Kenhing had seemed mildly sympathetic to Firebird's cause, back in the electoral chamber. Still, he wore his dagger. Tel clasped a little blazer deep in his pocket. He nodded over Esme's shoulder at his footman, who stalked out. Tel's hidden security staff could defend him against this pair, although if Esme had come from the palace, Shuhr "mercenaries" might have tampered with her, just as they had obviously brainset Burkenhamn. "What is it?" he asked, willing her to be sincere. "Kenhing, I thought you were in an emergency meeting."

"It ended half an hour ago."

Esme glanced around his library, at the volumes his fathers had collected and the portraits he'd purchased and painted. "Prince Tel, something is wrong with Father. He isn't acting at all like himself."

"We have also been assured," the duke said stiffly, "that Citangelo Base is about to be destroyed by our new so-called allies. Allies the Electorate did not call to Netaia, nor were we consulted about allying ourselves with them."

"Allies that Governor Danton just accused of setting Marshal Burkenhamn against Lady Firebird?" Tel demanded, clenching his pocketed blazer. "Allies who destroyed a city on Thyrica?"

Kenhing frowned. "We're in danger, Tellai."

Tel stepped closer. "Why did you come to me?"

"My staff tells me you recently raised a security force—"

"And you're Lady Firebird's friend," Esme interrupted.

"You want me to rescue your father." Tel stared down the countess, loathing the idea.

One heartbeat later, he guessed this was exactly how Caldwell had felt, four months ago when Tel asked him to rescue Phoena. The realization wrenched his gut.

Esme tilted her chin. The redness in her eyes brought out their green fire. "I know Father treated you shabbily. Please help us anyway. They'll destroy Citangelo, and he won't listen to reason."

Kenhing raised one hand as if in entreaty, but he seemed reluctant to lift it too far. "Tellai, I never would tell you this, except that I need you to trust me . . ." Trailing off, he glanced at Esme.

She straightened her shoulders. "I can be trusted with secrets, too, Kenhing."

The duke tucked his thumbs into his belt. "You will recall that my wastling brother Alef vanished some years ago. Lady Firebird was suspected of involvement."

Tel raised his head. "And?"

"She *was* involved, Tellai. I overheard a conversation. This is the first time I have ever mentioned it. I never incriminated her, nor Lord Bowman, when the incident was investigated. There are times to look the other way and times when we must act. Tonight, we have no choice." Straightening his tunic, he added, "Esme says there is talk of leveling your estate."

Tel whirled toward the countess. "Who said this?"

"Father's mercenary." Esme glanced from Tel to Kenhing. "Moda Shirak, or whatever his name is. The man with the cruel eyes. You're right, Kenhing. If Alef is alive somewhere, I don't care. In fact, I'm glad."

Esme had seen Micahel's infamous father? Tel wondered what kind of fears she'd been living under, with Shuhr haunting the palace.

Save Rogonin?

Save Phoena? Brennen hadn't scorned him but had gone to Three Zed. If Brennen could go to that planet, Tel might dare step into an occupied palace.

He ran his fingers through his hair. If the Shuhr threatened his own estate, he must not risk his servitors making multiple trips into the countryside, trying to save possessions.

But he must alert Danton. He'd seen what the Shuhr did to Sunton.

"Thank you," he told them both. "We won't have much time."

Her cheeks flushed. "Do you think you can do anything?"

"I will try." He motioned Kenhing and Esme to a lounger.

He rang for Paudan, gave a few orders, then paused to think. Firebird had finally admitted that Sentinels had infiltrated palace staff. Had they all left the grounds when she and Caldwell moved out?

Yes. If Shuhr were there now, all Sentinels had left. Maybe he could enlist a few of them at the Federate base. He could disguise them in Tellai livery.

He called the base again. "This is Tellai," he told the man who answered. "I need to speak with any one of the Sentinels. This is a Shuhr-related emergency."

CHAPTER 20

TRAITORS

precipitando
rushing, impetuous

Terza sat in a close, bare cell with the familiar dull scent of recycled air, watched by two keen-eyed Sentinels. Grim thoughts taunted her. *You thought he would value you. Already you've been ignored. They don't want you at all. He doesn't want your daughter, either. Traitor. Useless traitor. Do away with yourself, quickly.*

At least they'd let her change out of that uncomfortable palace uniform. The door opened. Her guards saluted someone in the hall.

Caldwell stepped inside, followed closely by the Sentinel she'd identified as his bodyguard. "I apologize that we haven't been able to speak with you sooner, Terza," he said. "We're going to move you. Since you believe you might be watch-linked, we're going to ask you to wear a sensory hood set to an entertainment display. You could help us by concentrating on it."

There was a presence to that man, an empathy, that was utterly different from anyone she'd ever known. She would've expected a former captive to be angrier, more vengeful.

A third Sentinel steered a mobility chair into the room. On its seat was a hood like ones she'd seen used for personal recreation. It had an eyepiece, earphones, and sensory pads on both sides of the nose.

She helped them adjust it for comfort, then took a seat on the mobility chair. When they switched on the hood, the eyepiece went opaque. Instead of her bare holding cell, she saw the view from an open-air mountaintop, a jagged horizon that seemed to stretch on forever. Pale blue sky darkened to azure overhead, and there was a scent of woodsmoke and . . . was that intoxicatingly sweet odor wildflowers?

"We just lost your sister," said a voice in Micahel Shirak's flight helmet.

"What do you mean, lost her?" he demanded, dancing on his rudder panels. *Just a little closer, Federate . . .*

He had penetrated Sitree Base with six of his father's voice-commanded lackeys. Only two had fighter experience. He sent the other four, loaded with incendiaries, into the other hangars. Four black smoke plumes rose behind him.

Evidently Sitree Base already had two fighters out on patrol. One was hot on his tail.

"Watch-link's still functioning," said his father's voice. "But they put a sensory hood on her. She's cooperating with them."

"*Can* she? Really?" Micahel sneered.

Modabah probably was in the new observation post under the palace's central public zone. "We've been trying to trigger suicide. So far, she's resisting. I'm not sure how. As long as we have her in link range, we can keep trying. But the sensory hood could mean they're taking her shipboard. If so, they could be headed—"

"To Three Zed," Micahel interrupted, firewalling his throttle as his left wingmate blasted the second pursuer. Caldwell, taking off with Terza, couldn't beat Modabah's messenger to Three Zed, not even if he launched quickly . . . but he might give Micahel a close race.

He wouldn't leave Netaia's atmosphere at all if Micahel got to Citangelo in time.

He vectored east, followed by his wingmates. They had taken off in three armored HF-class fighters, fully fueled and warhead-loaded. That weighted them for the deepest possible penetration at Citangelo.

"I'm turning you loose," said his father's voice. "We'll have to break a second-rate captive to get that RIA information. Crater Citangelo Base. Kill them both . . . what?"

The helmet voice became an unintelligible buzz. Micahel cruised east, accelerating over the midland corridor's irrigation grid, leaving a roiling wake of turbulence in thin clouds.

Modabah's voice came back. "Lift-off," he exclaimed. "One armored transport and four fighter escorts just cleared Citangelo. Cancel the base attack. Engage that transport. You're authorized to destroy, Micahel. I wash my hands."

Micahel shifted his hand on the Netaian fighter's control stick, arming a missile. From this range, his beyond-visuals couldn't pick up Caldwell's launch plume—but no transport could outrun heavy fighters. Not far.

The winter sun dropped in the southwest as the Angelo footman Tel knew as Paskel opened a side gate of the palace grounds. "I don't think the Shuhr have been here long enough to find all entry points," he murmured, "and we put down remote surveillance, but that might not last."

"Only gardeners use this gate," Tel said, waving Esme, Kenhing, and a column of liveried men and women through the vine-draped arch. Five Sentinels had appeared at his estate twelve minutes after he called the base. He reinforced them with ten armed Netaians. "We expected to need Esme's personal codes to open this."

One Sentinel, Thurl Hoston, had warned him: Either they would surprise the Shuhr agents, in which case this would seem all too easy or they would be taken captive and subjected to terrible violations. Tel had given all his new guards the option of backing down. Two did.

As Tel walked, he glanced up at the private wing's dark windows. So Firebird really had gotten Alef Drake offworld. He should've known! She had amazing courage.

The next time he was at Hesed, he would ask her permission to tell Alef's brother Daithi, Carradee's husband, what she had done.

Paskel shook his head, huffing as he kept up. His tight curls looked limp and sweaty. "The sensors on this side of the main building should remain down for six more minutes," he said. He pumped his arms as if jogging. "Palace staff is in turmoil. We're accustomed to taking orders from nobility, but something plainly has happened to the regent. The countess"—he nodded respectfully toward Esme—"left a message with her personal girl, which I intercepted. We lacked a leader, Prince Tel. Thank you for coming."

Tel glanced aside at Kenhing, who walked with his chief guard, Paudan. Kenhing might have sheltered Firebird's old offense, but obviously, he didn't dare to take responsibility this afternoon.

The footman, Paskel, halted the group at the edge of the grove of drooping evergreens. Tel checked the time lights at his wrist. They had four minutes to get inside.

Paskel strode up the lawn, up the colonnade steps, and spoke to a sentry. The crimson-liveried House Guard, sworn to defend the Angelo family, marched with Paskel to one of the huge white columns. He vanished behind it, and did not reappear.

Evidently the invaders hadn't yet taken time to mind-bend palace servitors. No wonder Paskel and the others had rallied around Esme. The sentry probably had agreed to turn his back.

Sure enough, Paskel peered around the column and flicked his fingers.

The group sprinted almost to the colonnade, then slipped in through a small side door. Paskel led down granite stairs into a corridor. "We need your Sentinels now," he murmured. "Stay on this side of the first door. That's the next surveillance zone."

Tel waved the Thyrians forward. Paskel was right—within a room's width or so, the Shuhr could detect other minds. Only the five Sentinels could shield their approach from the invaders and hope to surprise them.

Almost indistinguishable from Tel's own employees, all wearing black and indigo now, the other Sentinels crowded around Sentinel Hoston. "The intruders set up an observation post," Paskel explained. "Behind the fourth door on the left there is a storeroom. Behind that is a long chamber, directly below the palace's communication office. They tapped in between levels."

"Any other way out?" Hoston asked.

"Yes." Paskel pantomimed a long, invisible swath in the air. "The inner chamber can also be accessed by way of a second storeroom behind it, which connects with the next corridor south."

"We'll split up." Hoston looked hard at Tel. "Send your people to the next corridor. Paskel, can you show them the right door?"

The big servitor nodded. To Tel's surprise, he slid a blazer out of his white cummerbund.

Sentinel Hoston eyed Kenhing and Esme. "If we don't make it through that second door into the chamber, be ready for a violent counterattack. Noncombatants should wait in the stairwell." He raised a blazer, then donned a breath mask. "We're going to use gas." His voice came muffled through the mask. "Stay well back until we signal."

Tel nodded, wanting to help storm the chamber but knowing that was as unrealistic as when he'd wanted to enter Three Zed with Firebird. He didn't have the strength—epsilon, physical, or emotional—to carry a fight to this enemy.

Paskel led the Netaians toward the second passway, then the Sentinels moved out. As they passed the first door, Tel pulled a deep breath.

Twenty meters down the corridor, the Sentinels filed through a door on the left and out of sight.

Something touched Tel's hand. He looked into Esme's wide green eyes and turned his hand to grip hers. "Countess, you should be in the stairwell. We both should. Those people are professionals."

As they backed into shelter, she didn't pull her hand away. "Do you think they can—"

He heard three blazer shots, then scuffling noises. Finally, a *whump*. Full of dread, he tugged her back several more paces. The Sentinels would've warned them if that gas might spread, wouldn't they? Some chemicals broke down or dissipated quickly—

He peered out. One Sentinel reappeared at the door, slightly disheveled, her mask in one hand. She beckoned.

Tel led Esme and Kenhing through the uniform storeroom into a long, narrow chamber haphazardly crowded with subtronic gear, including three live observation screens and several unreadable consoles. The woman who'd waved them inside busied herself assisting another, who bent over someone leaning against the wall. It was Hoston, the senior Sentinel.

Paskel peered in from the south storeroom. "I can call for a staff med." He raised one hand. Tel spotted an interlink curled between his plump fingers.

Tel started to say, "Yes—"

"No." Hoston coughed, then explained, "There were only two of them down here. There must be more uplevel. Don't attract attention. We have biotape and topicals. It's . . ." He winced as his partner applied something to his chest, maybe a painkiller. "Just burned skin," he managed.

Esme backed out of the chamber, looking pale. "Stay with her," Tel murmured to one of his own men. "Don't let her tip them off."

The security guard nodded and followed her out.

"Look." An older Sentinel pointed. "That console was made by a Carolinian manufacturer." He moved his hand. "This display is from Inisi. That sensor array is Bishdan."

"Stolen," another Sentinel explained to Tel and Paskel. "Those are all Federate worlds that supply Regional command, Tallis."

Kenhing squeezed in alongside Tel. "Is that proof?" he demanded. "Proof of collaboration, admissible in electoral court?"

"Maybe not, but this certainly is." The Sentinel raised one of several recall pads. Tel squinted at the display. He couldn't read a word.

"Ehretan," the Sentinel explained. "That is our holy tongue of worship. Evidently *they* use it as their primary language. We have common ancestors. And that," he said slowly, "constitutes proof. So do these epsilon-fielded devices." He gestured toward the door. "If we hadn't caught this pair unaware, they would have sealed the room, and none of us could have gotten in."

Too easy, Tel heard in his mind. It had been their only chance of success.

Kenhing turned aside. "Wait," he exclaimed. He picked up another recall pad and passed it along. "How many of these did they leave lying around?"

Sentinel Hoston drew out a cloth square, took the recall pad inside it, and thumbed it on. His fingers tightened on its edges. "This is even better. These are orders to someone who accompanied Burkenhamn to the base." He read phrases that put ice water in Tel's veins. " 'Burkenhamn will be quick—a simple strangulation, a blow to the head—break her neck . . . but it must be his doing, not yours. Do not interfere. . . .' " The Sentinel trailed off. "This is next: 'Micahel is prepping two crewmen for the clean-up mission. Don't worry—we'll be far out on the plains in less than three hours—' "

"I've called Citangelo authorities and suggested evacuation," Tel interrupted.

The Sentinel glanced up at him. "Well done. I'll call this in, too. But here is the incrimination. 'Rogonin is cooperating fully.' " As Hoston's glance traveled down the screen, other Sentinels wheeled around and stared down at him. Tel wondered what Hoston had found. Something had brought up such a strong emotional reaction that he couldn't hide it, despite that infamous Sentinel emotional control.

Hoston pocketed the recall pad, though, so Tel refrained from asking further questions. Another Sentinel steadied Hoston on his feet.

"Will we recognize the Shuhr who are here?" Tel asked. "We mustn't harm innocent bystanders."

Paskel slid several thin tiles, printed with images, from inside his cutaway coat. "We've been using a camera recorder when we can. Several of our guests seem to constitute a core group. This appears to be the woman who defected." He laid a tile on the nearest console.

Tel had never appreciated servitors' cleverness or ubiquity quite as much as he did today. The dark-haired woman on the tile did look familiar from newsnet broadcasts.

So did the next image. It was the man she had killed on base.

The third image made his hands clench. "That's Shirak," he exclaimed softly. "Micahel Shirak, the assassin. I last saw him in gold." He passed the image to Hoston.

"Just so," said Paskel. "But he seems to answer to this one." He laid down the final image. The man resembled Micahel, somewhat older, with the same cleft chin and dark hair. "They call him Modabah, or Eldest. According to my sentry, he was down here for a little while, but he didn't stay long. He's with Rogonin in the main level private dining room." The big Netaian glanced up and north.

Moda, Esme had called him. *The man with the cruel eyes.*

Again the Sentinels exchanged glances.

Kenhing squared his shoulders, laying one hand on his dagger. "With this chamber secured, we should be able to get up there. Paskel, is the entire staff with you?"

"No." Paskel adjusted his cummerbund. "There are a few who can't imagine disloyalty in His Grace."

"Look," exclaimed one of Tel's own.

Tel glanced up. On one of the observation screens, several gleaming objects accelerated away from Netaia. Four small darts escorted a larger, blunted craft. Out of the west came a second flight, three darts pursuing the first group.

"Caldwell?" Tel demanded.

The Sentinel bent toward the console. He fiddled with controls, enlarging the image. Numbers scrolled across the monitor. "Probably. The others are Netaian heavy fighters. Origin looks like Sitree."

"Friendlies?" Kenhing asked.

"No!" Tel exclaimed. "That would be Micahel—he was to prep two crewmen for the clean-up mission! They're on their way here—"

"No," Hoston said, drawing a blazer to check its charge. "Citangelo isn't in any danger if Micahel has General Caldwell in sight."

"They're closing," the man at Sensors announced. "According to calcs, they won't reach intercept range before we can slip, unless they haven't fully accelerated yet."

Brennen answered, "I suspect they have." A suite of monitors enclosed his raised chair on *Sapphira*'s small command deck. The heavy Netaian fighters drew steadily closer on his aft screen. He had no doubt who was on board. He hated to run from Micahel, but this time he couldn't turn back and fight.

Unfortunately, even if *Sapphira* escaped being shot down, its north-spinward heading would leave Micahel no doubt of his destination. Those long-range fighters were slip capable, and Micahel wouldn't lose precious hours decelerating to rendezvous with a Thyrian battle group. Unless Brennen's pilot coaxed more acceleration out of *Sapphira*, Micahel would beat the Sentinel force to Three Zed.

From the previous messenger, the DS-212 launched from Arctica Base, Three Zed's defenders might even know exactly what threatened them. Shirak's home forces could have time to mount a fierce resistance, doubling or even tripling their fielding staff, even though Micahel might report that Brennen was coming with only this small force.

Brennen touched a com panel. "Engineering, can we safely exceed maximum normal speed? How long, and by how much?"

"I'll calculate and get back to you, sir."

"Push it while you calculate," Brennen ordered.

"Preparing to slip," Shields announced from the next seat over.

The slip-shields took hold. Brennen let himself relax slightly. Micahel wouldn't have time to catch them on this end of the slip.

The odd vibrational sensation nudged Terza out of her induced alpine reverie. At the same instant, a heaviness—something like her father's epsilon presence—slipped away from her. Along with it went all thought of suicide.

She had been taken shipboard, then, and they'd just escaped watch-link range. Shutting her eyes against the magnificent upworld view, she turned deep inside to hide behind her inner shields again. Was she free?

No. From this vantage, examining her own alpha matrix, she still sensed something unstable. She might be clear of watch-link, but Talumah had performed deep epsilon tampering, and she could do nothing to counteract it.

Then she hoped these people had locked her down securely. They'd promised they would do everything in their power to free her.

In the next moment, she knew where she was bound, and what her captors would want from her en route. Of course they meant to destroy Three Zed! They wouldn't take her to Tallis or Thyrica, and certainly not to their own fortress world. She'd faced that fact once today—what her defection could mean to others—but that had been under her father's compulsion. She had no emotional tie to anyone left in the Golden City.

Traitor! The accusation blasted through her mind anyway, from no source but her own stricken conscience.

She pressed her palm to the warm place below her belt. *This is for you*, she thought at her child. *It's the only way you ever will be safe.*

And, she realized, it was also for the Netaians—and others—that Juddis Adiyn would have infected with gene-modifying organisms.

On the observation screen in front of Tel, the blunted craft vanished, followed almost instantly by its escorts.

"They're away," murmured one Sentinel.

"Headed back to Hesed House, I'll guess," Tel said, doubly relieved. Caldwell had escaped, and Citangelo wouldn't be turned to a crater.

The two nearest Sentinels stared at each other, obviously speaking mentally. One said, "I hope so."

Hoston spoke up from the floor. "Don't frighten Countess Esme, but it's vital to get Rogonin in custody. He can be released from whatever they've done to him if he lets us try."

Tel remembered Firebird's assurances and Caldwell's self-restraint, proving that Sentinels could only use their gifts under special circumstances. "I understand," he said. "So you won't . . . dispatch him . . . without giving him that chance?"

"Not if there's any way to save him."

Tel rejoined Esme in the corridor, seizing her hand again. Her fingers felt cold between his. "Esme," he said, "listen. You were right. Your father is not himself. These intruders are Shuhr, and they've done things to his mind."

"Obviously," she snapped.

Tel didn't take offense. A frightened daughter would tend to snap. He glanced pointedly over his shoulder. "The Sentinels have promised me they will try to heal him—"

"Don't promise him," she demanded, glaring into the storeroom. "Promise me. You have no idea what a leap this is, trusting Sentinels."

Whatever they did behind his back, it must've satisfied her. She gripped his arm with her other hand.

"I promise, too," Tel said. "I will not harm your father." He drew his little blazer out of that deep pocket.

Esme nodded solemnly.

Hoston stepped toward the door. Now Tel saw that his livery jacket was burned open, low on the left side of his chest. Pale pink biotape showed through the gap.

The group followed Paskel up another service stairwell, placing feet softly, shifting weight carefully. With the observation post put down, there was less worry about being spotted, but "less" worry wasn't little enough for Tel.

He thought instead of the man with Rogonin. Modabah Shirak was probably the one who had ordered Firebird killed at the Hall of Charity. More than likely, he watched Phoena die. Tel didn't doubt he had the emotional strength to kill *that* man, if given a chance.

The Sentinel behind him must've picked up his determination or else spotted his small personal blazer. He nudged Tel's arm, silently offering a Federate service model butt-first. It looked twice as powerful as Tel's own, but Tel shook his head. He didn't want his life depending on an unfamiliar weapon.

The Sentinel returned his spare to an odd-shaped holster.

At the landing nearest the main-level kitchens, one more part of the palace Tel never had thought to see, the senior Sentinel halted the group again. "Have your people pair off with us," Hoston directed. "We'll have to hope we can shield your minds, so they won't sense us coming as we get close."

Tel passed the order down the line, then stepped closer to Hoston. Six of his own, unpaired, fell back.

Again he thought of Hoston's warning. This must seem utterly simple, or they had little hope of succeeding. The slightest alarm or mishap could doom them.

Tel and Hoston emerged shoulder to shoulder at one edge of a kitchen. Clattering noises covered their footfalls. A large man supervising kitchen machinery stared, wiping his hands on a floury towel. He barely nodded to Paskel, eyes wide, lips firmed.

Tel spotted a closed-down service window, where higher-ranking servitors out in the dining area would bring spent dishes to this crew for sterilization. He waved the others back. Hoston stayed at his elbow, breathing quickly but quietly. Tel edged closer to the window. The other four Sentinels, paired with four of Tel's guards, hurried to the main door. Tel's people held blazers. So did two Sentinels. The others drew silvery handgrips out of sleeve sheaths—their ceremonial crystaces, Tel realized.

Footsteps approached on the window's other side. Tel raised his blazer, steadied his elbows against the windowbar, and waited. He would have only one chance. The instant they saw him, they would attack.

Simplicity or failure, the quickest of surgical strikes or slow death. He would rather die here than live on a Netaia ruled by Shuhr.

The service window blinked like an eye, and Tel glimpsed the private hall. Several plainclothes men and women stood along the walls. Beneath a jeweled chandelier, two men sat at the table's near end. Tel recognized Rogonin's broad back. He knew the other man from the tile-image—Modabah Shirak.

In that moment, the intruder raised his head. Evidently Tel's escort couldn't shield his disgust.

Modabah would warn the others! Tel squeezed his trigger and held it down, pumping out three energy bursts.

Shirak toppled with a patch of his scalp smoking.

"Go!" exclaimed a voice behind Tel. Tellai-liveried Sentinels and Netaians spilled into the dining hall. Tel let the blazer fall from his hand, staring at that smoking hair. His gorge rose. He rushed to the corner, gripped the sterilizer's edges, and emptied the contents of his stomach. He vaguely heard shouts, eerie humming noises that had to be crystaces, the sharp crack of furniture and the duller sound of bodies falling.

By the time he turned back to the private hall, guards stood at every exit—his own guards, joined by several kitchen staff wielding knives and other kitchen tools. Bodies strewed the parquet floor. Six wore Tellai livery, and Tel cringed at the sight. Rogonin stood beside his chair under the chandelier. Scorch marks spotted the ceiling and walls.

He hurried out into the hall. "Call your med, Paskel," he ordered.

"On his way." The footman coolly covered one fallen Shuhr with his blazer.

I'd never make a soldier. He'd told Firebird and Brennen that months ago. Now he knew how true it was.

He joined Kenhing at the long table's near end. Rogonin spotted Tel and laughed shortly.

"Your Grace," Tel said, "I have the dubious honor of asking you to submit to arrest."

"Arrest?" As Esme suggested, Rogonin had a giddy light in his eyes, a defiant lift to one eyebrow. Even during the fracas back at Hunter Height, Rogonin had always maintained some dignity. "I'm a sovereign head of state," he declared. "You can't arrest me."

Tel drew up as tall as he could. "The sovereign answers to the Electorate, Your Grace, and there are several electoral charges that must be brought against you."

"What charges?" Rogonin put out a fleshy hand and grabbed the back of a chair. "In desperate times like these, strong leaders take stern measures."

A gilded entry opened. Three medical staff hurried in.

"First," Tel said, trying to sound firm and self-assured, "a charge of sedition against the noble house that you serve as regent. You have tried, consistently and illegally, to discredit and disempower House Angelo."

Rogonin laughed sharply. "The traitors deserve to be discredited. Every one of them—except young Iarla, of course." His lips curled in a smile. "And I don't think Her Majesty will be found soon."

Something like a cold hand gripped Tel's emptied stomach. "Do you know that for certain?"

"Of course not—"

"He's lying," said a voice behind Tel.

Aghast, Tel turned his head slightly. One of the Sentinels frowned at the regent. "He knows."

Rogonin had known Carradee's daughters would not be found, and he'd done nothing? That was treason! "What else did your . . . guests . . . tell you?" Angry now, Tel gestured toward the nearest body. Two servitors and a Sentinel crouched over it, draping it with kitchen towels.

"I am not on trial," Rogonin growled. "I only asked to hear what trumped-up charges you think you can bring against me. Speak carefully, Tellai. You too can be accused. So can you, Drake."

Tel exchanged dark glances with Kenhing. "Second charge," said Tel. "Subverting electoral procedures, by excluding House Tellai from two known electoral sessions, and probably others."

Kenhing spoke up. "That is an indictable offense," he added, "though not as serious. The Sentinel just accused you of the highest treason, Rogonin, and complicity with murder. Have you nothing to say?"

Rogonin lowered himself into his chair, then pushed the remains of his meal aside. "You're in on the uprising, too, Kenhing?" He laced his fingers across his stomach. "Go on."

Rogonin hadn't denied the charge! "Finally," Tel said, clenching his own hands in dark fury, "you will be charged with collaboration with off-world enemies of the Netaian state. The evidence is overwhelming, Your Grace." He looked pointedly at the nearest body—his own recruit!—and then laid Paskel's tiles on the table. "These individuals brought outworld gear into the palace and established an observation post downlevel. Much of it can be identified by world of origin. Some of it plainly—plainly, Your Grace—originated on Three Zed. This evidence also implicates you in the second attempt on Firebird's life, as well as a pending attack on Citangelo. On the people you are sworn to serve, Rogonin."

Rogonin's left cheek twitched. "You would have to convince twenty-six electors, Tellai."

Kenhing stepped forward. "I'm convinced. I don't think there will be any difficulty with the rest of them. You will be charged, Rogonin. You are plainly guilty. And if you're implicated in Iarla and Kessaree's disappearance, even by Sentinels, I will—"

"Traitors," Rogonin cried, clenching a fist. "Have you no idea what the Federatization of Netaia would mean? Workers displaced, commerce and government disrupted. Common influences taking over all arts and media, low elements ruling our schools, poisoning our children—"

Tel leaned both hands on the table, facing the regent. "Sir," he said sharply. He must try to show mercy.

Rogonin shut his mouth.

"Sir, these so-called guests of yours tampered with your mind. Let these Sentinels help you. They say they can undo Shuhr mind-work, but they will do nothing you will not allow."

Rogonin straightened. "Tell that to Caldwell," he barked. "He forced mind-access on me." He lowered his voice. "Who brought these creatures into my home? Wait—I think I know. Esmerield looked furtive at supper."

Tel flicked a glance toward the kitchens, where Esme hung back, hidden from view but not out of earshot. "She wants to see you healed, Your Grace. She loves you dearly."

"And she shows it this way?" Rogonin sprang to his feet, tipping his chair.

Tel backed away from the table. All around the room, liveried men and women stepped forward, brandishing whatever weapons they held.

Kenhing stood his ground. "If you refuse their help, Rogonin, and frankly I wouldn't blame you, then you will stand trial . . . and we *will* allow Sentinels to give evidence, if there is a charge concerning Her Majesty Iarla and Princess Kessaree—or any damage to Citangelo, including the Federate base." From the scabbard on his belt, he drew his shining dress dagger. He laid it on the table. "Or there is the traditional recourse, sir."

Rogonin glowered at Kenhing. Tel didn't expect him to let any Sentinel into his mind—but if he had only two choices, then for Esme's sake, Tel had to hope—

Then he thought of Firebird and all this man had done to her. To those adorable daughters of Carradee's. He wanted to see this man dead.

Kenhing stood stiffly. "Regardless of your choice, we will abide by the electors' designation of a new regent. Muirnen Rogonin, you are to be praised for your service to Netaia. On behalf of the Electorate, I thank you. But your service to this council has ended."

Two years ago, Tel had heard First Lord Erwin read those words over Firebird as she knelt between two redjackets. Geis orders, requiring her to seek a noble death.

"If you would prefer not to stand trial," Tel said softly, "I can send in your children to say their farewells. But the Sentinels are willing to help you."

Rogonin touched the dagger's hilt. "Traitors," he muttered, "in my own house. Leave this room, all of you." He opened his fleshy hand and seized the dagger.

INTERLUDE 8

Jenner Dabarrah, master of the Sentinels' sanctuary, wryly raised an eyebrow at Carradee. Seated on a bench in his medical office, within earshot of the reflecting pool's continual rippling and splashing, he crossed his long arms. "I did offer," he said gently. "Mazo Syndrome is treatable."

Carradee smiled. That syndrome, diagnosed in Firebird and treated on Thyrica, had kept the Angelo women from bearing male children and proved their kinship with the other Ehretan descendants. "Yes," Carradee answered. She reached aside to her husband's mobility chair and squeezed his hand. Yesterday, Daithi had taken a few hesitant steps out on one of the reflecting pool's green islands, where kirka trees were dropping their bud sheaths, revealing sticky, pale green needles. She could smell the fragrant sap from here.

New life was flowing in them all—

"Thank you, Master Jenner," she said. "We were grateful for your offer, and maybe we were foolish not to ask for treatment before we tried to conceive, but we are not disappointed. Nothing and no one will ever take Iarlet or Kessie's place, but we will be delighted to hold another daughter." *Thank you most of all, Eternal Speaker. I promise you, we will raise her to honor you.*

"Congratulations, then." Master Dabarrah rocked to his feet, stepped forward, and gripped Daithi's other hand. "You will have the very best of care."

Daithi's smile showed most of his teeth.

Carradee squeezed his hand even tighter. Let the gossips theorize about his chances of recovery now!

CHAPTER 21

CAPTIVE AND CONQUEROR

modulation
change of key

After Brennen checked on Firebird, he paused in the forward crew lounge to collect his thoughts. Shel sat watching her charge sleep. *Sapphira* was stable on course, and Engineering assured him it could run at fifteen percent past normal max for at least one shipboard day, pushing their acceleration well into military standards. The Luxian government had invested in an overengineered ship.

Uri emerged from the medical suite, where Terza had just been moved, again wearing her sensory hood. "Hancock's finishing a physical exam," Uri murmured. "Shouldn't take long."

Brennen nodded, listening to the soft drone of engines and ventilators. Twenty-four souls had squeezed on board, and he'd scheduled most of them for at least one daily watch on guard. Terza must be constantly observed by at least two Sentinels.

Uri took four steps back up the corridor, peered into the med suite, then beckoned.

Guide us, Holy One, Brennen prayed.

Uri settled on one of three stools alongside Terza's cot. Another guard sat near her feet. Over her head, a row of instruments gleamed with life signs. The corner readout indicated that a restraining field had been activated.

Med Adamm Hancock stood beneath the instruments, crowded against the inner bulkhead. His ash gray uniform looked rumpled from the hurry to board and launch. "Good general health," he told Brennen. "Mid first-trimester pregnant, as you said, with a female fetus. Are you sure you don't want me to administer a blocking drug?"

Brennen took the stool between Uri and the guard. Dispersing his shields, he felt a whirlpool of sensations—Terza's reluctance, chased by suspicion, anger, and dread.

"No drugs," he repeated. "If the child is in any danger, alert us."

The med nodded.

Brennen watched Terza's eyes for any sign of deception. "Is the child yours, too? Or a monoclone?" A male could have a monoclonal daughter if gene techs used two X-gametes.

"She is mine," Terza whispered.

Brennen exhaled, disgusted by their cruelty to her. "Sentinel Harris will breach," he said. "I'm sure you know I've been disabled."

"So we've been told," she said, "but no one believes it anymore. Not after . . ."

After several seconds, Brennen asked, "After what?"

"The Hall of Charity." She stared straight up. "She's alive. Unless that was *her* doing."

"How could it be?" Brennen demanded. He opened fully to Uri and sensed the gentle probe Uri was passing over Terza's alpha matrix, looking for natural flaws. It was easier and kinder to breach for interrogation that way, and this time it was also safer. Only the One knew what she might do by reflex if provoked.

"Polar's research," she answered.

Brennen frowned. "I don't recall much of Polar's research. I remember nearly nothing that happened at Three Zed."

"You'll see, then," she said, closing her eyes. "You know I was watch-linked. We're out of range, but I don't know what else was done to me."

More cruelty! No wonder the woman defected.

"Talumah probably placed other traps for you," she continued. "He is a master. But he never found my inner shields. I've kept them secret from everyone. I'll open them to you. If you stay inside that perimeter, you're probably safe."

"Thank you," Brennen murmured. Some Sentinels also had inner shields, but a skilled interrogator could find and break them.

Uri leaned away from her and drew a deep breath. Brennen took a moment to compose himself, too.

"There are already a number of rough breaches," Uri muttered.

"Surprise." Terza's bitterness came through strongly.

Brennen winced, observing, *Shirak, you may have doomed your own world by treating her this way.*

Uri leaned forward again. "Look this way, please," he said. "Can you open those shields?"

Brennen felt him stroke aside her bitterness and doubt, entering her alpha matrix on his first modulated thrust. She stared bleakly at Uri's eyes. As Uri maintained the breach, Brennen sent a follow-on probe. He swept gingerly over her surface emotional state, confirming her intention to leave her people, a motive so powerful that even their newer countercompulsion hadn't stopped her. Then he penetrated her memory and confirmed her claim to that hated name.

He saw how the girl-child was created and implanted, and he confirmed that the gamete carried his genes. This was a laboratory child, conceived not in love but in cold calculation—but his child nonetheless. Aware of Uri's intimate presence, he internalized Terza's shame, and how it intensified her latent wish to escape.

He'd felt the savor of Shuhr before, but that time he'd been the subject under scrutiny. Terza did not resist as he and Uri studied her personality. Now he sensed the shields, a protective secondary matrix surrounding his probe. They were unbelievably dense. On the Ehretan Scale of a theoretical hundred, this woman probably blasted off any cap. 110, 115?

The ones who'd done this to her were just as powerful. Her impulse to leave them was consistent with lifelong lines of character and intention. She'd always struggled with the demands placed on her. Her single desire now was to save the child she'd been forced to carry.

She had fixated on him, particularly. Once, she'd hoped to help Micahel kill him.

Her people did fear him. Some of them had started to seriously consider the prophecies given by Ehretan shamarrs. Respect for those prophecies had shaped so much of Brennen's life that it startled him to realize the Shuhr were just starting to believe.

And they did want him alive. Any Shuhr who destroyed him now would suffer excruciating consequences.

He sensed a call from Uri and drifted across her alpha matrix to recent memory.

Eldest Modabah Shirak had ordered Tallis attacked, in response to their suspicions about himself and Firebird. The order had gone out on the DS-212 messenger ship that was racing along, two hours ahead of *Sapphira*. They did suspect the Casvah mutation, and that it gave rise to exceptional power in the Angelo line.

Tempted to rush to the command deck, Brennen clung to his stool. He could not warn Tallis from slip-state. Instead, he double-checked their conclusions about the Angelo line. Terza had made the intuitive leap herself.

He couldn't fault her for observing and analyzing events. He probed deeper along that line of thought, into the complex web of long-term memory. The Shuhr did mean to seize other worlds, ostensibly to offer physical immortality. Wealthy Netaia would be first. . . .

In a laboratory, she'd seen evidence of Netaia's ruling family and its members' fates. The four-year-old queen and her sister were dead, just as she claimed. And Phoena . . . he'd forgotten watching her die, but his captors had taunted him about having failed to save her. Now Brennen saw her current status. Hideously crippled, skeletal muscles torn loose from their attachment points, she was incurable even by Shuhr technology, alive only by medical convention. Her physical brain could not recover. Held in cold stasis, at least she was not suffering.

Chilled, Brennen abandoned that thread and went deeper yet, beneath Terza's memory, to see if anything could be read at depth. Down here, the asphyxiating otherness of her core personality stole his breath, and he knew this was making her excruciatingly uncomfortable, too.

Studying the layer at depth, he found knots of suggestion—sabotage, deception, murder—a minefield strung with trip threads. Touching any locus at this depth would activate a deep, treacherous programming that would override any other intention, whether or not she truly hoped to escape. Neither he nor Uri had the skills to help her. Only psi-medical masters like Dabarrah or Spieth might make her safe.

Brennen pulled back, for her sake as much as his own. His chest ached with pity. His ancestors had created the skills that had allowed all this. His own people would have turned to domination just as surely as hers, without the Codes holding them back.

How many other Shuhr had doubts like Terza's?

Not many, maybe. She let him examine her inner shields at depth, where they arose. Now he understood how she'd hidden the compassionate side of her nature in order to escape Polar's vicious culling processes. Behind those shields he found a woman he could respect.

He withdrew for a moment, tiring. He would have a daughter. A half sister for Kiel and Kinnor. *Guide us,* he pleaded again. *Can I destroy her people in good conscience?*

As if in response, his epsilon carrier flickered out.

He opened his eyes, afraid Terza had attacked him. She reclined on the cot. Hancock attended to the flickering life-signs board, and Uri sat with eyes closed. Only the guard raised his head, catching Brennen's glance. Nothing seemed to have changed. . . .

Then he felt a nudge at the edge of awareness. This Voice never shouted but waited to be heard.

Brennen shut his eyes again. *Yes?* he asked urgently. *Yes?*

The Voice spoke in darkness this time, without giving him visual cues. *Take comfort in this,* Brennen heard. *There are no innocents in that city. Its iniquity is complete. Destroy them completely. You shall be a sword in my hand.*

The confirmation he'd wanted—the assurance he craved! He was free to attack evil in good conscience.

But . . .

Holy One, I am inadequate. Please restore what I was before. Crippled like this, I cannot serve you well.

The Voice answered, *I am strong when you are weak. Only in seeming death will you begin to live.*

Seeming death? In *Dabar*, that Ehretan term referred to physical death, which his people euphemistically called "the passage Across." *Is that my own call, then? To die at Three Zed after all? Show me, if I can bear it.*

He felt a deep love, a weight of eternal humor and terrifying sovereignty. Whether from the Holy One or his own imagination, he pictured the debris left from a terrible space battle. Pieces of a Thyrian Light-Five fighter tumbled, blasted open to space. He recognized a dead-on missile hit. *Even then*, said the Voice, *I will not forsake you. You are never alone.*

Brennen gulped air, naked before the Eternal. He remembered Mari's dream-vision, and the pronouncement that had been made over her, as the specter of wreckage drifted through his mind. Out of respect for the Presence, he strangled his terror of darkness and enclosed spaces and his very real, very human fear of dying. Of course the Holy One would not forsake him, even in physical death. But he'd hoped . . .

He could create other hopes. *I'll go wherever you lead*, he responded, *but please send Mari home to be a mother to our sons. Spare her from grief. Sustain her in your mercy.*

I will be all things to her, answered the Voice.

Terza had easily distinguished Lieutenant Colonel Harris's brisk, efficient probe from Caldwell's. Caldwell had a depth, an earnestness that settled the nausea of mind-access. After Caldwell's presence vanished, Harris withdrew almost immediately. She stared at them both, dissipating her own shields. Harris's confusion was easy to read and understand, but whatever was happening to Caldwell, it was nothing she'd seen before.

After several seconds, he opened his eyes, startling her. From this angle, there seemed to be a light behind his irises . . . an afterimage of something incomprehensible, something supernatural.

He moved his head, and the light vanished.

Maybe it was a reflection from the overhead panels.

"Are you all right?" Uri asked urgently.

Brennen nodded, though he felt more stunned than comforted. He wished he hadn't asked to be shown. Maybe his death would change the Federacy's attitudes toward his kindred. It was not necessary to understand, only to accept the holy call, and its cost—just as he'd gone to Three Zed. *You're certain I can bear this?* he prayed. "We're called," he murmured. "He . . . spoke to me."

Uri sat up straight, smiling as he lowered his eyebrows fiercely. "Was there more?"

"Not . . . yet. Go on," Brennen urged, to distract Uri. "We need to map Three Zed and find out how they mean to attack."

Uri adjusted his stance. "Terza," he said firmly.

The Shuhr woman's stare focused on Brennen just a little longer, long enough for him to understand that she'd seen something she couldn't comprehend.

Then she squinted at Uri again.

Brennen managed a turn. He felt Uri breach with one efficient probe. Piggybacking again, he drifted alongside Uri into a deep, golden city . . .

And he recognized it.

The nugget-textured corridors, the magnificent central chamber, the ancestors' hall . . . he knew them. Without hesitating, he led up a north-bound corridor to the fielding station. They had not taken him there, but he'd heard them refer to it. *This way,* he cued Uri.

An instant later, Uri seemed to be peering over his shoulder. *How did you know?* Uri subvocalized.

Brennen whispered, "I remember." Again he pulled out of access. Had the Eternal One granted his prayer, restoring everything he'd been? He spotted a writing stylus beside Hancock's elbow. His hand shook as he focused epsilon energy, then willed the stylus to rise.

It rolled, but it didn't lift.

He clenched his hand and dropped it in his lap. He'd received the confirmation he wanted, and an assurance that his attack would not kill the innocent alongside the guilty. Now he remembered that no children lived in the Golden City. They were raised in outlying settlements. His other memories from that place would be vital for the upcoming attack.

He did remember Polar's research now. He understood Terza's reference. He knew why pulsing red lights carried the terror of Three Zed: His cell door had been ringed with them.

He also remembered Phoena Angelo, writhing out her life in a pale yellow gown, sprawled on the glassy floor of a chamber full of exotic artworks. He recalled the unsettling temblors that had felt like distant explosions.

Rejoining Uri, now he saw areas where he had not been admitted. Terza knew little about its military sites, as he would expect, but enough to show heavy bombers where to strike. Enough that he and Mari should be able to find the fielding operators and blast them with fusion energy.

Uri pressed a final query, and now Brennen saw their abominable plans for Netaia, including the deliberate infection of every Netaian with gene-altering viral agents.

Tallis was in a more conventional danger.

Plainly, it was time to strike. Destroying the Shuhr stronghold would prevent both tragedies.

Uri rocked back on his stool, away from Terza. "Enough," he said. "Terza, unless there are other things you want to show us, we are finished."

She blinked, and Brennen sensed her surprise. "I thought you would take it all," she muttered. "Not just the colony, but my mind, my memories."

"Those belong to you," said Brennen. "We never take more than necessary." Now he recalled one other interrogation, when he *had* been ordered to go deep, to capture the Netaian mindset. Federate needs had led to the fulfillment of his own almost two years ago. That memory warmed the cold chill that had settled on him. "We serve a God of mercy," he added.

"So I hear," muttered Terza.

Uri raised his head, glancing up sharply.

Maybe he shouldn't have said that much. Terza hadn't asked any relevant question. *If I said too much, forgive me.* But in his urge to show mercy, Terza was the nearest in need. She'd done everything in her power to help them. *Accept that as her service to you, Holy One. Give her grace to receive you.*

"Pray for me, then," she muttered. "For my . . . for your child."

Stunned, he rested one hand on her shoulder and let the words come. "Show Terza and this child that mercy, Holy One. If Terza is a danger to herself or to us, protect us all by your power. Dispel her fears with your glory. So let it be." He barely pressed down on her shoulder, a reassuring gesture.

Terza lay motionless, clenching one hand over her chest as if seizing a new sensation. Her lips quivered. *So that,* she subvocalized, *is what faith feels like.*

Firebird pulled out of sedation by stages. First she sensed the deep contentment of lying in Brennen's presence. Gradually she became aware of a steady thrumming.

She opened her eyes. Brennen sat on the carpet beside her bunk, leaning against a richly embossed bulkhead, studying a recall pad. He finished making a notation with one finger, then reached up and laid the pad on the pillow of a second, luxuriously deep cot. "Good morning, Princess," he said softly.

"Don't call me that." She kept all venom out of her voice, though. The long, deep sleep had left her feeling extraordinarily refreshed. "Looks like you found quite a ship—" Or was this sense of peace something she felt in Brennen? "What is it?" she murmured. "What happened?"

He carefully released the humming arch and helped her sit upright. "I hardly know where to start."

That brought her fully awake. She stretched, careful not to twist her spine. "Then go from the middle. What happened?"

He told her about mind-accessing Terza, then about hearing the Voice again.

"The call your people have waited for?" she asked, laying a hand on his forearm. "What a relief! Now you can be certain."

"Yes. I made an announcement in the crew lounge. I wish you could've seen the change in attitudes. The new determination, the humility. And there's more." He looked directly into her eyes. "I have my memory back."

"That's why you feel different," she whispered. "You feel . . . complete again." Trying to will her pulse rate down, she leaned against him. "How did it happen? What did you do?"

"Only what I've been doing since Three Zed. I asked. This time, the answer wasn't 'wait for my time.' " His voice fell several notes down the scale. "My other abilities didn't come back, though. And He . . . didn't promise either of us would survive."

"Has He ever promised that?" she asked gently. She caught a faint feeling, almost a scent of mastered fear.

Brennen shook his head. "Only that in His country, we would be cleansed and restored. Remade as we should have been."

"With all our atonements made."

His eyebrows knit. "Mari, we don't make our own atonements."

"I know." She clenched her hands into fists on her lap. "But all you went through at Three Zed, doesn't that count for something? What I'm going through now?"

Brennen hesitated. Her Path instructor had explained this. *He* had explained it. Sometimes, she even seemed to understand.

But she'd been raised to believe she must sacrifice herself, and that her own actions must balance her shortcomings. Her willingness to give everything, her determination to serve at all cost . . . those were laudable, but . . . *Holy One, how can I make her understand that you will pay the price for what is inside her?* She'd learned so much . . . and at least the nagging notion of making her own atonement no longer roused her Angelo pride.

"He refines us, tests us, disciplines us. Sometimes He even lets the Adversary use pain, Mari. But we do not make our own atonement. You seemed to understand that, not long ago."

She spread her hands. "I can recite everything they taught me back on Thyrica. But this . . . idea that I have to do it myself, it keeps bubbling up out of my past, and I latch on."

"Don't give up," he murmured, twisting around so he could face her. His lips pressed against hers, warm and strong. Then came the smoky-sweet sense at the back of her mind . . . and it carried the memory of all the trials they'd shared, this time as *he* remembered them. She sensed the way her mental cry of grief over Veroh had sparked his eager curiosity, and she rejoiced in the way that his determination to see her recruited, possibly even converted, had been completed. Their sweet wilderness flight at Tallis, when she leaped off a mountainside into his arms . . . now she felt the passion he'd barely controlled at the time and his ecstasy in its consummation at their pair bonding. In memory, she stood inside his skin to face Phoena's death squad at Hunter Height, and then at the moment when Master Spieth told them they would be parents. She felt his anguished pride in the insane moments when Kiel and Kinnor emerged, and a regret almost as deep as his faith when they parted at Hesed House, as he left for Three Zed.

Truly, he was back! He leaned deeper into the kiss, tangling his fingers into her hair. She raised one arm to slide it around his shoulders, and a jolt of pain made her pull away.

It was only a little jolt, though. She was substantially better. With exquisite care, he helped her to her feet. "Ready to walk a bit?" he asked.

Before coming to the palace this morning, Tel had checked on Clareen Chesterson. Rescued from detention by two servitors, she was back at her own apartment. She'd answered his CT call in high spirits, assuring him she had enough song ideas to last into the next year.

A high-toned bell called the Electorate to order and broke off his thoughts. He stood beside the gold-rimmed table and then watched as a redjacket escorted Bennett Drake, Duke of Kenhing, to the gilt chair at the table's head. Newly sworn as regent, Kenhing held his silver rod along his forearm, close to his chest. Like Tel, he wore three narrow black wristbands. Esme Rogonin, her cheeks pale and her eyes red above her long purple mourning gown, held her head high. Her mother had declined to attend.

Kenhing took his new place. The electors seated themselves.

"Our first order of business," Kenhing said, "is to acknowledge Esmerield Rogonin as Duchess of Claighbro, head of House Rogonin. Our sincere condolences, Duchess. Your father's death was honorable."

"Thank you," she said gravely. "The holy Powers have surely received him into bliss, along with Iarla Second and Princess Kessaree." There was no bliss in her eyes, though, or on her trembling lips. Tel ached for her. Rogonin's allegedly honorable suicide was utterly unnecessary, just like the deaths of so many wastlings, but it had saved House Rogonin the humiliation of an ugly, protracted trial.

Yesterday, Netaia had added mourning bands for Iarla and Kessaree.

Kenhing—regent for whom?—touched Tel's arm. "Prince Tel," he said, looking up the table. "You asked to speak before we deal with the issue of succession."

Tel knew what they expected him to propose. Count Wellan Bowman already was glaring.

Tel laid both hands on the table and pressed slowly back to his feet. "First, my respects and congratulations to Your Grace." He turned to Esme and softened his voice. "My sympathies as well to you, Duchess." He paused, giving them place if they cared to respond.

Esme looked away.

"There are," Tel continued, resting one hand on the table, "unconfirmed reports that Second Commander Angelo Caldwell and General Caldwell are en route to Three Zed, the stronghold of those offworlders who brought this tragedy on House Rogonin. We are hearing rumors of an impending attack."

Young Duke Stroud Parkai swept out his arms. "We could lose House Angelo!"

"No," Tel said firmly. "For one thing, I witnessed her sons' birth. They do exist, under protection at the Sentinels' sanctuary world. They are in deadly danger if they go anywhere else, as long as the Caldwells' enemies have the power to strike."

Several sad stares turned to frowns. They'd never liked the idea of bringing an offworlder's sons into the palace.

"I urge you to . . . to pray," he said carefully, avoiding the customary *petition the Powers*, "for Firebird's safe return. Meanwhile, noble electors, I have received a communiqué from the Sentinels' sanctuary world, Procyel II. You may recall that Carradee and Daithi took up residence at Hesed House there. Daithi has been treated for his injuries."

He fingered the ends of his gold-fringed sash. "Noble electors," he repeated softly, "I have just been informed that Her Former Majesty Carradee is pregnant again. Before Lady Firebird left Netaia, she asked me to propose that the throne be restored to Carradee's line if Carradee conceived." He hadn't contested Firebird's instructions. He'd thought this was impossible.

Esme Rogonin tilted her chin. Winton Stele pushed away from the table, smiling broadly. Kenhing's sober frown faded. "Has Carradee given the child a name?" called the regent.

Tel nodded. "She has. Her third daughter will be Rinnah Elsbeth." *Rinnah*, a small blue Netaian songbird, was also the Ehretan word for *Adoration*, according to Carradee's communiqué. He shook his head. "I do suggest, for the sake of stability and a more rapid return to status quo government, that we acclaim Firebird instead."

"I would second that proposal," said Kenhing.

Reshn Parkai, Baron of Sylva and DeTar, gripped his writing stylus in a hammy fist. "A convicted criminal, the mother of a mind-crawler's heirs? When we could acclaim an innocent, pure-blooded Netaian?"

"Technically," said Count Quinton Gellison, "Firebird was not confirmed as an heiress. The ceremony was interrupted before that point."

"Rinnah Elsbeth," Tel answered the count, "has not been confirmed either."

Valora Erwin scowled. "Better a known monarch now, a woman who was raised among us, than a someday unknown who will probably grow up on the Sentinels' fortress world."

Tel clasped his hands on the tabletop as the argument heated up around him. This session would probably last far into the night. At one corner of his vision, Esme Rogonin stared in his direction.

He opened his hands, spreading his fingers in a diminutive shrug.

Esme smiled faintly.

CHAPTER 22

STORM'S EYE

allegro malinconico
fast, melancholy

Walking steadily, Firebird followed Uri across a docking tube onto the Thyrian battle cruiser *North Ice*. During her rest intervals, she'd spent hours developing a new visualization to help her stay conscious during epsilon fusion. Brennen had insisted they not try it—yet. From time to time, she caught a new depth, almost a desperation, in the small, kindly gestures he always made. There were hints, too, that he was shielding something from her.

She thought she knew what that was. If he'd been called to destroy the Golden City, his sense of duty had to be struggling with his compassion. Any trained soldier had doubtful moments, and he'd just regained memories of that place and its people. They must be haunting him, she guessed.

They probably ought to be haunting her. Terza had turned from Shuhr ways. Weren't others capable of changing?

"She's different," Brenn had explained. "Most Shuhr children with her disposition are culled in training—killed by their teachers. Either that, or they aren't admitted to train in the Golden City."

Firebird stepped onto the other ship's deck. A woman who appeared to be in her mid-forties, wearing midnight blue and a Sentinel's star, saluted Brennen. "Wing Colonel Janith Keeson, General. I relinquish *North Ice* to your command."

Brennen also saluted. "Colonel, I return *North Ice* to you with thanks. Carry on."

Sentinel Janith Keeson wore her chestnut hair short and curly, and her cheeks bulged like pink snow-apples. She turned to one of the few crewers in the docking bay who didn't wear midnight blue, and she gave a hand signal. Orders passed out of earshot, up the passway and onto a transpeaker system. "Shamarr Dickin sends greetings and a blessing," she added.

Firebird smiled at this news from Brenn's spiritual father.

"There's one important development," Brennen said. "We're called.

The Holy One has ordered us to strike Three Zed. There's no longer any question of following the Federate order."

"That's a relief." Colonel Keeson broke a smile, but it quickly faded. Firebird had wanted to see a Sentinel react to this news, and evidently the thrill of following a divine call didn't last long. Next came the sobriety of taking up holy responsibility.

Colonel Keeson stepped briskly up the corridor, and Firebird matched her pace. Under regen, her bruises had faded, muscles knit, and the last nerves were regenerating—though her ribs and spine still ached.

"How quickly can you secure and accelerate for Three Zed?" Brennen asked the colonel. "We're racing an advance scout."

Sentinel Keeson halted beside a wall console and called a string of orders. "How quickly can you prepare for acceleration, sir?" she asked.

Minutes later, Firebird sank onto another bunk, raised her arms as a new set of medics clamped down the regen arch, and then lay listening to the drive engines' pitch rise. Around her private cubicle, the meds anchored everything that was loose. "War is always like this," said Shel. "Weeks of boredom punctuated by minutes of panic, when only solid training means survival."

"Netaia has a similar saying." Brennen had assured her that *North Ice* would have flight simulator booths, and that her assigned Light-Five fighter would have an onboard sim-override program. She must be at her peak for this mission.

Brennen stepped into the small, private cubicle half an hour later, after gravidic compensators restabilized the deck. "Thank you, Shel," he said solemnly. "I relieve you."

The bodyguard slipped out.

"We sent a messenger to Tallis," Brennen said, standing close, "and general alerts to the Second Division. Terza's on her way to Hesed, under guard. There's no need to keep her in harm's way any longer."

"Good," Firebird murmured.

He laid a hand on her forehead. "Colonel Keeson just gave me more good news. When Alert Forces heard that Burkenhamn recommissioned you, they refitted a full-powered Light-Five for you with RIA and remote-pilot capacity. We're as well-equipped as we could hope."

"Good," she said again. Actually, as badly as she wanted to start her onboard sim training, she was scheduled to rest now. "Help me sleep." She shut her eyes. . . .

When she opened them next, Brennen had gone. A dark-haired woman had taken his place—a slender woman with keen dark eyes and a strong, shapely nose. Firebird knew that face. "Ellet," she exclaimed, tensing. Once, the Sentinel woman had been determined to claim Brennen for herself. Ellet had eventually pair bonded Brennen's friend Damalcon Dardy, though Brennen never adequately explained how *that* came about.

"I won't stay," Ellet said softly. "I only wanted to wish you well. To congratulate you on your new rank, and your survival. You're a tough woman to kill, Commander." Ellet barely smiled. She looked hesitant, unsure how she would be received.

Firebird couldn't resent Ellet any longer. "Coming from you," she answered, "that's a compliment."

Ellet's smile spread to her eyes, crinkling the skin around them. "I didn't just come with compliments." She slid a stool close to Firebird's narrow bunk. "I came to apologize. Firebird, I have been blind to your humanity. I owe you a debt, and I must ask for your forgiveness."

Marriage had certainly changed Ellet! Firebird could've easily gloated, but what would that accomplish? She was finally rid of pride . . . temporarily, she guessed. She would postpone its return as long as possible. She raised her arm, and Ellet clasped her hand. "Thank you, Ellet. What's your job here? Where's Damalcon?"

"I'm military historian for Colonel Keeson. Damalcon's on board the carrier *Weatherway*, and I transshipped over as soon as you arrived. He'll command the second flight, the heavy bombers."

"It's good to have you on board," Firebird said. This five-day slip might be Ellet's first separation. "Look me up if you get lonely."

Ellet Dardy raised an eyebrow. "You put me to shame," she said.

After Ellet left, Firebird checked the time. She had to spend another half hour prone, and she couldn't waste it. She must learn to stay conscious after achieving fusion with Brennen. He'd said that fusion stayed with him for as long as he could hold a turn, like keeping all mental circuits hyperactivated. If she could keep from fading out, then maybe she could actually do things with it, beyond simply setting off the explosion.

Brennen was probably on the command deck or down at Engineering. He'd spent most of his time on board *Sapphira* in one of those places. Struggling against the regen projector, Firebird loaded an off-white audio rod into a player Brenn's engineers had attached to the healing arch. Soft strains of a Netaian *largo* sprang up around her, amplified by net-cloth speakers draped over her pillow.

Before Ellet showed up, she'd been dreaming. Some kind of energy storm had descended on Hesed, and she'd cowered inside, protecting her babies with her arms and her body.

That dream, she'd be glad to forget.

Then she reconsidered. She'd run out of logical ways to visualize and control fusion. What about seeing it as an energy storm? Medical Master Spieth had warned, months ago, that if she played the wrong games with her epsilon carrier, she could go mad—but she would shortly face a fielding team that used madness as one of its weapons. She needed to stand against it somehow.

Pushing her head into the deep pillow, she tried to set the dream firmly in mind. The slow, somber bass line of the *largo* gave her a rhythmic framework.

Next, she imagined touching her epsilon carrier to Brennen's, and then she envisioned their fusion as a gale blasting over and through her imaginary wall. She heard its howl, smelled on the wind the warm-incense scent of Brennen's access—but hotter, fiercer, wilder—

Yes. She could imagine that.

She had no way of knowing if the image would give her any control, though. Not until she and Brennen actually tried it.

Now she must hit the simulators!

She rang for a med attendant.

The second slip passed too quickly for Brennen. *North Ice* and its carrier escort, *Weatherway*, hauled every fighter, bomber, or scout Thyrica had equipped with RIA equipment. Six light fighters were reserved in *North Ice*'s hangar-bay for Day Flight, the first attack wave. He'd ordered both ships' engineers to link the fighters' threat-assessor displays to firing overrides, going beyond standard ID procedure to actually prevent pilots from targeting friendly ships. That was one of the chief dangers of flying a group into a fielding defense. If engineers could make that impossible, Three Zed's defenders would have to fall back on direct mental attacks—amplifying enemy pilots' terrors or trying to induce madness. Those risks were sobering enough without destroying his own support group.

Another danger drove him to complete this project. If the vision he'd seen, the missile-blasted Light-Five, proved accurate—if he was destined to die at Three Zed—then he would do everything in his power to keep the Shuhr fielding team from voice-commanding Mari to fire that fateful missile.

Two days out from Three Zed, Firebird shook off drowsiness and tried to sit up.

Brennen stood over her. Last night, he'd reported on his other subcommanders' planning session. Sending a field general into combat flew in the face of all rules of engagement, but no other Sentinel would dare to fuse carriers with her.

So Day Flight, including her and Brennen, would launch the moment *North Ice* dropped slip-shields. Protected by their overlapped slip and particle shields, they would fly into fielding and RIA range. Brennen would initiate fusion by quest-pulsing to her, then try to overload the fielding site's circuits with fusion energy. They would have the combined power of two RIA ships, and if fusion left her unconscious, then her modified Light-Five could be flown out by a remote pilot while Night Flight—Dardy's heavy bombers—dropped their payloads.

Another Sentinel had volunteered to fly lead in Day Flight, where the enemy surely assumed Brennen would be. Firebird had to respect that man's courage. She prayed he would be spared.

"It's time we ran our own simulation," she told Brennen firmly. "High time."

"I'm afraid so." He reached toward a bulkhead. "I'll send Shel for a med, in case."

She had explained her new visualization. "Maybe focusing on the storm image will give me enough conscious time to fly out of the thick of things," she said. "You could press your attack while I pull out far enough to feel safe about activating the fighter's recovery cycle. I really don't want to use the remote pilot."

"I wouldn't either." He sank down beside her on the bunk and asked, "Are you ready?"

Firebird pressed her eyes shut, visualizing the wall, the carrier, the storm. "Ready," she whispered.

Brennen reached inside himself for his epsilon carrier. As he focused for access, he felt her carrier flicker, as if she'd been mildly dosed with blocking drugs. Twice, he tried to grasp and fuse with it. Twice, it blinked out of existence.

Had their fusion at the Hall of Charity damaged the ayin complex in her brain? She had managed to turn several times since then, but this was not a good sign.

Her eyes came open, dark and serious. "I can't turn," she exclaimed.

"Sickness or injury does sometimes affect us in unpredictable ways," he said. "We'll try again later."

After Brennen left, Firebird sat clenching her fists. Master Jenner had said that repeated fusion could scar her physical epsilon center beyond the ability to function—eventually.

Not before Three Zed! she prayed—but she hated the flaming darkness inside her. For all Shamarr Dickin's assurance that she was not actually using evil, but only seeing it clearly, she dreaded watching it spark the evil inside others . . . watching the evil, empowered by fusion, destroy them.

Brenn had been right all along. Epsilon talent carried responsibilities that no thinking person would want.

She hurried downship to her simulator.

A messenger ship's arrival called Juddis Adiyn away from his gene laboratory. Without waiting to hear progress reports from Netaia, he had ordered an accelerated primary fertilization program, enough to make a serious start at synthesizing enough genetic material to modify Netaia's next generation. Gametes were almost ready to be combined.

From his own rounded gold corridor, a gravity lift carried him up to the City's communication center, where he had a clear view of a bleak sunset. This courier should bring word of Firebird's demise and General Caldwell's captivity—or possibly his death. On the shebiyl, Adiyn saw him nowhere in the future. There should be no more Carabohd heirs until those twins grew up, unless his own lab produced them—but the shebiyl did sometimes shift, showing him the only safe course in the cruel nick of time. In those moments it seemed like a living evil, just as the Sentinels claimed.

Under the only sizable viewing dome in the City, he seated himself at a secure station, as the DS-212 pilot requested. He activated its sonic shield. "Acting Eldest Adiyn," he said into the transceiver. "What couldn't you send over general frequencies?"

"They failed." From the messenger's reproachful voice, Adiyn pictured a grimace. "Firebird survived. Caldwell appears to have saved her, and there's suspicion that they may have perfected an antipodal fusion technique. Reference Polar's research, if you don't recall—"

"I remember that project," Adiyn interrupted.

"Shirak orders immediate mobilization. Hit Tallis. Now."

"Slow down, slow down." People who hadn't reached their first century thought everything had to be finished now . . . or sooner. The shebiyl would tell him what must be done and when. "What exactly is the worry?"

"That Caldwell and his lady," said the irritated voice, "with the fusion ability Polar predicted, *plus* the RIA technology the Federacy just announced, could strike here. We would have no defense against that. Terza thought of the fusion idea. Maybe from a mutation in the Casvah line."

Adiyn rubbed his chin. "Our agents on Thyrica have turned up some RIA data. Its range is still finite, no more than a fielding team's." And yet—

Though RIA technology could explain how Caldwell and the lady got through the City's fielding net before, no theory adequately explained the power that blasted Dru Polar into the underground generator chamber's stone floor.

And what about Harcourt Terrell, killed under watch-link when he attacked Lady Firebird? The link supervisor, Arac Nahazh, was unfortunately dead. They would never know what killed Terrell. But definitely, there was more afoot than RIA development.

For years, his people had planned to set the Federacy against its Sentinel defenders. In the Shiraks' absence, Adiyn had continued the vital raids, relieving the Federacy of another half dozen fighters, two military transports, and even a small cruiser. Parked here in orbit, they could be sent against Tallis with only hours' warning, along a vector that would make it look as if the attack originated from a Sentinel world. The colony's commander-in-chief continued to conscript and train pilots out of the settlements. Adiyn wished the suicide-compulsion sessions weren't necessary, but weighed against humankind's immortality, already-limited lives had little value.

He had also sent signals to deep-cover agents on several worlds, including Thyrica. Those agents would trumpet to the Federacy that the Sentinels, with their terrifying new technology, must bear the responsibility for any further Sunton-style attack. Maybe nongifted Thyrians would respond to his own attack at Tallis by leveling the Sentinel College.

But what about this other development? He rubbed his chin. "What happened? How did they miss her?"

"I've transmitted a tri-D sequence, recorded off newsnet coverage."

Adiyn touched a control. "I see the file. And Terza?"

The messenger's hesitation prepared him for bad news. "Talumah's last set of subconscious commands appears to have failed. Her original orders kicked in, and she defected to them . . . by the old plan."

Against a new compulsion? The girl's Shirak genes had proved stronger than he suspected, stronger than the submissive maternal line that Modabah had ordered when he had her conceived.

Or was this a matter of human will—and did the girl have rogue epsilon talents? "Her deep linkages should remain," said Adiyn. "We have an agent among them now."

"Whether the old sabotage orders will activate, we won't know until potentially too late. But it's clear now that they were trying to trap one of us just as surely as we tried to get Caldwell for a full mind-access strip. Shirak wants you on highest alert."

Adiyn would do nothing without checking the shebiyl and the most likely paths the future would take. "Report to the communication center as soon as you're down," he said.

The courier signed off. Adiyn fed the burst-transmitted tri-D file to the secure booth's media block. As he watched, he smiled at the secondary explosions, minor—but noisy—charges Micahel must have planted around the nave, coordinated cues blaring that Firebird was about to die. As always, Micahel displayed a gift for showmanship.

But plainly, something unprecedented had happened on that carpeted stage. He shut down the projection unit and waved off all lights.

Terza! At least she'd left them with the idea that a Casvah mutation—not the Caldwell family at all!—produced whatever enabled Firebird to survive at that Netaian altar. This probably had destroyed Dru Polar, and Terrell as well.

Then they had a second formidable enemy. He must not underestimate Firebird again. He had already cloned breeder cells from the other Casvah-Angelo specimens. He would fertilize them immediately. Epsilon abilities usually matured at around twelve years old, but multiple ayin and hormone treatments could push epsilon maturity forward at the cost of other brain functions. In less than a year, he might produce laboratory creatures who could be epsilon-manipulated, but who could scarcely be called human.

Polar's offspring, he decided. Polar's strength, matched with the Casvah mutation. "Casvah, the vessel, a cup full of death," he'd called Phoena.

Polar and Phoena, then?

In the booth's darkness, he reached outside himself for the elusive shebiyl.

Firebird perched on the edge of her bunk in that narrow private cubicle. Medic Hancock returned his instruments to their case. Brennen stood behind him, leaning against a bulkhead, arms crossed over his chest. Shel stood just outside the door, with only her left arm and shoulder visible.

"Lady Firebird," Hancock said, glowering, "you've done an excellent job of sticking to your regimen, but under any other circumstances, I would not even consider releasing you to combat status."

"I understand," she said. "Under any other circumstances, I might have second thoughts, too. But I'm ready."

Hancock exhaled sharply, pulled a hand tool from his tunic pocket, and applied the tool to her wrist monitor. It fell free.

Firebird watched her medic leave. The countdown to drop point had begun. In twelve hours, *North Ice* would reenter normal space in the Zed system.

Brennen sat down beside her on the cot.

"Everything's under control, then?" she asked.

"Planned, replanned, and backed up with fail-safes," he said, running a hand over his face.

She felt his uneasiness. "I wish there were another way to end this threat, too," she said.

"No one is utterly evil." Brennen clasped his hands between his knees. "The One made us all. The same Ehretans who changed their genes changed ours."

"Is it harder," she asked gently, "now that you remember the place?"

"Yes and no. I was not treated well. But not all of them were as evil as . . . the ones who kept me in custody."

She nodded, staring across at the door, a meter away. "And the bio-weapons?"

He'd mentioned flash-frozen cultures, organisms that destroyed all remnants of life on Ehret.

"That," he said, "is the best reason to burn it down to bare rock. But they are exiles, too."

"They made themselves exiles. They declared the war, and they ended it with those bioweapons."

"But they also honor the memory of Ehret. Better than we do, in some ways."

"Not the ways that count."

"No," he admitted. "Their greatest pride is in rebellion. They want to make themselves into a higher species, something immortal in the flesh. That would be a terrible fate . . . to exist forever in a life that's tainted, growing more and more tainted ourselves."

"Or else stronger?" she suggested.

"Maybe. And when I think of the people who would love to see their artifacts—"

"That we're about to destroy."

"If we can." He said it like a sigh. "I would pray, if I knew I would survive this, that this will not haunt me the rest of my life."

A touch of that mysterious dread came through, and she seized one of his hands. "What have you seen that you still haven't told me?" she demanded.

For several minutes she felt the low rumble that meant he was struggling with his thoughts. She felt a faint engine vibration, too, and she breathed the acid tang of disinfected air. She edged sideways until her leg pressed against his.

"I saw a fighter," he said quietly. "My ship, though I'm not sure how I knew it was mine. It was in pieces. It looked as if it'd taken a missile hit."

She resisted the downward pull of his dread. "That wasn't necessarily a vision, Brenn. We often dream about our worst fears."

He gripped her hand. "I was not asleep. But you're right. And for decades, the shamarrs have told us that if we refused to pick up the sword when He called, then our enemies would slaughter millions. I can't wait for them to strike Tallis or Netaia." He reached over, twining both hands around the base of her neck. "What have we lived for, Mari . . . ourselves, our pleasures, our own wills and dreams? If I live for you, and you for me, we exist only for ourselves."

In this mood, he seemed utterly strange . . . yet he had always been vaguely alien, though he was half of herself. "I know," she murmured.

He massaged the back of her neck. "Whatever happens, it will be the highest good. Mari, if anything happens to me, I want you to be prepared. Tell Master Dabarrah I was told, 'It is time. Destroy my enemies.' He'll understand. He'll ease your grief, and Kinnor and Kiel will give you a thousand reasons to live."

"Tell him yourself," she murmured. *Didn't you order him to lead the fight, Mighty Singer?* "I'll be there with you." She craned her neck to kiss him, then let her mind go blank, her body limp, as they relaxed together on the cot. She concentrated on the warmth of his body. He wouldn't die out there in the cold. *Singer, he has done everything you asked him. You have no reason to punish him, and you've already disciplined me.*

He caressed her throat, then her jaw line, her lips. They'd hardly had an hour alone since her injury. She wondered how many other vital things they'd put off for "one day."

Life was a promise that had to break . . . break free of the physical, of space and of time. Tonight, she lay with her bond mate.

She slapped the cubicle's privacy control. The door slid shut.

Spent and unable to speculate any further, she pressed her head against Brennen's chest. His heart beat a strong, slow rhythm beneath her ear.

All her horizons slowly receded. It had been a spectacular hour. But in that Brennen-place at the back of her mind, she felt a certainty that tormented him cruelly. Whether or not they survived, this was the end of a part of their lives. If she didn't want a crown anymore, how did he feel about leading a holy war? *If there's some way to show mercy, spare him this*, she prayed. Then she drew a deep breath and raised her head. "Lock me down again, Brenn. We have eleven hours, and I'm entitled to one more regen session."

She rearranged her clothing, and then he clamped the field generator in place. He covered the humming arch with a pillow and rested his head on it. Waves of his drowsiness washed over her, dragging her down with her weary lover into unmeasured depths.

CHAPTER 23

SWORD'S POINT

furiant
a lively dance with frequently shifting accents

A deceleration alarm blasted Firebird awake. Brennen rolled off the bunk and released the healing arch. "It's time," he said softly, plucking his midnight blue tunic off a wall hangar. "Ten minutes to hard decel. Three hours to launch."

"Wait," she said. Closing her eyes, she envisioned the wall and pressed through, touching her epsilon carrier as smoothly as she'd ever done.

"Good," he murmured, closing the last clasp.

She seized his arm and pulled him into an embrace.

"I hate to see you risk this," he said. "I may not be able to ride your wing back in."

"I might be able to stay conscious."

"Do whatever is necessary. You must," he said, drawing back far enough to pierce her with the brilliance of his eyes, "no matter what happens. I will not build false dreams, and I won't run from what must be done."

"I won't either," she said firmly. "Take this." She fumbled with the little medallion's chain. "Wear it and think of me. And remember Tarance—"

"No," he said, and once again, she felt his lingering abhorrence of gold objects. "I gave it to you. Better grab a holdfast."

As the second decel alarm sounded, she seized a bulkhead loop with one hand and grabbed Brennen with the other.

As the cruiser started its stiff deceleration toward the Zed system, inertia momentarily pushed her toward the bulkhead. Something rattled inside a nearby storage bin.

Then Brennen pushed away. "See you shortly," he murmured.

Brenn had shown her where to find the uniform locker Burkenhamn had sent. In the cubicle's adjoining freshing room, after a fast vaporbath, she slipped into Netaian cobalt blue for the first time since . . . since not long after her capture by Federates, at Veroh.

A new insignia over her breast startled her: the gold-edged Fedorate slash. Like Burkenhamm, she was now Federate personnel.

Excellent.

Before closing her collar, she gingerly touched the ragged red entry-wound scar on her shoulder, then the fading surgical line across her chest. Both wounds were too deep for biotape to prevent scarring. "I owe the Shuhr for these scars," she told Shel's reflection in the mirror.

One inner pocket felt lumpy. She fished inside and pulled out the gold three-moon insignia of her new rank. An unfamiliar theater clip separated itself from the pair of three-moons. Veroh? she wondered. Was Netaia issuing theater clips for that disaster?

If so, she'd earned the insignia. She laid the clip and the three-moons back inside the locker, hoping she would survive to wear them on a non-combat occasion.

The quartermaster had included a hair catch. Hastily, she made a tail at the nape of her neck, then clipped the long gloves to her belt. At the bottom of the duffel was a heavy gray life suit and pilot's helmet.

Those were donned just this side of the cockpit. Carrying them, she walked up to the bridge.

She found Brennen there, conferring with his other subcommanders. *North Ice*, a light cruiser, had a large scan/sensor station and four transceivers, one inboard and three for command purposes. Between one subcommander's chair—occupied by Brennen at the moment—and the sensor station, engineers had moved one of the sim stations and linked it to Firebird's fighter controls, so that a remote pilot could steer her out of danger if fusion left her unconscious.

She hung back, leaning against a bulkhead while she waited for Brennen to finish. Threat axes, refuel procedures, med evacuations . . . as he'd said, every plan had been laid with excruciating attention to detail. He hadn't had any more time to dress than she had, but his jaw was clean and beardless, the line of it firm and straight.

She listened intently, glad for Brennen's steady nerves. If she ever wrote another clairsa piece for him, she must capture the tension of this moment, his calm acceptance of a pressure no one else understood . . . and the wisp of light red-brown hair that stuck out from having been slept on crookedly.

She spotted Ellet Dardy sitting at a bank of transcorders, uniformed as crisply as ever, ready to record and transmit the history they would make today. Ellet saluted, and Firebird returned the gesture.

Uri stood behind Brennen, still at his post. Brennen straightened his shoulders and reached for the subcommanders' hands in turn, finishing with Colonel Keeson. "Go with the One, General," she said.

"And you," he answered. Then he looked at Firebird.

He was her commanding officer now. She pushed off the bulkhead and saluted.

"Hangar-bay one," he said.

She embraced Shel. "Thank you," she murmured, then hurried out, leaving Shel on the bridge.

Uri also stayed behind. Their duties had ended.

Three men and a woman, the rest of Day Flight, stood in a briefing room near the hangar-bay's lift door. All carried life suits and helmets. Beyond a long window, crewers scurried through the bay, readying the fightercraft, performing final checks. Firebird sniffed an odor of ozone and fuel.

Brennen gathered his flight team around the table for final instructions. "There's some risk," he said, "of erratic asteroids in this vicinity. Watch for debris."

The man closest to Firebird—Major Hannes Dickin, a nephew of the shamarr—held his head erect. Since he had volunteered to fly the lead position, that would make him the Shuhr's number one target. She wondered if they could remote-manipulate orbiting rocks.

"To approach closely enough to strike," Brennen said, "we have to enter fielding range. Commander Caldwell, you will fly slot and hang back, since you are at greatest risk from fielding attack."

She nodded.

"We will remain within maximum shield-overlap range," Brennen went on, "take one pass at the fielding unit pinpointed on our targeting displays, and egress. Night Flight will follow three minutes behind us."

The woman beside Brennen tapped one finger against her helmet. Firebird wasn't the only nervous one.

"We have to destroy the fielding site," Brennen said. "If Day Flight fails, the operation fails. If you survive an aborted attempt, try to recover on *North Ice* before it accelerates outsystem for Tallis."

"Speaking for all of us, I think," said the stocky man on Brennen's other side, "I don't expect to have that problem, sir."

Firebird raised her head. That was a more typical pilot's attitude, a firm denial that anything might strike his particular craft, no matter how exotic the enemy's technology. She usually heard it after the mission, though . . . not beforehand.

Brennen smiled and kept talking. "Automatic recovery cycles and fire overrides are to be preactivated immediately after launch. If you find yourself acting irrationally, surrender operation of your ship. It will set a reasonably evasive course."

His voice softened. "One more thing. In an environment defended by fielding technology, any pilot who ends up extravehicular will be vulnerable to accentuating attack. Even at Hesed, we use that."

He'd discussed this with her privately. In a fielding zone, an EV pilot's fear and disorientation could be amplified by the Shuhr's coordinated, projected mental powers. This defense caused madness in ninety-nine percent of cases, even at Hesed. The Shuhr might have found ways to make that defense even crueler.

"Therefore, any pilot who goes EV will be moved to the second triage category for later recovery," Brennen continued. "Your EV unit has oxygen for more than an hour, but here, it will be kinder to let events take their course."

Simply falling asleep in the cold . . . Firebird had to agree. It wouldn't be such a terrible way to make the Crossing.

Was that what he foresaw?

No . . . he had described a missile hit. He'd said nothing about EV—

"Other questions?" Brennen stared at each pilot for several seconds. Firebird felt him send pulses of epsilon energy, and she guessed he was reinforcing the others' confidence. When he looked at her, her fears did drop away.

He dismissed the group, but she felt him urge her to linger. As soon as the others had left the briefing room, he broke uniform etiquette. He embraced her, one arm pinning her head to his chest, the other arm clenching her waist. She struggled to free her head, then thrust up her chin.

As he kissed her, the scent at the back of her mind intensified, as if he were pushing himself deeply into her memory in the last few seconds remaining to them. Emptied and panting, she shut her mouth as he drew back.

Neither spoke.

Firebird walked out into the main bay, then followed a crewer toward one of the small swept-wing fighters. The crewer halted beside a blocky starter unit and helped her into her depressurization suit. Proof against hard vacuum, with dozens of sealed inner compartments, the life suit would inflate automatically if she lost cabin pressure.

Why bother, she wondered, *if going EV means madness and death?* She'd trained in a life suit, though. She had always trained the way she meant to fight. It was the only way to survive.

She glanced up at the Light-Five fighter. She'd spent hours simming in this cockpit, first with an instructor and then alone. The fighter was nimble and well shielded. The RIA add-on system's energy demands limited its weaponry, but she did have four programmable missiles and excellent gravidics. She rounded it hastily, sliding her gloved hands along the little ship's smooth surface. Somewhere farther down the row, Brennen was checking out another such RIA fighter, but without remote-pilot capability.

Minding the connectors that dangled from her suit, she climbed aboard. Crewers fastened her in. In the seconds that took, she focused her thoughts beyond today, beyond her lifetime. If Brennen turned out to be the Carabohd descendant who wiped out the nest of evil, then obviously, the rest of the prophecies remained to be fulfilled by Kiel or Kinnor or their descendants. *All the Mighty Singer's power, in human form!* Maybe seen from a human perspective, stuck in the flow of time, the body of prophecy was something like a series of mountain ranges, with nearby peaks obscuring the distant ones. Only when you arrived at the first summit could you see that the second range was still far off . . .

Or something like that. She pulled at each of her suit-to-ship umbilicals and all five harness points, checked that they were secure, then turned thumb-up to her chief.

From far down the row, she sensed a call at the back of her mind. She stretched her neck to peer over the closest fighter's fuselage and spotted a helmeted figure looking her way.

She saluted him.

He touched one gloved finger to his helmet over his lips.

There were few things more useless, Shel Mattason decided, than a bodyguard whose employer was going out into battle.

Colonel Keeson had assigned her and Uri to bridge security, pending their reassignment to retrieval detail, post-combat. Really, both posts were gifts, excuses to observe. She sat on her assigned stool, following the glimmering break indicator's countdown to final decel. In her breast pocket was a heatsealed letter like many she'd carried before. This one was from Firebird, to be opened only if she and Brennen were both killed. Uri carried a similar packet. She almost hoped that if one of the Caldwells died today, both of them died.

She glanced around. Actually, they all might.

A Carolinian veteran of the Netaian campaign sat at the modified flight simulator, ready to override Firebird's flight controls and bring her back.

A com officer's voice rose. "One minute to drop point, at mark. Three, two, one. Mark."

Shel pressed her palms against her thighs.

Firebird pulled her splayed-finger RIA array over both ears, then stretched on her pilot's cap. Finally, she tipped her head into her helmet as the cockpit bubble dropped.

Her in-suit transceiver was already live. Brennen's tenor voice rose over a drone of more distant voices to call off final checks. His Federate terminology was significantly different from the orders in which she'd drilled, years before—but she'd used her sim time to reprogram her expectations. Brennen clipped out, "Day Leader, generator check."

"Two, check," she heard. "Three, check." She waited her turn, then answered, "Six, check."

Her seat vibrated as the engines lit. She scanned cockpit lights. When cued again, she answered, "Propulsion, shielding, go. Weaponry, countermeasures, go. All go, sir."

"Run-up," Brennen ordered the flight. "Full brake and throttle."

Firebird applied brake to the Thyrian craft, then gradually, she pushed throttle power fully forward. Still racing that Shuhr messenger—not to mention Micahel and his escorts—they must do everything at full speed, including launch. It would be a loose formation, with no dependence on cross-programming. Night Flight, on board *Weatherway*, would launch just as loose.

"Throttle check," said Brennen's voice in her ear.

She'd flown a personal fightercraft with him aboard over a year ago. She wished momentarily that she might ride out with him now, in a two-person trainer.

But that might not have done the job. They needed the power and versatility of two RIA systems.

She answered in her turn, then laid one hand on the brake lever. Seconds passed. Her heart thudded. She glanced down for her life-signs cuff, but it was gone now. Lights in the hangar-bay winked off. Ahead of her position, a force barrier shimmered with the chaos of quasi-orthogonal space.

"On my mark," said Brennen's voice, "brake release."

Go with us, Mighty Singer!

The shimmer grew brighter.

Seated in the communication bubble on the Golden City's south arc, Juddis Adiyn wrestled with the shebiyl. He had foreseen an attack, and that his forces were needed here before he sent any to Tallis. All probabilities showed strongly in Three Zed's favor today. Along several possible streams, he saw himself as Eldest of Three Zed colony. The Shiraks would not like that, but without his assistance, their line would die out anyway. His leadership might be best for the unbound starbred.

His reclined seat faced the transparent viewing bubble. On it, dozens of reflective display zones showed data, translucent against the backdrop of space. It had been a long day, and unless he'd read the shebiyl wrong, it would end well. At stations around him, other ranking officers called off orders. Adiyn had served some time in both fielding and command stations, so he knew battle language. The noise kept wresting his mind off the shebiyl. Tonight, he had the disquieting sense that something larger and more powerful than himself was controlling all paths of the future.

Someone shouted. He glanced at the overhead arc. A slip zone sprang into existence, entering the system not far from a cluster of asteroids, remnants of the colony's original defense. It showed on the arc of space like a set of concentric circles, dark red brightening to crimson at center, in the western sky.

Even closer in, three small ships—crewed by pilots who obviously knew where those asteroids would be—dropped slip-shields as they decelerated into normal space. "ID incoming," Adiyn shouted. "All of them."

Friend-foe analyzers whirred. New data appeared beside the red circles. "Polovia 85-B light cruiser," called a voice, "Thyrian. Also Thyrian, Polovia 277 fighter-carrier. Fighter bay opening."

Had Onar Ketaz's fearful illusion been a genuine glimpse of the shebiyl, after all? Uneasy, he demanded, "ID on the other three."

"Believe they're Netaian—" the voice started.

"Three Zed," shouted a static-charged voice over a room speaker. "Who's commanding?"

Adiyn recognized Micahel Shirak's voice. "Netaian fighter," he answered sternly, "this is Three Zed, Juddis Adiyn commanding. Micahel, what are you—"

"Listen to me." Micahel did not lower his voice or slow down. "Firebird Caldwell is in one of those incoming bogeys. She and Caldwell *have* learned to fuse carriers, just like Polar tried to do it. All the rest is only a diversion. Kill her, and Caldwell is helpless—and they can't use fusion against us. That order is from Modabah himself."

Commander-in-chief Ketaz relayed it into his link.

Polar, Adiyn reflected, would have objected. He would've liked to snatch the Angelo woman and conduct experiments—but Polar was dead, maybe at her hands. To Adiyn, her research value was genetic, and he already possessed cells from that strain.

There was also the possibility of recovering samples from her body. It should freeze quickly in space.

"Particle shielding down," announced a voice.

Firebird forced herself to go limp.

Drop point shivered the cruiser.

"Mark," Brennen called.

Firebird released her brake and hurtled forward along the hardened deck, through the collapsing shield barrier, and then out into starry space. Thrust compressed her insides against her spine. In the seconds before her head-up panel lit with route/risk data, she double-checked her position, starboard and aft of Brennen, and locked temporary tracking on the heat of lead pilot Dickin's engines.

For one instant, a spectral calm flooded her. Her husband sat on that gleaming engine at ten hundred low. He lived, and that was reality. His vision was only that—a vision, a glimpse, a chance to face down the worst possible outcome.

That was all the time she had for thinking. "Recovery cycles," she heard inside her helmet. The Zed star's arc shrank, falling behind the near planet's cratered horizon.

Next, she heard, "Firing control overrides."

She preactivated both cycles, then took a firm grasp on stick and throttle, each knurled knob solid and assuring through the life suit's gloves. If she let go of either for ten seconds, the recovery cycle would steer her back to *North Ice* and its pickup crews—or elsewhere, at the remote pilot's discretion. At least she'd be in voice contact with him.

Thrust made every move a struggle, even though she'd regained her strength. She checked energy shields again. Particle and slip both gave steady readouts.

Speckles appeared on her display. Four—five—six Shuhr defenders blinked into existence on one side of the targeted peak. The Shuhr commanders hadn't ordered blackout. Amber lights ringed the colony, presenting a beckoning target.

She recognized that symmetrical mountain.

From a northerly launch point came twelve, thirteen more defenders. Brennen hadn't guessed how many stolen ships Three Zed could command. *There just aren't that many Shuhr*, he'd said.

They would soon know.

"Four mark," said Brennen's voice.

Four minutes since launch? At this speed, anything might happen. She wished she'd had longer to tell Brennen good-bye. Illogically, she wished they were back at Esme's ball. She might never finish that dance with him.

As the cratered surface grew closer, blotting out thousands of stars every second, she realized that last complaint wasn't true. Here and now, she danced with Brennen in a realm where few mortals knew the music.

CHAPTER 24

DEATH GRIP

martele
forcefully

Brennen settled into awareness of surrounding space, as represented by six tiny screens on his console. Out here the claustrophobia didn't bother him nearly as much as it had in the hangar-bay . . . and no one could call the grand starfield *dark*. He pushed his vision of death deep into memory, where it wouldn't interfere with this mission. In less than a minute he would send a quest-pulse through the RIA apparatus to Firebird's craft, and link, and then would come the energy storm. Then he must strike.

He'd made his peace, first with fear and then with regret. At least he felt assured that the Shuhr would not take him alive.

At eleven hundred high, relative to his heading, several more engines burned to life, up in orbit—stolen Federate ships, activating against his force. His scanners showed two fielding satellites below.

"Six, lead," he directed his transceiver. "Mari, thirty seconds to range. Check pre-engagement on your recovery cycle."

"Pre-engaged," she answered.

"And the remote override." If only he could have done more, to protect her from fielding—

A new voice reverberated through his headset. "Thyrian battle group," it said, "break off. We have a hostage. Phoena Angelo is still here, and she is alive."

Firebird's throat constricted. Brennen had seen Phoena die . . . or was that another one of their deceptions?

No, he'd shown her the memory. She flicked a transceiver switch and transmitted privately, "Brenn, she may be alive, but only artificially. There's no hope for her recovery after what they did to her." The equation of right and wrong, justice and mercy, and the moral calculations that allowed this attack at all balanced only when Phoena's chance for survival—mindless— was discounted.

Still, Firebird was glad she wasn't in a Night Flight bomber loaded with incendiaries. *Singer*, she pleaded, *if she's finally about to meet you, show her how vast your mercy is.*

Brennen recognized Adiyn's voice. Now that he remembered the geneticist, he realized that Adiyn might be the Sentinels' truest enemy, the strongest and most stable Shuhr leader, skilled at mind tampering and steeped in *keshef*—sorcery. He transmitted back, "I am sorry, Mari—"

Then a foreign presence brushed his awareness. Hostile, inquiring, it probed deftly through his epsilon shields for his private fears. It echoed oddly, like multiple presences.

Fielding range! It was a Shuhr team. Quickly, before they could debilitate Mari, he focused to quest-pulse to her.

A missile-lock alarm pierced his attention.

Only part of their fielding attack, he told himself, *playing on my fears*— but he also glanced at his screens.

From eight hundred high, three Netaian heavy fighters closed on Day Flight. "Double shields," called Hannes Dickin, at lead.

The Netaian fighters trained their targeting lasers on Dickin, then poured energy into his slip-shields. As the trio passed, Dickin's ship exploded in a globe of debris.

There was no time to think, and grieving had to come later. Brennen activated his RIA unit, plunged into the RIA accord, and probed the lead bogey.

Its pilot must have expected exactly that attack. Like hooks driving into his mind, another presence attached itself to him. He tried to drive it off but couldn't.

Watch-link!

Welcome back, Carabohd. The words tore into his head. *I didn't think you'd be stupid enough to put yourself at lead. Where is she?*

The masquerade was over. Using all the epsilon strength he could muster, Brennen tried disrupting Micahel's consciousness with the sharpest possible probe.

Micahel only plunged deeper.

"There—that one!"

One Thyrian fighter started flashing on Juddis Adiyn's master board, as well as on the arc overhead. There she was, at slot position—the only real risk to them. He activated all communication frequencies, even Federate DeepScan. Let *them* hear this, too.

"All forces, bogey now designated FC on your targeting computer is Firebird Caldwell. Reconfigure targeting priorities. She dies first."

At the instant Firebird heard that, her controls went berserk. She wrenched stick and throttle in all directions. Nothing happened externally, but the nausea of mind-access threaded into her like ethereal tentacles. The fielding team probed deep.

"Activate remote," she transmitted, no longer reluctant. That pilot should be able to pull her back just far enough. As soon as Brennen got off a quest-pulse—

The nausea turned to a stab of pure terror. Out of her console came a hollow, silvery spike, aimed straight for her chest. It drove into her life suit, burrowing deeper to skewer her—

Only the fielding, she screamed to herself. *It's an illusion!* But they had found her irrational fear.

Next came sounds—screeching voices, instruments discordant and out of tune . . . and a vivid memory.

. . . Flailing frantically, she struggled against a much larger Phoena, who stood with both arms wrapped around Firebird's waist. Firebird had to be . . . three, four years old? A seemingly huge young man, dressed in natrusilk and velvette, grabbed for her flailing arms. His free hand held two injectors. . . .

Ignoring a host of needles and spikes now driving up out of her front and side panels, she managed a turn. She stretched out through the RIA unit and felt Brennen's ship, still in range. She tried to steady herself on his presence, blocking out everything her lying senses could shriek at her—the piercing, the cacophony. *Now*, she pleaded. He must quest-pulse, must initiate fusion.

It's no use. The leering young heir's lips moved, an ethereal face floating midcockpit. *You are about to die. But you can end it quickly, and suffer less.*

They must have found out about her odd epsilon carrier—

The voice dropped in pitch. *Yes. You are a freak, a mutant. Now that we know you, we can destroy you.* More needle-sharp illusions threaded through her life suit, burning in from all angles. More tone clusters of half and quarter and third steps whanged into her mind, exploding like sonic warheads, a hideous crescendo.

She tried reciting an Adoration, the way Brennen had beaten his new fears, but she could concentrate only on the metal horrors impaling her, pumping vile substances into her body. They were right . . . they would destroy her . . . poison her . . . deafen her. . . .

No! They would not! She felt her ship decelerate. She prayed that was the remote pilot, vectoring her out of fielding range.

Where was Brennen's quest pulse?

They had her, and Brennen saw nothing else. Decelerating, her fighter started to drop toward the planet's surface. Her remote-pilot connection was plainly defunct, overridden by the fielding team.

Now his fears pounced out of hiding—now, when he was most tempted to rely only on his abilities and not on his deeper anchor. He struggled against the watch-link. He knew who sat at the controls of that Netaian heavy-fighter. Micahel kept up a running attack, sending deeper and more vicious probes, distracting him. He could not focus a quest-pulse.

On his threat board, Micahel's heavy-fighter gleamed momentarily. Micahel was arming a missile.

Brennen gripped his stick, keyed over from ground-attack to dogfighting mode, and fired off a laser volley. It went wide. Micahel's missile streaked away, locked on Firebird's decelerating Light-Five.

The stabbing cut off, and he sensed his enemy's glee. *Watch, Carabohd. Watch her die.*

Finally free to go to quest-pulse, he saw nothing but one accelerating missile. He launched a pair of decoys, but an instant later, he comprehended the geometry of the situation. The decoys would fall short. She couldn't escape.

Now, Holy One. Now I see.

He fired all his remaining missiles at Micahel, lightening his ship. Then he shoved his throttle full-forward.

Firebird clenched her eyes shut, trying not to see the horrors she plainly felt. Through her RIA unit, she sensed Brennen getting closer again.

Maybe he couldn't quest-pulse. Their fielding team might have gotten a stronger lock on him. Surely Terza didn't know everything about their defenses.

She slitted one eye open. Beyond the silvery web of illusion, Shuhr fighters converged on her fore screen. Squadron mates' calls to Brennen echoed in her ears.

Her missile-lock alarm wailed. She wrenched her stick aside, evading. Through the RIA system, she sensed another strong presence. *Micahel?* she challenged him.

Greetings to you as well, Lady Firebird. Hail and farewell.

Brennen had meant to reach out for her, then strike. For some reason, he couldn't.

But Firebird had learned to quest-pulse. Letting her hands and feet control the fighter, she turned inward. This time, she resisted the impulse to shut her eyes and concentrate. Through doubled vision, she saw two worlds. She flailed along her lichen-painted wall even as the missile appeared on her aft screen, glowing red-orange. She held to her inner course and breached the wall. She thrust energy at it and focused her little energy surge. Then she fed that energy into the RIA system and directed it toward Brennen's presence.

Fusion!

Now, Brennen! Strike!

Light washed out her eyesight. It was an illusion, the onset of psychic shock. She flailed for her stick and seized it, but it didn't respond—and the cabin's interior seemed to be dimming. She was losing all sense of Brennen's location.

Take them down, Brenn—I'll wait for you in His country!

Surrounded by her own energy storm, she felt the shudder and tumble of impact, felt blazing heat wrap around her and burn deep. As she flew against her flight harness, Micahel Shirak laughed. A second impact blasted beneath her, pushing her seat into her thighs.

Had she gone EV? She focused on the outer world again. To her shock, she still plunged toward the light-rimmed city, strapped into her own Light-Five. On her aft screen, the remains of another Thyrian fighter tumbled wildly.

Those sensations had been Brennen's, not hers! She'd caught them through RIA, through fusion, and the pair bond itself. What had he done? Had he accelerated into the vector between Micahel's ship and her own—and taken the missile meant for her?

Strike, Mari. His words came through the RIA link, overlaid with the same kind of fielding-induced terror. *Take it down, take it down!*

Then *he* was EV! Aghast, she squeezed her eyes shut. A shrieking, howling gale surrounded her point of consciousness, but she found she could hold her turn. Her knotted, twisted epsilon carrier flared with unaccustomed energy. To grip it was holding fire. She wrenched energy through the breach in her inner wall and dove back out into the visualized energy storm for her splayed-finger RIA arrays.

A surging sense of hugeness meant she had reactivated RIA. Instantly, she flung energy—guided the storm—and rode with it toward Brennen and the circling Netaian craft. In her senses, the attacker gleamed with black lightning.

Micahel Shirak watched the biggest piece of Caldwell's ship tumble toward a cluster of asteroids. He savored Firebird's terror . . . and Caldwell's, as Three Zed's fielding team lashed out to shred the Sentinel's sanity and quench his life. Micahel's cockpit glimmered under battle-red striplights.

They both had only moments to live . . . and he'd done it himself. He had destroyed the last adult Carabohd, spinning off in his pitiful EV suit— and now he would take down the freak bond mate. Linked to her through their vaunted RIA system and his own watch-link on the dying Sentinel, Micahel thrust outward to batter her with epsilon power. His hands worked stick and throttle, vectoring closer. He armed another missile for the *coup de grace*.

He tore into her alpha matrix. His abhorrent otherness gagged her. She fled the cruel spikes and screaming disharmonies, drawing his presence inward. The pursuing storm swirled in, blasting her stony wall to rubble. As Shirak thrust through her mind, she clung to her twisted, flaming carrier, far less painful than the fielding attack. She felt him dive for its deadly darkness, evil drawn to evil.

Micahel's crimson cockpit lights turned black and burst into flame. Black fire surrounded him, hungering to consume him. . . .

Black fire? A part of him, only a glimmer, refused to believe.

. . . Gouts of flame licked into him, singing audibly, whizzing and whining, exulting in suffering and death. . . .

He fought the blackness and its searing pain. No one had ever breached his defenses like this. He struggled inside his own shields, trying to loose himself from Firebird Angelo.

The mutation! Was *this* what killed Dru Polar?

Before he could fire his second missile, his alpha matrix ripped. Streaks of blinding light drove from all angles into his center of inner vision. His epsilon carrier ruptured, flinging energy out against the blinding streaks. At the back of his head, down his spine, and then through every nerve of his body, ganglions withered in fiery heat.

He plummeted toward the planet.

Brennen flew wildly toward open space, curled by his inflated EV suit into a fetal tuck. The blast that blew him from the ship had distracted him from his turn. He'd lost fusion energy, and Micahel still held him in watch-link. He sensed Mari's fall into her own flaming darkness as the Shuhr fielding team amplified that heat to scalding torment. Gasping, he plunged down inside himself. He had only one defense against fear: his own focused dependence.

> *Mighty One, destroy my enemies.*
> *In you is truth, and life forever—*

The watch-link dissolved in a burst of agony as Micahel lost consciousness, but the fielding techs kept on pressing their attack. No human mind could endure this.

Three Zed's surface spun crazily. His enemies amplified that sensation, too. Bile rose in his throat.

> *Save me by your mercy,*
> *Cradle my loved ones in your mighty hands.*

He glimpsed the rest of Day Flight, engaging Shuhr fighters as Mari's ship plunged toward Three Zed, followed by Micahel's.

> *I will be with that remnant.*
> *I will refine and test them as meteor steel*
> *And make them a sword in my hand. . . .*

Focusing any original thought was a struggle now. *Catch and hold her, Holy One. Hold her. Keep her.* In his mind's eye he saw Kinnor and Kiel. *And them*, he managed. *And . . . Terza's daughter.*

Then he let his mind tumble into the remembered hymn.

> *. . . Where you are the light, and there is no darkness at all.*

Fresh terror blasted through him. What if it all was a lie, a figment of desperate human imagination?

> *No darkness at all.*

No Eternal Speaker. No reason to be dying. No country to Cross to.

> *No darkness at all.*

He had been a fool. Now he would die . . . insane . . . for nothing.

> *No darkness at all. . . .*

Firebird couldn't sense Brennen any longer, but Master Dabarrah had told her she'd know if pair bonding ever were broken.

This anguish must be something else. Must! She screamed and pounded her console. . . .

And then steadied herself. She was conscious after fusion, for the first time. She had to do this alone.

She refocused her mind's eye, thrusting the energy storm outside the ruins of her imagined wall. Massive spasms wrenched her chest. More long, silvery spikes drove into her forearms and up her calves.

"General?" someone else called in her headset. "Caldwell, come in. Come in, General."

She knew Brennen couldn't answer. The only transmitter in an EV unit was the rescue transponder, calibrated to an identifying frequency—for retrieval.

He'd given the triage order himself.

Infuriated, she fell into the fielding team's mental hold. She felt it tighten on her soul. This time, she deliberately did to them what she'd done to Harcourt Terrell, to Cassia, and to Micahel. If evil called to the Shuhr, she would call them deep. Let evil rise out of her tainted heart—and let it claim them! Anything at all to stop them from destroying Brennen.

The energy storm swirled around her, and she had the sensation that she couldn't slip out of her turn if she wanted to. Micahel had blasted down the wall. Black flames licked up, and a fire burned in the middle of her head.

"Remote pilot," she muttered, "you have firing control. I'm so close. Will my missiles launch?" Ground side guns fired up at her. On her targeting display, the fielding site flashed rapidly. She had it in range. She recognized a toothy crag near the entry she'd used before. Her fighter lurched as all four missiles fired simultaneously. As they accelerated, she plummeted behind them.

Seemingly in another world, she felt the fielding techs plunge deeper into her mind, stabbing as they came. She poured vengeful fury into the RIA link, pulling them in as all her other senses expanded, exploded, diffused. Focusing desperately on the task, unsure how Brennen would've accomplished it, she brushed aside their incinerated epsilon shields, traced the power lines that connected their flickering mental input with . . .

There. The fielding station's main energy banks.

As she poured fusion energy through the RIA unit, she felt the first of the fielding operators die. Her missiles pierced the mountainside. A moment's explosion burned after images on her brain. Out of sheer instinct, she wrenched her stick aside.

The fighter responded this time. The spiked silver mesh in her cabin evaporated. "Fielding down," she shouted into the interlink. "Night Flight, go in!" Compared with the Shuhr cacophony, the cackle of transceiver voices sounded like music.

Then she spotted Micahel's Netaian fighter. It kept falling, following her previous trajectory. Micahel might be dead on board, but his heavy-fighter was about to hit his own city.

Justice! But she didn't care. Brennen . . . was he alive, was he sane? Where had the blast sent him?

As if a fuse had burned down, the fire in her head exploded, wiping out all thought . . . and all awareness of Brennen.

The bond link was gone.

She collapsed across her flight controls.

Micahel groped back up to an agonized consciousness. He got an eye open, but no other part of his body responded. He recognized his trajectory. He couldn't work his hands. He couldn't pull out of his own suicide dive. Like one of his own voice-commanded pilots, he was headed straight into the target, accelerating.

The tightness in his chest surged out in a scream.

Shel glanced aside. Ellet Dardy sat at station, tears streaming down her cheeks. Uri remained at stiff attention.

"Remote pilot," barked Colonel Keeson. "Full override. She's gone unconscious. Her signs are critical. Get her out of there."

Like every other Sentinel who could see Firebird's life signs, Shel understood. Firebird was falling into bereavement shock.

Brennen was lost. For his sake, she hoped the blast had knocked him unconscious before the fielding team could torment him to death.

Behind Shirak's hijacked Netaian fighter, Night Flight dropped toward Three Zed. Thyrian bombers flew a steady course between their fighter escorts.

Juddis Adiyn stood over a tracking console, cursing under his breath as Micahel's fighter hit the city. The horizon flashed. The ground shook.

"Particle shielding holds," a voice announced. "Ninety-two percent of impact energy absorbed by planet's surface."

Adiyn pushed up from his console. Naturally, the colony's powerful defenses had drained most of Micahel's momentum away from the city itself. Caldwell was gone, but the Angelo woman vectored out and away. Adiyn reached toward his transceiver to alert the larger ships.

Then without any effort on his part, the shebiyl thrust itself into his mind. All of its stream-like paths unraveled like a vast web, flickering wildly—and then twined again, this time into a swift, unstoppable river of fire and light. A single figure straddled time's flow, robed in billowing, blinding white robes. He raised his left hand in imperious challenge. His right hand gripped a glimmering sword, poised to strike. His face was too brilliant to see.

Beneath Adiyn's feet, a throaty rumble answered the impact of Micahel's fall. The shebiyl faded and dissolved.

Adiyn tried to cry out a warning, but the ground shook again. Voices around him cut off in midsentence. He grabbed the console with hands that were suddenly slick with sweat.

There was one second's silence.

CHAPTER 25

HIS HAND

senza fiato
without breath

Shel stared at the monitor screens. Firebird's ship vectored back, escorted by three Day Flight pilots. Brennen's body had tumbled out of sensor range. Fragments of Micael's heavy fighter rolled out across Three Zed's basaltic surface.

Abruptly, the Golden City's amber external lights went dark.

Shel glanced over at Sensors, a fortyish woman in Tallan ash gray. "That impact shouldn't have knocked out the main generator," Shel said. Brennen had described that obsidian generator chamber, protected underground. . . .

"No, but it triggered a ground quake," Sensors answered. "Big one, getting bigger."

And those lights had probably been on auxiliary power.

Sensors gasped. *North Ice*'s boards painted a superheated plume rising into the mountain from beneath. "Magma," shouted Sensors. "No, it's gaseous!"

In front of Shel's eyes, the Golden City dissolved in a haze of scarlet dust, expanding like a bubble. Then it imploded, collapsing in on itself. Waves of blue lightning played back and forth over Three Zed's surface. A second blast sent fighter-sized globs of molten metal and stone into space. A glowing cloud of superheated air and ash flowed out along the planet's basaltic plain.

Shel shook her head, stunned. Basaltic lava didn't explode like this on a dry world. Either Three Zed was a geological oddity, or else the Shuhr had created an unstable situation. . . . *Or is it your wrath, after all, that destroys them?*

Colonel Keeson was already shouting orders. "Night Flight, all bombers, pull back. Fighters, break off. Pursue the ships they've launched."

Shel glanced down at Ellet, who was still working furiously over her transcorder, though tears spilled down her cheeks. Shel brushed her own cheek and realized it was wet, too. On screen, the ash cloud continued to flow away from the ruined city.

A flight of Shuhr fighters vanished. "Tallis vector," called Sensors.

Shel wiped her cheeks with both palms. Brennen had warned Tallis. Regional command would be on full alert.

On another display, the aft fuselage of Brennen's fighter spun toward a rogue asteroid cluster. Uri stared, setting his jaw.

Shel shut her eyes, not wanting to see the impact. His EV transponder had been sending for several minutes—but Firebird's life signs already told her everything she did not want to know.

Torment seared Firebird from her throat to her groin, and sweat rolled off her forehead. Someone bumped her, reaching into her Light-Five's cockpit. In the next instant, she recognized a crewer unhooking connectors. Brilliant light flooded the hangar-bay.

Her remote pilot had brought her back to *North Ice*, unconscious. Either the crewers had bumped her awake, or else the lights and fresh air roused her. Like the dying vibrations from a huge bell, her senses still rang with fusion energy. All of her senses except the bond-link to Brennen . . .

"No," she shrieked, "no!" She clutched the nearest arm.

"Don't move," she heard in her helmet. Someone pushed something hard against her shoulder. It stung. "Please, Firebird."

These were meds, then, not crewers, and they'd just hit her with a stimulant. Two more stood by with a heavy stretcher unit.

Pain throttled her, grief and fury so exquisitely compounded she could think of nothing else. She tumbled without caring how hard or far she fell. Someone, something, pulled her legs and torso straight and bound her to a flat surface. Something squeezed her upper arms.

Nauseating otherness flooded through her. Swallowing hard, she opened her eyes to see Shel's face. It bobbed as the Sentinel walked alongside her. "What was his vector?" Firebird cried. "Maybe he's alive, maybe he's still out there—" Talking drove new knives of pain into her chest.

The nausea intensified as Shel probed deeper. The Sentinel laid a hand on her arm. "Oh, Firebird, be strong. I'm so sorry. This is bereavement shock." Shel turned aside, speaking to a med in a yellow tunic. "I've been through this."

"No," Firebird groaned, "no, he can't be—"

Couldn't he? He had accelerated directly into that missile's path. Wouldn't she rather he'd crossed into the Speaker's country . . . than that he survived out there, deranged and terrorized?

And this time, she had deliberately used the evil inside her—wielded it like a weapon, instead of letting the evil ones be drawn in—

Forgive me, she pleaded, *forgive and cleanse me. Oh, Singer*—

"Be calm," muttered a med alongside her, "be strong, Commander. We'll help you." They propelled her around a corner into a passway.

Shel kept up, one hand gripping Firebird's shoulder. The tender gesture raked Firebird's agony into red-hot fire. "Firebird, I've been there. I remember. I won't leave you."

The meds transferred her again, this time from the litter onto one more sickbay unit. Another field projector dropped over her chest. Two meds clamped it down, binding her to a life she despised, if this really was bereavement shock—if Brennen was gone, and she'd done such an abhorrent thing.

Another med swept a translucent mask toward her face. "You have to rest," he said.

"Let me go!"

The vapors flooding her lungs smelled of Hesed House. "Breathe deeply," ordered the med.

She felt herself relax. The pain's knife-edge dulled. Her head started to clear.

He'd put himself in harm's way, dying in her place. . . .

It wasn't atonement, not the way Path instructors described it. But clearly, he had saved her with his own life—while she plunged into evil, fouling his sacrifice.

"He shouldn't have," she managed. It sounded and felt like a groan.

She barely felt Shel pull away.

"Major Mattason, this is Colonel Keeson."

Shel slipped out of Firebird's sickbay cubicle and raised her interlink. "Mattason here. Go ahead, Colonel." She glanced back into the cubicle. Firebird thrashed on her cot, plainly in the deepest throes of bereavement shock, her mental and emotional savor burning with loss.

"General Caldwell's ship impacted one of those asteroids. His EV transponder was still active when he tumbled out of range, but our people gave his final vector a thorough sweep and found no life signs. Other damaged fighters are sending positive signs. I'm sure you understand."

Shel's hand tightened on the interlink. "Yes. Yes, I do." *Welcome him home, Holy One. We will miss him terribly.*

"I'm sorry, Major Mattason. There are many other wounded to rescue. That's taking all our resources."

Shel slumped, wondering what Uri was feeling, as Brennen's personal guard. He'd already transshipped to *Weatherway*, ordered by Colonel Keeson to report to the battle group's chaplain. "I understand, Colonel. I'll tell her."

She slipped back into the cubicle and checked Firebird's monitor board. Plainly, she'd suffered a deep mental injury that endangered all her life functions. *We need to get her to Hesed*, Shel observed, *with the other bereaved*.

"Shel," Firebird pleaded, seizing her arm with both hands. Plainly, she'd heard some of that conversation. "Shel, if anyone could've survived that attack, he could. He might be in t-sleep. He could—" Her eyes widened, and Shel sensed her panic.

Shel turned around. A muscular young med advanced, brandishing a sub-Q injector. "I'll put her down," he said. "She'll kill herself if she doesn't rest."

Firebird's body arched against the field projector with terrorized strength. "No," she shrieked. "Shel, help! The Shuhr . . . the fielding . . . it was Phoena all along! Phoena and one of the other heirs—"

They play on our greatest fears. Firebird was making no sense, but Shel guessed how the Shuhr had tormented her. She thrust herself between Firebird and the med. "Wait," she said. "The woman is phobic. Let me talk to her."

"Shel, please." Firebird tried to grab her hand again, missed, then wedged both hands under the regen arch. "Aren't there med runners coming in with the wounded? Or isn't there some kind of a courier ship? Let me into one. Let me go out. I'm fit. I can fly. I have to see him. I must."

Shel shook her head. "Firebird," she murmured, "there's no need. And you're *not* fit. No one can think rationally in fresh bereavement shock. I couldn't. What would you accomplish out there? The forces will recover all the dead before we leave." There. She'd said it. Dead.

The med laid down his injector. "Please, Lady Firebird. You must rest. A retrieval crew will bring him to you. You've been through torments, and in your present state, stress could literally kill you."

"I wouldn't care," Firebird muttered.

Shel frowned. "You have to care. You have children. Brennen just gave you, and them, everything that was in his power. Don't throw that away as if it meant nothing."

Firebird tried once more to push the regen arch off her chest by bodily strength and adrenaline. Then she collapsed, surrendering.

Shel was right. If she couldn't accept Brennen's last gift, then she spurned him. Besides fouling his sacrifice, she called it valueless. . . .

She couldn't tell Shel what she'd done, though. She couldn't stop pleading. "Shel, Brennen survived so much at Three Zed. Couldn't he have lived through this?"

"I might have hoped so, when he was an ES 97." The tall Sentinel's chin lifted. "But Firebird, remember. Dying EV is just fainting in the cold. He wouldn't have wanted to survive mindless. Give him up to the Holy One."

Firebird envisioned his deep eyes blank, his dancer's body nerveless. "Master Jenner could help him," she managed, though she knew this was wrongheaded thinking. "Even if the Shuhr damaged his mind, even if . . ." She shivered. "Even if they destroyed it, I'd gladly spend the rest of my life taking care of him." *Just as Carradee will gladly care for Daithi. Let me atone for what I did, Mighty Singer.* "I'd make him happy," she promised.

Shel shook her head. "Firebird," she murmured, "he's gone."

"Then let me help bring back what's left," Firebird whispered.

Shel's eyes narrowed. She glanced over at the med, up at the life-signs display, and then to Firebird's surprise, she dropped to a crouch and gripped Firebird's hand. "Listen. Colonel Keeson did assign Uri and me to retrieval. There is a courier, and I'm cleared to use it if necessary. If you need . . ." She cleared her throat. "They wouldn't let me go back out for Wald. I never saw his body. Do you understand?"

"Yes," Firebird gasped, though she didn't.

Shel frowned. "Search-and-rescue has right-of-way over retrieval. We may have to wait for them to get a ship."

She understood that.

Shel's eyebrows arched. "And you mustn't hope he's physically alive. Let go. Think of him, not yourself."

"I'm trying," Firebird managed, but she could think of only one thing. Whatever remained of her bond mate, she must take him home to Hesed.

Most of an hour later, Firebird slumped against the little courier craft's starboard bulkhead and tried not to shiver. Stars seemed to quiver around her. Clearly, something was wrong with her senses. It could be bereavement shock. It could, but until she saw . . . until she was certain . . .

She shut her eyes and made one more promise. *Mighty Singer, I deserve nothing from you. If we can find him alive and whole, I'll give you the rest of my life in service. I'll serve wherever you send me.*

Just as at Hunter Height, though, it didn't feel right to bargain with the Almighty. She let go of all her pretended claims. *Truly, I owe you a life. One way or the other, it's yours.*

It always was, she realized.

Flying along Brennen's last known vector, far out of the search area, they finally got a weak transponder signal. It took several more minutes on thrusters to home in on the tumbling shape of an inflated EV suit. The pale gray curl brightened and dimmed as it rotated in the Zed star's feeble light.

"Four minutes to close approach," Shel murmured.

The stars kept shimmering. Firebird squeezed her eyes shut. There would be no way to go on, raising her children alone, except by accepting Brennen's sacrifice. She tried imagining him in the Singer's country, strong and whole, shining with new light.

Actually, that wasn't hard to imagine. *Bless him, Mighty Singer. Bathe him in your magnificent music. He has longed for that all his life. Give him back all he lost, down in the Golden City. And give me peace*, she finished weakly, *with whatever we find here.*

Really, she hadn't diminished his sacrifice at all.

Shel glanced aside. Firebird sat slump shouldered, her brown eyes dulled by pain medication—when they opened at all. She hadn't spoken since they launched. Shel hadn't mentioned the shivering. She remembered bereavement, with its mental and physical disorientation. Watching Firebird, Shel realized how far she had come, herself—how much she'd recovered.

Something old, hard, and cold seemed to be melting in her heart. Wald, long safe with the Speaker, would have understood what she was doing. Until Firebird saw Brennen's body, she would cling to false hope. She needed the assurance that Shel had been denied, the sense she had done all that she could, trying to save him.

Please, Holy One. Let us find that he went to you peacefully.

Shel matched her course with the spinning body, then slowly decelerated. The life suit didn't look as if it had been badly holed. *He probably did suffer, then*, she realized bleakly. The Shuhr must have tormented him.

Firebird roused. "Hurry," she whispered.

Shel took her time. At least Firebird would be able to see him here, against the chill beauty of space.

She activated the courier's low-power catchfield and tugged him closer. She and Firebird had both slipped into extravehicular suits on board *North Ice*. Now she pulled the umbilicals from her chest plate, attached a temp tank, and slipped a furled rescue bag over her shoulder.

Firebird disconnected too, and Shel didn't try to stop her. Instead, she double-checked Firebird's temp tank, shut down their ship's gravidics, and then helped Firebird steer herself into the airlock. As its outer hatch opened,

Shel tethered to the dull gray exterior. Firebird followed, moving weakly, like a half-charged automaton.

Shel caught his stiffly inflated arm. His faceplate was dark. She tried a quest-pulse and felt nothing.

She clenched and unclenched her hands, relieved for Brennen's sake, agonized for Firebird's. *Thank you*, she managed to pray.

"What can I do?" Firebird's interlink voice quavered.

"Anchor yourself to the hull and hold my waist so I don't spin," Shel directed. She wrestled the unwieldy life suit into her crinkly, reflective rescue bag, following standard procedure. Firebird hit the bag's pressurization control the moment Shel sealed it. It inflated swiftly, and then Shel towed the weightless bag back into the runner's airlock. She helped Firebird inside, then secured the silvery bag on one of the med runner's cots. Then she reactivated gravidics. Her feet settled to deck.

Firebird had already broken the bag's seal. She peeled it back, then wrenched off Brennen's flight helmet. Only his upper face showed behind his breath mask. Shel exhaled, deeply relieved. She saw not pain but an uncanny peace, his eyes and forehead relaxed.

Firebird pulled off her own helmet. Shel suspected the truth was finally sinking in.

Determined to play the comforter's role, Shel drew a deep breath. "If that's only tardema-sleep, I'll bring him up in a few seconds. But . . . Firebird . . . if I do, you have to be ready for the worst you can possibly imagine. If he's mindless, he could be violent. He might attack us both."

Firebird set her chin. "I understand."

"We can see he didn't suffer at the end." Shel groped behind his neck, found and toggled the deflation switch. The shape shrank to human size. She didn't bother to snug the restraint straps. Instead, she let herself fall into the standard rescue drill. She eyed the med runner's compartments, locating everything she might need for survivable injuries. She turned inward for her carrier, pausing to pray, *Holy One, have mercy on them both.* Then she stretched out an epsilon probe.

Firebird silenced all thought and emotion, trying to sense any change in Brennen. Where the pair bond had been at the back of her mind, she felt only a burned-out vacancy.

Maybe Shel was right. To be past all pain . . .

"Brenn," she murmured. She drew his breath mask away, shuddering as she touched his pale cheek. There was the scar where Phoena had kicked him. She brushed back a strand of light brown hair.

She laid her head on his still chest and shut her eyes. *Thank you, Mighty One. For all you gave us. For almost two years—*

"Firebird," Shel said softly, "I'm afraid—wait—"

Beneath Firebird's ear, Brennen inhaled hoarsely.

"Brenn," she gasped. Her pulse accelerated.

He struggled weakly against the cot's loose security bonds.

Looking horror-struck, Shel lunged forward. "Brennen, lie still," she ordered. "Brennen, can you hear me? Do you understand?"

Firebird seized both of his hands. She still felt nothing back at the Brennen-place in her mind.

What had she done? Because of her selfishness, would he live out his days mindless at Hesed House?

"Lie still," Shel repeated. "Brennen, lie still. You've been EV."

Brennen gasped. His right hand tightened on Firebird's, but his left hand hung limp. He tried to pull it away. "Shel," he said in a ragged voice, "bless you. Did you . . ." He coughed, then managed, "Did you rescue Mari, too?"

Brennen stared up through a medical scanner at Adamm Hancock. Every bone and muscle ached—except in his splinted left arm, both of his shoulders, and his neck. Pain blocks were in place.

Hancock eyed his scanner. "Headache gone?"

Brennen nodded cautiously.

The med finally smiled. "Your fluids are giving normal readings again. Six or seven hours on regen and you'll be free to go, but don't hesitate to call if the headache comes back. We'll fuse that fracture as soon as the swelling goes down."

Mari sat beside Shel on the next cot over, dangling her legs and watching Hancock finish. Pain lines still creased her forehead and cut between her eyes. He could see her worry, but even to him, at short range, the pair bond felt like a ghost of what it had been. Her symptoms—neural paroxysm, unfathomable grief, change in life signs—all indicated genuine bereavement shock.

Sanctuary Master Dabarrah would be able to tell them what had happened to her. For now, he could only thank Shel for showing such deep empathy toward her—and bringing him in before his EV suit's resources ran out.

He managed to smile at them both. Finally, he understood why the One had let him be weakened at Three Zed. His months of fighting irrational fears had taught him to fall completely into the Holy One's power. That strength had held against the fielding attack when his own strength would have shattered. Instead of destroying his own sanity resisting their attack, he'd slipped peacefully into tardema-sleep.

Meds and their assistants bustled around him. He'd asked Uri to stay on *Weatherway* and help debrief returning pilots. A memorial tonight would honor Hannes Dickin and the others killed.

Hearing footsteps, he opened his eyes. Colonel Keeson stepped into his line of sight. He touched his forehead to return her salute, cleared his throat, and asked, "What's the downside status?"

Colonel Keeson took a parade-rest stance at the foot of his cot. "The main city is utterly destroyed, full of magma and gas. Four small domes, which they call settlements, have asked to surrender. I need your authorization to answer. May I accept?"

At the edge of his vision, Firebird straightened her back. He saw fierce joy in her wide eyes and firm lips, and in the determined set of her eyebrows, even if he could not feel it in her mind.

The Holy One had spared his forces from having to slaughter their own kinsmen by destroying the Golden City. Would He not spare them from slaughtering the less guilty?

Brennen covered his face with both hands. *Lord of mercy, let this be the end. The city is burned to bare rock, as we were ordered. Your hand swept their power away. You spared us from—*

Yes. His answer came promptly. *You have finished. Well done, my child.*

"Yes," he told Colonel Keeson. "Accept!"

CHAPTER 26

CODA

calmato
quieted

Master Dabarrah laid his palm over Kinnor's wrinkled forehead. Immediately, the squirming child stopped bellowing and gazed up into the sanctuary master's face. He grabbed for Dabarrah's white-blond hair.

Firebird relaxed, too. "He dove off that chair like he thought he could fly," she explained, frustrated that after all she'd been through, she couldn't catch one leaping infant. Kin would give her heart failure—again—if she didn't keep a close watch.

"I biotaped this precocious little bird six times while you were gone." Dabarrah fingered the side of Kin's head. "You're right—he wants to fly, like his parents. Only a bruise," he assured her. "Not the first, and certainly not the last."

Kinnor struggled to be set down. Firebird looked around the med center, saw nothing dangerous within the little one's reach, and released him on the stone floor. He raised up on both arms and scooted toward the door.

His father caught him, picked him up by his padded hips, and aimed him into the room, toward the white-haired man in torn drillcloth overalls.

Brennen's spiritual father, Shamarr Dickin, had just come in from the gardens. Knowing that this was always his first stop upon arriving from Thyrica, Firebird had sought him out between rows. She'd bent with him over a pair of shovels and made a heartfelt confession. He assured her she had been forgiven the moment she asked for mercy, and that no one would blame her for the way she took down the Shuhr fielding team.

Now he crouched and held out both hands, beckoning Kinnor. "Since we are all here, Jenner," he said, "tell me the prognosis on this little one's parents."

Firebird edged closer to Brennen. These secrets couldn't be kept for long. Already, Brennen's masquerade had been exposed in Federate circles. Word would return quickly to Netaia, too. A messenger ship was decelerating toward the Hesed Valley with Tel Tellai on board, the only Netaian elector who could be allowed inside Hesed's fielding net.

Firebird had a terrible new respect for fielding technology.

Master Jenner opened a long hand in her direction and told the Shamarr, "Firebird's ayin is completely gone. Prolonged fusion scarred it through. She can no longer even turn."

—Visualization or no visualization! Micahel's blast of power and the repeated kills had damaged that tiny brain complex irreparably. She would do no more fusion killing, and there would be no further temptation to use evil against evil.

As Master Jenner explained it, the physical injury had traumatized other parts of her brain, combining with the prolonged fusion to disrupt her alpha matrix and interrupt the pair bond, creating genuine bereavement shock. As the trauma diminished, she felt Brennen's emotions again.

The bond had not broken.

"Then fusion," said Shamarr Dickin, "is riskier than we imagined."

Master Jenner answered, "I agree. No one will want to learn to do this, since the danger is so great." As the tall, thin sanctuary master eyed Firebird, a comforting wave of epsilon energy lapped through her mind. She welcomed Dabarrah's consolation, even as she fretted that Kiel or Kinnor might have inherited the reversed-polarity carrier, with its potential power and risk. That wouldn't make itself known for years. Raising that pair to training age would be a daunting job.

"And you, son?" asked the shamarr, eyeing Brennen.

Jenner spread his hands. "Full memory did return while they were en route to Three Zed. I verified that."

Dickin raised a bushy eyebrow. "Then there should be substantial restoration of ES potential."

That's right, Firebird wanted to shout.

Jenner nodded. "I can't perform fine calibration here, but my rough measurements put him nearly at the Master's range again."

The Shamarr took three long steps and wrapped his arms around Brennen. Brennen's hands clapped the shamarr's shoulders. Only someone who knew he'd been injured, Firebird observed, would see the slight stiffness in his left wrist. "I am glad," murmured Dickin, pushing away. "Well done, Brennen. Well done." He eyed Jenner again. "And I hear you have a fourth patient."

"Carradee?" Jenner smiled. "Yes."

Firebird sat down on a long stone bench. "I told Carradee to have Tel announce her pregnancy on Netaia. Kenhing can restore House Angelo to her new daughter. That shows on the simulations as a stabilizing factor, especially now. Without Rogonin in power, the Electorate can take a more long-sighted view."

"And?" asked the Shamarr. "Their reaction?"

Raising her head, Firebird glanced at Brennen. "Tel should be bringing us a report."

"This also looks significant." Shamarr Dickin pulled a message roll out of his dusty coveralls. "Brennen, this is for you. Tallis."

Brennen took it and thumbed the seal. At Tallis, Regional's First Fleet had wiped out the disorganized Shuhr attackers who fled Three Zed. Other Federate ships orbited Three Zed now, controlling all traffic as a committee of Sentinels oversaw the surviving settlements. Assisted by Shuhr survivors, Federate agents were searching the settlements' labs and data banks for bioweapons or gene materials.

Shamarr Dickin had also decreed that this other Ehretan remnant could be proselytized without waiting for inquiries—though already, Shuhr were registering as inquirers. After all, a Caldwell seemed to have done exactly what the holy books prophesied.

Maybe this union of remnants would bring about the true atonement, the new song . . . the Word to Come.

Firebird snatched Kinnor up off the floor and tried to hold him to her shoulder. He squirmed, giving out a groan that started to crescendo. She set him down once more. *It's going to be a battle of wills, isn't it, little one?*

She felt Brennen's shock—faintly—before his eyes registered it.

"What?" she asked softly. Shamarr Dickin hadn't given him the message in privacy, so it had to be news that could be shared.

Brennen raised a rolled scribepaper. "With the insubordination episode struck from your record," he read aloud, "the Federate High command has the honor of requesting that you accept the position of Battlefield Director, Federate Regional command . . . Tallis."

Firebird crossed her arms. Regional command, back on track toward his life's dream! *Thank you, Mighty One!* Tallis's MaxSec tower was no place to raise children, but with her new allowance, she and Brennen might buy a piece of prime land . . . something like the home she'd loved on Trinn Hill, in sight of the city but secure and secluded. She could set up her cultural exchange program right there at the Regional capital.

Brennen had told her, though, that he felt they had other priorities.

"Congratulations, Brenn." She slipped her arm around his waist. "Whether or not you accept it, this is a true honor."

He stared at Shamarr Dickin's eyes. "Yes," he said softly, "but I wonder what I could accomplish at Tallis, with the biggest threat to Federate peace ended."

"There will always be conflict," Firebird argued, glancing to the shamarr for support, "until the Word comes in power."

The white-haired man nodded solemnly.

"And this is your dream," she insisted. "If even the Federate bureaucrats are willing to set you back on track, think twice before turning them down."

"That doesn't compare to the need on Netaia," he reminded her. "Thousands of lives are still at stake." He laid a hand on Firebird's shoulder. "And you gave a solemn promise."

As Shamarr Dickin raised one hand, a shadow fell across the door. Carradee stepped inside, carrying Kiel against her shoulder. "He was looking for his brother," she said. "Is Kinnor going to be all right?"

"He will be, if he ever learns his limits." Relieved by the interruption, Firebird picked up her small explorer, raised her foot onto a wooden chair, and perched Kin on her knee where he could see Kiel. They reached for each other's fingers, communicating on some level that even Master Dabarrah couldn't sense.

Firebird didn't care squill for what she had promised First Lord Erwin, especially after he'd laid the Powers' blessing on her, but she *had* promised the rest of her life in service.

She'd come forward when Netaia needed her, but her desire to be a ruler had died with her pride. Even the desire to single-handedly save her people was utterly gone. In the future, if she could spare any attention from Kinnor and Kiel, she would rather develop her musical gifts than study those Federate simulations—and why should she spend her days sparring with the Netaian Electorate when she was no longer barred from proselytizing?

She was alive only because Brennen offered his life in her place. She was a flawed reflection of the divine image, with no cause to be proud.

She set Kinnor back on the floor and crossed the room, halting in front of the shamarr. "I defer to you, Shamarr Dickin. I owe a life to the One who saved Brennen. Please advise me."

The blue candles on both sides of Hesed's chapter room gave off the aromatic scent of kirka trees. Midday sun shone down through its skylight as Sentinels gathered to hear from Prince Tel. At Master Dabarrah's request, she and Brennen had taken seats in front, off to the left. Brennen looked resplendent in his dress whites. Firebird felt only moderately comfortable in her own pale blue sekiyr's gown. They'd let her keep this, even though all hope to train as a Sentinel was gone. From here, she had a good view of

Carradee, who sat next to Daithi's mobility chair at far right. Kiel perched on Aunt Carradee's lap, gazing up at the nearest candle sconce. Kinnor had finally curled up on the bench next to them both.

On the third bench back, Ellet Dardy waited beside her muscular bond mate.

Terza sat behind them with Sanctuary Mistress Anna. Terza's silhouette changed quickly these days. According to Master Jenner, who had healed the deep tampering on Terza's mind, she was as content as anyone could be while grieving so many of her people. Though she spent most of her time closed in her room, she did attend Chapter, and she worked in the gardens. Shamarr Dickin had sought her out as soon as he left the med center. Firebird remembered her nightly in prayer.

Behind Terza, the double doors opened. Tel strode in, dressed in elegant white velvette and carrying a papercase up the center aisle. He stepped lightly. Brennen raised an eyebrow, then bent toward Firebird's ear. "Tel seems pleased with himself," he whispered. "There could be a young lady."

. . . Or else something else that he'd wanted badly, Firebird guessed. Shamarr Dickin's counsel had been gracious but somber. If Tel called her forward, instead of Carradee, then she must accept. Even if she spent the rest of her life wrestling with the electors, she wouldn't face them alone.

Tel mounted the steps and turned toward her. "Lady Firebird," he said, "General, please join me on the platform."

Firebird pushed slowly to her feet and walked forward. *So be it, Brenn.* She felt him follow her, and she steadied herself by staring up at the star on the wall over the altar flame.

Standing beside tall Master Dabarrah, Tel opened his papercase. He plucked out a small, clear presentation box, then a certificate.

A soft, surprised grunt left Firebird's throat, though she tried to hold it back. Netaia's Triple Arrow was the highest military award the Electorate could bestow. *For Valor*, read the certificate.

She took a step backward, to the platform's edge. "Thank you, Your Highness," she said formally, "but the Golden City was destroyed by other forces, and I couldn't have touched its fielding station without Brennen. This was his doing, more than mine. Much more."

Tel reached into his papercase again. "So I've been told," he said. "So for the first time in Netaia's history, General Caldwell, the Electorate has also awarded this honor to an offworld born recipient."

Brennen stood at relaxed attention as Tel pressed the gold emblem to his dress whites—temporarily, she knew. Sentinels wore only the star. Even Master Sentinels. Surely Shamarr Dickin would give that back, no matter what else Tel announced. Brennen had pioneered a new, spiritual epsilon skill in addition to his recovery.

Firebird stood still as Tel fastened the other emblem near her neckline.

Then Tel stepped to the platform's center, blocking her view of the altar flame. Almost fifty Sentinels and sekiyrra had assembled when Master Jenner called them in.

"Now," he said gravely, "I have been asked to deliver a report from the Netaian Electorate."

Firebird kept her shoulders at a dignified military brace and caught Carradee's glance. Carradee smiled, but Firebird saw a pleading look in her eye.

Tel turned to Carradee and made a dignified half bow. "Majesty, as Firebird requested, the Electorate has acclaimed your daughter, Rinnah, as the next sovereign of the Netaian systems. Kenhing is willing to serve as her regent until she comes of age. It is our hope that you will agree to the acclamation. Will you give your consent?"

Firebird imagined she could feel the weight of a world slide off her shoulders and fall to the red stone floor.

Carradee inclined her head formally. Kiel reached up and snatched a curl of her blond hair. Carradee laughed softly and pulled it away from him. "I consent to the electors' wishes," she said, "as is my duty."

Firebird could barely keep from bouncing on both feet. She seized Brennen's hand instead, and he gripped hers back, flooding her with his own happiness.

Shamarr Dickin rose from the front bench and walked forward, mounting the steps. "Come here," he said kindly, drawing the blue-green vial of anointing oil from his side pocket. "Firebird, Brennen—and you, Carradee. It is time for new blessings."

AUTHOR'S NOTE

Due to circumstances beyond my control (writing fiction is like that), *Crown of Fire* developed a dual theme of pride and atonement. The issue of pride, raised in *Firebird* and continued in *Fusion Fire*, needed closure. Firebird's lifelong desires to excel and to be remembered aren't intrinsically sinful. We are commanded to do all things "heartily, as for the Lord rather than for men" (Colossians 3:23, NASB), which I understand to mean excellently, using all the gifts He gives us. As for Firebird's desire for remembrance—when Mary broke her jar of perfume and anointed Jesus for burial, He said, "what she has done will also be told, in memory of her" (Mark 14:9b, NIV). We can aspire to be remembered for the right reasons.

Pride was always Firebird's temptation, though, and mine. Whenever I do something well just to outshine everyone else, or I insist on getting my way while ignoring someone else's needs, or I refuse to do something that I know God wants, then I set myself up as my own little Power. Fortunately, our merciful God rarely finds it necessary to let the Adversary break our proud hearts quite as dramatically as Micahel shattered Firebird's—or as utterly as the One blasted Three Zed (Adiyn's final vision of the shebiyl is based loosely on Revelation 1:13–16).

I do not feel qualified to deal with such a vital subject as atonement, so I portrayed this seeming death and resurrection as a parable for Firebird's enlightenment, rather than as allegory. At this point in Firebird's story, she understands mercy, her flawed nature, and the necessity of dying to pride and self. In her universe, true atonement lies in the future . . . but she grasps the concept only when Brennen acts it out. His action saves her from being destroyed simply for who she is. Similarly, Christ submitted to death in our place, rescuing us from the inevitable consequences of who we are: His flawed but beloved children, created in the divine image but tainted by our propensity to sin.

Jesus was not miraculously saved from death, though. Even more miraculously, He satisfied the demands of justice and then returned triumphant from death. His resurrection proves the victory. Death has no claim on us, and we too can step out onto a new Path.

Kathy Tyers
Montana
Good Friday, A.D. 2000

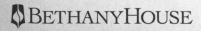